AUNTIE CLEM'S BAKERY 22-24

AUNTIE CLEM'S BAKERY 22-24

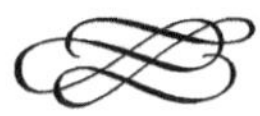

P.D. WORKMAN

ISBN: 9781774689462 (KDP Paperback)
ISBN: 9781774689455 (ePub)

ALSO BY P.D. WORKMAN

FIND MORE BOOKS AT PDWORKMAN.COM

MYSTERY/SUSPENSE:

Auntie Clem's Bakery

Culinary & Pet Cozy Mysteries

Gluten-Free Murder

Dairy-Free Death

Allergen-Free Assignation

Witch-Free Halloween (Halloween Short)

Canine-Free Christmas Caper (Christmas Short)

Stirring Up Murder

Brewing Death

Coup de Glace

Sour Cherry Turnover

Apple-achian Treasure

Vegan Baked Alaska

Muffins Masks Murder

Tai Chi and Chai Tea

Santa Shortbread

Cold as Ice Cream

Changing Fortune Cookies

Hot on the Trail Mix

Fateful Plateful

Cut Out Cookie

On the Slab Pie

Wedding Cake Crush

A Waffle Death

Murder Meringue Pie

A Fowl Play on Christmas Day (Christmas crossover story)

Cinn-Full Secrets

Muffin to Lose

Custard Cream Conspiracy

Mock Apple Alibi (Coming Soon)

Chocolate Eclairvoyant (Coming Soon)

Quiche Me Goodbye (Coming Soon)

Recipes from Auntie Clem's Bakery

Parks Pat Mysteries

Police Procedural Set in Canada

Out with the Sunset

Long Climb to the Top

Dark Water Under the Bridge

Immersed in the View

Skimming Over the Lake

Hazard of the Hills

Knows the Hills

Spanning the Creek

Sanctuary in the Stream

Echoes of the Engine

Bench with a View

Beneath the Icy Depths

Grounded in the Wind

Reservoir of Secrets

Peril in the Blooms

AND MORE AT PDWORKMAN.COM

CINN-FULL SECRETS

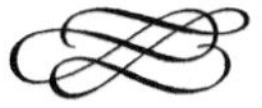

To all of those in toxic relationships.

CHAPTER 1

"All you need to do is tell me where she is," Simon growled. "Come on, you can help a guy out."

Erin shook her head. She continued to line up portions of cream cheese icing in tiny paper cups along the tray, deliberately avoiding eye contact with him. The rich, spicy smell of the freshly baked cinnamon rolls filled the bakery.

"Sorry, can't help you," she told Simon. As if she hadn't already told him a dozen times. She would just keep repeating it calmly as if he were a child and, sooner or later, he would leave. At least, that was the theory she was operating under. She hoped that it would unfold the way she planned. She didn't want there to be any trouble.

"You know where she lives," Simon insisted. "Where she works. You know where in town she might be."

Erin shook her head. "I don't keep track of Adrienne, sorry."

"Where's the other one? Bella? She would tell me where Adrienne is. She knows that we're back together again. You think you're protecting Adrienne from something, but you're not. We're together; I'm just wondering where she is right now. I need to talk to her."

Bella came out of the kitchen and stood back behind the counter with Erin. She was an older teen, still in high school. She had a brilliant business mind and wanted to own her own business after college. She was one of Erin's most dependable workers and always came up with good ideas. She was slightly heavy, with wavy blond hair and a ready smile.

At least, she usually had a smile on her face. Today, she was obviously not entertaining friendly thoughts about Simon.

"You and Adrienne are *not* together again," she told him icily, "and Erin and I are not helping you find her or talk to her, or passing a message to her, or anything else. Why don't you go back to Las Vegas or wherever you were? Adrienne doesn't want anything to do with you."

"My wife is in Bald Eagle Falls, Tennessee, so I am in Bald Eagle Falls, Tennessee," Simon said in a sharp, flinty tone. "And I'm not leaving here unless she and the kids are with me."

"That's not going to happen," Bella told him flatly.

Erin would never have had that kind of confidence as a teenager. She hated confrontation and would do just about anything to avoid it. But Bella was a dragon, standing up to a man twice her age, protecting Adrienne and her children.

Erin had been worried that Adrienne would get back together with Simon. Despite their efforts to keep Simon from tracking her down over the past few weeks, he had met up with Adrienne in town a couple of times. Bald Eagle Falls was not a big place; it wasn't that hard to find her if she were in town instead of at Bella's family farm, or wherever else she and her children might be squatting now. Erin wouldn't be surprised if Adrienne had moved her family deeper into the bush. Simon could find out from anyone in town where the Prost farm was if he knew that was where his wife and children were. People were always trying to be helpful and put families back together, even when you told them there was good reason to keep them apart. Friends and family members were notorious for feeling sorry for a wrongly done husband and father who just wanted to make things right.

They had looked pretty cozy when Erin had seen them together. Erin worried that Adrienne would take him back and put the children at risk. Adrienne had told Erin that she didn't want anything to do with Simon, but her actions didn't bear that out. It was obvious that she was attracted to him. They had been together long enough to produce several children —Erin didn't know if all of the children were his or not, but at least a few of them were—so the relationship was a comfortable place for Adrienne to return to. Being with Simon would feel natural. It would be easy to be seduced by his lies and believe that he was now going to support her. He was a changed man.

Only he wasn't. A leopard didn't change its spots.

Adrienne wanted to believe Simon would support her and her children now. That he wouldn't abandon them again, or do whatever other stupid stuff he'd done in the past. Adrienne admitted they had already broken up and gotten back together more than once. Erin was reminded of Adele, the gamekeeper who lived in the woods behind Erin's house and helped to keep them free of trespassers. Despite Adele's saying that she never wanted to see her husband again—and hadn't even told anyone she was married when she had first moved into town—Erin had seen how Rudolph Windsor had still persuaded her to take him in. He was bad for her and had a criminal past, but that had not stopped her from allowing him into her life again. Though, of course, it hadn't lasted.

Erin had her own history too. Would she have fallen back in with Brandon if he had shown up unexpectedly in Bald Eagle Falls and tried to woo her instead of stalking her? She would like to think that she would not have been tempted. She had lived with him out of desperation when she hadn't had anywhere else to go. It hadn't been a matter of loving him. She supposed that was the difference between her and Adrienne or Adele. It was a lot harder to resist a man you loved.

As far as Erin knew, Simon wasn't a criminal, just a lowlife. Someone who had abandoned his wife and kids one too many times. Gathering what she could from Simon's and Bella's words, Adrienne had finally decided to be tough and kick Simon to the curb.

And he was desperate to get back together with her now that she had money.

CHAPTER 2

*I*f you're not going to buy something," Erin told Simon, "please move on. Other people are waiting to be served."

Simon's small, black eyes flashed. He wasn't going to be put off that easily.

"Buy something? All of these empty carbs?" He looked over the items on display in the bakery case.

It wasn't like he was an athlete, keeping his body in pristine condition. He was on the short side for a man, with skinny arms and a gut. Not someone who worked out or watched what he ate.

Erin didn't bother to explain or excuse the preponderance of carbs in the display case. It *was* a bakery. Simon had known that when he had shoved his way through the front door.

"What are these?" Simon pointed to the sample cups Erin was preparing.

"Cream cheese icing for the cinnamon rolls. These ones are dairy," Erin pointed, "and these are vegan. Non-dairy."

"Non-dairy cream cheese?" he scoffed.

"Not everyone has the benefit of being able to eat dairy," Erin said evenly. "There are a lot of people who are allergic or intolerant. And they would still like to be able to enjoy their cinnamon rolls."

"They are cinn-fully delicious," Vic intoned from where she stood at the register.

Simon barely spared the pretty blond a glance. Most men would have at least given tall, slim, Vic a look of admiration. But maybe Simon had learned from Adrienne that Vic was trans, so he ignored her.

"All this stuff about everybody being intolerant or allergic to everything these days is just a crock," Simon asserted. "Sure, there are a few people who have celiac disease or will actually die if they eat something, but that's just a few people out of thousands. Everybody else," he shook his head in disapproval, "they're just being trendy. Pretending they are doing it to be healthy when they're just being difficult."

Wasn't he the one who had just complained about all the carbs?

"This is a gluten-free and specialty bakery," Erin pointed out. "If you don't want gluten-free, dairy-free, or another special diet, then there isn't anything here for you." Erin looked at the clock on the wall. "And I think it is time for you to go." Erin leaned to the side to see who was behind Simon, even though she knew very well who was behind Simon and didn't need to be so dramatic about it. "Mary Lou, what can I get you today?"

Mary Lou stepped forward, so she was beside Simon rather than behind him. She looked into the display case, smoothing her pantsuit over her hips.

"I'm sure Joshua would like to try some cinnamon rolls," she said. "The regular icing will be fine."

"Great," Erin agreed. "Do you want just a couple?" She knew that Mary Lou was on a budget. She wished she could do more to assist the family, but they wouldn't accept any "charity." Mary Lou also didn't usually eat any desserts and was very careful of the number of calories she ate to avoid putting extra pounds on her slim figure. Joshua, Mary Lou's son, and Roger, her husband, would each eat one. But six or a dozen was not in their budget.

"Yes, two should do it," Mary Lou agreed. "And a loaf of bread," she pointed to the multi-grain-crusted loaf she wanted. "And… maybe a pizza shell. The herb one."

Erin proceeded to serve Mary Lou, ignoring Simon, who didn't move out of the way.

"Do *you* know Adrienne?" Simon asked Mary Lou.

Mary Lou looked at Erin, raising her brows as if she didn't know how to respond to his question. Erin gave an infinitesimal shake of her head. Of course Mary Lou already knew not to tell him anything. Erin was confident that she wouldn't.

"I'm sorry, no," Mary Lou told him coolly.

"You don't know who Adrienne is?"

"I'm afraid not."

Simon didn't believe it for a minute. "In this small town? Everybody in Bald Eagle Falls knows everyone else," he insisted. "If they're not actually related to each other. I know who you are. You're the wife of the man who tried to—"

"Simon," Erin interrupted, trying to avoid a painful topic of conversation. "Did you want a cinnamon roll? You really need to buy whatever you're going to and get out."

Erin hated to be rude. She didn't routinely tell people to leave Auntie Clem's Bakery, but she was tired of Simon and his antics and didn't want him harassing all of her customers.

"You're the only one new here," Simon told Erin. "I know everyone else."

"I'm not exactly new," Erin pointed out. She had been there for a couple of years now, longer than she had lived in most places.

"You're new," Simon told her flatly, shaking his head. "Families like mine and Adrienne's have lived on the mountain for generations. We are real Tennesseans. Living here for a year or two doesn't qualify you to make any judgments about me or my family."

"I'm not making any judgments about you or your family," Erin told him, bemused. "And my family has lived here for generations; I'm the only one who has not. I don't see what that has to do with anything. You're in a bakery. Buy something and move on."

"You can't talk to me like that."

There were increasingly restless movements from the other customers. No one had come to get in the middle of some domestic situation. Mary Lou gave Simon a disapproving look and walked past him to the register to pay for her purchases.

Erin took her phone from her apron pocket, tired of dealing with Simon. She tapped the screen a couple of times to call Terry.

That is, Officer Terry Piper.

He and K9 would be happy to get Simon on his way. They were probably bored with a quiet patrol day and could use some excitement.

"Erin," Terry's voice was warm, but also concerned. She didn't normally call him when she was on shift at Auntie Clem's. "What's up?"

"I have a trespasser at Auntie Clem's who is causing some problems, Officer Piper," Erin told him, her eyes on Simon. "I could use some help."

"I'll be right there," Terry growled. He terminated the call.

Erin slid her phone back into her pocket. She looked past Simon again.

"Betty, what can I get you?"

Betty Thompson was a senior who usually came in with her husband and was notoriously slow in choosing what she wanted to buy. Best to get her up to the counter so she could start pondering her choices. At least now that she had been coming to Auntie Clem's for a couple of years, she didn't have to ask for the ingredients in each item or to ask Erin where each had come from or to debate the benefits and drawbacks of each.

Betty shuffled up to the display case to have a look, giving Simon a wide berth.

"Okay, give me a cinnamon roll," Simon snapped. "You see? I'm a legitimate customer. I'm not trespassing."

He'd been back in town for long enough to know that Terry Piper was, in fact, law enforcement and that he would be on Erin's favorite contacts list. It wasn't just a bluff.

Erin got a single cinnamon roll for him and put it in a sleeve. She did not ask him, as she would have asked any other customer, if he wanted her to warm it in the microwave for a few seconds so that the icing would soften and run into the spiral layers.

"Did you want the cream cheese or non-dairy icing?" she asked him politely, as if she hadn't heard his earlier diatribe.

Simon choked, swore under his breath, and then apparently decided that if he were trying to be a legitimate customer, he'd better watch himself. "Cream cheese," he snarled.

Erin nodded and added a plastic knife and a little container of cream cheese icing to his bag. She briefly entertained the idea of giving him the non-dairy icing to see if he noticed the difference. But she had seen enough people caused harm by restaurant employees "testing" to see if someone really would react to a small bit of a food they claimed to be allergic or intolerant to. She would never give someone anything other than what they had ordered. It just wasn't in her makeup.

She put the bag on the counter next to the cash register for Vic to ring up.

The bells on the door jingled as it was pushed open, and Terry came in, devastatingly handsome in his police uniform, a bit of a five o'clock shadow on his jaw after a long patrol. K9 walked briskly at his side, ears pointed alertly forward as he looked for any sign of trouble.

"You're having a problem?" Terry asked Erin, not seeing any immediate issues.

Erin indicated Simon. "Mr. Simpson is ready to leave."

Simon glared at Erin. "I'm a customer," he said, holding up the bag containing the cinnamon roll. "I have a legitimate reason to be here."

Erin folded her arms. "And now that you've completed your transaction, you're ready to leave."

He opened his mouth to argue. But where was that going to get him? If he had already purchased what he needed, then there was no need for him to stay around. If he was there for another reason, like to threaten Erin into revealing where he could find Adrienne or to cause problems with the other customers, he obviously couldn't do that in front of local law enforcement.

And even if he didn't happen to think that Terry Piper was a formidable force, he had to consider whether he would win or lose in an argument with K9. And most people Erin knew would choose not to be on the receiving end of a German shepherd bite.

"You're ready to go?" Terry asked.

Simon looked at Erin and Bella, then back at Terry and K9. There wasn't any way for him to save face or to stay there any longer, so he gave up.

"Yeah, I'm leaving," he agreed. He shook his head and departed the bakery.

A collective sigh went up from the remaining customers. And staff.

"That guy is trouble," Terry observed.

Erin nodded. "That won't be the last we see of him."

"Just keep calling me. Or the dispatcher if I'm not available. Don't try to argue with him or convince him to go. Just call me the second he walks in the door. It shouldn't take too long to discourage him from showing up here."

"Okay. I'll let everyone else know," Erin agreed.

But Erin was wrong, because it *was* the last time that Simon would set foot inside Auntie Clem's Bakery.

CHAPTER 3

"Wow, what a day," Vic sighed, stretching her arms and shoulders and letting her hair down from its bun now that she had her baker's hat and apron off. Few things were more satisfying than shaking off the day and heading home to relax.

Erin rubbed her shoulders and the back of her neck. She could tell that she had been holding herself tense for much of the day.

"I kept thinking Simon was going to come back."

Vic nodded. "Simon Simpson is more irritating than a mosquito bite on your backside. At least your man is willing to step in and take care of him."

"Yeah." Erin had to admit that she felt a lot better knowing that if Simon stepped through her door again, all she had to do was call Terry. She didn't have to try to talk him into leaving, misdirect him, or come up with something that would satisfy his demands temporarily without actually giving him any new information or leads. "Do you think he'll give up? I mean, sooner or later, he has to accept that he and Adrienne aren't getting back together, doesn't he?"

"Sure… sooner or later. We all know the only reason he's here at all is because Adrienne came into money. When he finally accepts that he isn't going to get his hands on it… he'll be gone again. Back to LA or wherever he's been since Sarah was conceived."

"Is Sarah his?" Erin asked tentatively. From what she'd heard, Simon had been gone for at least a few years, and Sarah was still an infant. Had Simon been back during the interim, or had Adrienne been with someone else?

"Uh…" Vic reddened. "I wouldn't want to say one way or the other. That's Adrienne's business."

Erin agreed.

"Do you know where the cake knife is?" she asked, hands on hips, looking around at the counters and anywhere else someone might have put it down. "I'm missing one."

"Are you sure?" Vic opened the utensil drawer and moved things around. "Yeah, you're right." She opened the fridge and looked inside. Sometimes things ended up in the oddest places. "I don't know. I'm sure it will turn up."

"I'm sure it will. Are you and Willie taking off anywhere this weekend?" Erin asked.

"I doubt it. He hasn't felt like going anywhere lately."

"Still not feeling very well?" Erin asked sympathetically.

Willie was undergoing chelation therapy for heavy metal poisoning and, from what Erin had gathered, the "flu-like symptoms" and "irritability" they had been warned to expect had been a lot more severe than the words suggested.

"No. And you know how men are when they are sick." Vic rolled her eyes. She looked at the clock on the wall. "I should be getting him something to eat before long… are you going to be much longer?"

"I want to do a few more things. Accounting, planning, all that kind of fun stuff. Charley and I are supposed to meet on Monday, and I should have everything caught up and ready to present."

Vic's eyes went to the clock again, and then the door. "So… do you want me to wait around?"

Erin shook her head. "Just lock the door on your way out. I'll be fine here."

Vic hesitated.

"Go take care of Willie," Erin urged. "You don't need to hang around here."

"Yeah, okay. Don't work too late, okay? Even if you don't have to get up for tomorrow's morning shift, you know you'll wake up anyway."

It was true. Try as she might to sleep in, Erin was never very successful in sleeping past her usual alarm time or going back to sleep once she had awakened.

"I won't be too long," she promised. "Maybe just an hour. Then Terry will be off his double shift and we can chill tonight and tomorrow."

"Sounds heavenly," Vic said a trifle jealously. Willie's demands must be wearing on her if "chilling" sounded that desirable. Vic usually liked being off adventuring, not just sitting at home.

"See you later," Erin promised. Since Vic lived in the loft over Erin's garage, they frequently had tea together in the evening, and it sounded like Vic might need the break even more than usual.

CHAPTER 4

On Sunday mornings, Erin held the ladies' tea for the church women who wanted to socialize after Sunday morning services. It was something that Erin's Aunt Clementine had done for them back when the bakery had been a tea shop, but she'd had to stop when she got too sick and frail to continue. Erin had been asked to reinstitute the practice when she inherited the storefront after Clementine's death.

It might seem like a strange service for an atheist to offer, but most of the ladies had accepted by now that Erin did not have any interest in their religion and they were not going to convince her to join them for church services. They were happy to have somewhere to go afterward to drink tea, nibble snacks, and gossip.

Teacups clinked softly as the women gossiped and discussed their week.

"How is Adrienne?" Erin asked Cindy Prost as she refreshed the platter of sweets at her table.

Cindy was not one of Erin's favorite people. Unlike her daughter Bella, who was endlessly positive and upbeat, Cindy usually had something to complain about. She was critical of pretty much everyone and everything. But Erin had seen her soften around Adrienne's children, transforming into an aunt or grandma figure who enjoyed doing things for them, feeding them, or playing with them.

Cindy turned her eyes on Erin, pushing a hank of blond and gray hair that had come loose from her bun back over one ear. She glanced at Erin as if about to assert that it wasn't her business. Then she gave her head a little shake.

"She'd be better off if that idiot was gone for good," she said, her mouth twisting into a snarl. "I don't know how he heard she'd come into money. Whoever told him has got somethin' to answer for. His kin were never anything but trash. She should have known better than to get together with him in the first place."

Erin nodded. She supposed she wasn't going to get a real answer from Cindy. The woman was just going to vent her spleen about Simon and his forebears, and Erin didn't really want to hear that.

She took a step away from Cindy to attend to another of the tables. Cindy put a hand on Erin's arm. She had a strong grip.

"She's going to be fine," Cindy told Erin. "As long as she stays away from Simon and he stays away from her, she'll be just fine."

The woman had been through a lot lately, and Erin hoped she was right. Adrienne deserved a break.

"I haven't seen Simon for a couple of days. Is he still around? Or did he decide to take off again?"

"I hope to heaven that he is gone. And that he never comes back again. She doesn't need his influence on the children. Adrienne always goes back to him. She needs to cut him off once and for all."

"Well… I hope she does. I hope that he's already gone and none of us have to deal with him again."

"Your lips to God's ears," Cindy agreed.

After the church ladies were gone, Erin and Charley did the cleanup. There wasn't much to do. Erin had learned to minimize the amount of preparation and cleanup needed for the ladies' tea so that she could have as much of Sunday to herself as possible, since they did not open for business on the Sabbath, as dictated by those same church ladies.

Erin checked to see if anything else needed to go out in the garbage. It looked like she had gotten all the used napkins and other detritus.

"I'm just going to toss this," she informed Charley and headed out the bakery's back door toward the dumpster.

Her nose wrinkled as she got closer to it. She knew her nose was more sensitive than that of anyone else she knew, but the bin smelled much worse than usual. Either the garbage hadn't been collected during the week, or someone had decided to dump their own garbage into the dumpster because there wasn't room in theirs.

The bakery did use eggs and dairy, so sometimes their garbage got pretty rancid by the time it was picked up, but what Erin was smelling wasn't the normal Auntie Clem's trash. It smelled like meat. Meat well past its prime. She gagged.

They rarely had any meat in Auntie Clem's. Erin didn't make meat pies or other prepared meals. Sometimes bacon for breakfast muffins or maple bacon muffins, but that was about it.

Someone had definitely put something in the Auntie Clem's bin that wasn't supposed to be there.

She held her breath as she approached the bin and threw her bag into it. She took a quick look for anything that shouldn't be there but could only see the trash she had previously disposed of. All of the trash bags were the same color and size.

Erin stepped back, shaking her head, and took several steps away before taking a gulp of air. She breathed in a few times through her mouth.

If the smell wasn't coming from something that someone had put into her bin—unless they had used exactly the same bags as Erin herself, then where was it coming from? She held her hand over her nose, looking around.

It was summer in Tennessee, which meant it was hot enough that her shirt was already sticking to her even though she had barely stepped out of the air-conditioned bakery. It might be an animal. A bird or mouse killed by a cat or something larger killed by a car going too quickly down the back alley at night.

She checked around the bins and back fences of each of her neighbors, but that seemed to be taking her farther away from the stench. Erin returned to her bin, looked in again, and still couldn't see anything to explain the stench. She leaned on the fence and looked into the space between the bin and the fence.

. . .

Charley looked over as Erin staggered back into Auntie Clem's Bakery, opening her mouth to ask a question. But when she saw Erin, whatever she had been about to ask was quickly forgotten.

"Erin? What's wrong? Are you okay?" Charley hurried over to her.

Erin tried to protest that she was fine but couldn't find the words. Her stomach roiled and she couldn't say anything or explain. She dashed for the powder room and slammed the door behind her. She luckily reached the toilet before she lost the contents of her stomach.

"Erin? Are you okay?" Charley shouted through the door.

Erin didn't hear what else she had to say. She wasn't okay, but she wasn't in any condition to talk. Charley was still speaking, but Erin couldn't make out any of it. Her ears were ringing and she was afraid she was going to pass out.

It was a while before she was able to calm her heaving stomach and consider standing up again. She eventually struggled to her feet and splashed cold water on her face. She was sweating like she had a fever. The cold water felt good and soaked down into the collar of her shirt.

When she opened the door, Charley was not in the kitchen, which she thought was odd. She knew Charley wouldn't have just gone home, leaving her throwing up in the bathroom. They were more than just partners in the business. Charley was Erin's half-sister and, even though they hadn't grown up together or even known of each other's existence until a couple of years ago, they cared for each other. As rough around the edges as Charley was, she wasn't the type to walk away from someone who was sick or in trouble.

There were low voices in the front of the store. Charley had let someone in through the front door.

Charley walked Terry and K9 into the kitchen.

"Erin? Are you okay?" Terry asked, going to her and putting his hands on her shoulders as he looked into her eyes. "Charley said you were sick. You don't look so good. Did it just hit you suddenly?"

Erin shook her head. "Out back," she croaked.

"Out back? What?" Terry looked toward the back door. "What are you talking about?"

"He's out there." Erin swallowed, trying to keep from reacting to the sight and smell again.

"Who is out there? Did something happen?" Charley demanded. "I didn't hear anything," she told Terry earnestly. "Erin, did someone hurt you?"

Erin gulped air and turned back toward the bathroom again, unsure she could keep her equilibrium.

"Simon." She gagged. "Simon Simpson."

"He was back there?" Terry hurried to the back door and looked out. "I don't see him now. What did he do?"

"Behind the bin. Behind the garbage bin."

Terry gave her a look that told her he thought she was off her head. He walked out the door. K9 led him unerringly to the new discovery, his doggie nose even more sensitive than Erin's.

Erin could see Terry through the doorway as he pulled out his phone and started making calls.

CHAPTER 5

"W hat's going on?" Charley demanded. "What are you talking about? Simon isn't back there."

They both watched Terry from inside the kitchen, not going out to join him. Did Charley have an inkling of what was going on, and that was why she was staying with Erin rather than going outside to see what Terry had found? Or was she just staying with Erin to keep an eye on her because she was sick?

Erin grabbed one of the stools she sometimes used in the kitchen when her legs grew tired, as it was tall enough to reach the counters comfortably. It took a couple of tries to get settled, and Charley helped her to make sure she was stable. Erin put her elbows on the counter and her face in her hands.

"It's Simon," she repeated. "He's back there between the dumpster and the fence."

"What's he doing back there?"

Erin had a sudden vision of what Charley must be picturing, rough-looking Simon crouched between the garbage bin and the fence, lying in wait for Adrienne. But that wasn't even close to what Erin had discovered.

"He's dead," she told Charley. Tears were leaking from her eyes but, with Erin's hands over her face, Charley wouldn't be able to see. "I could… I could smell something out there."

"Oh, yuck," Charley said. She patted Erin on the back and rubbed in slow, soothing circles. "How could something like that happen? I'm sorry, Erin."

How could something like that happen? It wasn't like it was the first death that Erin had discovered in Bald Eagle Falls. Or even the second. She didn't know how she always seemed drawn toward them. This time, it had been the smell. She should have known better than to look too closely, leaving it for someone else to investigate. Called Terry to look for her. Even if it had just been a dead animal, then who better than her boyfriend to find it and deal with it, protecting her from seeing what had happened or smelling the stench close up.

She gagged just thinking of it. She held her arm and then her shirt to her nose, checking to see whether she had carried the smell of the decomposition with her. She would have to wash everything. Shower for an hour to ensure it didn't cling to her skin or get into her hair.

"Can I get you something?" Charley offered. "A glass of water? Would that help?"

Erin nodded. "Maybe."

"Or some tea? I can heat a teakettle."

Charley was not the best in the kitchen. She had grown a lot and could now follow most of the recipes in Erin's big reference binder. Most of them. As long as she was careful and followed the step-by-step directions exactly. She was distractible and had been known to mess up an entire batch of dough more than once.

Erin nodded. Charley left her side to put the kettle on to boil. Erin sniffled.

"You might as well use the big boiler. If the police want anything…"

"Oh, yeah, I suppose," Charley agreed. She turned off the kettle and looked at the big boiler they used for the ladies' tea and other events. "This thing always scares me a little."

"You just need to turn it on and make sure the tank is full."

Charley looked at the boiler dubiously, but followed Erin's instructions. The boiler started to tick, warming up.

"Ginger?" Charley asked, looking at a selection of teas in the ladies' tea basket. "That's supposed to be good for stomachs."

"Yeah." The pungent smell would help clean the smell out of Erin's nose as well as the tea reducing the nausea. There wasn't anything left in her stomach to throw up, but that didn't mean she couldn't try.

The sound of approaching sirens reached into the kitchen, tinny and far away at first, but quickly homing in on the bakery and its latest, deadest customer. The wails rose to an unbearable level before finally stopping outside and cutting off abruptly.

Terry spoke to the sheriff for a couple of minutes. They both walked behind the fence, looking down at the ground, their heads close together as they discussed the discovery.

They were both experienced law enforcement officers and it certainly wasn't the first time they had been faced with a decomposing body. Still, she couldn't understand how they could stand that close to the remains without covering their mouths and noses. Or getting sick.

After a few minutes, Terry left the sheriff there and he and K9 returned to Auntie Clem's, joining Erin and Charley in the kitchen just as Charley was putting a mug of ginger tea in front of Erin.

Terry stood a few feet away from her, unsure of how to approach the subject or treat Erin. She was, she supposed, a person of interest by virtue of being so close to the dead body. And the fact that Simon had been harassing her about Adrienne and then he had disappeared, only to turn up dead.

Surely, he knew by this time that there was no way Erin could have killed Simon or anyone else. And there was no way that she would have put herself in the position of having to see and smell the body in that condition. If Erin were to commit a murder, she would be more likely to kill and dispose of someone in a big walk-in freezer like the one in Buttermilk Biscuits, a restaurant in Whitewater Junction, than she would leave a body out in the Tennessee sun to putrefy outside her back door.

"Erin, are you okay?" Terry asked, still a couple of steps away from her. Did he maintain that distance because he was still acting in his role as a law enforcement officer, separate and emotionally distant from Erin? She had thought the sheriff would have taken him off the case.

"Mm-hmm," Erin murmured. She took a tiny sip of the ginger tea and waited for it to start working before filling her stomach. One small sip at a time, until she could get the whole cup down. Then she should feel much better.

"Can you tell me what happened? How did you discover the body?"

Erin shook her head.

"You can take your time," Terry said. "If you're not ready yet."

"She was just taking the garbage out," Charley informed him. "We were cleaning up after the ladies' tea."

Terry nodded. He looked at Erin for more details, but she just shook her head. There wasn't much else to say about it. She didn't want to relive the experience. If she kept going over it, the discovery would just be indelibly impressed upon her memory, so she could never forget it.

"It isn't exactly in plain sight," Terry pointed out. "How did you end up looking behind the dumpster?"

"The smell."

"It is pungent," Terry admitted. "But you didn't think it was just the garbage?"

Erin shuddered and shook her head. "Does it smell like garbage?" she challenged.

"Well, yes. To me… it doesn't smell any different than any other rotting garbage."

Erin shook her head. "Ugh. Rotten garbage doesn't smell like that."

Terry looked at her, his face a study of concentration. "I'm glad I don't have your sense of smell," he told her, not for the first time.

Erin nodded her agreement. As delightful as it was to have her sense of smell when there were cookies or a nice turkey dinner in the oven, her sense of smell was more often an inconvenience than a helpful tool. It might be fun to identify the ingredients in a tea or recognize what brand and variety it was, but garbage, dead bodies, and other terrible smells were not things she enjoyed.

Erin took another sip of her tea. She could hear the muted voices of the other law enforcement officers talking or yelling back and forth as they secured the scene and looked for any forensic clues that would tell them what had happened there.

Erin, Charley, and Terry said nothing for a while, each pondering their own thoughts.

"When was the last time you saw Simon?" Terry asked. "Before this, I mean. The last time you saw him alive."

Erin swallowed. "The same time as you did. When I called you to get him out of the bakery."

"You had to call him to get Simon out of the bakery?" Charley repeated, not having heard this detail previously.

Erin nodded and looked at Terry. "He was harassing me. Wouldn't get out. Blocking the other customers or asking them uncomfortable questions. I asked him to leave and he wouldn't, so I called Terry." She nodded to him. "He got Simon on his way, and that was the last I heard from him. I was expecting him to come back... he kept coming back to demand to know about Adrienne. Where she was or if I could get her a message."

"But he never came back after that?" Terry asked.

"No."

"That was... Friday afternoon."

Erin nodded. She thought about the state of decomposition of the body. It wasn't a fresh kill. Someone had made sure that Simon would never come back to the bakery to harass Erin again.

"I guess that's about right," Terry admitted. "He must have died soon after that. It's been more than a few hours. More than a day, I would say, but we'll have to see what the medical examiner has to say about it."

"Who would do that?" Erin demanded. Who would kill Simon? Who would leave him right outside Erin's back door, rotting behind the dumpster like that? There were so many questions whirling through her head as she tried to make sense of it.

"How was he killed?" Charley asked sensibly. She was the only one of the three of them who had not seen the body, so she would need to be filled in on the details of the murder.

Because Simon *had* been murdered.

CHAPTER 6

erry looked at Charley and didn't answer the question, obviously trying to keep the details of the investigation under wraps.

He was the one who was required to keep the details confidential, not Erin.

"Stabbed," Erin told her. "That's what it looked like."

They both looked at Terry for confirmation. He just shrugged. No comment.

"Stabbed," Charley repeated. "Up close and personal, then. A face-to-face confrontation." She looked at Erin. "Was it face-to-face?"

"Stabbed in the front," Erin agreed. "Chest or stomach… maybe more than once, I didn't get close enough to investigate."

"Anger," Charley deduced. "Rage? How many stab marks?"

"Don't know," Erin reiterated. Charley looked at Terry, but he didn't help out.

"He was so well-liked," Charley said sarcastically. "It's going to be hard to find anyone who wished him dead."

Terry snorted. K9 looked up at him with a doggie expression of concern.

"Who did you see around here Friday?" Terry asked Erin. "After I left.

Who was around the bakery in the next couple of hours? Customers, employees, anyone you saw walking down the alley?"

"I didn't see anyone walking down the alley. I don't stand out there watching for people to go by. The only time I open the back door is for deliveries or to take stuff out to the garbage."

"Did you have any deliveries Friday afternoon?"

"No."

"Anyone come by for the day-old bread?"

That was another thing that people came to the back door for, and Terry knew that. Anyone who needed help with their groceries, who couldn't afford the bread that the family needed, could come by Auntie Clem's to get day-old bread and baking from the freezer. Whatever they needed, no questions asked.

"No. Not Friday."

"Did Adrienne ever come to the back?"

Erin shook her head. "Not on Friday."

"Did she ever?"

Erin balked at revealing anything sensitive to Terry. "I don't see what that has to do with it. That's confidential."

"If Simon knew that sometimes she came by for day-old bread, he might have camped out there to watch for her."

"And then stabbed himself?" Charley asked sarcastically.

"And then… had a confrontation with Adrienne or someone else."

"Adrienne didn't come by," Erin repeated.

"No one else came by?" Terry verified.

"No."

"And you didn't… hear anything strange out there Friday or Saturday?"

"It's a heavy door. And we often have machines or water or fans running back here. So we don't really hear anything from outside."

"Did you hear anything?" Terry repeated. Erin could hear the frustration in his voice. She didn't mean to answer ambiguously; she just felt that his questions needed more context. She meant to answer.

"No. I didn't hear anything."

"Any of your employees? Anyone mention hearing or seeing anything unusual?"

Erin looked at Charley and shook her head.

"I don't know of anything," Charley confirmed. She wasn't in the bakery very often but, hopefully, her confirmation reassured Terry that Erin was telling the truth and not just trying to brush him off.

Sheriff Wilmot entered the kitchen. He stomped off his shoes at the door in case they were dusty and wiped his sweaty forehead. It was evening, but it was still pretty warm out.

"Miss Erin," he greeted. "Mind if we have a chat?"

Erin nodded. "Of course."

She was glad that he had come in himself to interview her rather than assigning the job to Rodney Stayner, whom Erin had never really gotten along with.

He nodded toward Erin's tiny, closet-sized office and asked, "Shall we take your office?"

But there really wasn't room in there for two people. There was no guest chair and Wilmot would have to stand or sit on the edge of the desk. And it would be very close and warm.

"Why don't we grab a table at the front instead?" Erin suggested.

The sheriff nodded his agreement, and he and Erin sat down at one of the small wrought iron tables in the front of the bakery that they used for the ladies' tea and that customers occasionally used if they needed a quiet place to have their tea or cookies before going back to the office. Everything was clean and tidy. Erin and Charley had just wiped everything down, swept, and wet-mopped.

Sheriff Wilmot sighed as he sat down opposite Erin. "So... Another day, another body," he joked gently.

"I think it's time for someone else to take a turn," Erin said ruefully.

"Yes. You seem to have had to deal with more than your own share, haven't you? How are you feeling? You're a mite pale."

"Well... I was sick. But I guess I'm okay now. As long as I don't think about it too much."

"We'll try to avoid that the best we can, under the circumstances. I'm sure you've already walked through it with Officer Piper, but if you could outline things once more for me..."

"I was just taking the garbage out. I could... smell the decomp. I looked around, thought it might be an animal. And then... I saw him."

"Quite a shock. Despite your experience in these matters."

"It's always a shock. And it's not something that I go looking for."

"Certainly not," he agreed. "Was there anyone else around when you found the body?"

"Just Charley. And she was inside the bakery, not out there."

"Anyone walking by? Did you hear anyone out there earlier? Yesterday?"

"No."

"I'll need a list of your employees and when they were on shift."

Erin thought about that. She wasn't sure how knowing the bakery shifts would make any difference. If someone were working a shift, did that make them a suspect? Or did that mean that they had an alibi? It could go either way.

"Okay," she agreed. But she didn't really think it would help him.

"Have you seen Adrienne the last few days?"

Erin shook her head. "No. She hasn't been around town very much." She gave a little grimace. "Almost as if she was avoiding someone."

Wilmot chuckled. "Almost as if she were," he agreed. "Do you have a phone number for her that works?"

"Um… I might."

He frowned, brows drawing closer together. "Miss Erin. Do you have a number for her or not?"

Erin sighed. "Yes. But it is supposed to be private. I'm not supposed to share it with anyone."

"You're going to need to give it to me. We need to get in contact with her to notify her of Simon's death and discuss the circumstances with her. We can't get around that."

Erin nodded. "Okay. But can you not put it on anything that others will see? If it leaks out to other people in the town… then it's not exactly private anymore."

"It is going to need to go into our official records." He held up his finger to stop Erin from objecting. "Again, no way around that one. We have to keep accurate records. It won't be available to anyone outside of the police department."

Unfortunately, Erin knew the police department had at least one very large leak.

She pulled out her phone and found the number for Wilmot. "Just please… keep it as private as you can."

"Isn't the danger already past? Wouldn't you say that the one person she needed to keep that number from is past being able to use it?"

Clearly, Simon was dead. But was he the only person who would show up interested in Adrienne's windfall? She was reclusive and liked to keep herself and her family apart from mainstream society. She wouldn't want just anyone calling her.

"It's not a public number," Erin reiterated. "Keep it as quiet as you can."

Wilmot nodded his agreement. "When was the last time you saw Simon?"

"Friday. When I called Terry to get rid of him."

The sheriff raised his brows. "To get rid of him?"

"From Auntie Clem's. He was making a nuisance of himself and wouldn't leave when I asked him to. So I called Terry, and he saw him on his way. That was the last I saw of him. I expected him to come back, but he didn't."

"Very good. That's helpful. And you didn't see or hear anything else in the back?" He gestured again.

"No." Erin tried to think of whether she had heard the trash pickup or whether she had seen or heard anything else over the past two days. "No, I can't think of anything at all."

"How late were you here Friday night?"

"Uh… maybe seven. I'm not sure."

"And you didn't hear anything out there? Shouting? Anything like that?"

"No. I was in my office, and you really can't hear anything in there."

"Who else was here? Miss Vicky?"

"No. I was… just by myself. The bakery was closed. I had some accounting and planning to do while it was quiet."

"You were here by yourself."

"Yes." Erin swallowed and tried to meet his eyes. "Is that really a problem? You don't think I did it, do you? I wouldn't take on someone like Simon physically. That would be stupid."

"People do stupid things. And desperate things. And they even up the score with weapons or other advantages. No, I don't think you had anything to do with Simon's death. But I still have to follow up and make sure I have everything documented. I still need to follow proper investigative procedures."

"I know."

"What time did Victoria go home?"

"Six o'clock, maybe. Roughly that. And she said she was going to cook dinner for Willie, so she had an alibi. She wasn't hanging around waiting for Simon Simpson to show his face."

Wilmot nodded. "Fair enough. I will talk to her and confirm that. As well as the rest of your employees. What about other people you saw in the bakery that day? Who was around?"

"Friday and Saturday? That's a pretty tall order… I can make copies of the sales for you. But I can't tell you everyone that we sold something those days. Or that might have come in with someone who bought something."

"You have a lot of turnover," Wilmot joked.

"No, we're out of turnovers this week," Erin deadpanned. "We've been focusing on cinnamon rolls."

"Mmm. I might have heard something about that. Cinnamon rolls with cream cheese icing." He licked his lips.

"I'll pack you some to take home."

Wilmot grinned. "I would be much obliged, Miss Erin. Although my wife might have something to say about my expanding waistline."

"She'll have to take you for a walk."

He guffawed at that. "She will indeed."

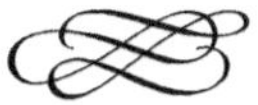

*B*y the time Erin and Terry got home, word of Simon's death had spread over the Bald Eagle Falls grapevine, and everyone wanted to talk to Erin. Her phone kept ringing until she turned it off. When she arrived home and went to put tea on in the kitchen and scrounged for some leftovers from the fridge, she was counting the seconds until Vic descended the stairs from her loft apartment, crossed the yard, and showed up at the back door. She was not disappointed. The motion detector lights went on, and Erin went to the back door to disarm the burglar alarm and open the door for Vic. Vic had her own code for the alarm, of course, but Erin thought she would eliminate any concerns Vic had about intruding during a difficult time by opening the door for her.

"Oh my word," Vic exclaimed, fanning her face. "I can't believe it! Simon Simpson is dead?"

Erin nodded and let Vic in. Willie was just a few steps behind her.

"Are you okay, Erin?" he asked.

Erin nodded. "I'm tired," she admitted, shaking her head. It wasn't quite bedtime for her yet, but it was close, and being interviewed by the police always tired her out. "But other than that... I'm just fine. Peckish." She turned to look at the fridge again, feeling too exhausted to do much more than defrost a couple of cookies, which wasn't a good idea for her figure.

"Shoo. You sit down," Vic ordered, waving her hands at Erin. "I'll pull something together for you. The least Officer Handsome could do is take you out for something to eat after he interrogates you." She raised her voice to make sure that Terry would hear her.

"I just put in a double shift," Terry shot back. "I'm going to shower off the sweat and dust from the day, and then there'd better be something on the table for me."

Vic laughed. "What does he think, I'm his servant?"

Erin smiled. She melted into the chair—as much as one could melt into a straight-backed kitchen chair—and mentally reviewed the evening. It had dragged by but, at the same time, it was all blurred together. She couldn't have put everything into a perfectly coherent timeline if she'd had to.

"But you're okay?" Vic asked as she worked at the counter to pull the leftovers into something appetizing.

"Yes. I'm just fine. It isn't like they think I had anything to do with it. They have to investigate all avenues of inquiry."

"That sounds like something that came out of the sheriff's mouth," Willie observed.

"Yes… him, Terry, everyone. It's just one of those things. If they didn't get all of my information, the investigation wouldn't be complete, and they could be in trouble. Or might end up missing something important."

"With the number of deaths around here, you would think they'd had plenty of practice," Willie said. "This should be a cinch for them."

Erin shrugged. She looked around. "Where is Orange Blossom? Usually, when I'm late getting home, he has a fit." The noisy orange cat had not put in an appearance when Erin had opened the door. He might be sleeping in one of the bedrooms, pouting because she had neglected him.

"I came over and fed him a couple of hours ago," Vic assured her. "I figured you wouldn't get home until late."

"Oh, you're the best. And now you're over to feed me, too! What did you guys have tonight? Do you want anything? Dessert?"

Vic glanced over at Willie to see what he thought. He sat back in his chair, arms folded across his chest, and shook his head. "I'm supposed to be watching what I eat," he advised. "No junk food or sweets."

Erin admired him for sticking to his diet. "Good for you. I don't know if I could give up sweets," she admitted.

"Well, it's not forever, but while I'm in treatment… to tell the truth, I want it to be over as soon as possible."

"It's been pretty rough, hasn't it?"

Willie looked over at Vic. "It has probably been even harder on Vic than me. I can grouse around or sleep half the day and everyone just accepts that I'm sick and puts up with it. But they don't have to be around me all the time like she does."

"You *have* been a grumpy old man," Vic agreed cheekily.

Erin laughed. Vic put a sandwich and bowl of soup in front of her. Looking over at the stove, Erin could see that there was more waiting for Terry when he finished his shower.

"This is really nice, Vic. Thanks for the help."

The soup was warm and soothing. Erin closed her eyes and savored it.

"So…?" Vic sat down at the table. "Spill. What are all of the details of Simon's death? There are so many rumors going around right now, I have no idea what to believe."

Erin sipped her soup, thinking about it. She had gone over it and over it with the police. That was how they worked, repeating the same material over and over again and seeing how much each repetition varied. Digging up more details. Examining anything she might not have been entirely forthright about. Although there was no reason for her not to be completely forthright about it. It wasn't like she had anything to hide. Everyone already knew about the animosity between Simon and Erin. And that the reason she was at odds with Simon was because she was protecting Adrienne. She didn't have any previous contact with him or any other reason for arguing with him.

"Someone said he'd been dead for a long time," Vic prompted. "It didn't just happen today."

Erin nodded. "I guess that depends on how you define a long time. But yeah… the body was in pretty bad shape."

She had to swallow and take a few deep breaths to fend off the nausea.

"But we saw him on Friday. So it was after that," Vic contributed.

"Probably pretty soon after that, they're thinking. I don't know; we'll see what the medical examiner says and who had seen him since he was at Auntie Clem's. But in this heat…" She swallowed again and shook her head. She sipped more soup. She hoped eating would help settle her queasy stomach rather than making things worse.

"How was he killed?" Willie asked. "Finding him in the back alley like that… was he hit by a car? Thrown to the side? I'm not sure how he wasn't discovered right away. It isn't like it's a big town. People use that back alley."

"Stabbed," Erin told him. "And he was… out of sight. Back behind our dumpster. I guess… maybe someone dragged and dumped him there. To where no one would see him right away. But I could smell something that wasn't just the garbage…"

"Erin and her super smeller," Vic said.

"It isn't the first time I've wished I didn't have a good sense of smell. Believe me… there are many things I would rather not *ever* have to smell."

Willie chuckled. "I can believe that."

Erin went back to her soup, inhaling the savory scent deeply before taking another spoonful.

"So, stabbed," Vic said meditatively. "I'll bet there are a lot of people who would have liked to have stabbed him. I know I would have."

Erin nearly choked on her soup. She swallowed her mouthful and looked at Vic, shaking her head.

"You can't just go around stabbing people."

"Well, I *know* that. That's why I say, I would have liked to have stabbed him. But I didn't do it. I controlled my homicidal instincts." She looked at Willie. "I have a lot of practice with that."

"You see, there is a benefit to me being a cranky old man," Willie teased. "If you didn't have all of that practice restraining your homicidal impulses, you could be in jail right now."

"I could be," Vic agreed.

"It's a good thing you're not," Erin told her. "I'm going to need some extra help the next few days. You know how crazy Auntie Clem's gets when something like this happens. And I don't know how well I will sleep tonight."

"That's right," Vic agreed. "We should call someone right now for the morning shift so you don't have to worry about getting up early. You can sleep however late you need and just come in when you feel up to it."

"People will want to talk to me."

"No problem. We'll just feed them a bunch of wild gossip until you get there to keep interest high. We always get the best business when there's something juicy to talk about."

Erin laughed. "You are *not* going to feed them a bunch of lies until I get there to tell them the truth."

Vic shrugged and fluttered her lashes at Erin, putting on an innocent schoolgirl act. "Well, we'll just have to see what happens until you get there."

CHAPTER 8

$\mathcal{E}$rin knew that Vic was only joking about spreading gossip about the murder until she got there to answer people's questions about what she had discovered. But she still couldn't help feeling like she had to be at the bakery to make sure that there weren't any false rumors spreading about Simon's death. She had seen how quickly stories could spread through Bald Eagle Falls. No one seemed to care whether a story were true or not. They just wanted something juicy to chew on.

Erin would prefer that whatever was circulating was the truth. She didn't want to spend the next few days or weeks trying to quash false rumors about what she had seen or done.

So, despite a restless night, she was up early as usual the next morning and was in the kitchen dressed and ready to go, fresh hot coffee in her travel mug, when Vic made her way down the stairs from the loft.

"I thought you were going to sleep in," Vic teased. "You didn't get enough sleep, did you?"

Erin shrugged. "Enough to get by for one day. I'll get Charley to close and come home for a nap."

Vic laughed. "No, you won't."

"I could."

"Yes, you could, Miss Erin. In fact, you could have slept in this morning. But you didn't."

Erin handed her the second mug of coffee. "This sounds like a discussion that could be carried on at Auntie Clem's while we get ready for the day."

Vic took the mug, and she and Erin climbed into the yellow bug for the drive to Auntie Clem's Bakery a few blocks away.

Erin had called in Cheyenne the night before in case she couldn't make it, so there were three of them to get the ovens going and to prepare for the morning rush, which was bound to be even busier than usual with the news of Simon's murder.

They were all familiar with all of the morning routines and recipes, so they worked together efficiently and had the display case filled and labeled well ahead of opening the doors, and were able to sit down for a moment to finish their coffee and fortify themselves for the flurry of activity that was a few minutes away.

Then Erin arose and unlocked the front door, flipping the sign over to Open. A number of customers were already waiting, gossiping over their morning coffees and eager to hear the details of Erin's discovery from the horse's mouth.

Erin didn't want to rehash the details of what she had seen—and smelled—over and over all day long, but she knew she would. And their sales would skyrocket because of it. A murder in Bald Eagle Falls was like free advertising. Especially one that happened right behind the store.

Erin was not surprised that Melissa Lee was the first one in the door. Melissa was one of the worst—or best—for spreading gossip in the town. And since she worked part-time for the police department, she often had little snippets of information that she should not, and was eager to share. She liked to make a splash and would take every opportunity to do so.

"Oh, Erin," she gushed, reaching for Erin's forearm and squeezing it as if comforting her for a terrible tragedy. "I couldn't believe it when I heard what you had found." She had a broad smile, as she always did while spreading gossip. She shook her head, dark spiraling curls bouncing in every direction. "How do you do it?" She laughed.

"Don't ask me," Erin told her dryly. "You're welcome to spread the word that someone else could take over the honor any time now. I'd be quite happy to have someone else stumbling over the bodies."

Melissa giggled. "I'll make sure people know."

She made a show of looking over the display case. "Everything looks so good. And I always love the smell of fresh bread first thing in the morning." She took a deep breath of the sweetly scented air. "If you could make that smell into a drink… you could make a fortune. Because that's all I want to do, just drink it in."

"I made some of the white chocolate chip brownies you like," Erin pointed out the brown bars with white dots of chocolate chips. "Not what you want for breakfast, I don't suppose, but you'll need something for dessert tonight."

"Yes," Melissa agreed, "I'll take a couple of those. And I should probably take something in for the police department. Maybe a muffin assortment."

Erin nodded. "Sheriff Wilmot has money on account for the police department. So you don't have to pay for those."

Melissa's brows rose. "Sheriff Wilmot?"

Melissa had recently complained that she was the only one who ever brought treats in for the department, and paid for them out of pocket. Erin had spread the word and ensured that Sheriff Wilmot had liberated some funds from the department budget and donations from the other members of the police department to ensure that Melissa did not have to continue to pay for them herself.

"Yes. You don't need to pay for them. They're covered."

"Oh!" Melissa's cheeks flushed pink. "Well, thank you, Sheriff! I'll be sure to thank him."

"No reason you should have to pay for them all the time, especially when you are only—when you only work part-time hours there."

Melissa nodded. "It's so nice to have someone else step forward."

For a moment, she had been distracted by the food but, as soon as she had picked out the muffins for the department, her thoughts returned to the latest gruesome discovery.

"I can't believe that Simon Simpson was killed right behind your bakery," she told Erin, making sure that her voice was loud enough to carry to the other customers. "What are the chances of that?"

Erin had no idea what the chances were. It seemed to be a fairly common occurrence since she had moved to Bald Eagle Falls. Bodies in the bakery itself or on the property were more common than she wished.

"I didn't have anything to do with it," she pointed out.

"Oh no, of course not. I wouldn't suggest that. Even though…"

Erin eyed her. She wasn't sure she wanted to hear Melissa's latest news.

"Even though what?" she asked eventually, since Melissa would not go on until she'd leaked whatever information she had come to share.

"Well… I wouldn't want to say. The body was picked up by the medical examiner's office this morning, so it isn't like we have his report yet. He hasn't even looked at it. But some things were obvious…"

Erin shrugged. If they were obvious, then she probably already knew them. But Melissa hadn't really come to share her observations with Erin, who had seen the body. She had come to share them with the rest of the town.

"Well, I couldn't help noticing the knife Simon was killed with," Melissa said.

CHAPTER 9

*E*rin's stomach tightened. She didn't want that news to get out. But the police department was bound to find out exactly where that knife had come from. And they probably wouldn't hold the news back from the public.

Nor would they be able to if Melissa was going to announce it in Auntie Clem's.

"Do you really think you should be sharing that?" a voice behind Melissa asked.

Melissa turned partway around to look at the speaker. Erin was surprised to see that it was Lottie Sturm. She was more used to Lottie stirring things up than her being the voice of caution.

Melissa's mouth hung open for a minute as if she were astounded that Lottie would suggest such a thing. She closed it and shook her head. "Everybody is going to find out anyway," she pointed out.

"What if the police aren't ready to release it yet? As someone who works in the police department, aren't you required to follow their lead?"

"Nobody has said anything to me about it being kept quiet," Melissa informed her. "I'm not doing anything wrong."

"Aren't you?"

There was silence in the front of the bakery while everyone waited for

Melissa's answer. Erin could hear Cheyenne in the kitchen, pulling pans off of oven racks.

Melissa's generous mouth twisted into a grimace. She tried to blank her expression, but still looked like she was pouting. She stepped over to the cash register to pay for her order, which Erin placed on the counter. Vic rang up the brownies, and Melissa paid and left, scowling at Lottie as she walked past her.

Vic rang up the muffins separately and put the receipt to the side for Erin so she could keep track of how much money was left in the police department's charge account.

She raised her brows at Erin. Erin recognized the expression of disbelief that Melissa would listen to what Lottie had said instead of just steamrolling over her, as Erin would have predicted.

Erin shrugged in response. They would have to discuss it later.

Lottie approached the counter and looked over the baking in the display case, her expression serious. Erin didn't know whether to make a joke or thank her for her intervention, or to go on as if nothing had happened.

Since Lottie didn't look at her or say anything, Erin decided that the best thing was just to let it go. Whatever Lottie's reasons were for jumping in and stopping a discussion she would normally have encouraged, Erin wasn't going to argue.

Lottie ordered what she wanted in a clipped, no-nonsense tone. She paid for her treats and shot each of the remaining patrons an angry look as they parted to let her pass back out of the store. Erin shook her head and smiled at the next customer.

It was early afternoon, after the lunch rush had passed, that Terry stopped in with K9. Erin refilled his water bottle and offered him a cookie, which he declined. He was trying to stay in shape despite always having multiple desserts available at home. Erin always had the freezer packed with bread, rolls, cookies, and other treats. He was trying to hold himself to one small dessert after supper, and that was it. Erin knew how hard it was to resist the allure of the baking. She felt it too, but didn't want an ever-increasing waistline to take over her life and threaten her health.

Terry didn't leave again immediately after Erin handed him his water. He lingered. There was only one other customer in the bakery. Erin served Mrs. Peach, her next-door neighbor, and Terry was still there after she left.

"Was there something else?" Erin asked. "Are you sure you didn't want a cookie?" She couldn't think of what else he might want.

"No, not a cookie. I just wanted to talk to you alone for a minute. I was hoping that you could help me to find Adrienne."

He stood there looking at her expectantly. Erin opened her mouth and didn't know what to say. Nothing came to mind. She just shook her head. "No… I don't really know where she is right now."

"No?" He studied her. "Are you sure?"

"I know some places she could be, but no, I don't know for sure where she is staying or where she is right now. You know that she's hoping to build a place of her own. I don't know if she has picked out a property yet. She might have."

"Nothing has been registered at Tennessee Land Title. There's nothing in her name. And I somehow doubt that she has set up a shell company while she has been squatting."

Erin shrugged. "Well then, I really don't know."

"What about Bella? Is she here?"

"She won't be here until after school. A few more hours. She'll help with closing."

"Can you call her? Ask her where Adrienne is?"

Erin shook her head. "She's at school. I can't call her while she's in class. They're not allowed to have their phones out during class and I don't want to get her in trouble. You'll have to wait until school lets out. And then… I don't know if she'll talk to you about it."

"We need to talk to Adrienne."

Erin nodded. "Uh-huh."

"Do you have a phone number for her?"

Erin looked for a way around the question. Terry was a law enforcement officer and she was always careful not to lie to him. She sometimes left him with the wrong impression, but she tried not to actually lie. Unless there was no way around it. And then not if it was part of a police inquiry. If it were something about her private life… she felt she still deserved some privacy. But this was a police investigation. A murder investigation.

"A phone number?" Terry repeated. "One that works?"

"I have one, but I don't know whether she will answer it. Or if it is still good."

"Give it to me and I'll see."

Erin reluctantly pulled out her phone and gave him the number she had for Adrienne. Which she very well knew *was* the right number and that if Adrienne didn't answer it, it was because she had it turned off or didn't want to talk to whoever was calling.

"Why don't you call her and see if it works?" Terry suggested. "If she answers, you can give it to me."

"No!" Erin was appalled at the idea. "I'm not setting her up."

"No one said anything about setting her up," Terry said reasonably. "We just need to get in touch with her. We haven't even been able to do the death notification yet. She is the next of kin."

"I'm not calling her for you. If she wants to talk to the police, she can answer when you call."

"What are you protecting her from?"

Erin rolled her eyes. She didn't know why he even bothered to ask. It was perfectly clear what she was trying to protect Adrienne from. She didn't want the police to pursue her as a suspect. It was ridiculous to think that Adrienne had left her children to come into town and stab her estranged husband to death behind the bakery.

There was a pain in her chest when she thought about it. She knew that Adrienne couldn't possibly be involved. Adrienne was very thin. She couldn't have a lot of strength. Her husband would have been able to fend her off easily. Statistics might say that the likeliest suspect was the spouse or ex-partner, but that wasn't always the case. There were plenty of people who were killed by strangers, enemies, or in the course of committing a crime. It wasn't hard to imagine Simon as a criminal. He was a tough character.

"Will you let her know that the police would like to talk to her?" Terry asked.

Erin thought about how that conversation would go. They hadn't yet done the death notification. Did Adrienne know that Simon was dead or not? Erin certainly didn't want to be the one to tell her. If she had already heard it from someone else, maybe from Bella, then she would know why the police wanted to talk to her. She was already dodging them.

"You'll just have to try to reach her," Erin said. "I don't want to get involved."

Terry shook his head. "*You* don't want to get involved. You, who I have to keep out of every other murder investigation in Bald Eagle Falls, you don't want to be involved in this one."

"No. I don't want anything to do with it."

"What about Cindy?" Terry asked.

Erin was thrown. "What about her? I don't remember if… I don't think she was in the bakery that day. But you were there. What do you remember?"

"Cindy is not being helpful either. I'm sure she knows exactly where Adrienne is, but she won't say a word about it."

Since Adrienne had been living on the Prost farm the last time Erin had seen her, Erin was sure Terry was right. Cindy probably had a very good idea of where the family was. She was probably one of the few people who knew exactly where Adrienne and the children were staying.

"I'm sure that when Adrienne is ready to talk to you… she will."

He grunted, not liking her answer. They were impatient to find out where everyone had been at the time of the murder and to be able to pin it on someone.

"You were quite likely the last one to see Simon alive," he told Erin.

"If I was the last one to see him alive, then you were too. Everyone in the bakery Friday afternoon was. Because I didn't see him again after that."

He stood there, looking like he would say more. Maybe he, like Melissa, wanted to talk to her about the murder weapon. Get her take on it. Lay the evidence before her and see what she had to say about it then.

Eventually, K9 whined and nudged against Terry's leg. Terry petted him and scratched his ears. "I'd better be getting on my way."

"See you tonight."

"See you then."

Erin did not wish him luck as he left.

CHAPTER 10

*E*rin had expected to be the one to run out of energy before the
end of the day, but she caught Vic yawning several times in the
afternoon and eventually sent her home. She could nap before having to
make supper and look after cranky-pants Willie. Or maybe Willie could
step up and take care of Vic. Make her a nice dinner and show her how
much he appreciated her.

Erin understood that there was a reason for his irritability and mood
swings. A real, physical explanation. She had fully expected that Willie
would not feel well and would have problems with brain fog, focus, and
being able to follow all of the routines that had previously been easy for
him. But that would all go away quickly enough, and then he would have
more energy than ever and be able to go on with his life.

She had not anticipated the extent of the problems that Willie would
have. She had expected that he would go on just as before, only with a
little more difficulty. But he seemed more like a cancer patient—little
energy to do anything, weight loss, no concentration, always upset about
something. Vic found him difficult to cook for. He said that everything
tasted like metal.

It was a wonder that Vic was still putting up with him and hadn't just
kicked him out until he could be civil again. He had his own house. He

didn't need to hang around the loft. Vic was a better partner than Erin would have been if Terry had behaved the same way.

So Erin and Bella were alone at the bakery at the end of the day, counting up the day's deposit, sweeping the floors, wiping down the counters, and prepping the batters that they would put into the ovens first thing the next morning.

There was a knock on the back door. Erin checked the peephole, worried that it would be a reporter or a cop or someone else with questions about the murder. She didn't want to talk to anyone about it.

But it was not someone in uniform. Or a reporter. Erin slid back the bolt and opened the door.

"Adrienne!"

Adrienne looked around quickly, head tilted, like a little bird. She made a motion with one skinny arm that Erin took as a request to enter, so Erin stepped back and let her in. She closed the door and threw the bolt again. If anyone had followed Adrienne, they were not getting in.

"Adrienne, how are you? Are you okay?"

Adrienne's eyes were rimmed with red and her face was blotchy. She had obviously been crying.

"I can't be long," she said. "The kids are watching Sarah."

Sarah was her baby, far too young to fend for herself or be watched by preteen siblings.

"I guess…" Erin trailed off awkwardly, unsure what to say to the young woman. "The police must have managed to get ahold of you."

"The police?" Adrienne's eyes widened. "No, I've been able to avoid them so far."

"Terry Piper… he asked me for your phone number. I hope you don't mind that I gave it to him. I didn't know what else to do. I didn't want to be guilty of impeding an investigation."

"It's not even on most of the time. Just when the kids might need to get me." Adrienne sniffled and wiped her red eyes.

"But someone told you… about Simon."

"Yes." Adrienne nodded. She sniffled again and shook her head. "I don't know why I'm crying about it. Do you know how many times I wished that man dead? He was so aggravating. I just couldn't deal with him and his nonsense anymore. I wanted to be done with him." She quelled a sob. "And now I am. No more problems from Simon."

"I'm so sorry." Erin wanted to hug her but wasn't sure how it would be received. She touched Adrienne's arm lightly, then withdrew.

55

CHAPTER 11

should get some bread," Adrienne said abruptly. "Could I get some bread?"

"Of course. Let's get what you need from the freezer."

She escorted Adrienne to the freezer full of day-old bread and baking that Erin did her best to give away to those who needed it. She had been able to give some of it to Adrienne before. And she had also donated some through Adele when Adrienne was still too shy to have anything to do with Erin directly.

Erin pulled out several loaves of bread. Straight white bread. She knew what kids liked. They wouldn't want the multigrain or herb stuff. They would want snowy white, evenly sliced bread that they could use for peanut butter and jelly sandwiches. "And some muffins," she murmured. "And cookies. What else do you want? Some pizza shells? Tortillas?"

Adrienne nodded. "Not too much," she cautioned, "I don't want to take more than my share. Just a few things to keep us going."

"There's plenty more; you're not taking too much. Anything I can't find a place for in Bald Eagle Falls, I have to take to the city. I would rather get rid of it here."

Adrienne helped herself to some more muffins and a couple of bags of waffles. "Everything is always so good. You're an angel."

"I'm a baker. That's all."

"You're a good baker. The kids always love your stuff."

"How are they all?"

Adrienne shrugged. "They're okay," she said tentatively. "They don't know yet about Simon. I don't know how I'm going to tell them."

"Are they all his?"

Adrienne hesitated, then nodded. "Yes... we had such an up-and-down relationship. He would be out of my life and I would think I was never going to see him again, and then one day he would show up and... I just couldn't tell him no. I especially couldn't keep him from the kids. It wouldn't be fair to them. But now... I guess I didn't do them any favors letting them develop a relationship with him. Now they will all be upset that he is never coming back again."

She swallowed, and she and Erin filled up a couple of grocery bags with the baked goods.

"Maybe I just won't tell them," Adrienne said. "They're used to him taking off. They'll think that he's just skipped out again. And that one day, maybe he'll come back again."

"I don't know if that would be the best thing," Erin ventured. But what did she know? She wasn't a mom. She hadn't raised any kids. Not with a partner and not by herself. She didn't have any right to think she knew better than Adrienne about how to raise her children.

"I know," Adrienne admitted. "But it's just not fair. It is... so unfair. They're just little children, and now they'll grow up without any dad in their lives. Ever. Do you know what that's going to be like for them?"

"I grew up in foster care," Erin told her. "At least they still have you. They don't have to be passed from one family to another, thinking no one wants them."

"How am I going to raise them by myself? How can I be everything to them? What if something happens to me? Then what?"

"Don't think about the worst. It won't help them. You were raising them by yourself anyway. Before Simon came back. And you were going to kick him out, not let him stay around to raise them."

"I was trying. I don't know if I would have been able to keep saying no. He always... wore me down sooner or later. That was why I was trying not to even see him. If I didn't respond to him, he couldn't find me in town or anywhere else, then he would give up eventually and go somewhere else."

And what would have happened if Simon had refused to give up? If he had waited back behind the bakery watching to see if Adrienne came by to collect some day-old bread for the family? What if there were a confrontation and Simon wouldn't just give up and go somewhere else?

But it still didn't fit. Nothing that she had thought of so far had worked.

"It's better with him out of your life," Bella told Adrienne, her voice sharper than Erin would have expected. "Now you can move on and you can be in control of your life and your family. You don't have to worry about him tracking you down and showing up. You don't have to worry about his influence on the kids or him taking all your money." Her voice was angry. "Can you imagine if he had cleaned out your bank account with all the settlement money sitting there?"

Adrienne's face was already pale. But at Bella's words, she looked even whiter. The money was her one chance to build a home for her children instead of living in a tent in the woods or with other people. It was her one chance to have a permanent home and the stability the children needed. If Simon had taken that away or threatened to…

"When did you see him last?" Erin asked. "He was in here on Friday looking for you, but I just kept shooing him out. Even called Terry to get him out of here the last time. Then he stopped coming."

"He was persistent," Adrienne said. "He didn't like to give up. He always had dreams, ways he was going to make it big. He would go from one thing to another, but he always had something… some kind of plan to finally get all the money he wanted, or the fancy car, or watch, or whatever the new thing was. He had it all figured out, and this time, it was all going to work out. But if it worked out… it was never enough. He'd go on to the next scheme and he'd lose it all. He always bragged that he'd made millions." Her mouth twisted into a tight grimace. "And I don't think he'd made that much. But he always said that he had made millions but lost millions, too. He said it wasn't so hard, making a million dollars. The hard thing was hanging on to it."

"I think if I ever made a million dollars, I would be able to hang on to it," Erin said. "I think I'd hold on to it pretty tight."

"The man never made a thing," Bella said. "Forget making millions. He hardly ever even walked away from the table with a profit. If he made ten bucks on one hand, he'd lose fifteen on the next."

"You don't know all of that," Adrienne said, looking away from Erin, clearly embarrassed.

And she was probably right. When had Bella ever had the opportunity to watch Simon playing cards?

"I have ears," Bella countered. "I hear people talk."

"Well, people exaggerate," Adrienne said. "Even me, if I was mad at him. You can't assume that everyone is telling the absolute truth."

"I know he wasn't good for you and the kids. I know that he left you high and dry, that he didn't even look after you when you were having a baby, just left you like that. No money. No home. Four little ones and a baby on the way, and he just left. Didn't bother coming back for two years!"

Adrienne looked at Erin, spots of color appearing in her cheeks. "Bell. You need to watch what you say. You'll get me in big trouble."

Bella closed her mouth. She looked at Adrienne, then at her boss, then went back to cleaning up and prepping for the next day.

"Erin would never do anything to get you in trouble," she said. "I'm just blowing off steam. She wouldn't repeat it." Bella looked at Erin over her shoulder. "Would you?"

"No. But you do need to be careful what you say and who you say it around. Adrienne is going to have enough trouble with the police looking into Simon's death without either of us saying anything to anyone. And you..."

Erin looked at Bella, chewing on her lip. She didn't like to think that Bella might have lost her temper with Simon and done something she couldn't take back. But Bella was fiercely protective of Adrienne and the children. And sooner or later, the police would put everything together and come knocking at their door again.

"Just be careful, Bella. Be careful what you say and do. I wouldn't want you to get in any trouble."

CHAPTER 12

*I*t had been a long day, and Erin didn't feel much like making a meal, even just for herself. It was easy enough to prepare a sandwich or open a can of soup, but she didn't feel up to even just that. She suspected Terry would be engrossed in the Simon Simpson case and wouldn't be able to join her for dinner. She called him from her car after closing up.

"Erin, is everything okay?"

There had been enough drama in Erin's life, especially around untimely deaths in Bald Eagle Falls, that she supposed he could be excused for immediately worrying that something might be wrong. Had she found another body? Been threatened by someone? Heard something in the parking lot in the dark?

"Everything is fine," she assured him. "I just wanted to see if you wanted to go out to dinner. Can you take a break from your work?"

"I'm supposed to be off."

"I know. But are you actually going to put everything aside and come home?"

There was a pause while Terry considered this. Maybe he had been planning to go home but, looking at everything on his desk now, realized that there was no way he would be getting out of the office until late.

"Uh… you're probably right," he admitted. "I have a few things that still need to be done. Avenues of inquiry that need to be followed up on before the trail starts to go cold."

"Right," Erin agreed. "So, do you want to come home for supper or stop for something at the restaurant…?"

She hoped he would understand that her suggestion of a restaurant meant she didn't want to cook. He should know her at least that well.

"Uh… a restaurant is fine. I was probably just going to order something in."

If he ordered takeout, he wouldn't have to interrupt his work. He could just work at his desk. Or he and the rest of the police department would eat a pizza or two in the boardroom while discussing the case. It would mean that she wouldn't see him all night. Probably not before she went to bed. She had an early bedtime due to the need to rise early in the morning to bake before the opening of Auntie Clem's.

"Of course I'd love to see you," Terry said, his thoughts following these same lines. "I'm sorry. Yes. We can go to a restaurant."

"It will probably be good for you to get away from the office for a little while. Give you a new perspective."

"That's true," Terry agreed. "Sometimes stepping away from a case for a few minutes is just what you need to make a breakthrough."

"So you can take a few minutes for supper?"

"Sure. What are you in the mood for tonight?"

"I don't even know. I'm too tired to make a decision."

"Sure," Terry agreed. "I don't think you got enough sleep last night, and the gossip at Auntie Clem's probably has you all worn out."

"It's been quite the day," Erin admitted. She thought about Bella and Adrienne. With the right encouragement, she might learn more about the progress of the investigation from Terry. His investigation might be focused in another direction altogether. Maybe she didn't have to worry about the two young women.

"How about Chinese?" Terry suggested.

"Sure. Whatever you like is good for me. As long as all I have to do is sit there and eat it."

"Okay. Are you leaving now, or are you still closing up?"

"I'm in the car. I'll be there in five minutes."

"I'll see you there, then."

~

In a few minutes, they were seated at a table in the Chinese restaurant. Erin just motioned to Terry when he asked her what she wanted. He knew what she liked, and she was in no mood to have to choose. He ordered their favorite dishes.

"You shouldn't have gone in today," he said. "You really look worn out."

"I'll be fine. It was a long day, though. I sent Vic home early."

"You should have sent yourself home early."

"I like one of us always to be there, not just a couple of the part-time employees. Other than for the ladies' tea."

"A couple of hours in the afternoon wouldn't hurt."

"No… it wouldn't hurt," Erin admitted. It wasn't a rule that was set in stone. She didn't mind leaving Charley in charge, even though she wasn't the best baker, because she was the half-owner of the bakery. And she had sometimes left Bella in charge. Though in light of the current circumstances, she probably wouldn't do that again if she could help it.

Terry's head was cocked. Erin looked at him as if she were coming out of a dream. "Sorry, did you ask something else?"

"No. Just wondering where you are."

"Nowhere. Just tired." She didn't want him to read the truth in her eyes and averted her gaze. She had a sip of water. She was probably dehydrated. She had been talking a lot and had not thought much about taking care of herself. She was sure she had stopped for lunch but couldn't remember what she had eaten; it seemed like a long time ago. Her stomach ached with hunger.

"So, how is the investigation going?" she asked.

Terry paused to take a drink himself. He would have had a beer if he had been at home but, since he was still returning to the office, he had settled for an RC instead.

"I know that discussing the case over dinner is not ideal. And you're already tired, but…" He trailed off, watching her.

"What?"

"You saw the body. You saw the murder weapon."

Erin swallowed. She just nodded, not answering.

"I didn't ask you anything about it that day because I didn't realize it was special."

"There was something special about it?"

"I thought it was just a knife out of a block set, like you would get at the department store. Some kind of chef's set that any household might have."

Erin nodded. She hadn't said anything about it then, hoping that was the direction the police department would go. It was just a regular knife that anyone could have bought or had in their kitchen. Just an average, run-of-the-mill kitchen knife.

"But I'm told by the techs who were helping me to identify it that it is a cake knife."

Erin nodded. "Anyone could have a cake knife."

"But it isn't one that someone would have just picked up at the department store."

"A kitchen store would have them, though."

"It's a high-end knife. The type of thing that a bakery would have. High-quality materials and workmanship."

"But anyone could have one. It doesn't have to be a bakery."

"I suppose you have one at Auntie Clem's."

Erin nodded. "Sure. Of course."

"So you could show it to me."

Erin took a deep breath in and let it out again.

"You've checked to make sure that you still have yours at the bakery?" Terry pressed.

"I have more than one. I could show you."

He studied her as the waitress delivered their dishes, arranging them on the table.

"Then I guess the question is… are you missing any? Are they all the same brand and model?"

"I bought them at different times. They're not all identical."

"You didn't say whether you are missing any."

Erin sighed and rubbed her forehead, where a knot of tension was gathering.

"Just one," she sighed.

CHAPTER 13

Terry gazed at Erin steadily.

"I see. And how did your missing knife end up in Mr. Simon Simpson?"

"I certainly didn't put it there."

Terry chuckled, but he didn't sound amused. K9 looked up at him and readjusted his position, putting his head down on his paws.

"Who had access to the knife?"

"Anyone in the kitchen. Me, Vic, Charley, and any of the part-time employees. We don't allow the public into the kitchen, but sometimes there are other people… deliverymen, repairmen, people picking up day-old bread."

"Who does that include for the past week?"

Erin hadn't had any repairmen in. All of the employees had taken at least one shift. She didn't discuss who used the day-old bread program.

"I already gave Sheriff Wilmot the list of employees and their phone numbers. So he knows everyone who was on shift. I don't think… I can't remember anyone else that we've had in the kitchen in the days before Simon was killed. A few deliveries, but they're in and out pretty quickly."

"Adrienne?"

Erin shook her head. "Not in the week or so before Simon was killed."

"How long was the knife missing?"

"I'm not sure. Like I said, we have others, but Vic had noticed that one had gone astray around the middle or end of the week. It's hard to know when something isn't there anymore. You don't necessarily miss it right away. I figured it would turn up sooner or later. Sometimes people put things away in the wrong drawer or put it on top of the fridge or something silly like that while juggling things."

"You allow people to juggle knives in the kitchen?"

Erin rolled her eyes and gave a tired laugh at the way her words had come out.

Terry was still serious, and he also looked tired, but he was trying to lighten the mood and keep them from getting bogged down in the investigation. It was too easy for them to get tangled up in the immediate, in something that was pressing like a murder investigation, and to forget to take care of their relationship. They had not arranged to eat dinner together just to further the investigation. It was supposed to be their chance to connect.

"I know it looks bad," Erin said, "But couldn't it have been an outsider? A vagrant or someone who was passing through and argued with Simon? I mean, he didn't exactly steer clear of trouble. He liked to threaten."

"How did that person get your cake knife?"

Erin rubbed her forehead. She dished up a little food from each of the bowls. "I don't know. Maybe…" She tried to think of a scenario in which the cake knife had been taken from Auntie Clem's for an innocent reason, and then someone else had gotten their hands on it. Just one of those things, a bunch of things happening at the same time to cause the perfect storm. A murder that looked like it had been committed by an employee of Auntie Clem's when it had not. "I'll have to think about it," she admitted.

"I would be willing to entertain the possibility that it was someone else in Bald Eagle Falls or someone else from outside of Bald Eagle Falls," Terry said. "But we would have to be able to explain how a knife from your bakery was used as the murder weapon."

"I can't believe any of my employees could have done something like that. And if it was someone from the bakery, why would they leave the knife there? They had to know it would point right back at the bakery employees. Why not take it back into the bakery, clean it off, and put it in the drawer? No one would know the difference."

Terry shrugged. "Criminals are famous for doing some very stupid, self-incriminating things. If he was killed in the heat of the moment, I could easily see an unsophisticated killer leaving the weapon behind even though it pointed back at them. That's how we catch people. He—or she —panics and runs away, leaving it behind."

"But the body was there for two days. They could have returned to get it when no one else was around. If it was an employee, she would have a key and could let herself in when no one was around. Wash the knife off and put it away. Or put it on top of the fridge or in a place where it didn't belong so everyone would think it had just been misplaced for a few days. No one would connect it to the murder."

Terry's lips compressed together. "I think we would still have figured out that it was the murder weapon. There aren't a lot of knives around that fit the profile. That wide spade shape is pretty unique."

Erin shook her head. She ate some of the noodles on her plate, even though she felt more tired than hungry. "I just don't think it could have been anyone at Auntie Clem's."

"There's another possibility."

She looked at him hopefully.

"What if it was Simon who took it?" Terry suggested. "One of the dangers of arming yourself is that your weapon could be used against you. What if there was a struggle and someone else ended up with his weapon?"

"Yeah…" Erin liked that idea. She tried to figure out how Simon could have gotten his hands on the knife. He'd been in the bakery several times asking about Adrienne. He had come to the back once and his body had been found behind the bakery.

What if the back door had been left unlocked at some point? An employee going out to smoke and then forgetting to lock it again? A delivery man who brought in more than one load and had left the door propped for five minutes while he returned for his second load? Or what if an employee had used the knife in the front of the shop and had put it down on the counter where Simon could reach when he had been in?

She tried to picture each time she had talked to Simon. Had she kept her eyes on him the whole time? Watched every move that he made? She probably hadn't. She had tried to show him she wasn't interested in helping him by going on with her other work as if he hadn't been there. She had deliberately ignored him, hoping that would make him leave sooner.

"I guess it's possible," she said. "And if Simon was the one who stole it, then the killer could have been anyone. Not just an employee." She felt lighter at the possibility. The idea that the killer could be one of her employees had been tying her gut in knots.

Terry sighed. Having a larger pool to draw on was not necessarily good for him. It was much easier for the police department if they only had a few suspects. Or only one.

CHAPTER 14

*E*rin couldn't help smiling at his dismay. "Simon wasn't such a nice guy," she pointed out. "Did he have a lot of enemies?" Bella and Adrienne had implied that he was a gambler, swindler, or both. He had abandoned his family, which probably meant he'd had interests elsewhere. Maybe he was the type who had "a girl in every port" as he gambled his way around the country. For long-suffering Adrienne to say that she'd wanted to throttle Simon more than once, he must have really pushed the limits.

"We'll have more suspects than we know what to do with," Terry admitted, "if we don't find a way to narrow the pool."

"Well…" Erin ate a few more bites of her dinner, hungrier now as she considered unknown suspects instead of her friends and employees. If they could prove it was someone else, she wouldn't have to worry about Bella or Adrienne or anyone else. They could all go on as usual and forget that Simon had ever been a part of their lives. "What do you know about the time of death? Did you get anything from the medical examiner?"

"We're looking at Friday afternoon or evening, shortly after you kicked him out."

"After *you* kicked him out," Erin corrected.

"After *we* kicked him out."

Erin frowned.

"He had eaten part of the cinnamon roll he bought from you," Terry contributed, giving her more details. "He wouldn't have carried it around for several days."

"No," Erin agreed, nodding. He must have been killed within a couple of hours of leaving Auntie Clem's. Had he been interrupted after eating part of it? Had he gotten hungry after standing around watching for Adrienne and started picking at it, or had he met his fate within just a few minutes of leaving the bakery?

"Did the ME examine the stomach contents?" she asked. "They can pinpoint the time of death from that, can't they?"

"Only if they knew what time he ate the cinnamon roll. And it will keep dissolving in the stomach acids after death so, when the body has been there for two days already, it's pretty much useless. But..." he frowned and stopped himself. He shook his head. "Nothing."

"What?" Erin demanded.

Terry concentrated on a sweet and sour chicken wing. "These are really good."

Erin watched him, waiting. He wasn't doing a good job distracting her from the fact that he had nearly told her something and then taken it back. She knew that he was holding something back, and she was going to wait until she knew what it was.

Terry looked at her after a moment. "So how *was* the gossip at Auntie Clem's today? I assume everyone now knows everything there was to know about Mr. Simpson and how he was killed?"

"*But* what?"

He raised an eyebrow. "Hmm?"

"But what about the stomach contents? They found something else? He'd had pizza for lunch? Swallowed an SD card? Was muling drugs?"

Terry was shaking his head, but didn't fill in the facts. Erin stopped eating and sat back.

"I'm sorry," Terry said, "you know there are things I can't tell you. And that there are things that we hold back from the public."

Erin reviewed the conversation in her mind. He hadn't said that the ME had finished the autopsy yet or had examined or not examined the stomach contents. He had just made general statements about it. Statements that Erin figured would have been replaced with details if he had known them.

Yet there was still something about what Simon had eaten or not eaten or the time of death that Terry had been about to tell her and then had thought better of.

"This is something about what he ate?" she asked. "About the part of a cinnamon roll...?"

Terry gave no sign, positive or negative.

Erin didn't like to think about what she had seen in detail; she didn't want it to be lodged in her long-term memory. But she had seen Simon's body. She had stood near enough to smell it so clearly that she had been sick. The horrible smell of decaying meat, the offal, and the faint smell of... cheese?

Erin steadied herself on the table and took a quick drink, forcing the water down and hoping it would not bring anything else up.

No, not the smell of cheese. The smell of Parmesan cheese always made her think of vomit. She had looked it up once, curious as to why the two should be connected in her mind.

"Butyric acid," she said finally, her stomach back under control.

"What?" Terry was bewildered. He shook his head with no idea what she was talking about.

"It's what makes vomit and Parmesan cheese stink."

"Okay... and you're telling me this because..."

"Because I could smell it on Simon. Not very well, because of... you know... the decomposition. But that means he had vomited, doesn't it?"

Terry closed his mouth and shook his head. But he wasn't denying it. He just couldn't believe that Erin had figured it out without his telling her.

"So..." Erin tried to follow the fact to its natural conclusions. "He didn't have anything in his stomach because he'd already thrown up? So stomach contents aren't going to help establish time of death."

Terry shrugged. "I didn't tell you any of this."

"Okay," Erin agreed. "I never heard anything from you. I figured it all out by myself."

Terry nodded his agreement. Erin continued to eat her dinner. She really shouldn't be talking about such things while she was eating. She got nauseated easily enough without trying to remember how Simon's remains looked and smelled. She wasn't the kind of person who could just shut off her body's natural reaction to such things. It was like a poison. Once exposed to the scene, there was no way to stop her body's reaction.

"Poison," Erin murmured. Looking across the table, she met Terry's eyes.

"What?" He broke eye contact, looking out the window beside the table.

"He threw up. Why? Do you think… he was poisoned?"

Terry cleared his throat. "There's no way to know that at this point. The ME needs to do an autopsy and lab tests have to be done. All of that will be determined eventually. For now, all we can do is speculate. It is… *suggestive* of poisoning."

"Someone poisoned him and then stabbed him?"

"It's been known to happen. Many times, poisoning doesn't work exactly how the killer expected, whether it is attempted suicide or murder. The victim gets sick and then recovers. The victim throws up, expelling the poison, or enough of it that he doesn't die. Or it is a long, lingering illness and the would-be killer gets impatient. He ups the dose, changes the poison, or changes the method. You find a lot of cases once you start looking."

"On TV shows or movies, they poison someone and they die. Or have a really close call and end up in the hospital with their stomach pumped and recover."

But Erin knew the details of more than one case of poisoning where death had not been immediate. Terry's words should not come as a surprise.

"Just like any method, there are many different ways it can go wrong," Terry said. "And it is usually a long-term method. Not the immediate frothing-at-the-mouth thing you see with cyanide poisoning shown in movies."

"So what killed him? The poison didn't work, so the killer switched methods and stabbed him?"

"We have to wait for the ME's findings. But that would be my guess. Or…"

Erin cocked her head and looked at him curiously, wondering whether he were going to tell her this time or try to keep it a secret again and make her guess.

"Or what?"

"Or it was two different people. One who poisoned him and one who stabbed him. Two different suspects, two different motives."

"What do you think the chances of that are?"

"I wouldn't want to guess. I'm assuming there was only one killer, but have to stay open to other possibilities, especially considering his reputation. Someone who has an alibi for the stabbing might not have one for the poisoning, and vice versa. Ditto access to the poison or the knife. We may have two killers."

*E*rin enlarged the text on her computer and read the short obituary for Simon Simpson. The Bald Eagle Falls weekly would be out in two days and would probably contain a longer obituary and maybe an article or two on the murder. Still, she would have to make do with the bare-bones obituary that the funeral home had posted on their website until a more comprehensive version was published. Erin imagined that the funeral home had quickly put together a short-form biography to stave off the calls that they were getting until the family provided them with something else. And they would refer any inquiries about how he had died to the police.

There wasn't much to be gleaned from the obituary. Adrienne and the children were mentioned, although Erin noticed that not all of the children's names had been listed. Both baby Sarah and another of the children had been omitted, despite Adrienne's assertion that they were all Simon's.

But there was also a sister living in Bald Eagle Falls. If Simon's family were really multigenerational residents of Bald Eagle Falls and the surrounding area, it made sense that he would have some family around. Families were much smaller than they had been a few decades ago; it was not uncommon to have only one or two siblings now instead of six or eight. A lot of lines were dying out.

Simon's sister's name was Scarlett Simpson and, with a few quick searches, Erin managed to find her address. Erin had found that the residents of Bald Eagle Falls were not as concerned with protecting their addresses as city-dwellers were. People in Bald Eagle Falls went to school, church, and other community events together. They all knew where the other members of the community lived. There wasn't any way to keep it a secret.

She quickly arranged a plate of cookies, tarts, and dessert bars using what she had in the freezer. They would defrost quickly once she got into the car. By the time she arrived, they would be thawed through. That was one benefit of the Tennessee summer heat.

There were a few other cars in front of Scarlett Simpson's home. She'd probably had a pretty constant stream of visitors since the news of Simon's death had spread through the town.

It was an older house. A hundred years or more, Erin would guess. Older than Clementine's house, which Erin had inherited. It had, she assumed, housed several generations of Simpson family members. It appeared to be in pretty good shape. Carefully maintained rather than falling into disrepair after so long.

Erin walked up to the door and rang the bell. She knew that the proper etiquette was probably to knock or yoo-hoo and enter, allowing Scarlett to stay where she was instead of answering the door whenever another visitor arrived—no point in running her off her feet.

The door opened within a few seconds. It was an older woman, not someone Simon's age. Erin did a double-take and realized that it was Betty, an elderly woman who was a regular customer at Auntie Clem's.

"Oh, Erin," she greeted. "No need to ring the bell. Come on in."

Betty took Erin by the arm and escorted her first to a table piled with a mountain of casseroles and platters, exclaiming over the sweets, and then took her into the cool, dimly lit parlor where the mourners were gathered. There were murmured conversations, sniffles, and soft sobs.

"Scarlett, dear," Betty addressed a woman in her thirties at the center of the gathering. "I don't know whether you know Erin Price? She just brought a lovely plate of desserts. She runs Auntie Clem's Bakery. You know? Dear Clementine's great niece."

"Hi," the woman with long, sleek, dark-brown hair nodded. "Thank you so much. That was very thoughtful."

"I hope I'm not intruding," Erin said awkwardly. "I didn't really know

Simon, but I'm very sorry for your loss and wanted to express my condolences."

"You're very kind. Why don't you come sit down and we'll tell you some of our stories about him?"

Betty nudged Erin toward an empty chair, and she sat down. Betty headed back toward the front door to man her post.

"She's so nice," Scarlett said. "And I happen to know she didn't even like Simon. I don't know exactly what he did to her when he was younger, but she's still holding on to a grudge. Or she was. I guess it's over now."

"Oh," Erin didn't know what to say to this revelation. "Well… I've always admired Betty. It's very nice of her to help you out."

"Some people just know what to do," Scarlett said, nodding.

Erin felt like she was the opposite. One of the people who never knew what to do. She always seemed to bumble through things until someone showed her the right way. She was grateful for Betty being at the door and helping her through what might otherwise have been awkward.

"I only met Simon when he got into town a couple of weeks ago. But I guess you guys grew up here?" she asked Scarlett.

"Yes. We lived here with our parents and grandparents. I stayed on. Simon… always had somewhere else to go. He had some big thing he had to try… some new venture or sure thing… he hated staying in one place."

"Wanderlust?" Erin suggested. "I moved around a lot from the time that I was young. Got used to it. This is the longest that I have ever stayed in one place."

"I guess some people are homebodies and some just have to be out adventuring. I always knew that Simon would be the one to leave. I thought he'd come back after a while, but…"

"I guess he must have returned a few times, with Adrienne being here," Erin suggested.

Scarlett rolled her eyes. "Adrienne is a lovely person," she said, "but I wish she and Simon had never met. He was always so… entangled with her. They were either all goo-goo eyes and making plans, or he'd had enough and was taking off."

And cleaning out the bank account before he left.

"And Adrienne wasn't from around here?"

"Not exactly. It would have been better if she had just stayed away."

CHAPTER 16

*D*o you think…" Rae Young, a woman Erin didn't know well, leaned forward in her seat, her voice low, "Was she the one who…?" Her meaning was clear, even if she didn't finish the question.

Scarlett rocked back in her seat.

"I can't see Adrienne doing something like that," she proclaimed, shaking her head. "She loved Simon. She was the only one who put up with all his crap." She continued to shake her head adamantly. "I can't see her doing anything to hurt him."

"But he wasn't faithful to her," Rae pointed out. "A woman scorned… even Adrienne couldn't ignore it when he took up with someone right under her nose."

Erin sat listening, eager to hear the gossip about who else might have a motive. She hoped that Scarlett was right and that Adrienne hadn't had anything to do with Simon's death, but she still had that worried knot in her stomach, that feeling of dread that at any moment, the whole world might come crashing down around her and Adrienne would be arrested for the murder.

If there were another woman, then that woman would have just as much of a motive to kill Simon. Well, maybe not just as good as the woman struggling with raising his five—or three—children on her own and worrying that he would somehow get his hands on the money she had managed to get to build the house.

But still a good motive. People killed out of jealousy all the time. Maybe Simon had told the other woman that he was going back to Adrienne. That he wasn't going to divorce her as he had promised, but instead needed to take care of his children. When, of course, he just wanted to worm his way in to get the money.

"Who was he seeing in town?" Scarlett asked. She ran her fingers through her long hair, sweeping it back over her shoulders away from her face. "I thought… he was always pretty good about at least keeping his affairs out of town."

Rae shook her head. "Emily Johnson," she pronounced, drawing muffled gasps of shock—real or pretended, Erin wasn't sure which—from the other mourners.

"The schoolteacher?" Scarlett shook her head in disbelief. "She was here yesterday. Brought a casserole. She didn't say… are you sure? I don't think Simon had anything to do with her."

"Not after he was finished breaking her heart, maybe," the gossip said, "but I saw them together. There's no doubt. And if I saw them, then other people did, too. I'm sure Adrienne would have heard about it from some quarter."

"Did you tell her?" Scarlett asked.

"Me? I wouldn't do that!" The woman gave a little head shake. "I did ask her if she knew Emily. I thought that she should at least have her eyes open. Someone would tell her sooner or later, and she might as well be prepared for it."

"Simon and Emily Johnson? She's always been so quiet. When was this? Recently?"

"Last time he was in town. When was that? A year ago? Two?"

Scarlett didn't answer the question.

"Why would Adrienne do anything about it now?" Erin asked, unable to keep quiet. "If it happened a year or two ago, and Adrienne wasn't getting back together with Simon, then why would it be an issue now?"

"Do you really think any of that matters?" Rae challenged, black eyes sparkling. "When you hear that your man has been messing around with another woman in town, right under your nose, does any of that come into it? I would be furious. They were still married. She was raising his children. And instead of stepping up and taking responsibility, she discovers he's catting around on her. He probably didn't even come back to see Adrienne. He probably planned to take up with Emily again."

"No," Erin disagreed. "It wasn't because of another woman that he came back here."

Everyone turned their eyes toward her, curious to find out what she knew.

"You don't know why Simon came home," Scarlett challenged. "He wanted to see his family. Me. His children. I know that Adrienne turned him out, but they were talking for a few days; there was the possibility of them getting back together up until Friday." She dabbed at the corners of her eyes. "Oh, if he could just have settled down. Maybe this wouldn't have happened if she had taken him back."

Erin didn't want to badmouth Simon before his sister and the other mourners and supporters. She had no intention of being unkind and hurting anyone.

"He wanted to see if he could work things out with Adrienne," she said, agreeing with Scarlett's statement. Simon had sought out Adrienne. He had been trying to work things out with her. Whether it was because he genuinely wanted to be with her and with his children or was just trying to get his hands on the money, Erin didn't know. But Simon had been trying to reconcile.

Her words hung in the air. Everyone was expecting more. To hear some dirt. Scarlett eyed her. Had Simon told Scarlett about the money and she was waiting to see if Erin would bring it up? Or was she completely innocent as to the reason Simon had really come back?

"But I don't blame Adrienne for not taking him back," she asserted. "And I don't think that she had anything to do with his death. Adrienne couldn't do something like that. Even if she was in a jealous rage… she has the children to look after. She wasn't even in town that day."

"How do you know that?" Rae challenged.

"Simon was looking for her and she wasn't around. She was lying low, trying to avoid seeing him."

"Would have made more sense to just *off* him," Rae said. "Why sneak around and have to limit her life to avoid seeing him? Easier and cleaner to just get him out of the way. Not have to worry about him coming back to town again." She looked at Scarlett. "I don't mean it was justified. I'm just saying what *she* would have thought."

"Simon was a pretty bad husband," Scarlett admitted. "He was a good daddy, cared about his kids, but he wasn't a very good partner to Adrienne."

He was a good daddy? Erin didn't challenge the assertion out loud, but she couldn't help wondering where Scarlett was coming from. Maybe he loved his children. But abandoning them didn't show that love. It wasn't okay to be an attentive father for a day or two, buy the kids milkshakes, and then disappear again for a couple more years. With all the family's savings.

"Well, it isn't like Adrienne didn't do some… exploring of her own," one of the other women provided. "She was no innocent babe waiting for him to come back home to her."

Sly looks passed between some of the women. Erin shifted uncomfortably. She didn't know anything about Adrienne's private life. She had never seen Adrienne with a man. She was with her children, at work, or with Bella. It was rare for her to even be without the children. On the occasions when she had come to see Erin on her own, the children were playing in the park nearby, left alone for just a few minutes. When did she have time to have an affair?

"I didn't know that Adrienne was seeing anyone," she said as neutrally as she could, trying not to show her bias for Adrienne and against Simon. It wasn't really the place to show her antagonism for Simon.

"She's had her… relationships," Rae asserted. "Don't let her fool you."

"Is there something wrong with her having relationships with someone else when Simon was gone? It wasn't like he was off to war or something like that."

He had abandoned her. Why would anyone expect her to wait for his return and put her social life on hold indefinitely?

The women seemed shocked at the suggestion. A double standard. Fine for Simon to leave her behind and have a girl at every port. But not okay for Adrienne to find solace with someone else?

"She was a married woman," Scarlett insisted. "Any virtuous married woman would have waited for him to return. She wouldn't have sullied herself with other men."

Virtue. A concept Erin didn't know if she would ever understand.

Why it was okay for a man to have whatever relationships he pleased and it was just brushed off as men having needs or boys being boys, yet for a woman to have a relationship before marriage or outside her failed marriage was somehow seen as a major character flaw and a disgrace.

"It's too bad that no one stepped forward to help her take care of those kids," Erin said. "Since Simon wasn't willing to do it."

There was silence in the room. Erin had done what she had just told herself she wouldn't do, pointing out the dead man's flaws. But it wasn't like everyone didn't already know them.

"He was such a scamp as a boy," Scarlett said, either changing the subject or turning those flaws into something boyish and silly instead of admitting her brother had some major character flaws and had been a deadbeat. "He was always getting into trouble one way or another. Schoolteachers, church, running around with other little hooligans around the neighborhood. How many times did they break Mr. Hanes's front window with a baseball? I'll bet that man regretted moving into a house across from the park!"

"Do you remember how they used to chase the little girls at school?" Rae asked. "Cooties! The boys and girls were always teasing each other. Funny the way that they fight all the way through the early grades, and then all that attention turns into... a different kind of attention in the teen years."

"It's all just practice," Scarlett agreed. "He never stopped chasing the girls. It was just that when he caught them..." She gave a high giggle.

"The only reason he liked Adrienne was because she was the new girl," Rae declared. "She was something different, novel. She wasn't someone he had known his whole life like the other girls. That was why he pursued her."

"And caught her," Scarlett pointed out.

There were indulgent chuckles from around the room. Erin closed her eyes, trying to remember something from months ago. Back when she had first met Adrienne.

"*Were* they married?" she asked Scarlett.

They had asserted that Adrienne was a married woman and that Simon was a poor husband, but Erin had lodged in her mind the idea that Adrienne was not, in fact, married. She was an independent person. She had fallen for Simon Simpson, but had they actually tied the knot? Or had Adrienne refused to be tied down to a man, just like she had refused to move to the city where there were homeless shelters available because she didn't want her children put in that atmosphere? She wanted them to be outside, running and playing in the fresh air, not cooped up in some program where they had to follow strict rules, go to school in a classroom, and be exposed to street people with TB, fleas, and lice.

Scarlett looked at the other women, hesitating. Erin knew that the church ladies would still consider it a sin if Adrienne had been with other men while unmarried. But maybe a little less than cheating on her husband while they were married.

"No," Scarlett admitted finally, "they were never actually officially married."

"Adrienne didn't want any part of it," Rae said flatly. "Maybe if she had tied the knot, Simon would have stayed home."

But Scarlett shook her head. She knew that it wouldn't have made any difference to her brother.

CHAPTER 17

*T*here was a knock on the door and, a moment later, Betty escorted Mrs. Foster in with her two youngest children. She relieved the woman of a casserole dish and put it on the table with the rest of the offerings.

The Fosters were some of Erin's favorite customers. Peter, the oldest, was her special friend. He was a very serious and mature child and had celiac disease. He was delighted to be able to go to a bakery and pick out whatever he wanted, just like the other kids he went to school with, instead of being limited to whatever stale boxed cookies or bread sat languishing on the shelves of the Bald Eagle Falls grocery store. Before Auntie Clem's, one of his parents had occasionally made the drive out to the city and could pick up a specialty item, but that was rare. And Mrs. Foster did not have much time to bake special foods for him.

But it was a weekday and school had just started up again. With none of the bigger kids to help, Mrs. Foster had her hands full with Traci and baby Allan. Traci was a very active, very strong-willed preschooler, and Allan tended to be fussy and fretful. His disposition was improving as they identified what foods he reacted to and eliminated them from his diet. Erin would have been grumpy if her stomach hurt all the time too.

"You know Abigail Foster," Betty said to Scarlett, "and her children."

Mrs. Foster shook hands with Scarlett, and Betty helped to shuffle people around to make space for her and Traci. Allan was still small enough to cuddle in her lap if he would stay quiet. Mrs. Foster settled her diaper bag between her feet and pulled out a gluten-free teething biscuit from Auntie Clem's, tipping it toward Erin in a salute before giving it to Allan.

"I don't know what I would do without Auntie Clem's Bakery," she told Erin and the rest of the room. "You are such a lifesaver."

"How is Allan doing?"

"Not bad," Mrs. Foster said, "He's sleeping better, which is a great blessing."

Erin nodded. She could only imagine the difficulty of raising five active children on insufficient sleep.

Traci homed in on Erin and darted away from her mother before Mrs. Foster could grab her.

"Cook-kie!" Traci demanded, walking right up to Erin.

Erin laughed while Mrs. Foster tried to correct Traci and get her to come back to sit down, but Traci refused, repeating her demand for a cookie from the woman she knew to be the cookie lady. It was perfectly logical that Erin would have a cookie to give her, since she always had one when Traci came to Auntie Clem's with her mother. And Allan had a teething biscuit. Traci should get a treat too.

Erin gathered Traci to her to give her a hug. "Do you mind if Traci has a cookie from the table?" she asked Scarlett. "I brought some with me, and it looks like a few other people did, too."

Scarlett nodded. "Of course, help yourself."

Erin stood up, picking Traci up with her. "Is it okay?" she asked Mrs. Foster.

"Sure. Thank you. Traci, you tell Miss Erin 'thank you.'"

"Cook-kie," Traci insisted.

"I think she's going to wait until she has it in hand," Erin observed. She took Traci over to the table and let her choose from the available plates of cookies. "Which one would you like, sweetie?"

Traci considered, her lips in a pout as she considered her options carefully. Finally, she pointed. "Dat one."

Erin knew that if Traci didn't get the exact cookie she had identified, she would have a fit. It didn't matter if it were the same variety. She had to have the specific cookie she pointed at. Erin moved closer to make sure she knew which one Traci was pointing to and pulled back the plastic wrap to retrieve it.

"This one?"

Traci kicked excitedly. "Dat one! Dat one!"

"Let's get a little plate," Erin suggested. "We'll play tea party, okay?"

She put the cookie on a small plate and grabbed a couple of napkins as well. Traci was not a tidy eater; Erin knew from experience. She returned to her seat and sat Traci on her lap, whispering in her ear and setting the plate in her lap.

"Tell Miss Erin thank you," Miss Foster reminded.

"Tank you," Traci obliged this time.

Erin gave her a squeeze and wondered how Adrienne and her children were faring.

Erin had stayed at Scarlett Simpson's longer than she had planned to. But she had not wanted to leave Mrs. Foster alone to take care of both Allan and Traci, so she stuck around until Allan started to fuss and Mrs. Foster decided it was time to take him home. She thanked Erin for helping to keep Traci quiet and occupied as they stepped outside into the furnace-like heat of the summer.

"They are quite a handful, I'll tell you!" Mrs. Foster said. "It was one thing when Allan was happy being in the sling, but now that he is older, he wants to be moving around and more independent, and you know Traci…"

"They are a going concern," Erin laughed.

"They're going!" Mrs. Foster agreed.

Erin drove her car over to the mechanic. She had finally gotten around to setting up an oil change, which she knew she was late taking care of. Things got so busy with the bakery that sometimes other priorities slid.

But she couldn't let her car be one of them. She needed it to get her around reliably, both in town and out to the city. She knew how hard it was to manage without a car, even in a small town like Bald Eagle Falls.

She greeted Darryl Wilson, the quiet, unassuming mechanic who seemed to have a magical touch with cars. Erin had always pictured "car guys" as being burly, rough-and-tumble, constantly cussing men with pin-up girls in their lockers and grease under their nails.

But Darryl was soft-spoken and endlessly polite. Erin couldn't imagine him cussing over anything less than a car rolling over his foot and breaking his toe. His garage and the waiting room were spotless, and the coffee in the waiting room always fresh. He worked diligently to stay on time and under budget, and if he did go over, was always sincerely apologetic for it, even if it were due to someone else's emergency situation.

Erin pulled her car into the two-bay garage and slid out. She looked at the car in the next slot over.

"Is that Adrienne's car?" she asked curiously. She had only seen Adrienne drive a couple of times, but thought she recognized the rusting old station wagon. It was probably older than Adrienne.

Darryl looked at the car, color coming to his cheeks. He looked uncertain about whether to answer her. Erin didn't think there was such a thing as mechanic-client privilege but, like Erin, he probably wanted to protect Adrienne and make sure that no one could find or harass her.

"It's fine," she said. "I think it is Adrienne's car, but you don't have to say anything. Adrienne and I are friends. I'm not going to tell anyone that she's here. Or coming back here when you've had a chance to get her car fixed up."

Darryl nodded gratefully. "She's had enough to go through without more people coming after her."

"More people?" Erin repeated.

"Simon. And then the police. And unsavory-looking out-of-towners."

Erin frowned. "What out-of-towners?"

Darryl shook his head slowly. He didn't answer immediately, thinking about it and composing what he wanted to say. Erin had learned he was a very deliberate speaker and did not handle it well when he was hurried, so she waited for him.

"A couple of rough-looking guys were by asking where her place was, asking for directions to get there. They were quite upset when I wouldn't help them. Not the kind of guys I would want hanging around here." He looked worriedly at Adrienne's car. He clearly did not want it to be there when he knew that people were out looking for Adrienne and she couldn't be far away.

"Not mechanics?" Erin teased.

"No. Might know something about cars and bikes, but... not professionally. These guys were more the kind who are in the *collections* business."

Erin knew what that meant. She had been through enough lean times to know the allure of getting a loan from someone who offered to help and then the terror of being unable to pay it back by the deadline. Those guys could be scary. Of necessity, they *were* scary. Even if they didn't utter any threats and just politely informed her that they were there to collect and would take whatever she had that had any value. Which, unfortunately, was nothing. Erin had always lived close to the bone, perhaps with only one suitcase containing all her worldly goods. Maybe you couldn't squeeze blood from a stone, but Erin wouldn't put it past one of those guys to try it.

"Adrienne doesn't owe anyone any money," Erin told Darryl.

He looked grateful and nodded his agreement. "I know she doesn't," he agreed. "She won't borrow or overextend herself. She's very careful. But they wanted Simon and, since he's not around anymore..."

"They can't collect it from her," Erin said firmly. "She doesn't owe them anything."

"They can still come after her."

"Not legally. Not unless she signed for it."

"These folks don't always do *legal.*"

"Did you warn her that they were around looking for her?"

He nodded. "Sent her a text after they were gone."

"Okay. Good. I'll let Terry know too, see if he can move them on their way."

"Thanks."

Erin started to walk to the customer waiting area. She could pull out her planner and work on Auntie Clem's upcoming campaigns.

"Miss Erin?" Darryl said.

She turned back to look at him.

"Adrienne is a good person. She didn't do this."

Erin took a deep breath in and let it out slowly.

"I don't think she did either. I hope not."

"She loved Simon. She knew that she couldn't live with him or let him back into her life again, but she still loved him. She wouldn't have done that."

Erin gave Darryl a long, thoughtful look before nodding and turning away.

CHAPTER 18

*E*rin was still in the waiting room when Adrienne returned for her car. Erin could hear her talking to Darryl in a low voice for a couple of minutes, probably just about the car and settling up, before Adrienne appeared in the doorway, peeking in at Erin.

Erin straightened in her seat and smiled. "It's just me," she promised. "How is it going? Did Darryl get your car all fixed up?" She kept her voice as light and cheerful as possible. Adrienne had enough negative drama going on in her life. She didn't need Erin dragging around like Simon's death was a huge tragedy that Adrienne might never recover from.

"Yes, it should run for a few more days now," Adrienne sighed.

Erin laughed. "That good, huh?"

"It seems like just when you fix one thing, something else breaks. I keep saying, 'This will be it; there isn't anything else to fix after this. Everything has been replaced.' And then something that I've never even heard of before breaks. If I didn't know how trustworthy Darryl is, I would think he was intentionally bringing me back here just so we could chat." Her smile seemed forced and plastic.

"I think he does have the tiniest crush on you," Erin teased, remembering how Darryl blushed when Erin asked him about Adrienne's car. Maybe it was true.

Adrienne swallowed and shook her head. "Be careful what you say," she warned. "Half the town already hates me. If they found out about Darryl and me, they'd never forgive me."

"You and Darryl…?" Erin repeated.

"We're just friends. Maybe. Now that Simon is gone, who knows? But you have to keep your mouth shut. They already think I'm some kind of… loose woman. You think I'm loose when I stayed with Simon for ten years? That's a long time."

"It is," Erin agreed. "And I don't care what anyone else says. I don't care who you were with. Or whether you were married. That's their hang-up," Erin made a motion waving them all away. "Not mine."

Adrienne looked at her for a moment, frozen like a rabbit that has been startled.

"You know what it's like," she told Erin finally. "They don't know. They've always had whatever they need, never had to hang on to someone just to survive. And then for him to take off, to take all that stability with him and leave me with nothing!" She spat. "He could be so aggravating. Come back here, treating me as sweet as honey and courting me. But I knew that it would all fade away again. As soon as he got the itch, he'd be out of town and probably all my money with him."

Adrienne went to the coffee station and looked down at the coffee supplies as if she didn't know what to do with them.

"I couldn't let him do that to me again. I couldn't let him take the one chance we had to make it. To build a place of our own, someplace that would be ours, that no one could take away from us. I could start to build a real life here instead of one where I have to keep moving every few months when someone chases us off."

"So you…" Erin was breathless, worried about what Adrienne was about to reveal. She did not want to know if Adrienne had killed Simon. She didn't want to have to cover for Adrienne. To lie to Terry. Her heart pounded hard and she felt nauseated.

"So I told him no," Adrienne finished sharply. "I told him he couldn't play daddy anymore. He couldn't take anything else from me. He couldn't hurt the kids. Make love to me and then take off. I wouldn't stand for it anymore."

Erin nodded. She sipped her cold, bitter coffee, hoping her relief was not too noticeable.

"That's good," she told Adrienne. "I wish that it had worked out differently. That he'd just gotten the message and… taken off."

"Me too." Adrienne scrubbed at her eyes. "Please… don't say anything to anyone about it. Or about Darryl. I just need… some time to figure things out. And to let people get used to the idea of Simon being gone. His sister, Scarlett…"

"I was over there today," Erin said. "Took some cookies from the freezer for her. I would come out and visit you too, but… I don't think you want anyone near your place."

"No," Adrienne agreed. "We need to stay out of sight. Especially when thugs are looking for someone to pay off Simon's debts." She shook her head. "Good for you for seeing Scarlett. I'm sure she needs the support just as much as anyone. But don't expect her to be warm toward me."

"I know. She's protecting the memory of her brother."

Adrienne laughed bitterly. "The memory of her brother. The way she wished he'd been, maybe. They never got along in life. She hated him as much as she hated me. Maybe I even got the warmer shoulder now and then. She was not a fan of Simon."

"Really?" Erin was shocked. "She kept going on about him. Childhood memories. All of the scrapes he used to get into. How *people* hadn't treated him fairly." Adrienne probably knew Erin meant that Adrienne had treated Simon badly, but she wouldn't say that to her face. "I thought they were close."

Adrienne shook her head, chuckling. "They could never get along. Fought like cats and dogs. I actually tried to get the two of them to reconcile. But Scarlett would have nothing to do with him. I think Simon would have made up with her and would have apologized for all of the stupid stuff he did to her growing up. But there was no way."

Maybe Scarlett was covering up her real feelings so that no one would think she had a motive to kill Simon. But would anyone kill over sibling rivalry? Erin thought not but, as soon as she thought it, she remembered Davis Plaint killing his brother Trenton over their inheritance. She reconsidered. Maybe Scarlett was a viable suspect.

But could she tell Terry or the sheriff that? She didn't feel like it was fair to accuse one of the chief mourners. Especially when she had no proof. Scarlett had said one thing and Adrienne another, and Erin was more inclined to believe Adrienne. But she didn't have any evidence either way. But it would be a lot harder for Adrienne to work around her five children to find a time to kill Simon without anyone finding out about it.

"Where *are* the children?" Erin asked abruptly, looking around.

"Playing in the park," Adrienne said, startled. They both studied each other. "Bella's watching them. She's good with them. Hope idolizes her."

Erin nodded. She sighed, thinking of Bella. She did *not* want to believe that Bella was mixed up in this, either in committing the act or enabling Adrienne to do it.

She couldn't let herself think that.

Adrienne fiddled with the coffee machine for a moment before saying anything.

"You've been a good friend, Erin," she said finally in a voice as whispery and unemotional as a dried reed. "I hope… you stay that way. Don't turn on me in the hardest time of my life."

Erin swallowed.

"I won't."

CHAPTER 19

*E*rin was relieved when Adrienne was gone and she was sitting by herself in the waiting room again. She was sure that Adrienne was innocent. How could she have killed Simon even if she wanted to? She couldn't leave her children alone and, if she left them with someone else, then they would know that she had been gone during the time that Simon had been murdered.

Of course, if that person were Bella, she would never tell Erin, the police, or anyone else that Adrienne had no alibi for the time of the murder. She would protect Adrienne to the bitter end. They were close friends despite the difference in their years. Erin thought that they were probably distantly related—all of the old mountain families were, to some extent—not just friends, but cousins of some kind. They had probably known each other since Bella had been a little girl. And neither was going to do anything to implicate the other.

Erin looked up at the sound of footsteps, surprised that Darryl could be done so quickly when he had just finished with Adrienne's car. Or maybe he wanted her authorization for some extra work that her car needed.

But it wasn't Darryl who appeared in the doorway. Nor was it Adrienne, coming back to ask Erin again not to say anything that would bring any more attention to her as a suspect. It was Joshua Cox. Mary Lou's younger son, a friend of Bella's at high school, and intrepid investigative reporter, who had gotten himself into trouble with his investigations more than once. And had also rescued Erin from a dangerous situation when no one else had figured out where she was.

Erin knew that Mary Lou didn't like her talking to Josh or encouraging his investigations but, after all they had been through together, she couldn't just turn the boy away. She did her best not to "encourage" him, but how well she did that was a matter for discussion.

"Oh, hi Josh."

He smiled. "Miss Erin." He entered the room and took a seat near hers. "I didn't know you were here."

Erin shrugged. "Just getting an oil change."

He nodded. "Mom asked me to bring the car over for Darryl to have a look. It's making a noise."

"Well, he shouldn't be too long on mine. Adrienne just left, so he should be doing my oil change now."

Josh nodded. "How is she doing?"

"Adrienne?" Erin realized she probably shouldn't have mentioned Adrienne's name. The woman had just told her not to make things more difficult for her, so Erin promptly informed the investigative reporter that they had been talking? Not exactly the smartest way to honor Adrienne's request. "She's okay, I guess," Erin tried to brush the topic aside. "As well as can be expected under the circumstances."

"It must be tough for her." Joshua had been through his own trouble with suspicion falling on his family. Or with a family member being guilty of harming someone in Bald Eagle Falls. He knew what it was like to be the center of negative attention during a time of tragedy. He knew how the townspeople happily spent hours speculating on the goings-on in Bald Eagle Falls.

"Yeah," Erin agreed. "I think she'd rather not talk about it to anyone."

He raised an eyebrow at this. "I've already talked to her."

"Oh." So much for Erin discouraging him from talking to her. At least Adrienne couldn't hold her responsible for a call from Joshua that had happened before Adrienne had asked her not to interfere or draw any attention to her. "Well, that's good. You're out ahead of this story. I guess the paper probably needed more information from her for the obituary."

Joshua looked at her for a moment, then nodded. "Yeah. That and other articles."

"The obituary put out by the funeral home doesn't even have all the children on it."

"Maybe there is a reason for that."

Maybe Simon wasn't the father of all the children, he meant. Erin shook her head.

"I don't think now is the time to be airing dirty laundry in public."

He gave a little smile at that. "Is there ever a good time to air dirty laundry in public?"

"Well… no, I guess not," Erin admitted. The whole point of the saying was that private matters should be kept private.

Joshua pulled out his reporter's notepad and settled more comfortably into his chair. Erin took her planner binder from her oversized purse and pretended to be hard at work planning the following week. She really should be working on it. But she was finding it difficult to focus on the things that she needed to. With everything that was going on in Bald Eagle Falls, she didn't know how she could be expected to stay focused. Yet work went on. If she didn't stay on top of business at the bakery, who would?

"So, what did you think of Simon Simpson?" Joshua asked after they had both flipped pages for a few minutes in silence.

"I don't think anything of him now. He's dead and gone, and good riddance."

"So you didn't like him."

Erin shook her head. "I didn't know the man, other than knowing that he was trying to separate Adrienne from her money. I didn't find that endearing."

"I guess not. What made you think that it was about money?"

"His timing. He has five kids with Adrienne, and I'd never even seen him in town before! Then she gets a settlement—" Erin didn't know how much, if anything, Joshua knew about the settlement with Fontainbleau's estate. "—and he shows up in town looking for her? It was obvious that he was only here to try to get his hands on that money."

"How did he know about it?"

CHAPTER 20

That gave Erin pause. The payout hadn't exactly been public record. Certainly, there was nothing on the records of the estate or with the probate court. Neither Adrienne nor the woman who had effected the payment would be spreading the news.

"I don't know." The only thing that made any sense was that Adrienne had told him. But why would she? Had she wanted to draw him home, but then had decided after his arrival that she couldn't take the chance on letting him into her life and the lives of the children again? Had she discovered something else about him that made her change her mind?

"If you came into money and knew someone like that, would you have told them?" Josh asked.

"No. I probably would have left town. Gone somewhere that no one knew me, and he wouldn't be able to find me."

Just like Erin hadn't told her ex-boyfriend about moving to Bald Eagle Falls. But he had still had his ways of finding out where she had gone. And eventually, he had caught up to her. Simon hadn't had to figure out where Adrienne was. He had known that she was somewhere around town and would show up there sooner or later, even if he couldn't find the campsite out in the wilds.

"If she told him about the money and asked him to come back, then why would she kill him?" Erin challenged. "That doesn't make any sense."

"I didn't say she did. I'm just making observations."

"Adrienne did not kill her husband. Simon, I mean. It was… probably some stranger from out of town. Someone we've never even heard of before."

"Why?"

"I don't know. Simon's past caught up with him. His gambling debts or a jealous woman. Who knows what else he was into? He didn't exactly look like the most reputable-looking guy."

"You can't judge a book by its cover," Joshua reminded her. He was probably thinking about Willie, who had always looked like a dirty, homeless man when he was really one of the most industrious members of the town. Or Beaver, who was involved somehow with Joshua's brother Cam and was an undercover federal agent. Neither one was what they looked like.

But Erin hadn't judged Simon by his looks. He could have been a perfectly respectable man and still looked like a thug. But Simon's behavior had told Erin much more about him.

"He was asking after Adrienne when she didn't want to be found. Came here looking for money that wasn't his, but was the only way to guarantee his children's future. Made threats. And the things I'm hearing about him from around town do not indicate that he was a *respectable* man," Erin insisted.

Joshua wrote down a few notes. Erin needed to be more careful what she said to Josh rather than giving him more ammunition.

"It wasn't Adrienne," Erin asserted again.

"Of course not," Joshua agreed.

"Have you looked into Simon's sister? Apparently, there was no love lost between the two of them."

"What did you hear?"

"No specifics. Just that he was a hellion when they were growing up and the two of them never got along very well."

"He was a prankster," Joshua said.

"Apparently. Although 'prankster' implies that it was just silly little pranks. And that's not what it sounded like to me. It sounded to me like he was cruel."

"What specifically did he do to her?"

Erin had to shake her head. "I don't know. I didn't hear any specifics.

Adri—I just heard that they didn't get along, and Scarlett could never forgive Simon for how he had treated her. That sounds pretty serious to me."

"So you think that she's a suspect."

"I guess…" Erin shrugged. "But she's not the only one. If that is the kind of person he was, and he grew up in Bald Eagle Falls, then there are probably a lot of people with grudges against him. I mean, even Betty Thompson. She's such a nice old lady and I've never heard her say an unkind word about anyone, but Scarlett was surprised that she showed up at the house, because she had never forgiven Simon for something that happened when he was younger."

"Betty Thompson?"

Erin nodded. "You know her? She's an older lady, friends with my neighbor Mrs. Peach?"

Joshua nodded. "Yes, I know who she is."

"And there are ex-girlfriends. I guess Simon gambled. There were people looking for him that he owed money to. That are still hanging around thinking they can get money from Adrienne."

Joshua bit his lip as he scribbled down some notes. "How do you know that?"

"Da—someone told me. Sounds to me like he must have owed a lot."

"Must be, if they are chasing him around the state for it or across the country…" Joshua agreed. "If they're willing to spend money looking for him." He made a couple of notes. "Do you know who they are? Where I could find them?"

"I don't know. Out-of-towners. I don't know where they are staying, if anywhere. Just that they're asking around after Adrienne."

"I hope they don't find her."

Erin cleared her throat and nodded. Adrienne was tough. Despite her attraction toward him, she'd been able to stand up to Simon. But could she stand up to thugs? Could she protect herself and her children if they got violent or made threats?

Had she stood up to Simon's threats?

"And you think Simon had affairs?" Joshua asked Erin. "I know he ran around a lot… but he wouldn't get together with someone here in town, would he?"

"From what I hear, yes."

"Do you have names?"

"I think I should probably leave that to the police."

"Come on," Joshua coaxed. "The great Erin Price is going to leave it up to the police department? You know they won't hear all of the gossip you do. They're going to be three steps behind."

"I'm not a detective. Just a baker. It's up to the police." Erin pushed aside the misgivings she had about the police department and the number of times that she had scooped him on a murder investigation because they were just a little too far behind. It had put her in danger more than once. And not because she was a meddling, interfering snoop. No matter how hard she tried to stay out of an investigation, it came to her.

$\mathcal{I}$f Erin wanted the police to investigate people other than Adrienne and to know what things she had encountered about Simon so far, then maybe she should talk to them. It wasn't like she didn't know anyone inside the police department.

She stopped by Auntie Clem's to make sure that everything was going smoothly. It was getting close to closing, so she grabbed a selection of the sweets that remained in the display case before heading over to Town Hall, where the police department offices were.

Clara, the receptionist, had apparently left for the day. Erin could see through the glass doors that no one was handling the reception desk, and the glass doors were locked. Erin knocked on the door, hoping that someone would still be there and would hear her.

There was no immediate answer. Erin juggled out her phone to call Terry. Then she saw someone emerge from the hallway to see who was at the door.

Stayner.

Of all the law enforcement officers who worked in Bald Eagle Falls, he was Erin's least favorite. She sighed, the knot in her stomach tying even tighter.

Stayner, a square-jawed rookie with limited people skills, opened the door and looked at her inquiringly. Erin proffered the box of treats. "I just brought some baking by. I was hoping that I could talk to someone. Terry's not here?"

He took the box of treats from her. "No, he's out on a call."

The crime rate in Bald Eagle Falls was pretty low. It always surprised Erin when Terry was actually out on a call. She hoped that it was something minor—nothing involving weapons or domestic violence.

"Oh, okay."

"Did you have some information to share?" he asked, surprising Erin. She had thought that he would just put her off. Let Terry take care of it when he got back to the office.

"Well… there are a few things that have come to my attention. I don't want to take you away from something important, but…"

He opened the door the rest of the way. "Come in."

Erin's mouth was dry and her stomach was doing all kinds of acrobatics. Stayner led her, not to the small office he and Terry shared, but to one of the interview rooms. That was probably just because the office was so small, Erin assured herself. He wanted to have more space, not be cooped up in a tiny office with avalanches of stacked files and papers all around them. Terry didn't mind getting cozy with her, but Stayner was another story.

Stayner motioned for Erin to take a seat. He opened the box of treats on the table within reach and invited her with a gesture to help herself. Erin didn't. Stayner fell into one of the sturdy chairs with a grunt. He rubbed the back of his neck and rolled his shoulders. Too much time sitting in front of the computer.

"How is the Simon Simpson case going?" she asked him tentatively, knowing he would not share anything with her.

Stayner shrugged. "Lots of avenues to investigate. Did you have some information on it?"

"I heard there were some rough-looking men in town looking for Adrienne, his wife—domestic partner. I guess Simon owed them some money and they were hoping to recover it from her."

Stayner frowned. "We don't like people like that hanging around town."

Erin nodded. "I was hoping that you would be able to… encourage them to move on."

He wrote it down in his notebook. "I'll have someone look into it," he agreed.

Erin glanced around. She didn't like being cooped up alone with Stayner in the interview room. The door was still open, but she felt anxious. "Are you the only one around tonight?"

"Right now, yes. Terry's still on duty, as you know. If he finishes with any active calls, he will come back here."

Erin tried to turn her attention back to the matter at hand.

"Right. Of course. I wondered about… other suspects in the Simpson case. Whether you are investigating other avenues…"

He would just brush the question aside, she knew. He wouldn't share anything with her about an active investigation.

Stayner studied Erin. "Suspects other than you?"

CHAPTER 22

*E*rin caught her breath. She swallowed, mouth drier than ever, and looked around for a bottle or glass of water. Even cold coffee would be better than nothing. But Stayner didn't offer her anything. He sat there, staring at her, analyzing every movement or change in her expression.

"I'm not a suspect… am I?" Erin asked, her voice squeaking and barely louder than a whisper.

"Let's see." He looked up at the ceiling as if trying to remember a long list. "There is the murder weapon. That's yours. And he was found outside of Auntie Clem's Bakery, your business. By you. You had hoped that someone else would discover him before he had decomposed too much, but you couldn't stand the smell anymore, so you called it in. *And then* we find out that he was also poisoned."

"Terry mentioned that," Erin said in a tiny voice.

"Poisoned by a cinnamon roll from your bakery," Stayner said. "So… everything points to the baker."

"It wasn't me," Erin said, "That's ridiculous. Why would I kill him? What motive did I have?"

"He was harassing you. Showing up at your place of business. Maybe at your home. You wanted to protect your friend. To keep them apart. Eventually, you decided to do something about it."

Erin shook her head. "No, nothing like that. The last time I saw him, when he wouldn't leave the bakery when I asked him to, I called Terry to send him on his way. I didn't need to resort to violence."

"But he came back after that. When no one else was around. When you didn't have time to get to your phone before he came after you. You grabbed the nearest knife and you stabbed him."

"But first I poisoned him," Erin said sarcastically.

"Everybody saw you sell him the poisoned cinnamon roll. You had done that earlier in the day. You hoped that it would do the job for you. Women prefer poison, death from a distance instead of having to do it face-to-face. But he threw up. Ejected most of the poison out of his system. So that didn't work. He came after you, whether because he realized what you had tried to do or he was trying to bully the information he wanted out of you."

"No. That's ridiculous. Why would I open the door to him?"

"He came in while it was unlocked. You had been out to put the garbage in the bin. Or he ambushed you while you were still outside. He knew that if he waited out there, you would come sooner or later."

"And I took the garbage out with the cake knife in my hand?" Erin demanded. "Trust me, I don't arm myself for an ambush when I take out the garbage!"

"Then he followed you back in. You grabbed the knife from the counter to confront him. And presto, Simon Simpson is dead, and you are responsible."

Erin looked around again for a drink of water, but none had materialized.

"No way," she said. "Never happened. And if it had, I would have called the police."

"You drag the body out behind the dumpster—"

"Do you know how much strength it takes to drag a dead body?"

He gave her a little smile. "Do you?"

Erin felt a chill. She shook her head. "You know I didn't do this. Why would I kill him? I would just call Terry again. He hadn't been physical with me."

"There's nothing to say that he didn't escalate to violence. I'm sure if I talked to Mrs. Simpson, she would tell me of a time or two that he had gotten physical with her. I know how guys like that operate. I have no doubt he would have put hands on you if he thought that would give him what he wanted."

Stayner was probably right about that. But Erin wasn't going to let him treat her as a suspect. As his primary suspect, from the sounds of it. He had already had her in mind because of the knife and the location of the murder. It seemed clear that it had been an employee of the bakery, or else someone who wanted to implicate them. But as soon as Stayner had seen the results of the autopsy and knew that Simon had been poisoned, he had decided that it was Erin. She was the baker and proprietor. She was the one who was responsible for whatever went into the baking.

Her stomach lurched at the thought of her baking being used to poison someone. She had been accused of poisoning before but, of course, she had been exonerated. It wasn't her fault if someone used her baking to kill someone who was allergic to the ingredients.

She looked daggers at Stayner and didn't tell him he might just be at the top of her hit list. She had come to the police department offices to help with the investigation, to offer her insights, and to see where they were on the investigation. She had even brought cookies.

As if hearing her thoughts, Stayner's eyes strayed over to the box of baked goods.

Oh good grief.

Did he really think that she would try to poison the police department as well? Or even just him?

She admitted that it was a tempting thought. Just Stayner. After hours. When they were alone in the interview room. There would be no record that Erin had been there. No one would know.

Except that the poison would be in his stomach and they would know what he had eaten. She wouldn't get away with anything.

Erin reached over and selected a classic chocolate chip oatmeal cookie. Stayner watched her take it out and bite into it.

"If this is your version of a cyanide capsule, I'm going to be very disappointed," he told her.

"Disappointed? Why?"

He shrugged. "I'm always interested in your... *unique* take on a case. No one can question your solve rate."

He folded his arms and sat back in his chair, watching her. Was he waiting to see if she would drop dead from eating a poison-laced treat? If so, he was going to be waiting for a long time.

She pondered on what he had said. If he really thought that she had poisoned someone, then he wouldn't be concerned with her solve rate or *unique* view on this murder case or any other.

"You don't think that I did it."

He gave a slight smile. "It seems a little heavy-handed," he admitted. "The cake knife. Behind the bakery. Poisoned baked goods. The baker as the victim of Simpson's harassment and protective of her friend."

"You think everything was intended to point to me? That I was targeted and framed?"

"It would certainly appear so, don't you think?"

Erin blew out her breath in a long, slow stream, relieved. "Yeah. It does," she agreed. "But why would anyone target me?"

He held his hand, palm up, and moved it toward her as if handing the problem back to her. "Why do you think?"

"I don't know..." Erin thought about it, closing her eyes and picturing the different people that might have had motive to kill Simon, but also to frame her. What could they have against her? She was a baker. She tried to be kind and fair to everyone. As far as she knew, she hadn't stepped on any toes lately, and any that she had stepped on previously were healed and she was forgiven.

Several people in the state penitentiary might have a grievance against her, but they were locked up. They were not running around Bald Eagle Falls planting clues.

"I don't know... maybe someone got the idea because I've helped out with other murder cases in the past. They associated me with murder, and just..."

"An unconscious association? I don't think so."

"Maybe... they were afraid that I would figure out who did it, so they wanted me out of the way?"

He considered. "Possibly," he grunted. But he didn't seem too excited about the idea.

"I don't know of anyone who would want to put me in prison for murder. Not anyone who could be in Bald Eagle Falls."

Stayner reached over and selected a white chocolate chip brownie. "Melissa always steals all of these."

Erin's stomach and chest muscles relaxed. Stayner would not eat the brownie if he thought that she was involved in a poisoning. In trying to decide whether she was really considered a suspect, that brownie tipped the balance. He did *not* consider her a viable suspect.

CHAPTER 23

"I hear you were by the office to see me this evening," Terry said casually as he and Erin started to work on dinner, Terry setting the table and Erin starting some soup stock simmering while she cut up vegetables.

Orange Blossom came yowling into the kitchen, loudly complaining about how Erin had neglected him and hadn't given him anything to eat today. Erin got the can of kitty treats out of the pantry and skimmed a couple along the tile floor for him to chase and devour.

K9, lying beside the table waiting patiently, looked up with interest. Erin got out one of his gluten-free doggie biscuits and offered it to him. Unlike his feline rival, K9 was the perfect gentleman, never harassing her for food or snatching it away. He took it from her with his lips, and then lay down again with it between his front paws to munch on.

Hearing the other animals getting treats, Marshmallow lolloped into the kitchen with long ears pricked up and looked at Erin for his share. Erin took a handful of the ends of the vegetables she was cutting and offered them to the soft brown and white rabbit. Marshmallow munched happily.

"So…?" Terry prompted.

Erin looked at him. "What?"

"I missed you at the office this afternoon. I was out on a call."

"Oh, yeah." Erin looked sideways at Terry, wondering how much of the conversation Stayner had relayed to him. "I left you some brownies."

"Yes, they were as good as always. I tried to leave enough for the rest of the staff when they arrive in the morning, though it was a hardship."

"You can always come by Auntie Clem's for more if they run out."

After adding the chopped vegetables to the simmering stock, Erin glanced over her shoulder at Terry. He was smiling, the dimple in his cheek prominent.

"Make sure you ask for the ones that aren't poisoned," she told him.

Terry chuckled. "I was going to talk to you about the poison tonight. But Rod beat me to the punch."

"He had me believing I was the prime suspect. Again."

"You have to admit that on paper, you look good for it. If we didn't know you as well as we do, there might have been reason for concern. Even now… we're being very careful and trying to document everything. Explain why we did not believe you were a viable suspect. There's no guarantee that whoever acts for the defense in the case won't present you as the suspect in an alternative theory of the murder and demand to know why you were not arrested."

Erin wasn't as worried about that. It was still concerning but, at that point, it would mean that they had the actual killer in custody, and she was sure that they would be able to dig up enough evidence to convict him—or her—and Erin wouldn't end up fighting charges herself.

"Do you know what kind of poison it was?" Erin asked. "Rat poison? Something that had to be ordered on the internet?"

Terry shook his head. "Mushrooms."

Erin was taken aback. "Mushrooms? Poisonous mushrooms?"

He nodded. "Apparently… death cap mushrooms."

Erin thought of the pictures she had seen of the innocuous-looking white mushroom. "Do they… grow around here?"

Terry nodded. "Yes. They are native. Untraceable."

"Anyone could have picked them…" She frowned and shook her head as she stirred the soup. "But mushrooms in a cinnamon roll? Someone would notice if there were pieces of mushroom in a cinnamon roll."

"Apparently, it is pretty easy to prepare a liquid extract."

Erin shivered in the summer heat of the kitchen. Someone could be walking around right now with a vial of death cap poison in his pocket. It would not take very much to poison a person. The mild mushroom flavor could be covered up with the intense sugar and cinnamon spice of the cinnamon rolls. Topped with cream cheese icing, of course. A little of the slightly nutty-tasting death caps would be undetectable.

Simon was lucky that he had thrown up the death cap toxin. Maybe he would have survived if it hadn't been for being stabbed in the chest with a cake knife.

"How could someone have poisoned him? Do you think it was in the cinnamon roll or something else? I don't see how anyone could have poisoned the cinnamon roll between me giving it to him and him eating it."

"Someone must have had access to it at some point," Terry said. He grimaced. "I know you didn't poison it. Of course not. But if you could think about what was happening at the bakery when he bought it… who handled it, who was near it? Whether anyone could have contaminated it before he left the bakery."

Erin was shaking her head. She tried to remember who had been in Auntie Clem's at the same time as Simon. She was sure that she was the one who had handled the cinnamon roll, taking it out of the display case and sliding it into a sleeve for him. And then… had she put it on the counter next to the till? Who had rung it up? Had Simon picked it up or had someone handed it to him? And then there was the cream cheese. Erin couldn't remember who had handled the little condiment cup full of icing.

"I don't know." She rubbed her forehead. "I'll have to think about it."

Terry nodded. "We'll ask the others that we know were in Auntie Clem's at the time. I'm afraid I had a bit of tunnel vision—I really didn't look at anyone other than Simon."

She was glad that Terry's recollection wasn't any better than hers. It would have been embarrassing if she could remember nothing and he could reel off the names of everyone who had been in the bakery and every move they had made. Terry was trained to notice things, and if he had missed whatever opportunities anyone had had to poison him, then Erin didn't have to feel inferior for not being able to either.

"If it wasn't poisoned at Auntie Clem's, then he must have met someone else between the time he left the bakery and when he ate the cinnamon roll," Terry said, "We're trying to trace all of his movements during that time. If someone saw him with his killer… Any meeting between them probably looked completely innocuous. If Simon let himself be poisoned, then he wasn't suspicious of the person who killed him. It might have been a friend or casual acquaintance, but not someone he was worried about."

Erin pictured Simon meeting with a friend in a cafe or on a park bench. Somewhere, Simon had felt comfortable sitting down, spreading the icing on the cinnamon roll, and eating a portion while he sat and visited with some unknown person.

He had been completely unworried about the person having access to his food. Like the woman who left her trusted friend to watch that no one mickied her drink while she went to the ladies' room, giving him the opportunity to dose it with his date rape drug of choice.

"It couldn't be anyone at the bakery," Erin said. "No one knew that he would be there or would decide to buy a cinnamon roll. I pushed him to buy something or move on, or he wouldn't have."

Her face warmed.

"I suppose that makes me look like the killer, but I didn't put anything in it. I would never poison my own baked goods. It's like… desecration. My whole goal is to provide people with baking that they can eat without it making them sick. Besides—it would be stupid."

Terry nodded.

"But it couldn't have been any of the employees," Erin reiterated. "No one knew ahead of time Simon was going to order it. They wouldn't have had time to poison it. And someone else in the bakery…" She shook her head. "You think someone was following him around with a vial of poison just waiting for the opportunity to poison him? And that they would have time to poison the roll before he picked it up? It must have been done later."

Terry scratched K9's ears. "I can't completely eliminate the possibility that it was dosed while he was at Auntie Clem's. But you're right… it seems unlikely."

Erin couldn't help thinking about Bella. She took the soup off the burner and left the pot in the center of the stove while she got out the soup bowls and ladle. She tried to fix in her mind where Bella had been each moment Simon had been in the bakery. She had been in the kitchen. She had been behind the counter. She had argued with Simon about his right to know where his wife—or domestic partner—was. And then…? Erin didn't think she had been close enough to tamper with the roll or the cream cheese, but she couldn't swear to it. After Simon had left, Bella had clocked out. She had needed to study for a test.

"Stayner thinks that someone wanted to frame me or someone at Auntie Clem's. He thought that it was…" She tried to remember the words he had used. "That it was heavy-handed. An obvious frame job."

She looked at Terry expectantly as she placed the soup bowls on the table.

"We are all in agreement," he admitted. "We know you and the other employees at Auntie Clem's. And you're not stupid. You've been involved in enough murder investigations." He shook his head. "Using a knife from the bakery and leaving it in the body? Calling the discovery of the body in yourself and *still* leaving the knife in the body? Poisoning your own baking? Yes, heavy-handed is a good word for it. Based on that evidence, it might seem like you or your employees are good suspects. But I can't see you leaving that much of a trail. And the same applies to your employees."

Erin sat down. While her stomach was still tight, she felt like she could manage the soup and the biscuits she had already set on the table. She wasn't that worried about herself or about Terry or the other law enforcement officers, assuming that she was the one who had poisoned and stabbed Simon.

But she was still worried about Bella and Adrienne. More worried than she would like to admit.

CHAPTER 24

drienne was still the main suspect in Simon's murder, and she and Erin both knew it. Erin kept telling herself that there was no way that Adrienne could have left her children to kill Simon, but she knew she was looking for reasons to exclude Adrienne as a suspect. She hadn't dared to ask Adrienne about her alibi.

"I know I don't have any right to ask," Adrienne told Erin over the phone. "You helped me out when Mr. Fontainbleau was killed… and I just… I don't know who killed Simon, but it wasn't me."

Erin made noises of agreement, though she wasn't sure what to say to Adrienne. It would make sense to say that she believed Adrienne and knew she hadn't had anything to do with Simon's murder. But she didn't think she could make her tongue form those words.

"What can I help you with?" she asked finally, after fumbling about for some response.

"I just thought you might be able to help me figure out who did it. Maybe… it was probably something to do with something he did when he was out of town. I know that Simon was no saint," she admitted. "If he thought he could make a buck without too much work… he was always running one scam or another. Maybe someone wanted to get back at him."

"Maybe," Erin agreed.

"He was crook… I didn't want to know what he was involved in. I never wanted to know what he was up to, how he was bringing in the money when he did. And it wasn't very often he actually brought something for me and the kids. When he did, I knew it was best not to ask where it came from."

"I'm not sure how I can help," Erin protested, when Adrienne trailed off.

"When I finish work this afternoon, I'll be over at Prosts'. Cindy said I could use her computer, but I'm crap when it comes to computers. I thought maybe you could help me to… see if we can figure out some stuff about Simon's past while Cindy watches the kids. If there are—were—people looking for Simon… it might explain what happened."

Erin wasn't the best on computers herself, though she had grown more proficient in the time she had been in Bald Eagle Falls.

"I shouldn't ask," Adrienne said again. "I know you're busy with other things. But if you could help me…"

"Okay," Erin agreed. "Of course. I'm not sure I'll be able to do much, but we can try."

She got the details from Adrienne as to what time she would be at the farm and agreed to meet her there.

Erin had been to the Prost farm before, off in "the sticks" outside Bald Eagle Falls. It was a goat farm. They circulated the goats through a couple of pastures, and Erin didn't see any of them close to the house or old barn. They were probably in the upper pasture or the newer barn.

After pulling into the driveway, she stayed in the car, looking for the guard dog. Adrienne came out of the house a minute later and motioned her in.

"Dog's tied up behind the house," she said, noticing Erin looking around for it. "He won't bother you."

Erin could hear the shouts of the children as they played, and hoped they knew enough not to get too close to the dog. But maybe he knew them well enough now that they could approach him and could talk and play with him without any danger.

"Thanks for coming," Adrienne told Erin. "Can I get you some tea?"

Erin nodded. "Sure. That would be nice."

They would ease into the computer searches. It would be best to get more background from Adrienne before they started so Erin had a better idea of what to look for. Adrienne probably knew more about Simon's past than she was willing to share initially.

Adrienne took her into the kitchen and Erin sat at the table while she watched Adrienne put the kettle on to boil and put a little basket of tea bags on the table for Erin to sort through. She picked out a ginger peach tea. She smelled the tea bag before putting it in front of her. It smelled like summertimes with Clementine. She could remember her great-aunt making them iced ginger peach tea as a special treat on hot summer days.

"How long did you and Simon know each other?" she asked.

Adrienne considered. "About… ten years, I guess. We met each other in high school when my family moved into town. I was… I didn't make friends easily. I was kind of an outsider. But Simon was nice to me. He would talk to me and didn't make fun of me for being from away. I guess… I fell for him because he was one of the few people who accepted me."

"That's nice. I'm glad he was welcoming."

"Simon was always eager to meet the new girl," Adrienne said, unsmiling. "I'm not sure it was a demonstration of his good character."

CHAPTER 25

*A*drienne brought the teapot over to the table. She poured for Erin and then herself, selecting a green tea.

"But the two of you stayed together," Erin observed. "A lot of couples don't."

"I probably shouldn't have. I should have just dumped him and gone on with my life. But I kept taking him back when he showed up again. Pretending that it was going to be different. That I believed he was going to be different every time. That this time, he would stay, and help to support the children. Help raise them so it wasn't just me all by myself."

Adrienne sighed and swept her thin, straight hair back over her ears and behind her shoulders. She looked not just exhausted after a busy workday, but world-weary. She was younger than Erin, yet had been through so many trials with her children and Simon. Erin had been through her own tough times, but at least she'd only had herself to look after. She couldn't imagine going through it all with young children to look after as well. Putting a roof over their heads and food in their mouths. Trying to take care of them or arrange for childcare. Erin didn't know how she had managed it.

"What did he do when he was away? Do you have any idea?"

Adrienne sipped her tea, frown lines between her eyebrows. "He would go off, saying he'd heard of an opportunity. Or saying that he had a job interview or had gotten hired for something. But I knew that most of the time, he didn't have a new job. He just had… an idea of something else he could do. A new scheme. Or scam. I always wanted to believe him. But after a while, I knew it was just… him getting tired of the quiet life and chasing rainbows. He loved the kids, and I'd like to think he loved me too, in his own way. You always want to believe that a man really loves you, don't you?"

"Yes," Erin admitted. She too had dealt with that longing. That wish or pretense that the man she was with really loved her, was devoted to her, and would do anything for her. She hoped that she'd found that with Terry, but she often found herself doubting either his devotion or that, this time, she had found something different, and she and Terry were in it for the long haul. It had lasted longer than most of her relationships, and Terry really was a good guy. But sometimes she worried she was just lying to herself.

"I know that there were other women," Adrienne said. "I knew that when he went off somewhere for weeks or months, that he wasn't keeping himself for me. He would come back and sometimes I would be able to smell her on his clothing, until everything had been washed a few times. It wasn't just hotel soap."

She sniffled and wiped her nose with a tissue tucked in her pocket.

"When he was with me, I wanted to believe that he'd realized the error of his ways and had come back to me for good. But after a while… I realized how bad that was for the kids. And I tried to change. To be tough and not just take him back. Sometimes that made him mad and he would take off again. Others… he would try to prove himself. Try to show me how much he had changed."

"But it didn't last."

"It never did. If it lasted longer than the time before, I would get to thinking that it might stick this time. But it never did."

Erin wished she could hug Adrienne and make her feel better. But Adrienne was not a touchy-feely person. She kept herself aloof most of the time. Even asking Erin to help with the computer work and have tea together was very unusual. And Erin found shows of affection awkward enough without trying to judge whether Adrienne would accept her ministrations. She wished she had someone like Betty Thompson there to tell her what to do next.

Adrienne took another sip of her tea and looked at her watch. "We'd better get started. I want to be done by the time Bella gets home."

Erin waited for a more thorough explanation, but Adrienne didn't clarify. Maybe Bella would need the computer for homework when she got home.

Adrienne brought her cup with her and motioned for Erin to do the same. They climbed the stairs to the small bedrooms, and Adrienne led her to a tiny computer station wedged into one corner of the master bedroom.

"Internet here is pretty slow," Adrienne warned. "Someday maybe they'll get that satellite connection here but, right now, it's just over the phone lines."

They sat down, Erin taking the computer chair and Adrienne perching on the corner of the bed, close enough for her to see most of what Erin was doing on the computer.

"So I'm not sure exactly what you want," Erin said tentatively. She typed Simon's name into the search bar, and most of the results on the screen were obviously for other people. Erin scrolled through them, looking for Simon's face. She found him on one of the social networks and clicked his name to pull up his profile. She and Adrienne skimmed through the last few entries he had made before his death.

"I guess…" Adrienne leaned forward, looking at the details. "Does it say where he has been? Who his friends are? That kind of thing. Then maybe there will be something on their social media… maybe some pictures of him or things he was involved with."

Erin looked through the pictures and entries on his timeline. She opened a new document and started noting the places and people with their profile links. Simon's timeline was pretty innocuous. Only a few posts a year. There was a picture of him with Adrienne and some of the children crowding into the frame. Erin looked at the date. Two and a half years previous. That might have been the last time he'd been home with them. Erin could see the joy in Adrienne's eyes at the family being together.

And then he had left.

She followed the links to some of his friends. Some of them posted more actively than Simon. Others had profiles that were completely locked down so that only their few close friends would be able to access anything.

They were generally a rough lot. Erin glanced at Adrienne's face to see if she recognized any of them. Were any of them the men who were looking for Simon, who wanted to collect his debts from Adrienne?

Adrienne just shook her head. "No one from around here."

Drinking pictures. Pictures of them with barely clad girlfriends. Trucks and motorcycles. Off-roading holidays.

Erin went back to the initial search that she had done and started clicking on some of the results that didn't have pictures beside them. Some of them were obviously not him. Erin accidentally clicked on another profile on the social network she had found him on and hovered the mouse cursor over the back button.

"Wait," Adrienne held up her hand. They both watched the page load over the slow internet connection. It was Simon's picture, but it was not the same profile as they had already looked at. Erin looked at the details along the left side of the page. "Arizona," she pointed out, shaking her head. "Maybe it's one of those fake profiles? He got hacked?"

A picture appeared on his timeline. Simon holding a couple of children on his knee. Towheaded twins about two years old. The comment posted with the photo said that he was grateful for his family and professed his love for them. Erin scrolled down a little to look at other comments, puzzled. She glanced over at Adrienne, who was staring at the screen, her face white.

A picture of Simon with a short-haired blond woman with an angelic face in a flowery cotton dress.

A picture of two red-skinned twins in a hospital bassinet.

CHAPTER 26

$\mathcal{E}$rin swallowed. She copied his girlfriend's profile to her document and glanced through the few posts for any friend mentions. She pressed the back button and the pictures disappeared.

"He has another family," Adrienne said hollowly. "A newer one."

Erin shook her head in disgust. "That's really dirty," she said sharply. "That's really unfair. If he's going to go off and start another family, what's he doing coming back here and trying to work things out with you?"

Adrienne shook her head. "He wouldn't stay. He never did before. He just wanted the money." She took a couple of large gulps of her tea. "I kept telling myself that it wasn't about the money. But look at her. She's not going to be satisfied squatting or living out of her car or some shelter. And those babies…" Adrienne's voice broke.

"Oh, Adrienne." Erin wished there was something she could say. She had nothing to offer to comfort her. Adrienne had been taken by a scoundrel. Taken in by him over and over again. She had trusted him even though she knew what kind of a person he was. She had allowed him back in and he had just kept taking from her, someone who had nothing. Meanwhile, he had started another family somewhere else.

Erin typed Simon's name into the social media search bar and clicked the search button. The profiles with matching names were listed on the screen. Simon Simpson was not uncommon, and there were a number of them scattered across the world. Erin narrowed the results to just the United States. Simon wasn't a jet setter. He hadn't been traveling to other parts of the world. Just the United States. There were still a lot of profiles. She started scrolling down the list, looking at the profile pictures. Some of them had only avatars. Some of the photos were not clear at thumbnail size. Erin clicked on one and, again, Simon's face appeared on her screen.

Erin wished she could take it back. What was she thinking, searching for him again? She had already discovered the first two profiles. What need was there to find any more?

Adrienne swore under her breath.

This time, the woman Simon was with was a redhead. She was tagged as Tate Banks. Erin wrote down the name. She scrolled down the timeline. As with the other profiles, Simon hadn't posted very often. Once or twice a year and, sometimes, it wasn't even a picture or explanation of what he was doing. Some were just memes or Christmas graphics that said nothing about him.

But there he was, several days' growth of beard, cheek pressed against Tate's, and a little boy below their chins. Maybe a five- or six-year-old. Black hair. Darling little dimples as he grinned up at his parents. Erin felt sick.

"No, no, no," Adrienne murmured, looking at the little boy. She shook her head. "How many more are there?"

Erin shook her head. "I don't know. And there is no saying how many he might have never created profiles for. He might have told them he didn't like social media, and these are just the ones who talked him into it. There's no way of knowing."

"I knew there were women. I didn't think… I never knew that there were children. And so many of them… I thought there was another woman. Maybe two regulars. And the others were just… one-night stands. Just… satisfying a physical need. But this…" She closed her eyes to block it out and shook her head.

"It's too much," she told Erin, waving it away with one hand. "I don't want to see any more. Now I know what he was doing… fine. He was a worse kind of dog than I ever imagined."

Was it worse to establish multiple families than it was to pursue one-night stands? Erin supposed it was the children who made the difference. Not the length of the relationship. Adrienne had always thought that her children were the only ones. That he would always come back to her because she had the children.

"I don't want to see any more of that," Adrienne insisted. "You can give that to the police. Have them chase every one of these women down and talk to them. See if they have alibis. If any of them knew about me. Maybe one of them followed him here."

"Okay. Is that it, then?" Erin glanced around for a printer to send her document to.

Adrienne shook her head. "I want to know what else he was doing. I know the police are going to come after me. Who else is a better suspect? They know I had a motive. And he would have met me anywhere if I called him or sent him a message. I was the one who could get close to him, who had something that he wanted. So they're going to come after me."

Erin didn't deny it. But she still wasn't sure what Adrienne wanted her to do next.

"All of those different places," Adrienne said, motioning to the list Erin had typed up. "All of those friends. I want to know what else he was doing. If he was involved in something." She hesitated. "I never wanted to know what he was doing. I didn't want to know where the money came from. It was better if I didn't know, if I didn't have anything to do with it. I know there is no way that he would have given me all of his money, but sometimes it was thousands of dollars. We had credit cards that had to be paid off, vehicle loans with back payments due. He had bookies and loan sharks. A couple of times, we had houses where back rent was due. He would sweep in, pay everyone off, and leave me with a little spending money. It was never enough. But it was something. And I knew how much other stuff he had to pay off. I never believed it was one big win. I think… it was something else."

"Some other scheme or scam," Erin repeated what Adrienne had told her earlier.

"Yeah. There was always something. Another way to make it big. And sometimes… it paid off. But I didn't want to know what."

"And now you do." Erin stared at the computer monitor. "I have no idea how to find anything. It isn't like he would post about it online if it was some scam or something illegal."

"But people do," Adrienne insisted. "The police catch them—drug dealers, fraudsters, murderers—because they post about it. Brag about it. They want everyone to know what they did."

"Well… when was the last time he came home with a lot of money?"

Adrienne thought about it and gave her an approximate date two years earlier. Erin wrote it down.

"Don't look," she told Adrienne.

Adrienne looked bemused but obeyed, looking away from the computer screen. Erin searched for posts by Simon around that date. Which profile had he posted on?

She found one close to the date that Adrienne had provided, professing love to his family in Ohio. She double-checked that the picture on the profile was Simon's. A charming smile, photo taken while he played with a train set on the floor, a child's feet extending into the picture beside him.

"Okay. Ohio," Erin said. She clicked away from the social profile and returned to the search engine. Adrienne looked back at the screen.

"Ohio?"

"Yeah. Did he ever say anything to you about Ohio?"

"I remember him saying that he had a job out there. I forget what nonsense he told me about it. But he had money when he came back. Samuel Andrew was sick in the hospital and we couldn't afford the treatment he needed."

"Well, I don't know if I can find anything, but…"

Erin tried a few different searches. First with Simon's name and then broader searches. Combining "police" with the town name. Trying different words like "scam," "fraud," "drugs," and "cash."

A few different possibilities floated to the top. Erin clicked on the various stories. Most of them led to arrests by the police, but no pictures or names to indicate that Simon had been one of those involved. She clicked on a report on a bank robbery. It wasn't the kind of thing that she thought Simon would be involved in. He was a small-time crook. Someone who had not, as far as she knew, done any hard time.

She looked at the detailed news reports. Four armed gunmen had held up a bank in a town in Ohio close to the one Simon lived in with girlfriend number four. Or were they up to five or six? They had gotten away with thousands of dollars but, in the process, they had killed a bank security guard when he had opened fire on them. Both he and one of the four gunmen had been killed in the exchange, but three of the gunmen had gotten away cleanly with their haul.

And then Simon had shown up in Tennessee to see Adrienne, money in hand.

Adrienne swore as Erin read the details out to her. "Tell me you wouldn't have done anything so stupid, Simon," she said softly. "Tell me that wasn't you."

"There's no way to know," Erin told her. "They don't have pictures of the robbers. They were wearing masks."

"Maybe I don't want to know this," Adrienne said. "I thought I did, but…. if he was involved in stuff like that, I don't think I can face it." She cleared her throat. "There's a reason I never demanded to know where the money had come from. There's a reason I never wanted any details."

"Did you suspect something like this?"

"I don't know what I thought it was. I hoped it was just gambling. But the guys he met with sometimes, the men he hung out with… I never trusted any of them. And I never wanted to know what Simon was doing with them."

There was a sketch of the robber who had been killed. Erin guessed that an actual photograph of the dead man would have been too gory to print in the paper or post on the internet. The sketch was softer and would not give children nightmares. Erin displayed it full size on the screen and showed it to Adrienne.

"Did you ever see him with this man?"

CHAPTER 27

*A*drienne could not get any paler. Her expression was pinched. If she weren't already sitting down, Erin would have taken her to a seat. She felt guilty for uncovering what she had. She felt like she should have stayed out of it. Not looked so hard. Just reassured Adrienne that yes, all Simon had ever done was gamble. The only person he had hurt was himself. And Adrienne and the children.

But now Adrienne knew he had been involved in much worse than that. At least once. Erin tried to convince herself that it had only been a one-time occurrence. She had only found one heist, so maybe that was the only time Simon had done anything like that. It hadn't turned out well, so he had never attempted such a thing again.

But Adrienne said that he had shown up other times with thousands of dollars to pay off his growing debts. What were the chances that all of those times, it had just been gambling winnings and he had only ever pulled off a robbery at gunpoint once?

There might be dozens of other incidents that Erin hadn't found yet. Now that she knew what to look for, she might find more. But there might be a lot of robberies that were smaller and never made it to the news as well—a convenience store, a home invasion, a gas station—there were a lot of crimes that were too commonplace to make it to the papers.

Adrienne stared at the sketch. She shook her head.

"Simon, oh Simon…" Her voice was soft and rough. Not only had the man she loved died, but her perception of who he was had been killed too, violently struck down by Erin.

"You knew him?" she asked Adrienne unnecessarily.

"Reggie. I met him a few times… he would pick Simon up and they would go out for a 'guys' night.' Go to a bar and watch the game. Just the boys hanging out for the evening…"

Planning a heist or maybe even breaking into a closed business or invading someone's home. While Adrienne had thought that he was having a good time with his buddies, they had been committing violent criminal acts.

Unless the bank heist was a one-off. An ill-thought-out job that they had regretted afterward and never attempted again.

But Erin suspected that was not the case. And Adrienne didn't think so either, judging by her expression and the tone of her voice.

"What do I do?" Adrienne asked in barely more than a whisper. "Do I tell the police about this? Give them someone else to look at? A different avenue to pursue? I don't want anyone to know this. I want to bury it and not have anyone know… what kind of a man I took up with."

"He was from Bald Eagle Falls stock," Erin pointed out. "If they admit he was bad, they're putting a black mark against the community. They're more likely to romanticize him. You know how everyone likes a bad boy."

Adrienne nodded, sniffling.

"Scarlett was already doing that when I went to see her," Erin said, "Talking about the scrapes he got into as a kid. Laughing about what a troublemaker he was. Even though you told me how much they fought and that she wouldn't forgive him. He's dead now, and they'll pretend he was just… high-spirited."

Adrienne grimaced, attempting to force a smile to cover the mask of grief.

"I wish I could say that. I wish I could just pretend. To the town, the children, myself… I wish he could just be…" She sniffled and rubbed the corners of her eyes. "Like a pirate. Not the modern kind from Somalia or in the South China Sea. But you know, the ones in Disney movies."

Erin nodded her understanding.

"What if they don't romanticize him?" Adrienne demanded. "What if they say that I made him into a criminal? That it was because of some-thing I did? Because I entrapped him and he had to find a way to provide for his family. Or that my out-of-town friends pulled him into something?"

Erin looked back at the pencil sketch. A guy friend of Simon's or an old friend Adrienne had introduced him to?

She didn't want to ask.

"I think… you should give this information to the police," she said. "It might take the focus off you. You need to be able to concentrate on the children and not worry that the police could be coming after you at any time. That's why you wanted me to find this."

"But… I didn't think it would be so bad. I thought we might find some unsavory people… out-of-towners that we could point at to keep the focus off me. But I didn't think it would be something like this. They killed one of the bank employees. They killed someone, Erin! That bullet could have come from Simon's gun."

Erin nodded in agreement. She couldn't deny it. But she felt so bad for Adrienne.

"Well, we don't have any proof that he was actually there or ever pulled the trigger of a gun. It's only a guess based on where he was and who he associated with. The police in Ohio will know more. They might have suspects or be able to eliminate Simon. This is just a news article and only has a few of the details. They'll know a lot more than that."

Adrienne nodded. "I suppose. He might have just been involved in the planning. Or not involved at all and those were just gambling winnings. Just because he knew Reggie, that doesn't mean that he was involved in the bank heist. *I* knew Reggie, and I wasn't involved." She gave a wild laugh.

Downstairs, the front door banged. Adrienne and Erin froze, listen-ing. Erin expected the voices of one or more of Adrienne's kids. Maybe one of them had skinned a knee and needed a kiss from his mother. Or they were hungry for a snack.

"Anyone home?" Bella's voice floated up the stairs.

Adrienne looked at the computer. She shook her head at Erin.

"I'll be right down," she called to Bella, hoping that she wouldn't come upstairs to see what Adrienne was doing.

"I'll email these links to myself," Erin said, copying the information she had jotted down and switching to the email app. "Do you want me to give it to Terry? Or do you want to think about it? I won't do anything until you say."

Adrienne bit her lip. "Give it to him," she said recklessly. "If Simon did this… if this is the kind of thing he was up to, then there are other suspects. People who are much more likely to be violent than me."

"Are you sure?"

Adrienne nodded. "Yes. Do it."

"Okay. I will." Erin pressed Send to route the links to her own inbox and closed all the windows that she'd had open.

CHAPTER 28

*E*rin wasn't in a rush to tell Terry everything that they had found. She wanted to give Adrienne a chance to change her mind. Adrienne had made the decision in a hurry and might regret it afterward. Erin couldn't do anything about it if she had already passed the information on to the police. But if she held back, then, if Adrienne changed her mind, there was no harm done and she and Adrienne would be the only ones who knew what she had found.

So she didn't tell Terry when she returned home. She let Adrienne sleep on it and didn't go over to the police department offices until after her early shift at Auntie Clem's.

She hoped Terry would be in the office and not out patrolling. Her hopes were rewarded by Clara's nod.

"Yes, he's here. Let me see whether he is free to see you."

Erin knew that he would be. Clara liked to play the gatekeeper and bar Erin from entry, but Terry never refused Erin unless he was right in the middle of a call or interview.

Once upon a time, Erin would have just gone in, waving at Clara as she passed or leaving her a box of treats to keep her busy for a few minutes. But after a couple of unfortunate incidents where Erin had been caught snooping where she shouldn't have been, Clara was now charged not to let her past without an escort.

But Erin wasn't there to snoop; she had legitimate information to pass on to Terry to aid him in his investigation.

"He will see you," Clara said in a slightly disapproving voice as she hung up the phone, which meant that Erin could walk over to Terry's office. It was a worse mess than usual—maybe the investigation into Simon's death was producing a lot of paperwork—and the tiny office, made for one person and occupied by two desks, was claustrophobic.

"Uh, let's grab a meeting room," Terry suggested as he came out from behind his desk and stepped around a couple of stacks of paper on the floor. There was no more room on his desk or credenza.

Erin looked curiously at the paper but was too far away to make anything out. Terry took her to the same interview room that she and Stayner had occupied while he told her about Simon's poisoning and all the clues that pointed to an employee of Auntie Clem's Bakery, Erin in particular.

"Coffee?" Terry offered.

"No. I'm good."

"What can we do for you today?"

Erin had printed out a few of the web pages that she had found while working with Adrienne.

"I have some additional information for you about Simon Simpson."

"Oh, really? Where did this information come from?"

"Public internet search. Nothing confidential. Nothing shady."

He nodded and leaned forward, keen to see what she had.

Erin first showed him the social profiles. All of Simon's little families. Or all the ones that she had found. She didn't doubt that she might have missed some additional social profiles, maybe ones where he used a different name or an avatar rather than his own picture, and kept the security settings locked down so that pictures of the children could only be seen by close friends or family members.

Terry gave a snort of disgust. "Unbelievable. What a jerk. He can't make a clean break with Adrienne. Or any of these women, apparently. Just keeps stringing them each along, making her think she is the only one."

Erin nodded.

"Well, it certainly widens the pool of suspects." Terry's eyes flicked from one picture to the next. "We'll have to see whether there were any strange women seen around town before Simon was killed."

"You've probably already been on the lookout… but men more than women."

"True. The men you reported looking for Adrienne seem to have either left town or gone quiet. None of us have been able to catch sight of them. Which is both good and bad."

"Good because maybe they're gone, but bad because you don't know for sure?"

"And if they are still here, we don't know where they are or when they might pop up again. Or who they were or if they had something to do with Simon's death. I'm glad that Adrienne is out of town where she is safer… but if she's isolated and someone with bad intentions figures out exactly where she is, she is vulnerable."

Erin too worried about Adrienne being alone. She knew that the Prosts kept an eye on her, but they weren't with her all the time and, if something happened to her, either an accident or an attack by someone who wanted her out of the way, they might not know anything was wrong until hours later.

"Oh, there's Tom. Tom!" Terry called out to Tom Banks, who was walking by in the hallway.

Tom stopped in the doorway of the interview room and nodded to them. "Hey. What's up?"

"You see any sign of the out-of-towners who were looking for Adrienne?"

"Nope. No luck there. I talked to Darryl to get detailed descriptions, but I haven't been able to find them or where they are staying. I suspect they're probably staying in the city until they can get a better lead on Adrienne's location."

Terry nodded his agreement. Tom's eyes flicked over the papers on the table. "What's this?" He stepped into the room for a look, though he paused for a second before approaching to see if Terry would shoo him away.

"Some more background on Simon. All the women he was stringing along. Lots of little Simons running around out there now."

Tom made a noise of disgust. "Always hated that guy. What's amazing is that he wasn't killed sooner. By one of these women when they found out about his philandering ways. Or a brother or other family member that found out what he was up to." Tom's eyes blazed.

"That's not the worst of it," Erin advised. "I was just about to show Terry... this." Erin took a breath before she placed the article about the bank heist in front of Terry. "This went down in Ohio shortly before Simon showed back up in town with thousands of dollars to pay off his debts. This man..." she pointed to the sketch of the dead bank robber, "was a known associate of Simon's. Adrienne says they hung out and did things together. Went for 'guys' night out' when she thought they were watching TV at a bar."

Terry skimmed through the article, his face serious. He swore under his breath. "I knew Simon was a lowlife, but I never envisioned him being involved in something like this. They never caught any of the other robbers?"

"Not that I could find. But if you talked to law enforcement in Ohio, they could probably tell you more. Stuff that wasn't released to the papers."

"Yeah. They'll at least have approximate heights and builds. Maybe a recording of their voices. This is serious stuff. Not just penny ante misdemeanors. I never would have picked Simon for something like this."

"Adrienne is sick about it all."

"She didn't know at the time?"

"She didn't know anything until I found this yesterday. She thought the money was gambling winnings."

"And the other women? Did she know about that?"

"She thought that there were other women, but she thought they were just one-night stands. Didn't realize that he had families sprinkled all over the country."

Tom, standing beside them, was red-faced with fury. "How could this be going on and her not know about it? She must have had some inkling."

Erin shook her head. "He would leave for months at a time. How was she supposed to know what he was doing when he was halfway across the country? She had children to take care of. She had to eke out her own living. It hasn't been easy for her, you know."

"I know, I know. But Adrienne should have known. He comes home with thousands of dollars and she doesn't ask where it came from? Doesn't question him more closely to see if he is telling the truth? If she knew he was cheating on her, why did she keep taking him back? I guess she liked the convenience of that money every now and then."

Erin had never known Tom Banks to be anything but kind and compassionate. His sudden accusations surprised her.

"The person who is at fault here is Simon. Not Adrienne," she told him firmly.

Tom clenched his jaw.

Terry gave a little nod. "We know that, Erin. It's sometimes hard for a cop to see how citizens ignore what's right in front of their own faces. Law enforcement would be much easier if people told us what they saw or suspected and didn't try to protect family members or friends who break the law. But it's easy to say that you should report everything you know. It's another to actually do it."

His eyes met hers. This wasn't the first time that Erin had been a suspect in an investigation he had a part in conducting. She could only imagine how hard it was for him to be open and honest with his team, even if what he said implicated Erin in some way.

At least the fact that he hadn't been kicked off the case meant that she wasn't a serious suspect in Simon's murder. If they believed that Erin had done it, Terry would not have been able to take part in the investigation.

The problem with Simon's murder wasn't a lack of suspects. It was that there were too many of them. And Erin had just widened the pool further.

CHAPTER 29

*E*rin headed over to Auntie Clem's after she was finished at the police department offices. She knew that it would be closed and locked up tight. But she wanted to make sure that everything had been properly prepared for the next day and to get something put together for her advertisements in the next week's newspaper. She was always either preparing for a new sales campaign or analyzing the last one. When she'd decided to open a bakery, she'd had no idea how much administrative work would be involved. She had just pictured herself going in to bake bread every day. All other parts of the business would somehow sustain themselves.

But that wasn't the way it worked.

Erin reached for the burglar alarm panel when she stepped in the door, but saw that the green light was on rather than the red, indicating that the alarm had not been armed. She frowned at that. The employees were normally very good about ensuring the bakery was properly secured when they left at the end of the day. Of course, it was still possible to lose track of things and for an employee to think she had armed the alarm when she had not, but the failure was a major breach that she would have to talk to everyone about.

She reached for the light switch instead and flicked on the three switches for the kitchen.

She stopped, a scream stuck in her throat and her heart racing. She stepped back out the door into the parking lot, scrabbling for her phone in her purse. It should have been in her hand. She shouldn't ever go in the door of Auntie Clem's without the phone in her hand, ready to make a call if something were wrong.

She swiped and tapped frantically, but the screen rewrites were slow, and she kept hitting the wrong buttons. A call went through to Vic when she had meant to call Terry. Erin wanted to hang up and try again, but Vic would see the missed call and wonder what was happening. And Erin wasn't confident that she would be able to hit Terry's name on her second attempt either. It was like one of those nightmares she had when everything went wrong, and the more she struggled to right them, the worse and more confusing it became.

Maybe it was a dream. Had she gone home and gone to bed? What day was it? If she could wake herself up, she could go to the bathroom or silence her alarm—whatever it was that had disrupted her sleep and brought her into that panicked dream state.

"Hello? Erin?" Vic's voice was tinny and far away. Erin drew the phone up to her ear with great effort, as if it weighed a hundred pounds.

"Vic?"

"Are you okay? You sound funny."

"Call the police, Vic. Call Terry. I need him."

"Where are you?" Vic demanded, her voice forceful.

"Auntie Clem's."

"Are you okay? I'm going to hang up and call him right now."

"Yes."

"Okay, stay put. He'll be right there."

There were two beeps as the call ended. Erin let her arm fall back to her side again, the phone still heavy in her hand. But she didn't drop it. Once her arm was back at her side, she couldn't even feel it anymore. Erin felt like she was drifting, lost in space somewhere.

There was a siren far away, carried by the cooling breeze. Goosebumps prickled on Erin's arms. She was rarely cold in Tennessee, but she was now. She started to shiver deep down in her stomach, the muscles quivering uncontrollably.

Terry's truck pulled into the parking lot and skidded to a stop a few feet away from her. He jumped out of the car and hurried toward her, one hand on his hip, head swiveling to look for any danger. K9 was at his heel, ears pricked forward, nose scenting the breeze.

"Erin." He didn't touch her, didn't immediately sweep her into his arms. "What is it? What happened?" He turned his attention to the open door.

They'd been there before. Erin had a strong feeling of Déjà vu as he stepped over the threshold of the bakery door, drawing his gun.

The lights were still on, so he could immediately see what she had seen. He stayed in the doorway, gun drawn, frozen like a statue. Erin wondered why he didn't go in. But she knew why. He was waiting for additional law enforcement officers to arrive. He knew better than to rush into a dangerous situation without backup. They all knew what could happen. It wasn't TV, where everything would turn out well in the end. An officer who ran into a building without backup might never come back out alive. No amount of sharpshooter or ninja skills would protect him from an ambush by a criminal or criminals with multiple weapons.

Erin tried to control her breathing. She could hear it rasping in the dark, like a bad horror movie. But she couldn't feel it or control it. Two squad cars pulled into the parking lot, and the sheriff and Stayner jumped out.

"Rod, go around front," Terry ordered. "See if the front is locked and keep an eye on it. We'll wait until you're in place."

Stayner hurried down the block. The stores were interconnected, so he couldn't just go around Auntie Clem's, but had to go down to the end of the block and around. In a few minutes, Erin heard his voice crackle over the radio.

"Erin, I need you out of the way," Terry told her. "Can you go stand behind my truck?"

She didn't move. She was fastened to the concrete.

"Erin." He took her arm and gave her a little tug. Erin's feet followed. "Over behind my truck."

She had trouble getting her feet to obey but, eventually, she was on the other side of his truck. She couldn't see clearly as he and Sheriff Wilmot entered the bakery through the back door and searched it for intruders. He was back at her side a few minutes later.

"There's no one there," he assured her. "You are safe. Whoever was there is gone."

Erin nodded.

"Why wasn't the burglar alarm armed?" Terry exploded. "What is the point of us putting an alarm in there if no one arms it? This is exactly the kind of thing that we are trying to prevent from happening!"

"I didn't close today. But we always arm it. Every night."

"Was it armed when you got here? Did you disarm it?"

"No." Erin shook her head. "It was green."

"So whoever closed didn't arm it. Who was on this afternoon?"

Erin tried to remember. Her brain moved as slowly as a rusty bike chain.

"Bella. And Charley."

He shook his head. "They both know better," he growled. He turned to Sheriff Wilmot. "Can you get them both back here? I want to know what happened tonight."

Wilmot nodded agreeably. Even though he was in charge, he wasn't offended by Terry taking over and giving the orders. He worked in partnership with his officers, confident in letting each play to their strengths. And anywhere Erin was concerned, that was Terry's wheelhouse. Unless she was a suspect.

"I can go in?" Erin asked, wrapping her arms around her body in a hug, shuddering with cold.

"You can go in, but you can't touch anything," Terry warned her. "Hold on." He went to the truck and pulled a blanket out of the back seat. It had collected a lot of dog hair. He unfolded it, shook it, and wrapped it around her so that the dog hair was on the outside. "You wait inside," he told her. "Just don't touch anything."

"I won't," she assured him.

She walked inside and through the kitchen with her eyes half-closed, determined not to see anything in the kitchen. She would sit at her desk in her office. There wouldn't be anything disturbing in there.

The first thing she checked when she entered her office was that her computer was still there. Then the backup drives in her drawer. She had another backup drive at home that she rotated out every week so that no one could ever make off with all the data vital to the bakery's running—once burned, twice shy.

She closed her eyes, cuddled in the blanket and pretended that she was at home on the couch, warm and cozy, and everything was right with the world.

She wasn't sure how long it was before Vic was allowed in. She brought Erin a thermos of hot tea.

"Be careful," she warned. "Don't burn yourself."

Erin sipped it. Hot and sweet, like Vic's mother would have told her. Southern first aid.

"Are you okay?" Vic asked.

Erin nodded. "Yes." Her voice came out as a whisper at first. She cleared her throat and tried again. "Yeah, I'm fine."

"Why did you call me?" Vic asked curiously. "Why didn't you call Terry directly?"

"Stupid phone refreshed the screen and my fat fingers hit the wrong number." Erin shook her head. "I meant to call him. Thanks. For everything."

"Of course," Vic said. She rubbed Erin's shoulder. "What happened? How did someone get in? Was it left unlocked?"

"No. I don't know. Terry is calling Charley and Bella back in. They closed."

"I can't see either of them forgetting to close properly. They're usually great at following procedures."

"I know."

It wasn't long before Erin heard Charley's strident tone as she objected to answering any questions and insisted on being allowed inside to see Erin. Terry apparently did not bar her entry, and Erin heard Charley swear as she saw the state of the kitchen and walked through to Erin's office. Vic moved out of the way. There wasn't enough room in the office for two people, let alone three.

"Erin? Are you okay?" Charley demanded. She swore again. "What happened?"

"I don't know. Did you lock up?"

"Of course I locked up," Charley said irritably. "I don't know how to lock a door?"

"Someone… got back in."

"Yeah, obviously." Charley was growling. Her eyes flashed. She looked back toward the kitchen and then returned to Erin. She was looking for someone to attack. Someone to blame. She was action oriented. She didn't want to talk about the crime. She wanted to do something about it. Retaliate or catch the culprit.

Erin shook her head. "I don't know how. I just came in to do some work and…"

"Was the alarm set?"

"No."

Charley huffed. "Then someone disarmed it. We set it when we left."

"Who did? You or Bella?"

"Bella. She was right behind me."

Bella. Erin sighed.

"Where is she?" Charley demanded. "Why isn't she here?"

"She was probably all the way home. It takes a while for her to drive in."

"She should be here," Charley grumbled.

There was another voice in the kitchen, but it wasn't Bella's. It was a calm, drawling voice that Erin recognized. Beaver. Rohilda Beaven was an agent with some federal agency, though Erin wasn't sure which one. Beaver always seemed to show up when something interesting was going down, whether she had a professional interest in it or not. She and Vic's youngest brother, Jeremy, were a couple. Beaver didn't live in Bald Eagle Falls. But she was at Jeremy's often enough.

Erin stood up, pulling the blanket more tightly around her and taking the thermos of hot tea with her. She didn't want to be cooped up in the tiny office any longer and felt strong enough to be in the kitchen again. She watched Beaver come into the kitchen through the outside door. Beaver took in all the knives stabbed into the drywall, the red gel icing dripping down the walls and smeared into a messy message.

MURDERER

Beaver stared for much longer than Erin expected her to. What was she thinking? Did she see things that Erin didn't? Did she recognize the vandalism as someone's signature? Did she know why it had been done? Was she profiling the person who would have done such a thing?

Eventually, Beaver turned to Erin, her jaw working hard at the omnipresent wad of gum.

"You do seem to attract interesting characters," she said casually.

CHAPTER 30

*E*rin shook her head helplessly. "I can't understand who would do something like this!" she told Beaver, trying to keep her voice from cracking with her overflowing emotions. "This… why would someone target the bakery? Target me? Do they really think that I did this? Is this the person framing me for the murder? Or someone who believes that the evidence all points at me? Why would anyone believe I would do something like this after all that has happened?"

Beaver nodded slowly. "Lots of questions to be answered yet. First and foremost, how did they get into the bakery?"

"Terry said that the alarm must not have been armed. Charley said that it was. We're waiting for Bella to get back. She was the last one to leave the bakery. Charley said Bella was the one who armed it. If Bella says that she did… I don't know where that leaves us."

She couldn't imagine Bella intentionally leaving the bakery unlocked. It didn't make sense that she'd want anyone to get in while they were gone. Bella was just as much a suspect as Erin. The "murderer" accusation might just as easily be intended for her as for Erin.

But had she been so distracted by everything going on that she had accidentally left without arming the alarm?

Or locking the door? Surely the door hadn't been left unlocked too.

Charley would have been watching to ensure everything was properly secured.

"Someone must have broken in," Vic said firmly. "This wasn't anyone's fault."

"It's possible," Beaver agreed, looking at the burglar alarm panel. "These systems aren't completely foolproof. An experienced burglar could find their way past it pretty quickly."

"Terry said it was a good system."

"It is. Adequate for most places like this. You just want a deterrent. Thieves will go for the easy targets. If a good security system is in place, they'll go on to the next store. But that doesn't mean that it can't be defeated. Nothing is that secure."

"Nothing?"

"You don't have armed guards here. Guard dogs. Biometrics. Just a security alarm with a six-digit passcode. I could probably get around it given enough time, and burglary is not my specialty."

"But why would someone even want to?" Erin gestured at the damage to the wall. "Why break in here to accuse me of being a murderer? I didn't kill Simon Simpson. The police don't even think so."

"The Bald Eagle Falls residents know enough to make you a viable suspect. Most of the people who know you won't believe you had anything to do with it, but those who are just gossips and don't know you… it's fun to speculate."

Erin didn't consider it much fun.

"But people who are just gossiping about who killed Simon and whether I'm a good suspect are not going to be skilled enough to get by the burglar alarm."

Beaver chewed for a few minutes. "Then maybe the burglar alarm wasn't set and the door wasn't locked."

"It was locked," Charley insisted. "I watched Bella lock it. Everything was secure. I don't care what you think; you're wrong." Charley looked at Erin. "We all know that there have been break-ins at Auntie Clem's before. That's why the security system is in place. We're super careful to arm the alarm and lock the door every time we close. We didn't want anything to happen."

"And all of the tunnels were blocked off?" Beaver asked.

It had been a long time since Erin had thought about the old tunnel system beneath a number of the Bald Eagle Falls businesses that they had discovered was being used for drug trafficking shortly before they had moved Auntie Clem's Bakery to its new location. Erin had been sure to wall everything off securely so that the tunnels could no longer be used to access the bakery basement.

"Of course," she told Beaver. "What's the point in putting locks on the doors if you allow free access through another entrance? We didn't want anyone to be able to get in here that way."

Beaver shrugged. "Sometimes people ignore the obvious. Barricade the front door and leave the back insecure."

"Maybe we should have Terry look at it anyway," Charley told Erin. "Or maybe someone like Willie. He might be able to see if someone has messed around with anything down there. Maybe someone reopened the tunnel and hid a door you don't know about…"

Erin remembered the one that had been hidden behind a stock shelf before. None of them had been able to see it until the release button was pushed. "Or K9. He was the one who found it when…" She looked over at Vic and didn't finish. *When Vic had been on the other side of that door.*

Vic didn't seem to be disturbed by the allusion to her kidnapping or Erin's deliberate avoidance of mentioning it directly. "I'll get Terry and K9 to recheck it," she offered, and headed back outside.

Sheriff Wilmot came in. He looked at them. "Sorry ladies, I need you to clear out so we can take pictures and gather evidence. Terry and Rod can take your statements if you are ready."

Erin and Charley headed back outside to the parking lot. Beaver trailed them out, though Wilmot would probably have allowed her to stay. Bella was pulling into the parking lot and stopped behind the police vehicles. She got out of her car quickly.

"What happened?" She demanded. "There was a break-in?"

Erin nodded. "Yeah. Someone got in after you and Charley left. I just came by to do some desk work, and…"

"What did they do?"

Erin looked toward the bakery door. If the sheriff hadn't just kicked them out, she would have told Bella just to go in and have a look. But that was out of the question while they were documenting the vandalism.

"They… stabbed all of the sharp knives into the drywall and used food coloring to… write a message."

Bella shook her head. "Why would anyone do that? I'm so sorry, Erin."

"The burglar alarm must not have armed properly when you left," Erin said, blaming the system rather than on Bella herself.

Bella shook her head. "It did! I always make sure that it beeps and turns red. Sometimes it takes twice if you do it too fast and it doesn't register the first time. I always wait for the confirmation that it is armed."

"Maybe this one time, it didn't work."

"And the one time it isn't armed properly is the one time it gets broken into?" Bella asked. "Just coincidentally, it happens not to be armed and someone comes along and tries the door?"

Erin considered this. Bella was right; it was a pretty big coincidence if the one time they forgot to arm the alarm was the one time someone had broken in to vandalize the place. Maybe Beaver's scenario was the right one. Someone who knew what they were doing had defeated the alarm.

But how many people in Bald Eagle Falls could do such a thing? Maybe Beaver, by her own admission. Maybe Willie. He knew a thing or two about security systems and electronics. There couldn't be too many more in a town the size of Bald Eagle Falls. And what had they gotten out of vandalizing the bakery? Why would someone break in to do that? Was it someone who really thought that she was a murderer or just someone who wanted to make trouble? Why go to all the work to break into the bakery? That made it seem like it must be something important to them.

Erin watched Terry go back into Auntie Clem's after talking to Vic. K9 heeled sharply. He was very well-trained and, even when off-duty, he rarely did anything silly or naughty. Did she want him to find something in the basement or not? Erin would welcome the knowledge that the vandal had not defeated the security system. But she didn't want to worry that even if they blocked off the tunnels, someone could still get through them again and attack from an unexpected direction.

And the burglar would still have had to override the system to unlock the back door. The password was needed to disarm it. If the vandal had just come and gone through a tunnel entrance, the alarm would still be armed. But it had been disarmed and the outside door accessed. Whether he had entered through a tunnel or not was immaterial. He had still cracked the alarm system.

"I promise I armed the alarm and locked the door," Bella reiterated. "Charley was there. She knows."

Charley nodded. "I told Erin that already."

Bella looked at Erin, her eyes worried. "I'm always careful," she insisted. "I never wanted something like this to happen."

Erin closed her eyes and shook her head. "I'm sorry they made you come back here. There isn't really anything you can do."

"Erin?"

Bella's voice was insistent. Erin opened her eyes and looked at her again. She recognized how young Bella was for the first time in a long time. Erin always considered Bella an equal; she had such a good business mind and was so responsible. Erin accommodated Bella's high school schedule and knew that Bella had plans to go to college and to start her own business, but she still somehow forgot how young she really was. Bella looked at Erin with big, tear-filled eyes, looking for reassurance.

"I believe you, Bella," Erin told her. "Like I said... I'm sorry they called you back. You should be at home relaxing or doing your homework."

"I want to help."

"Nothing you can do right now. Once you've talked to the police, just go home. I don't want to be in trouble with your mom for keeping you from studying!"

"I can help clean up." Her eyes darted toward the bakery. "How bad is it?"

"It's manageable. No permanent damage. Nothing stolen. At least, not that I've noticed yet. The computer and everything important are still there. I didn't count the knives or anything."

Bella looked down at her feet, her face getting red. Erin's heart sank. She knew which of her employees had taken the cake knife.

Why would Bella do such a thing? Had she taken it for protection because Simon was threatening her or one of Adrienne's kids? Had she been the one to stab him? Was she the poisoner too, or had that been someone else?

Originally Erin had thought it would be a weird coincidence if two people had been trying to kill Simon using two different methods. It would have to be the same person. She had just changed methods because poisoning was taking too long or because she was afraid that Simon had thrown up all the poison.

But now that she knew more about Simon, she wasn't so sure. Erin did not doubt that he could have a dozen people trying to kill him. There were undoubtedly more than that who had good reason to want him dead.

"Is there anything you want to tell me?" she asked Bella.

Bella shook her head. She forced a smile. "I'm just tired. And worried about Auntie Clem's. I hate to think of anyone doing anything to harm it."

Erin nodded. "Of course."

Charley looked at Erin, frowning. Erin didn't know whether she would tell Charley about Bella having taken the cake knife from Auntie Clem's once they were alone. Charley was Erin's partner in the business, and she liked to know what was going on. She might not work as hard as Erin thought she should, sleeping in too late to be able to take anything before the afternoon shift, always wanting to try new things before waiting to see how the last campaign or change had turned out, not showing the customers the deference Erin thought she should.

But she was still a good partner. She let Erin have the final say on things they had a different opinion on, since Erin was the original owner and the one who ran all the day-to-day operations. And Charley did work hard when she was there and could take over management in a pinch. Erin had the feeling that Charley would have grown even more in the management of Auntie Clem's if Erin hadn't kept such a tight grip on the reins. As it was, she was like a smothering mother who wouldn't give her kids enough freedom to explore and make mistakes on their own. Because it was her business, she didn't want anyone experimenting and making mistakes with it. Other than herself.

Erin would tell Charley about Bella and the missing cake knife. Eventually. When they were alone. Charley should know what was going on.

CHAPTER 32

$\mathcal{E}$rin had done the best she could to get in enough sleep before her next shift at Auntie Clem's. She knew that it wouldn't be easy. She had wanted to wait until the police were finished with the kitchen and get it cleaned up, but Terry wouldn't let her.

"You'll be too exhausted to work tomorrow, but you'll get up for it anyway. You don't want to make yourself sick or make mistakes at work. I will clean up when we are done. You go home, have a cup of sleepy tea and go to bed. I'll be home later."

Erin knew that it wasn't the job of the investigating officers to clean up a crime scene, even the stuff they had done themselves, like smudges of fingerprint powder. There were companies a person could hire for crime scene cleanup. At least, in the city there were. There weren't any such companies in Bald Eagle Falls. Though she could hire a regular maid service and handyman to clean up and repair the vandalism. Terry shouldn't have to do it after putting in a full shift.

Of course, Erin had put in a full shift too, getting up a few hours before he had, and she was exhausted, physically and emotionally wrung out after the discovery of the burglary and vandalism.

She finally obeyed Terry's order to go home, take care of herself, and leave him to do the cleanup. She had her cup of sleepy tea with Vic, who would also take an Ambien to ensure she could sleep and be ready for work in the morning. She was lucky enough not to get groggy and hung over from sleeping pills. Erin would prefer being regular-tired from not getting enough sleep to the fogginess and nausea she felt the morning after taking a sleep aid.

The next morning, even though Erin knew that Terry had cleaned up the kitchen for her, she still dreaded opening the door and seeing what it looked like. Would there still be red stains? Would the word "murderer" still be visible? She knew that Terry would have removed all the knives from the wall, maybe even keeping some of them for evidence, but the handles of the knives protruding from the walls were imprinted in her brain and she didn't really believe that they would be gone.

Vic gave Erin a sympathetic look when she stalled at the back door of the bakery, her hand on the handle, afraid to open it.

"Let me go first," Vic offered.

Coward that she was, Erin stepped back and let Vic go ahead. Vic opened the door, disarmed the alarm, and turned on the light in rapid, efficient movements. Erin waited to see what her reaction would be.

"They did a really good job," Vic told her, motioning her in.

Erin reluctantly entered the kitchen.

She exhaled as she looked at the clean, white walls. The red gel coloring had not permanently stained the paint. From a distance, Erin could not even tell where the knives had been stabbed deeply into the wall. She stepped closer to examine the surface.

Terry—and the other members of the police department, if Erin was not mistaken—had carefully applied drywall filler to the cuts from the kitchen knives. The surface was smooth, but the filler could be seen on close examination. It would need to be sanded and painted. They hadn't been able to do that during the night because it needed time to dry and cure. Erin made a mental note to give Terry a call when he was up to thank him for taking such good care of Auntie Clem's for her.

"You're right, it's a nice job," she told Vic.

"We'll sand it and paint it on the weekend," Vic said. "You won't be able to tell anything ever happened."

Erin nodded. There was a lump in her throat that made it difficult to speak or swallow. Vic gave her one pat on the back and then got to work. Erin was glad to jump into the routine and distract herself from the break-in and Simon's murder. If she just focused on her baking, nothing else existed.

~

Erin hadn't told anyone about the break-in at the bakery but, of course, everyone knew about it the next day anyway. Even if no one had seen the arrival of the police cars, Melissa Lee was eager to spread the news to everyone she could, dramatizing it as much as possible while pulling a tragic expression so it didn't look like she was enjoying herself too much.

Erin caught several people craning their necks to see into the kitchen to catch sight of the knives and garish red letters that were no longer there.

All the interest and activity was good for sales, but mentally exhausting.

Business had slowed after the lunch rush. Vic was in the kitchen taking care of a few sheets of cookies. Erin smiled at the next customer and found it was someone she didn't know. She held the smile firmly in place.

"Welcome to Auntie Clem's Bakery. I don't think you've been here before…?"

The young woman didn't respond at first. She looked around. "I was actually here once before, but someone else was on."

"Oh, okay. So you already know that everything is gluten-free. If you have any allergies or sensitivities, please let me know and I can help you to pick out baked goods that are safe for you."

"I had the cinnamon roll with cream cheese icing. It was really good."

Erin smiled. "They're so decadent, aren't they? I just love making them."

"Just perfect," the customer agreed.

"I didn't catch your name?"

"It's Juliet."

"Juliet. Glad to meet you. I'm Erin Price."

"You're the baker?"

"We all bake, but yes, I'm the proprietor and head baker."

"The other girl I talked to couldn't tell me… I'm looking for Adrienne. Do you know how I could reach her?"

"Oh. Sorry, no. I can't help you there. I could give her your name if she comes by. Will she know how to reach you?"

"Uh, no…" Juliet hesitated. "She doesn't actually know me. We have… mutual friends. I was hoping to be able to connect."

Erin's senses were all on alert. Juliet didn't know Adrienne but wanted to meet her? Was she a reporter? A curiosity seeker? Someone who wanted to see the dead man's widow and possible murderer?

"What did you want to talk to her about?"

"That's… sort of personal," the woman said.

Erin studied her. The woman's mane of red hair flowed down to her shoulders. She was slim—not as skinny as Adrienne—with big blue eyes. They were similar in age. After looking at the pictures on Simon's various social profiles, Erin should know whether he had a "type" and whether Juliet fit it. But she wasn't sure if he preferred a certain look or was indiscriminate in his affairs. Maybe any pretty face would do.

"Were you and Simon involved?" Erin asked.

The woman's eyes widened. Her mouth dropped open. She didn't look quite as cute and innocent with her mouth hanging open like that. "What?"

"I know that Simon was seeing other women. Are you one of them?"

The redhead just looked at Erin. She was probably trying to figure out whether it would be to her advantage to admit it or to protest. Would she have a better chance of getting Erin's help if she were one of those unfortunate women? Or should she pretend to have some other relationship or reason to be looking for Adrienne?

"You are, aren't you?" Erin prompted. She shook her head. "Why would you come here looking for her? Why don't you just leave her alone? Don't you think she's been through enough without you coming around here?"

She couldn't imagine what the woman hoped to accomplish. Did she think that she would be friends with Adrienne because of what they had each suffered? Did she want to throw her relationship into Adrienne's face and claim he loved her more? Maybe she had a child or two and hoped to beg money from Adrienne, thinking that a portion of what Adrienne had should be hers. She probably had no idea where that money came from. It had nothing to do with Simon.

"I just wanted to talk to her," Juliet said.

"About Simon?"

"About… things that happened."

"If you want to leave me your number, I can have her call you the next time she's around. But I'm not just sending you to her. She deserves her privacy. She needs time to grieve."

"She doesn't know what kind of a person he was," Juliet said darkly. "No one here knows what he was."

"We're starting to get a pretty good idea. But it's not Adrienne's fault. He scammed her too. Took all her money more than once. So you're not getting to see her unless she says."

"She deserves to know about him. Why… things happened the way they did."

"Just go home to your kids," Erin suggested gently. "Go be with them and forget about Simon."

Juliet closed her eyes and shook her head slowly. "I don't have any kids." She opened them again, the blue irises burning brightly. "He took everything."

"I'm sorry." Erin couldn't think of anything else to say to this. She still wasn't going to put Juliet in touch with Adrienne. "Would you like another cinnamon roll? On the house?"

Juliet looked into the display case, a slight smile on her face. "With cream cheese?"

"Of course. I'll even warm it in the microwave for you. Make it nice and drippy and syrupy."

"*Mmm.*" Juliet groaned. "Okay, you've got a deal. And you'll give my number to Adrienne; tell her to call me?"

"I won't tell her to call you. She can decide whether to call you herself."

"Deal."

Erin got out a big cinnamon roll while Juliet wrote her phone number on a scrap of paper.

Vic looked up as Erin entered the kitchen to warm up the cinnamon roll.

"Everything okay?"

"Just warming up a roll."

"Who is out there? I didn't recognize the voice."

"Someone named Juliet. Out-of-towner looking for Adrienne."

"Everyone is looking for Adrienne. I wish they would all just leave her alone."

Erin nodded her agreement. "I understand people wanting to connect with her because of what happened. But these folks from out of town… seems like all they want is money. And it isn't like Adrienne even has that much. She has what she needs to build her house and give the kids somewhere to live. To have a little security. And that money doesn't have anything to do with Simon."

"I know," Vic agreed.

The microwaved beeped and Erin removed the warmed roll. It was just the right temperature to remain soft and fluffy like it had just come out of the oven and to melt the cream cheese icing so that it seeped into the spiral of dough.

"Those smell so good," Vic said. "It should be illegal."

CHAPTER 33

erry wandered into Auntie Clem's about the time they were getting ready to close. Coincidence? Erin thought not. There were a lot of good reasons for stopping by the bakery as it closed. One was that it was a good time to get a free handout as they cleared the display case and put the leftovers in the freezer for the day-old bread program.

Or Terry might want to get to work on the next step of the wall repair and sand the spots he had filled the previous night so that they could be painted over without showing any sign of the repair job. Or he might want to supervise the closing so that he could be sure that Erin was on her way home and the bakery was locked up tight and properly monitored by the security alarm.

But both guesses, though good ones, appeared not to be the case. Terry's expression was grim.

"Is everything okay?" Erin inquired.

"I wish I could say it was. There have been developments in Simon's murder case, and I don't like the direction they are going."

Erin swallowed, wondering if they were once again pointing the finger at her. Maybe the police department had decided it wasn't just an attempt to make Erin look guilty, but that she actually was.

"What's wrong?"

"Do you know where Bella is?"

"She wasn't on today. It was her day off."

"So would she be at home now? Or does she study in town or have late after-school activities?"

"At home. She helps with the farm work. And helps with Adrienne's kids when they're there." Erin glanced around, ensuring no one was within earshot. She was getting paranoid about everyone wanting to know where to find Adrienne.

Terry nodded. He stood there with his thumbs in his belt loops, watching Erin clear out the display case.

"Why? What's happened?" Erin asked. She handed him an apple tart, one of his favorites. He took it with a nod of thanks.

He didn't answer immediately, and Erin began to marshal her arguments for why he should tell her what was going on. She would find out anyway once it went public. Or when Melissa leaked it. She could help him to brainstorm and think of whether there were any other explanation for the new evidence. Clearly, he wasn't happy with whatever it was or how he interpreted it.

"Bella's fingerprints were on the murder weapon," Terry said abruptly, eliminating the need for her arguments.

Erin shook her head. She rubbed the back of her neck.

"It couldn't be Bella," she said. "It just isn't her nature. And if it was… it would have to be something like self-defense or trying to protect one of the kids. She is not a murderer."

"I agree that she isn't the typical killer. But who is? We have had plenty of unlikely killers. Just because she's young and because she seems to be nice, that doesn't mean she is innocent."

"If the cake knife came from here, then any of our fingerprints could be on it. We all handled them."

"Of course. I'm not saying that it's proof she did it… but there have been… other things."

Erin avoided saying anything. She didn't want to agree that there were things that pointed to Bella, or protest and make herself sound overly defensive.

Terry looked at her, waiting.

"What other things?" Vic asked from the doorway to the kitchen, obviously having overheard the conversation.

Erin should probably have asked that too, and Terry was wondering why she hadn't.

"Bella and Cindy are very close to Adrienne, physically and emotionally. They are very protective of her and her kids. Bella has been known to be confrontational with Simon or others who might have threatened Adrienne. We know that threats were made."

"She's a teenager," Erin dismissed. "Teenagers say things they shouldn't. So do plenty of adults, for that matter. It doesn't mean they plan to do anything to hurt anyone."

"I can't see her doing anything violent," Vic agreed.

"I still need to talk to her about it. An alibi would go a long way to eliminating her from suspicion."

Erin wondered fleetingly if there were anything she could say to alibi Bella. Say that she had seen Bella somewhere else around the time of the murder. Say that they had been together. That Bella had gone straight from Auntie Clem's to… where?

She would need to talk to Bella before Terry to find out the details and ensure they had a story that would hold up under examination and persistent questioning.

Vic and Terry were both looking at Erin with an expression that told her that her thoughts were an open book to them. She turned her face away, heat blossoming in her cheeks.

"I'm sure Bella will be able to tell you where she was and what she was doing around the time of the murder," Erin assured Terry. "She is *not* a killer."

"I'm sure she will," he agreed. "So you figure she is probably on the farm?"

"I'm sure. She doesn't spend much time in town other than to go to school or work."

He nodded and ate the apple tart with his fingers. "Do me a favor and don't call her to tell her I'm on my way."

CHAPTER 34

After Terry was gone, Erin looked at the clock and then at Vic.

"I'll be in my office. I have some phone calls to make."

Vic looked at her doubtfully. Erin never shut herself in her office to make phone calls. She sometimes made calls on her cell phone on Bluetooth while she and Vic closed. Or sometimes she sat at her desk to make calls to suppliers or her accountant while she sat in front of the computer and could see her orders or numbers while she talked. But she didn't shut her door.

"Personal calls," Erin said.

As if that explained anything. She and Vic talked about everything. Erin often bounced ideas off Vic or discussed her problems or troublesome thoughts. Vic generally knew what was going on in her life—even more than Terry.

Not that Erin didn't have her secrets. She liked to keep the past in the past. But that was different. Everyone deserved their privacy about some things.

"Terry knows what he's doing," Vic said slowly. "You know he's not going to railroad Bella."

Erin smiled, though the expression felt strange on her face and she was worried it would look more like a grimace of pain. "Terry is good at his job," she agreed pleasantly. "I'm sure that he will do everything he can for Bella. But… that also means that he needs to follow certain policies and procedures and, if he or Sheriff Wilmot feel like there is enough evidence pointing to Bella killing Simon, they will have to act on it." She paused, trying to decide whether to say more to Vic about it. "Sometimes, the law needs a little help toward the right outcome."

"You don't want to get in trouble for interfering with an investigation. And you don't want… Terry told you not to tell Bella he was going out there to talk to her."

"Which is more important? Keeping Bella out of prison or keeping Terry happy?"

She didn't relish the idea of his being angry with her. And he would be, even though he was the one who had come to her in the first place.

"I'm not going to tell Bella he's on his way out there," Erin assured Vic. "But why would he come here and tell me that her fingerprints are on the murder weapon and that she needs an alibi if he didn't want me to do something about it?"

Vic's mouth worked for a minute, opening to speak and then discarding what she had been about to say before the words finally came out. "He told you that because he felt bad about what he had to do. Because he's worried about Bella. Not because he wanted you to interfere and… invent an alibi."

"I'm not inventing anything." Erin stepped into her office and reached for the door. "I just have some business calls to make."

She ignored the look of concern on Vic's face and shut the door before she could make any other arguments. She sat down at her desk, picked up the phone, and looked at it for a moment, trying to figure out what she would say to Bella. She wasn't sure how to initiate the conversation or tell her what was going on in a way that she could defend in the future. Because she was pretty sure she would have to defend her actions very soon.

She forced herself just to dial Bella's number and trust that she would be able to come up with something on the fly. It was one of those times when, no matter how much thought she put into it ahead of time, she wouldn't come up with the perfect script. And the longer she took to initiate the call, the harder it would be. She didn't want to end up just sitting there staring at the phone for an hour. She needed to talk to Bella before Terry arrived at the farm, which only gave her a limited amount of time.

"Hi, Erin," Bella answered the phone. Her tone was calm, but tentative. She probably had an idea of what was going to happen. They had both been fighting against Bella being identified as a serious suspect for some time. Ever since Erin had discovered Simon's body. "What's up?"

"I just wanted to see how you were doing. I know… things have been pretty crazy lately. Since Friday…"

"Friday?"

"Friday was when Simon came to Auntie Clem's that last time. I guess you remember that."

"Of course," Bella agreed, sounding confused about why Erin was calling her.

"And you remember what you were doing after that," Erin suggested. "How you spent the rest of the time you were in Bald Eagle Falls."

"Umm…"

"You know where you were and what you were doing."

There was a long pause. Erin looked at her phone, trying to reassure herself that Bella was still there.

"Erin, you know that I wouldn't—"

"Of course I do," Erin cut across Bella's protest and anything she might not want to hear. "You and I were…"

"No." It was Bella who cut Erin off this time. "I wasn't with you. I was with Josh."

Erin breathed out. "Joshua Cox?"

She didn't know of any other Josh. She just needed to reassure herself that Bella understood and would be protected.

"Sure. We were studying," Bella said. "We've got a big test and needed to prep for it."

"So you were studying… in the library? Or at the school?"

"No, just… like, in the park, out of the way. Enjoying some fresh air."

Not in the library or school where the other students might have seen or not seen them. Erin swallowed, nodding to herself.

As long as Bella had Joshua to back up her alibi, she would be fine. As far as Erin knew, the two of them were not romantically involved, so the police couldn't accuse him of just covering for his girlfriend. He was more objective—a better, more reliable witness.

"Okay, good," she told Bella. "And as far as the equipment at Auntie Clem's goes… it would be perfectly natural for your fingerprints to be found on anything. You work there. You wash and put cutlery away in the drawers. Why wouldn't your fingerprints be on them?"

"Well… yeah," Bella agreed. Her voice sounded choked and Erin wondered if she had pushed it too far. She didn't want Bella to shut down before Terry got there. If Terry arrived to find her hysterical or defensive before he even said anything to her, it would look a little suspicious. Bella needed to be strong and confident. She couldn't be tentative about her alibi or her explanation of why her fingerprints were on the murder weapon.

"You use all of the tools at Auntie Clem's," Erin told her firmly. "You do the washing up and put stuff away."

"Yeah. I do. Almost everything will have my fingerprints on it," Bella said faintly.

"It's perfectly natural," Erin reiterated.

"Sure," Bella's voice gained strength. "That's right."

"Good. I guess I'd better get off the phone. You might have some calls of your own to make. Soon."

"Yeah," Bella agreed. "Thanks for calling… I guess I'll see you tomorrow."

"See you then. Take care."

Bella murmured something and ended the call.

Erin pushed her breath out slowly, trying to remain calm and in control of her emotions. She didn't need to worry about Bella. Bella understood and would have a good alibi for Terry. Terry would accept it and report back to Sheriff Wilmot and the other law enforcement officers that Bella could not be the killer despite any other evidence of her involvement.

CHAPTER 35

When Erin hung up the phone, she could hear voices in the kitchen on the other side of the door. Vic and a male voice. Had Terry come back for some reason? It was a good thing she had shut the door to talk to Bella. Erin stood up and returned to the kitchen.

It wasn't Terry, but Tom Banks, another member of the police department. For a moment, Erin let her anxiety take over. Was he there to execute a search warrant? Was there some other piece of evidence they hoped to find in the bakery implicating Bella or someone else?

She couldn't think of what else might be a problem.

Tom smiled and lifted his hand, showing her a can of paint.

"Just stopped by to put a coat of paint over those patches," he explained.

"Oh, you don't have to do that!"

They had already gone way above and beyond what an ordinary police department would have done. A coat or two of paint and the wall would look perfect. There would be nothing to remind Erin of the vandalism.

"We take care of our own," Tom assured her.

"You guys have been so good about all of this." Erin's eyes burned with tears. "You could have made things really difficult for me with the cake knife and the cinnamon roll and everything." She rolled her eyes to the ceiling, trying to keep the tears from escaping. "And I know you don't have to do all of this, but you've all done such a nice job."

Tom smiled. "Why should you have to suffer because some lunatic decides to target your bakery? You've had enough trouble here. You don't need that. Don't worry." He waved this aside. "We'll take care of this."

Erin helped Vic get the last few jobs of the day done.

"Do you want me to stay here?" Vic asked, glancing over at Tom. "Wait until everything is done?"

"No, you go ahead. I'll stay a bit longer. This won't take long."

Tom looked at them. "I can lock up after I'm done, if you like. You don't have to stay to supervise."

"I've still got a few things to do," Erin said. "It's fine."

Vic nodded. "Okay, well, if you've got this covered, I'll see how Willie's day has been. Call me if you decide you need anything."

"Go ahead. You've done your duty today. You still need to give Willie some time and attention."

"Yeah," Vic massaged her neck and shoulders. "I hope he's not too negative tonight, or I might have to take drastic measures." She shot a look at Tom. "You didn't hear that."

He chuckled. "You do what you gotta do."

Vic and Erin laughed, and Vic left.

"It's a good thing someone finally took care of Simon Simpson," Tom said as he started to slowly roll paint over the sanded patches.

Erin was working on the schedules laid out on the whiteboard on one wall of the kitchen. "I thought that as a law enforcement officer, you would be against any kind of violence."

"Normally, yes. But I can't say I feel bad when a lowlife scumbag like Simon is removed from circulation. Some people just don't deserve to be a part of decent society."

She probably shouldn't have been surprised. She'd heard him mutter a few things about Simon when he'd found out about all the different women that Simon was stringing along in what they thought was a long-term committed relationship. And he'd been there when Erin had shown Terry the information she'd found about the bank robbery that went bad. Tom knew as well as anyone what "lowlife scum" Simon was.

He might appear to the women he was stringing along to be a decent family man but it was far from the truth. He would have kept taking everything he could from them. And she didn't believe that the bank heist was the first violent robbery he had committed. That didn't just come out of nowhere. Someone didn't just wake up one day and decide to rob a bank at gunpoint with three accomplices. It had all been set up ahead of time. And there had undoubtedly been smaller crimes leading up to it and other jobs that followed.

That hadn't been the only time Simon had gone home to Adrienne flashing plenty of cash and making good on his mountainous debts.

"I feel bad for the girlfriends especially," Erin said. "Or the wives, if he was actually married to any of them. I can't believe that he just kept stringing women along, having babies with them, taking their money, and they kept taking him back."

"He got them so twisted around, they thought it was their fault if he didn't come home. Or he convinced them he was off on a job that paid well and would get them out of the hole. But of course it never did."

Erin frowned at Tom. She kept working on the schedule while he painted, and she turned his words over in her mind, trying to get a handle on what was bothering her.

"How well did you know him when he lived here? It sounds like you knew him pretty well… or is this all just from your investigation of his death?"

Tom wasn't of the same generation as Simon. He was an older man. Old enough that he could have retired from the police force, but he kept serving part-time because they needed him, and he enjoyed still having his hand in and knowing what was going on in the town.

Tom considered, a long pause between Erin's question and his answer.

"He took up with my niece," he said finally. "I told her to stay away from him. But when did warning a young lady about a scoundrel ever produce the desired results? They have to find out for themselves. They think that you're an old fogy and don't know the way the world works anymore. They think that things are different now and they're more sophisticated."

He *tsked* while he continued to roll the paint in long, slow strokes that didn't cause any drips and covered the wall evenly.

"Oh, I'm sorry," Erin said. "I didn't know."

She vaguely recalled one of Simon's social networking profiles with a

Banks. What had her name been? It had also started with a T. A funny sort of name. Tara? Something more masculine.

"Tate," Erin remembered, "Tate Banks."

Tom turned his head to look at her over his shoulder, sheepish. His face turned slightly pink.

"I saw it that day when you had them all on the table for Terry." He stopped painting for a moment, thinking about it. "Up until then... I thought he was just two-timing her. Splitting his time between Adrienne and Tate. Maybe some time on his own as a swinging bachelor. I had no idea that there were so many of them." He shook his head. "Unbelievable. Why did they all do it? I never could see what Tate could see in him. He was a troublemaker from early on. It wasn't like he appeared to be a nice, law-abiding guy. Why are women attracted to that type?"

Erin didn't know if Tom had ever been married or had a long-term relationship. He hadn't been for as long as Erin had been around, but that had only been a couple of years. Men naturally slowed down as their testosterone flagged.

"Some girls are just attracted to bad boys," she admitted. "I don't know if it is a rebellious thing or what... but it's not uncommon."

"Did she think she was going to reform him? That he was going to turn around and become an outstanding citizen?"

"Women marry men to fix them," Erin said, quoting a foster mother. "But you can't change someone else."

Tom nodded, grunting his agreement.

Erin tried to remember what she could about Tate Banks from Simon's posts.

"Was she a redhead?"

Tom nodded. "Yeah. Carrot top. We always teased her when she was little."

He didn't say what had happened to her after that. She had left for other climes. Had she run away with Simon? Gone away to school or to a job? Had she felt she wasn't taken seriously or respected by her family members and wanted to show that she could stand on her own two feet?

"And she has a little girl? No, a little boy. Do they ever visit?"

"No, not very much. Her mother, my sister, lives in the city, so sometimes Tate makes it there. But not back to Bald Eagle Falls." He sighed.

"Too many memories, I guess. Her mother was never happy here either. Small-town life isn't for everyone." He shook his head. "I wouldn't give it up for anything. You think I want to live in the city where no one knows your name unless it's to give you a bill? No thank you, ma'am. Here, where I'm known, if anything was to happen to me everyone would know about it. The community pulls together when something bad happens. You've seen it with Adrienne. With Simon's sister, Scarlett, even though people hated him. They still draw in to comfort her."

"She didn't… Tate didn't come here for Simon's memorial, did she? Or to see Adrienne or you?"

"No. I don't think she'd come here to see him off after everything he did to her. And I'm not going to be the one to tell her that he's dead. She's better off if he just disappears from her life."

"She doesn't know that he's dead?"

"I haven't told her. Maybe one of her old school friends will tell her, but I won't."

Erin thought about the woman who had come to the bakery. She had been a redhead. She had as much as admitted that she was one of Simon's women. Had that been Tate? That wasn't the name she had given and she said she didn't have any kids, but what if she hadn't wanted to tip off Tom or other old acquaintances that she was in town? What if she knew Adrienne wouldn't see her if she gave her real name? Did they know each other? Did they know about each other? Or had they before Adrienne had seen Tate's picture on Simon's other profile?

"So… you haven't seen her lately? She doesn't come to Bald Eagle Falls?"

Tom shook his head. "What's here for her, other than her old Uncle Tom? She didn't have the best experiences growing up in Bald Eagle Falls. Why would she come back here? Especially if anyone else knows that she left with Simon? Or that she was still with him? And Adrienne here with five children of his?"

Or three, if the obituary were to be believed. Who had given them the information? Scarlett? It couldn't have been Adrienne because she would have included all the children's names. Did Simon have anyone else in town? That schoolteacher, Emily, or another woman? His mother?

Erin put the finishing touches on the schedule and pondered whether to leave Tom on his own to lock up or to stay until he was finished. He only had a few more minutes to go and he would be finished with the repair job on the wall.

CHAPTER 36

It had almost been a week since Erin's discovery of Simon's body back behind the bakery dumpster, and things were starting to quiet down again. There had been a full spread in the Bald Eagle Falls weekly newspaper, with articles contributed by several different reporters or civic leaders. Joshua had put together a "crime beat" article listing the facts of the case and the clues that he thought important. He didn't say who his suspects were. Obviously, he didn't think that Bella had done it since he had been with her at the time. And Erin hoped that he knew it hadn't been her, either. The clues pointing toward the bakery were too heavy-handed and the vandalism of the kitchen hadn't exactly been subtle.

Erin smiled at Mrs. Foster as she entered the bakery with her little crew. The children swarmed around other customers to look in the display case and began to debate which cookies they should get. As the older girls' debate got louder, Traci started banging on the glass, shouting "cook-kie, cook-kie, cook-kie!" at the top of her lungs. Peter bent over her, trying to convince her to quiet down, and pointed out to the little girls that the louder they got, the louder Traci was getting. Eventually, he got them to settle down and shot a look at Mrs. Foster, who smiled tiredly and nodded at him.

"Thank you," she mouthed.

Peter grinned and looked proud. Erin gave him a thumbs-up. He was such a good big brother.

She served the next couple of customers and then smiled down at the little girls as Mrs. Foster took her place at the counter.

"Have you girls chosen what you want for the kids' club yet?"

Traci pounded the glass again, with her usual demand of, "dat one!"

"Please," Mrs. Foster prompted tiredly. "Be polite, Traci. Say 'please.'"

Traci pounded harder, "Please, dat one, please!"

Peering at Traci from the back of the display case, Erin tried to determine which exact cookie she wanted and put it in a sleeve for her. The other children were easier to deal with. Allan was still working on teething cookies and not old enough to choose his own treat from the display case.

Once everyone was happily munching on their cookies, Mrs. Foster could select the baking she would need for the rest of the weekend and the beginning of the following week.

"I heard you had some trouble," she murmured as Charley rang up the purchases at the till, indicating the kitchen with a slight jerk of her head.

"Yes," Erin admitted. "But nothing serious. It has all been taken care of."

"I can't understand why anyone would do anything like that," Mrs. Foster said, shaking her head. "What's wrong with people who have to be so destructive? And the violence…" She was always careful not to mention murder or specific examples of violence in Bald Eagle Falls in front of the children. "We live in such a fallen world."

Erin wasn't entirely sure what that meant, but she nodded sagely, deferring to Mrs. Foster's judgment.

"You can't make other people's choices," she said. "All you can do is choose not to do things like that."

"You're so right," Mrs. Foster said emphatically. "All we can do is make our own righteous choices."

The conversation was more religious than Erin was comfortable with, and she was glad when Mrs. Foster paid and motioned for the children to follow her to the next store. Peter helped to herd them along, waving goodbye to Erin.

"That one's a little…" Charley grimaced and didn't specify whether she thought Mrs. Foster crazy, overly concerned, or too religious. "Doesn't she know you're an atheist?"

"Yes, she knows. But people forget. Or they think everyone still has the same Christian values even if they aren't Christian."

Charley snorted. She'd been raised by strict Christians and was still a little rebellious about it.

"But she's right about there being too much senseless violence," Erin offered. "Trying to make sense of it is…"

"A lost cause."

Erin nodded. She looked at Charley curiously to see if she had any comments about violence in the world. Charley had been part of one of the organized crime families before meeting Erin. While she wasn't part of that scene anymore, Erin imagined she had some very different ideas about the acceptable use of violence.

But Charley kept her mouth shut and didn't offer anything in front of the customers waiting to be served.

One of the next customers was Mary Lou. She looked her usual unflappable self with a helmet of gray hair that was never out of place and a professional-looking skirt suit that showed not a single wrinkle.

"Hi, Mary Lou," Erin greeted. "I don't think I've seen you since… what, last Friday? You must have had a busy week."

Mary Lou nodded. "When I left here, Roger's aide called to say that he was having a meltdown, so I had to go straight home to try to settle him down."

Roger was Mary Lou's husband, not a fractious toddler. He had some challenges following his near strangulation several years earlier. He was home again now, but he needed to have someone there to watch him any time that Mary Lou or Josh couldn't. Their lives revolved around his home care schedule.

"Oh, I'm sorry. Was everything okay?"

Mary Lou shook her head. "He was really agitated. I could not get him settled down. I had to call Josh home. Sometimes, he can distract Roger with talk of fishing or some other father-son thing. And he's stronger than I am if Roger tries to leave."

Erin winced. She didn't like the sound of that. Roger was strong and could do a lot of damage if he were out of control. They had him on medications that usually kept him calm, but it sounded like something had really triggered him.

"Neither of us slept," Mary Lou confessed. "Saturday, we took him into the city to the hospital. It turned out he had an infection. Apparently, that can really throw people off. Cause a lot of psychiatric complications."

"It really can," Erin agreed. She had done home care for elderly people herself, those whose families wanted them cared for at home and not at a nursing home. They didn't always pay well, but offered room and board, which reduced her other living costs. "I've seen that with elderly people and UTIs. If someone suddenly starts hallucinating… lots of times, it's a UTI, not a stroke or drug overdose."

Mary Lou shook her head. "You learn something new every day. So that was our weekend, and we've been recovering from it since. Roger is finally back to normal, so I thought I'd better sneak out while I could and get some supplies."

Erin assembled the baking Mary Lou requested and wrapped everything up for her. "There. Charley will ring it up for you. You take care and don't try to do too much. You think you should be able to jump right back into everything, but you probably need recovery time just as much as he did. Especially if he's been keeping you up nights."

"We've been alternating nights, Josh and I, but it will be good to get caught up again. I won't deny that."

Charley took care of Mary Lou's purchase, and Erin looked at the next customer.

It wasn't until later that she realized the real impact of Mary Lou's words.

CHAPTER 37

*B*ella looked critically at the wall that had previously been defaced. She nodded her approval. "It looks really good. Even knowing that's where it was all messed up, I can't see any sign of the vandalism. Terry fixed it?"

"All of the police had a hand in it, I think," Erin said. "Tom Banks was by last night to put a coat of paint on it." Erin studied it. "I don't think it's going to need another coat."

"No. It looks really good."

"New schedule is up," Erin told her, pointing to the whiteboard. "Let me know if there are any problems with it."

Bella looked it over and took a picture with her phone. "Looks good. And, um…" Her voice faltered at first, then strengthened. "Thanks for the call yesterday. Officer Piper came by, but we were prepared for him."

"Good." Erin was glad that disaster had been averted. She didn't need one of her best employees being arrested for something Erin was pretty sure she hadn't done. "I'm glad you had someone to back up where you…" Erin stopped.

Bella turned around and looked at her after a minute. "Erin? What?"

Erin pressed her knuckle to the front of her forehead. She had as much as offered Bella an alibi, but Bella had said that she had been studying with Josh. And that was presumably what she had told Terry when he had visited her.

And Terry had been satisfied with their alibi. He'd probably talked to Josh to confirm it and been happy to eliminate Bella as a suspect. Her fingerprints on the weapon could be explained and she hadn't been anywhere near Simon at the time of his death.

But if he talked to Mary Lou to confirm Joshua's story, then Mary Lou would tell him what she had told Erin that morning.

That Roger had suffered a crisis and they had been with him all afternoon and night and had spent the following day at the hospital. Joshua had not been with Bella. He'd been helping take care of his father.

Bella took in Erin's look of dismay. Her face turned white. "What?" she demanded. "Why are you looking at me like that?"

"You lied about your alibi."

Bella shook her head. "I needed to study for a test. Joshua and I—"

"You weren't with him."

"We were by ourselves. You weren't there. You couldn't know."

"I know where Joshua really was."

Bella looked uncertain about this. "What do you mean where he really was? We were together. That's what he told Officer Piper. He believed him. I have an alibi. He knows I didn't do it."

"Until he talks to Mary Lou."

Bella shook her head. "What? What did Mary Lou say?"

"She said that there was a problem with Josh's father, and Josh was helping her. Simon was here, at the bakery and, when he left, Mary Lou got called home to see to Roger. And she had Joshua come home to help her too, because he was so agitated and she hoped that Josh could get him calmed down."

"Maybe it was after that… or she got her days mixed up."

"They were with him all night and took him to the hospital Saturday morning. And then they were at the hospital all day. So Josh can't give you an alibi for any of the time of death window."

Bella shook her head. "But… why didn't Josh tell me that?"

Erin held up her hands palms-up, at a loss. "I don't know. He's short on sleep. Maybe he got his days mixed up. If you put him on the spot, maybe he didn't remember. Maybe he looked at his calendar and there wasn't anything there, so he thought he was safe saying he was with you."

Bella pulled at her hair, distressed. "Or maybe he just thought that he could get away with it. I mean, so far, it has worked. I don't think that Officer Piper... I think he wanted me to have an alibi. I don't think he cared what it was."

Erin had gotten the same feeling from Terry. That he knew that Bella wasn't the one who had killed Simon and wanted to be able to pursue other avenues to find the real killer. Even if all the clues pointed toward it being a bakery employee, and now Bella in particular due to her fingerprints being found on the murder weapon, he knew that it wasn't one of them.

To think that Bella could have killed Simon was ridiculous. Bella was cool-headed and smart. She wasn't someone who was likely to be provoked into doing something violent and stupid, even by Simon. Even if she had been angry at him and threatened him, that had just been words. It wasn't the same as physical violence. Erin had never seen Bella be physically violent toward anyone. Not even a push or a playful slap.

But Bella *was* guilty of something.

Erin breathed out slowly. "Tell me about the cake knife."

Bella shrugged. "It was just the same as the other cake knives."

"Why did you take it?"

"I didn't!" Bella protested. Then her eyes met Erin's, and she dropped them to the floor. "I'm... I'm sorry. It wasn't like that."

"Wasn't like what? I didn't say anything. I asked why you took it."

"How did you know it was me?"

"The way you've been acting. I thought it was you right from the start. But I couldn't figure out why. I still can't figure out why. So you need to tell me what's going on. I can't keep covering for you without knowing why."

"I didn't even mean to take it."

Erin tried to imagine it just falling into Bella's school bag as she cleaned up at the end of a shift. *Oops.* It just fell in there and she didn't realize it until she got home.

But then how had it ended up in Simon's chest?

CHAPTER 38

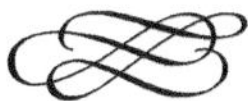

I would have said something to you," Bella's voice was tearful. "I would have told you; things were just crazy here and I didn't get the chance. I was just borrowing it and I would have brought it back here and put it back in the drawer on Monday."

But by that time, it had already been in the decomposing body.

"It was my Home Ec teacher, Mrs. Parker. We were talking about different kinds of kitchen knives in class, about the different shapes and what they were used for, and how to recognize them. But she had never seen a cake knife like that. She had only seen the long skinny ones, with a rounded or blunt end."

Erin nodded, following Bella and suspecting she knew where Bella was going with the explanation.

"She hadn't ever seen the spade-shaped one that can be used as a lifter as well as cutting with it," Erin contributed.

"It's so handy," Bella agreed. "A really sharp tip for piercing or starting a cut, the blade edge, and the wedge shape to serve the slices. It's like three tools in one."

And it was apparently nice and sharp and sturdy enough to be used as a weapon, too.

"So you took it to show to Mrs. Parker."

"Yes. I was just borrowing it. I didn't mean to *take* it, and it wasn't a secret. I just wanted to show her. When she asked the class what a cake knife looked like, and I said it was wedge-shaped, she said I was wrong, and everyone laughed because I work in a bakery, and I should know. So I was going to show her." Bella finished lamely. "I just wanted to show her."

Erin nodded. "And then what happened?"

She probably shouldn't ask. She knew she should probably encourage Bella to confess to the police what had happened and stay out of it herself. But Erin couldn't help feeling protective of Bella. She needed to help Bella sort it out and ensure that she would be okay.

Bella bit her lip and didn't answer.

"Did he come after you?" Erin asked. "How did you end up…"

"It wasn't like that. That isn't what happened."

"What, then?"

"Simon *did* come at me again, demanding to know where Adrienne was and saying I had to take him to her. Saying that money was his just as much his as it was hers. He'd given her lots of money in the past, and this was his chance to finally get something back from her."

Bella wiped at her nose.

"He was just so… awful. All he cared about was himself, and he had no idea what Adrienne and the kids had been through. Because of *him*. He acted like he'd given her this wonderful life, always giving her whatever money he had, and she just spent it all. But I know what it was like. All of Adrienne's money went into caring for the kids and herself. She didn't spend it on stupid stuff. Simon was the gambler."

"He wasn't very nice," Erin agreed. "So what happened when he went after you demanding to know where Adrienne was so he could get the money from her?"

Tears spilled down Bella's cheeks. Erin tried not to be affected by them. Guilty people still cried. Even if someone didn't feel sorry for the person she had hurt or bad for what he had done, she still cried about getting caught, and how a conviction would mess up her life. Bella swiped at the tears.

"He was threatening. He was pushing me around and threatening me… and I remembered the knife in my bag. I held the bag between us to try to block him, and then I felt it through the bag and remembered it was there. I took it out and…"

Bella gulped and tried to get her tears under control. It took all of

Erin's self-control not to take Bella in a protective hug and tell her that everything would be okay. She needed to hear the story. She needed to know exactly what had happened to formulate a plan.

"Just tell me what happened."

"I didn't stab him," Bella insisted. "I got the knife out to show him I could protect myself and he needed to leave me alone. I just wanted him to leave me alone."

Erin nodded. "And?"

"I wish I'd had what it took to actually stab him. But I've never done anything like that. I've never hurt anyone or threatened anyone with a weapon. He just laughed. He tried to grab it from me. I pulled back… I stepped back from him. He pushed me up against the wall. He grabbed my wrist and pinned it." Bella shook her head in disgust. "I wish I could say I was a ninja, but I'm not. He got it off me."

"He took the knife away?"

Bella nodded. Her eyes were swimming in tears. "Just like taking candy from a baby. I couldn't do anything to stop him. I outweighed him. I'm not some helpless little girl… but I was. I wanted to fight him. Not to stab him, but to hold him off… to show him that I had some teeth and he couldn't just push me around like that."

Erin thought about that.

Then Simon had been the one with the knife. Had someone wrestled it away from him and stabbed him with it? Or had he trusted his attacker and handed him or her the knife willingly? Had he attacked someone and had the knife turned back on him?

"You're going to need to tell Terry or one of the other law enforcement officers the truth."

"No, Erin…"

"They're going to figure it out. It's better to come forward and tell them what happened willingly. Say that you panicked and told a lie, but you realize they need to know the truth to investigate this killing properly. If they catch you in a lie… it's not good. It's going to make them more suspicious. And you don't want to get Josh in trouble too. You guys are young. Just tell him that you made a stupid mistake."

"If they know I took the knife from here, they're going to think that I murdered Simon."

"They already know that you had it in your hand. That you were one of the last people to hold it."

"I thought you said that you would help me."

"Well, it's too late for me to give you an alibi. They need to know that Simon himself had the knife. It changes things. Someone didn't go after him with the intent to kill him. He started something. Or he got into a heated argument and pulled it out."

"What does that matter?"

"It puts a completely different spin on who killed him. It might have been an accident or manslaughter or self-defense. It wasn't necessarily a premeditated murder."

The death cap toxin kind of argued against that viewpoint. But maybe there were two killers, one who planned things out and one who was opportunistic or who had killed him in self-defense.

CHAPTER 39

It was not unusual for Erin to show up at the police department offices with a box of treats in hand. Sometimes it was because she wanted something, and sometimes it was just to pamper them or to thank them for some action they had taken. Between Erin's deliveries and the muffins or other treats that Bella picked up, the police department usually had treats from Auntie Clem's once or twice a week.

It was unusual for Bella to show up with Erin, however. Clara looked at the two of them over the top of her glasses rims as she wrote something out on a yellow legal pad.

"Yes...?"

"Is Terry in?"

"No one is in at the moment." Clara looked at her watch. "Terry will be off soon. I don't think he'll be back here before he heads home."

Erin wasn't sure what to do. Take Bella home with her? It would be more comfortable for them to have a living room conversation than sitting on the hard chairs in an interview room. But would Terry agree to that? Or would Sheriff Wilmot insist that the interview had to occur at the station with cameras rolling?

Clara was waiting for her response. Erin handed her the box of cookies while thinking about it.

"Bella needs to talk to someone… if no one is in, then I guess we may as well go home…"

"You could see someone tomorrow. Is it urgent?"

"Well…" Erin looked at Bella, who looked miserable. She did not want to be there. And making her wait until morning the next day? Making her stew overnight and then drive back in on a Saturday? At least she didn't have school to get through before she could talk to someone.

Bella had already been holding on to her story for a week, bearing that burden alone. It was too much for a teenager, especially someone as sensitive as Bella.

"Do you want to come over for supper?" she asked Bella, at a loss for what else to do.

"I don't think I can eat," Bella protested, one hand over her stomach.

"Would you rather talk to Terry tonight or tomorrow?"

"Can't I just… I don't know. Next week, sometime. Maybe. When I run into him."

"No." Erin was firm. Bella couldn't keep putting it off. That wouldn't help her, and the police would just be that much more suspicious when they realized that she had lied. "Tonight or tomorrow morning?"

Bella moaned, hand over her stomach.

"Erin…"

Clara looked sympathetic, but didn't say anything to interrupt the decision-making process. She set a couple of cookies on a napkin beside her keyboard and took a bite of the first one before she began typing.

"I guess tonight," Bella finally conceded. "I'd better call my mom and tell her I'll be late getting home. She won't be happy about it," she warned Erin, as if that might make her change her mind.

"The other option is tomorrow morning," Erin reminded her. "Maybe that would work better for Cindy."

"No," Bella sighed. "I have chores to do in the morning. I was supposed to help take care of the kids tonight."

"Well, maybe you'll still get to, and it won't take long to talk to Terry."

But they both knew that wasn't very likely. Police interviews took a lot of time. They always made her repeat the whole story at least three times. Erin knew it was a way of checking details, making sure that the interviewee was not lying, and teasing out any more information that the witness or suspect might have.

Bella just shook her head.

"Thanks, Clara," Erin told her. "Sorry to leave you with all of those cookies." She winked. "Take them home to your family or give them to the boys tomorrow."

"Will do," Clara agreed, taking another bite.

After getting back in the car, Erin texted Terry to warn him they would have company, but she didn't say why.

Although Bella and Erin were home before Terry, he arrived home not much later. He greeted Bella pleasantly without realizing she was there to see him, and went to shower and change into street clothes before dinner. Erin thought it best if he were nice and relaxed and didn't see it as an interrogation. She hoped that would help to put Bella more at ease. But Bella didn't look very comfortable.

"Sorry," Erin said. "Won't be much longer."

Bella gave her a look that told Erin she was looking forward to the conversation about as much as a firing squad. Sooner was not necessarily better.

Erin cooked and Bella paced around the kitchen and helped with a few small jobs like setting the table. She enjoyed giving the animals their treats but was not distracted from the reason for being there for very long.

Eventually, Terry joined them in the kitchen. "Should I come in?" he asked. "Or do you need more time to get ready?" He would happily go through his news and social media feeds if she weren't ready for him.

"We're ready. Come on in."

Terry sat down in his usual chair at the table. Erin brought the hot dishes over and motioned for Bella to sit down. She didn't dish anything up. Terry looked up after a moment, noticing that no one else was dishing up or eating.

"What's up?"

"Bella needs to talk to you."

Terry looked at Bella. He chewed and swallowed. "Okay. What can I help you with, Bella?"

He flashed a look in Erin's direction that told her he was not happy about being ambushed with the interview. Though he had no way of knowing yet what it was about.

Bella folded her arms. She rubbed her forehead. Placed her elbows on the table and her hands over her eyes.

"Bella might want to revise her statement on what happened Friday afternoon."

"Oh?" Terry looked at Bella, his expression serious. "Okay."

He pushed himself back from the table and patted his chest where he normally had a notepad in his shirt pocket. He settled on finding his phone in his pants pocket and putting it on the table. He tapped the screen a few times to start recording. Bella stared at it dubiously.

"What happened on Friday afternoon?" Terry prompted. "After Simon had left the bakery and you left for the end of the day."

CHAPTER 40

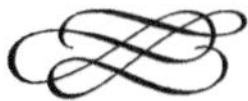

Bella rubbed her face. "I… do I have to start there? Can I start with what happened before that?"

"Sure. Of course."

"Before I left Auntie Clem's… I put a cake knife in my school bag."

"I see. Why did you do that?"

"I just… was going to take it to school to show to one of the teachers. Because it is a unique kind of knife that she hadn't seen before."

"And how did that come up?"

"It was my Home Ec teacher. We were talking about different kinds of knives in class, and she knew about the long kind of cake knives, but not those ones. The wedge-shaped kind."

Terry nodded. That was something he could check. "Okay. So you put it in your bag to show her."

"Yeah. Erin didn't know about it," she told him. "I was just borrowing it, but things were so busy at the bakery that I didn't ask. I just assumed it would be okay."

Erin appreciated Bella's effort to let Terry know that she hadn't been holding this knowledge back from him.

"Sure," Terry agreed in a neutral voice. "You were just taking it for a short time to show someone, and then you were going to return it."

"But… well, that's not what happened."

The tears started again. Erin had been hoping that Bella would find it easier to tell the second time around or that talking to Terry would make her calmer and more objective. Erin stood up to get a box of tissues from the living room and put it on the table. Bella nodded her thanks and wiped her eyes and nose.

"Simon came after me. He knew I was Adrienne's friend and someone had told him I knew where she was or could give him her phone number. So he insisted that I stop blocking him and help him get in touch with Adrienne. He said they were family and I had to help him get what was his."

"What was his?"

"Her money. Simon had given her money in the past, so he figured that now that she had money, she owed him part of it to pay him back. Never mind the fact that he had stolen all her money half a dozen times." Bella's eyes snapped and her words were clipped and hard.

Terry nodded. "So he came after you. He was angry. Making demands."

"Pushing me around. Threatening." Bella's eyes shifted toward Erin. "Smacked me a couple of times."

Did she add that for Terry's benefit because she wanted to make Simon look more violent? Or did she not tell Erin that part because she hadn't wanted Erin to see her as a victim of violence?

Erin kept her mouth shut. It was Bella's story. Bella's witness testimony. Erin had not been there and could not say what was true and what wasn't.

Terry waited for Bella to go on.

"I pulled the knife out of my bag. I wanted to make him stop. To scare him away."

"And how did he react to that?"

Bella shook her head, fresh tears spilling from her eyes. "He just laughed. He grabbed it from me and threatened me. Said that he could kill me if he wanted to. I didn't... I didn't know what to do. I couldn't do anything. So I... I just ran away when he let me. Left him there, with the knife, laughing and shouting after me."

"I don't know how Simon attracted so many women," Erin said. "He was such a nasty guy."

"I'm sure he wasn't that way when he came on to a woman," Terry answered. "He might have let some of his 'bad boy' edge show, but he would be sweet, making her think she could see his vulnerable side. Talk about how no one had ever really given him a chance. And then he would reel her in."

Bella stared at Terry, her eyes widening. Had she been taken by Simon, too? Had he been nice to her to begin with? But then, when she refused to help him talk to Adrienne, he had shown his true colors, threatening and scaring her.

"Where was Simon when you ran away?" Terry asked.

"Kind of back behind the general store."

Not far from Auntie Clem's, but not where Erin had found him. Something or someone had brought him closer to Auntie Clem's.

"And what time was that?"

"I don't know. Six-thirty, seven. Not any later than that."

"And then what did you do?"

"Went to the store. Got something to eat. Went home."

"And was your mother at home?"

"No."

"Adrienne? Anyone?"

"No. Mom took them into the city." Bella's eyes were averted. Another lie? Or just embarrassed by her previous lie and her inability to fight Simon?

"What did you get at the store?"

"What? Oh. Chocolate. A frozen dinner. I knew Mom wouldn't be home and I didn't want to make anything."

"Who did you see there?"

"I don't know. Don't remember."

"You remember who was at the checkout?"

"No."

"Stop to talk to anyone?"

"No."

"How about outside? Was there anyone around when you were arguing with Simon? Did you see anyone after that? Anyone who would have seen him alive after your fight?"

"I didn't kill him."

"Answer my question."

"I don't remember seeing anyone else. I don't know. There wasn't anyone around when we were fighting, or he wouldn't have touched me. And I wouldn't have pulled the knife on him."

Erin believed that. Simon would have behaved in front of witnesses. And Bella would have gotten away on her own or shouted for help. But they had been alone for the confrontation. No one to stop Simon from abusing Bella. No one to vouch for the fact that she hadn't killed him.

"Did you call anyone?" Terry asked. "Tell anyone that this had happened? Adrienne? A girlfriend? Erin?"

He didn't look at Erin when he asked the question.

"She didn't tell me," Erin said. "Not until today, when I told her she needed to come to you."

Terry kept his eyes on Bella. "Anyone, Bella?"

"No. I didn't want to tell anyone. I just wanted to forget about it. Pretend it never happened."

She'd bought chocolate and dinner and gone home to lick her wounds and put it all behind her. It sounded just like what Erin would have done.

"So when you left Simon, he was alone. There was no one else around. And he had in his possession the knife that would kill him."

Bella nodded. "Yeah."

"And you have no idea who was around. Who he might have talked to after you were gone."

"No."

Erin watched Terry, waiting to see what he had to say. Whether he was going to get aggressive with Bella and tell her that she was a suspect unless she could give him more information that pointed to someone else. Threaten to arrest her and send her to prison for life for killing Simon in a premeditated attack. Somebody had killed him, and she was the last one to admit to seeing him alive.

But Terry remained calm and relaxed as if he were still off duty rather than taking a witness statement. Maybe this was the story he had expected to hear from Bella all along. He had just been waiting for it. He took a couple of bites of his dinner, chewing slowly.

"You know that if you killed him in self-defense, that is different than murder," Terry suggested. "There *is* justifiable homicide."

"I didn't do it. I swear I didn't."

"I will need to get your statement transcribed, and then you need to come in and sign it."

Bella nodded. "Okay."

"Is there anything else you want to tell me?"

"No."

"Anything that you want to revise? That might not have been quite true?"

"No. It's all true. That's really what happened."

"Why did you lie to me about it before?"

"I… I didn't want you or Erin to know I had taken the knife. I knew that he was killed with it after I took it… I knew it would look like I killed him. So I just wanted… I didn't want anyone to know about it."

"Even when you knew we had found your fingerprints on the knife."

Bella nodded, her face getting pink. "I just thought… it was natural that my prints would be on it anyway." She looked at Erin. "I handle all the implements at Auntie Clem's. I help to wash up and put stuff away. You can't do that without getting your fingerprints on them. So I just thought… it didn't prove anything."

"And you called Joshua Cox to give you a fake alibi."

"Well… I know. I shouldn't have done that. I was scared when I knew you were coming over, and I knew I needed to cover myself because I didn't have a good alibi for that evening. I was just… with Simon and then by myself."

Erin avoided looking at Terry when Bella indicated that she knew that Terry had been on his way over to talk to her. Hopefully, that would just go over his head. Or he would accept the fact that, yes, if one of Erin's employees or friends were in trouble, of course she would do whatever she could to help.

Whether he liked it or not.

Erin was intensely loyal. Maybe that was why she felt so betrayed by Bella lying to her. Bella should have told her the truth from the beginning. She should have asked to take the knife to school. She should have gone to Erin as soon as she had problems with Simon. She should have come forward and let Erin know of what had happened as soon as she knew about Simon's body being found. But despite all the time they had spent together, all the confidences, everything Erin had done to protect Adrienne in the past, Bella still hadn't trusted her.

CHAPTER 41

Eventually, Terry sent Bella home, reminding her that she would need to come in to sign her statement, but not threatening her with anything. He thanked her for coming forward with the information she had provided. Bella's shoulders were slumped, finally relaxed after a week of walking around expecting the whole world to blow up around her.

Erin knew what that felt like. Holding back information that she hoped no one would ever find out about, but knowing that in the end, it would somehow come out. Dreading what people would say. What they would think. No matter how she tried to protect herself, the secrets seemed to eventually come out.

She hoped that she was stronger because of it. But that was probably just empty words, something people said to make themselves feel better. People were not better because of the trials they had gone through. They were just more beaten up. Tireder.

"She's just a kid," Terry said.

Erin tried to push her dark thoughts to the back of her mind and to focus on Terry, sitting on the couch next to her and yet far, far away. She hadn't paid any attention to him all night. When they were together, she should give him her full attention. If she ignored their relationship, it would fall apart. Partners needed to spend time together. To be seen and heard.

"What?"

"Bella is still a teenager. You can't expect her to behave like a responsible adult. I know that most of the time she does, making it hard to see her for what she is. But she is still a kid. Her brain isn't fully developed. She hasn't had the experience you and I have."

Even with all of Erin's experience, she had still done the same thing as Bella and tried to hide the things that she had done in the past. Even during murder investigations, she had tried not to let Terry or the other law enforcement officers or Bald Eagle Falls citizenry in general know all that had happened, even when it was far in the past. She couldn't very well fault a teenager for doing the same.

"I know. I just feel… betrayed that Bella didn't trust me. That I had to figure it out myself; she just lied to me and tried to keep me from finding it all out."

"It's hard, isn't it?" He didn't rub her nose in it, but Erin still felt the sting. It *was* hard when someone she loved lied to her like that.

"I'm sorry," she said with a little laugh. "All the stuff I've done and haven't told you about. Kept a secret from you. I'm sorry."

Terry put his arm lightly over her shoulders and, when Erin snuggled into him, he tightened his grip and held her close.

"I know. It's fine. We've gotten past all of that, haven't we?"

Erin thought about it. How many more secrets did she feel she needed to keep from him? Could she just let them go, talk to him about her life before they met, her growing up years and her lonely adult years? She had started fresh when she had moved to Bald Eagle Falls, and she thought she could put all of that behind her. Would the past ever truly be behind her?

Sunday afternoons were one of the few times that Erin could be sure to have time to rest and recover from her week. With Auntie Clem's closed for Sunday, only opening for a couple of hours to serve the after-church ladies' tea, Erin could focus on herself and whatever other things the week required. She tried not to fill it up with planning marketing campaigns or any other bakery-related business, though sometimes things popped up that she had to deal with anyway. It was usually a nice, quiet time when she could daydream, spend time with Terry, or read through Clementine's family history books and files. She didn't get much "me time."

Sitting on the couch with her planner binder and tablet, Erin tried to relax and let the week's trials fade behind her. It was not a huge surprise that her mind kept returning to Simon Simpson and his murder. It seemed like it had been ages since she had discovered his remains. But it hadn't been. It had been just a week. So much had happened since then. She thought the police should have enough evidence to figure out who the killer had been. Yes, Simon had a lot of enemies, but it was someone who had to be in Bald Eagle Falls recently, and it wasn't that easy to sneak in and out of town without being seen by anyone.

Had it been one of the men who had been looking for Simon or Adrienne, people he owed money to? A Bald Eagle Falls resident, maybe even someone Erin thought she knew well, who had a grudge against Simon for something that had happened long ago or because of one of the women he had taken up with? Even sweet Betty Thompson had nursed a grudge against him for many years. While Erin didn't think an old woman could have driven the cake knife into Simon's chest, Betty was just one example of the resentment many Bald Eagle Falls residents probably nursed against him despite the intervening decades.

Not Betty. Simon would just have taken the knife away from her, as he had from Bella. Though maybe at that point, he had been suffering from the poisoning and had been weak or disoriented. Erin couldn't eliminate someone he would have easily been able to fight before being poisoned. She had no idea how disabled he might have been by the death cap mushrooms.

Something stirred at the back of Erin's mind. Something that she had thought of before and had wanted to look up. But life was so busy that it had been driven from her mind and overtaken by other, more immediate concerns.

What had it been?

She thought that she had been at Auntie Clem's at the time. That was a time when thoughts often came to her and fled just as quickly when she had to deal with customers and didn't have time to stop and write down an idea while it was still fresh in her mind.

Had it been something that Mary Lou had said? Erin was pretty sure not. Mary Lou had given away that Joshua had not been with Bella during the window of time that Simon had been killed. But Erin didn't think there was anything else.

Other than that she should check in with Mary Lou to see how Roger was doing and if there was anything else the family needed. She worried about the hospital bills that they would have incurred. The Coxes didn't have extra money. Mary Lou counted every penny and was very frugal. They had lost their life savings and home before Roger's hypoxic brain injury. And who knew how many other debts Mary Lou was trying to pay off while taking care of herself and Joshua. And Roger, since he was home again. Erin hoped that the paper was paying Josh well for the articles he was writing for the newspaper, but suspected not. Josh was still very new to investigative journalism and, even though he had written some excellent articles on breaking news or developing situations within Bald Eagle Falls, the paper probably didn't have the budget to pay him very well.

Erin should drop a care package off for Mary Lou. A box of baking from the freezer that would last her for a few weeks so that she didn't have to worry so much about the grocery bills. It might not be a lot, but it was something she could do to help.

It came to her as Erin jotted a note to herself in her planner. It hadn't been Mary Lou she had been talking to. It had been Tom Banks. When he had been talking about his niece. What was her name?

CHAPTER 42

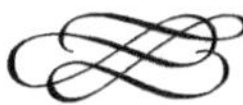

*E*rin tapped the screen of the tablet and searched her email for the notes she had made while doing the research with Adrienne. She had jotted down the various names associated with the social profiles Simon had created for himself.

There was a lot of stuff in her inbox that she needed to deal with. Why did it seem like the more she did, the more emails appeared in her inbox?

She found the email and skimmed over it.

Tate. Tate Banks.

Was that the woman who had shown up at the bakery asking after Adrienne? Tom had said that she had not been in town, but he could have been covering for her. Or he might not have had any idea that she had been in town. If she were there for nefarious purposes, she wouldn't exactly call her uncle the part-time cop to tell him about it, would she?

Erin searched for the woman's profile. It took her a few minutes to dig down and find the right one. She would not have thought there would be so many people named Tate Banks on one social network. She eventually found the one that was associated with one of the Simon Simpson profiles. She clicked through and looked at the pictures of the woman on the profile avatar and timeline. She breathed out a sigh of relief. It was not the woman who had introduced herself as Juliet. She was a redhead, but not the same woman.

At the same time, she was disappointed. She didn't want someone that Tom knew and loved to be a killer, but she also wished she could move the case forward and help identify the real culprit. It would be a big relief to Adrienne and everyone else if they arrested someone. The rumors would die down and Erin, Bella, and Adrienne could go on with their lives without whispered accusations following them everywhere.

She went painstakingly through each of the other Simon Simpson profiles she had found with Simon's picture on them, and then searched for more, trying to make sure that she had all of Simon's identities. He was a busy man. Lots of girlfriends with children scattered across the country. But she couldn't find the red-haired woman who had come to the bakery.

But some profiles were locked down so that all the pictures and friends were hidden from Erin. Women who were more careful of their online security or who didn't even use social media. Any one of them could be the redhead who had shown up at Auntie Clem's.

Erin hadn't seen her since then. She hadn't continued to come by, asking for Adrienne's information. Did that mean she had gotten it or given up?

Eventually, Erin had to concede that the social networks were a dead end.

What about other crimes? She had found the bank heist. Maybe she could find other criminal acts that Simon had been involved in. Looking at the various posts he had made, she tried to match the cities he had been in with police activity reports. But she didn't have much success. She'd been lucky the first time. But then, Adrienne had given her the timing of Simon showing up with money to help pay the hospital bills. If she hadn't known when he had come into money, she wouldn't have been able to match it up with a successful bank robbery or other heist in the area.

Maybe that bank heist had been his only one. That would explain why things had gone so badly. Maybe it wasn't his area of expertise, just a one-time job. And then he hadn't done it since because he'd lost a man in the process.

Erin searched for reports on the bank heist and read through them, looking for the name of the robber who had been killed. Maybe she could find out who his online friends were and then see if any of them had been arrested for anything else. Chances were, it wasn't the first crime he had participated in.

A few minutes later, she was plugging the name Denny Martin into her search field. Again, there were far more of them than she would have expected. But none of the faces on the social profiles she could find matched the sketch that had been published. But as she was scrolling through search results, she found a recent obituary.

Would his family publish an obituary when he was killed in the crossfire at a bank heist? Erin had assumed they would not want to draw attention to the family members and would not publish anything.

But the picture of the smiling man beside the obituary was a match for the sketch of the robber who had been killed. Erin focused on the small, dense text next to the picture and tried to work her way through the description of how he had grown up in Ohio and the long list of family relationships. Reading was not her strong suit, but it probably helped that she had been going through Clementine's family history files, which included a lot of dusty and faded obituaries, some much smaller than the type on the screen.

She zoomed in on the text, but it became too wide for the screen and she had to scroll back and forth to see it all. Then she lost her place when she pinched it to make it smaller again. She skimmed over the words, trying to find her place.

Juliet Marsh.

The woman who had come to the bakery had said that her name was Juliet.

Erin read the words again.

Survived by his spouse, Juliet Marsh.

Juliet was not one of Simon's partners. She was the dead bank robber's wife.

CHAPTER 43

*E*rin stared at the words, trying to figure out what that meant. Why had Juliet come to Bald Eagle Falls? What was she looking for? Juliet had asked after Adrienne, so she knew that Adrienne was Simon's partner. What did she want with her? Did she think she was owed part of the money Simon had given Adrienne from the bank heist? If so, she was out of luck because it was long gone. But Adrienne did have money of her own. Would Juliet distinguish the money she had earned herself from the bank take?

Erin tried to figure out what to do with the new information. She should let Terry know, of course. He was sleeping after a double shift and Erin wasn't going to wake him up. It wasn't actually urgent, even though it had set her heart pounding like a train engine. Erin hadn't seen Juliet since Friday when she had come to the bakery. She had probably given up and gone home. She'd realized that it was a wild goose chase and that even if she found Adrienne, she wouldn't give her any money.

Except that after she had traveled all the way from Ohio to find Simon or Adrienne, it seemed unlikely that Juliet would give up after just asking around.

Erin tried calling Adrienne on her phone, but there was no answer. It was not surprising. When she wasn't using it, Adrienne kept it turned off for privacy and to conserve her battery and minutes. Because it was turned off, Erin wouldn't be able to text message her either. The text might go through, but it wouldn't wake the phone up. Adrienne wouldn't get the message until she turned the phone on next.

Erin tried Bella's number. It rang through to voicemail. Was Bella avoiding her because she was embarrassed about her confession? Or because she was angry with Erin for making her talk to Terry and tell him the truth? She might just be studying or doing something with friends, but Erin had never had a problem reaching her before.

She tried Cindy Prost's number. Even though she didn't get along particularly well with Cindy and avoided talking to her if she could help it. This was different. She felt increasing concern over not being able to reach anyone. What if Juliet were out there? What if she had done something terrible to Adrienne, Bella, and Cindy? And what about the children? Surely Juliet wouldn't do anything to hurt the children.

Erin tapped Bella's name again. She listened to the ringing, a knot growing in her stomach. Maybe she would have to wake Terry after all. He could judge whether it was important enough to call in the other law enforcement officers. Whether he should go to the Prost farm to see if anything had happened to them.

"Hello?"

Erin blew her breath out in relief. "Oh, Bella. Thank goodness you're there. Is everything okay?"

"Uh… yeah, everything is fine," Bella said cautiously. "Why? What's wrong?"

"I couldn't get any of you. I was worried that something might have happened to you."

"Something like what?" Bella's tone took on a tinge of fear.

"I just figured out who Juliet is."

"Juliet? Who is that?"

Bella hadn't been at the bakery when Juliet had come around looking for Adrienne. "Juliet is—" Erin cut herself off. "Did Adrienne tell you about what Simon did?"

Bella grunted in exasperation. "What are you talking about, Erin? I know who Simon was."

"But did she tell you what she discovered about him… in Ohio?"

"Oh…" Caution entered Bella's voice. "About… that bank thing?

Yeah… she said it was the only time, though, that it had never happened before. That was the only time."

And how did Adrienne know that? She couldn't know what Simon was doing when he was across the country. She hadn't known about all the other families. She certainly hadn't known what he had been up to with them.

"Maybe it was," Erin said flatly, not expressing her doubts. "But here's the thing… one of the other robbers was killed in that heist."

"I know," Bella agreed.

"Juliet was his wife. The wife of the guy who was killed!"

"Okay…?"

Erin realized that Bella was still missing a step. "Juliet is in town. Or she was a couple of days ago. She's been looking for Adrienne."

"Why would she be looking for Adrienne?" Bella sounded more alarmed, the situation starting to become more clear.

"That's exactly my concern. All I can think of is that Juliet wants the money. Just like Simon did. Just like the other guys who were looking for Simon and then Adrienne. Everyone is looking for Adrienne because they want her money."

"But it isn't the bank heist money. It's Adrienne's settlement. It doesn't have anything to do with Simon. She wasn't even going to give any of it to Simon. It's for the children. For building a house."

"I know, but no one cares about that. They think that since Adrienne has money, she should give it to those Simon owed money to."

"Why would Simon owe anything to Juliet?"

"I don't know. Maybe they didn't give Denny Martin's share to his wife. Maybe she never got anything for that heist, even though she lost her husband because of it."

"Maybe," Bella said doubtfully.

"Where is Adrienne?" Erin asked. "Is she with you? We need to let her know about this."

"No. She's not here. She was going into town."

"Here? What for?"

"I don't know. She needed to pick some things up from Scarlett."

"Why didn't she turn her phone on?"

"Adrienne never does," Bella sounded irritated. "She doesn't want anyone to be able to trace her movements, so she never has it on when she's driving. She only turns it on if she needs to make a call."

"She was going to Scarlett's? Was that the only place?"

"I guess. Everything is closed on Sunday. She knows that. She couldn't go to any of the stores."

"Did she have the kids with her? Could they be going to the park or anything?"

"She has Samuel Andrew. And the baby, of course."

So they probably weren't at the park and couldn't be at any of the stores. Scarlett's house. Maybe some other errand that didn't involve going to a store.

"I'm going to try to find her," Erin decided aloud. "I'll have my phone on. Would you please call if she gets back before I find her?"

"Yeah, sure. What are you going to tell her? I don't understand."

"I think Juliet could be dangerous."

"Why?"

Erin tried to find the words to describe the feelings she'd had from the instant she realized that Juliet was not one of Simon's past lovers, but the wife of the dead bank robber. "She doesn't exactly have any reason to feel kindly toward Simon or Adrienne. Her husband died. She might have blamed Simon for what happened. He might have bilked her out of her share of the bank take. I just… if she is going after Adrienne and I don't do anything about it, I could never forgive myself."

"I'll come into town and help."

"It will take you half an hour to get here," Erin looked at her watch. "You'd better stay there and make sure nothing happens to the kids."

"Get help from Terry. Don't go after her yourself."

Erin looked impatiently toward the bedroom where Terry was sleeping. She wanted to get out of the house, and he would make her wait while he woke up, got ready, and called the police dispatcher or Sheriff Wilmot to let them know what was going on.

"I won't," she agreed and ended the call.

CHAPTER 44

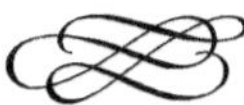

Erin really hated to wake Terry when he had just put in a double shift. She should probably call the dispatcher or Sheriff Wilmot instead, to get someone who was fresh and could be fully alert for the job.

And what? Leave Terry there sleeping while she went off following a lead? He would want to be there. First and foremost, he would want her to be safe, and she could be by taking someone else, but he would also want to be there. He would want to be the one going in with her. He'd be really upset if he woke up to find that everything had gone down while he had been asleep and no one had bothered to wake him and at least let him make his own decision.

Erin nudged Terry's shoulder.

Terry didn't move or make a sound at first. She gave him a couple more nudges. Terry groaned in his sleep and pulled away from her.

"Terry. Wake up. You need to wake up. I need to ask you something."

"Whatever you want," he mumbled. "Jus' go ahead."

She laughed to herself. Wouldn't he be ticked if she took him at his word and went ahead based on his sleep-talking?

"Terry." She shook him harder. "Terry."

K9 had followed Erin into the room and started to whine. He didn't like this unusual behavior.

"It's okay," Erin told him. "He'll be awake in a minute. Then you can go out for a walk with us."

K9 sat back on his haunches, panting. He seemed to think this was a good idea.

"I guess I'll just call the sheriff," Erin said, looking down at Terry.

He stirred. "The sheriff? What's wrong?"

"You need to wake up. I need to talk to you."

Terry rubbed his eyes. "Erin? What's going on?"

"Are you awake?"

"Well, I guess I am now," he said grumpily.

"I'm worried about Adrienne. We need to find her and warn her."

"What?" He rubbed his eyes again and shook his head, trying to wake himself up. "You need to go out?"

"Adrienne might be in danger."

"What's going on?"

She watched his face, waiting until she knew that he was truly awake and paying attention to her. He was still tired, but he wasn't just going to drift back into sleep.

"It's Adrienne. The woman looking for her isn't one of Simon's other women. She's the wife of the dead bank robber."

Terry blinked at her, processing this slowly. "She's the…"

"The bank robber that was killed when Simon robbed the bank in Ohio."

"We don't have any proof that he was one of the men who committed that robbery."

"I know," Erin said impatiently. "But there are enough connections that he could have been. And the woman who was here trying to track down Adrienne was the wife of the man who was killed. Why would she be here if Simon *wasn't* involved in the bank robbery?"

"How do you know she was his wife?"

"I found his obituary. And she was listed as his wife. It says right there, Juliet Marsh. And that's how she introduced herself to me. Juliet. I looked for her photo online, and it matches. She is the dead bank robber's wife. It doesn't matter what else we can prove. I know she's his widow."

"It *does* matter what else we can prove. We can't just arrest the woman or ask her to come in for questioning based on the fact that she is the widow of someone who *might* have known Simon and been involved in a bank heist with him. There's absolutely no evidence of that yet."

"I don't care about arresting her right now. I just want to protect Adrienne!"

He rubbed his hand over his face. "Where is Adrienne?"

"She turns her phone off, so I can't call her. Bella said that she was coming into town. To get something from Scarlett."

"Coming into town? When?"

"She's probably here already. I want to go over there, but… certain people think I should wake you up first."

He gave a quick smile at that. "Yes, certain people would be right. Give me a minute to dress."

"Just pull on some pants. I'm worried."

He slept in his boxers and t-shirt, so it wasn't like he was indecent. He would want to pull on his full police uniform, and Erin was raring to go. It would take time to get on his full gear.

He gave her a look and climbed out of bed to get dressed.

"Running into something like this without being fully prepared can be dangerous," he warned. "Taking a few extra minutes to ensure I am properly prepared can be the difference between failure or a successful outcome."

Erin groaned.

"I'm getting ready," he pointed out. "I'll go, but not in a panic or only half ready."

She noticed that he said "I" and not "we."

"I'm coming too."

"If you think that Adrienne is in danger, then you have to acknowledge that it could also be dangerous for you. And I'm not taking you into a situation where you could be hurt."

"I'm the one who told you what was going on."

"That doesn't mean I'm going to put a civilian in harm's way."

He was quick and efficient in getting dressed and assembling his equipment. He put in a call to the police dispatcher to warn that he was going to Scarlett Simpson's house to look for Adrienne and a possibly armed suspect, Juliet Marsh.

The dispatcher promised to send one of the other LEOs over to back him up.

At least he still let Erin in the truck. She had been beginning to wonder if he would just leave her at home and expect her to wait for him to report to her when it was all over.

~

Adrienne's car was not in front of Scarlett's house. Terry parked his truck and called K9 out behind him. He leaned back in the window to address Erin.

"Just stay here. I'll check to see if Juliet is inside or if anyone has seen either. Don't come in, even if you think it is safe. Do you understand? Stay outside and out of the way."

Erin sighed and nodded. This was becoming an all-too-familiar situation. It was her own fault for doing what she was supposed to. She knew that Terry was absolutely right to be cautious and she *didn't* want to walk into a dangerous situation. But she did wish that she could see what was going on inside. If she could see what was happening *and* be safe from any violence...

She watched Terry and K9 walk up to Scarlett's door and knock. The door opened a few seconds later and they walked in, looking relaxed and casual. No drawn weapon, no tensing as Terry looked around and realized that his quarry was there.

One of the marked squad cars pulled up, and Stayner climbed out. He reported in on his radio, looking around for anything out of place, then returned the mic to its holder. He saw Erin sitting in the truck and nodded at her but did not come over to talk. He walked around the house and entered the backyard, out of Erin's line of view.

There were no fireworks. Within ten minutes, Terry was back at the truck. "Everything looks fine," he told Erin. "Scarlett does have some things for Adrienne, but she hasn't shown up to pick them up yet. Scarlett doesn't know Juliet, but said she'll keep an eye out and report any unusual activity. Any strangers in the area, male or female."

Erin looked around, wishing that she could spot something herself. It was a letdown. She had been expecting a lot of action and drama, and all was quiet. It was good, of course. Adrienne was safe. Scarlett was safe. Erin was safe. She blew out her breath.

All was quiet.

"What about Adrienne?" Erin asked. "You need to find her and let her know about Juliet so she isn't taken off guard."

"I don't think anyone is in any danger. I'll contact Adrienne when I can, but she isn't answering all the calls from the Bald Eagle Falls police department right now. You might have better luck reaching her."

Erin frowned. "I can at least talk to Bella. Some of the kids are at the farm right now, so Adrienne will be going back there."

Terry nodded. "Talk to Bella. That's probably the best approach right now."

He walked over to talk to Stayner at his squad car for a few minutes before going home. Erin wondered whether they would put any surveillance on Scarlett's house to see if Juliet Marsh would show up there.

Eventually, Terry returned. He opened the door for K9, who jumped up into the cab. Terry climbed into his seat and rubbed his face tiredly before starting the engine.

"I'm sorry... I shouldn't have woken you up," Erin apologized. "I really did think that they would both be here. And I don't know what Juliet wants from Adrienne or what she might do if she doesn't get it. Do you think she's the one who killed Simon?"

"Why would she kill Simon?"

"Because of the bank heist... she blamed Simon for her husband's death, or because he didn't give her Denny's share."

"Well..." He nodded. "It's as good a reason as any, I suppose. We'll investigate it further. But like I said... we don't have any evidence that Simon was part of that bank heist."

"Except that Juliet Marsh showed up asking for Adrienne. That's pretty good evidence that Simon was involved."

"A couple of leaps of logic there. We need to tie it up nice and neatly to get any warrants or to make an arrest."

They drove home in silence. Erin was sorry she had gotten Terry out of bed. Hopefully, he would be able to get back to sleep right away and would not be too wound up because of the interruption and checking out Scarlett's house.

"Sorry, I won't bother you again," she told him as he settled down to go to bed again.

Terry gave her a peck on the cheek. "You did the right thing. I'm glad you didn't just go out there yourself."

She waited until she was sure he was asleep again, listening for his heavy sleep breathing before leaving the house.

CHAPTER 45

Erin couldn't wait around and do nothing. She knew that Bella would call her when Adrienne returned to pick up the kids, but she couldn't sit waiting at home. She took her own car and headed out on the route she had followed several times before.

Hopefully, Bella wouldn't be doing a lot of chores. Morning was the usual time for farm chores, wasn't it? Though Erin knew Bella might have to move the goats to a different pasture or their barn for the night.

Bella should be watching TV or doing her homework. Or maybe having a late dinner. She and Erin could talk while they waited for Adrienne to get home. Perhaps Bella had been wrong and Adrienne had not been going to Scarlett's house. Or maybe she had a series of errands and was going there last. There were a lot of reasons that Adrienne might not be where she was expected to be.

And Juliet might be gone. Maybe she had already talked to Adrienne and then headed back for Ohio. Just because Adrienne hadn't chosen to talk to either Erin or Bella about it, that didn't mean she hadn't seen Juliet. She might prefer to keep that information to herself. She certainly wasn't required to tell anyone else her private business. Erin was sure Adrienne didn't want everyone to know that Simon had been involved in such nasty business. The citizens of Bald Eagle Falls already had a low enough opinion of him, with the little they knew. If they knew everything, they might shun Adrienne. The woman was already considered an outsider. She didn't need to be alienated further.

The day was cooling, the sun going down. The scenery was green and peaceful. Erin should be getting ready for bed if she were going to take the early shift at Auntie Clem's.

But she couldn't stop thinking about Juliet and what she was doing in Bald Eagle Falls. Had she killed Simon? If she had, why was she still there? Because she wanted to kill Adrienne too? Because she wanted her money from the bank heist?

Or was there something else, another piece of the puzzle that Erin hadn't yet put together?

Erin was nearing the Prost farm when she saw a vehicle pulled into the ditch on the other side of the road.

Adrienne's car.

At first, Erin was filled with relief at the sight of it. That was why Adrienne hadn't shown up at Scarlett's. She'd had car trouble and hadn't been able to get into town.

But if she'd had car trouble, why hadn't she turned on her phone and called Bella for help?

Even if her phone was out of power or out of minutes, it wasn't that far back to the Prost farm. She could have turned around and walked back in the time since she had left.

And maybe she had. She had probably left the car there, walked back to the farm, and was there now with the children. Bella hadn't called Erin back to tell her, but she didn't really have to. Maybe she had been busy and hadn't had the chance to yet. There were a lot of kids to be managed.

Erin pulled over and crossed the quiet highway to the other side to examine Adrienne's car.

The beaten-up old thing wasn't pretty, but it didn't have to be pretty to get them from one place to another. It just had to be running. Which obviously it wasn't, now. Adrienne would have another unexpected expense to deal with. But at least she had some money now. It wouldn't mean the kids wouldn't be able to eat this week.

Erin wouldn't have let them go hungry anyway. She would have made sure that they got all the baking they needed from Auntie Clem's freezer.

The driver's door hung open. Adrienne must have intended to return immediately to deal with the car. She'd had two of the kids with her, Bella had said. Sometimes, that could be two too many. It was hard to deal with whining kids and car troubles at the same time. She had probably taken the children back to the farm and then would walk back or drive one of the tractors back to take care of the car.

As Erin got closer, she heard the thin cry of a baby in the distance. Adrienne must still be close by with Sarah. Could Erin hear all the way to the farm from there? Was she on her way back, having dropped Samuel Andrew at the farm? The night was quiet. There were no traffic sounds to cover up the noise.

Erin looked up the highway but couldn't see Adrienne or anyone else walking on the shoulder. Then where was she?

Erin covered the distance to the car and looked inside. Her heart sped as she saw that Sarah was still in her baby seat in the back. Her face was red and streaked with tears.

Erin hurried around the car and opened the back door. She poked her head in.

"Hey, Sarah," she said with a big, reassuring smile. "Hi, baby! How are you? It's okay. Everything is going to be fine. Let's get you out of there."

She wasn't used to the buckles on child seats. They always seemed awkward and difficult to get the child out of without bending her arms in strange contortions. But Erin was as calm and reassuring as possible, smiling and cooing at Sarah and working the straps and buckles until she could finally pull the girl free from the car.

"There! Doesn't that feel better?" Erin asked. She cuddled and bounced Sarah, looking around and trying to figure out what had happened. Why had Adrienne left Sarah behind in the car? Where had she gone?

Sarah's wails settled down to quieter sobs. Her little baby fists grasped Erin's shirt tightly, pulling herself into Erin's body and clinging to her. Her thin face still showed her distress, and she was as light as a bird in Erin's arms. She'd been thin since she was born. Erin had often worried that she wasn't getting the nutrition she needed.

"There, there. It's okay," Erin reassured her, patting and rubbing her back.

She looked around for some sign of Adrienne. She couldn't imagine that Adrienne would have returned to the farm without her baby.

"Adrienne? Adrienne, are you here?" she called out, trying to project her voice into the trees. Maybe Adrienne had taken Samuel Andrew into the trees to relieve himself. Perhaps they had been waiting for a tow, but Samuel Andrew couldn't wait and didn't want to go right by the road. So they had left the car for two minutes to take care of business.

But it felt like Sarah had been alone for longer than that. There were a lot of tears on her face. Her diaper was heavily saturated.

But they could have been sitting there for a while, waiting for someone to rescue her. Maybe Adrienne hadn't been able to call Bella and couldn't walk that distance because of the children. It was one thing to make a hike like that by herself. Another to do it with two children, one a babe in arms. Erin got the feeling that Samuel Andrew was frailer than the other children. If he couldn't make it that distance, Adrienne couldn't very well carry him.

CHAPTER 46

"Adrienne?" Erin called again.

She strained her ears and thought she heard a faint reply. That was reassuring. Adrienne was close by. They could all pile into Erin's car and go back to the farm. Adrienne would be grateful for the rescue. And grateful to be warned about Juliet. Everything would be fine,

There was another distant cry. Erin looked toward it. Was Adrienne coming back? Did she want Erin to go to her to help her with something? Sarah was still sobbing and prevented Erin from being able to hear the call very clearly. She felt her phone in her pocket, wishing that Adrienne would turn hers on so they could talk to each other and Erin would know what to do.

She held Sarah against her to muffle her sobs for a second to try to get a fix on where Adrienne and Samuel Andrew were.

"Adrienne?"

Another distant cry. Erin started to walk toward it. Toward the farm and into the trees, if she were pinpointing the voice correctly. Erin wasn't sure what she would do when she got there. Call for help, probably. She had a working cell phone, and Adrienne apparently did not. Erin would drive everyone to the farm, and they would get Bella to tow Adrienne's car with the tractor. Adrienne would feed Sarah and Samuel Andrew and put them to bed. Then they could have the talk that Erin had come out for.

To tell Adrienne about Juliet and discuss what precautions they could take to prevent her from finding Adrienne and bothering her.

Covering the rough ground while carrying a baby was more challenging than Erin had expected. She couldn't always see where she was putting her foot down and would land on a rock or thick tuft of grass that threatened to trip her. And despite how skinny and light Sarah was, she got heavier the farther Erin walked.

"We're almost there," she reassured Sarah, trying to keep herself calm at the same time. "You'll get to see your mommy again. You'll be really glad to see her, won't you?"

She could hear voices. Adrienne talking to Samuel Andrew. Maybe he was sick and couldn't go anywhere, and that was why they had failed to get back to the car. Poor guy, getting sick out in the middle of nowhere, when all he probably wanted to do was lie in his bed and sleep.

Erin could see something large in the clearing ahead. At first, she thought it was another car, though it didn't make sense for it to be back there so deep in the woods, so far away from the road. Then she realized she was looking at a tent. She laughed at herself for being so worried about everything. It was Adrienne's camp. Her tents. Erin had known that it was somewhere close to the Prost farm, but Adrienne didn't like people to know exactly where she was. They'd been harassed by those who didn't like the little family squatting, even if they had the owner's permission to be there.

And of course, Adrienne hadn't wanted Simon or anyone else who was interested in her windfall to be able to find her. He had succeeded in seeing her when she was in town, but she had been able to keep her campsite hidden from him. That was why it was so far back in the trees instead of somewhere she could pull the car up. Moving the heavy tents and tarps over that distance must have been difficult. She must have borrowed a wagon or dolly from Bella. Erin couldn't see her being able to carry all of that equipment that distance by hand.

"Adrienne?" she called out to let the woman know she was approaching the camp. It wasn't good to walk into someone's campsite unannounced. Especially if that someone might happen to have a rifle for hunting wild game and protecting them from visitors.

"Erin?" It was the first time Erin could make out what Adrienne was saying. She was relieved.

"I'm here. I've got Sarah."

"You probably shouldn't come any closer."

Erin froze.

Not come any closer?

Her mind flashed back again to the idea of Adrienne holding a hunting rifle, protecting herself from intruders.

"It's Erin," she repeated.

"Erin Price," another voice observed, "the baker who doesn't know to mind her own business."

Yes, that was probably an apt description.

Erin looked around, trying to spot the owner of the voice. She sounded like she was close by. There was a movement in the trees, and she focused on the shape of a woman.

Juliet.

Of course.

No one had believed that Juliet might be a danger to Adrienne, and now here she was at Adrienne's camp. She had figured out where it was despite everyone's attempts to keep her from finding out.

"Juliet," Erin tried to make herself sound surprised. She had a role to play. If she could keep Juliet off balance and make her think that Erin didn't know what was going on, maybe Erin or Adrienne could find a way to overcome her. "What are you doing here?"

"You people think you are all so smart," Juliet sneered. "You think that I'll just give up and go home. You don't know anything about me. I'm patient. I plan things. I think. It's the power of the brain. People like you just don't understand." She looked toward where Adrienne was standing. "People like Simon."

Erin moved closer, hoping to be able to see them more clearly and figure out what to do. Maybe there wasn't any danger at all. Juliet just needed to be heard. And when they heard her and made her understand that Adrienne's money was from a settlement and was for a house for the children, she would go home. She would leave them alone and that would be the end of it.

Adrienne wasn't standing. She was sitting on a stump. Samuel Andrew was in her lap. Juliet stood nearby, looking threatening, though Erin couldn't see if she had a weapon.

"I don't understand what you are doing here," Erin told Juliet, feigning ignorance about Juliet's connection with Simon and the robber who had been killed. How would a baker in Bald Eagle Falls know anything about that? "Do you and Adrienne know each other?"

"Oh, we know each other all right," Juliet said in a threatening tone. "We know each other all too well."

"Did you go to school together?"

Juliet looked at her, scowling. "You need to just stay out of this. I don't know what you're even doing here. I expected that cow Bella to show up, but not you."

"Bella said that Adrienne had gone into town. But when she wasn't there, I thought I would come out to the farm and talk to her when she got back."

"What about?"

About her.

But Erin didn't say that. She shrugged. "Just gossip. See how she was doing since her husband died."

"Her husband," Juliet snarled. "Simon was never much of a husband. Or he was too much of one, all over the United States." She looked at Adrienne. "Only, he never married you, did he, dear?" she asked snidely.

Adrienne just stared at her and said nothing. Erin watched the two of them, trying to decide what was going on and if they were in any danger or if Adrienne had just been forced into an awkward conversation.

But Sarah had been left in the car. Adrienne would not have chosen to leave Sarah in the car by herself.

Adrienne held herself rigidly, not moving a muscle. Her face was pale. Erin couldn't tell whether she was holding on to Samuel Andrew to comfort him or to keep him still.

What exactly had she interrupted?

CHAPTER 47

$\mathcal{E}$rin felt her phone in her pocket, trying to figure out what to do next. How to de-escalate Juliet or to get the help that they needed. It was pretty hard, coming into the situation blind, to know what would help and what would make things worse. For the moment, Juliet did not appear to be violent or threatening. But anything Erin said might change that.

She felt for the home button on the phone. She was going to have to take a chance.

"Is everything okay, Adrienne? Do you want me to… call the police?"

"No," Adrienne shook her head, her face pale and pinched. "Don't do that."

"Yes," Erin acknowledged. "I understand."

Juliet gave her a confused look, frowning. "You just stay out of this," she told Erin. "No one asked you to come here. You're not a part of this."

Erin cuddled Sarah and kissed the top of her head. "Well, when I saw Adrienne's car stopped beside the highway on the way to the Prost farm, I had to stop and help. And I couldn't leave baby Sarah in the car, could I? I'm glad that Adrienne and Samuel Andrew are okay. I'm glad you didn't hurt them, Juliet."

"Shut up," Juliet said crossly. "I don't like the sound of your voice. Adrienne and I were just having a woman-to-woman talk about her husband's responsibility in the death of my husband. She owes me. She owes me big for her part in Simon taking my Denny from me."

Erin swallowed. She had wondered whether Juliet blamed Simon for what happened to Denny. Now she had her answer.

"You mean in the bank heist?" she asked. "Adrienne didn't have anything to do with that. She was here in Bald Eagle Falls. Simon was off in Ohio."

"Is that what she told you?" Juliet demanded. "You think that this is all just on Denny? He would never have been in that bank if it wasn't for Adrienne."

Erin looked at Adrienne but just got a frozen stare from her. She didn't fill in any details to make it easier for Erin to understand.

"How is it Adrienne's fault that Denny was in the bank?"

"Because she's the one who called Simon and told him that she had to have money. That the baby was in the hospital and he was going to die if she didn't get the money for his treatment."

This squared with Adrienne's comment that Samuel Andrew had been in the hospital two years ago when Simon had brought her the money. He hadn't been a baby, but he was still a toddler or a preschooler, and Erin supposed that they probably referred to the youngest as a baby even if he wasn't an infant anymore.

"Adrienne couldn't help it if Samuel Andrew was in the hospital. And I'm sure she didn't tell Simon to go rob a bank to get the money."

"She might as well have," Juliet snapped. "Suddenly, Simon needs money and he needs it fast. Too fast to put a proper plan in place." She shook her head, jaw clenched in fury. "I've put together dozens of jobs, and nothing ever went wrong. And do you want to know why? Because I know how to plan. I know how to put together the right crew, to research and reconnoiter the target, to make a plan to get us in and out of there safely. But no, Simon has to have money right now. There isn't any time for us to set it up properly. He has no patience. Goes in there with no plan. He's participated in enough jobs to think he knows how it all works. And you know what happened?"

Erin knew what happened. They had gone in without a proper plan and there had been a firefight. Denny had died. The security guard had died. They got out with the money, so Simon had been able to get back to Tennessee and pay for Samuel Andrew's medical treatments, whatever that had involved. And Adrienne never knew the heartache she had caused by insisting she needed money from Simon right away.

"It wasn't Adrienne's fault," Erin tried to use a calm, soothing voice that would persuade Juliet of the injustice of her accusation and make her see that Adrienne hadn't really had anything to do with it. "She was just trying to take care of a sick baby."

"She shouldn't have pressured him like that. The hospital wouldn't have let the baby die just because she didn't have the money. They have to give lifesaving treatment whether the patient can pay or not. Do you think I don't know that?"

"They won't do everything," Adrienne argued. "They'll do emergency procedures, and they did, but he needed more. And you know what they did? They told me to set up a crowdfunding campaign. If I want to be able to afford the antibiotics and everything he needs, then I have to raise the money myself. And not just the medicine, but the room at the hospital. Meals. Supplies. Doctors. They charge for everything. And they just keep racking up the charges. If I could raise the money for it. If not, they would send him home. He could be treated as an outpatient at some public clinic."

Adrienne looked down at Samuel Andrew and gave him a squeeze.

"They were going to send him right back to the hole we lived in. The place that made him sick to begin with. They would call public health to report it and get it shut down. Then we'd have nowhere to live. But we could go to the clinic for the treatments," she sneered.

Adrienne shook her head emphatically.

"He would have died. He wasn't strong enough to be released from the hospital. He was still coughing. He could hardly move. And they said the danger was over. As long as he stayed on the drugs, it would eventually clear up. Do you know how long they said?"

Erin shook her head in answer. "No. How long?"

"It might take months or years. They would have to keep cycling through other antibiotics if it was resistant. We're not talking about a week of amoxicillin for strep!"

"Maybe he wasn't meant to live," Juliet said cruelly. "Maybe you should have just let him go. You had enough other kids. And Simon had loads. Why should he care so much about one little sick baby? He should have planned the job properly! He should have listened to me! Instead, he insists that we go in there blind. He says that he's scoped the place out and it is a piece of cake. Walk in and walk out."

But Denny had never walked out.

Juliet laughed, sounding a little hysterical. "A piece of cake," she laughed. "Well, I showed him. *A piece of cake!* You'll think of him the next time you're cutting up and serving a cake with one of those knives," she told Erin.

Erin swallowed, feeling sick. She forced the words out of her mouth, even though she wished she could blot out what Juliet had just said. She didn't want to remember it. She didn't want to think of Simon and his rotting remains behind the bakery whenever she cut and served a cake.

"*You* killed Simon?" she asked in a tone of disbelief. "Why?"

"I just told you why," Juliet shrieked. "I killed him because he killed my husband! He thought he could just walk away from there! He got what he wanted, and he never had to see any of the rest of us again. He could just walk away."

"Were *you* part of the heist too?" Erin had a hard time wrapping her head around this thought. She had never imagined that one of the bank robbers had been a woman. How sexist was that? She had simply assumed that all of the bank robbers were men.

Juliet hadn't just lost her husband in the bank job. She had seen him killed in front of her eyes. On a job that she knew if she had planned herself, would have gone off without a hitch. But Simon had rushed things through too quickly and had screwed everything up.

"You think I would let Denny go in there without me?" Juliet asked. "I would never send him into a job that I wasn't taking part in myself. We were partners in every sense of the word. I thought that if things went wrong, I would be able to get him out of there safely. I'd done more jobs than he had. Before we even met. I thought we'd be able to get out."

"I'm sorry," Erin told her sincerely. Her mouth was dry and she wished she had a bottle of water. A drink of anything. "But... Adrienne couldn't have known that any of that would happen. She didn't know that Simon would commit a bank robbery to get the money!"

Juliet stared at Adrienne, who remained sitting as still as a statue. "Of course she knew."

CHAPTER 48

*E*rin didn't know whether to believe it or not. Adrienne had said that she had never wanted to know what Simon was involved in. But sometimes people knew and refused to admit it, even to themselves. It was too hard, so they just curled up into themselves and, like a possum, pretended they had seen and heard nothing.

"Adrienne knew what she was asking when she called to demand money from Simon," Juliet insisted. "She knew it would be a bank. And she knew it would have to be a rush job. That it wasn't one we could spend weeks planning. She wanted that money *now*. No time to set everything up properly. Adrienne knew. And when it went bad, she knew she'd killed my husband."

Adrienne shook her head. "No. No, I never knew anything about it. Simon just brought me the money. He didn't tell me where it came from. He didn't tell me what had happened. I thought maybe…" she trailed off, trying to decide what to say.

What she had told Erin previously? That it was some scam or scheme? Gambling? Had she really known that Simon was involved in armed robbery?

"I didn't know any of this," she insisted. "I wouldn't have asked Simon to do something like that." She hugged Samuel Andrew to her tightly, making him squirm. "I just wanted to save my baby. I needed money for the drugs to make him better. They weren't cheap, and it was months before they said it was all cleared up and he wasn't testing positive anymore."

She loosened her grip and stroked his hair back from his face.

"He's always been fragile. If anything was going around, he would be the one to get it. They were all positive, but he's the one that got sick. The nurse said that it was because of the place that we were living in. Those tiny, moldy rooms in a flophouse… I thought it was best for them to have a roof over their heads, but it turned out it wasn't. They need space and fresh air. No more confined spaces. No more disease-ridden rooms where they can't breathe."

And so Adrienne had turned to living outside in tents instead of flop-houses or shelters. Trying to provide the children with the best, healthiest environment to keep them well and strong.

"You're stupid," Juliet railed. "If you can't afford kids, can't afford to raise them, then why are you having them? How many of the little rug rats do you have? Five? Six? Why did you keep having them if you couldn't afford them?"

Adrienne just looked at her, saying nothing.

Erin's anxiety was rising. She had hoped that her distress signal would bring help, but there was no sign that anyone was coming to rescue Adrienne and her children. Darkness was falling rapidly. She could hear the hoot of an owl nearby. In the dark, no one driving down the highway would notice Adrienne's abandoned vehicle. No one would know there was anything wrong and come looking for them.

Except for Bella, and would she know to look at their campsite? She had the other kids with her and thought Adrienne had gone into town. She wouldn't know where to find them. Even if they raised the alarm, the police would search for Adrienne and the children in Bald Eagle Falls, not the wilderness.

But Erin's yellow bug was out there too, it would stand out like a beacon if they realized something was wrong and searched for them. *When* they realized something was wrong.

Sarah was fussing in Erin's arms. She could hear her mother close by and wanted to go to her. She was wet and probably hungry. The air was getting cooler, and she would need a sweater or blanket.

"Why can't you keep that one quiet?" Juliet asked irritably. "I don't know why you brought her here. I told Adrienne to leave them both in the car."

Erin looked at Adrienne holding Samuel Andrew and understood. He was big enough that he wouldn't stay in the car when she left him behind. He had followed her. Sarah, of course, was not independently mobile and could not get out of her seat.

Erin couldn't imagine Adrienne obediently leaving her children behind in the car without a physical threat. She eyed Juliet, but it was getting harder to see her in the failing light. Erin still didn't know what kind of weapon Juliet had. A gun? Another knife? If she had performed the dozens of armed robberies that she claimed, then she was used to handling a gun, and it could easily be held at her side where Erin couldn't see it. She had to assume that Adrienne knew what she was doing. If she had decided that the best thing was to sit frozen on the stump, Erin had to assume any movement on her part could draw fire.

Especially if the baby kept fussing and irritating Juliet.

"Juliet Marsh." The amplified voice made them all jump.

Juliet looked all around, her face an angry mask. She couldn't spot anyone. Erin finally saw the handgun. Juliet had been holding it at her side, but now that she was cornered, she needed to identify the soft spots in the net closing around her, and she held it in front of her as she completed a full circle.

Erin was relieved to see Juliet beginning to back toward the woods instead of threatening Adrienne. Erin didn't want a hostage situation. She couldn't stand to see the gun held to Samuel Andrew's head. After all Adrienne had done to save the boy's life when it had been threatened by disease, it would be unfair for them to lose him to this madwoman.

Juliet was heading deeper into the bush, and Erin had a sudden sinking feeling that she had been here before and she knew exactly what Juliet was about to do. Erin dashed toward Adrienne and handed her Sarah. "Quick, take her!" She fumbled the pass, but Adrienne managed to get a good grip on Sarah and avoided dropping her.

Erin raced after Juliet.

"Erin!"

She ignored the call behind her. They might not know what Juliet was doing, but Erin did. She wasn't concerned about the gun. She couldn't let Juliet get away.

Adrienne or Terry might tell her that she should just let Juliet go. At least if she were in the wind, she wouldn't bother Erin or Adrienne.

But that hadn't been true of Theresa. When Theresa had escaped, she hadn't stayed away. She had harassed all of them, causing as much pain and fear as possible. Juliet was cut from the same cloth. She hadn't stayed in Ohio where she was safe. She had chosen to come after Simon and Adrienne instead. She had demonstrated she could hold a grudge for two years, without any apparent cooling.

CHAPTER 49

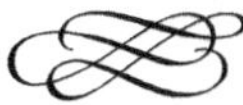

*E*rin wasn't the fastest runner. But she put everything she had into it, moving as quickly as she could after Juliet without tripping over the rocks, tufts of grass, sticks, bushes, and logs. It was an obstacle course, but she gave it her all.

She was right behind Juliet when she broke into the clearing where she had parked her motorcycle. Erin had known that it would be there. Juliet was a planner. Of course she had arranged for a way to escape and wasn't just randomly running into the forest thinking she could hide behind a tree. Just like crazy Theresa, she figured she could escape through the goat trails and back roads that the police couldn't block off. It had worked for Theresa. But Juliet had to be able to get on her motorcycle to escape and Erin wasn't about to let her.

Apparently, neither was Beaver.

As Erin chased Juliet wildly through the trees, breathing raggedly, her lungs feeling like they were about to burst, Beaver leaned lazily against the bike, her strong jaw working away at the gum in her mouth.

Juliet stopped abruptly. "Who are you?" she demanded, breathing almost as heavily as Erin. She fumbled to raise her gun, which she had holstered before running. Apparently, she knew enough about firearm safety not to go belting through the woods with the gun in her hand.

But Beaver was already holding a large gun herself. She trained it on Juliet.

"I wouldn't do that if I were you."

Juliet stared at her and tried to decide what to do.

"You're under arrest, Juliet Marsh. How about you take that gun out with two fingers and drop it on the ground? Kick it away from you. Then lace your hands behind your head."

Juliet's mouth opened and shut. "You can't do that! You have no reason to arrest me. Where is your cause? This is a licensed weapon and I can carry it wherever I want to."

"Well, let's start with the murder of Simon Simpson. We can go from there. I am sure there are other charges we can lay, but I don't want to take all of the Bald Eagle Falls PD's fun away. Gotta leave them something that they can charge you with."

Juliet just stood there, thunderstruck. Beaver chewed away on her gum, waiting for Juliet to react.

"You have no proof I murdered anyone," Juliet asserted.

"I've told you you're under arrest, ma'am. I suggest you do what you're told if you don't want to end up with a hole in your belly."

Juliet's face turned red with fury as the implications of what was happening started to click into place. But she followed Beaver's instructions and dropped her gun to the ground.

"Put your hands behind your head," Beaver told her in a bored, lazy tone. Erin knew that despite Beaver's relaxed demeanor and exaggerated laziness, she was alert to every movement and fully aware of how dangerous Juliet might be. Beaver's act was just that, the act of a highly trained special agent who occasionally made Bald Eagle Falls her home.

Juliet laced her hands behind her head and, by the time any of the law enforcement officers who had arrived to rescue Adrienne and Erin made it to the clearing, Beaver had her handcuffed and was checking her pockets and person for any hidden weapons.

Stayner was the first to arrive, apparently a better runner than Terry, who was close behind him with K9 at his side. K9 could have run faster, but Terry had apparently not sent him on ahead despite the fact that his girlfriend was running pell-mell after an accused murderer with a gun.

Terry and Stayner both stopped and watched Beaver, who gave them a lazy grin. "Little late to the party, aren't you, gentlemen?"

"How did you get here?" Terry demanded.

Beaver shrugged. "Just out doing some hunting." Her smile made it clear that she was teasing him. Beaver looked at Erin and raised her brows.

"You followed me?" Erin asked.

She thought back to her drive toward the Prost farm. She couldn't remember seeing any other vehicles behind her. But apparently, Beaver had followed her at a distance. Either that, or she had some kind of tracking device on Erin's car. Or maybe her phone. It would appear that Erin had led Beaver right into the hostage scene.

"If you followed me here, why didn't you help Adrienne and me? She could have killed us!"

"You seemed like you had things under control for the time being." Beaver shrugged. "And I knew that the PD was on their way, since you managed to get a call into the Bald Eagle Falls dispatcher before I did."

Erin let out her breath. She hadn't known at the time whether it would work. She couldn't key the police dispatcher's number into the phone while it was in her pocket. Not with a touch screen rather than hard buttons. But she could hold down the home button and give voice commands. She had held it down while asking Adrienne if she wanted Erin to call the police, so that the command the phone received was "call the police." Of course the voice assistant wouldn't call the emergency number without confirmation that it had heard the command correctly, so Erin had told it "yes" despite the fact that her response hadn't exactly made sense in the conversation.

After that, she did her best to give the police dispatcher the necessary information. Where she was, having found Adrienne's car by the road on the way to the Prost farm. The presence of Adrienne and her two young children, in addition to Juliet. The fact that Juliet had not hurt them.

Juliet had also obliged by admitting that she had been involved personally in the bank heist and that she was the one who had killed Simon Simpson for his part in Denny's death.

Apparently, the dispatcher had been able to hear enough of this information through the muffling effect of Erin's clothing, and the police had quickly arrived on the scene.

Erin looked at Terry, his eyes red-rimmed with dark bags underneath. He had been awakened shortly after getting to sleep again. That was twice she had woken him up after he'd put in a double shift. He must be about ready to drop.

"I'm sorry…"

"Sorry for what? That you managed to get yourself into the middle of this? You came out here on your own without anyone to back you up? Why would you do that? You know that I went with you to check out Scarlett's house. You knew that any of the Bald Eagle Falls police department would back you up even if I was unavailable. Why would you come out here all on your own?"

"I didn't come out here looking for Juliet. I didn't think she knew where Adrienne was. I just wanted to talk to Bella and wait for Adrienne to get back so I could tell her about Juliet. So she knew to be careful of her."

Terry studied Erin closely, looking for any sign of deception. Erin didn't drop her eyes or look away. She hadn't been looking for trouble. She hadn't planned on meeting up with Juliet and ending up a hostage at gunpoint along with Adrienne and her two young children.

"But then you ran after her instead of leaving it up to the police. Why would you do that? You knew she was armed and you aren't. What were you going to do? Tackle her? You should have waited for the police department to take her down. Stayed with Adrienne where it was safe."

"I was afraid she would get away. Like Theresa."

"We would have…" Terry looked at the motorcycle, maybe reconsidering. When Theresa had gotten away, he had been disabled, knocked unconscious and tied up. He hadn't seen how quickly she had disappeared into the trees, but he knew the results. He had read all of the reports of what had happened that night. He knew that despite all of the law enforcement officers who had been dispatched to the scene, they had lost her when none of them had been able to follow the motorcycle through the trees and onto the trails and back roads that led away from her family farm.

"I didn't know that Beaver would be back here," Erin pointed out. "I was afraid Juliet would get to the motorcycle and get away."

"How did *you* get here?" Terry asked Beaver.

"Followed Erin in," Beaver advised around her wad of gum.

"What made you think she was going to lead you to Simon's killer?"

"Erin had already been targeted twice, which was a good sign that she was close to figuring out the identity of the killer."

"Twice?" Stayner repeated. "You mean the vandalism of the bakery?"

"That and the evidence left behind that linked the killing to Erin or the bakery."

"You think Juliet was the one who vandalized the bakery?" Erin repeated.

Beaver looked at Juliet. "Well, you were, weren't you?"

Juliet remained tight-lipped, exercising her right to remain silent.

"She was trying to point to me as the killer?" Erin asked.

"I think she already did that by leaving the cake knife in the body and the body behind Auntie Clem's Bakery. But I think that the vandalism of the bakery was more subtle. I think," Beaver looked at Juliet for confirmation, "She wanted people to know that *Simon* was a murderer. That he had gotten Denny Martin killed in the bank heist."

"You all act like Simon and Adrienne were innocent bystanders," Julie snapped. Her venom was aimed at Erin rather than Beaver. "It was Simon's fault that Denny was killed. And Adrienne's fault. You can hold her up as a model mother all you like, but that isn't who she is. She is culpable in the killing of my husband, just as if she had been there. She signed his death warrant herself."

"She was trying to get her son medical treatment," Erin pointed out.

"She is a cold-blooded killer. She killed him for the money. She admits it."

Erin shook her head. Adrienne had confirmed that she had been trying to save her baby. Not that she had intended anyone to die getting him medical help.

"Why did you come over here instead of rescuing Erin and Adrienne?" Terry challenged Beaver.

"She was doing a good job. When I called for backup, the dispatcher already had her on the line and patched me in so I could listen in. Things were staying calm and she had Marsh talking, so I didn't think I needed to interfere. But I didn't want her to get away."

"You knew about the motorcycle?"

"I knew they used motorcycles to escape after the heist. Motorcycles have several advantages over cars in traffic or densely wooded areas like this. Even an ATV would have a challenge getting through here. But a motorcycle will outstrip a runner even at low speeds and, with all the back roads around here… it would be very easy to slip away."

Terry looked at Erin. "Did you know that they used motorcycles to get away from the heist, or did you just guess that she might have one?"

Erin shrugged. "There wasn't a second car with Adrienne's. Juliet had to have gotten here somehow, but there was no other vehicle around. I guess she could have been dropped off by an accomplice. But I just… I remembered Theresa getting away, and I didn't want to go through that again."

Well, enough chatter," Beaver said. "Let's get this sweetheart booked and secured for the night." She grasped Juliet by the arm and, though Juliet attempted to pull back, she did not appear to be any match for Beaver's strength. Though Beaver's arms were currently covered by her camo jacket, Erin had previously seen how well-muscled they were. They were impressive. Beaver guided Juliet away from the motorcycle and the clearing back toward Adrienne's campsite.

Sheriff Wilmot and Tom Banks were there. All of the members of the Bald Eagle Falls police department were out in force. Adrienne was nursing Sarah, Samuel Andrew standing at her side, cuddled close to her rather than in her lap. Adrienne watched the police march Juliet past her, back toward where Adrienne's car and the police cars were now parked. Her eyes went to Erin.

"I guess I owe you one. Again."

"You don't owe me anything," Erin said. "I'm just… glad that I could help."

Adrienne stroked Sarah's head and cuddled her and Samuel Andrew close. "Thanks to you, they are both safe, and she will…" Adrienne looked in the direction Juliet had gone. "She will be put away, won't she? She'll go to prison?"

Erin nodded. "She admitted to murdering Simon and being part of the heist—and dozens of others. They got all of that on tape. And then kidnapping you and holding you at gunpoint. They'll be able to put her away for a long time."

Of course, things didn't always work out the way they were supposed to. No one could guarantee that Juliet would be put behind bars forever and that there would be no problems with convicting her on all counts. But Adrienne didn't need to hear that. She needed to hear that she and her children would be safe.

Adrienne nodded her appreciation.

More people were coming out of the woods into Adrienne's campsite and, at first, Erin thought they were professionals there to process the crime scene or offer medical care to the hostages. But as they got closer, she saw Bella and Cindy Prost. Cindy looked grim and Bella concerned, her eyes wide.

"We need to talk to Adrienne. This is my property," Cindy insisted when the sheriff attempted to keep her at a distance.

But there wasn't any evidence to be collected or any reason to keep Cindy and Bella from Adrienne. The sheriff would need to get Adrienne's statement as to what had happened, how Juliet had gotten her out of the car and held her at gunpoint, but that could wait. They already had a recording of what had happened while Erin was there and there were plenty of other charges to file against Juliet.

So Sheriff Wilmot conceded, stepping back and letting Cindy and Bella approach.

"Adrienne, are you okay?" Bella asked worriedly, leaning over her immediately to give her a hug. She reached down and tousled Samuel Andrew's hair. He made a noise of protest but didn't pull away or look frightened. He knew Bella.

"We're okay," Adrienne confirmed. She looked at Erin. "No one was hurt. Erin came and… how did you call the police? Did you call them before you showed up? When you saw the car?"

On reflection, Erin realized she probably should have. Instead she had gone waltzing into a probably dangerous situation.

"Uh, no. I called them while I was talking to you. In my pocket."

Adrienne shook her head. "I didn't even know you could do that."

"Well, you have to turn it on first," Erin said pointedly.

Adrienne looked down at Sarah as she nursed. "I have good reasons for keeping it off most of the time. Not everyone can afford big phone bills, and I need to keep it charged when I'm out here." she made a motion indicating the tents in the clearing. "I did have it on when I left the farm, but... Juliet made me turn it off."

Juliet was a good planner. It was lucky she hadn't forced Adrienne to drive the car deep into the trees where it couldn't be seen from the road. Or fortunate that the forest was too dense to drive the big car into.

Without a word, Cindy put her arms out for Samuel Andrew. He launched himself at her. Cindy picked him up and held him to her shoulder, not interrogating or babying him, just holding him close. His arms closed around her and he settled his face against her neck.

"We need to get back to the house before long," Cindy declared. "Hope is looking after the others, but it is bedtime and they won't go to bed on their own. Is everyone ready?"

Adrienne detached Sarah from one breast and turned her to nurse on the other side. "Just give me five more minutes, and then we can go."

CHAPTER 51

$\mathcal{E}$rin didn't know whether to expect Bella to make it for her shift
the next day. Bella didn't have to be there early, of course; her
shift was never during the school day. But after all that had happened,
Erin thought she might want to go home after school and just be with her
family. The last week had been hard on everyone, but especially Bella. She
had been under suspicion, worried about whether she would be found out
or arrested. She also carried the burden of concern for her friend and had
to face the aftermath of the break-in and vandalism at the bakery. It had
been hard for Erin, but not nearly as hard as it must have been for the
teenager.

But Bella was there on time after school, her smile uncertain but
otherwise seeming like her usual self. She did some pre-closing tidying up
in the kitchen, then took over the till from Vic for the rush of customers
that always took place between school letting out and the bakery closing,
as people made last-minute purchases before suppertime.

It had been a busy day. Not as busy as the day after a murder, maybe,
but people were still excited to hear all of the details they could get about
Juliet taking Adrienne and the children hostage and Erin rescuing them.
At least, that was the way they wanted to spin it. Erin wasn't sure she had
actually been a hero. She had been at the right place and managed to
place a call to the police department but, other than that, she had done

nothing heroic. She hadn't disarmed Juliet or put herself between Juliet and the hostages. She had never really been in danger.

Those who were regulars at Auntie Clem's knew that if they wanted to see Bella, she would be there between school and closing, so the pre-dinner rush was even busier than usual as people showed up to see her and to talk to her about what had happened. Erin had been there, but Bella was friends with Adrienne and could offer the best insight into what had happened and how she felt being held hostage.

Not that Bella had much to say about it. She was trying to protect Adrienne's privacy, just as they had all been doing both before and after Simon and Juliet had shown up in Bald Eagle Falls.

At closing time, Bella went up to the door to lock it, then let in one last customer. Cindy Prost led Adrienne's four oldest children into the bakery. They looked around with wide, interested eyes.

"They're here for their kid's club cookies," Cindy said sharply. "And… I'll have a couple of pizza shells. We'll have a treat for supper tonight."

"Yay!" the boy who was older than Samuel Andrew cheered. Erin couldn't remember his name. The children gazed into the display case with wide eyes and wanted to know which they could choose. Erin had been running the kids club for a couple of years, but Adrienne's children had never participated. Adrienne generally kept them away from the bakery and either Adele or Adrienne picked up the baking they needed from the day-old bread program. Erin understood Adrienne wanting to keep the children out of the bakery, where they would beg for all the sweets they were looking at in the display case now.

But they were well-behaved and didn't make demands for all of the different treats they saw.

"You can have one cookie each. Whichever kind you choose," Erin told them.

"Chocolate chip?" the boy demanded, pointing at them.

"Yes, chocolate chip. Is that what you would like?"

"Peanut butter?" one of the girls asked.

"Sunbutter," Erin corrected. "Yes. Whatever you would like."

The children each pondered the cookies they wanted and Erin handed them out. Bella rang up the order for the pizza shells. Erin was tempted to tell Cindy there would be no charge since they were for Adrienne, but she refrained. Cindy might be insulted at being offered "charity." She worked and owned the farm and had the money needed to buy a couple of pizza shells for dinner.

After paying, Cindy gathered the children around her like a mother hen. It always warmed Erin's heart to see Cindy interacting with the children. On her own, Cindy was blunt to the point of rudeness. She was judgmental and had targeted Erin more than once with her critical comments and Vic with religious condemnation. But in her interactions with the children, she was almost grandmotherly.

"Tell Miss Erin thank you," Cindy instructed the children.

As the children chorused their thank yous, Cindy nodded to Erin and spoke over their piping voices.

"Thank you for everything," she said, and no critical comments followed.

MUFFIN TO HIDE

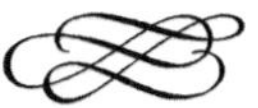

*For those at the center of controversy
they never sought*

CHAPTER 1

*D*o you really think there is a possibility that Gerald Montgomery would come all the way to Bald Eagle Falls?" Vic asked. Her tone was doubtful, but her eyes were bright. She was, Erin thought, trying to tamp down her excitement over the idea, not wanting to get her hopes up for something she considered to be unlikely.

"I didn't think it was possible," Erin admitted. She and Vic sat at the table in Erin's kitchen with their heads together, going over their plans for the next week. "It seems like a stretch that anyone would want to come way out to rural Tennessee to a little bakery like Auntie Clem's. But my sources say we are on *Montgomery's Muffin Mania* tour route." She shrugged, holding her hands palms up. "If he's going to be in the area, then he's coming to Auntie Clem's. It's the only bakery around that makes gluten-free muffins. Even in the city, only one place makes its own gluten-free cupcakes and muffins. Everyone else either orders from them or gets commercial stuff shipped from Nashville."

And that meant that they weren't fresh. Gerald Montgomery wasn't interested in something pulled from the freezer or sitting on the shelf for a couple of days. He had criticized restaurants or bakeries in the past for trying to pass something off as fresh when it was a day or two old. It wasn't worth his attention if it hadn't just come off the stove or been baked in the last few hours.

"Your sources?" Vic swept her long blond hair back, tucking it behind one ear. "How reliable are these *sources?*"

Erin Price couldn't blame her young assistant for being skeptical. Rumors that came over the grapevine in Bald Eagle Falls were plentiful but not necessarily accurate. The women of the town—and many of the men, too, Erin suspected—enjoyed gossiping about their neighbors. If there wasn't anything legitimate to discuss, they didn't seem to have any scruples against speculating or flat-out making something up. Some of the rumors that got back to Erin about herself or Vic or another friend or employee of Auntie Clem's Bakery were so far from the truth that Erin wondered whether the person who had started them was testing to see just how bizarre a rumor had to be before people would begin to question what they were hearing.

"Well, you know Cherise, the woman who runs the restaurant supply store in the city?"

Vic nodded, leaning forward with interest.

"Well, her nephew works in Gerald Montgomery's office. He saw Montgomery's travel itinerary for this tour and Bald Eagle Falls was on it. He figured she probably knew the bakery he would visit, so he called to share the news."

"And Cherise called you."

Erin nodded. "She knows I run the only bakery operating in Bald Eagle Falls and that everything here is gluten-free, so it was a no-brainer that if Montgomery is coming to Bald Eagle Falls, he is coming to Auntie Clem's Bakery."

"How did her nephew know he was coming through Bald Eagle Falls rather than just staying in the city? His itinerary is that detailed?"

"He's staying at the B&B."

"Which one? Mrs. McClung?"

Erin nodded. She had already confirmed the booking with Mrs. McClung. There wouldn't be any reason for Montgomery to stay at the B&B in Bald Eagle Falls unless he was planning to go to Auntie Clem's Bakery. If he wanted to go to the bakery in the city that made gluten-free muffins, he would have stayed in the city. The accommodations would be more convenient than staying in Bald Eagle Falls.

"Well…" Vic drew the word out long in a drawl. "Don't that beat all. He's coming to Auntie Clem's Bakery!"

"Who's coming to Auntie Clem's Bakery?" a male voice asked.

Erin didn't need to look up to know it was Officer Terry Piper, her… significant other. She really hated the word boyfriend. Partner sounded too much like business. Spouse wasn't right since they were not married, much to the dismay of the church ladies who patronized Auntie Clem's Bakery.

Erin sat back in her chair and stretched her back and shoulder muscles. Terry entered the kitchen to fetch a bottle of beer to drink while he watched the game on TV. Erin wasn't sure what game he was watching or even what sport. He had told her, she was sure, but she had been too distracted by the news of Gerald Montgomery's tour to retain any details.

"Just Gerald Montgomery," Vic said, her voice high and dramatic. "Just one of the most famous food critics in the country, coming to taste muffins at Auntie Clem's Bakery."

Terry looked at Erin. "Really? That sounds pretty prestigious."

"If he likes it, yes. If he doesn't like what he tastes… a review from a guy like Montgomery is enough to make or break a bakery. And he's very tough."

"Sounds like the plot of a Hallmark movie," Terry said. "If you can just find the right recipe to impress him, he'll give you your five gold stars and you can save the bakery from certain ruin and pay off the mortgage and fix all of the appliances in need of repair…"

"Well, there's no mortgage to pay off or appliances needing repair, but we *do* need to figure out what to serve him when he gets here. We can't just serve him an everyday rice bran or blueberry muffin and expect him to be impressed."

"Why not?" Terry challenged, "Your baking is the best. You shouldn't need to do anything special to impress him."

He removed the cap from the beer and had a swig.

"He'll be expecting something special," Erin said. "The everyday fare at Auntie Clem's is just fine—"

"Outstanding, even," Vic inserted.

"—But this guy is testing gluten-free muffins all across the country. You think he will be impressed with just any old muffin?"

"I don't think you sell 'any old muffin.'" Terry said generously. "You can't even tell them apart from a muffin made with regular wheat flour. And when you dress them all up with icing and other little bits…"

"Decorate them," Erin advised.

"When you do that, it takes them to a whole new level."

"Those prepackaged gluten-free blueberry muffins you can get at the store," Vic said slowly, "they don't even have real blueberries in them. They have *simulated blueberry nuggets…*"

Erin shuddered. "Well, anyone can make a muffin better than that. But we have to make a muffin that's better than them all."

Terry and Vic both looked at her. "That's a pretty tall order," Terry said. "You're not baking these muffins in the fires of Mount Doom."

It was Erin's turn to stare. "What?"

"Lord of the Rings," Terry advised. "The one ring to rule them all…"

"Oh." Erin gave a nod. "Yes, you're right. I won't be baking them in the fires of Mount Doom." she paused for dramatic effect, "but it *will* be the one muffin to rule them all."

CHAPTER 2

hat kind of muffin are you going to make?" Terry asked.

"I don't know, that's what we need to work out. We need to create something truly special. He'll take some of the other varieties, too; he always explores your range, but we need something that is… new, different, and special." Erin looked at Vic. "What do you think?"

Vic nodded, pursing her lips. "We should probably look over what he has liked at other restaurants and bakeries. Get a feel for what he likes or dislikes. Some people like a lot of rich sauces or rare ingredients, and some really like simplicity and making sure you have a solid grasp of the basics."

"Good," Erin nodded. "That will give us a good place to start. I've heard he also has allergies, so we'll need to get a list of what he can't eat. We want to have lots of options available to him. It wouldn't do to have a specialty bakery where he can't eat anything."

"It must be hard for him to be a food critic if he has multiple allergies. It can be really hard for some people to find anything they can safely eat."

Vic had learned all about how complicated it could be working with Erin at Auntie Clem's Bakery. People who needed to eat a gluten-free diet due to celiac disease often had other food allergies as well, and Vic knew of a few customers who came to Auntie Clem's—some from quite a distance—because they knew that Erin would work with them to find or create something they would be able to eat.

The Fosters were among their favorite customers in town. The oldest child had celiac disease and was very sensitive to any traces of gluten, and they were still trying to sort out all of the sensitivities of the youngest Foster child, Allan, to figure out what he could eat without digestive distress.

"I guess it would give him a chance to test out the service level of the restaurant, too," Erin suggested. "He can get a feeling for how they treat people with allergies or special needs, whether they have the right protocols in place to protect people who have allergies. Or else if they are sloppy and act like they don't want to deal with a customer who is particularly demanding."

Vic nodded. "I'll do some internet research and start pulling together a dossier. We'll get it all pinned down so we have plenty of safe choices for him."

Terry nodded at the two women and headed back to the living room as the commercial break ended and his game started up again.

"He *shore* likes his football," Vic drawled, drawing the word out.

"Is that what he's watching? I wasn't even paying any attention."

Vic laughed. "Growing up with so many boys, there was no escaping the almighty pigskin in the Jackson family. And I was right in there with the rest of them. My poor ma!"

Vic was transgender and had grown up as one of the brothers in the Jackson family before running away at seventeen to live as Victoria instead of James. Even knowing Vic as well as she did, Erin had a hard time remembering that the pretty young blond had once been a rough-and-tumble, shotgun-toting farm boy in the Jackson clan, one of the notorious organized crime organizations in the area. Vic had certainly transformed her life in the short time she had been living in Bald Eagle Falls.

"Did you want to go check the score?" Erin offered.

"I'm fine!" Vic assured her. "I'll watch the highlights with Willie later."

Erin nodded and glanced across the backyard toward the loft apartment over her garage, where she assumed Willie was sleeping or doing computer work. Willie still had his own house but hadn't been there much lately. Since he had started chelation protocol to reverse heavy metal poisoning, he had been in Vic's apartment most of the time, too tired and ornery to see to his own meals and other needs. Willie had always been totally independent, and none of them had expected the chelation to affect him as much as it had.

The doctors had suggested he would be dealing with "flu-like symptoms." But Erin felt like it was more like going through chemotherapy. He was constantly exhausted and nauseated, along with a whole host of other symptoms, not the least of which was "irritability." Vic was a saint for putting up with his whining, demands, and moodiness.

"How is he doing?"

"Well, William Andrews ain't the best patient in the world. But he *does* try my patience."

Erin chuckled. "I'm sure he does."

Vic looked at the clock on the wall. "He should be good for a while yet. Let's spend a few more minutes on the muffins and Mr. Montgomery before he wakes up from his nap."

"Have they said how long it will be before Willie is done with the chelation and can return to normal?"

"They just say he's progressing, still clearing heavy metals from his system, and sooner or later..." Vic sighed and held her hands up in a gesture of surrender. "Sometime..."

Erin grunted. Wasn't that the way it always worked? The doctors had a prescribed protocol, but how long it would take and what the side effects would be were far less predictable than they would have liked.

"So this Montgomery," Vic insisted on turning the conversation back to the critic, "I've seen the guy on TV. He's tough. You sure you want him coming to Auntie Clem's?"

"Well, it isn't like I can tell him not to! I didn't arrange for him to come and can't exactly turn customers away. If I told him I wasn't interested in a review, he'd just give me a bad one."

"You have the right to decide who to serve."

"And he has the right to say whatever he wants to in his show."

Vic grunted and nodded. "Do we at least know when he's coming?"

"We know *Montgomery's Muffin Mania* has already started, though they're not revealing where he has been or where he is going next. I have the dates that he has reserved a room at the B&B, but I'm sure he doesn't plan to be here more than one night, so he must not be sure exactly when he will arrive."

"So we need to be prepared that whole time."

Erin nodded. "And it's not so bad. We can make a special muffin several days in a row and just not roll it out until he gets there. I want it to be a surprise, for him to be the first person to try it out. If we make a batch each day and those just go into the freezer if he doesn't show up, that's fine. Then when he comes, we roll them out and he gets to tell the world what he thinks of them."

Even though Erin said it casually, breezily, her stomach tightened at the thought of it. What if Montgomery didn't like them? What if he *really* didn't like them and gave them one of his trademark horrible reviews and everybody thought that Auntie Clem's Bakery was sub-par?

"Everybody here knows Auntie Clem's is a great bakery," Vic assured Erin, reading her expression. "They love your baking. If moody Montgomery doesn't like the baking, that won't change."

Erin knew that was true. Her customers already knew her product. But it would cut down on the number of people out of town who made the trip to see what she had to offer. If Montgomery gave her a rave review, the traffic from the surrounding areas would increase. Maybe by quite a bit.

"We'll get a good review," Erin declared, making a positive statement like all of those build-your-success books said to. She didn't know if she believed in all of the positive-affirmations-lead-to-success stuff. But it couldn't hurt. "He'll give us a great review, and it will be great for the business."

CHAPTER 3

The next few days were a blur as they learned everything they could about food critic Gerald Montgomery. They read about him, stalked his online profiles, and watched his shows, making copious notes about everything he ate and what he liked and disliked.

On the one hand, Erin liked how the man forced the restaurants and bakeries he visited to 'up their game,' putting out new offerings, pumping up what they had, and changing ingredients based on whatever demands Montgomery might make. She and Vic quickly discovered that Montgomery never informed the restaurants and bakeries in advance about his allergies, instead expecting them to adapt on the fly. Which was really difficult when he came for muffins that had already been baked as opposed to table service at a restaurant. But Montgomery was adamant that the restaurants he visited not share what his allergies or requests were so that it was a level playing field. It was apparent what special requests he had made in some episodes, especially if the restaurant did not follow them correctly. But they never specified on TV which foods were allergens and which requests were just show challenges. Auntie Clem's Bakery would not be given the list of Montgomery's allergens until he arrived.

"But we know some of the restrictions," Vic said, looking down at her latest list as they sat on stools at the counter in the kitchen of Auntie Clem's during their early lunch break. The room was redolent with the aroma of baking cinnamon rolls. "We know that this particular tour is for gluten-free muffins. That's not hard since everything we make is gluten-free, and we always have at least three varieties of muffins available each morning. He's not vegan, so the maple bacon muffins should be okay. Sometimes, he demands dairy-free but, sometimes, he allows it. He usually allows eggs in baking but not cooked egg dishes."

"We always have at least one egg-free, dairy-free muffin."

"I think this special muffin you develop should be egg and dairy-free. Just in case Montgomery decides not to allow either."

"Baking that is egg, dairy, and gluten-free can be pretty challenging," Erin said, thinking over her favorites and trying to decide what seemed to match Montgomery's tastes the best. "At least muffins are pretty forgiving, and he's not going to ask for the near-impossible, like egg-free angel food cake or meringue."

"You've made that aquafaba meringue," Vic pointed out.

"I know… but some people just can't tolerate it, so I don't use it too much. Muffins are a lot easier to adjust for multiple allergens."

Vic nodded. "Yeah. I'm glad it isn't going to be anything fussy. Because… he's fussy enough without adding another challenge."

"I like his show," Erin offered. "I like watching him work and learning about the foods he is exploring and the different ways to prepare them. But all of the stuff I've read about him that talks about how disagreeable he is… above and beyond being harsh with his criticisms… I'm terrified to meet him. I'm sure he's just a normal guy like anyone else, but the image I have of him from TV, with the addition of all of the other criticisms and accusations that fly around about him online… he's kind of like a supervillain in my mind. And I don't think I want to meet a supervillain in real life."

"You've got the baking superpowers," Vic assured her, grinning. "You'll come out okay. I'm sure he won't shoot lasers at you or anything."

"I hope not. I don't think I'm laser-proof."

"Just remember, in a few days, it will all be over."

Erin wasn't sure she found that any more comforting than the thought of meeting Montgomery face-to-face.

CHAPTER 4

$\mathcal{E}$rin didn't have long to wait.

The day Gerald Montgomery showed up, she was glad Vic was there to back her up. The other employees were wonderful, but Vic was the one that Erin really depended on and who put in almost as much time at the bakery as Erin did. Even though Charley was part-owner of the bakery, she didn't put in a lot of hours.

Bella was also on duty. She was a high school student, a few years younger than Vic, a curvy girl with wavy blond hair and a good nose for business. She hoped to get a degree and start her own business after graduating. Erin suspected that most of the money Bella made at the bakery went directly to her college fund. Would she want to open a business in Bald Eagle Falls or another small town? Or did she dream of opening something in the city with its noise, bustle, and plenty of walk-by traffic? Erin wasn't sure what kind of a business Bella hoped to open. Whatever she chose, Erin was sure it would be a success.

Bella was on the heavy side and, when people saw her round face and youthful appearance, they tended to underestimate her intelligence, experience, and people skills.

Erin didn't see Montgomery enter the bakery. It was the lunch rush; so many people were hurrying in during their breaks from work or school to grab something to go along with their lunch or maybe buy a muffin or trail mix bar that would serve as a meal replacement.

But as Erin finished serving Lottie Sturm and looked up to see who the next customer was, she was startled first to see an unfamiliar face, but then realized that she did, in fact, know who he was even if he hadn't ever been in her bakery before.

Montgomery wore a suit and tie and had a short beard and permanent frown lines between his eyes. He looked a little too thin to be a food critic, making Erin worry that he was even more critical than she had seen on TV. The camera really did add ten pounds. Which didn't make Erin feel good about how *she* would look on the show. But it was too late to worry about losing weight now.

"Oh!" Erin's mouth went dry, and she couldn't think of anything to say at first. After a few seconds of awkwardness, habit kicked in. "Welcome to Auntie Clem's Bakery. How can I help you?"

Montgomery's crew tried to be as unobtrusive as possible. Still, they carried extra lights, microphones, and handheld cameras, spreading out to get the different angles they wanted for the show. Erin licked her lips, wishing she had a water bottle handy. She kept a smile pasted on her face.

"I am Gerald Montgomery, food critic," Montgomery announced self-confidently. "You may recognize me from Montgomery Meals and Reels online or on network TV. I am on the *Montgomery Muffin Mania* tour, looking for innovative twists on this delicious staple that are available for the gluten-intolerant or sensitive. Or even people who are just trying out a gluten-free diet."

He paused. Erin wasn't sure whether he was expecting her to answer or whether it was just a dramatic pause or where they would make a cut when they were producing the show.

Montgomery looked down at the display case. "I understand that everything at Auntie Clem's Bakery here in Bald Eagle Falls, Tennessee is gluten-free. Is that really true?"

Erin nodded. "It was my dream to offer a wide variety of gluten-free products to those who are unable to eat conventional baking and always end up with few, if any, choices at a regular bakery. Instead of being given the option of one kind of gluten-free cookie sitting on the shelf at the grocery store going stale and having to go into the city to special order things like birthday cake, my gluten-free customers can come in here and choose anything they see. Unless they have other allergies, of course. But everything that is made strictly follows a recipe and avoids cross-contamination, so we know the exact ingredients in everything we sell."

She took a deep breath and considered what else the at-home audience would need to know about the bakery.

"By only using gluten-free ingredients and offering gluten-free products to our customers, we avoid the problem of pans or other tools being contaminated with gluten, even in microscopic amounts."

"I'm sure your customers who must follow gluten-free diets appreciate that."

Erin nodded.

"I understand you run the only bakery in town. Do you get many complaints from those who don't want to be forced to eat gluten-free and would prefer that you offered both?"

"New customers are sometimes surprised but, after they've tasted the baking, I usually win them over."

Montgomery gave her a sardonic smile that made Erin feel guilty for bragging about her baking. But she wasn't about to be cowed by this food critic before he even tasted the goods. What Erin said was perfectly true. It didn't matter if she was blowing her own horn.

"So, what muffins do you have on offer today?" Montgomery asked.

Erin indicated the varieties in the display case. "In addition to these, I actually have a new muffin variety that I am just debuting today," Erin informed him. "If you choose, you can be the first person other than me to taste it."

Montgomery raised an eyebrow. "Are you telling me that purely by coincidence, you have a new variety of muffin for me to test today?" He looked around at his crew. "Do I have a leak inside my organization? Did someone tell you I would be here today?"

"I heard a rumor you might be going through this part of Tennessee," Erin said, "But I couldn't get any information from your office as to when that would be."

Montgomery nodded. "Good. Well, what is this new variety of muffin, then?" He turned his gaze away from Erin to Bella. "If you could please package up one of each of these." He gestured to the display case.

"Sure," Bella agreed. "Of course." She was flushed around her neck but kept her composure. Hopefully, she wouldn't drop anything on the floor.

Hopefully, Erin would not drop anything on the floor either. She could just picture herself tripping as she retrieved the special muffins, sending muffins flying off of the tray and rolling across the floor in all directions.

She hoped she hadn't jinxed herself by thinking of it. She gave Montgomery and the cameras a nod that was not as confident as it looked. She gulped as she turned around and went into the kitchen. She went to the sink first and got herself a glass of water. She drank a few swallows, taking it slowly so she wouldn't inadvertently choke and end up coughing uncontrollably.

Calmer after the drink, she retrieved the fresh muffins, centered the little card at the front of the tray, and walked them slowly out to the front of the bakery. She took a deep breath, savoring the sweet vanilla smell of the fresh muffins. They were still warm from the oven.

Vic had the ingredient Bible out and was comparing the ingredients for each muffin she had packaged up for Montgomery to the card she now held in her hand.

Erin set the new muffins on top of the display case and looked around Vic at the small print on the wallet card. It was headed *Food must not contain*, followed by a list of ingredients. Most of them were gluten-containing ingredients. A few nuts. She didn't have to worry about gluten or nuts since they didn't use either at the bakery. A few other random fruits, additives, and shrimp.

Erin nodded. "Yes, these are all safe."

"And what do you have here?" Montgomery looked at the new muffins. "Morning Sunshine Muffins." He looked over the golden-brown tops.

"They're a—" Erin started, but Montgomery held up his hand to stop her.

"Since you have not named them descriptively, the flavor is intended to be a surprise. Please check the list of prohibited ingredients to ensure they comply; if they do, don't tell me anything more about them. I will taste-test them without any preconceptions."

Erin dutifully took the wallet card from Vic and read through it again. As she already knew, they were completely safe for Gerald Montgomery.

He could taste-test them at his leisure, knowing that she had checked and double-checked the ingredients.

"Yes, you're good to go," she told him, smiling. "I hope you really enjoy them!"

He nodded. "Yes, we will see. Please ring those up," he told Bella. He looked down at the wallet he still held in his hand, fingers poised over the credit cards, then shook his head. "I forgot. Michael, would you…?" He flicked a hand at one of his crew to direct him to pay for the muffins.

CHAPTER 5

In a few minutes, they were all gone again. Montgomery and his crew cleared out of the bakery, leaving it feeling suddenly empty and quiet despite the customers who were still gaping at what had just happened and whispering to each other.

"I can't believe you had Gerald Montgomery here!" Lottie exclaimed. "In Bald Eagle Falls—in our bakery!"

It was probably the first time Erin had ever heard Lottie say *our* bakery. She had never been complimentary about Auntie Clem's. She often complained about it being the only bakery in town. Despite what Erin had told Montgomery, the bakery did have its detractors. Those who, even after tasting her baking, still felt like there should be another bakery operating in Bald Eagle Falls or that it was Erin's duty to offer both gluten and gluten-free options rather than subjecting all of the townsfolk to her gluten-free creations.

Lottie was not someone who had ever been thrilled with the idea of a gluten-free bakery or supportive of Erin and her business—even though, voting with her dollar, she continued to shop at Auntie Clem's rather than going into the city to a conventional bakery.

Erin suppressed a smile at Lottie's sudden turnabout in now referring to Auntie Clem's Bakery in the possessive.

"It's quite something, isn't it?" she agreed. "I was excited when I heard he would be coming here."

Lottie fanned herself with her hand. "Lordy, I thought I would faint when I saw him. And all of those cameras and lights. You don't realize when you see him on TV all of the equipment they use to film those scenes. I always thought of him as being incognito, but you really can't hide all of the equipment, can you?"

"It's all part of the fantasy," Vic said knowingly. "It's the same thing when you watch *Survivor* or *Manhunt* or any of those shows. You feel like you're the only one watching, that you just have this little window into what's going on on the island, and the participants have completely forgotten that anyone is watching them. But they've got a whole camera crew and production team following everyone around, as well as whatever surveillance or hidden cameras they have around the place. The participants can't forget that everything they do and say is on tape."

Lottie shook her head. "I never even thought about it. I guess I thought there was just one person with a camera on their shirt button that everyone could forget was even there. Isn't it amazing?"

She looked over the items in the display case, but it seemed like she was still dazzled by having witnessed Montgomery's appearance, and she didn't focus on any of the items she usually bought.

"I think—why don't I try those Morning Sunshine Muffins? They look really good."

In other words, she wanted to share the experience that Montgomery was having. To be the first to say she had tasted the muffins right after Montgomery. Or even before. She could get a review and comments on social media before Gerald Montgomery and show off to her friends.

"Actually, the Morning Sunshine Muffins will not be on sale until after Gerald Montgomery's tasting airs," Erin advised. "Then they'll go on sale and everyone else can see what they think."

Lottie stared at her. "What do you mean they're not on sale yet? Didn't you just say they are debuting today?"

"They are. But only to a limited audience. After Mr. Montgomery gets his review up, everyone can try them out."

"But that's not fair."

Erin could feel Bella laughing beside her and didn't turn to look at her, keeping her focus on Lottie, but also making the announcement to the rest of the customers as well.

"I'm sorry you feel that way, but this is a special event, and we're making the most of it. The Morning Sunshine Muffins will not be on sale until after Montgomery Meals and Reels airs the tasting."

"Well," Lottie huffed. "You're getting a mite big for your britches. If there was anywhere else in town to go for my bakery needs… you can bet I wouldn't be spending my money here."

But there wasn't. So Erin just smiled pleasantly and waited to see if Lottie would place an order or walk out in a snit. Lottie eventually picked out the bread and other items that she wanted.

"And you can bet I won't be coming back here tomorrow to buy any of your precious Morning Sunshine Muffins," she declared.

But Erin figured she would be, just like everyone else.

After Lottie was gone, Erin served the next couple of customers. Lottie had drawn enough attention to herself that everyone understood that the new muffins would not be available until after Montgomery's tasting aired and, though they cast interested and longing glances in the direction of the tray holding the remaining muffins in the batch Erin had made that day, they did not demand the right to purchase them.

Erin had seen Peter Foster enter the bakery, opening and closing the door quietly with the bare whisper of bells, and moving in behind the adults. She was surprised at the lack of his usual exuberance and his solemn expression when it was his turn to approach the counter.

Erin raised her brows and gave him a tentative smile.

"What's up, Peter?"

He looked listlessly over the goods in the display case. Usually, he was excited to be able to choose from all of the gluten-free wonders Erin baked. He was a celiac, and it was for people like him that Erin had opened Auntie Clem's Bakery. People who couldn't have gluten-containing baking. People who had no choices at a conventional bakery and just a few prepackaged goods on the shelf at the grocery store.

"I don't know. I just wish…" He looked at the baked delights before him and sighed.

Erin waited for him to finish his thought, but he didn't. "What's wrong?" she asked after a moment. "Are you not feeling well today?

Or…" A thought occurred to her. Maybe he didn't have any money for a treat today. His family had gone through some rough patches with work lately, and they had a lot of children to support. Maybe he didn't have the pocket money that he'd had other days when he had come to Auntie Clem's after school. "Did you want your Kid's Club cookie early this week? I could sneak in an extra one for my very favorite customer."

He looked surprised. "No, that's okay. I'll come with the girls for Kid's Club. I have money today." He jingled coins in his pocket. Erin suspected he did chores for neighbors to earn a little spending money.

"Okay…?"

"I just wish… that I could eat normal stuff."

Erin couldn't help feeling a little hurt that he would say such a thing when she had dedicated her life to opening Auntie Clem's and serving people who couldn't eat gluten a wide variety of "normal" baked goods. With no other bakery in Bald Eagle Falls, Peter had precisely the same choices as anyone else.

"Is there something specific I could make you that you wish you could have?" she suggested.

"No. You make all of the gluten-free stuff I need."

"But you still wish you didn't have celiac disease."

He nodded. He looked at the customers behind him and moved closer to Erin, speaking quietly so that she could hear him, but the others wouldn't.

"Kids at school say that the reason Auntie Clem's is gluten-free and they have to eat all gluten-free baking is because of me. If it wasn't for me, you would just have a normal bakery and they could eat normal food with wheat flour in it because you wouldn't have to worry about making anyone sick."

Erin's anger rose at the cruelty of the other children. There was just enough of the truth in what they said to hurt Peter and make him feel guilty and bad about himself and his condition. What did it hurt them to eat gluten-free baking? It was just as good as what they would find at a conventional bakery. Most people couldn't tell the difference. It didn't hurt them to have the tables turned so that they were the ones who had to make a special trip to find a conventional bakery, if it made that much of a difference to them. That was what celiacs and others with food sensitivities had to do all the time. The rest of the townspeople had choice. They could eat the gluten-free goods if they wanted to. A celiac couldn't choose to eat conventional baking if they planned to stay healthy.

"Peter… you aren't the only one in town who has to eat gluten-free. Other people need this kind of baking, too. And baby Allan probably has celiac disease. You know how much trouble he's been having with his digestion and being unhappy all the time."

"He's a lot better now."

Erin nodded. "It makes a difference when you eat stuff that doesn't hurt your tummy. You know you aren't very happy when you're sick."

"I know it's not just me," Peter admitted. "But wouldn't it be good if no one was celiac and had to eat gluten-free? If we could all just eat the same things?"

Erin shrugged. "I guess so. But that's not the way it works. Did I ever tell you about my foster sister Carolyn? The one who was celiac?"

He shrugged with one shoulder. "You've mentioned her, I guess."

Erin considered what to tell him about Carolyn. He was just a kid, and his mother would not appreciate Erin telling him that she had died because she had refused to follow her special diet. That was a pretty harsh reality for a child.

"It was because of my sister Carolyn that I wanted to open a gluten-free bakery," she said. "Because when we were growing up, she didn't have any good choices for gluten-free baking, and it made her really sad. Sometimes, she snuck gluten foods so that she could eat with her friends. It made her sick, but she was so sad about not having any good food to choose from and not being able to eat with her friends that she didn't care."

Erin was aware that other customers were waiting behind Peter. She reached into the display case and grabbed him a chocolate chip cookie, which she put in a wrapper and handed it to him.

"The name of the bakery might be Auntie Clem's Bakery after my aunt Clementine, but it could just as easily be called Carolyn's, because she's the reason I opened it."

"Does she ever come here?"

"No, she passed away a long time ago. But I still remember how hard it was for her, and I wanted to make it easier for people like her. And you."

Peter took the cookie and dug in his pocket for his money.

"This is a special occasion," Erin said. "No charge. I just want you to know that there are a lot more people than you think who need Auntie Clem's Bakery. People with celiac disease, gluten intolerance, and other food allergies. And people who want to share with you and their other friends. People who only want to eat gluten-containing baking can eat wherever else they want to."

Peter nodded. "I guess."

"Bella," Erin motioned to the next customer. "Can you take over here for a minute? I'm just going to walk Peter over to the Book Nook. Is that where you're going, Peter?"

His father worked at the Book Nook now, so Peter was usually on his way there when he stopped in at Auntie Clem's after school.

He nodded. "I can go by myself," he pointed out.

"I know. I just wanted to talk for a minute longer."

Bella took Erin's place at the counter and invited the next customer forward. Erin walked around to Peter and they exited the bakery together.

"The people saying those things are just being mean," Erin told Peter. "Or they don't understand about celiac disease and other sensitivities. We have to educate them."

"We do?"

"Just like your mom taught you to look after your own health and find out what is in the food you eat to make sure that it is safe. She taught you really well, didn't she? So that you know all of the questions to ask about the ingredients."

"Yeah."

"You're really smart, and you learned that stuff pretty quickly. But these friends of yours who are teasing or bullying you… they need to be taught about what celiac disease is and how many people have celiac disease or gluten intolerance or other allergies or sensitivities like Allan. It isn't their fault that they don't understand. Their parents didn't teach them because they didn't need to know, like you did, or because their parents don't know it themselves."

Peter pondered this as they walked into the Book Nook and looked around for Mr. Foster.

"Do you think it would help?"

Erin sighed, thinking about Lottie in the bakery. If adults didn't know how to behave themselves, how could they expect the children to? There were still too many people who thought that allergies and intolerances were just over-dramatization. People looking for attention.

"Maybe one day they'll see," she told Peter. "I hope so."

CHAPTER 6

*H*aving watched several episodes of Montgomery's show online, Erin knew that he did not use a crew to film the actual tasting. He was very particular about being alone and undistracted when he tasted the products. He had a tripod stand for his lights and cameras and operated them himself.

Erin didn't know if this was some kind of OCD or sensory issue, or if it was just his own little dramatic twist to make his show unique. It was very interesting to watch him take a bite or two of a dish or baked good, chew or roll it around in his mouth, staring off into space or closing his eyes as he considered the taste and texture. At times, his reactions were intense, spitting and wiping his mouth in disgust, even though the dish seemed perfectly edible and likely received praise from other customers.

And sometimes he was more thoughtful, making notes to himself as his face moved through several different expressions, considering what he had just consumed.

His video would not be shown to Erin until his crew and producer had viewed it and discussed how it would be presented to the public. It wasn't like she had seen in movies about food critics, where the owners were peeking out the kitchen door to watch the critic take his first few bites of the meal, or the staff was lined up in front of the critic's table, watching his expression as he tasted it for the first time.

No, she would have to wait. Not just a few minutes or hours, but overnight, and then as long as it took in the morning for everyone involved to view the video and have an opportunity to pass on their comments on how it should be showcased for the best dramatic effect.

Until then, Erin and her employees would have to wait and wonder.

CHAPTER 7

From the time she woke up, Erin was on pins and needles waiting for word of the results of Montgomery's tasting. She knew it would be hours before she knew what he'd had to say about the muffins, particularly the new recipe. He would send the recording to his people, and they would take time to look at it, review it, and discuss the treatments and approaches they would use. Eventually, someone would get back to her.

At least they didn't make her wait until it aired for her to find out what Montgomery thought. They didn't film her reaction live on the air, letting her find out in front of millions that he'd found them too dry or too moist, that they didn't have a perfect crumb, or that he thought them cloyingly sweet.

Instead, she would find out today, in the privacy of her own bakery, whether Montgomery's review would have a chilling effect on her business or bring a rush of new customers from the surrounding areas.

She supposed that either way, there would be new people coming around to check out Auntie Clem's Bakery, the bakery that had been on Gerald Montgomery's show on TV and the internet. He had millions of followers. Some of them would check out any restaurant or bakery in the state that had appeared on Montgomery's show. Maybe any bakery in all of Appalachia. Or the country.

Were there groupies who traveled the country to visit every restaurant he had reviewed? He had enough followers. There probably were. If it were a negative review, would they actually order the Morning Sunshine Muffins to see if they were as bad as Montgomery said they were and render their own opinion? Or would they laugh and refuse to buy anything from Auntie Clem's, just coming to gawk at her and the little backwoods bakery that had attracted so much attention?

"You'll find out soon," Vic said.

Erin looked up from the pan of apple crumble dessert bars she was cutting to look at Vic, who was watching her from the sink, where she was washing out several mixing bowls as they prepared to open.

Vic raised a brow, smiling. "You're off in your own little world, boss," she observed, "but I know what you're thinking."

Erin rolled her eyes and didn't deny it. "I'm sure it's pretty obvious."

Vic chuckled. "I want to know just as much as you do. It feels like everyone in town is holding their breaths, waiting. I'm as anxious as a cat in a room full of rockers."

"I just can't help wondering if it will be great for business... or devastating. What if it's a bad review and I end up having to shut down?"

"That's not going to happen. Even if it was a bad review—and that's not going to happen—everyone in Bald Eagle Falls already knows how great your baking is. They won't stop coming here because some internet celebrity decides he doesn't like a muffin. And you'd probably get a bunch of lookie-loos who just want to see the place just because it was on TV. Or to try out the awful muffins for themselves. Either way, you're golden. You won't have to shut down the bakery because he gives you a bad review. And he's not going to give you a bad review."

"He could. He's ruined plenty of other people who were really popular and had lots of great reviews saying how wonderful their food was. Then Montgomery comes along and says how crappy it is, and they lose too much of their customer base and have to close their doors."

"That's not going to happen to you. For one thing, you're the only bakery in town. Where is everyone going to go? You think they're going to drive into the city to go to a bakery there? Or start buying their bread and muffins off the shelf at the grocery store?"

"People do eat grocery store bread," Erin pointed out. "Lots of it."

"Well, people who are used to your baking will not want to go back to grocery store bread. They will keep coming here, whether some ninny has said that your baking is good or not."

Erin smiled and went back to cutting the apple crumble bars.

Mary Lou was one of the early-morning customers. She liked to hit the bakery before she opened up The General Store and started her own workday. On occasion, she would join the before-dinner crowd after closing The General Store, but she was tired after work. No one liked to shop when she was exhausted.

Mary Lou touched her gray bob to ensure there wasn't a hair out of place—there never was—and smoothed her pantsuit over her hips.

"Have you heard anything from your critic yet?" she asked Erin. All of her regular customers, and the church ladies in particular, knew about Montgomery; that he had been coming, what kind of a personality he was, and that he had been there the afternoon before. News spread fast in Bald Eagle Falls. It was not an easy place to keep secrets. Even things that had happened years ago tended to pop up again sooner or later.

"No, no word yet," Erin told her, as she had told everyone else.

"I'm sure he'll give your muffins a good review," Mary Lou assured her. "They're perfectly normal muffins." She decided she might have come across the wrong way and amended it. "What I mean is, they are no different than normal, non-gluten-free muffins. There's no difference. So when he tastes them, he'll say the same. And they're good. You always have a nice variety on hand, and you even developed a new recipe just for him."

Erin nodded. "I'm having second thoughts about that," she admitted. "Why would I try something new instead of sticking to the old favorites? A recipe needs to stand the test of time; you need to know that it works for everyone and to make little adjustments here and there until every-thing is perfect. But I didn't go through that process. No one else has tasted them other than me."

Mary Lou looked at Vic. "And Victoria, I'm sure."

Vic shook her head. "Not even me. Erin wanted Mr. Montgomery to be the first person to taste them. I'm as eager as everyone else to get my chance at a Morning Sunshine Muffin."

There were, in fact, a couple of batches baking in the ovens as they spoke. Erin figured she would sell out in short order. People would be eager to try the new muffin that Montgomery had reviewed, whether his review were good or bad. She had been counting on it being good for the publicity. But what if she had been wrong and it didn't move the needle? What if nobody cared and Montgomery's audience of millions didn't make any difference to a tiny bakery in the Tennessee backwoods?

"Do you have them on sale yet?" Mary Lou asked, looking over the offerings in the display case. "I don't see them."

"Not yet. Not until I see Montgomery's review," Erin said.

She had a whole marketing plan surrounding the Morning Sunshine Muffins and Gerald Montgomery's review. She had read everything she could get her hands on about marketing after a celebrity endorsement. She was doing everything she could to build the excitement and anticipation.

"It's all very exciting," Mary Lou said. "I suppose I must come over after work to snag one. Though you'll probably have sold out by that time. Would you set one aside for me? I'll pay now."

Mary Lou's request was a testament to the success of Erin's marketing. Mary Lou rarely bought anything sweet for herself, very careful of what she ate in order to maintain her slim figure. If she was going to eat one of the muffins, or even just have a few bites of one, it was a special occasion.

Erin shook her head, feeling bad about the decision. "I've already said there are no reservations," she explained regretfully. "I'd like to make an exception for you, but I really can't."

"You're very clever," Mary Lou said with a smile. "You'll get a lot of people in when you finally release them. I'm sure everyone is just as excited to try them out as I am."

"I'll try to keep up with the demand. So you might luck out and still be able to get one after you finish at The General Store."

"If not, then maybe tomorrow."

Erin was glad that Mary Lou didn't resent or take the policy personally.

"We'll have some in the oven first thing tomorrow," she promised.

"I look forward to it."

CHAPTER 8

It wasn't until Mary Lou had picked out her week's baking and was counting out her change for Vic that she mentioned offhandedly, "There's something going on down the street. Did you see the police cars?"

Erin looked at her. "No, what police cars?"

Even though other customers were waiting, Erin went around the counter and to the front door. She couldn't see the police cars until she opened the door and leaned out, and then she could see them a couple of blocks down the street.

"Are they at a house? What's going on?"

She resumed her place behind the counter and continued the conversation with Mary Lou even though she was finished. It was time for Erin to serve the next customers waiting there patiently, Betty Thompson and her husband.

"Yes, one of the houses just past the commercial district," Mary Lou confirmed. "Maybe something at the B&B?"

Erin froze. "At the B&B? Where Gerald Montgomery is staying?"

Mary Lou shrugged. "That doesn't mean it has something to do with him. Though, of course, being an outsider, he is probably behind any disruption. He's a celebrity; maybe someone was harassing him. Tried to get into his room to get a picture of him."

That could be it. Erin didn't have to assume the worst every time something happened in Bald Eagle Falls. It might be a slow, sleepy little town, but it still needed a police presence. People still broke the law; it didn't have to have anything to do with her or anyone she was associated with. Erin let out her breath slowly.

That was it. Just someone who was stalking Montgomery, wanted an autograph, or had been getting in the way of his crew while they were trying to get things set up. Undoubtedly, his presence in Bald Eagle Falls had attracted some outsiders who didn't necessarily know how things worked in a small town. They thought they could get away with things, that there wouldn't be any scrutiny because they were such a small place. There wasn't even 9-1-1 service. People might think that there were no police.

Erin pulled out her phone to look at it and ensure that Terry hadn't messaged her. Officer Terry Piper, also known by Vic and some of the other ladies as Officer Handsome, might have some insight for her into what was going on. But if an active crime investigation were underway, he wouldn't be calling or telling her anything about it until the crisis was over. Then, she might hear some inside information about it if she approached it correctly.

"Tell me if you can see anything when you go to The General Store," Erin told Mary Lou. She wouldn't be walking as far as the B&B, but she might be close enough to see what was happening there.

Mary Lou smiled at Erin and raised her brows. "Oh, now you want a favor from me. Maybe we could trade."

"Trade?" Erin echoed, not following her train of thought.

"Barter," Mary Lou said, leaning closer and speaking softly. "A favor for a favor."

It took Erin a moment too long to connect the two conversations. Mary Lou wanted a Morning Sunshine Muffin put aside for her. Erin wanted information on what was going on at the B&B. They were both in a position to offer the other person something if they wished.

Erin looked at Vic to see what she thought about this. Vic had been on board with Erin not letting anyone have a Morning Sunshine Muffin until after the results of the critic's tasting were known. Should Erin stick to her guns or bargain with Mary Lou?

Vic shrugged. "It's up to you," she murmured. "They're your muffins and it's your plan."

"Well..." Erin considered, then finally nodded. "All right. I will put a you-know-what aside for you. You don't get one before they go on sale, but I'll make sure there is still one here for you when you can get back. And..." Erin made a twisting-key movement at her lips.

If others of the church ladies found out that Mary Lou had been given special treatment over them, there might be a mutiny. She couldn't give away that she had given Mary Lou a special favor over everyone else.

"Deal," Mary Lou agreed, giving a firm nod. She walked to the front door and put her hand on the handle. "I'll let you know."

She pushed open the door and left. Erin turned back to Vic before serving Betty Thompson. "Have I just sold my soul to the devil?"

Vic snickered. "Well, I couldn't say no for sure. But I think your soul is safe for now."

Erin blew out her breath dramatically and turned to Betty. "And what can I get for you today, Mrs. Thompson?"

"How about one of those lovely muffins I keep hearing about? You know, the..."

"The ones that aren't available yet?" Erin challenged.

Betty smiled. "Well... I'm not sure about that. You must have sold one or two, Or I wouldn't be hearing about them."

"No, they're not available yet. But I'll be sure to let you know when they are. From what I have in the case today... is there anything I can get you?"

"Oh, dear. I was hoping for a muffin today..."

"Today, you have the options of a blueberry muffin, raisin bran, or chocolate chip duo." Erin indicated each in the case as she spoke. She hoped Betty could be distracted from the Morning Sunshine Muffin, much like a toddler from his favorite toy.

"Chocolate chip duo?" Betty asked, leaning closer to get a good look at it. She was a retired lady, older like Mrs. Peach, still vigorous and in good shape. Erin hoped that she would be doing as well at seventy or eighty.

"It has milk chocolate and white chocolate chips," Erin told her.

"Ooh. That sounds very good."

"Shall I get you half a dozen of those?"

Betty looked back at her husband, resting with his hands on the bars of his walker.

"Those sound great," Mr. Thompson encouraged. "If that's what you want."

"The doctor said I should be watching my chocolate intake."

"They don't have a lot in them," Erin pointed out. "The muffin itself is vanilla, so there is no cocoa in them. And just a few chips to make it more decadent. It couldn't be more than… a tablespoon of chocolate chips per muffin. Maybe two."

"That doesn't seem like very much," Betty agreed. "I'm sure the doctor would say that a tablespoon of chocolate chips every now and then would be fine."

Erin didn't want to put words in the doctor's mouth or to give Mrs. Thompson medical advice. For all she knew, Betty's doctor had told her not to have *any* chocolate.

"Well, let's go with that," Betty said finally. "And six of the blueberry muffins. Blueberries are very high in antioxidants."

"So is chocolate," Erin laughed. She packaged the chocolate chip and blueberry muffins for Betty and passed them over to Vic to ring them up.

Erin's phone vibrated in her apron pocket and then, the next time she went into the kitchen to take a batch of the Morning Sunshine Muffins out of the oven, she took the opportunity to check the screen. Mary Lou had texted her as promised.

They are at the B&B. Can't tell what's going on. Several police cars.

Several police cars likely meant all of the Bald Eagle Falls police department. So it was something big. They had even called in the off-duty officers.

It seemed sort of a waste to have promised Mary Lou one of the muffins when all she had provided was the information that there were police at the site, which they already knew. But Erin put one of the hot muffins to the side for her anyway. If she physically separated it from the rest of the products, then none of them would accidentally put it out for sale when Erin had promised to hold it.

She sent Terry a quick text asking him what was happening at the B&B, then returned to the front of the store where Vic was manning both the counter and the till. On Erin's return, Vic moved back over to the till.

Even not knowing the results of Montgomery's taste test yet, people's curiosity brought them to Auntie Clem's Bakery in a steady stream all day long.

CHAPTER 9

$\mathcal{I}$t was late afternoon when Erin glanced over the customers waiting for service and saw that, with the last jingle of bells, Terry had entered with K9. She smiled at him and kept serving the customers ahead of him. He waited patiently to get to the front of the line, and Erin handed him a biscuit for K9 and offered to refill his water bottle.

Terry shook his head. "I need to talk to you."

"You need to talk to me?" Erin shrugged. "Okay."

"It would probably be best if this was done in private."

Erin looked at the other customers who were still waiting to be served. "Can it wait until closing? It's been busy all day and we don't have much longer."

He stood there unmoving, considering it. "You asked about what happened at the B&B. Why everyone was there."

"Yeah, what was going on over there?"

"I'd like to talk to you about it. In private."

"Oh. Okay." Erin's stomach knotted. It obviously wasn't good news, but she didn't know what to expect. Maybe it wasn't just a fan crowding Montgomery. Or breaking in. Maybe they had made threats.

She tilted her head to indicate she was going to the back. The door opened with another jangle of bells, ringing wildly this time.

Erin thought she recognized this dramatic entrance. People were usually pretty quiet coming into Auntie Clem's. People who came to pick up a loaf of bread or pizza shell for supper were usually not dealing with emergencies. A few last-minute shoppers would always be rushing against the clock at closing, but it wasn't quite six o'clock.

Erin looked at the new arrival and saw exactly who she had expected. Melissa Lee, her spiraling dark hair in disarray, red-faced from her excitement and rush to get there. She stepped around the waiting customers to address Erin directly, then saw Terry. She froze.

"Miss Lee," Terry greeted gravely. "Or should I say Missus Plaint."

"Oh," Melissa flushed further. "You know I don't usually go by that. Just… for special occasions."

She had recently married Davis Plaint, a resident of the nearby penitentiary, and preferred not to attract too much attention to the fact in the course of normal conversation.

Terry and Erin waited for Melissa to say something. She closed her mouth and stood there awkwardly, pretending to be studying the contents of the display case.

Melissa was a member of the administrative staff of the police department and their biggest leak, and both Terry and Erin knew very well why she was there. She was there to tell Erin whatever it was Terry had come to tell her, hoping to be the one to break the news to her. But she had been foiled by Terry's arriving before her, and would now have to buy something chocolate to soothe her injured spirit and justify her presence in Auntie Clem's. She couldn't very well say that she had come only to fill Erin in on the latest gossip.

Erin looked at Vic, raising her brows, then turned and entered the kitchen. Terry walked around the counter and followed her in. They moved away from the doorway but didn't go into Erin's office, which was closet-sized and claustrophobic.

"Well?" Erin asked, looking around the kitchen for something to keep her hands busy while they talked, and settling on filling a sink with water to start soaking pans. Maybe turning on the water wasn't the best choice of activities, since it was loud and Terry waited until she turned it off again before attempting to speak to her.

"I'm sure you know that Gerald Montgomery was staying at the B&B."

Erin nodded. "Sure. I thought he must be involved in whatever all of the police were there for. Maybe he was being harassed? A stalker or threat?"

Terry nodded. "That would be a good guess—"

"I figured as much."

"—But not correct," Terry finished.

Erin looked at him, startled. "Oh. What was it then?"

"Montgomery died last night."

"He died?" Erin gaped. She couldn't remember how to breathe. "What?"

Terry nodded. He walked over to the other sink and filled a glass with cold water. He handed it to Erin. She took it carefully, unable to feel it in her hand, and took a long drink of the cold water before looking at him again.

"How could Montgomery be dead? Was he sick? He looked okay yesterday. He wasn't… sweating or coughing. He didn't look sick."

She had held a number of elder care jobs. She might not be a doctor, but she recognized more quickly than others when someone was sick.

"No, I don't think he was sick when he saw you."

"Oh, well. An accident, then? Or…" Erin hated to suggest it, "It wasn't homicide, was it? I mean, celebrities… they can be vulnerable to stalkers when they spend so much time in the public eye." Erin swallowed. "How horrible…"

"Why don't you sit down?" Terry suggested, motioning to one of the stools Erin used when she had work to do but couldn't be on her feet any longer.

Erin didn't have a good feeling about this. She grabbed the nearest one and sat, looking at Terry for his revelation of the bad news.

K9 was tired of waiting for Terry to give him his biscuit and gave a little whine. Terry looked down at him and offered him the treat. "I'm sorry, boy. Here you go. Chew on that for a minute."

K9 took the biscuit from his fingers and lay down on the floor with it between his front paws. Off duty for a few minutes. *Code seven*, in cop talk.

"Erin, it looks like Montgomery died from an allergic reaction."

"Oh, dear."

"Did you know that he had allergies?"

"Yes. It was known, and he gave us a card with his allergies on it when he was here."

"Do you have that handy?"

Erin looked around, trying to remember where she had put the card after Montgomery had left. Of course, she didn't have any paperwork out in the kitchen. The only thing they used in the food preparation area were her recipe and procedure books.

"Uh… probably in my office. I don't remember putting it down."

"Do you remember what his allergies were?"

Erin tried to picture the card and remember her thought processes as she had looked over the ingredients in the Morning Sunshine Muffins. She recited the ones she could remember to Terry and he wrote them down in his notebook.

"Was it something he was served at the bed and breakfast?" Erin asked, thinking of how Mrs. McClung must be feeling if something she had fed Montgomery had killed him. "Or did he order something from one of the restaurants?"

There was a delay of several seconds before Terry answered her.

"Erin… we think it was your muffins."

"What?" Erin's eyes went wide with shock and she felt the blood drain from her face. She held on to the counter to steady herself. This was why Terry had told her to sit down. He hadn't wanted her to collapse when he told her the news. She fought back against the black spots and flashes of light that obscured her vision. She knew Terry was looking at her with concern, but couldn't see him clearly through the visual disturbances.

"Have another sip of water," Terry suggested.

Erin shook her head. She didn't know where she had put the cup of water down and couldn't find it now.

"How could it be…?" Erin fumbled for words. "It couldn't be the muffins. I checked the ingredients against his list. There's no way it could have been something on his list."

But she knew there were other possibilities. A new allergy that he hadn't had to deal with before. Cross-contamination of an ingredient in the field or factory before it had made its way into her kitchen. Something that Montgomery had added when he sat down to eat. Maybe a snack he had gotten out of the mini-fridge in his bedroom. There were many possibilities, none of which were Erin's fault. She had followed proper procedure when she had made the muffins. And she had checked the ingredients against his card. There was no way it had just slipped by her.

"We won't know all the details for a few days," Terry told her.

Erin knew from past cases that Montgomery's body would have to be sent to the city for autopsy and testing. Those things took time. Sometimes weeks or months, not just a few days. It wasn't like on TV, where everything was wrapped up in a few hours.

"No, of course not," Erin said faintly. "But… you think it was the muffins… that was the last thing he ate?"

It wasn't enough that someone had poisoned one of Erin's cinnamon rolls? Now someone had to tamper with her muffins too?

But poisoning was different from an allergic reaction. People could react to totally innocuous ingredients. Things that you thought no one could be allergic to.

"Yes," Terry confirmed. "He went back to the B&B, and then I guess he does a private tasting. No one else is allowed to be around."

Erin nodded numbly. "Yes. That's his usual procedure. Always alone."

Terry shook his head. "It seems counterintuitive that someone with serious, possibly life-threatening allergies would put himself in a situation where he was eating something potentially dangerous all alone, with no one to help out if he had a reaction."

"Well, you can't be with other people all the time. I don't know; it was just one of his quirks. Or one of the things his show had set up to catch people's interest."

"Doesn't seem like a good idea."

"In retrospect… no," Erin admitted. "And I did watch some of the shows where he had an allergic reaction to something he had been fed. He handed out these allergy cards to ensure the chefs or bakers didn't include any of his allergens. But sometimes people did anyway, and he always failed them if they did…"

"I would guess so," Terry said dryly.

"But the shows I watched… He would recognize that a dish contained one of his allergens, and he would take an antihistamine. Or epinephrine if it was one of the bad ones."

"This had happened before? So why didn't he change his protocol? Make sure someone was in the adjoining room with the door open?"

"I guess he figured he'd always been able to handle it by himself before."

Terry shook his head. But he didn't argue the point. It wasn't Erin's opinion; she wasn't the one who had set up Montgomery's protocols. She was just suggesting what his thought process might have been.

"I suppose. But it seems so stupid. Like playing Russian roulette. Just because you've never killed yourself before, that doesn't mean it isn't going to happen eventually."

Erin nodded. She was glad not to have to deal with any life-threatening allergies herself. She had seen what had happened to Angela Plaint when she had been poisoned with wheat flour. And her son, when he had been exposed to dairy. It was not something Erin treated casually.

And she *knew* she had checked Montgomery's allergens against the ingredients for the Morning Sunshine Muffins. And Vic had checked them against the ingredients for the other muffins Montgomery had bought. And there hadn't been anything unusual in his allergen list. Not anything that Erin could see being cross-contaminated in the kitchen.

"Do you know what he was allergic to? What did he react to?"

"Our best information at this point is strawberries."

"Strawberries?" Erin repeated in horror.

The Morning Sunshine Muffins were filled with a strawberry compote.

CHAPTER 10

Terry read Erin's expression easily. He put a steadying hand on her shoulder.

"It's okay. Just stay calm."

"He was allergic to strawberries?" Erin demanded. "Why weren't they listed on his allergy card? What's the point in handing out an allergy card if you don't list everything you are allergic to?"

"They are listed on his card."

"No," Erin shook her head adamantly. "I read the card. Vic read the card. It didn't include strawberries. We would never have let him have those muffins if it had said that he was allergic to strawberries."

Terry knew how careful she was about customers' allergens. Sometimes, it seemed like she knew them better than the customers themselves, who sometimes forgot to check for a particular allergen when making a purchase, and Erin had to stop them. She would never let anyone purchase anything that contained one of their known allergens. Unless, of course, they told her it was for someone else. But that was how Trenton Plaint had been killed. With a cupcake purchased from Auntie Clem's Bakery.

She tried to wipe the memories of those events out of her mind. That had been beyond her control. Joelle had known exactly what she had bought. It had all been planned out. It hadn't been Erin's fault. No more than it was the shopping mart's fault if someone poisoned their spouse with antifreeze or eyedrops purchased there.

But people in Bald Eagle Falls had still blamed Erin.

And now they would blame her for Gerald Montgomery's death.

And he wasn't just some backwoods hick. He was a national celebrity. Internationally known. He had followers all over the world, and they would all know soon that Erin had given him the food that had ended his life.

She covered her face, trying to compose herself.

"I can't believe this. How could something like this happen? Why didn't he list strawberries on his wallet cards? That doesn't make any sense."

"Do you still have it?"

Erin looked around her again. Of course, it wasn't there in the kitchen. They would not have left it out in the food preparation area.

"It's probably in my office. On my desk somewhere. My inbox."

"You didn't throw it out?"

"No… I don't think so. I wouldn't have needed it anymore, so maybe, but I thought I hung on to it. In case he came back and wanted something else. Or as a souvenir of his visit." She took a deep breath, trying to keep her voice steady. "Thinking that I would want to record and remember him coming here, doing the review. I might want to put it in a scrapbook or journal if I ever got around to making one."

She shook her head. But now this was a nightmare. She wouldn't want to remember it. She wouldn't look back on it fondly as the event that made her baking career—a highlight of her professional life.

How could she have ever thought that it could turn out well? With the trail of broken chefs and closed restaurants Montgomery had left behind him, what were the chances that he would give Auntie Clem's Bakery a stellar review? That people would flock from all over Tennessee and the United States to taste her gluten-free products?

She scrubbed at her eyes and rubbed her forehead, a tension headache gathering right in the center of it.

How could she be mourning her lost dreams when a man was dead? Killed by something she had given him. She had packed those muffins into a box and wished him well and, instead of enjoying the taste test, he had died at her hand. Terry might as well lock her up now.

"If strawberries were not on the card he gave you, you can't be blamed for his death," he told her consolingly. "It isn't your fault."

"Why did you say that strawberries were on his card? I saw it and Vic saw it." Erin visualized it, trying to see every word on it in her head. The colors, the layout, the various items listed so that she would not give him anything that might kill him. "Gluten, nuts, some fruits, but not strawberries."

"We saw his wallet cards. There were some in his luggage in the room. They did include strawberries."

Erin shook her head.

She knew she would never have given him those muffins if he had handed her a card stating that he was allergic to strawberries. Why would she? She didn't want to kill anyone. It would be the end of her career if she did so. As well as seriously curtailing her freedom when she was locked up in prison.

"Talk to Vic."

He looked toward the front of the bakery. "We'll wait until she's closed. I don't want to interrupt her duties."

Neither of them would be able to go back to serving customers after hearing the news of Montgomery's death. Erin knew Terry was right about that.

"Why don't I call his office?" Terry offered. "Maybe he had more than one card."

"And he gave out one that didn't include all his allergens?" Erin demanded.

That didn't make any more sense than anything else.

Terry shrugged. He pulled out his notepad and checked a number on it, then dialed his phone. He put it on speakerphone while it rang. It was picked up after just a couple of rings.

"Montgomery Meals and Reels," a woman announced crisply. "Mavis speaking."

Terry announced himself. Mavis had apparently already been given his name and had known to expect his call.

"Yes, Mr. Piper. How can I help?"

"I had some questions about Mr. Montgomery's wallet cards. The list of allergens."

"Yes?"

"I found a stack of them in his room at the B&B. They included strawberries."

"Yes… do you think that's what killed him?" she asked with a catch in her voice.

"Well, that's the most likely scenario at the moment. But I'm not sure why he would be given anything with strawberries after giving someone his wallet card stating that he was allergic."

"It happens all the time. Even when Gerald would tell people he was allergic to a certain ingredient, he would be served something unsafe. Chefs would think that a little bit wouldn't matter or that he was just making up the fact that he was allergic to something to make the challenge harder. Or they would forget that the ingredient was in there. Some foods go by a lot of different names, and they didn't check the ingredients of the ingredients."

"The ingredients of the ingredients?" Terry repeated, baffled.

Erin opened her mouth to explain the woman's meaning, then closed it again and waited for Mavis's answer.

"Well, for example, if you were making a stir fry and sauce, and Gerald told you he was allergic to gluten or wheat, you might think that your stir fry and sauce was fine if you served it over rice instead of noodles, and not think about the fact that one of the ingredients in your sauce was soy sauce, and one of the ingredients of soy sauce might be wheat. You need to check all of the ingredients of the ingredients you put into the dish. Soy sauce isn't just soy. Potato chips aren't just potatoes. They might have all kinds of wheat or dairy ingredients but, as someone who does not have to deal with multiple allergies, you don't have to think about that. You just think potatoes."

"Ah," Terry said. "I understand."

"People just aren't careful about allergies," Mavis said. "They think that they aren't really a big deal. That people who have multiple allergies are just being dramatic or attention-seeking."

"There's no possibility that the bakery was given a card that didn't include strawberries on the list of allergens?" Terry prodded.

There was silence for a few seconds.

"Well…" Mavis didn't come back with a flat "no," which Erin took as a good sign. "Strawberries were a recently developed allergy. We had to add them in and reprint the cards."

"So it is possible he still had one of his old cards and gave it to the bakery."

"I really don't see how. We were careful to replace them everywhere. It would have been dangerous for him to be passing out incomplete information. Especially with how severe the strawberry allergy had become."

"What about the cards in his wallet?" Terry asked, looking at Erin questioningly.

She nodded to confirm that the card Montgomery had given to her had come out of his wallet.

"Yes, I changed out his wallet cards myself. I know that he had the new cards. Is that what these people are claiming? That they were given a wallet card that didn't include strawberries?"

"We're just investigating," Terry told her. "We don't have any statements to release yet."

"Well, I'll tell you," Mavis said with emotion filling her voice. "Those people ought to be charged with murder. I can't believe someone did this to him. They should be in prison for the rest of their lives."

Erin heard Vic lock the front door to the bakery and then she came through the kitchen door. She looked concerned about Erin and Terry not having returned from the kitchen. Then her gaze fastened on Erin.

~

"Oh, my stars. What's happened? What's wrong?" she demanded, her hand going to her throat.

Neither one of them bothered to ask how she knew something was wrong. Erin knew she must look like a wreck. She certainly felt like one.

She just shook her head, unable to speak the words. To break Vic's happy bubble and tell her the devastating news. Auntie Clem's would be ruined. They would all have to find work somewhere else. But worse than that, a man was dead. And Erin might be headed to prison for it.

"Gerald Montgomery is dead," Terry told Vic. "An allergic reaction to the strawberries in the muffins."

"Dead?" Vic's mouth opened and closed like a fish's as she attempted to find the right words. "Are you kidding?"

People always said that, going first to disbelief.

"I'm afraid it's the truth," Terry told her gravely. "I believe it was an accident. But we are conducting an investigation to sort out all of the details."

"Strawberries? Did he even know he was allergic to strawberries?"

"They were on the allergen card," Terry asserted.

"No siree," Vic disagreed. "Erin and I both read the allergen card."

Erin motioned to Vic, nodding at Terry. Vic had just confirmed what Erin had already said. They had two witnesses that the allergen cards had not included strawberries.

"We would never have given him the muffins if he had put strawberries on the card," Vic asserted.

"Do you have the card?"

"No. I gave it to Erin," Vic looked at her. "Didn't you show it to him?"

"I don't remember where I left it. Or if I threw it out. I thought I kept it, but…"

Vic looked toward Erin's little office.

"I can check—"

"Leave the office," Terry told her. "We'll check it out ourselves. We don't want anything touched."

"You think that we would mess with evidence?" Vic growled.

"I know I have to follow certain protocols," Terry said mildly. "We have to do everything we can to preserve the chain of evidence."

Vic folded her arms, her jaw jutting at a stubborn angle. "I wasn't going to touch anything."

"Of course not."

Vic looked like she wanted to argue further, but Terry wasn't giving her the opening she wanted. So she left it alone, giving a curt nod.

"We would never have given him those muffins if we had known about his strawberry allergy. And you know that we are very careful here about allergies."

"From what I've seen, yes," Terry agreed. "And you haven't had any accidents, as far as I am aware." He glanced at Erin for confirmation. She nodded. "That's a pretty good track record."

But Erin knew that wouldn't stop the rumors.

CHAPTER 11

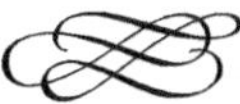

"You should proceed with your usual closing procedure," Terry suggested. "Do I have permission to search your office?" he nodded toward the closet-size room.

Erin hesitated. She didn't like other people to be in her office. She didn't like other people to touch her things. She knew that it was silly to be so worried about her privacy or the possibility of someone else messing with her stuff, blaming it on her upbringing in foster care, where she had never had her own place or her own stuff that was safe from the other children in the home. She had always known that at any time she could be moved to another home and that she might be able to take nothing but the clothes on her back with her. Sometimes she was allowed to throw a few special things and changes of clothes into a plastic shopping bag or garbage bag before she was taken out, but sometimes the parent or social worker would pack while she was out of the house and she wouldn't have any choice about what she took with her. Or she would be taken in an emergency apprehension and would never see anything from that home again.

It wasn't because she had secrets from Terry. None that would be revealed by a search of her office at Auntie Clem's Bakery. Most of her secrets were locked away in her head, with no written records anywhere.

That was the other thing she had learned in foster care. How to keep her thoughts and feelings locked up where no one else could read them. Her memories were her own if she were careful to share them with no one. Her private thoughts and feelings were no one else's business.

It didn't make for good relationship-building, and Erin was trying to share more of herself with Terry, Vic, and the other people she wanted to be close to. It was hard to be vulnerable.

And vulnerable was how she felt when she considered Terry searching her office. It was silly. There was nothing there but receipts, recipes, and newspaper ads. Nothing the least bit shocking or private. Nothing she needed to worry about Terry seeing.

"Erin?" Terry prompted. "I won't shut you down. I won't search the entire bakery. I just want to look in your office for that allergy card. It's a critical piece of evidence."

"I'm not even sure it is in there."

"I'll look. If it's not there, it's not there. I won't touch anything else. Whether it is there or not, I'll be in and out. Done in ten minutes and out of your way."

Erin swallowed hard. She glanced over at Vic, who was watching, but didn't jump in with any suggestions or tell Erin that she should or shouldn't allow the search.

"Don't tell me you're going to force me to get a search warrant," Terry grumbled. "For an allergen card you want to share with us to prove that you didn't know about his strawberry allergy. You *want* me to see it, Erin."

She nodded. "I know."

"So I'll look," he motioned again to her office. "And then I'll get out of your way."

Erin finally nodded. "Okay, but… shut the door."

Frown lines appeared between Terry's brows. "After I'm done, you mean?"

"No. While you're in there. Just shut it so I don't have to see you going through my stuff, okay?"

Terry nodded slowly. "Okay," he agreed. The frown lines didn't disappear. He hesitated, maybe thinking that she would give him more instructions or some explanation, and then he walked into her office and pulled the door shut behind him.

Erin tore her eyes from the door and tried to ignore what was happening inside. She couldn't see it, so it wasn't happening. But she imagined she could hear him rustling papers as he went through things.

"Why don't you put some music on while we close?" she suggested to Vic, trying to keep her voice light and casual, like this was something they did all the time.

"Sure," Vic agreed. "Any special requests?"

"No. I just need… I don't want silence."

They usually talked while they closed, so it wasn't exactly silent. But Erin didn't want to explain how jarring it felt today. At least as long as Terry was in her office, she needed music on.

Vic pulled a keychain-sized Bluetooth speaker from her purse and cued up a playlist. The kitchen, with its hard, reflective surfaces, immediately filled with sound. Pounding drums, harmonies, and a quick, energetic pace. It was just what Erin needed to get herself moving. She smiled at Vic in relief and gratitude and gave her hips a little shake.

"Perfect. Let's get to work."

Focusing on their usual closing routine and moving to the beat, she was able to shut out the worst of the thoughts about Terry looking for the evidence of her innocence. The tiny card that would prove to the world that she hadn't negligently killed the world's most famous food critic.

There was a lump in Erin's throat when Terry broke the news that he hadn't been able to find any sign of the allergy card in Erin's office. She nodded, forced a plastic smile, and pretended it didn't matter. Terry believed her anyway. He knew that she would never have been so careless. And Vic had seen the allergy card and read it and knew that it hadn't had strawberries on it. But of course they would both say that in the wake of Montgomery's death.

There would be other ways to prove her innocence. The facts of the case would be revealed and she and her bakery would be cleared and everything would go back to normal.

"I'll just check…" Erin said, and went into her office to check. There was no sign that it had been searched. Terry had carefully placed everything back just the way he had found it.

Erin was messier, ripping through stacks of paper and letting them fall back into place skewed and rumpled. She picked up bunches of paper and shook them violently to ensure that the card hadn't gotten stuck between the pages. But she knew that it wasn't there.

She could see at a glance that she hadn't left the card on her desk, where it would have been one of the top few items in her inbox. But she kept looking anyway. It must have fallen out. Gotten buried. Accidentally been clipped to something or slipped in between the pages.

After thirty seconds, she knew it wasn't there. After ten minutes, she had proven it several times over. She had checked every stack of paper, every file folder she had touched in the last week. Every drawer in her desk.

She grabbed her purse and, with tears burning in her eyes, returned to the kitchen.

"I'll see you at home," she told Terry calmly. "You won't be too late tonight? You don't have much more to do, do you?"

"No," he admitted. "There isn't much more that we can do today. We need to wait for responses on test results, people from his office, family members. An investigation takes time, even when it is something like this that looks like it was just… an unfortunate mishap."

Erin nodded. "You may as well get your sleep tonight. Be fresh in the morning."

She couldn't remember his shifts for the rest of the week. But his schedule would have changed. If there were a big investigation like this, his old shift schedule would be out the window while everyone put in all the time they could to break the case.

Terry nodded and looked at the clock on the wall. "I'll try to be home in an hour."

"Okay." Erin agreed. They all walked to the back door. Erin, Terry, and K9 went out first and turned to watch Vic arm the burglar alarm and turn off the lights before shutting the door behind her.

They would have to be extra vigilant. Who knew what kind of people might be coming by the bakery looking for a thrill after what had happened? She didn't want anyone to be able to get into the bakery to vandalize it, shoot some kind of on-the-scene video there, or steal something as a souvenir of the experience.

Erin climbed into the driver's seat of the yellow VW Bug, and Vic got into the passenger seat. They headed for home as usual, leaving Terry and K9 to find their way back to his vehicle and the police department offices or the B&B or wherever he was going next.

CHAPTER 12

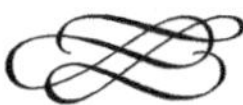

*I*t will be okay," Vic said unnecessarily when Erin pulled into the garage. "Everything will turn out all right."

Erin nodded. "I'm sure it will."

She knew she couldn't bluff Vic. She would see through the facade and know exactly how Erin felt about the whole thing. And probably she was feeling the same way. She was just covering it up with talk about how everything would work out in the end because that was how God or the universe would make it happen. But Erin didn't believe in that stuff.

"Really," Vic insisted. "Everyone knows how careful you are. They know that you do this for a living, that you do it because you want to. You do it because you want to provide safe food for people, not because you want to make a million dollars. You would never jeopardize anyone's safety, and everyone in Bald Eagle Falls knows that."

"Unfortunately... this is going to have far-reaching consequences beyond Bald Eagle Falls," Erin pointed out. "This will be shared around the world. Everyone from here to Timbuktu will know what happened and that it was my fault."

"It wasn't your fault."

"Maybe I made a mistake."

"I saw that card. You didn't make a mistake."

Erin looked at Vic for a moment.

Vic held her gaze fiercely. "I saw that card," she insisted. "It did *not* have strawberries on it."

Erin took a deep breath and let it out slowly. "Unfortunately, there is no way for us to prove that now."

Vic followed Erin into her house rather than taking the stairs up to the apartment over the garage. She watched Erin disarm the burglar alarm there and turn on the lights. Erin was immediately targeted by a large orange cat with a raucous meow. Orange Blossom wound his way around her legs, yowling loudly and telling her how long he'd had to wait for her to get home and how his food dish had been empty all day.

Erin laughed despite herself. "You are *not* that hungry," she told the cat. "You aren't going to starve to death in a day. And I fed you this morning."

He kept complaining and, with him trying to trip her up, Erin made her way over to the pantry to get the can of kitty treats. She grabbed a few bits out of it and skimmed them along the floor. Blossom went rocketing after them and gobbled them up in an instant. After a few more, she filled his bowl, and he settled down to eat his dinner, his rumbling purr filling the room.

Marshmallow, the brown and white rabbit, made his way into the kitchen to see what all of the fuss was about. Actually, he knew what all of the fuss was about, since this was the way Orange Blossom behaved every day when Erin got home. Marshmallow waited patiently while Erin got a carrot out of the fridge and then hunched over it eating while Erin moved around the kitchen, putting the kettle on and looking through the fridge and cupboards without any interest in the contents.

"Gerald Montgomery is the one who is responsible for his own death," Vic told Erin firmly. "He is the one who ate alone even though he knew he put his life at risk by doing so. Montgomery is the one who chose a career putting his life on the line every time someone put a dish in front of him that he hadn't prepared himself. He's the one who told you *not* to tell him what was in the muffins and gave you a card that didn't list strawberries as one of his allergens. He should have asked you specifically about each of the ingredients that might make him sick. Read the ingredients list from the Bible himself. Looked at the card that he gave you to make sure it was the current one. It's his fault, not yours. He's the one who did not take care of himself."

It was a long speech. Erin watched the kettle and listened to it tick as it heated up, pondering Vic's words.

Everything Vic said was true. Montgomery had eliminated a lot of the safety nets that he should have kept in place. He had undoubtedly thought that if he had an allergic reaction, he could treat it himself. He had antihistamines for a mild reaction. He had epinephrine for anaphylaxis. How many auto-injectors did he carry? Erin knew that they might stop an allergic reaction for only fifteen or twenty minutes, and then he would need another shot. It took an hour to get to the city hospital. He might need as many as four or five shots to get him safely from the B&B to the hospital. Had he even considered that?

Or had he been flirting with death all along, just daring it to take him?

"He's had allergic reactions from foods he has tasted before. The woman at his office said so. Why would he keep doing this if it put his life in danger? Over and over again? Why wouldn't he take the proper precautions?" Erin asked.

Was it the same as Carolyn, who had refused to look different in front of her friends? To her, eating "normal" food had been about being accepted in her community. It had been more important for her to be normal and acceptable than it had been to protect her health. Even though she had been told that eating that normal diet could kill her, she had kept eating the food that would damage her intestinal tract. Her death had not been quick like Montgomery's, but had been long and drawn out over a period of months of starvation.

On the surface, Montgomery wasn't someone who had been obsessed with looking the same as everyone else. He was in-your-face. He was famous. He had millions of followers. But he had thrown up roadblocks to things that might make him look different in front of his fans. Refusing to disclose his allergies ahead of time. Insisting that his dietary needs be addressed on the fly, putting pressure on the restaurants he attended, which might result in mistakes or resentments and intentional sabotage. Had he just been a child inside, refusing to acknowledge his own vulnerability and mortality? Unable to fathom the consequences of his risky behavior?

"What are you thinking?" Vic asked, as Erin poured the boiling water from the kettle into the teapot and prepared to take the tea service to the table.

"Did they publish the recordings of the tastings where he had allergic reactions?"

"Yeah, they did. That's how I knew some of the ingredients to watch out for. Do you want to see? Hang on." Vic sat at the table and pulled out her phone to search. Erin put everything they needed on the table and sat down with Vic. She didn't have any appetite and her brain was whirling with a hundred different questions about Montgomery's death and what the police would be investigating. She picked a soothing ginger and chamomile tea. That would help to calm her digestive system and promote calm before bed and sleep in a few hours.

Vic drew in her breath sharply. About to pour the hot water into her cup, Erin looked at Vic to see what was wrong.

A problem at home, maybe. Willie was sick and needed to be taken into the city to see a doctor or be admitted to emergency. Or she had just remembered an appointment she was supposed to be at. Or that she had been planning to take her dog, Nilla, out for a walk right after work and now she might be faced with an unpleasant clean-up job when she returned to the loft.

Vic tapped her screen a few times, her face white and expression frozen. Erin didn't want to intrude, and waited for her to share what was wrong. Or to say that she had to go because she had something to take care of.

Vic stared at her screen for a few long seconds and then turned away, looking nauseated. Erin couldn't wait any longer.

"Vicky? What is it?"

"It's the video of Montgomery tasting our muffins," Vic whispered.

"What?"

"His company has posted the video of him tasting the muffins."

Erin gulped. "All of the muffins?"

Vic was staring at her phone, face as white as bone. "Yes, finishing with the Morning Sunshine Muffins. Including... his reaction to them."

"What? You don't mean..." Looking at Vic, Erin knew that she didn't mean that Montgomery broke out in hives on the video or expressed concern over the scratchiness in his throat.

Vic covered her mouth and shook her head. She didn't turn the phone to show it to Erin. Erin was torn between horror that the company would post such a thing and a need to see what had happened. She knew that she didn't want to see Gerald Montgomery die from anaphylaxis on the screen. That was just too horrible.

Erin took a few sips of her hot tea. Too hot. It burned her mouth and throat. But she was glad for the pain that made tears leak from the corners of her eyes.

"Are there… has anybody watched it? Do you have to search for the right thing to see it? Is it behind a membership wall?"

Vic shook her head. "The view numbers are in the six digits right now. Be into the millions before long."

Millions of people watching Montgomery die on the screen after eating Erin's muffins.

The ginger tea could not take away the nausea.

CHAPTER 13

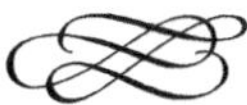

"This is terrible," Vic said, staring at her phone, unable to take her eyes off the screen.

Erin reached over and took it from her. Not to look at it, but to get it away from Vic and turn it off. She did not need to keep watching it.

Vic clutched at it at first, then let Erin take it and watched while she turned it off. She sagged in her chair and put her face in her hands, murmuring words of what Erin thought might be a prayer to herself.

Erin put her hand on Vic's arm for a minute, then tapped Terry's contact record on her own phone.

Terry didn't answer. Erin hung up rather than leaving a voicemail message and called him again. There was no answer again.

Maybe he already knew. Maybe he was dealing with it and couldn't stop to take her call because it was more important to get the horrific video removed than it was to answer Erin's call. As far as he knew, she just wanted to know what he wanted for supper or something equally unimportant.

She found Sheriff Wilmot's number and called him. It went to voicemail. They were probably all in a meeting. None of them would answer. But someone had to be available for emergency calls.

Erin hung up and called the emergency dispatcher, though she felt guilty for doing so. It wasn't the kind of emergency where someone's life was in danger or a child was missing. But she knew the police would need to know about the video if they didn't already.

"Bald Eagle Falls emergency dispatch," a woman answered.

"It's Erin Price. Who is on call?"

"What's the nature of your emergency, Miss Price?"

"I need to get ahold of Terry or one of the others. About a piece of evidence in the Montgomery case."

"Leave a message on his phone."

"It's urgent."

"Is this piece of evidence in danger of being destroyed?"

"No…"

"Then they can deal with the case in an orderly manner—"

"A video of Montgomery's death has been posted online."

There was a second or two of silence as the dispatcher considered this.

"Is this the number you can be reached at?"

"Yes."

"Stay by your phone. Someone will call you right back."

Erin blew out her breath. "Thank you!"

She terminated the call and put the phone on the table beside her teacup. It would only be a minute or two, she was sure, before the phone rang and Terry or one of the other police department members was asking her the details.

"Are you okay?" she asked Vic, looking at her with sympathy.

"I hope never to see such a thing in my life again," she mumbled through her hands.

"I know," Erin agreed. She had seen things in her life too, things that she wished she could erase. To forget she had ever seen them, the images and all of the circumstances surrounding the memory wiped out of her mind. And not just the sights, but the smells, too, and the feeling of horror that went along with a gruesome discovery.

"Try not to think about it," Erin told Vic, picking out a bag of valerian tea and hanging it over the edge of Vic's cup. "Think about something else. Willie. You remember what it was like when you first met him? I know he's being a pain in the behind right now, but you remember what it was like in the beginning?"

Vic pulled her hands away from her face and looked at Erin like she was crazy.

"What?"

"Before you knew Willie really well? You remember how nervous you were about him? About how he felt about you?"

"Yeah...?" Vic said tentatively, clearly wondering where Erin was going with this. But it was just as Erin had told her. She wanted Vic to think of something else. Something with strong emotions attached to it so that it would hold her brain's attention and let her pull still further back from the video. If Vic kept replaying it mentally, it would be more likely to stay in her brain permanently, vivid and sickening. It would be less traumatic if she could pull back and move her mind on to something else.

"He's come a long way since then," Erin commented. "And you too. You're a lot more comfortable in your own skin now."

Vic's expression softened. She nodded her agreement. "Yeah, I am. I'm much happier with who I am now, and Willie has been a big part of that."

"I'll sure be glad when he's through the chelation therapy. Happy for you, I mean. He hasn't been much fun to live with the last little while."

Vic's gaze went to the window, likely checking to see if the lights were on in her apartment, or whether Willie was sleeping or out.

Erin's phone vibrated, making both of them jump. Erin took a deep breath and picked it up.

"Erin," Terry's voice was urgent. He didn't waste any time on preliminaries like asking her how her evening was going or what she was having for supper. "What's this about a video of Montgomery's death?"

"He always recorded himself during a tasting. He didn't want anyone else there, which was risky considering his food allergies and the reactions he'd had before, but he wanted to be alone."

"Yes, we know all of that."

"So I guess he recorded himself for the muffin tasting yesterday. And..." Erin faltered, but pushed herself on, wanting to be strong for Vic and save her as much mental pain as possible. "They got everything. His allergic reaction to the Morning Sunshine Muffins..."

"You saw it?"

"Vic did."

"Where is it? Who posted it?"

"Someone at his company, I guess." Erin looked over at Vic. "It was posted on the show's website?"

"I guess," Vic said, "and their social media. I just saw a video. I thought it would be one of the reactions that he had previously. He's always pulled through okay before…"

"On their social media," Erin repeated to Terry. "Vic said there were already hundreds of thousands of views."

Terry swore at this.

"How did they get that footage? It was Mrs. McClung who found his body, and she called us right away. No one else was allowed in the room."

"Then I guess…" Erin tried to think through the logical possibilities. "Maybe he did have someone with him? Or someone found him before Mrs. McClung and took the video but left him there…" She frowned. None of that made any sense. The company would have to know that the police would discover they had the footage and know that someone had been in the room. Maybe it was just someone who had happened by? But who would go into his room? And if they did, it wouldn't have been the production company that posted the ghoulish footage.

Vic was shaking her head. "It probably uploads to the cloud automatically. They can access it remotely. They don't have to be anywhere near the room."

Terry swore again. "Well, it will be fun trying to force them to remove it. We'll have to get a court injunction. That takes time, even in an emergency."

"Are you allowed to post something like that?" Erin asked. "Isn't it against the terms and conditions of the social media sites to post a video of someone dying?"

"Yes," Terry agreed. "We'll try that first. But getting them to pull it from their own site might be more difficult. And if it is still there, people will just keep downloading it and reuploading it to social media under different accounts."

"Have you seen the video?" Erin asked him.

"No. The video equipment was handed off to the forensic techies in the city for review. We're not allowed to mess around with electronics on our own. In case someone ends up destroying evidence."

"So now several hundred thousand people know more about how he died than the Bald Eagle Falls police department does."

Terry grunted, not sounding too happy about the fact. "We'll have to watch it before we get it pulled down. Have you watched it?"

Erin shook her head vigorously, even though he couldn't see her on the phone. "No way. I want to know what happened… but I don't want to see him die. Vic saw it. I know I don't want to."

Vic shook her head in agreement, her eyes looking hollowed out as if watching the video had affected her physically, drained some of the life out of her. Erin felt bad that she'd had to see it. All because Erin had suggested that she wanted to see footage showing what had happened when Montgomery had suffered an allergic reaction previously. If Erin had kept her mouth shut then, at least, Vic wouldn't have had to be the one to see it. She put her hand over Vic's, making an apologetic face. "Sorry," she mouthed.

Vic nodded her acknowledgment.

"We'll get right on this." Terry's voice was clipped. "Thank you for letting us know."

"Yeah. Of course."

"And Erin…?"

"Uh-huh?"

"I don't know when I'll be home. Don't expect me early."

He would probably be dealing with the video, Montgomery Meals and Reels, and the various social networking platforms that it had been posted to for hours. Terry wasn't the only cop in town, but Erin suspected that he and Stayner were probably the only ones with any technical savvy.

CHAPTER 14

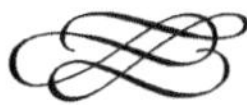

The next morning, fortified with plenty of caffeine, Erin looked at the Morning Sunshine Muffins they had baked the day before, still sitting on the counter awaiting their debut. She had planned to serve them as soon as Montgomery's tasting aired.

Well, now it had aired and she wasn't sure what to do about them. She couldn't serve them, could she? Serving the muffins that had killed Montgomery would be in poor taste.

Wouldn't it?

Vic followed Erin's eyes to the muffins and her mouth formed a grim line.

"What are we going to do?"

"Should we just throw them out?" Erin asked. "I hate to waste food, but… it's macabre, isn't it?"

"You still sold chocolate muffins after Aunt Angela died, didn't you?"

"Well, yes. But they weren't a special kind of muffin made just for her… they were just chocolate muffins. And everybody didn't see her die."

"Yeah, I guess that's a bit different."

"I can't just throw them out. I could freeze them for the homeless shelter. Not call them Morning Sunshine Muffins. Instead, they can be… Strawberry Surprise Muffins."

Vic raised her brows. "Strawberry Surprise?"

Erin thought about Montgomery's surprise when he tasted the muffins and regretted the suggestion immediately. "No, no… Strawberry Compote Muffins."

Vic nodded. "That's better. Do you think they'll still know? They know that the donations come from Auntie Clem's, don't they? They'll hear about all of this in the news and know that the Strawberry Compote Muffins are what killed Montgomery."

"The administrators will know. But the diners won't. I think it's okay. I don't think they'll be upset about getting them, do you?"

"I think it will be okay," Vic said slowly. "Let's think about it, though, and make sure we both agree by the end of the day. We'll just leave them for now and put them in the freezer at the end of the day if we still think the same thing."

Erin nodded her agreement. "Yeah. No need to make a rush decision. They'll still be good at the end of the day."

They moved through the familiar morning routine. Erin was fighting brain fog after a very restless night. She hadn't settled down by the time Terry had gotten home and joined her in bed. Caffeine had helped to get her going, but she knew enough to anticipate a crash within a few hours unless she kept herself wired all day.

The caffeine also ramped up her anxiety. She knew it was going to be a trying day. Everyone would want to talk about what had happened to Montgomery, and some of them would have seen the video before it was pulled down.

How would people react? Would they be sympathetic? Accusatory? Even if they were nice to her, Erin knew she would feel guilty, embarrassed, and vulnerable. Maybe more so if they were nice. If people were rude, she could get angry and defend herself. She had done nothing wrong, after all. But she wasn't sure she could hold it together if they showed sympathy.

"You didn't set the timer," Vic observed as Erin put bread in the oven and walked over to the fridge for the next batch of batter. Erin looked at her, then the timer on the stove. Vic was right.

"Well, you just saved that batch of bread." Erin walked back to the oven and set the timer.

"You would have noticed," Vic said, brushing it off.

"On a normal day, maybe. Not today."

The first batches of baking were out of the oven, and Auntie Clem's was filled with the yeasty smell of freshly baked bread and the savory spices in the muffins and herbed pretzels and pizza shells. When Erin went to the front door, flipped the sign over to Open, and turned the bolt, she was surprised to see how many people were waiting for her to open.

Familiar customers stood around with their coffee cups as usual, getting the baking they would need for the week before work started, or a nice muffin or pastry to start the day. Their eyes were bright and excited and they were ready to ply Erin with questions, she could tell.

But there were other people there too. Faces that were unfamiliar. A group of young people was sitting on sleeping bags and blankets on the sidewalk, making Erin wonder how long they had been there. They hadn't been there when she had closed the night before, but they appeared to have been camped there for a few hours, anyway. They were like fans camped out in line to get tickets for their favorite band when they went on sale.

Erin looked at them for a moment through the glass, then opened the door to let her regulars in and ignored the trickle of strangers who mixed in with the group as she walked back to her place behind the counter to greet them and see what they wanted.

One of the young people pushed her way in front of everyone else who had been there waiting, snarling at them as if they had somehow stolen her place in line rather than the opposite. Her eyes went over the contents of the display case. She shook her head and pushed a lock of greasy black hair over her ear.

"Where are they?" she demanded. "The Morning Sunshine Muffins."

"Well…" Erin looked nervously at the other customers. "I didn't think anyone would want them after what happened."

"What do you think we came here for?" the girl asked, aggrieved. "It wasn't for a rice bran muffin, I'll tell you that!"

Erin felt a little embarrassed about the bran muffins in the display. There was nothing wrong with bran muffins, but the girl made her feel like she had been dishonest to put them out or that she was trying to fool people into thinking that nothing had happened the day before.

She didn't mean to cover up what had happened to Montgomery.

That wasn't why she had left the Morning Sunshine Muffins in the kitchen.

"Well, I have some in the kitchen. I just didn't think people would want…"

"We all want the Morning Sunshine Muffins," one of the other young people said loudly, making sure Erin knew she'd better bring all the muffins out rather than just one. Erin glanced over the crowd. The strangers nodded in agreement.

A few of Erin's regular customers nodded too.

"It wasn't like something was wrong with them," the girl pointed out. "That wasn't why he died. But we want to taste… the last thing Gerald Montgomery tasted. We want that experience."

They didn't want the whole anaphylaxis experience; Erin could assure them of that.

But they wanted the Morning Sunshine Muffins. The muffins wouldn't be going to the homeless shelter at the end of the day.

CHAPTER 15

*E*rin looked over the crowd of customers before stepping into the kitchen to get the muffins they had baked the day before. She was sure that the customers in this group would not be the only ones wanting to taste the muffins. If they wanted to, then everyone else would, too. She had badly misjudged in thinking that people wouldn't want anything that would remind them of Montgomery's death or how he had died.

It wasn't the first time she had misjudged how people would respond to a tragedy. Maybe by now, she should have figured out the way that people reveled in the news of an untimely death. She'd seen it enough times to have figured that out by now.

"I'm going to limit the Morning Sunshine Muffins to one per customer," she said as she looked them over. "And we'll get more in the oven as soon as possible. But we don't want to run out in ten minutes. I should have enough for everyone here, but if I do not, please come back this afternoon, and I'll have some more fresh out of the oven."

There were grumbles from a number of the visitors, but most of them nodded their agreement anyway. They could see how many people had come to eat the muffins. They wouldn't have camped out on the street if they hadn't thought the muffins would be in short supply and they would need to be there first thing in the morning to get a taste.

Vic nodded at Erin, telegraphing a look of understanding. Instead of one manning the counter and the other handling the till, they would divide their tasks between the kitchen and the customers. One would mix new batches of Morning Sunshine Muffins and get them into the oven while the other sold the finished product.

Erin was glad to get away from the eager eyes of the customers for a moment. She looked at the muffins, contemplating them for a few breaths. She could do this. She was a strong, capable person, and she had been running her own bakery for two years. She had gotten through worse challenges than this. She could put on a cheerful yet sympathetic expression and deal with the customers one at a time.

It should be a piece of cake.

She gathered the Morning Sunshine Muffins and collected them on a tray. She had known that there would be a run on the muffins after Montgomery's tasting. Now, it was time to put her plan into action.

Erin squared her shoulders and returned to the front of the bakery. People were chatting with each other, enjoying the warm bakery and the comforting smell of fresh-baked bread while they waited. Erin put the tray of muffins near the cash register, bumping Vic out of the way. Vic headed toward the kitchen to start on a new batch of muffins.

"Call around and see who else can come in," Erin told her. "I think we're going to need an extra baker or two today."

Vic nodded her agreement. "I'm on it, boss," she agreed.

Erin looked at the customers. "Okay, how many people are here only for a muffin and don't need anything else?"

Several people put up their hands or nodded their heads.

"Okay, I am going to sell one muffin to each of you and get you on your way as quickly as possible." She gave an apologetic look to her regular customers. "That will help to clear the bakery out quickly so that those who need longer to choose or have larger orders will have time to decide without feeling pressured."

Everyone seemed amenable to this. Not that it mattered. Anyone who had an argument about it would just have to put up with her plan of attack anyway.

The pushy girl who had camped out the night before was the first one at the counter and Erin didn't argue with her about having forced her way to the front of the queue. The best thing was to get her out of the bakery as quickly as possible. After paying for it, the girl held the muffin aloft, showing it off to everyone.

"The first Morning Sunshine Muffin to be sold since the one that killed Gerald Montgomery," she announced.

There was a murmur from the crowd. There was no cheer. It was more an expression of reverence than one of delight. The girl removed the wrapper from the cupcake and took a big bite. Everyone watched, not moving or saying anything. She turned it around to display the strawberry compote filling.

Everyone waited. The girl didn't have an allergic reaction or show any ill effects. She chewed, swallowed, and took another bite.

"It's really good," she told them in a calm, slightly wistful voice. "I think he would have liked it, if he'd had the time to enjoy it."

Was it a worthy last meal? Erin sighed and turned to the next person in line, quickly checking the single-muffin purchases through. People laid down twenty-dollar bills and told her to keep the change, not bothering to wait for her to ring them up. Many, like the first girl, unwrapped them and took their first bite or two in the bakery. A few gathered at the wrought-iron tables at the front of the store to have quietly murmured conversations.

Of the customers who remained after the single-muffin purchases, some were regular customers from Bald Eagle Falls whom Erin knew well, and others were not.

An Asian woman stepped forward with a friendly smile. "I'm Olivia Morgan," she announced.

"Nice to meet you," Erin said politely. "Are you from near here?"

"No." The woman laughed. "You've never heard of me?"

"Uh, no. Sorry, I haven't. I don't..." She was going to say, "watch a lot of TV," because she thought the woman looked like another TV celebrity and she obviously expected Erin to know who she was.

"You're a gluten-free baker," Olivia interrupted, shaking her head. "I would have thought you would have read one of my books. Tried out some of my recipes."

"Oh. Oh, *that* Olivia Morgan," Erin said, trying to act as though she were familiar with the woman's books. "Didn't you write..."

"*Baking Liberation: Set Yourself Gluten-Free?*" Olivia offered. "*Footloose and Gluten-Free?* I'm sure you must have read some of them.

Anyone in the gluten-free baking business is bound to have read at least one of them."

"Of course," Erin agreed with a smile. She had heard the name before; she was pretty sure of that. She had developed her own baking methods primarily by watching other people in online videos and testing out the characteristics of the various flours and other ingredients that it was necessary to combine to replicate the properties of wheat flour. Before coming to Bald Eagle Falls, she wasn't a big reader and had only had what possessions she could fit into her suitcase and backpack. No books.

Olivia seemed to sense that Erin was not telling the truth and had not, in fact, read any of her cookbooks. Her smile dimmed, and she shook her head slightly. But she went on without pointing out to the world that Erin had never read any of them. After all, if Erin was now a famous gluten-free baker who had appeared on Gerald Montgomery's show and had invented the muffins that everyone was now flocking to taste and she hadn't ever even heard of Olivia Morgan, then what did that say about Olivia and her celebrity?

"What can I get you today?" Erin offered. "I'm afraid I don't have anything made from any of your recipes on offer today, but maybe you would be interested in…" Erin trailed off and looked down at the display case, unsure what Olivia's specialty was and what she would be interested in sampling.

"Well, let's try a variety," Olivia offered. "I'll have a blueberry muffin as well as the Morning Sunshine Muffin. And maybe one of those double chocolate chip cookies. They look good. A loaf of your regular white sandwich bread and then one of those artisan loaves… the rosemary and sun-dried tomato looks really tasty. What else do you sell a lot of?"

"The pizza pretzels are popular," Erin pointed to them. "And maybe a pastry? A turnover or tart?"

"Of course," Olivia agreed. "Get me a pretzel, whichever variety sells the best, and a lemon curd tartlet."

Erin gathered everything together and boxed it up for Olivia Morgan, famous published gluten-free baker.

"You should go next door to the Book Nook," she told Olivia. "See if they have copies of any of your books that you could sign. People always love getting signed copies…"

Olivia gave her a smile that seemed forced. "I'm not sure if the bookstore in a little place like Bald Eagle Falls would have much demand for gluten-free baking books. Especially with such a lovely gluten-free bakery right in town. People don't have to make their own."

"I suppose so," Erin agreed. "Well, I'll be sure to order some in now that I've met you. Replace my used copies and suggest them for those in town who want to do some of their own baking as well as buying from Auntie Clem's. People do still like to do some of their own baking as well. Some people really enjoy it."

"Do you?"

"Of course," Erin was surprised. "I love to bake."

"Some people don't, once they have to. Running a bakery can take the joy out of it."

"Oh, no. I still enjoy it. There are days when I wish I was just baking for myself again, because of the pressure of running my own business, but I still love to bake and experiment. In a business like this, you don't get ahead by just following everybody else's recipes."

After she said it, she wondered if she was being tactless, somehow telling Olivia that she wasn't good enough or current enough to be of interest. She smiled and tried to reassure Olivia. "I mean, I always start with a basic recipe, but then I try out new stuff. Different ingredients, new techniques; soaking or fermenting or different oven temperatures…"

"I'm sure," Olivia agreed, looking irritated by Erin's explanation. As if she felt she were being patronized. "If you could just ring those up…"

Erin ducked her head, rang up the items Olivia had ordered, and gave her the total. Olivia paid.

"I hope you enjoy everything!" Erin said brightly.

She was a little nervous that Olivia would find her goods to be substandard or would tell people they were even if she didn't think so. Of course, she couldn't ascribe evil motives to someone she had never even met before. She could be totally misjudging Olivia; she didn't know anything about her. The woman had been friendly in her approach, and she had told Erin who she was, not pretended to be a regular customer and then ambushed her with a bad review like others might have done.

Olivia nodded coolly and left with her purchase. Erin turned to the next person in line, a bouncing Melissa Lee, who was obviously there to tell Erin the latest developments in the Montgomery case. There had been so many people that Erin hadn't even seen her come in.

"Oh, Melissa. How are you?"

"You wouldn't believe how tired I am." Melissa affected a yawn. "I was up all night worrying about this case and how it would affect you."

"Oh." Erin motioned to the display case to direct Melissa to make her selections. "Well, I don't think you need to be worried about me. I'll get through this."

"I knew how devastated you would be that Mr. Montgomery was killed by one of your muffins. It's too awful for words. And then to have the whole thing broadcast online like that. Did you watch it?"

"No. I didn't want to see it. Vic watched it," Erin glanced over her shoulder toward the kitchen. "It really freaked her out. I don't see any reason to expose myself to that, no matter how curious I am about what happened."

Melissa leaned forward. "I hear you. But I don't understand how you could *not* look. How do you resist something like that? I mean, don't you *want* to know? Can you just imagine it without checking to see if you were right in how you pictured it? I didn't want to watch it, but I couldn't not watch it. I had to look."

Erin shook her head. "What do you want? Like I said, I'm curious. But I'm too afraid to look. I don't want to see him die."

Melissa nodded sagely. "But it is evidence," she pointed out. "And if you want to solve what happened to Mr. Montgomery, then you need all the clues you can get."

"We know what happened to him. He had an allergic reaction to the strawberries."

"But why? Why wouldn't he tell you that he was allergic to strawberries, if they were that dangerous to him? They would be on his list, wouldn't they?"

"His office said that strawberries were on the list. And Terry said they were on the list he saw at the B&B."

"But not on the card that he gave you. You and Vic both said so. You wouldn't say that if it wasn't true."

Erin appreciated Melissa's support but knew that wasn't how law enforcement would look at it. They would be looking at ways to prove that she had intentionally poisoned Gerald Montgomery. They couldn't just believe what she had to say if it weren't substantiated by hard evidence. Maybe they would be more inclined to believe her since Vic supported her story, but anyone looking into the case would know that Vic and Erin were best friends, so of course they would back each other up.

Erin rested her elbows on the display case and looked at the customers waiting patiently behind Melissa. Or those who were not so patient, fidgeting and whispering behind their hands to each other.

Melissa looked at the people behind her and smiled, but decided she'd better make her selections and move out of the way.

"Okay. You still have a credit for the police department, right?"

Erin nodded. "Yes, would you like some pastries for them this morning?"

"Everyone has been working hard," Melissa declared. "Lots of hours put in on this case already. So I think they deserve a little something sweet." She looked slyly around her. "How about the Morning Sunshine Muffins?"

Erin just stood there looking at her. Melissa had presumably been there when she gave her little lecture on how she would only allow one Morning Sunshine Muffin per customer.

"Half a dozen," Melissa suggested. "That's only one per person, like you said."

"No, not one per person. One per customer. You can have one, but not every person in the department unless they all come in here personally. There will be more muffins later and over the next few days until the demand settles down. So… what would everyone like for breakfast today?"

Melissa rolled her eyes, but apparently decided there was no point in trying to cajole Erin any further on the Morning Sunshine Muffins. She sighed. "How about six Danishes and six assorted muffins? Including one Morning Sunshine Muffin."

Erin could imagine them cutting the Morning Sunshine Muffin into pieces so that everyone could examine one piece and then eat it.

But they could do whatever they wanted to with the Morning Sunshine Muffin, including sending it into the lab in the city to analyze the ingredients. Though of course if they asked, she would give them the list of ingredients. It wasn't that much of a secret. And they wouldn't bother asking her for the ingredient list because they already knew it was the strawberries Gerald Montgomery had reacted to.

"All right." Erin assembled an assorted Danish and muffin pack for Melissa, rang it up, and put the receipt aside to be charged against the police department's prepaid account. "And did you want anything for yourself?"

Melissa considered, then shook her head. "No, I'll just grab one from the box since I will be working there all morning today." She paused before leaving. "You really should watch that video, you know."

Erin shook her head. "No, I really don't think so."

Melissa laughed, her dark curly hair bouncing wildly, and she left.

CHAPTER 16

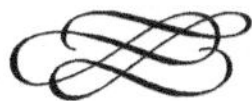

*V*ic returned from the kitchen. "Couple more batches in the ovens," she announced.

"Great, thanks for doing that."

Vic looked over the customers who remained. "You were able to clear people out of here pretty fast. How did you do that?"

"A lot of them just wanted one of the muffins. I took care of them first so that I would have more time to spend with everyone else."

"Good. How are we doing on muffin supply?" Vic looked at the tray on which the Morning Sunshine Muffins had been laid. "Just a couple left. We'll have some fresh out of the oven in fifteen minutes, so we're doing quite well. You want me to take till?"

Erin always felt more comfortable with Vic on the till. Both because she was better with the computer and making change quickly, and because she was good with the customers and made sure that no one left without feeling like they had been seen and their needs taken care of. Vic was just that good with people. Erin always felt like she was fumbling around in the dark, trying to figure out what people wanted when Vic knew instinctively.

And Vic seemed happy to deal with the till. She didn't think that Erin was just giving her the crap jobs that she didn't want. If neither of them had liked till, Erin would have been sure to change off with her regularly so that no one got stuck with the majority of the grunt work.

"Thanks, that would be great." Erin turned the cash register over to her. "Okay, who was next?"

She'd had a feeling it would be busy all day. It was a challenge to close down for their early lunch break. Vic had to man the door to let everyone out as they finished and not let anyone new in, advising them that they would be open in half an hour for the lunch rush. Eventually, they managed to lock the door and sit down on stools in the kitchen to take their own repast. She'd only had coffee and a piece of toast for breakfast and, by the time their lunch break rolled around, Erin was ravenous. She was in the mood for a treat, so she grabbed a couple of pizza pretzels as well as the sandwiches they had made. And another cup of coffee.

Vic eyed Erin, knowing she didn't usually have any coffee after her morning wake-up cup and that she'd already had extra coffee that morning.

"Are you trying to give yourself a heart attack?"

Erin laughed. "No. Just trying to come down gently." She inhaled the rich aroma of the fresh coffee. "If I don't have anything, then that post-caffeine crash is going to hit me in the middle of the afternoon and I'll be paralyzed. This will keep me going until I get home, and I might have another half-cup at supper."

"Having more coffee to avoid crashing sounds backward."

"I know, but it's what works for me. It's like weaning off of a drug."

"I guess it is, at that," Vic agreed, nodding.

They split up the sandwiches and pizza pretzels and were happy to take a load off for a while. Erin had comfortable shoes, but she still felt a lot of leg and foot fatigue by the end of the day if she put in both the morning and the afternoon shifts.

"Charley is going to come by and bake more muffins in the afternoon," Vic said, "And Bella will be out of school early so she can take the last half of the afternoon shift. I figured that by then, we'll be ready to go home. Charley and Bella can close and we can crash."

Erin always felt guilty going home early, even if she was the boss and had made sure that everything was covered, but she knew Vic was probably right to arrange it that way. Neither of them had slept much, if at all, the night before. They would need to spend the evening unwinding and go to bed early to start catching up.

CHAPTER 17

When they finished their lunch and opened the door again, there was a lineup outside the door. The man at the front of the line looked disgruntled.

"What kind of business is this that closes in the middle of the day?" he demanded.

"An owner-run business that starts very early," Erin told him evenly. "And we need a break and our own lunch if you want the bakery to be open into the afternoon."

He stared at her for a minute but eventually nodded and backed down.

"Fine. I suppose you're running on limited staff. This is a small town and maybe the demand isn't as big as it would be in the city."

"Or maybe people here are more considerate," Vic suggested tartly.

The man's neck grew rosy. "I'm not being inconsiderate," he objected.

"Telling us that we can't take time for lunch? That we must be some minor league operation if we need breaks?"

He swallowed and gestured toward the door. "If you're open now…"

Erin opened the door and stepped back. Vic followed her example, making space for the customers to come in.

Erin looked the stranger over. She didn't think she'd ever seen him in town before. One of Montgomery's followers, she suspected. There to get a Morning Sunshine Muffin, and then she would never see him again.

He was tall and stylish, well-dressed; not the kind of guy she usually saw around the bakery. Most men who came in were dressed in work clothes, picking something up for lunch or break or on the way home to their wives. Or maybe dressed casually, stopping in for a cookie or a trail mix bar before or after a workout.

"What can I get for you?" she asked, indicating the baked goods in the display case. Things were starting to look a little spare as they kept making more muffins and didn't have a lot of time to refresh the rest of the baked goods. But the man didn't seem to care.

"I understand you're restricting purchases to one muffin per order."

Erin nodded. "For the Morning Sunshine Muffins, yes. Other muffins are not restricted. But we are limiting order to the Morning Sunshine Muffins until the supply and demand have stabilized."

"I guess that's what I'll have then. One muffin."

Erin got one of the fresh muffins out and put it into a single-serving box. "Can I get you anything else? Are you in town for long?"

"No, I'm not staying around. No reason to hang around here."

Erin nodded and smiled as if he had been friendly to her. "Were you and Mr. Montgomery friends?"

They were probably around the same age. Erin had no other reason to think they might have known each other personally. He was probably just a follower, as she had first thought.

"Friends?" His voice was gruff, resentful. "I should say not! I wouldn't associate myself with such an immoral, unethical fraudster."

Erin's mouth dropped open as she tried to think of a response to this. There were several gasps around the bakery at this accusation. Around Bald Eagle Falls, most of the church ladies tried to follow the maxim of "speak no ill of the dead."

"Well, I'm sorry to hear that," Erin told him lamely. She was just the baker. He certainly couldn't expect her to do anything about the past wrongs done by the dead man. She'd barely even met him. Practically all she knew about him was what she had learned from watching his shows. And he had produced those shows, so the chances that they would reveal any immoral or unethical behavior were pretty low. He didn't mind being portrayed as harsh, judgmental, or bad-tempered, but there were a lot of famous chefs who were those things. It was pretty much to be expected of a food critic.

"The man was a crook—a cheat. You can bet that over the next week, everyone will be writing about his life as if he were a saint. But I'll tell you, that was not the case."

"Well," Erin swallowed. "You're entitled to your opinion and can say what you like about him. I only met him one time."

"He built his empire on the backs of hundreds of honest and hard-working people. Creatives, chefs, bakers. People who put in the work and the time, only to have everything stolen from them by Mr. Magical Montgomery and his Meals and Reels mythology."

"Okay…" Erin drew the word out. "I'm so sorry for whatever happened to you. If you could pay over here, Vic will take care of you."

Vic encouraged him over and, even while Erin tried to help the next customer, she could hear him complaining to Vic, baring his soul as she tried to help him check out.

"My name is Mark Thompson, and I'm not the only one that fraud stole and plagiarized from."

"Can you plagiarize a recipe?" Vic asked.

"Of course you can. If it's someone else's and you copy it, that's plagiarism. Doesn't matter whether it is a book or a recipe."

Vic looked over at Erin. "Well, a lot of chefs get their ideas from other people's recipes, and then they make changes to it, the ingredients, the method… then it becomes theirs, right? I mean, there are going to be a lot of really similar recipes around. You can't tell who wrote the first one or who used whose as inspirations."

"I'm not talking about inspirations," Thompson argued. "He stole from me. Flat-out took my recipes and passed them off as his own. Copied my recipes, my ideas for setting up his company and TV tours. They were all my ideas, and he just decided to take them for his own."

Erin didn't think that ideas were something that could be protected. Company structure, concepts, viewpoints, how Montgomery conducted his tours and tastings, none of it could belong to one person.

But that didn't mean Thompson couldn't be angry about it. No reason he couldn't resent Montgomery just as much as if he'd stolen his wife or his manuscript.

Vic was nodding, clucking sympathetically, and trying to get

Thompson to move on. Eventually, he found his way out of the bakery. There was a collective sigh of relief.

"Wow." Erin blotted her forehead with a napkin.

"Don't that beat all," Vic drawled.

"It sure does. I knew the guy wasn't very well-liked, but it seems like it might go a little deeper than that."

"I would say that is an understatement," Cindy Prost commented. "Seems like someone your boyfriend might want to make the acquaintance of."

Erin looked at her. "Terry? Why?"

"Seems like he isn't too broken up about Montgomery's death. Maybe he had something to do with… wanting him that way."

Erin shook her head, bemused. "But we know what killed Montgomery. It wasn't murder. It was… just accidental exposure to an allergen."

"Unless it wasn't."

Time seemed to stand still.

Erin stared at Cindy, trying to follow her train of thought. No one had suggested that Montgomery's death might have been caused by anything other than anaphylaxis.

Was there any other possibility? Could it have been poisoning? What would make Cindy think it had been something other than what it had appeared to be? Did she actually know something? Erin glanced over at Vic.

"I didn't see the video. It *was* an allergic reaction, wasn't it? It couldn't have been… something else."

"It was an allergic reaction," Vic insisted. "It was just like you hear about. His throat swelled up; he had hives on his face, and he couldn't breathe. It just happened really fast. Like super-fast. He didn't have a chance to do anything about it, like he had when he'd had accidental allergic reactions before."

"You see?" Cindy shrugged as if this supported her theory of Thompson being the cause of Montgomery's death. "It happened too fast. Hadn't been like that before. So he must have gotten an extra-large dose of his allergen, or it was something even more lethal, like cyanide. It could have been, you know."

Erin was pretty sure that cyanide poisoning didn't look that much like anaphylaxis. Not from what she had seen on TV. Of course, crime TV wasn't a reliable source of medical information, but cyanide didn't cause hives, did it? Maybe an amateur observer couldn't tell the difference between his throat swelling from an allergic reaction and not being able to breathe due to cyanide poisoning, but the medical examiner would be able to tell, wouldn't he?

"I'm… no one has said anything about it being something other than an allergic reaction," Erin asserted. "I don't think… they're looking for suspects."

"They wouldn't have to look far, would they?" Cindy observed, and chuckled.

Erin's face burned. She knew better than to let Cindy get to her. Maybe it was because she was so short on sleep, but she wasn't willing to put up with Cindy's nonsense this time.

"If that's all you came here to say, then I think it's time for you to go now."

Cindy's mouth opened. "Well, no, I came here for…" She looked at Erin's face and perhaps thought better of asking for a Morning Sunshine Muffin. She looked past Erin at the kitchen. "Is Bella here yet? I need to talk to her."

Erin looked behind her. She hadn't heard Bella come in, but checked to be sure. Cindy was Bella's mother and, if Bella had heard Cindy talking the way that she was, she would have had something to say about it.

"No, not yet. You can send her a text to give you a call. She's going to be busy when she gets here."

Cindy's eyes went to the Morning Sunshine Muffins and then back to Erin. She clenched her jaw, and then stepped back, toward the door.

"I'll talk to her later," she said in a clipped tone, then let herself out.

CHAPTER 18

$\mathcal{E}$rin blotted her face with a napkin again. Despite the air conditioning in Auntie Clem's, she was sweating heavily after the interactions. She did not like confrontations. She wanted the atmosphere in Auntie Clem's to be pleasant and friendly. She wanted it to be a place where people felt happy and warm when they arrived, where they could talk comfortably with each other or Erin and the employees and experience being nurtured emotionally as well as physically.

She looked at Vic and shook her head. "Things are a bit... dramatic today."

Vic nodded, her eyes wide and round. "Things will settle down now, I'm sure..."

Erin hoped she was right. She was used to dealing with gossip, but Thompson's behavior was over the top, and Erin couldn't deal with Cindy's digs after being stirred up by that conversation.

She took a deep breath and smiled at the next woman in line. Another out-of-towner. A tall, slim woman with dark hair tucked behind her ears, one strand lying loose across her cheek. Erin reached for one of the Morning Sunshine Muffins.

"Hi, welcome to Auntie Clem's Bakery. Do you know what you want, or did you need a minute to look?"

"You are despicable," the woman spat. "Do you have any idea what you have done?"

Erin froze, her hand hovering over the muffins. She looked for a way to defuse the situation.

"I'm sorry…?" She struggled to give the woman a warm, reassuring smile. "I'm just trying to sell some baking here…"

"You killed him. You don't even feel bad about what you did. All you care about is the money. A brilliant man died because of what you did, and you don't even care."

Erin swallowed. "Of course I care. If I had known Mr. Montgomery was allergic to strawberries, I would never have sold him that muffin. It's a terrible tragedy and I am very sorry for what happened."

"Oh, it sounds like it," she snapped. "It really sounds like you care about him. You're pushing those muffins like a crack dealer. Capitalizing on people's grief. Making this whole thing a circus and you're selling tickets to the show."

Erin tried to think of what to do or say to calm the woman down. She was obviously grief-stricken over the loss of Gerald Montgomery.

"I wasn't going to sell any more Morning Sunshine Muffins," she felt the need to defend herself. "It was the fans who asked for them. I wouldn't have… but there's a huge demand. People really want to… share something with him. To taste what it was he tasted before… you know."

"Before you killed him. Don't act like you didn't have anything to do with it. It was all your doing. You took him away from us. He was a brilliant foodie, and now he's gone. I can't believe you could be so cold and callous. Killing the guy just to sell a muffin. Despicable. That's what you are."

"Let's move things along," Vic said in a hard voice, lower and gruffer than normal, "It's time for you to leave."

"You can't kick me out of a public place. If you don't like what I have to say, that's just too bad. I have every right to say it."

"You can get out now or we'll call the cops."

"Do you even have cops in this town?" she challenged, nose wrinkling up as if she'd smelled something bad.

"The nice thing about such a small town is that they're always close by," Vic told her.

There was a short pause while the woman considered this information. But her brief contemplation about the possibility didn't make her any more cautious. "I don't care if you do have me arrested. I'm here and I'm going to say my piece."

Vic pulled her phone out of her apron pocket and dialed a number. Erin wasn't sure whether she was calling the police dispatcher or Terry or was bluffing, but the woman didn't seem to care.

"People like you should be locked up," Montgomery's fan told Erin venomously. "People can come and look at *you* and point and laugh. And you wouldn't be a danger to someone like Gerald, who deserved to live a long, fulfilling life and to keep contributing to the world like he was."

"I'm just a baker," Erin protested weakly. She knew she should be more assertive and stand up for herself, but she understood the woman was hurting. She had suffered a loss. Maybe she was a close friend or relative of Montgomery, thrown for a loop by what had happened, reacting before she had a chance to think about the appropriateness of her behavior. "I'm just trying to make sure that people who need a gluten-free diet have choices. I'm just trying to nourish people…"

"What did Gerald Montgomery ever do for anyone?" Lottie Sturm challenged the newcomer. "You think anyone other than you really cares about him being gone? He was the one who was only trying to bring everyone else down. He was happy to destroy other people for the sake of his pocketbook."

The two women faced off against each other. Erin clutched the counter, worried that they would come to blows. It was one thing if they had to get Terry in there to cajole a disappointed woman into leaving the store without causing any more trouble. It was quite another to have a fistfight in the middle of Auntie Clem's.

"Ladies," she protested. "I understand you're upset and disappointed… but this is not the place…"

"Who do you think you are?" the other woman demanded from Lottie. "What does this have to do with you? I was talking to the proprietor."

"I'm a customer, and you're not. So why don't you move on so the rest of us can get our baking?"

"I won't be treated this way!"

CHAPTER 19

Terry must have been close by when Vic called because he opened the door and marched in, the bells ringing loudly, and K9 close beside him, ready to take on any criminal he might encounter there.

The woman had turned to confront Lottie instead of Erin, so she was facing in the right direction to see Terry enter the bakery, his dark uniform and dog making it very clear who he was.

"I have a right to be here," she snarled. "You can't kick me out. You have no reason to detain or arrest me."

Terry's expression was inscrutable. "Is there a problem here, ma'am?"

"Yes, there's a problem. Why is this woman still here after she poisoned and killed Gerald Montgomery? Are the police here so incompetent that they can't even arrest her for that?"

"At the moment, Gerald Montgomery's death is considered accidental. We are looking into it, but I can't comment on ongoing investigations."

"An accident? She deliberately gave him those muffins. She wanted them to be famous, and now they are. Everyone wants one of the Morning Sunshine Muffins from Auntie Clem's Bakery now. They'll be taking orders from Japan and shipping them around the world next thing you know. His death is being made into a circus, with millions of viewers watching his death. And this woman is profiting from his death. Doesn't that tell you something?"

"Ma'am, I'm going to ask you to step outside. We can continue this conversation out there."

She folded her arms over her chest. "I'm not going anywhere. I came here to say my piece. And I'm not leaving until I'm finished. And I will decide when I am finished, not anyone else."

Terry raised his brows. He pulled out his citation book. "Can I get your name, ma'am?"

"Becky Chalmers."

"Do you have identification on you?"

"If I say my name is Becky Chalmers, that is who I am. You don't need my identification."

"It is an offense not to supply identification when asked for it by law enforcement officers."

She considered this for a moment and then dug into her purse. "I haven't done anything wrong," she asserted. "I have every right to be here."

"As a customer, ma'am. It doesn't appear that you are here to buy anything. The proprietors have every right to evict you or deny you entrance at their discretion. They don't have to have a reason or explain why. But if you come here or remain here after you are told to leave, you are guilty of trespassing. And I don't want to have to cite you for that."

His pen hovered over the page.

Chalmers found her wallet and opened it up to display it to Terry, taking several steps closer so he could see it. People moved out of the way to avoid being caught between them.

K9 growled when Chalmers got too close for his liking, and Terry hushed him. He looked the woman over.

"Do you have any weapons on you?"

"Weapons? Me? Of course not. I came here to talk. To tell that woman what she has done!"

"Are you sure?" Terry glanced down at K9. "My dog seems to think otherwise."

"Well... I have a weapon, yes, but I'm not going to use it."

"Drop your purse there, please, and put up your hands," Terry told her sharply.

The other customers drew farther back, worried. Erin reached out for Vic to herd her into the safety of the kitchen, but Vic stood her ground, one hand under her apron. Erin knew she used a bra holster and wasn't sure how easy it would be to draw with the apron on, but Vic was apparently prepared to do so. Knowing Vic, she had probably practiced the action regularly.

Chalmers didn't act as quickly as Erin would have liked but, looking at Terry, his eyes hard and one hand on his holster, Chalmers decided she'd better take him seriously. She lowered her purse to the floor and raised her hands.

"Where's your gun?" Terry demanded.

Erin wondered how he knew it was a gun or if he were just guessing. Chalmers might have meant that she had a knife or a taser. Some women carried personal tasers in their purses and might not have considered it a weapon since it was only for self-defense. Maybe K9 had given Terry a sign that it was a gun, or maybe Terry was assuming the worst. Better to be prepared for a gun than surprised by it.

"In there," Chalmers looked at the purse beside her. "In my purse."

"Kick it toward me. Keep your hands up."

She did so. The braggadocio was leaving her posture. She wasn't quite so brash and self-righteous now, maybe starting to comprehend the serious situation she was in.

Terry grabbed the shoulder strap and pulled the bag out of the way so it was beyond the woman's reach.

"Turn around and lace your fingers behind your head."

Chalmers obeyed.

"Get down on your knees."

"It's in my bag," she protested. "I don't have anything on me."

Terry didn't back down. "Get on your knees."

The woman was young and athletic enough to do so. Erin winced at how the hard floor must hurt her knees, though. As Erin got older, she found it harder and harder to be comfortable kneeling on anything.

"Lie face down."

"I can't do that with my hands behind my head."

Terry stepped forward. His hand left his holster and helped her transition from kneeling to lying prone on the floor.

Erin couldn't help but feel bad for Chalmers. She had undoubtedly not left home this morning expecting to end up face down on Auntie Clem's Bakery's floor with customers standing around her gaping as Terry frisked her thoroughly.

Vic's position relaxed and her hand came out from behind her apron.

Terry secured the woman and went to her purse to investigate it. He pulled out a handgun that was larger than Erin had expected.

"I didn't come here to shoot anyone," Chalmers protested. "I just came here to talk. I never threatened anyone or took that out of my bag!"

"Do you have a permit? Is it registered?"

"I've been using guns since I was a child. I know what I'm doing!"

"So it's not registered? Do you have a permit?"

"Not… as such."

Erin didn't even want to know what that meant.

"I'm taking you in on firearms violations. Do you want her charged with trespassing?" Terry asked Erin.

"No. I think… she's had a bad day. I don't want to make things worse." Erin tried to meet Chalmers's eyes as Terry lifted her to her feet. "I'm sorry about your friend. I hope you believe me when I tell you that I never meant anything to happen to him. I wouldn't have given him those muffins if I had known about his strawberry allergy. And as far as selling them… people want to buy them. It's an… homage to him. A way to remember his passing. I'm not doing it for the money."

She felt a twinge of guilt saying so, because she had put together a marketing plan to sell the muffins, fully expecting people to be interested in them after Montgomery released his review. And she would continue to sell them as long as there was a demand.

But she wasn't capitalizing on the man's death. She was just selling gluten-free baking, like she always did. She had marketing campaigns around Christmas and Easter and Founders' Day, and every other observance with a good hook to bring people in. She made different shapes of cookies and different recipes suited to each holiday. And now she was selling Morning Sunshine Muffins around Montgomery's death. She had to admit that it did sound a little ghoulish when she thought about it that way.

"No, I'm sure you're not making any money on it at all," Chalmers mocked. "You're just doing this out of the goodness of your heart."

"I can't just give them away. I would lose all kinds of money."

"Yeah, that's what I thought," she sneered at Terry as he marched her toward the door.

"I'll see you after work," Terry told Erin. "I'll be around for closing to make sure that nothing unexpected happens."

Erin appreciated it but, at the same time, dreaded the possibility that anything else could happen today. She just wanted it to all be over and for things to go back to normal. What was wrong with normal? Why had she been so excited about Montgomery patronizing Auntie Clem's Bakery to start with?

CHAPTER 20

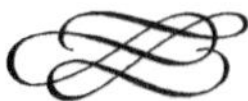

fter work, Erin normally had some alone time to decompress and relax from the rigors of the day before Terry came home or it was time to go to bed.

And she was getting off early, as Vic had arranged extra shifts to come in so that she could get caught up on her sleep.

But Terry came by before Erin left to ensure that no one was hanging around the bakery or the house who shouldn't be. He walked a patrol around the block with K9, checking out both the front and the back of the bakery and making sure no one was lurking in parked cars nearby. He nodded, signaling that it was safe for them to go out to the car, and watched as they climbed in and buckled their seatbelts.

"I'll follow you home," he told Erin when she rolled down the window.

"You don't need to do that. You already checked to make sure that everything was safe."

"There could still be people around that I'm unaware of. I can only see so much."

"You don't think that Chalmers or someone else is really any danger, do you?"

"Let's talk about that when we get back to the house."

Erin hadn't been expecting all of the attention. He and the other law enforcement officers must think there was reason for concern if they were letting Terry off to watch over her, checking out her route as if she were a dignitary, escorting her home, and then sitting down to discuss the possible dangers.

She didn't like it.

It was good that she had a law enforcement officer who was so concerned about her, but she did not like the idea that he thought she was in danger.

Erin rolled up her window and drove home without any conversation with Vic, whose brow was wrinkled in a frown and seemed to be in her own world thinking things through.

When they got home, Terry suggested that Vic grab Willie and meet them in the living room so that they could all sit down for a talk together.

"Willie needs to be a part of this too?" Vic asked doubtfully.

"Best if everyone gets the same message. Firsthand news is always more clear and definitive."

Vic grumbled and headed over to the loft to see if Willie were there. Erin thought longingly of her bed and the afternoon nap she'd hoped to have. But it looked like this day was not going to go the way that she had hoped. She'd gotten their shifts covered at Auntie Clem's, but she still didn't get to relax.

"Should I make some tea?"

Terry shrugged. "I could use a beer."

Erin walked over to the fridge to get him one. "You're not still on duty?"

"Technically, no. Practically… I still want to keep an eye on things here and see if we can make any progress. I can manage one beer without it affecting my judgment."

He must have had a pretty rough workday. He normally would not have a beer unless he were truly off for the day and just planned to couch-surf with Erin. Or maybe while they were on a date. She didn't think there was any danger in his having a beer; as he said, he wouldn't be impaired by just one. But it was out of character.

Vic returned with Willie, who also helped himself to a beer despite Vic's glare. He wasn't supposed to be drinking until he was fully recovered from the heavy metal poisoning and chelation. Erin didn't know how significant the risks were, but she knew Willie had been told no alcohol.

CHAPTER 21

hey all sat down in the living room.

"Did Vic tell you what happened at the bakery today?" Terry asked Willie.

Willie looked over at her. "She said something about a customer causing a fuss, but… it didn't seem like anything concerning."

"It wasn't," Vic agreed. "The woman was angry and upset, but no one was in any danger."

"That's not quite accurate," Terry said. "She had a concealed, unlicensed weapon. She would not listen to reason and was behaving erratically. All of those things together present a very serious situation."

Vic shrugged. "One crackpot."

Terry took a swig from the beer bottle. "The problem is that she was not just one crackpot. Montgomery seems to have had a whole following of crackpots. And they are all intent on getting to Auntie Clem's Bakery and eating a Morning Sunshine Muffin."

Erin laughed. "Could be worse things."

"Could be. Most of them will just buy their muffin and leave. Film themselves tasting it, post it to social media as hashtag Morning Sunshine Challenge, and go back to their lives. But you get some like this woman from this afternoon, who are not happy with just buying a muffin and who blame Erin or Auntie Clem's for killing Montgomery, and that's a whole different story. She wasn't much of a threat—unless she decided to use that gun."

Willie was leaning forward, elbows on knees, listening to Terry intently. He looked at Vic, nodding his agreement. "This isn't the kind of thing you want to ignore."

"But we can't have an armed guard on duty at the bakery."

"I'm there," Vic said. "I'm there for at least one shift most days, and I'm armed. I can take care of any threats."

Neither Terry nor Willie looked happy with that.

"It will blow over," Erin said. "In a day or two, it will all trickle off, just like it always does when there is a death. It won't keep going on for weeks or months."

"Are you planning to close down until it does?"

"Well, no. I can't do that. They're coming for the baking. Or at least the muffins. If I closed down… what good would that do? It would just get them riled up."

Terry shook his head grimly.

"How is the case coming along?" Willie asked. "You must be ready to put it to bed soon. It's pretty clearly an accident. An open-and-shut case."

"There are… complicating factors."

Willie grunted. "Like what? Seems to be a pretty straightforward case to me."

"Well, for one thing, the number of enemies this guy had. The number of people who were quite happy for him to be dead. There are online forums on which it is discussed in extensive detail."

"What is discussed?" Erin asked.

"The best way to kill him."

"Oh." Erin looked at Vic, then at Terry. She hadn't anticipated that.

"Yeah. And a lot of those methods involve his allergies. Somehow slipping him something that he is allergic to."

"That's horrible." Erin couldn't believe someone would discuss such a thing openly, even if the forum was supposed to be private and password protected.

"Has the medical examiner identified cause of death?" Vic asked. "Was it an allergic reaction?"

"Yes, it was. A massive allergic reaction that occurred too fast for him to be able to get help. He did manage to get his auto-injector but, by the time he injected, it was too late. It wasn't able to reverse the reaction."

Vic nodded.

Erin had wondered why he hadn't used his auto-injector. Now she knew. He had. But unlike the magical effects epinephrine always had on TV, a single dose wasn't always sufficient to reverse a reaction. Or time ran out and it was too late to recover.

"What else?" Willie asked. "The fact that people wanted him dead did not make this a murder instead of an accident. It's an interesting fact, but…"

"There is also the fact that Erin and Vic swear that strawberries were not on the wallet card listing of allergens that they were given. The corporate office confirmed that strawberries were a recent addition. Older wallet cards would have omitted strawberries as a trigger."

Erin tensed. Neither man acted like they doubted it was true. They seemed to believe that if their partners said it was true, it was.

"So he accidentally gave them an old card," Willie offered with a shrug. "That's believable."

"The office manager said that she changed over his wallet cards personally. She took the old ones out and put the new ones in. So how did Montgomery give them an old one?"

They all considered the possibilities.

"Maybe she is mistaken," Erin suggested. "A year or two ago, when I got a new credit card, I accidentally cut up the new one instead of the old one. I had to get them to send me another one. I've talked to a ton of people since then who have done the same thing. So maybe it was the same. She takes the old cards out of the wallet. Something distracts her. She puts the old cards back into the wallet and trashes the new ones. It could happen easily."

Terry nodded. "Yes," he allowed. "But there were no old cards in his room. Everything we could find listed strawberries."

Erin immediately wanted to defend herself and assure him that the card they had received from him had not had strawberries on it, even though he hadn't accused her of anything. She bit her tongue, but it was hard to keep from objecting.

"So he just had one of the old ones left," Willie said. "It was in his suit pocket, not his wallet. Or he had them in two different slots in his wallet and the executive assistant didn't realize it and only replaced the ones in one slot. There are a lot of different possibilities. If you've had two different versions of the same card printed, that will happen. You'll end up leaving the old ones somewhere without realizing it." He shrugged. "How many times have you had new business cards printed, gotten rid of all the old ones, and then two years later more of them show up somewhere? The briefcase you use for business conferences. A coat you haven't worn lately. A monogrammed card holder in a drawer that you never bother to carry with you. It's like they reproduce."

Terry sighed and sat back. He took a pull on his beer. "Maybe I'm imagining things," had admitted. "There are a lot of strangers in town; we're getting all kinds of calls from reporters, his office, other jurisdictions, and fans to find out what we're doing about it. People who think that there was foul play. That he was killed intentionally. We have this woman showing up in the bakery yelling and carrying a weapon. Maybe I am just reacting to outside pressure."

"How many people knew that he was allergic to strawberries?" Erin asked tentatively. "I don't think it could be really well known because we researched it before he came here, trying to figure out what was safe and what wasn't. Vic watched a lot of his old shows and I watched a few. We did a bunch of searches and avoided anything that it seemed like he didn't eat or that he was reported to be allergic to. Montgomery had this thing about people not sharing his allergies. I wondered if the list he gave us was a complete fiction. Like if it was just part of the game. An additional challenge to see who could stick to it and who screwed up."

"That would be a dangerous game if you really were allergic to multiple foods," Terry observed.

"Yeah. I know. I keep wondering why he didn't just put the list on his website. Let everyone know. Why keep it a secret? The only thing I can come up with is that he was ashamed of it. Felt like it meant he wasn't a man. But it was really risky behavior."

"Some people get off on risks." Willie leaned back in his seat and rubbed his forehead. He was obviously fatigued and fighting a headache. And he hadn't yet had supper. Vic would need some time to make him something. Alcohol on an empty stomach probably wasn't doing him much good.

It reminded Erin how tired she was. She was also hyped up and was afraid that when she finally did get a chance to crash, she would lie awake staring at the ceiling, passing a long, sleepless night as she tried to figure out whether someone had intentionally killed Montgomery.

"Maybe he liked the feeling of risking his life whenever he tried a new food," Willie said, eyes closed. "Maybe that's why he did it by himself instead of with someone who could help him if he had a reaction. Maybe that was why he decided to do it in a town without a hospital. Where the nearest hospital is an hour away."

"He was suicidal?" Erin asked.

"A risk taker. Not necessarily suicidal. Maybe he just liked the rush of danger."

A quote came into Erin's mind. For a few seconds, it floated just out of her reach and she tried to pin it down and to remember where it came from. Peter Pan, she thought. Maybe.

To die will be an awfully big adventure.

CHAPTER 22

Terry looked at his watch. "I'm going to head back to Auntie Clem's for closing. Just to ensure there is no more trouble and everything gets locked up properly."

"Charley is there. She'll make sure."

Terry grimaced. Charley was not his favorite person and he obviously did not trust her to ensure that everything was properly secured at the bakery. It could have had something to do with the fact that before they had met, Charley had been operating on the wrong side of the law, part of the Dyson Clan, an organized crime family. Or at least, dating a member of the Dyson clan. She was pretty young and Erin didn't know exactly how involved she had been in any illegal activities with the Dysons. Enough that she knew her way around a gun and had been in and out of trouble with the law. But she hadn't done any time, and Erin thought that said something about her.

"Charley is fine closing up," Erin insisted.

"I'm sure she is. But I'm also going to make sure. Just part of my services as the friendly town law enforcement officer." He stood up and hitched up his duty belt. "I'm sure they will feel much safer with Officer Piper on the scene."

It wouldn't hurt anything, so Erin didn't argue it any further. What harm was there in his keeping an eye on things? There *were* a lot of strangers around town since Montgomery's arrival.

"Okay. We'll have dinner when you get back. I think that right now… I might have a hot bath or a nap. I haven't decided which one yet."

"Better not be a nap in the bath," Vic warned. "You don't want to drown yourself."

"I wouldn't drown. That only happens if you are drunk or something. Otherwise, the water wakes you up!"

Vic eyed her, shaking her head. "Don't do it. Pick one or the other or I'm going to have to supervise."

Erin gave a sharp laugh at the suggestion. "You need to go back to your apartment and feed Willie." Erin gestured to him. "Can't you see that this poor man is wasting away?"

Willie chuckled and opened his eyes. He tried a forlorn expression. "She's right, darlin'."

Vic laughed and motioned for him to join her. They went in their separate directions, leaving Erin alone with the animals, trying to decide her course of action.

~

"Erin?"

Erin startled awake, splashing the water and realizing that it was cooling down and the tub needed to be refilled if she were going to stay in any longer.

"I'm not asleep!" she told Terry, who was poking his head in the door. "I was just thinking with my eyes closed."

"It's time to get out. Why don't you come cuddle on the couch? Or head to bed. You don't want to fall asleep in there."

Erin moved drowsily. The water swirled around her, waking her up more. She rubbed her face.

"Yeah, I'll come cuddle," she agreed. She might just fall asleep on the couch and stay there. "How was everything at Auntie Clem's? Went smoothly?"

"There are still too many outsiders hanging around. I don't like it. But they were able to close without any incidents. And I made sure that the burglar alarm was set and everything was locked up tight."

Erin nodded. They'd had a break-in recently and, while Terry thought it was because the burglar alarm had not been set, Erin was sure that it had been, and that the burglar, a professional thief, had known how to bypass it. Beaver had told her that it wouldn't be that hard for someone who knew the system. But Terry felt better having supervised the closing and seen for himself that the burglar alarm had been set, and it didn't hurt to have him double-checking and making his presence known. Outsiders would notice that the police were keeping a close eye on the bakery and its employees and would be less likely to cause any trouble.

If they were actually there to cause trouble. Erin hoped that most of them were just there to try out the muffins and not to threaten her. Even Chalmers hadn't threatened to use the gun she carried. She seemed shocked that anyone would even think that. Erin thought she just felt better having a gun in her purse for self-defense, even if she never used it.

In a few minutes, Erin was out of the tub, had slipped into her comfy nighttime t-shirt and shorts, and joined Terry on the couch while he surfed for a movie to watch on the TV. Erin was wider awake than she had expected to be. Maybe the almost-nap in the tub had been all she needed to refresh herself for the rest of the evening.

"I made a snack," Terry pointed out unnecessarily, pointing to the chips, pretzels, and drinks he had assembled. Not really a good replacement for supper, but Erin didn't have the energy to make anything and Terry probably didn't either. They both just wanted to sit down and relax after a long and taxing day.

Half an hour into a drama that Erin wasn't following very well, K9 suddenly sat up, ears pricked, and looked toward the door. Erin looked out the window and waited for someone to approach the front door and ring the doorbell. She couldn't see anyone, but K9 could clearly hear someone out there. He got to his feet, sniffed the air under the bottom of the door to get their scent, and paced back and forth, waiting to be let outside.

"What's going on out there?" Terry asked him. "Something wrong, K9? What's going on?"

K9 sat down and whined to be let outside. Since his dog run was out the back of the house, not the front, Erin knew he didn't just want to go out to relieve himself or play with Nilla.

"Terry, do you think something is going on?"

He got up from his seat on the couch and went over to the door. K9 stood up when Terry put his hand on the doorknob, alert and waiting to be released. Terry patted his hip before appearing to remember that he was no longer wearing his duty belt.

"I'll be right back," he muttered, and went down the hall to the bedroom to retrieve his gun. Erin watched K9, worried about what might be going on. She had brushed Terry's concerns off as an overreaction, but maybe she had been wrong.

Terry returned. With his gun in one hand, held down and out of the way, he used his other hand to slowly open the door, telling K9 to stay where he was so that he wouldn't dart out.

"Somebody out there?" he called, holding the gun out of view, inside the house. Not like some cop show on TV where he would have jammed it out the door ahead of him without knowing who might be in the yard.

Erin heard the yell of "murderer!" and some shouting back and forth that she couldn't make out.

"Get out of here, or you're going to end up in jail," Terry warned. Erin stood up to join him, but he caught her movement in his peripheral vision and motioned her to stay back.

There was laughter and more catcalling, and then whoever was out there seemed to have run off, footsteps and laughter and shouting fading off into the distance.

Terry muttered something under his breath and started to close the door again; then, something caught his attention, and he stepped out onto the front steps to look at the other side of the door and the front of the house. He swore.

"What is it?" Erin asked, moving forward, then stopping because he had told her to stay put just a moment before. She pressed him further. "What's going on? Who was it? What did you see?"

Terry called K9 out of the house and nodded to Erin. "It's okay. You're safe. Our friends just decided to buy some eggs before coming over here."

"Oh, really?" Erin shook her head. "Why would anyone do that?" She joined Terry on the steps to look at the mess the raw eggs had made when they had struck the house.

"I guess they wanted a concrete way to express their displeasure," Terry advised.

K9 sniffed at the vandalism and began to lap up the raw eggs that were within his reach. Erin giggled. K9 was going to think that the vandals really were his friends. They had brought him this nice treat of raw eggs.

"I'll get the hose and rinse off the ones K9 can't reach," Terry advised. "Why don't you just relax while I take care of it? It's easy to clean up while it's fresh."

"Did you see who it was?"

"Out-of-towners. No one I recognized."

"More Montgomery fans."

"I guess so."

"Do they think I killed him on purpose?" Erin shook her head. "How could anyone think that? Why would I do such a thing? How would that benefit me?"

"Well, you are getting a lot more business, especially people who want to buy the new muffins."

"Really?" Erin rolled her eyes at Terry. "Don't you think I would have gotten a lot more business if I'd actually managed to get a good review from him? A positive review would have been better than him dying."

"You don't expect people to be logical about it, do you?" Terry asked. "They aren't acting from a place of logic. They know that you're the one who gave him the muffins he was allergic to so, therefore, you must have wanted to kill him for some nefarious purpose."

Erin shook her head. "I can't believe people think I would do something like that on purpose. My whole reason for running the bakery is so that people with gluten-free diets or food sensitivities have a variety of good food to choose from. I didn't set up shop to murder people."

Terry shrugged and walked over to the end of the house to get the garden hose, which he uncoiled so he could wash off the rest of the raw egg.

As he'd pointed out, the fans weren't acting logically. It was all just an emotional reaction.

Hopefully, in a few days, all would be forgotten and everything would return to normal.

CHAPTER 23

*S*unday was Erin's day to rest and relax, to take some time away from Auntie Clem's and make sure she was prepared for the next week. Auntie Clem's was closed every Sunday. Everything in town was closed on Sunday for the sabbath. But they did hold a ladies' tea following Sunday services, for the women to get together and gossip and have some tea and treats. Erin rather liked the tradition now, though she had been a mite put out initially when the church ladies had insisted that, atheist or not, she couldn't run her business on Sunday, but that they expected her to reinstitute the ladies' tea that Clementine used to hold at the tea shop that had been the predecessor to the bakery.

Most of the time, Erin had other employees run the ladies' tea so that she had all Sunday off. But she had been worried about problems from the Montgomery fans when they discovered that the bakery was closed and they were being barred from ordering more Morning Sunshine Muffins. And that only the usual attendees of the ladies' tea were being allowed to attend.

With Sheriff Wilmot on the back door and Terry screening attendees at the front and only allowing Bald Eagle Falls residents in, they had managed to keep the disruption to a minimum. However, Erin was still happy when it was finished. She could go home and sit down with her planner to work through the next week's activities and make sure she stayed on top of the birthday orders, holidays, specials to be advertised in the weekly paper, and whatever else she needed to keep track of.

She let out a long breath of relief, settling into the little attic office in her house, which was the perfect retreat away from the busy world. Terry and Vic both knew that if Erin was in the attic, she was not to be disturbed.

She had her cup of tea, planner, colored pens, highlighters, and flags. An hour or two of solitude in her attic room, and she would have everything laid out for the upcoming week. Things would undoubtedly change, but that was just the nature of planning. She would do her best and then adjust as real life happened.

Erin arranged her pens the way she liked them and opened her planning binder. She started to flip through the planning pages for the previous week, recalling how she had expected the week to unfold and evaluating how many of her set goals she had been able to achieve and where things had not worked out as expected. Gerald Montgomery dying had definitely not been in her plans.

But she had still been a part of the show. There had been a tasting but no review, and she had made the new muffins available to the general public, so those things had unfolded as expected. There had been a bigger run on the muffins than she had anticipated, and they were still going strong. Montgomery's fans were making a pilgrimage to the town where he had died and eating the last thing he had eaten as a way to connect with his memory and to honor him.

Erin's finger caught against a smooth card tucked into the front pocket of the planner a couple of times before she turned the pages all to a closed position to see what it was.

Gerald Montgomery's allergy card. Erin held her breath as she inched it out of the slot, sure she would see what everyone had told her must be there—the inclusion of strawberries in the list.

She pulled the card all the way out and read it another time.

She had read it three times before she could believe what she saw.

"Terry?"

She wasn't usually one to bellow across the house. She didn't like shouted conversations and preferred to be in the same room as the person she was talking to.

Terry didn't even hear her over whatever game he was watching on TV.

Erin whistled. "K9," she called, "get Terry."

A moment later, she could hear Terry chastising K9, trying to get him to lie down and be quiet. But then his manner changed. The sound was muted on the TV.

"Erin? Are you okay?"

"Come up here. I need to show you something."

She could imagine his rolled eyes. He sighed heavily as he got up to deal with whatever Erin wanted to show him, sure that nothing was more important than his game. It was his day off. Time to relax, not to deal with an addition to his honey-do list. But he didn't make any complaint as he walked down the hall and up the pull-down stairs.

"What's up?" he asked in a flat voice, attempting but not quite succeeding in hiding his irritation at his game being interrupted.

Erin pointed to the card on her desk. Terry got closer to see what it was, and his brows shot up.

"Where did you find it?" he demanded.

"It was in my planner. I guess I tucked it inside and forgot about it."

"You've touched it?"

"Around the edges. Sorry, I didn't think about fingerprints until I got it out and realized what it was."

"That's okay. I have your fingerprints on file. We can eliminate those and see if we pull anyone's prints other than yours and Mr. Montgomery's."

"And Vic's. He handed it to her first."

Terry sighed and shrugged. "That's a lot of people handling it. But maybe we can find a print that doesn't belong to someone with a good reason for having handled it."

"Does that mean you think it was intentional? That someone made sure that we got this card instead of the right one?"

"Well, no. The simplest explanation is that it was just a mix-up. An accident. Like we discussed before, it's easy to mix up two nearly identical cards."

"It doesn't have strawberries on it," Erin pointed out. She knew that he'd already looked at it and doubtless noted this fact, but she felt the need to draw attention to it. She and Vic were vindicated. Montgomery *had* given her a card without strawberries on it.

"No," Terry agreed. "It is one of the old cards. Identical, with the exception of strawberries."

"He should have looked at it," Erin told herself. "He should have looked at it before he handed it to us to make sure that it had been updated."

Terry nodded. "He should have been more careful. I know that his fans are trying to put this all on you and say that you did something wrong, but the responsibility was on Montgomery himself. He should never have eaten unfamiliar, untested food alone. He should have kept his auto-injectors closer at hand. He shouldn't have been so far from a hospital. He should have checked to make sure he gave you the right card, even read the list of items to you out loud and then noticed that it was missing strawberries. He should have looked at the list of ingredients for each food he ate instead of being surprised."

Erin nodded. She knew all of that was true, but she couldn't help feeling like she was just as guilty as Montgomery for what had happened. It had been an accident, but she could have done more. She could have insisted that he read the ingredient lists. She could have specifically asked about strawberries, which she knew had high histamine levels that could aggravate someone allergic to multiple foods, even if they hadn't been identified as a specific trigger.

She was sure there were other things that she could have done. But she had been flattered by Montgomery being there to review Auntie Clem's and hadn't wanted to do anything that would jeopardize the review. When he had said she shouldn't tell him what was in the muffins, she should have anyway, as a responsible baker who knew she was dealing with someone with multiple allergies.

She could have called them Strawberry Sunburst Muffins. Nothing in the bakery should be a surprise.

"It isn't your fault," Terry repeated. "He should have been more careful of his own health."

"I know."

Terry's expression told her he understood that even if she didn't admit it, she still felt like she was the responsible party.

"This shows that it was accidental and not malicious or negligent," he told her, pointing to the card.

"But you never thought it was."

"Of course not. After getting to know you, I knew there was no way. That's just not you. And if you did want someone dead—and I have no clue why you would want Montgomery dead—you wouldn't do it with food. I just know that."

Erin couldn't imagine how she would kill someone if she wanted to. She wasn't a violent person, and stabbing or shooting seemed far beyond her abilities as a moral and compassionate person. It was one thing to protect herself. But premeditated murder? She couldn't see herself ever doing it. But if she did, Terry was right; she would never intentionally feed someone poison or an allergen.

"Leave it there," Terry instructed, pointing to the card. "I'm just going to grab gloves and a bag."

He went back down the attic stairs.

Erin took a picture of the card on her desk and texted it to Vic.

Vic immediately texted back a stream of startled emojis.

You found it! She texted after the emojis. *Where was it?*

In my planner

A laughing emoji. *I should have known*

The planner is the key to all knowledge Erin agreed.

CHAPTER 24

*E*rin went to the bakery with a lighter heart the next day. Despite her worries about people still thinking that she had killed Montgomery intentionally or had been careless in giving him something she should have known was an allergen, she was happier just being cleared in her own mind. Whether anyone else believed her or not didn't matter.

The fans would keep coming to the bakery; some would believe her and some would not. If they didn't, they were just wrong. Too bad for them. Erin wasn't responsible for what anyone else thought.

She had always been a people pleaser. At least as long as she could remember. She wanted people to believe her, to like her, and to think the best of her. But she was beginning to see that none of that really mattered. She could live with it as long as she knew she had not done anything wrong. And as Terry had said, Montgomery was largely responsible for his own death.

Erin was in the kitchen of Auntie Clem's when her phone vibrated with a text message, so she took a moment to pull it out and check to see what the message was. She would never do that out in front of the customers. She asked her employees not to text or do other things that would distract them while working in the kitchen but, as she had finished her kitchen tasks and was just heading to the front, it seemed like the ideal time to take a quick peek at the message.

It was from Melissa. She must not have been able to get away from the police department and didn't dare let anyone hear her phoning Erin to tell her the latest news.

Erin's eyes flashed over the words.

ME's decision is in

Erin knew that Melissa was hoping for a reaction. And that she should not encourage this kind of gossip and drama from Melissa.

But she wanted to know. She had to know. And that was exactly why Melissa had texted her.

She hesitated, not leaving the kitchen and taking her place at the counter. She decided to take one more minute before resuming her place at the counter.

What?

Melissa kept her hanging, not answering immediately. Had she been interrupted by someone she didn't want to see her texting? Or was she trying to increase the tension?

Erin refrained from any response to try to hurry Melissa along. If Melissa wanted Erin's reaction, she would have to spill the beans. And she had to do it before Erin went back out front.

Finally, her phone vibrated again.

Accidental death

Erin gave a sigh of relief. That was it, then. The case was over. It was decided. It was an accidental death, and she didn't need to worry about the police coming after her. They knew that it had just been the perfect set of circumstances that had unfolded to cause Montgomery's death. They knew Erin had been given the wrong information about his allergies and had no way of knowing it was strawberries.

It was all over.

She couldn't stop thinking about it, but she kept reminding herself that the case had been decided and she didn't need to worry about it anymore.

Charley was working the afternoon shift and Erin told her the results. Charley pursed her lips and looked thoughtful, but didn't raise any objections.

"So you're okay now?"

Erin nodded. "Yeah. I'm good. Everything is decided. I don't need to worry about anything."

Charley indicated the customers with her eyes. "Only about any more wackos."

"I'm sure we won't see too much more of that. People will get bored with the muffins and move on to the next big thing."

"Probably... sooner or later..."

"Soon," Erin said. "We've seen... *unusual deaths* here before, and once people have had a chance to talk about them... they just kind of drift away again. People only stay interested for a few days, and then they move on to something else."

Charley nodded. She had been involved in her own case and had seen Erin work her way through several more since then. She knew the pattern as well as Erin.

"Did you drop this?" One of the customers Erin didn't recognize bent down to pick up an envelope from the floor.

Erin frowned at it. "No, what is that? Does it have a name on it?"

The woman turned it over and back again. She handed it over the display case to Erin. Erin took it and saw that her name was handwritten on one side. She shook her head and put it into her apron pocket.

"I have no idea what that is. I'll take a look at it later."

She sold the woman a Morning Sunshine Muffin, and the next couple of people too. Then, a familiar face, Mary Lou.

"What can I get for you?" Erin asked. "Do you want one of the—" Erin started to point out the Morning Sunshine Muffins and then stopped herself. "Oh! I never did give you your reserved Morning Sunshine Muffin. What happened to that? Someone must have taken it, but it was labeled with your name..."

Mary Lou held up a hand to stop her. "No, it's fine. Don't worry about it. I told them to give it to someone else. I really... didn't want it after Mr. Montgomery..." Mary Lou shrugged, looking away. "After he passed, I really didn't have any interest in having one of those muffins. I'm sure they're just fine. They sound perfect, but I couldn't. Not knowing that they had caused a man's death."

"Oh. I see. I understand."

"I'm sure they're fine," Mary Lou repeated. "I'm not big on sweets and, after hearing the news, I really didn't have any appetite for them."

"That's actually how I expected *everyone* to respond," Erin said with a small laugh. "I didn't think I'd have this big run on them. It really surprised me."

"It seems… a little morbid, to be honest," Mary Lou said with a note of relief in her voice that Erin hadn't overreacted to her rejection of the Morning Sunshine Muffins.

"I thought so too," Erin agreed. "I mean, I'm happy to make them and have people buy them. But I didn't expect so many people to want them. Not because they're a great muffin, but because someone died after eating one." Erin shuddered. "It's more than a little creepy. But if that's what people want…"

"Give them what they want," Mary Lou agreed. "I've learned to be a salesperson at the General Store. If people want a particular product… sell them that product. If there is a run, get more. Encourage fads, challenges, viral sales, whatever. If that's what people want to spend their money on, then give it to them."

"Yep," Erin agreed. She had learned the same thing. She couldn't predict what would be hot but, if people came in demanding Morning Sunshine Muffins, she would give them Morning Sunshine Muffins. "Now, what can I get for you today? What would *you* like?"

Mary Lou looked over the offerings. "Two loaves of bread, twelve rolls, and… how about brownies? Roger and Joshua both like brownies."

"Sure," Erin agreed. "How many do you want? Four?"

Mary Lou wouldn't likely eat them herself. So Erin calculated two each for her husband and son. Mary Lou was frugal, but liked to get them a little treat each week. Just something small to make them happy.

"Yes," Mary Lou nodded. "That should be good."

Erin packaged up her order, and Mary Lou counted the money out for Charley on the counter next to the cash register.

Erin didn't think about the envelope again until they were nearly finished closing. Her hand touched her apron pocket and she felt the envelope and looked down at it again.

"Oh, right." She pulled it out and looked at the handwriting again. She didn't recognize the writing. Who would have written her a note and then carelessly let it fall to the floor in the bakery? Had she handed it to Erin or placed it on the counter for her, and Erin had been thinking of other things and brushed it to the floor while filling the next customer's order? She couldn't remember anything like that happening. She didn't recall seeing the envelope until the customer had handed it to her.

"What is it?" Charley asked as Erin slid her finger under the flap to tear it open.

"I don't know. We'll find out in a minute here…"

She slid the folded white copy paper out and flicked it open. There was only one sentence handwritten in block letters in the middle of the page.

I did you a favor

Erin shivered despite the heat of the kitchen.

"What is it?" Charley repeated, approaching her this time to look at it. Erin held it for her but, when Charley reached for it, Erin pulled it back, not letting her touch it. Charley read it and looked at Erin's face.

"Who did you a favor? What's that about?"

"I don't know. It doesn't make any sense. But what if it's about… Montgomery's death. What if it means…"

Erin didn't finish the sentence. Her brain was already racing ahead, calculating all of the possibilities.

"Montgomery's death? You mean that someone intended for him to die?" Charley asked, shaking her head and frowning, brows knitted together.

"I don't know. What else could it mean? It sounds like… it almost sounds like a threat. Or the beginning of some blackmail scheme. 'I took care of your problem. Now it's your turn to take care of mine.'"

"But there isn't any demand."

"Maybe that's coming next."

Charley shrugged and nodded, agreeing that it was possible.

"You'd better call your sweetheart, then."

Erin realized it was true. She resisted the idea. The Montgomery case was closed. Why cause trouble?

"But there hasn't been any threat or ask, so maybe I should just wait until there is. And I don't know who left it for me. It could be anyone. Shouldn't I wait until we know who sent it and why?"

"Sure, if that's what you want to do," Charley said. A little too fast. Erin always had to check herself if Charley agreed with her too quickly.

"I can't really tell the police anything yet."

"You have physical evidence." Charley indicated the piece of paper. "They could test the paper. Test it for prints or DNA. Analyze the handwriting. Match it if they can find a suspect."

Charley was right, unfortunately. The police department would want to analyze the letter.

If they believed it was related to Montgomery's killing or another crime. But they believed that Montgomery's death was an accident. The ME had just closed the case on it. Why reopen it again without any evidence that it was something else? Anyone could have left the letter. It didn't have to be someone who had any connection with Montgomery or his death. She had seen the kind of things his fans did, things that made no sense to her.

They came into the bakery throwing around accusations, calling her a murderer. They egged her house. And they came to buy the muffins that had killed their idol, as if it were some kind of sacrament that would transform them and bring them closer to Montgomery even in death.

How could she make sense of someone like that? How could she predict their behavior or what they intended by leaving her the note?

Erin sighed. "I guess I'd better let Terry know. But maybe he won't want it."

"Maybe," Charley said, though it was clear from her tone of voice that she didn't think this likely.

Terry answered his phone almost instantly when Erin called. Maybe he had been watching the clock and worrying that she would run into trouble around closing.

"Erin. How's it going?" His voice was deliberately casual.

"I'm fine. Everything is fine," she assured him immediately. "I just... Charley thought I should call you. I got this strange letter... message... I don't know what it means. But it isn't threatening. It isn't clear what they intended by leaving it here..."

"What letter? What are you talking about?"

"It was just something that was left in the store. It was on the floor. And I'm not worried about it. I know the Montgomery case is closed, so you don't want anything else that might be related to that, right?"

"Well, if it is, then I guess we need to know about it. What does it say? What makes you think it has something to do with Montgomery's death?"

"It just says, 'I did you a favor.'"

"I did you a favor."

"Yeah."

"And that's it?"

Erin nodded impatiently. "Yeah. That's it. Like I said, it doesn't mean anything… or I don't know what it means…"

"Charley is right. I should probably have a look at it. At least log it into evidence, just in case."

CHAPTER 25

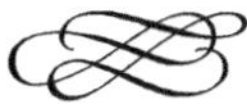

erry took the message into evidence and promised to check it for fingerprints or other clues, but he didn't seem to think it was too important.

"There are a lot of crackpots in town right now, making the pilgrimage here after Montgomery's death, wanting to walk in his footsteps." Terry shrugged and shook his head. "Can't say I understand it or his popularity. From what I have seen, he wasn't a very pleasant person and had a lot of enemies. But he had his fans, too. This…" he indicated the unfolded sheet of paper. "This is probably nothing. Just a prank. Someone who wants some attention. He wants to see if we panic over it. But… we will follow up on it, just in case it is serious."

"But you don't think it is," Erin looked over at Charley. Just as she had expected, Terry didn't think it was anything of importance. He said they would follow up on it, but that probably didn't mean anything more than checking it for fingerprints.

Charley made a face at Erin. "I told you that you should call him."

"But they're not going to do anything about it."

"Erin," Terry frowned and used an exasperated tone, "I told you that we *would* follow up on it."

"Yeah. But you don't think it is anything to be concerned about."

"Well, no. But that doesn't mean I won't take it seriously. We will still follow up on it."

Erin shrugged. She wasn't expecting much. "You don't think it has anything to do with Montgomery's death."

"I don't think…" Terry's brows knitted as he tried to put together the words he wanted. "It may be *because* of Montgomery's death. It may be one of his fans. But I don't think that anyone did anything to cause his death. It was just an accident, an unfortunate set of circumstances. You know that. It was determined to be an accidental death. The police department and the medical examiner's office in the city agree on that point."

"It *could* have been engineered."

"Whose idea was it to put strawberries in the muffins?"

Erin opened her mouth, then closed it again. She thought about it. "Well… mine."

"And what was the one thing left off of the allergy card?"

"Strawberries."

"So unless *you* took strawberries off of the allergy card, this wasn't engineered. No one meant for this to happen."

"They might have taken strawberries off the list and just hoped that sooner or later someone would feed him strawberries."

"And that he wouldn't know it? That they wouldn't be billed as strawberry compote muffins? What were the chances, really, that someone would feed him strawberries not knowing about the allergy and that he would eat them not knowing that they contained strawberries?"

Erin had to admit it was a stretch.

Whoever had written the note was just playing games with her. Or they had meant something completely different, and she just thought it had something to do with Montgomery's death because that was what was foremost in her mind these days.

"Okay… you're right. I don't see how anyone could have engineered that."

Terry nodded, satisfied. "I don't want you worrying about this, Erin. I know we have had a lot of crime in Bald Eagle Falls since you moved here, a lot of violence and death, which is unusual for a little place like this. But not every death is a murder. This was just an accident and you don't need to worry that it was anything more. It was unfortunate, but you can put it behind you. Okay?"

Erin nodded. "I'll try. I think… I don't know. Maybe it is a little bit of PTSD still. You know… hypervigilance. Thinking that there is danger where there is not. Maybe from the other deaths. Maybe just from the way that I grew up, with my parents' death and then growing up in foster care, where I couldn't really trust anyone else to keep me safe."

"Well, you're with me now. And I promise I will keep you safe. I would tell you if this was something to be worried about. But I don't think it is. I think that we still need to be careful of all of the visitors in town, especially the ones who are riled up over his death. But whoever wrote this message, whether they intended you to think that it was from someone who had something to do with Montgomery's death or not, I don't think they did. I can't see how anyone could have influenced enough of the factors involved in this case to have caused his death."

"So you don't think this has anything to do with Montgomery's death."

"I don't think that person had anything to do with Montgomery's death."

"I was afraid that they were going to ask me to do something for them. Since they did me this favor, whatever it is."

"How would killing Montgomery be a favor to you?" Charley asked. "It doesn't benefit you at all. In fact, you've got people calling you a murderer and throwing eggs at your house."

"Well… it has gotten me a lot of business with people coming here to taste the muffins."

"But how could anyone predict that? They didn't do it for you."

"They could still see that it was a benefit afterward and then decide to use that against me. Or… to get something from me. I don't know yet." Erin looked at Terry. "Do you think I'll get another one? Telling me to do something that is… illegal or unethical?"

"Maybe, maybe not. It probably depends on how you respond to this one. If you don't appear affected, maybe they just let it go. I don't know if they intend to follow up with a 'part two.' You can't expect these cranks to act logically."

"I know," Erin agreed. But she was wondering whether it really was a crank, or whether it was someone who had planned everything out carefully.

Terry had convinced her that if Montgomery's death had been intentional, the killer had been very clever in setting it up.

CHAPTER 26

I love it when we can get to the community market," Vic declared. She took a deep breath of air laden with the scents of baking, scented candles, flowers, and fried food. "There's nothing like a country market to whet your appetite and make you glad to be alive."

"And to make you spend your money," Erin added.

Vic grinned. "Well, you don't have to, but how else are you going to get a taste of those little fried donuts and the harvests coming in from the fields? If you get those fresh fruits and veggies, it offsets anything bad you eat."

"It is a lot of fun," Erin agreed. "And a great way to get super fresh ingredients. I'm going to put fresh blueberries in the muffins this week instead of frozen. They're so ripe right now that they practically pop when you put them in your mouth. So sweet and juicy..."

Vic mimed wiping her face with the back of her hand. "You're making me drool!"

"I love fresh berries."

"I'm hoping the Jam Lady might be back in business this year. I sure have missed those wonderful jams since the Jam Lady went out of business."

Erin thought about Mary Lou's husband Roger, the cook behind the Jam Lady label, though very few people knew it. She didn't know if he still had the ability to make the wonderful, flavorful jams that he had made before he'd had to go to the institution for treatment. Now that he was back, on fairly heavy medication, she could only hope that he would still able to produce another batch of his beautiful, jewel-tone jams.

"That *would* be good," she agreed. "Good news for everyone."

Vic nodded.

They made their way down the line of stalls, examining all of the wares. Everything from fresh fruits and vegetables to preserves and handicrafts, to quilts and furniture and harvest tools that cost hundreds of dollars. They really did have everything. It was hard not to go all -out and spend way too much money. Erin had learned that she needed to be critical and fight the urge to get everything that looked good.

It was midafternoon and the weather was hot despite the umbrellas and awnings that shaded most of the booths and tables from direct sunlight. Erin had her water bottle with her but, before long, she was looking for somewhere to refill the bottle and get into an air-conditioned space for a while.

"Maybe we could stop in at the General Store."

"They have a booth," Vic pointed out.

"I know. But I need to get out of this heat."

Vic refrained from saying, "But it isn't even hot out." She looked at Erin. "You're looking a mite red," she admitted. "We'd best get out somewhere cool for a bit."

Erin led the way to the General Store, and they entered. Like Auntie Clem's, the shop had bells over the door that tinkled quietly when Vic and Erin entered.

They browsed until Mary Lou came out from the back room to see who was there.

"Oh, Erin and Vic. I didn't know you were stopping in today."

"We were at the market, but I was getting overheated," Erin explained. "I need your air conditioning."

"It's always nice to shop out-of-doors," Mary Lou observed. "Until you need to get away from the out-of-doors."

Vic chuckled. "Ha. You're right."

They continued to browse through the shelves of the General Store, which boasted a wide variety of practical and decorative items, some of which were made or sourced locally and others special-ordered. Erin could always count on being tempted by something when she went to the General Store. Like going to a candy store, toy store, or little corner market when she was a kid.

"It's funny, we were just talking about Jam Lady," Erin told Mary Lou. "Wondering whether there would be any new stock coming in."

"Well, you never know," Mary Lou said. "Not yet, but… things change from one day to the next. I'm never quite sure what to expect. I am hopeful that he will improve enough to start cooking again… but as it is…" Mary Lou looked around the store to ensure no other customers were within hearing distance. "He can't be left in the kitchen. And for one of us to be there to supervise… well, we need the time."

"We sure would love it if he could produce another batch," Erin told her with a warm smile. "But of course we would never push. It all depends on what he can do and what you have the time and energy for."

Mary Lou nodded her agreement. "And how was the market? Were you enjoying yourself? Before you got too hot?"

"Definitely." Erin lifted her canvas bag bulging with goodies. "Too much!"

"Ah, that's good. I look forward to whatever ends up in your baking."

"Me too. I like my own baking just a little too much," Erin confessed, putting a hand over her stomach, which was definitely thicker than it had been when she had arrived in Bald Eagle Falls.

"You work hard," Vic dismissed. "You look just fine."

Erin rolled her eyes and looked for a way to change the subject. She wished she could stay as slim as Vic, but her body had other ideas. She didn't want to complain to Vic, who had body image issues of her own to deal with. But she didn't think she looked "just fine."

"It's too bad that strawberries are out of season. We've been going through so many in the Morning Sunshine Muffins. I still have some more preserves that we bought earlier in the season. But we'll be out soon."

"How long do you think this run on the muffins will last?"

"Who knows? It's crazy. I had no idea so many people would want to eat Gerald Montgomery's last meal." She shook her head.

"You might be able to pick up some more preserves at the B&B. Mrs. McClung was saying that she had such a bumper crop. She put up dozens of jars."

"Oh, I'll check it out! Thanks for the tip."

"If you're going over there…" Mary Lou hesitated.

"What?"

"I just have an order for her. She hasn't been able to stop by to get it yet. Like you, she's been overrun by sightseers and hasn't been able to get away."

"I'd be happy to take them over," Erin said immediately.

Vic looked at her with surprise. They had planned to spend several hours at the market, not running other errands.

"You don't have to come," Erin told her. "I was just thinking… I've never actually been there. Maybe Terry and I will take a little vacation there one day. Who says you have to go out of town for a getaway?"

"I thought it was implied in the name," Mary Lou said dryly. "A getaway?"

"Well, we would get away from the house and hopefully away from work for a day or two."

Vic was looking at Erin with a frown. "I've never heard you or Terry talk about going to the B&B."

"Well… I guess we haven't talked about it around you."

That didn't clear up the frown on Vic's face, but she didn't argue. Mary Lou looked thoughtful.

"Maybe there is something else you wanted to check out at the bed and breakfast,"

"Oh," Vic's face suddenly lit with understanding. "You want to snoop."

Erin's cheeks got hot. She couldn't very well deny it. But she didn't like the slant that the word "snoop" put on it. "I just want to… have a look around. See where it happened."

"What is that going to tell you?" Vic demanded. "You aren't going to find out anything new by looking around there."

"Who knows?" Erin shrugged. "Maybe it's just morbid curiosity, like all of the people coming to buy muffins at Auntie Clem's. I want to be where he was. I want to have a look around. I know I won't be able to figure anything out… but I still want to see."

"What is there to figure out?" Mary Lou asked. "Montgomery was killed by an allergic reaction."

"I know, I know," Erin agreed, not wanting to have to argue it with anyone. She had already been thoroughly put in her place by Terry.

There was no way that the allergic reaction could have been planned. No one had known what Erin was making. Nothing had been added to the muffins to poison Montgomery. He had just had a reaction to one of the ingredients Erin had included. And she hadn't known because he had given her the wrong card. It would never have happened if she had not been given the wrong card.

But no one had put the wrong card in his wallet intentionally. And no one had known that by doing so, Erin would give Montgomery something with strawberries in it. She rarely put strawberries in muffins. It wasn't a common muffin ingredient.

"I know it wasn't deliberate. It wasn't poisoning or something that anyone set up. But I still want to see, to understand what happened."

Vic was standing slightly behind Erin, and Erin had the feeling that Vic had made a gesture or facial expression to Mary Lou, warning her not to push it any further. They were humoring her. Letting her have her crazy theory in hopes that sooner or later, she would drop it on her own.

"I would be happy to help by taking your order to Mrs. McClung," Erin told Mary Lou firmly. "And I can ask her about strawberries and see if I can buy some extra preserves from her. If she has that many, she probably won't mind parting with a few jars."

She looked at Mary Lou and then back over her shoulder at Vic. Neither of them disagreed. Erin had two perfectly legitimate reasons for going to the bed and breakfast. It didn't matter whether she was just curious or had serious theories about how Montgomery's death could have been staged. She didn't need any other reason.

"Well, that would be a big help to me," Mary Lou declared. "Thank you so much for your kind offer. You make sure you stay inside here until you have cooled down enough to be outside again. And let me fill your water bottle."

Erin handed it over with a smile of gratitude.

They continued to browse and chat until Erin felt cool and relaxed and didn't think she would have problems walking over to the B&B with Mary Lou's delivery. Erin bought a few little items from the General Store to pay her way for standing around using their air conditioning for so long.

CHAPTER 27

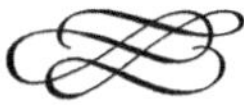

$\mathcal{E}$rin had never been inside the bed and breakfast. She had only heard it referred to. Of course, most of the Bald Eagle Falls residents had never actually stayed there because, as Mary Lou said, when people wanted a getaway, they left town. They got away.

Since the closing of the Inn, the B&Bs had picked up the slack and, from what Erin heard, were usually booked up.

The house was similar in age to the one Erin had inherited from Clementine, but it was two stories tall, with bedrooms upstairs instead of on the main floor. Probably twice as many square feet as Erin's house.

She recognized the curly-haired woman who answered the door, looking questioning.

"Mrs. McClung. I brought you over a delivery from the General Store. We were just over there, so I thought I would pop by with it."

Mrs. McClung took the box from her slowly. "You're Erin Price, aren't you, the baker? You aren't working at the General Store now?"

"No, we were just saying hi to Mary Lou. She said that you had a bumper crop of strawberries this year."

Mrs. McClung looked even more confused by this segue.

"Yes, it was a very good year for strawberries."

"I am running out of strawberries, and she suggested you might have a few extra jars you would like to get rid of."

"Oh!" Mrs. McClung laughed and shook her head. "I had no idea what this was all about. So you came here to give me the delivery and find out if I had any strawberries you could buy?"

Erin nodded. "That's pretty much it," she agreed. Of course, she was still hoping to go in and look around but, if Mrs. McClung didn't invite her inside, she would have to find another credible excuse to ask.

"Well, that was very nice of you." Mrs. McClung opened her door wider. "Why don't you come in while I get you a few jars? You too, Miss Victoria."

Vic gave her a smile and followed Erin into the house. She looked around.

"I've never been in here before. This is very nice, Mrs. McClung."

Mrs. McClung looked at her and didn't say anything. Erin had found that some of the Bald Eagle Falls residents really didn't know how to talk to someone who was transgender, or disapproved of her and didn't think they should speak to her, as if they might somehow be contaminated with her "sin." At least she had invited Vic into the house and hadn't made her wait on the porch.

Mrs. McClung left them to go find the jars of strawberry jam and Vic rolled her eyes at Erin.

"Sorry," Erin apologized. "Some people are just… stubborn."

Vic nodded. "I'm a bit stubborn myself sometimes," she admitted. "Can't blame others for the same fault."

Erin snickered. Vic being a "bit stubborn" was like saying that Everest was a bit tall. She and Willie had some real set-tos when they disagreed, neither one willing to back down.

Erin glanced around to see if anyone else were around, maybe other guests of the B&B, but they seemed to be alone. She wandered around a bit rather than staying at the door where Mrs. McClung had left them. Vic watched her but didn't raise any objection about how rude Erin was being snooping around while Mrs. McClung fetched the strawberries.

Erin went to the bottom of the stairs but couldn't think of a good excuse for ascending them to look at the other rooms. Mrs. McClung returned with a box containing several jars of strawberry preserves. She looked askance at Erin.

"I was wondering about coming here for a sort of a date night," Erin said, not waiting for her to ask. "You know, a sort of a couples getaway. I know it's silly, vacationing in town instead of going somewhere more exotic, or at least to the city," she said, remembering Mary Lou's argument, "But I don't like to be too far from the bakery in case something goes wrong, and you know how Officer Piper has to be on call at all times…"

Mrs. McClung forced a smile. "Well then, going somewhere in town sounds like the perfect solution," she agreed.

"Do you think I could see the rooms? At least, the ones that aren't in use right now?"

"I don't know. I don't usually do tours. There are pictures on the website."

"Oh, of course," Erin acknowledged, but she didn't return to the front door. "What was it like having all of the police here? That must have been a unique experience."

"Yes, it certainly was," Mrs. McClung admitted. "I can't say I've ever had a guest die before. I guess it must happen sometimes, especially in bigger places. Big hotels. But it's never happened here before. I didn't know what to do. Who do you call when something like that happens? It isn't exactly an emergency, is it? Nothing the police or doctors can do when the man has been dead all night."

"How did you know he'd been dead all night?"

"Well, heavens… people were calling me trying to reach him all night. Very rude, some of them. They said he wasn't answering his phone and I should wake him up and make him talk to them. Do you think it's my job to wake guests up to make them answer their phones? Ridiculous!"

Erin nodded and made encouraging noises.

"But he didn't come down for breakfast in the morning, and it was getting late. The people from his office were getting upset about it. When he checked in, I told him that I clean the rooms at eleven every morning. By that time, breakfast is over and people are up. They're either sightseeing or want to get started on their trip to the next place, so they want to get an early start. People don't usually stay in bed past ten."

"So you finally decided you'd better check on him and make sure he was okay."

"Yes. I wish now that I had done it sooner, but I really can't breach a guest's privacy that way. People come here to relax and turn off. Honeymoons," she nodded to Erin, reminding her of her fictional plans to come there with Terry. "You can't just interrupt people because they're not answering their phones and certain other people don't like it."

"I would expect my privacy to be protected, too," Vic agreed.

Mrs. McClung gave her a look that clearly stated that Vic would not be allowed to register as a guest at the bed and breakfast. No such hanky-panky would be permitted while she was in charge of the place.

Vic's face got pink, but she didn't say anything.

"What time did Mr. Montgomery get in? And when did people start complaining that he wasn't answering his phone?"

"He was here early in the evening. He brought home a box of goodies from the bakery and didn't offer to share them. He went up to his room. He didn't go out for supper, but I guess he had all those pastries to eat."

"And then people started complaining that he wasn't answering his calls…?"

"A couple of hours later, I guess. Eight, maybe."

"Who was trying to reach him?"

Mrs. McClung favored her with a glare. "Your boyfriend may be a police officer, but I don't think you are, Miss Price."

"No, I'm sorry. I didn't mean to pry. I'm just another of those annoying rubberneckers, I guess. A curiosity-seeker. It is just so bizarre to think that he died right after I saw him. Right after he bought my muffins."

"Because one of them poisoned him," Mrs. McClung pointed out.

"Not poisoned," Vic objected. "He had an allergic reaction to it. There wasn't anything toxic in it. Just… for him."

"Yes, and he was poisoned by it, wasn't he?"

"How big are the rooms?" Erin tried, hoping that if she asked enough questions about them, Mrs. McClung would tell her just to go upstairs and have a look.

"The size of standard bedrooms. There are pictures on the website."

"And Mr. Montgomery's must have been the largest? The master bedroom?"

"Yes."

"Do the rooms all have their own keys?"

Mrs. McClung gave her an odd look.

"Yes, of course. How else would guests keep their rooms secure? I mean, we don't have people wandering in and out of guests' private rooms, but you can't ensure that if they don't have any way to lock their rooms."

"Are they regular keys or key cards like at hotels?"

"Regular keys. And a chain on the inside. We want people to feel safe."

"But Mr. Montgomery didn't have his chain on?"

"What makes you say that?"

"You were able to get in… you didn't say you had to break down the door or get someone to help you with it, so I assume the chain wasn't on."

"No, it wasn't."

"Where are the keys kept? The ones that have not been given out to guests?" Erin assumed there were at least three keys per door. Two keys for double occupancy and a key for Mrs. McClung herself. Maybe another for the maid. Or maybe there was a master key that opened all of the doors, and Mrs. McClung had one, and a part-time maid, and a handyman. There might be half a dozen people who could get into each room easily.

"The keys are kept in my locked drawer," Mrs. McClung said, wrinkling her nose at Erin as if she smelled bad. She pointed at a writing desk. A little faux antique number with a large keyhole on the front of the drawer that could probably be popped open with the long, slim letter opener on the writing surface.

"Did Montgomery have any visitors?"

"He had a TV crew. I don't know how many people. They were coming and going the whole time he was here."

"Or until he came back that evening. Were they coming and leaving from his room after he came back with the muffins?"

"I was told that he was not to be interrupted after that. It was his *artistic process.*"

By her tone of voice, she didn't like artistic people much better than transgender people. Erin rolled her eyes to make Mrs. McClung think that she identified with her on this point.

"I'll bet he was a pain in the neck. All of those artist types are, aren't they?"

Mrs. McClung nodded her agreement. "They always need something else. Making demands. It's like they don't understand that this is my *home.* I'm happy to give them a room and make them breakfast. I keep my house nice and clean and welcoming for them." She spread her hands to indicate their surroundings. "But I'm not a servant. I'm not there to see to every request and serve them hand and foot. *Get me an aspirin for my headache. Take these flowers out of my room. I thought this was a fragrance-free facility.*" She rolled her eyes and shook her head. "Fragrance-free? Where did he even get that?"

It was an odd comment. "Is that what Mr. Montgomery said?" Erin asked. "People with multiple allergies often have environmental triggers. But if you don't advertise the B&B as fragrance-free, I don't know where he would have gotten that."

"Somehow, it's *my* fault that there are flowers in his room? They came to him from his fans. I mean… talk about privilege. I'm supposed to read his mind and know what to put in his room and what not to. Of course I will put any deliveries that come while he is out into his room. I'm keeping them safe and ensuring he gets them right away, and then I'm a bad guy for putting flowers in his room. Good heavens."

"He got a flower delivery?"

"He was getting deliveries all day: flowers, wine, cards, chocolate. I don't know what all of them were. From the time that he booked the room, they were coming. I don't know how so many people knew where he would be staying. It was supposed to be a secret, or so I understood. He made the booking, and no one was supposed to know which days he would be here."

CHAPTER 28

$\mathcal{I}$t must have been very exciting to know that such a famous person was going to be coming to the B&B," Erin observed. "I'll bet you were tied in knots trying to make all the arrangements to make it perfect for him."

"I wasn't supposed to go to any trouble for him. Just keep things the same as they always were. They didn't want anyone tipping people off that something unusual was happening. They weren't even supposed to know he was coming to Bald Eagle Falls, but someone obviously leaked that."

Erin nodded. "Yeah, I heard about it from a couple of different directions before he came. That's how I knew to be prepared for him at the bakery."

"By preparing something for him that he was allergic to?"

"Well, no. I didn't know Mr. Montgomery was allergic to strawberries. That wasn't included in his list of allergies, so I didn't know to avoid it. I wanted to make something special for him, and the strawberries this year were so good…" Erin motioned to the bottles of preserves that Mrs. McClung had brought out for her. "It just seemed like a great choice. Something that I didn't usually use in muffins, so it would be a surprise and so nice at the end of the summer. I looked through all kinds of recipes online to figure out what to make for him. And Vic and I watched videos of his past shows online."

Erin tilted her head toward Vic to try to keep her in the conversation despite Mrs. McClung's apparent opinion of her.

"And the videos didn't mention anything about him being allergic to strawberries," Erin went on, "Just like he didn't tell you ahead that he was allergic to flowers or fragrances."

"It would have made things so much easier if he had just been upfront about all that stuff from the start," Mrs. McClung's voice was aggrieved. "To expect me to know anything without telling me... well, that just wasn't fair. If he didn't want flowers in his room, he should have let me know. They were *his* flowers."

"Exactly. How were you supposed to know that?"

"He complained about everything. A light in his room was flickering. His neighbor was playing music he didn't like. He kept getting phone calls. Could *I* help it that he got phone calls? On *his own* phone? How is that my problem? He says he's never had issues like that before. So it must be my fault?"

"Issues like what?" Vic asked, unable to resist participating in the conversation.

"Some prank calls. I don't know. Do you think I asked him for any details? I just nodded and made sympathetic noises, but I couldn't do anything about the calls he got on his phone. He should complain about those to his phone provider or to whoever at his office was giving out his phone number. That woman is here." Mrs. McClung rolled her eyes upward, indicating the rooms on the floor above.

"What woman?"

"The one from his office. The one who is so demanding, constantly calling me up to make sure that I've made this or that arrangement. After telling me that I wasn't supposed to do anything special to prepare for Mr. Montgomery's visit"

"Is that Mavis?" Erin took a stab at it. She remembered the name from Terry's conversation about the business cards.

Mrs. McClung nodded. "That's the one," she agreed. "Mavis. I could think of a lot of other names for her, bless her heart. The woman was a thorn in my side. *Is* a thorn in my side. When is she going to go home? Mr. Montgomery isn't here anymore, so why is she here? Shouldn't she be back at his office taking care of things there? There isn't anything for her to do here,"

"Why *is* she here?" Erin asked curiously. It did seem strange that anyone from Montgomery's office would stay at the bed and breakfast.

"She says she needs to be here for public relations, because of all the fans. Do you know those people keep showing up at the door? Expecting to get a tour of the house? Thinking that I'll take them up to look at the room he died in?" She shook her head in disbelief. "What ghouls! I was afraid I wouldn't be able to rent that room out anymore after someone died there. You know how buildings get a reputation for being haunted, or for being bad luck. I wouldn't want someone else to think that it was a death room, that if they stayed there, they might die."

"That's exactly what I thought about the muffins," Erin told her. "I didn't think I would be able to sell the Morning Sunshine Muffins. Everyone would think they were murder muffins. But they all want them. Everyone who comes into town to mourn Mr. Montgomery's death, or whatever they are doing by coming here."

Mrs. McClung nodded vigorously. "I didn't think I would ever be able to rent that room out again. Or I would have to change its look completely and change the name so no one would know it was the same room."

"But you've already rented it out?" Erin guessed.

"I've had so many inquiries after it that I hardly know what to do with myself. But I don't want to rent it to all those ghouls. What if they rip it all up for mementos? Take the lamp and the bedsheets and the clock? You know how these people are."

"They'll strip it like piranhas," Vic contributed.

"The company has still reserved it, so I haven't had to make a decision about it. But what would you do? They're offering outrageous amounts for it. I could redecorate it for what they're offering to pay. They can have the lamp and the clock for that price; I'll just get a new one. But what if they damage it structurally? Or do some damage that takes hundreds of dollars to fix?"

"It's still reserved by the production company?" Erin asked.

"Yes, that Meals and Reels. Until next week."

"And Mavis is staying in his room?"

Erin supposed that eliminated any hope she had of being able to see the room where Montgomery had died.

But did she really want to? Maybe it was best if she didn't have the option. She wouldn't have nightmares about it.

"No, she is staying in one of the other rooms. The one that he died in is still sitting empty."

"And it's the big one? You don't think I could see if it is what I want for my getaway with Officer Piper?" Erin suggested. "You can come with me, and I promise I won't strip it down. I just wanted to see if it would be... suitable."

Mrs. McClung frowned. "Maybe some other time."

CHAPTER 29

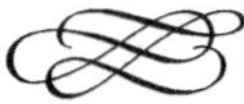

*E*rin nodded slowly. "I guess you're probably run off your feet with all this stuff. I don't want to add to your work."

Mrs. McClung nodded. She motioned to the box of strawberry preserves jars. "We can settle up for these." Her eyes went to the box Erin had brought from the General store. "And I do appreciate you bringing this over for me. That was a very nice thing to do."

"Mary Lou knew how busy you must be and wanted to make sure you got it," Erin said with a nod.

Mrs. McClung ran a key through the tape at the top of the box to slice it open, then pulled it open. She took out a couple of fat white candles and held them up to her nose. "I just love these vanilla candles that the General Store carries. They are so nice, give a room such elegance and atmosphere."

"I'll bet Montgomery loved them."

Mrs. McClung shook her head. "Fragrance-free. That means no scented candles. No flowers. No room freshener. Even the sheets were too heavily scented from the laundry detergent. Can you imagine that? Not being able to use laundry detergent?"

"Well, they do have unscented detergents. But a lot of people like scented sheets."

"They smell *fresh*," Mrs. McClung agreed. "If they don't smell like anything… people think they haven't been washed. They are always washed between guests. Always. But if people can't tell, they get upset."

"You can't win," Erin said sympathetically.

Mrs. McClung put the candles aside and peeked into the box to see what else it contained, but she didn't remove anything else.

"The strawberries are five dollars a bottle."

"I'll take all I can get."

"Six jars in there and, when you run out, give me a call and see how much I've got left. I'm sure I won't be through my stocks before you are ready for more."

As Erin settled up for the jars of preserves, there was the sound of footsteps on the stairs, and she looked up, expecting to get her first look at Mavis from the production company but, instead, it was a face she had seen before.

"Olivia Morgan," Erin said effusively. "The cookbook author! I didn't know you were staying here."

The woman looked pleased at being recognized. She looked at Erin for a moment before placing her.

"The baker. What are you doing here? You live here in town, don't you?"

"Yes, I just needed to pick up some more strawberries, and Mrs. McClung had a bumper crop from her garden this year."

"Well, that was lucky, wasn't it?" Olivia asked. "Well, not for Gerald Montgomery."

Erin felt like she'd been kicked in the stomach. "None of us knew that he was allergic to strawberries."

"No, I guess you didn't," Olivia agreed.

"So you're staying here?"

"Yes. Nice little place. A bit rustic, but sometimes you want to get away from all of the pressures of the city. Be somewhere you can chill and enjoy the country atmosphere. It's a nice little place. Mrs. McClung puts on a nice spread for breakfast, so that's one less thing to think about during the day. I'm going to leave her with one of my recipe books so that she can see how easy it is to prepare gluten-free baking for any guests that follow a special diet."

"Or she could just get baked goods at the bakery," Vic pointed out. "Which is entirely gluten-free."

Olivia looked at her for a minute, then turned back to Erin without acknowledging Vic's comment.

"Do you think I could see your room?" Erin asked. "I've never stayed here and I'd love to see one of the bedrooms, but they are all booked up."

"Well, of course," Olivia agreed. "I'm just on my way out right now but… well, I guess you could grab a quick peek before I go."

She turned around and climbed the stairs. Erin followed close behind her. Vic followed a few steps behind, leaving Mrs. McClung to watch them from below. But apparently, she didn't need to do anything upstairs and didn't see the need to supervise the visitors when Olivia herself had taken them up to show them the room.

Olivia used her key to unlock her door and opened it. "There you go," she offered. "It isn't anything unexpected. Once you've visited a few of these places, they all look the same. Some different quirks from one to the other, but mostly white bread…" She lifted her eyebrows. "And not gluten-free white bread."

Erin chuckled. She wasn't quite sure what Olivia meant, but smiled along with it anyway. She looked around at the room, which wasn't that different from a hotel room, with some homey touches. There was a bed, writing desk, flat screen TV anchored to the wall, a quilt rack which probably held the colorful quilt displayed there twelve months a year, and a small table with two chairs. Breakfast would be in the dining room downstairs, but Mrs. McClung didn't offer three meals a day so, if guests wanted to take it to their rooms, they had a place to eat it instead of sitting on the bed getting crumbs in the sheets.

There was a bud vase with a flower, some doilies, little shelves and plaques on the walls with funny or sweet sayings. The bed wasn't just the usual sheets, cheap blanket, and scratchy bedspread that Erin was used to seeing at cheap hotels; it was spread with a bright, hand-stitched bedspread and sheets that looked expensive.

Olivia caught her eyeing the unmade bed. "I wasn't expecting anyone," she said, laughing at herself. "My mother taught me always to make the bed… and I hardly ever do."

"It looks comfy," Erin observed. "How is the noise? Do you hear everything your neighbors say in the next room?"

"It's not soundproofed, but it isn't too bad. I've had a lot worse in hotels. These old houses were well-built with heavier materials. Not as much deadening as concrete walls, but not paper thin."

Erin thought about Montgomery complaining about the noise. Who had been next to him? One of his camera crew? A stranger? A fan who had managed to figure out where he was going to be staying in time to book the adjacent room before anyone else could?

"So, it's just you up here now?" she asked Olivia, knowing it wasn't the case.

"Oh, no. Not just me. One of Montgomery's staff is staying here, and she and the rest of the crew are coming and going at all hours. There's supposed to be a curfew, you know, so that you aren't keeping the other guests up, but it doesn't seem like it applies to Mavis from Meals and Reels." Her tone was sarcastic.

"I guess Mrs. McClung feels like it is a special case."

"I won't be here much longer. I'll be happy to get home, I guess."

"Why were you here? Just for a vacation? To see Mr. Montgomery?"

"You don't know him at all, do you?" Olivia questioned. "I mean… you don't know anything about him. The kind of person he was. It was like he went out of his way to bring other people down. I was doing great with my books and becoming known as a gluten-free chef. Had a good gig at a respected restaurant. And then he comes in, and…" Olivia trailed off and shook her head.

"He did what Gerald Montgomery does," Vic suggested from the doorway. "Insulted your cooking skills and wrecked your reputation."

Olivia nodded and spread her hands out in mute appeal. "I couldn't believe it. I hadn't ever done anything to hurt him. He had no idea who I was. I was just some faceless chef who had prepared his meal. He said… it was bland and tasteless. I can assure you it was not! He was out to get me. He wanted to hurt someone, and I was just a convenient target."

"I'm sorry." Erin touched her on the arm, just lightly, then let her fingers trail away. "That must have been really hard to deal with."

She tried to reconcile what Olivia said with her actions.

"Then… why were you here? Why would you follow him and stay at the same place?"

"I wanted another chance. I wanted him to taste some baking, to see that he'd been wrong about me. He just happened to be in a bad mood when he tasted my food before. So I hoped to get him to… give me another try."

Erin had a feeling that Gerald Montgomery didn't give anyone a second chance. You had one shot to impress him and, if that failed for some reason—whether because the food was bad or he was just a jerk in a bad mood—then that was it. You got what you got. Erin was glad she hadn't known more about him and his reputation before he had arrived. She would have been a wreck when he showed up at Auntie Clem's. It had been bad enough when she had thought he was just hard to please.

"But then you never got your chance. Did you stay here hoping someone else would take over for him? That you could get someone else on his crew to review it?"

Olivia shrugged in a way that Erin thought meant that had been her hope, but it hadn't worked out. She felt bad for not recognizing Olivia's name when she had first shown up at Auntie Clem's and for saying that she didn't work from cookbooks. Olivia had been through the wringer with Montgomery's review and was trying to get her name out there now. Erin's ignorance had just made her feel worse.

"Well, sorry it didn't work out," she sympathized. "I hope you can see some success… now that he's gone. Maybe people will forget about all of his reviews now. Move on to the next famous critic or chef."

"We can all hope so," Olivia agreed.

She motioned to the door, indicating that they should go. She had said she was on her way out, so Erin didn't want to hold her up any longer.

"Which room was Montgomery's?" Erin asked as they walked back into the hallway.

"The one in the middle. That one," Olivia indicated a doorway at the end of the hall, "is where Mavis is staying now. I think there might be a connecting door between them, but I'm not sure. I haven't gotten in to take a look."

Erin looked at Olivia, wondering if she were implying that Mavis or someone else from the crew might have had access to Montgomery's room from another direction. But it didn't matter. Montgomery's death had been ruled an accident, not homicide. There was no way anyone could have known that Erin was going to serve him muffins containing strawberries.

"Thanks for letting me see your room. I appreciate it."

"You should go over and talk to Mavis. I'm sure she could answer any questions that you have about how Montgomery died."

"I don't really have any questions…"

Olivia gave her a look that said she didn't believe a word of it, and then continued down the stairs.

Erin looked at the door. She was right there. Olivia had said that she should talk to Mavis. Erin assumed that Olivia and Mavis must have talked in the hallway or over breakfast, and Olivia knew what kind of a person Mavis was and how she would respond to questions from Erin about Montgomery.

She hadn't gotten the feeling that either Mrs. McClung or Olivia liked Mavis from Meals and Reels. But that didn't mean that Mavis couldn't answer a few questions. She had helped Terry with his questions about the allergy cards. She was probably the stereotypical type A personality—driven and efficient, but pushy and not terribly considerate of anyone else.

Erin could handle that.

CHAPTER 30

"Are you ready to go?" Vic asked, taking a step toward the stairs.

Vic hadn't wanted to go to the B&B to begin with. She had wanted to go shopping at the market. Then she went into the General Store with Erin to make sure that she cooled off and was okay. Then she came over to the B&B even though Erin told her that she didn't have to. Probably to keep Erin out of trouble and ensure she didn't get too over-heated on the way over there or the way back, carrying a box full of jars. Erin hadn't considered how awkward and hot it might be to walk back to the bakery with a box of jars of jam. They wouldn't be light, and it wouldn't be any cooler out.

Vic probably wanted to get back to the market before everything closed.

"If you want to go back, go ahead," she encouraged. "I think… I just wanted to ask a few more questions." Erin took a few uncertain steps toward the door at the end of the hall.

"More questions?" Vic shook her head and followed Erin. "What about? We already know what happened. I mean, you could watch the video and see it with your own eyes. I saw it, and I'm telling you, no one killed him. He had an allergic reaction and he just couldn't stop it. It all happened *so fast*," Vic got glittery-eyed as she considered it. "I never saw anything like it."

"I don't want to see it. I know that it was just an allergic reaction. But... someone sent me that message saying they had done me a favor. And what else could they mean?"

"How could killing Montgomery be a favor to you if it was actually done on purpose? Unless they knew that he was going to give you a bad review? And why would he? Your baking is fantastic. Everyone loves the muffins. He wasn't going to give you a bad review. So killing him... was probably the worst thing they could have done for you. They should have let him broadcast how good the muffins are. People would flock to Auntie Clem's. Killing him with your muffins had a better chance of shutting you down or putting you in prison than triggering this pilgrimage of everyone coming to taste the muffins."

"Is someone there?" came a voice from within the room.

Erin and Vic looked at each other, trying to decide what to say. There were footsteps, and the door opened.

Erin had been expecting an older, gray-haired woman. Mavis was an old name. Erin didn't think she'd ever met anyone under sixty by that name.

But the woman who opened the door was young, in her thirties, earnest-looking. In a dark gray tailored suit and white shirt, she looked like Erin had predicted—a type A corporate executive—just a very young one.

"Can I help you?" she demanded. "I didn't hear you knock."

"Uh, we hadn't yet," Erin said, feeling awkward. "We were just trying to decide whether or not to disturb you. I know you must have a lot to do here. Things are very disrupted. But..."

Mavis looked questioning, waiting for Erin to get to the point of what exactly she wanted. Why was she standing outside Mavis's door discussing whether to disturb her?

"Okay, well... I'm Erin Price."

Mavis looked at her for a minute as if she had no idea who that was or why Erin was there. Then the light came on.

"Erin Price. Auntie Clem's Bakery. You're the baker that Gerald was supposed to be reviewing."

"Yes," Erin agreed, looking down. "It was my muffins... my muffins that he was eating when... it happened."

"Your police chief said it was an accident," Mavis said. "Case closed.

No one blames you for what happened. I'm just as guilty for what happened as you are."

Erin shook her head. "Why?"

"I was the one who had the new cards made up and put them in his wallet. I told that detective who came by. If there were still old ones around that didn't list strawberries on them, then I am the one to blame. I was supposed to have swapped all of them out. And I thought I had. I don't know how he managed to give you an old one. He must have had some in his pants at home or somewhere I never thought of."

She threw her hands up, tears welling in her eyes. "It was my fault."

"He should have noticed, and he should have told me," Erin said. "He shouldn't just rely on someone else doing it. It was his life that was at stake. And he shouldn't have stopped me when I was going to tell him what was in the Morning Sunshine Muffins. He said he wanted to be surprised. But if he hadn't stopped me, it never would have happened. I was about to tell him they were filled with a strawberry compote. If he hadn't stopped me, he would have known."

"Oh, what a mess. Who would ever have thought that something like this could happen."

"Were you with Mr. Montgomery for long?"

"No, only a few months. And I was the one who insisted that he had to have the allergen cards so that he wouldn't end up sick or in the hospital from an accidental exposure."

"Did you like working with him?"

"Well… he wasn't the easiest guy to work with, I'll admit. But if you ignored the personality… and the criticisms…" Mavis gave a little laugh. "Well, it was a good job."

Erin wondered what would be left to be good about it. Maybe when Montgomery was away and out of her hair, there were other parts of the job that Mavis liked. Or perhaps it paid well. She hoped so. Mavis was young and inexperienced; maybe she didn't know how to be assertive with Montgomery and insist that she be paid what she was worth.

"Will you be staying on with the company now that he is gone?"

"I don't know yet. We'll have to see what happens. I assume they'll get another personality to take over for Mr. Montgomery, but he may come with his own staff, and then I'll be gone."

"How much longer will you be in Bald Eagle Falls?" Vic asked.

"Well, I guess that now that the police investigation is closed, I'll be moving out of here pretty soon. I needed to be here to take care of anything the police or anyone needed. The company wanted to make sure that we were fully cooperating with the police and to control messaging."

"Do you think we could see Mr. Montgomery's room on our way out?" Erin asked as they turned back toward the stairs.

Mavis frowned. "Why would you want to do that?"

"Well, I suppose it might sound a little gruesome," Erin admitted while trying to figure out how to make it sound less so. Did she really want to see the place where Montgomery had died? It was better than seeing the video of him dying. She had no desire to see that. "I just… want to be able to put it all together in my mind. What happened to him. It all started with my muffins… I wish it hadn't. I wish this had happened to him somewhere else, with someone else's strawberry dish. Or maybe he would have seen the strawberries in something else. But I just…"

Mavis didn't seem to need a more coherent explanation. Maybe the fact that Erin was vague and rambling was to her benefit.

"I suppose," Mavis said reluctantly. "It isn't like it's a shrine or still a police scene or anything like that. It's just… a bedroom. And it's booked until I tell Mrs. McClung the company doesn't want it anymore."

Mavis exited her room and walked past Erin and Vic in the narrow hallway to the middle bedroom.

"Did Mr. Montgomery complain a lot?" Erin asked. "Mrs. McClung said something about the noise, but it seems pretty quiet up here."

"I think that other woman, the gluten-free author, kept doing things that irritated him. I doubt she was that loud. That was before I got here. He kept calling me and telling me that it was untenable. The noise, the smells, people coming and going all the time, his phone constantly ringing." She shrugged. "He was a celebrity. What did he expect?"

"His phone?" Erin repeated. "What did he expect Mrs. McClung to do about the phone? Do you mean the phone in his room kept ringing?"

"No, his cell phone. That wasn't a complaint he made to her. Or if he did, you're right; there isn't anything she could do about it. But he wanted me to track down who kept calling and hanging up on him. It was his personal cell phone and no one was supposed to have the number, but someone must have gotten it, somehow. He lost his wallet one night, so maybe he had something in there that someone traced… I don't know. It's not like I am a cop or some CSI tech. I asked the phone provider for a list of the numbers he'd been talking to, but the one that kept hanging up on him was a blocked caller. It didn't show who it was on his phone activity statement either. The phone company says they don't share information like that. If it's blocked, it's blocked. Only the police can subpoena it."

Mavis put her key in the lock and opened Montgomery's bedroom door.

CHAPTER 31

*E*rin looked around. She didn't know what she had been expecting. There was nothing menacing about the room. It was bright and pleasant. The same type of furnishings and decorations as she had already seen in Olivia's and Mavis's rooms. Old fashioned, homey, the restful atmosphere Montgomery had probably sought.

It wasn't dank or dusty. Erin had been braced for the smell of death, even though she knew it had been several days since Montgomery's body had been there, and he had only been there for a few hours after death.

"Can I go in?"

Mavis shrugged. Erin entered the room and moved slowly around, taking in her surroundings. She didn't know what she was looking for. Nothing, really; she just wanted to reassure herself that, as everyone kept telling her, this had not been an intentional death. No one could have known or predicted it. No one could have planned it.

Montgomery's suitcase and equipment were still there. Mavis would take them back with her, presumably. And give them to whom? Was there a next of kin? Someone to take his personal things and whatever money he had made? Who benefited financially from his death?

Erin imagined Montgomery in that bedroom, sitting down at the table, which was slightly larger than the one in Olivia's room, and setting out the muffins for tasting. Had his auto-injectors been close at hand?

Across the room in his luggage? What had made this allergy attack so fast and severe that even with his epinephrine at his table, he'd been unable to stop it?

And why hadn't he had anyone with him? He'd had a camera crew and a number of people who had come into the bakery with him. Why not keep one of them on hand during the tasting of any unfamiliar food to make sure that he was safe and didn't come to harm?

Erin heard the stairs creaking and footsteps as Mrs. McClung made her way up. She flashed a quick look at Vic and decided they had seen enough of the bedroom and it was time to get out of there. She didn't want to give the proprietor any reason for concern. They were out of the room and shutting the door when Mrs. McClung reached the top of the stairs.

Erin smiled at Mrs. McClung reassuringly. "We were just coming back down."

The woman did not return her smile. She looked around as if to see what havoc the two young women had been raising since they had come up with Olivia and then not gone back downstairs again.

"This is a private residence," she pointed out. "I did not give you permission to have the run of the place. I told you earlier that you could look at the bedrooms on the website. You didn't need to come up here. There's no reason for you to harass my guests. I can't understand why you would do such a thing."

"No, we weren't doing anything to harass them." Erin looked at Mavis for her to confirm that they hadn't been doing anything intrusive. "We just... I thought I would talk to Mavis while we were up here. We didn't even knock on the door; she just heard us talking and came out to see what was happening. I didn't mean to disturb anyone."

Mrs. McClung looked significantly at the door to Mr. Montgomery's room. "And you had to go in there? Why? Don't try telling me that you just wanted to have a look at it because you might want to honeymoon here with your sweetheart. I wasn't born yesterday, you know. I know when someone tries to pull the wool over my eyes."

"We just wanted to see it," Erin said. She didn't have a good explanation. She didn't even understand why she found the need to go in there and have a look around. She knew what had happened. If she wanted to, she could even see a video of what had happened. The police and the medical examiner had ruled it an accident, and that was the best outcome for her. She didn't want to be held responsible for having given Montgomery something that had harmed and ultimately killed him. So what was she doing messing around now? Giving them a reason to look at her further?

"I'm sorry. I didn't mean to cause you any problems. I didn't think there was any harm in just looking at the room."

"My guests have their right to privacy. That room is still rented by someone else. Not either of you." She turned and looked at Mavis. "And not even you. You just work for the company that has it booked. You have the right to be in there if there is something you need, but that doesn't mean you have the right to let other people in there, not without the approval of your company. Why would they want Erin Price in there?"

Mavis blushed. She shrugged her shoulders and looked down. She had looked young before; now, she looked even younger. She looked like a child taken to task for helping herself to a cookie before supper. Shamefaced that she had taken advantage of the privileges she had been given and had made a wrong choice.

"Now," Mrs. McClung said heavily. "It is time to take your jars of preserves and go. I appreciate you bringing me my delivery from the General Store, but I hope not to see you again any time soon."

Erin felt her face getting red. She didn't like being treated like a child in front of the others either. She had thought that she was being subtle about her investigations, but she had obviously not been. Mrs. McClung had seen right through her, and probably everyone else had, too.

"Yes, of course," she agreed, heading down the stairs with Vic as if this had been their next planned move, not that they had been caught with their fingers in the cookie jar and had them slapped. Vic looked embarrassed enough for them both, and none of it had been her idea. Erin felt bad for leading her into trouble, and murmured an apology on the way down the stairs.

Mavis returned to her room. They heard it click shut behind them as they returned to the main floor.

As they reached the front room, there was a quick knock on the front door, and then it opened. Erin saw Terry on the threshold with K9.

"Mrs. McClung?" Terry called before seeing them all there. "Oh."

Terry's lips thinned and his face tightened as he looked at them. "Erin. What are you doing here?"

"I just brought Mrs. McClung a delivery and was picking up some more strawberry preserves," Erin told him quickly, picking up the box filled with jars. She glanced around. "What are you doing here?"

"There's been a complaint."

Erin looked back at Mrs. McClung, her face flaming even hotter. She had called the police on them? Even knowing that Terry was Erin's partner?

It was bad enough that she had called the police, but then for Terry to be the one to answer the call… Erin tried to swallow her embarrassment.

"We were just leaving."

"Good. You and I can talk about this later." Terry looked back over his shoulder. He groaned and shook his head. "And you have the press to deal with, too."

Advancing to the door, Erin saw a reporter and camera crew approaching the house. She had seen them around town, but she had refused to talk to them at Auntie Clem's and had sent them on their way. Now she didn't have the advantage of being able to kick them off her property. And she couldn't even jump into her car and escape, because it was still parked back at the bakery, where they had left it while shopping at the street market.

Erin looked at Terry for help, but he just shook his head. What was he supposed to do about it? He was there as a law enforcement officer responding to a complaint, not as her friend or romantic partner. He couldn't take either of those roles in front of the reporters. He didn't need the Bald Eagle Falls police department taking any flak because he had treated a possible offender like a friend.

Erin marched past Terry and K9 with the box of jars. She flinched at the furnace-like summer heat. Vic followed in her wake. Erin didn't imagine Vic felt any better about the situation than Erin did, and none of it had been her doing.

"Miss Price," the reporter called. "What are you doing here at the bed and breakfast where Gerald Montgomery was killed? Why would you want to be here after what happened? After what you were responsible for?"

"I wasn't responsible for his death," Erin protested, over Vic's declarations of, "No comment, no comment!"

"It was your Morning Sunshine Muffins that killed him. Isn't that true?"

"It isn't my fault because he never told me he was allergic to strawberries. And that's been proven. I turned in the card he gave me to the police, and they can confirm that it doesn't include strawberries."

"Has that been proven?" the reporter immediately asked of Terry, turning the microphone toward him. Terry gave Erin an angry look.

"Gerald Montgomery's death was determined to be an accident. That's all the police department has to say about it."

"But just *how* accidental was it?" the reporter pressed. "Shouldn't Miss Price have known his allergies before cooking for him? Wouldn't that have made more sense?"

"I can't speak for Mr. Montgomery or his company's practices," Terry pointed out.

"You have been in contact with his company during the course of the investigation, haven't you? What did your investigation show? Was there negligence on the part of Auntie Clem's Bakery staff?"

"If you don't want to be sued for slander, I would be very careful what you say."

"It was only a question. We haven't made any accusations of wrongdoing."

"You're blocking the sidewalk," Terry told the reporter and his crew. "If you would please step aside and let people through."

Under Terry's stern eye, they did move aside and make room for Erin and Vic to walk by them to head back to Auntie Clem's.

The box of jars was already heavy and Erin knew that by the time she got back to the bakery, her arms would be aching and she would be soaked with sweat. She really didn't like Tennessee summers.

CHAPTER 32

*E*rin knew she was going to be under fire when she and Terry both got home that evening. They were in the kitchen, where Erin had hoped to make a cup of tea that would help to keep things calm and civilized. But Terry had been embarrassed by being called to the scene where it had appeared that Erin was the guilty party, and by having to face the press over the incident. His ego wasn't going to be soothed by a cup of tea. He wouldn't sit down with her, but paced back and forth across the kitchen trying to deal with all of his burning energy.

"What were you thinking, Erin?" he demanded in frustration. "I can't understand you going over to the bed and breakfast and making trouble over there. What was the point of that? The whole thing has been declared an accident. You are in the clear. There will be no consequences. And then… this. I don't understand you at all."

"I wasn't… I didn't go over there to make trouble," Erin said hotly. "And I wasn't doing anything wrong. I just took a delivery over to Mrs. McClung and asked her about getting more strawberries. The rest… just happened. I was there anyway. I just talked to the people who were there, who knew something about Mr. Montgomery and what had happened. I wasn't doing anything to bother anyone. They talked to me freely. It was only Mrs. McClung who got her panties in a twist."

Erin had never even used the phrase before. That just went to show

how upset she was about the whole thing. She shouldn't need to defend herself. She hadn't done anything wrong.

"It wasn't Mrs. McClung. Just because someone didn't tell you to your face that you were bothering them or file a police complaint, that doesn't mean that you *weren't* bothering them. It just means they were too polite to tell you to take a hike."

"Olivia and Mavis were *fine* with me talking to them. I wasn't pushy. I just asked them a few questions…"

"You shouldn't have been there and you shouldn't have been asking any questions. Why can't you let this go?"

Erin hated raised voices. She hated confrontation. That didn't mean she was a shrinking violet and couldn't express her opinion, but she hated arguing with Terry over anything.

"Because it was my muffins that killed him!" she growled at him. "Why can't you understand that?"

"It was an accident. It wasn't done intentionally, I know that. The police department knows that. It's been declared an accidental death. So why would you want to stir things up more?"

"I don't want to. I want to… understand it. I want to know what happened and understand why it happened, because it doesn't make any sense to me. I know how to cook for allergies. I know how to take care of people. This shouldn't have happened!"

"Of course not," Terry said, dropping his volume and trying to sound sympathetic. "I understand that it was a shock. It was a terrible thing, and you would have done anything to avoid it. But it happened. It was more Montgomery's fault than anyone else's because he didn't take proper precautions. But you need to put it behind you and stop making everybody else miserable. You're getting the press and others in town stirred up, thinking that there was more to it. And there wasn't. It was just an accident."

Erin gritted her teeth, trying to ignore his tone and deal with what he was telling her. She knew it was true. She had been obsessing too much over Montgomery's death, and there was nothing she could have done to prevent it. It had been Gerald Montgomery's responsibility to tell her what he was allergic to, not hers to figure out or guess at. She had followed the directions he had given her and that should be the end of it.

She had been worried that the police would find that she had some culpability in it or the company or estate would sue her.

All those worries had been resolved, but she still felt like she needed to do more. Everyone else was satisfied with the answers that the medical examiner and police department had provided. Why couldn't Erin be?

"I just... I don't know. I don't understand it myself," Erin told him, shaking her head.

Terry looked in the fridge and then slammed the door shut, frustrated by her responses. Erin knew he wanted to solve the problem, to fix things for her, to actually do something to make everything better. But he couldn't do that. No one could.

"I'm sorry," Erin told him.

"You don't have to apologize for your feelings. I just wish I could... you need to understand that even if you aren't happy with it, you can't keep pursuing this. You can't stir everyone else up. We want this to blow over and things to return to normal. As long as you are providing the media with fodder and his fans are coming here for muffins... it isn't going to happen. Can't you just let it go?"

Erin opened her mouth to respond, though she didn't know what she was going to say to him. But there was a quick knock at the back door, and Vic burst in.

CHAPTER 33

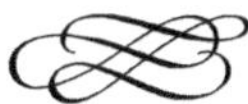

Strands of her hair were pasted to Vic's face. Even when Erin had been soaked in sweat that afternoon, Vic had looked as cool as any southern belle. But now, everything was in disarray, and her eyes were wide and frightened.

"Vic! What is it?" Erin sprang to her feet, the lethargy she had been feeling a moment before disappearing in a flash. She was on her feet before Terry finished turning around to look at Vic.

"It's Willie. Something is wrong. I need to take him into the hospital, but..." Vic shook her head. "I can drive, but you know I don't have a... car." At the last moment, she looked at Terry and replaced "license" with "car." She didn't have either one, but Erin could see that she had been about to say she didn't have a driver's license, but then didn't want to admit it in front of Terry. As if Terry hadn't already figured it out.

"We'll drive," Erin said immediately. "I guess one of the trucks. The bug is too small." She looked at Terry. "We could use your lights and siren."

"Of course," Terry agreed. "Do you want me to drive it around back?"

Vic nodded. "Yeah. That would be really helpful. Thanks. I'll bring him down."

"Do you need help?" Erin asked Vic.

"No… I don't want too many people on the stairs; someone will trip and fall down."

Erin nodded. The staircase was steep and wasn't made for three people walking together. She hoped that Willie could walk on his own, not wanting him to rely on Vic for support as they descended the stairs. There was a sturdy railing.

Terry left by the front door to get his truck. K9 was immediately at his heels, eager to know what was going on, ears pricked up alertly. Erin shut the door behind him and locked it. Then she went out the back door, setting the burglar alarm and waiting anxiously for Vic to bring Willie down the stairs.

Willie was able to walk under his own power. He held on to the handrails on both sides of the stairs, moving down them slowly ahead of Vic. Erin could hear Vic arguing that she should go first to help Willie if he fell. Willie, in turn, argued that he didn't want to fall on her and injure her. Two hard-headed people wanting to help each other.

When they reached the bottom of the stairs, Erin could see why Vic was so concerned. Willie was pale, with a number of welts on his face and neck. He was scowling and didn't give Erin his usual reassuring smile. Once he was at the bottom of the stairs, Vic hurried forward to steady him in his walk to the truck, which Terry was pulling around the back. Willie struggled to maintain his balance but, with Vic's support, he managed to stay on his feet. She wasn't carrying his weight, but providing a steadying shoulder.

Terry jumped down out of the truck to give Vic a hand. "Let's get him into the front seat. That will be the quickest to get him in and out of."

"I don't need help," Willie protested, swatting at Terry's hand to start with, but then taking the proffered shoulder a few seconds later. "It's just a headache," he insisted. "They said that was one of the side effects of chelation. I'll just sleep it off."

"You've been trying to sleep it off all day," Vic told him sternly. "This is serious. I can feel it in my bones. I'm not going to let you argue me out of this."

Willie allowed them to guide him into the cab of the truck. They boosted him up onto the seat.

"Erin, why don't you and K9 take the back," Terry suggested. "I'm sorry, I just think it's best if he is in front with me and Vic."

"Of course it is," Erin agreed. She had CPR and first aid training, but Terry's training was more extensive than hers, and Vic had a better chance of recognizing the instant anything changed and worming out of Willie what he was feeling.

Erin climbed into the back seat and called K9 to her. He sat on the seat beside her and watched the activity in the front seat with interest. As soon as Vic's door was shut, Terry reversed the truck and flipped on the lights and siren, heading for the highway.

He waited until he was on a straight section of the road before looking at Willie and asking him a few questions to evaluate his condition.

"So, you've been having headaches?"

"It's perfectly normal," Willie said, slurring slightly. "I've been having headaches after every treatment. And between treatments. In fact, I have a headache almost all the time."

"But this one is worse," Vic contributed. "It isn't usually this bad. He's been nauseated and throwing up."

"That's all part of the treatment. Sometimes it hits me the wrong way. This isn't the first time I've been sick from it." Willie rubbed his forehead slowly, but it didn't seem to be giving him any relief.

"What else?" Terry asked. "You look like something that crawled in from the swamp."

Willie chuckled at this. He fingered one of the welts on his face. "They said I could have rashes or hives. My system is full of toxins. It's not unusual to have a skin reaction to the toxins or chelation agents."

"Any trouble breathing?"

"No." Willie's head shook back and forth ponderously, as if it were very heavy. "Breathing just fine."

But Erin had noticed him breathing hard when he had come down the stairs. It wasn't surprising that he would be tired climbing up the stairs, but it was unusual for him to get out of breath going down a single flight of stairs.

Terry's foot was pressed to the gas pedal, and they were moving down the highway faster than Erin would have been comfortable driving. As Terry asked Willie questions, his attention was split between the road and his passenger's condition.

"They're gonna tell you everything is fine," Willie told Vic. "I should have just stayed home and slept."

"You've been sleeping all the time lately," Vic told him, "I'm kind of worried about it, if you want to know the truth."

"Sleep is the best thing for me. The body's way of healing."

Vic didn't repeat that it had been too much. That would just aggravate Willie further, but she glanced back at Erin to see what she thought. Erin shrugged. She happened to agree that the amount of time Willie had been sleeping lately was excessive. But people who were sick often slept. She agreed with Willie too, that it was probably what his body needed. That and good food to nourish and strengthen his body.

"How have you been eating?" she asked, thinking about his having a beer with Terry the other day. She knew he had been specifically counseled to stay away from alcohol.

"Vic's a good cook," Willie said. "Everything has been just fine."

"You've been following the instructions the doctors have given you for what you should be eating? Or not eating?"

Willie rubbed his forehead. "More or less."

Erin looked at Vic, but Vic didn't meet her eyes or make any comment on whether Willie had been following the diet instructions given to him by the clinic doing the chelation therapy.

"I'm doing what I'm supposed to," Willie told Erin, his eyes closed and head back. "You might think you would do better, but it's not easy trying to follow all the instructions. They said that the symptoms would be mild, but I can tell you they are anything but mild. And I'm no wuss as far as being sick goes. I'm not one of those people who whines and takes to his bed at the first sign of a sniffle."

"I know you haven't been feeling well," Erin told him. "I'm not trying to say that's because you haven't been 'doing it right.' Just wondering… if there's anything we can do to help. To make it easier on you."

"How about letting me sleep instead of dragging me to the hospital?"

Erin looked at Vic. Despite Willie's assurances that everything was fine and he just needed to sleep, he looked like death warmed over. And Erin knew that Vic wouldn't insist that Willie needed to be taken to the hospital without good reason. She had seen the look of panic in Vic's eyes when she had burst into the house. She was really worried.

"What is it you were the most worried about?" Erin asked her.

Vic hovered over Willie, watching him like a hawk. She stroked a lock of hair on his temple. "He's just not himself… he was having chest pains and palpitations. And the headache… it's not just a headache." She shook her head. "He hasn't had one like this before."

"I've had plenty of headaches," Willie said, eyes still closed.

"I know. And this one isn't like any you've ever had before, is it?"

"I just want to go to sleep."

Vic looked at Erin and shook her head helplessly. Erin nodded her sympathy and gave Vic's shoulder an encouraging squeeze. She didn't know what to do about Willie's symptoms, but they would be at the hospital in record time at the speed that Terry was driving. When Erin thought about Willie's pallor and everything else Vic had mentioned, she got a knot in her gut that wouldn't go away.

Willie was still. His breath rasped noisily. He had apparently gone to sleep as he had wanted to. Vic stroked his hair lightly so as not to wake him up. She shook her head.

"I worry about him so much. This whole thing has been much worse than they ever told us. I know they said that his levels of heavy metals were so high it was hard to believe he was still working normally and wasn't obviously sick. I thought he would just fly through the detox. He'd go from feeling a bit irritable and moody to being calm and mellow. I wasn't expecting all of the physical symptoms. It's like he's a chemo patient."

Erin didn't like the sound of Willie's breathing, growing louder and raspier. She touched his carotid and felt for his pulse.

Vic looked at her worriedly. "What is it?"

"I don't like his breathing. His pulse is… fast and irregular. If he's sleeping, it should be slow."

"I told you he was having palpitations. I was worried he was going to have a heart attack."

Erin nodded. "We'll be at the hospital before too long and they'll take care of him."

They were all tense and didn't know what to say to make the others feel better. Terry was occupied with driving, so it mostly fell to Erin and Vic to stay on top of Willie's condition. They listened tensely to his breathing, waiting for each new breath to be regular and whether it would be better or worse sounding than the previous one.

It seemed like it took forever to reach the city limits, even though Erin knew Terry had been pushing the truck as fast as he could safely go. Erin breathed a sigh of relief.

She remembered Willie running her to the hospital when she had been poisoned. He had sung to her, trying to keep her awake and alert. His singing had been terrible. But he had gotten her there in time for the doctors to treat her. And they would see that he got the treatment he needed too.

Terry weaved through the streets and, eventually, they reached the hospital's emergency entrance. Vic put her hand on Willie's shoulder and shook him gently.

"We're here, Willie. Time to wake up for a few minutes."

He didn't respond. Vic shook him harder.

"Come on, Willie. Wake up!"

Erin knew what it was like to try to rouse someone who would never wake up. Heart in her throat, she pinched Willie hard and he stirred, swatting at her. "Ow!"

Vic repeated that it was time to get out, and he managed to slide himself across the seat to the door and land without collapsing on the sidewalk outside the truck. Erin climbed out behind him. It was easy to see that he was leaning on Vic for more than just balance this time. Vic struggled to hold him up. Erin hurried to his other side to support him from there.

"I'm just fine," Willie protested. "Don't need to be treated like an invalid. I'm just fine."

But even as he protested, he leaned on Erin as well, and the two of them together were still straining. They staggered forward a few steps, and an orderly outside for a smoke break quickly put out his cigarette and grabbed a wheelchair. He efficiently settled Willie into it, quelling his protests.

"It's procedure," he insisted. Once Willie was sitting, the orderly grabbed the handles of the wheelchair to push Willie into the emergency department, walking briskly past the lineup at triage and swiping his card to get past a locked door to jump the queue. A few nurses and other professionals hurried in to help him, asking questions and leaning over Willie to check his vitals and talk to him.

Vic leaned against Erin, sniffling. "Now what?"

Erin took in a deep breath, sucking in the smells of antiseptic, cleaners, and the faint smell of fries.

"Now we wait and see what they can tell us. They won't be able to tell us anything right away. But they're going to need to ask you questions. Whatever Willie can't answer himself."

"He can answer all of them. They won't need me for anything."

But Erin had seen how Willie was and knew he would not be answering many questions. He might be able to answer the basics about who he was and that he was going through chelation therapy, but Erin didn't think he would be able to manage much beyond that.

"Come on. Let's get over to where they can find you when they need you."

She led Vic over to the triage area. The heavy nurse triaging patients looked at them and pointed in Willie's direction, raising her brows questioningly. Erin nodded in response. The nurse gave her a nod in return and continued talking to the patient before her. When she had dealt with him and sent him back to wait in the chairs area, she motioned to Erin and Vic. Erin pushed Vic forward.

"They need to talk to you."

Vic looked over her shoulder at Erin as she stepped forward, looking uncertain and abandoned. But Erin knew how strong she was and that she would be able to handle it once the nurse started asking her questions. Erin went back to the waiting area and found Terry. One of the benefits of driving an emergency vehicle to the hospital was that he could park in the reserved area, nice and close to the doors. He didn't have to search for a parking space and pay an arm and a leg for it.

"They took him straight in?" Terry asked, looking past Erin to see Vic talking to the triage nurse.

"Yeah."

"That's Good. They'll stabilize him, and then can start to figure out what's going on with him."

"Do you think it's all because of the chelation therapy?"

"I'm sure that's probably the trigger—or rather, the heavy metal poisoning is. And that can cause all kinds of problems. I read all about it when we were looking into Fontainebleau's death. It can affect all of the body's systems."

"It's good we got him here when we did." Erin gazed toward the triage area. "I don't know what would have happened if they had waited any longer."

CHAPTER 34

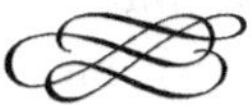

Erin knew it would be hours before they would have any real news about Willie and what had gone wrong with his treatment. Terry offered to drive her home and then to return for Vic when she was ready to come home, but Erin shook her head. She wanted to be there for Vic, just as Vic was always there for her. And Willie was a good friend. She wouldn't be able to sleep without knowing that he was stable and out of danger. She wanted to hear that they understood what was happening and were treating him for it.

That was a lot to ask. How often did people get sent home from the hospital without the doctors having the slightest idea what was happening? Hospital shows on TV might give the impression that hospitals can always effectively diagnose and treat even the most obscure diseases, but real-life experiences were far less impressive. Erin knew plenty of people who had been sent home without a diagnosis or with the wrong diagnosis or treatment.

They would be able to help Willie.

He was important to Erin and Vic. The doctors would be able to find out what had gone wrong and teach them how to keep it from happening again.

She hoped.

In the meantime, Erin had to call the various employees to make sure that someone could cover for her and Vic in the morning. Erin would be back in the afternoon, she assumed, but those early hours would have to be covered so that Auntie Clem's could open on time in the morning and serve the early customers their morning muffins.

K9 lay by Terry on the floor, occasionally sighing or groaning and shifting to another position. He didn't like lying around, and Erin didn't suppose the cold hard tiles were much fun to sleep on. She took him outside a couple of times to stretch his legs and sniff all the interesting nighttime smells. She and Terry took turns. It was, Erin thought, a little like keeping a toddler entertained—a very smart toddler who didn't have much to say.

Eventually, Vic came out to the waiting room.

"The doctor said that I was right to bring him in," she told them, as if she needed to justify her actions, though neither Erin nor Terry had given her even the suggestion that they thought she was overreacting to Willie's condition. "He was having irregular heart rhythms, as well as the rest of the stuff. He shouldn't be having this bad a reaction to the chelation therapy, but some people do. Especially if the poisoning was very bad."

"And we know Willie's was," Erin put in.

Vic nodded. "They should have told us back at the beginning that the worse the poisoning, the worse the chelation side effects would be. Then, at least, we might have been prepared for some of what had gone on instead of being blindsided when they said that the side effects of chelation are usually mild."

Erin and Terry nodded. Erin leaned forward in her seat. "And his breathing? They got that sorted out? I was really worried about how he sounded. He doesn't always sound like that when he sleeps, does he?"

"No. A bit of snoring now and then, but not that breathing he was doing in the car. The doctors said it was anaphylaxis."

"Really? I thought that it would be a lot more severe if he had anaphylaxis."

"His throat was closed almost all the way by the time we got him here. They had to put a tube down to help him breathe. They said it will be taken out soon, they don't expect him to need it for a long time. But I guess not all anaphylaxis is fast like you see on TV. Or like it was for Montgomery. Sometimes it can take a few hours, and it doesn't always involve breathing problems." Vic shook her head to try to accustom herself to this new information. "I guess it's like a Hollywood heart attack. We expect it to look one way because that's how it is always portrayed in the media, but there are different kinds, and it can look really different."

Erin nodded. "Anaphylaxis is a life-threatening allergic reaction. It might be less obvious symptoms. If you have a reaction that causes symptoms in several body systems—skin, digestive, respiratory, circulatory—then it is considered anaphylaxis. But what was he allergic to? Did he have a different treatment than usual? Did they change things around?"

"They said sometimes it can be triggered by stress or exercise, not necessarily an allergen. Or that if he is stressed out, that could turn a normally mild reaction into anaphylaxis."

"I thought anaphylaxis was always caused by an allergy."

Vic shrugged. "Apparently not. I guess sometimes people get it just from exercise, like an asthma attack. Willie's had side effects from the therapy right from the start. I guess those can indicate a mild allergic reaction, but they don't worry about it too much if it isn't life-threatening or keeping him from getting further treatment."

"Maybe he should have gotten treatment for the side effects earlier."

"Maybe. But you know how men are." Vic looked at Terry. "They don't like to ask for help. Don't like to admit that they might not be able to handle things on their own. And Willie prides himself on not being a whiner about getting sick, like some guys."

Erin appreciated that Willie didn't become a helpless infant when he got a cold or flu bug, but he still needed to take care of himself and talk to his doctor about his symptoms.

"So why do they think this happened now? Was it all of the treatments adding up, or the amount of metals being pulled from his body now? Or do they think it is from a different allergen trigger or stressor?"

Vic sat in one of the plastic chairs across from where Erin and Terry were sitting.

"Doctor said that we might never know. They'll do their best to figure out the trigger so we can avoid it happening again."

"How are they going to figure it out?"

Vic flourished a stack of papers. "Questionnaire time. Full history since he started treatment, any previous medical history, especially any previous reactions or allergies, things that have been going on in his life lately. All of the medications he had taken, not just the chelation agents but any over-the-counter medications, herbs, vitamins, or alternative treatments. Changes in diet, samples of his dietary plan…"

"Wow. Can I see?"

Vic raised her brows and handed it over to Erin. "You want to fill it out too?" she teased.

"I don't think so." Erin was not sure why she even wanted to look at the papers. She wasn't a big reader, and there was a lot there to digest. She promised herself that she only needed to skim. She didn't need to read everything. "I just wanted to take a quick look."

Before the night was over, Willie was moved to a room so they could visit him briefly before heading back to Bald Eagle Falls.

He had more color in his face, Erin noted. The welts she had noted earlier, hives from the reaction, had disappeared. He was hooked up to a pulse oximeter so that his vitals were shown on the screen on the monitor beside him. Everything seemed to fall into normal parameters, except his blood pressure seemed slightly low. Erin knew that lower blood pressure could be normal for Willie, either genetic or because he was in good physical condition. With all of his physical work and caving, Erin assumed it was because his body was working efficiently, not because of anaphylaxis. They would be watching for any recurrence of those symptoms.

"Hey, Willie," she greeted, giving him a warm, reassuring smile. "How are you doing?"

"Feeling a lot better," he admitted. "Whatever they gave me is working."

"You're looking much better, old man," Terry observed. "Not like you're at death's door anymore."

Willie rubbed his head. "It wasn't *that* bad."

"Who do you think you're kidding?" Vic demanded. "You had to be intubated to keep you breathing. Your heartbeat was irregular. Your blood pressure was barely registering. If Terry hadn't kept the pedal to the metal and used his lights and siren, we might not have gotten you here fast enough. You should be thanking him for getting you here before you died."

"It wasn't that bad," Willie grumbled. "I would have slept it off."

Vic rolled her eyes and shook her head at Erin.

Men. So stubborn.

"How long will you be here? Have they given you any idea?" Erin asked Willie.

"I don't think it will be long. I don't need to be here now; they just want to monitor me for a while to make sure that I don't… start having trouble again."

"You'd better stay for a day or two," Vic told him sternly. "This was serious, and if I hadn't been home or Terry hadn't been able to get you here quickly enough, that might have been the end of the road for you."

"But I'm okay now. And we know what to watch for if it happens again. Time is money."

"Your business can wait for a day or two. What would have happened to it if you had died? Or been so disabled by this that you couldn't do anything anymore?"

"They charge an arm and a leg to stay here," he grumbled, "I'd be just as good recovering at home."

Vic shook her head adamantly. "You're staying here until I'm sure they've got everything sorted out."

Willie rolled his eyes. But Erin could see his affection for Vic and that he would do as she said and stay there until she was convinced that it was safe for him to go home again.

"What about one of those watches?" Erin asked. "A lot of the sports watches now will tell you if you are having heart trouble. I'm always hearing about how it saved this person or that one who didn't even know that they had a problem."

Willie's eyes gleamed. He was a tech guy, and the idea appealed to him. "I can get one of those. They can send out alerts, too. So even if I was asleep or couldn't get to a phone, it would let everyone know."

Of course, *everyone* in this case was Vic.

"That sounds like a good idea," she agreed. "But it doesn't replace doctors. You're going to have to have your heart checked. Make sure this was just a one-time reaction, not some disease or disorder needing treatment or regular monitoring."

Erin couldn't help grinning at the young girl ordering Willie around and telling him what he needed to do to take care of his health. Willie nodded his agreement and promised to get the help that he needed.

"I plan to be here for a long time," he told Vic. "On this planet, not in the hospital. I don't plan on leaving any time soon."

Vic nodded, her eyes glistening with tears. "You'd better. If you up and died, I would kill you!"

Willie was home from the hospital, but Vic still wasn't ready to leave him alone, so the other employees covered her usual shifts during the week. The furor from Montgomery's death was starting to dissipate, with fewer Morning Sunshine Muffins being ordered each day and not so many strangers hanging around town.

Terry was happy to see that Erin had abandoned her obsession with what had happened to Montgomery and that things were getting back to normal.

Except that they weren't. Erin had managed to stay out of trouble and to keep Terry from noticing that she still had something on her mind. Or maybe he noticed that she was still troubled but just happy that she wasn't drawing attention to herself by questioning random Bald Eagle Falls residents or talking to the media.

But that didn't mean Erin was done.

"I've been thinking about Gerald Montgomery and how he had such a severe reaction to the strawberries," she said to Vic over tea one evening.

Vic raised her brows. "Oh? I thought you had decided to leave the subject alone."

Erin shrugged. "No. I know Terry doesn't want me involved in it, but..."

"But you are," Vic finished. She shook her head but didn't try to dissuade Erin. "So… you're wondering about his reaction. He was apparently *really* allergic to strawberries."

"But when we looked at his stuff online, that's not something he had ever reacted to before. So it had to be a recently developed allergy or one that had gotten more severe over time."

"Okay…?"

"And the videos where he'd had a reaction, he'd always been able to handle it before. I mean, I know we keep saying that it was his own fault because he didn't have someone in the room with him or have every ingredient checked like he should, but he'd never had a reaction that was that severe before. Had he?"

"I don't know if he ever had, but not on any of the videos we watched. And certainly, nothing that was *that* bad, or he wouldn't have been around to have another one."

"So it was a lot more severe than any reaction he'd had before. So fast and serious that the epinephrine didn't work, even though he took it."

Vic agreed. She took a sip of her tea. "But what does that tell us? We've known all of that from the start."

"There must have been factors that made it worse. Like Willie's reaction. All of those things that you filled out in the questionnaire that might have contributed to him getting so sick."

Vic's eyes widened. "Yeah. That makes sense. We were all wondering why he reacted so violently."

"All those things on that questionnaire—stress, exercise, another allergen that he was already reacting to…"

Vic nodded eagerly. "Let me pull it up…" She tapped and scrolled on her phone. "I took pictures before I gave it to the doctors so that I have a record and don't have to look those things up again down the line."

"Good thinking."

Vic scrolled through a few pages. "Okay… other things that they said could make a reaction worse. Alcohol. He hadn't had any of that. Willie, I mean."

"Not that day," Erin pointed out. He hadn't been avoiding alcohol as strictly as he'd been told to. "Mrs. McClung said Montgomery had gotten deliveries. Including wine."

"Okay, so check that box for Montgomery. Medications that can make an allergic reaction worse… non-steroidal anti-inflammatories."

"Like aspirin or naproxen," Erin said, "He was complaining about headaches and asking for aspirin."

"And about the flowers and fragrances… the doctor said that if Willie was already having an allergic reaction to something, then a new reaction could be more serious."

"And *stress*. The show must have been stressful. Having to make a decision about how to review the muffins."

Vic wobbled her hand back and forth in a "maybe" gesture. "He thrived on that, really enjoyed that part of it. Even though it would have been stressful for me or you, that was the part that made the whole thing worth it."

"Hmm." Erin thought about it, pressing her lips together. "Yeah. You're probably right."

"But it did sound from Mrs. McClung's description like he was stressed. He was complaining about the fragrances and the music. His headache. The hang-ups on his phone."

"Right." Erin pointed to her. "So he *was* stressed. Stressed, drinking, taking something for his headache, reacting to other allergens…"

Vic nodded slowly. She stirred her tea absently while she considered it. "So it was like the perfect storm. All of those things together that would make an allergic reaction worse. So when he happened to be exposed to the strawberries in the muffins… it was a much more severe reaction than he would have expected. He thought he could handle any reaction with a shot of epinephrine and some antihistamines, but it was too severe this time because of all of the other factors."

Erin agreed. She sipped her tea, which was getting too cool and needed to be refreshed.

"So now you know," Vic said. "It wasn't just you. And it wasn't just Montgomery. There were all of these other factors too, things no one could have predicted. And it was all of them together that resulted in Gerald Montgomery's death."

"Yeah."

"So that makes you feel better? That you can relax and know that it wasn't your fault? It was just all of these chance things happening at once?"

Erin took another sip of her tea. "But *was* it all coincidental? Just by chance? What if it wasn't?"

CHAPTER 36

There was still one other piece of the puzzle to put together. As Vic had told Erin more than once and Terry had also brought up, it had been pure coincidence that Erin had served Montgomery strawberries. Especially in muffins. She made plenty of blueberry muffins. That was a traditional flavor, but there were not a lot of strawberry muffins around. It wasn't something that she saw when she went to other bakeries or to the grocery store. She read a lot of recipes and looked at a lot of baking brands online, and it just wasn't a usual muffin flavor.

If someone had been trying to engineer Montgomery's death, they could not have been relying upon Erin to deal the fatal blow. Whoever the culprit was that had arranged for all of the other *coincidences* that Vic had noted, had to have another plan in mind. Had someone sent Montgomery something spiked with strawberries, perhaps the wine, without his noticing? Maybe the wine *had* been spiked with strawberry juice, but it wasn't enough to put him over the edge. Not until he'd had the muffins as well. Maybe just drinking the rest of the bottle would have had the same effect, and the mastermind had simply been lucky that Erin had stepped in with her strawberry muffins and finished the job.

She might have believed that, except that if she were right about everything else, Montgomery's death had been carefully planned. It had been a very detailed, methodical approach. Nothing left to chance. Except for the introduction of the allergen.

It didn't make sense that someone would plan everything out and leave the last step to chance.

So Erin sat in front of her computer in her tiny office at Auntie Clem's Bakery and tried to reconstruct in her mind the thought processes that had led up to her creation of the Morning Sunshine Muffins for Gerald Montgomery's tasting.

She had her browser history, and that was a good start. She wasn't a very technical person and she wasn't aware of any utility that could have shown her everything she had done in the days before she started experimenting with a recipe for strawberry compote surprise muffins. It would have been nice to have Willie's help with the project. He was very good with computers. But he was still recovering and she didn't want to do anything that might take away from his energy and the healing process. He needed to be at home in bed relaxing until Vic said otherwise.

Erin searched her browser history for the word *strawberry*.

There were more hits than she would have thought. Apparently, strawberries had been on her mind quite a bit. She narrowed the timeline and studied web pages that came up. She consulted several when looking for the best sugar ratios and cooking time for the strawberry compote. It was important for the compote to be sweet and thicken properly but to avoid overcooking the strawberries or losing the tartness of the berries. It was a balancing act, and she looked at other recipes for the starting point, which she then experimented upon.

Erin went back before that, looking for the genesis of her idea for the muffins. There were a few baking forums where she had discussed possibilities for an impressive muffin to serve to a critic. She had posted anonymously so that no one would know she was the one asking about it or that Montgomery was the critic in question. In those discussions, people had talked about several ways to incorporate strawberries into a muffin recipe.

Going further back in the browser history, Erin found a series of emails she had received the week before she started playing with ideas for a strawberry muffin.

- Before Strawberry Season is over…
- Everyone loves strawberries
- Strawberries in muffins? Yes, please!
- Surprise your guests with strawberries
- Win over even the toughest critic with these strawberry recipes

Erin stared at the subject lines. She didn't even remember receiving any of those messages. She was subscribed to a lot of baking newsletters and blogs and only read a fraction of the emails she received from them. It was entirely possible that all she had read of these emails was the subject lines. She might not have ever even opened them. But they had arrived in her inbox and she had read at least a portion of the subject lines in order to decide what to do with the emails. To read them, save them for later, or delete them.

She opened each of the emails in turn. They looked like what they appeared to be. Chatty, informative newsletters that attempted to sell a brand or to get readers to buy something based on what they had offered in the email.

But she didn't recognize the senders or the branding of the emails. They were not emails that she got regularly. She tried following links and searching the senders' names to get a better handle on who they were. Chances were, she had subscribed to them at some time or another. But too many of the links ended up with 404 errors, and she didn't recognize the faces or websites of the signatories she managed to find. Even though she got a lot of emails, that seemed odd. If she didn't ever read what someone was sending to her, she generally unsubscribed after a few weeks.

She tried the unsubscribe link in each email, but only one worked. The rest returned errors of "not found."

Erin clicked on the selection box for each email and forwarded them to Terry's police department email address.

Call me, she wrote to him.

There was no immediate response, but she didn't expect one. If everything was going well, he was on patrol somewhere with K9. If there was a lot going on, then he was at a trouble call and wouldn't be checking his email. She might have to wait until later in the evening or the next day for a response. And then she would have to explain herself to him, which she wasn't looking forward to.

Erin got up from her desk to stretch her legs. She kept reading about how dangerous it was to sit at a desk for hours on end. Bad for one's health. Increased rates of heart attack, diabetes, and other lifestyle diseases.

She checked the burglar alarm while she was walking around. The bakery was very quiet. Normally, she liked that. She loved the peace and quiet of sitting in her office in the deserted bakery, making plans for the upcoming week or reviewing how the previous week had gone.

But tonight, it was creepy. Erin wanted Terry to call her back. She wanted to know that he was okay out there and that no one was hanging around near the bakery to vandalize it, break in, or do her any harm. It had happened in the past, and she was vulnerable, there alone, even with the burglar alarm armed.

As she paced, she thought about who the email sender might be. What if someone had sent all of those emails to her to intentionally influence her choice of what to make for Montgomery's review? "Strawberries in muffins" and "Win over even the toughest critic" were not exactly subtle. But with those emails buried among others, and reading only the subject lines, Erin might easily have absorbed them subconsciously and then they had come to the forefront as she considered what kind of muffin to make for Montgomery's tasting.

Erin didn't like to think that she could be as easily manipulated as that but, when she looked at the history and considered how soon after those emails she had started experimenting with strawberry compote, she couldn't very well deny the possibility.

There was a sharp knock on the back door of the bakery. Erin's heart leaped in her chest. It raced as she pretended to herself she could walk calmly to the door. She looked through the peephole, one hand on her phone as she prepared to call Terry to get him to run off whoever had shown up now to harass her.

As much as she hated that he kept insisting she move on with her life and quit obsessing over the Montgomery case, Erin had to admit that it would be really nice if his rabid fans didn't keep showing up, either demanding muffins or calling her a murderer and saying she should die. Or both.

It would be nice to return to normal and not worry about them again.

She let out her breath slowly and unlocked the door. "Come on in."

She let Terry and K9 enter and rearmed the burglar alarm. "I wasn't expecting it to be you. I'm glad it was."

Terry pulled out his phone and tapped the screen. "What's all this about? Why are you sending me these emails?"

"I think Mavis engineered Montgomery's death."

CHAPTER 37

Jerry rolled his eyes. "No one engineered Montgomery's allergic reaction. We've talked this to death, Erin. No one could have done that. No one could have known that the muffins had strawberries in them unless you told them. No one could have engineered it."

"Did you look at those emails? Someone was sending me emails about strawberries. About putting them into muffins. About giving them to food critics. They were trying to influence my thinking!"

"It was strawberry season and you are on a million mailing lists. Of course you got emails about using strawberries."

"I know, that's what I thought too. But none of those are from legitimate mailing lists. Someone is trying to make it look that way, but they aren't. I thought maybe your forensics guys in the city could track down the IP address that is sending them, or whatever, and verify who was trying to get me to put strawberries in those muffins."

"The case has already been closed. We don't need to look into anything else."

"Listen. I think it was Mavis. She was the one who had easy access to his cards. She was probably the one who booked the B&B and then sabotaged Montgomery's stay so that he was stressed out and having a low-level allergic reaction to the flowers and whatever other fragrances, and a couple of other things that would increase his reaction. She might have told him it was a fragrance-free house so he would stay here."

Terry just stared at her.

"And why is Mavis still here?" Erin demanded. "She's the one who called the police about us being at the B&B asking questions, wasn't she? She calls the cops about us harassing people there and then tries to keep us there longer. She was the one who opened the doors and invited us in. And let us see Montgomery's room. She was keeping us there until the press and police arrived."

"Why would she do that? Keep you there?"

"So that she could get the police and the press involved, so that we would stay away after that. Embarrass us so we would stop asking questions." Erin realized she was implicating Vic in all of this. "Me, I mean. Vic wasn't in on me asking people questions."

"Why would she attract police attention when she wanted us to close the case?"

"You had already closed the case. Mavis didn't need to worry about that. She just wanted to keep us away."

Terry shook his head. "So you think Mavis, who worked for Montgomery, set him up? Made him think he had the new cards when he had cards without strawberries on them. Then emailed you to make you put strawberries into the muffins. And sat back to see what happened."

"*And* made him react more strongly to the strawberries by exposing him to stress, other allergens, and other substances that would increase his allergic reaction. That's why it killed him so fast, even when he tried to use his auto-injector to stop the reaction."

"How could she do that?"

Erin explained the various factors she and Vic had discussed: the wine delivered to him, aspirin for his headache, the phone hang-ups, and other stressors and allergens.

"I just don't know," Terry said, reluctant but not saying it was entirely out of the question, which was progress. "It all sounds a little... out there."

"Will you at least look into it? If those emails about strawberries came from Mavis, then you know something weird was happening, right? If they were all legitimate, then you just tell me. I'll accept it."

Terry smiled with good humor. "You will never accept it until you are completely satisfied that it was an accident. And I don't know if that is even possible."

445

CHAPTER 38

Terry promised he would look into the emails, extracting from Erin a promise that she, in turn, would not approach Mavis through any means, ask her any questions, or send her any messages, letting Terry take care of things through proper channels.

"If Mavis did have something to do with engineering Montgomery's death, then she could be dangerous. Not the type of person that you want to get involved with."

"No," Erin agreed. "I'm not going to do anything to put myself in her crosshairs. Right now… she has no reason to think I suspect her."

"Keep it that way," Terry agreed, voice firm.

Erin felt better knowing that he was looking into the emails. That would be a real, concrete answer. Not just Erin guessing about what was going on. She didn't have the technical know-how to tell where those emails had come from. Maybe it was just an inept mailer who had entered the wrong information in his links. Or let his web hosting account or security certificate expire. Or his server's web host had gone down for some random reason.

That kind of thing did happen. It happened all the time. Erin could just be looking for something that wasn't there. The mailer or mailers had just been looking at the bumper crop of strawberries that year and making suggestions accordingly, without knowing that their website was about to go offline.

Whatever the case, she was happy to have Terry looking into it. From the beginning, he had not considered Montgomery's death anything but a tragic accident, one that only involved Erin by pure coincidence. Now he was finally looking into it. She just hoped that it wasn't too late. They could reopen investigations, couldn't they? They did it all the time. They even looked at cases that had already been adjudicated and people were serving prison time for.

What if Terry was right, and Erin was just seeing conspiracies where there were none? What if she was seeing patterns or motives where there weren't any because she wanted to make herself feel better about being the cause of Montgomery's death? What if Mavis was completely innocent and Erin was just imagining things? The young woman had certainly not done anything that had seemed suspicious to Erin. She hadn't acted like someone who had just engineered the death of her boss.

But a sociopath wouldn't.

Vic was still looking after Willie and making sure he didn't jump back into work too soon. Erin covered extra shifts at the bakery and had the other employees come in more often to cover Vic's usual shifts. It was an extra hassle, but everyone was happy to help out despite the inconvenience.

It was the quiet point in the afternoon, when Erin spent as much time as she could in her office working on accounting and planning, and in the kitchen cleaning up and prepping for the dinner rush before closing. She could hear the bells if someone came into the bakery, unless she were running a mixer or blender, which she avoided.

The bells at the door drew her out of her contemplations about Mavis's possible involvement in Montgomery's death. Erin tried to push it all aside. She had customers to serve.

Walking out to the front counter, she saw Olivia.

"Oh, hello! I didn't expect to see you again. I thought you would be on your way home by now."

"I was supposed to be doing a tour, but they've delayed the next event, so I'm stuck here. Well, not stuck. I could go home in between, but I would be backtracking, and I don't really want to go home just to turn around and go back out again in another day or two. I thought I would extend my stay here, enjoy the fresh air and atmosphere, and be nice and relaxed and mellow for the next appearance."

Erin nodded. "Sounds like a plan. I'm sure you're not happy about having your plans disrupted, but it's nice to have another day or two to relax."

Olivia nodded. She looked over the offerings in the display case.

"The thing is, I've got itchy fingers. I want to cook. But I can't exactly take over Mrs. McClung's kitchen. I offered to make her and Mavis dinner tonight, but she seemed… rather horrified at the idea of someone else being in her kitchen to tell the truth. It was funny, actually. You would think a busy woman like her wouldn't mind having a nice home-cooked meal in her own kitchen. But…" Olivia shrugged. "I guess I can understand not wanting someone else to come into your territory, too. Her kitchen is her own private place, and some people really don't like other people touching their stuff."

"I wouldn't mind someone making me a home-cooked meal!" Erin laughed. "I'm always so exhausted by the end of the day; it's mostly just warmed-up soup or freezer meals."

Olivia smiled. She pointed to a rustic loaf of hand-shaped bread. "That looks lovely. If it was winter, I would suggest pairing it with a nice, hearty beef stew. But in the summer… maybe with a couple of salads and the bread toasted and topped with bruschetta…?"

"Yes," Erin agreed. "That sounds wonderful."

"How about it?" Olivia said. "I will come to your house and cook you an extra-special meal. All you have to do is sit back and enjoy it."

Erin considered. She knew that Terry was on the evening shift and wouldn't be home until it was nearly time for Erin to go to bed. She was always so tired at the end of the day. But maybe she wouldn't be if she had a chance to relax and be pampered by Olivia's top-notch cooking. Erin had looked at some of her recipes and demonstrations online, and it all looked delicious.

"That sounds really nice." She considered how she felt about someone banging around in her kitchen and decided she was okay with it, considering the outcome. "But I have pets… are you okay with a pesky cat underfoot? I would lock him up while you're there, but he's really loud and would ruin the evening."

Olivia laughed. "Yes, of course. I love cats. No dog?"

"No. Terry has K9, but he will be on duty. And there is a rabbit, but he won't cause you any trouble."

"Wonderful. Can I do it, then? Come by and cook for you when you're off?"

"Sure." Erin laughed. "It's an offer I can't refuse!"

"Awesome." Olivia looked happy about this development. Erin wondered if she would go stir-crazy and want to go to other peoples' houses to bake if she weren't able to do it for a week or two. She just might.

"I'll take that loaf, then." Olivia pointed.

"On the house, since you're providing the supper," Erin told her. "What other ingredients will you need? I have the basics in the kitchen, but if there is something in particular that you are thinking of…"

"No, I'm going to shop to entertain myself. What time are you off tonight?"

"I should be home about six-thirty. Does that work?"

Olivia nodded. "I'll see you then. What's your address?"

Erin gave her the details and packaged up the bread for her.

*E*rin was excited when it was time to head home. Vic was her best friend and they often saw each other multiple times a day. Erin could always talk to her and they shared everything. But Vic was busy with Willie's medical crisis, and she hadn't had time for Erin lately. Erin had been feeling alone and neglected, even though she knew Vic had a perfectly good reason for not being around.

The dinner date with Olivia was the perfect solution. Erin was looking forward to being pampered, not making her own supper, and having a great discussion with Olivia about gluten-free cooking, restaurants, cooking, and even Gerald Montgomery, if his name came up. Olivia got her kitchen fix and Erin got socialization and a free dinner.

Olivia was at the front door with bags of food a few minutes after Erin arrived. Erin shut off the burglar alarm and let her in. "This is going to be so much fun," she told Olivia. "Now, can I help you in the kitchen?"

"Just show me where things are and I'll get on myself. This is your chance to rest, remember? Just sit and chat with me and we'll have the time of our lives."

"Whatever you want," Erin agreed. She showed Olivia to the kitchen and gave her a quick tour of the cupboards, pantry, and fridge. Orange Blossom came into the kitchen warily, not sure what he thought of a stranger being there. He yowled at Erin, telling her how hungry he was. Olivia would think that she had been neglecting him for days; the poor thing sounded so mournful. But then, she could see by his size that he wasn't actually on a starvation diet.

"Oh, he's lovely," she told Erin as she watched Erin feed him. Hopefully, that would quiet him down for the night and he would stay out of Olivia's way. Marshmallow pattered into the kitchen a few minutes later, ready for his supper as well.

"And this is Marshmallow," Erin introduced. "They are both rescues. Marshmallow was injured when we found him, and rabbits are really prone to going into shock, so that even if their injury is treatable, vets often lose them anyway. But he pulled through just fine and has been here ever since."

"He's very nice. And he gets along with Orange Blossom?"

"They're really funny when they get to play with each other. Blossom will chase him around the house until Marshmallow decides he's had enough, and he turns around, kicks Blossom in the nose, and chases him instead. If you've never seen a rabbit chasing a cat…"

Olivia's peals of laughter filled the kitchen. "That must be hilarious. I hope they do it while I'm here."

"I don't know. They might, but usually it's when it's just me and Vic around."

"That's the young lady you were at the B&B with, right? The two of you seem close."

"Yeah. She lives back there." Erin waved a hand at the loft apartment over the garage. "And we work together. So we're together all the time, but we love it. We don't get tired of each other and are happy just to sit around and do nothing together, too—planning, crossword puzzles, journaling, genealogy, whatever. But her partner had a medical crisis this week, so she's staying with him, making sure that he's feeling better before she comes back."

"Oh, that's too bad. What happened?"

"He's going through some treatments for a medical condition, and they think that he might have reacted to one of the medications, or it might just be the stress that he's under. He went into anaphylaxis, and that's never happened before so he didn't have epinephrine. We barely got him to the hospital in the city in time."

"That's scary. Especially after seeing Montgomery die from the same thing."

"Well, we didn't know at the time that was what it was, luckily. I didn't have to worry about that as we were taking him in. But I could tell that his breathing and pulse were bad. It was pretty scary."

"It must have been. I understand Vic's wanting to stay home to care for him for a while."

Erin nodded. "Okay, well, the beasts are fed, so the kitchen is yours. If you need anything, just ask." Erin sat down on one of the kitchen chairs. It was strange to be a guest in her own kitchen. She wanted to jump up and help Olivia with the preparations. But it was nice to sit back and watch someone else cook, too. Like having her own cooking show right in her kitchen.

"This is very cool," she told Olivia. "I've seen you on the internet, so it's like having Celebrity Chef right here in front of me. Tell me about what it was like running your own restaurant."

Olivia talked about it as she chopped and measured and stirred. She had clearly enjoyed the restaurant business, no matter how stressful it must have been. She spoke of her kitchen staff as if they were family, the same way Erin felt about her employees. They weren't just people who worked together; they really were her family, whether they were related like Charley, distant cousins, or not at all. They were the people she loved and trusted and spent her day with, and they didn't let her down.

Many of the challenges that Olivia had faced were similar to what Erin had experienced at Auntie Clem's. There were always supplier issues, customers who weren't happy, and malfunctioning equipment. But there was a lot more to deal with in a sit-down restaurant, dealing with thirty or a hundred diners there for an hour or two, supervising the prep of hundreds of orders in the kitchen, and ensuring people were happy.

But Olivia sounded like she had been right in her element. It had been her dream job, despite all the ups and downs.

"Things were going really well. All of the kinks worked out, stable employees, good location, everything working smoothly… and then along comes Gerald Montgomery," Olivia told her as she bussed serving dishes over to the table. She had spread garlic butter on the bread from Auntie Clem's; it smelled so good, Erin could hardly wait to dig in.

Olivia told Erin about each dish and its ingredients and preparation, though some of it was repeated from her comments as she had cooked. They dished up and tasted each of the salads Olivia had prepared and Erin raved about the bruschetta on garlic toast.

Olivia returned to her discussion about Gerald Montgomery.

"He shows up at my restaurant one day out of the blue. Like these guys do. They love a surprise. And you're supposed to pretend you don't know who he is, even though he is surrounded by cameramen and equipment. I mean, it's not exactly covert. So you're trying to prepare something for this critic, and to get everything just right, but not neglect anyone else's meals either, because if he hears other people complaining, that is going to go into his show as well."

"So stressful," Erin commented. Even just having Montgomery walk into Auntie Clem's, only having to deal with him for five minutes at the counter, had been stressful. She couldn't imagine what it would be like to have him in her restaurant for an hour or more, while still trying to maintain service to the rest of the customers as well.

"It was. And, of course, you aren't ever going to have a day when everything goes perfectly. Something is going to be off. He's going to be able to find something to complain about. And throw his allergies into the works as well..." Olivia shook her head. "Well, of course, I am the Queen of Gluten-Free Cooking; just ask my fans, so that part of it really wasn't a challenge. But he was in a bad mood, so it didn't matter what I did or said; he was going to find something negative to say."

They ate in silence for a minute.

"In fact, most of what he said was negative," Olivia confessed. "I can't think of a single nice thing that he said. Maybe that the gluten-free baking was 'adequate' or something to that effect. It was just... a roast. He called me out. Said I wasn't a good baker, or chef, that the cooking at the restaurant was bland, tasteless, and unimaginative. We *had* good reviews. People loved the place. It had a good reputation, regular clientele, good write-ups in the papers and foodie review sites. It was a good restaurant."

Erin indicated her food. "I believe you. I can see—taste—what you can do. This would be a hit at any restaurant."

Olivia nodded appreciatively. "We were doing so well. I thought when Montgomery came in that it would be a challenge, but we would be able to impress him and it would just be another feather in our caps. I hadn't dealt with him personally before, and I didn't realize how unreasonable he could be. That he wrote reviews based on how he felt at the moment, which wasn't anything to do with whether the food was good or not. If he was in a bad mood, he wrote a bad review, even if he didn't have anything specific to say about the food. He would just… burn everything down, if you know what I mean. Write a review that said that everything about the restaurant was bad."

Erin shook her head slowly. "That's terrible. A critic should be very specific, and his personal feelings should never enter into it. It should be a balanced, unbiased review. Not just some… drunken rage because someone cut him off in his car on the drive in."

"Exactly," Olivia agreed. She pointed at Erin and then emphatically thumped her finger on the tabletop. "That's exactly right. You hit the nail on the head."

"But other people didn't see that side of him. They thought that a bad review really meant that the restaurant was bad," Erin suggested.

Olivia sighed and nodded in agreement. "And that was the beginning of the end. Things went down pretty quickly from there. He has—had— so many followers that word just spread like wildfire across the internet and into the real world. Before long, everyone was badmouthing the restaurant based on what Montgomery had said, without ever experiencing it themselves. Pretty soon, all the review sites had negative reviews and reposts of Montgomery's review. And the clientele just dried up. Even those who had been repeat customers before acted like we had the plague. They stopped coming. It didn't matter what advertising or promotional efforts we attempted, they wouldn't come back, and nobody new would try us out. We changed the name a few times, tried new promotions to bring people in, tried changing the cuisine and menu, but nothing we did made any difference. As soon as we reopened with a new name, it would be posted online and people would copy what had been posted before. We all put our own money into it and tried to keep it running, but eventually… none of us had anything left to put into it and we had to admit that it was dead. That dream was gone."

"I'm so sorry. That sounds just awful."

"And the reviews still follow me. Whenever I try to get a new job at a restaurant, they look me up, and they find the 'boring, bland, and uninspired' garbage and won't hire me as a chef. I've done some restaurant work, but it's impossible to get any traction or get promoted above line cook. My book sales bring in some money, but not nearly enough."

"Why won't people trust their own taste buds? Give you a chance, and if they like what you cook, hire you. Why does it have to be based on some stupid review that will never go away?"

"I wish I knew the answer to that. I've considered changing my name —not just using a pen name, but legally changing my name so that people will give me a chance."

Erin, who had gone by many different names in many different circumstances, could certainly understand that desire. Sometimes, a person just wanted to shed the past and start over again. To start with a fresh slate. What Montgomery had done to Olivia was reprehensible. It was awful that one person should have so much power over another's life.

"Now *you* are a good gluten-free baker," Olivia told Erin, indicating the serving dish with the toasted garlic bread. "You wouldn't want to be limited by a bad review from Gerald Montgomery. You wouldn't want the same thing to happen to you as happened to me."

"No," Erin agreed. "I guess I dodged a bullet on that one. I thought he would probably give me a good review but, even if he didn't, I could still weather it. I didn't realize how much weight people would give to someone else's opinion over their own."

"You're lucky that he died."

Erin made a face. "Maybe. But not so lucky that it was while eating my muffins."

"Do you think so? Seems to me like you've had quite a run on those muffins. On the social networks, they are still promoting hashtag Morning Sunshine Challenge. The people who can't make it here to eat one of your muffins are trying to duplicate the recipe and make them at home so that they can participate. You might not like it, but your muffins have become a touchstone for his followers. That doesn't hurt you."

"I've been lucky," Erin admitted. "But I'd just as soon it never happened."

"Sometimes fate has a way of stepping in."

Erin took a long sip of her tea, wondering whether to tell Olivia about her thoughts about Montgomery's death being engineered by Mavis at

Montgomery Meals and Reels. She took another piece of garlic bread and considered.

"You look like you have something serious on your mind," Olivia said. "Is the bakery having problems? I thought that with all of the new business after Montgomery's death, things would actually be going pretty well for you. You're the only gluten-free baker in this part of the country. You've got a captive audience."

CHAPTER 40

"It's not that," Erin told her. "I am doing well, and Montgomery's followers have brought a bunch of business to the bakery. His death has definitely brought us more attention than we would have gotten any other way. I was thinking about Montgomery himself and that it's too bad it had to end that way."

"He was a nasty, judgmental person. You're better off having only had a very brief encounter with him. And with him bringing business after his death—I don't see how you can complain about that."

"I'm not complaining. Like I said, the bakery is doing well. It's just… I'm not sure that his death was as accidental as everyone thinks."

Olivia dropped her fork with a clatter. She quickly picked it back up and said nothing about her clumsiness.

"What do you mean, not an accident? Did you know about his strawberry allergy?"

"No. I didn't know about that. I wouldn't have given him something I knew he was allergic to. But I'm afraid that someone might have known that and tried to engineer things so I would make muffins with strawberries without knowing he was allergic."

Olivia shook her head, bemused. "How could anyone make you make him strawberry muffins? If they even knew in the first place that he was allergic to strawberries?"

"His office knew."

"His office? How many people knew that?"

"I know one in particular."

Olivia didn't answer at first, looking at her plate and worrying her salad with her fork.

"Which one? Mavis is the only one I know personally, and she seems like a nice girl."

"Yeah, Mavis. I know that she knew about the allergies because she was the one who made the new allergen cards and replaced them in his wallet. She says that she was the one who thought of doing the wallet cards in the first place."

"And you think that… she made a mistake on them? Put the wrong cards into his wallet?"

"I think she put the wrong cards in his wallet. But I don't know if it was an accident."

"Intentionally? You think that she wanted Montgomery to die? She was trying to make it so that no one would know about his strawberry allergy?" Olivia's voice rose, disbelief in her tone.

"I know it sounds crazy," Erin admitted. "I haven't had much luck getting anyone else to believe it."

"I'm not surprised." Olivia gave a little chuckle.

Erin's cheeks heated. She didn't want Olivia to think that she was crazy, but that was probably how she was coming off.

"I'm not just making it up," Erin told her. "I may not have proof—yet —but think about it. She was the one who had the best access to the cards. She didn't have to do anything but mix one or two of the wrong cards into the stack. So it would look like he only had the right ones, when Montgomery was handing out cards with the wrong information, making it more likely that people would make him something he was allergic to."

"Sure. But other people might have had access to his wallet. People he worked with, a girlfriend or wife, whoever he lived with. Or people lay their wallets down, maybe even leave them unattended for a minute or two. He wouldn't necessarily know if someone had been touching it."

"But the wallet isn't the only thing. I think they were trying to force Montgomery to have a more serious allergic reaction, too."

"How is that even possible?"

"Because of Willie's allergic reaction, we had a bunch of information on what can make a reaction worse. Like stress."

"And how would she cause him extra stress?"

"Phone call hang-ups. Someone kept calling him and hanging up. Who knows what kind of business stresses she might have caused him. She could have screwed up all kinds of arrangements for him. Mrs. McClung said that he had a lot of complaints. Things like expecting the B&B to be fragrance-free when it was never advertised that way. He was bothered by the smells of the flowers and linens and who knows what else. They gave him a headache and caused him extra stress. And he probably took aspirin, too."

"And is that bad? That would help, wouldn't it?"

"It could intensify an allergic reaction. And if the flowers and fragrances were causing him a low-level allergic reaction, then he's starting at a higher level of histamines. It wouldn't take as much to put him into anaphylaxis. He was already well on his way there."

"But you don't have any proof that Mavis was doing any of this."

"The flowers were sent from somewhere. Maybe we'll be able to trace who sent them. And there were the emails, too!"

"Someone was sending him threatening emails?"

"No, no. Someone was sending *me* emails."

"Why would they send you emails? And what effect would that have on Montgomery?"

"They were trying to get me to put strawberries into the muffins."

"Blackmail? But why would you do it if you knew he was allergic? Did you think that he wouldn't have a big reaction? That he would just get a little bit sick? But then he wouldn't give you a good review."

"No, I didn't. It was more subtle than that. Sending me emails about strawberry season, about putting strawberries in muffins, about silencing the critics with strawberry recipes..."

"Well, you certainly accomplished that."

Erin's cheeks flamed hotter. She hadn't even thought about how it would sound before the words came out of her mouth.

"I didn't mean that. I mean what the email said. That everyone would think they were great, that there wouldn't be anything about them to criticize. And I must have taken it all in subconsciously. I don't even remember reading those emails."

Olivia shook her head. "Well, I'm not sure how you would prove to anyone that you were subconsciously tricked into making something that Montgomery was allergic to."

Erin's phone rang and she took it out of her pocket to see who the caller was.

CHAPTER 41

Terry's email dinged and he opened the inbox to see what he had received. Surprisingly, the techs from the electronic forensics lab in the city were getting back to him with preliminary results.

He opened the email and skimmed through it.

The first revelation was that all of the emails had come from the same sender.

Since all the emails had different headers and sender information, Terry had initially dismissed Erin's suspicion that they might all be from someone trying to engineer Gerald Montgomery's death as paranoia.

What were the chances that someone had been trying to engineer Montgomery's death? And even more, that they had succeeded? Erin's theories had sounded far-fetched.

He dug deeper into the report and tried to sort out what they had found. They needed to reach the sender's ISP to find out the name of the account holder. And what if it turned out to just be public Wi-Fi? Then, the address and account holder wouldn't get him anywhere.

Erin had suggested that the person who had set Montgomery up was Mavis, Montgomery's assistant, so that was who Terry needed to talk to next. Hopefully, she was at the bed and breakfast and not out sightseeing.

"Come on, K9." Terry stood up and gestured for K9 to heel. "Let's go check out the B&B."

~

In a few minutes, he was knocking on Mrs. McClung's door. She seemed confused as to what he was doing on her doorstep.

"I didn't call the police," she told him, shaking her head.

"I know. I'm here to talk to Mavis. Is she in?"

"Uh… yes, I believe she is in her room. It's the supper hour, and she should be going out to dinner soon, but she hasn't left yet."

"What can you tell me about her?"

Mrs. McClung looked at him questioningly. "What do you mean?"

"How much do you know about her? I know Mavis works for Meals and Reels, but that's about it. She arrived with Mr. Montgomery? As his personal assistant?"

"No," Mrs. McClung shook her head. "She didn't come here until after he died. To see to arrangements."

"Oh. She wasn't here at the same time as he was?"

"No. I had talked to her on the phone when she booked the rooms, but I hadn't seen her face-to-face. She was just a voice on the phone."

"Who was here with him, then?"

"I don't know. There was a whole mess of them. Camera crew, microphones, I don't know what all of those people are called. I never did understand all of those technical positions they list after a movie. Gaffers and grips and all of that. He had a lot of people, and they used the second room. Came and went. They didn't sleep here; they used it for equipment and meetings. Then after he died, they didn't need the crew here anymore, but wanted someone here to deal with… the body and the press, I suppose. There's a lot to do when someone dies. And it's more complicated when that person is out of town. Transporting the remains back to his family."

"And there has been a lot of press surrounding his death."

Mrs. McClung nodded her agreement. "It has not been fun trying to keep them out of here. They keep trying to sneak in, bothering me and the other guest and all of the fans who keep coming into town to see where he died."

Terry knew that Mrs. McClung had made several trespassing complaints. He and the others had each been there at least once to disperse a crowd or get rid of some fan who thought they had the right to go wherever they liked.

"They're quite a nuisance."

"You're right about that," the old woman agreed, nodding. "Think they should have the run of the place. Olivia said that I should just start charging admission for them to come and see where he died. I could make a lot of money doing that."

"I suppose you could."

"But I am not the type to take advantage of a person's death. That's just not right. They are ghouls. I'm not going to encourage that kind of behavior."

"Good for you." Terry nodded. "But I imagine it does make things disruptive for you. You can't escape them."

"Well, I'm sure it will only be a few more days now. You've decided it was an accident. I'm sure Mavis will be packing everything up and moving on. You have released the body…?"

"That would be the medical examiner in the city. I don't know what arrangements have been made. I assume it has been released. Mavis will be able to make arrangements for its transport."

"It's such a strange thing when you think about it. Dealing with the shell of the person you have lost. They aren't there anymore, but their husk is still important for our rituals. It's the last thing that we can hold on to physically."

"I guess so," Terry agreed. "I haven't thought much about it. I'm involved with the other end of the business. I'm not the one dealing with the body after it has been released. It must be difficult for such a young woman. I don't imagine she has much experience with that kind of thing."

"She is a very competent young person. But it has been very hard on her. I don't think people have much compassion for a girl who just worked for someone who has died. But the tragedy has touched her, too. This is probably her first real job, and what happens? Her boss has a terrible accident and dies."

"You're right. I didn't think about how it must affect her personally. Though I gather he wasn't a very nice person, so it wouldn't be as bad as if she were close to him."

"That would be a real tragedy," Mrs. McClung agreed. "The poor girl. She thinks she can hide her red, puffy eyes with cold compresses, but I sometimes see her when she gets up in the morning before she's had a chance to put anything on them. I see how it's affecting her."

In Terry's experience, those who had intentionally killed someone did not generally spend the night crying their eyes out. Even if they felt guilty afterward, that usually led to increased drinking, agitation, or moodiness —not tears.

CHAPTER 42

"So Mavis wasn't even here before Montgomery died," Terry mused, thinking through Erin's theory. How many of the things she had suggested would Mavis have needed to be present for? Obviously, Mavis could have sent the emails from anywhere. She could have changed the wallet cards when Montgomery had last been at the office. Wine and flowers could have been ordered over the phone or internet from anywhere in the world. Nobody would be looking at them with suspicion. Would Mavis have needed to be present for any of the set-up Erin had suggested?

"Who was it that booked the room? I supposed that was done several weeks before he arrived."

"Yes. They had to make a reservation, but no one was supposed to know when he was actually going to be here. They booked it for a couple of weeks, but no one knew what day he would arrive."

"Including you?"

"Including me," she said with a nod.

"And was it Montgomery or Mavis who made that reservation?"

"It was Mavis," Mrs. McClung said with certainty. "And it was a good thing, with Mr. Montgomery canceling his credit card."

Terry had been looking at K9 and preparing himself mentally to go upstairs and talk to Mavis, but Mrs. McClung's words pulled him back down to the present.

"What?"

"It was Mavis."

"No, what was that about the credit card?"

"His card was canceled. So he would not have been able to pay for the room."

"Why was his card canceled?"

"He had lost his wallet, so he canceled his credit cards and was in the process of finding out how to get his identification reissued."

"This happened right before he died?"

"A few days. Maybe the day before he got here. But it was turned in. He got it back. He was just missing his cash so it turned out he didn't have to get his identification reissued. But he'd already canceled his credit cards."

Terry pondered this new information. The wallet had been out of Montgomery's possession for long enough for him to notice its absence and start canceling credit cards. Certainly long enough for someone to add a couple of old cards in with the new ones, or take the new ones out and put the old ones back.

"I imagine he'd had plenty of practice getting cards reissued," Mrs. McClung told him. "He didn't keep track of it very well. He left it on the desk down here one day and I had to take it up to him."

"Really. Do you remember what day that was?"

"Some people are like that, you know, they don't pay attention to what they are doing. Leaving wallets, phones, keys—you wouldn't believe the number of times I have to return things to guests that they've just carelessly left here or there."

"Mmm-hm. Do you remember what day it was? That you found his wallet and returned it to him?"

She considered it for a moment. "Probably that last day. The day he died."

"In the morning or the evening?"

"Oh, the evening. Definitely. And there were so many people coming and going with that film crew of his. It was just chaos here. He should have booked all of the rooms so that there weren't any other guests around to bother. I was very concerned about him upsetting Olivia. But she didn't complain. I guess what's good for the goose is good for the gander."

"What do you mean by that?"

"Well, because she was the one who had been making noise and bothering Mr. Montgomery the day before that." She widened her eyes at Terry and anticipated his question. "Playing her music. Opera, mostly. I went up to talk to her about it after a couple of hours, told her how inconsiderate she was being of the other guest and that she needed to wear earphones if she was going to continue to listen to it. But she just laughed. Said that she and Mr. Montgomery were old friends and he could deal with it." She rolled her eyes. "He kept complaining about it. I tried just to put him off to begin with, said that I had already talked to her, and if he wanted to try appealing to her directly, he was welcome to. I heard the two of them arguing, and him banging on her door, but she was not to be reasoned with."

Mrs. McClung shook her head.

"Up until then, I thought that she was very charming and an excellent guest. I can't understand why she behaved that way. But I guess some people are very particular about their music. She said that it was meant to be listened to in open halls, not on tinny little earphones. She had it on very late the night before he died. And then again early in the morning. Last night, she had it on again after dinner, but only for a little while, and Mr. Montgomery wasn't complaining, so…"

She trailed off, the blood draining from her face.

"Is that why he didn't complain about the opera music? Because he was dead? Oh, my stars…"

Terry patted Mrs. McClung on the arm and looked for somewhere for her to sit down. She looked like she might faint dead away.

"Try not to think about it," he told her, steering her into a chair. "Can I get you a cold glass of water? That usually helps."

She didn't answer. Terry looked around and found the kitchen. He ran cold water into the sink until it was icy cold, then filled a glass and took it out to her.

"So it was Olivia who played the music that gave him a headache."

"Yes. He was whining and complaining like a baby. He couldn't work like that. He needed to have quiet and solitude for the tasting." Mrs. McClung stuck her nose up in the air and spoke precisely, obviously mimicking Montgomery. "If he wanted absolute quiet for his little show, he should have used a recording studio. In a bed and breakfast, people come and go, they talk, they play music, they make noise. It's a home away from home. Expecting it to be silent so you don't get any outside sounds on your tape is ridiculous."

Terry nodded. He waited for Mrs. McClung to take another sip of her water. She was pinking up again. "You're right. People need to be reasonable. Practical. If he needed a soundproof room, he should have booked a place with soundproofed rooms."

She nodded emphatically.

"And if they want fragrance-free rooms, then they should book a room that advertises that," Terry added, watching her closely for her reaction.

"Exactly. I would never go to someone else's house and insist that they remove all of the smells!" She looked affronted at the idea. "I understand that some people are very sensitive, but then those people should know to ask ahead and only book rooms in places where their *needs* can be accommodated." She sneered out the word needs.

"Mavis didn't say anything about Mr. Montgomery's allergy to fragrances on the phone when she booked the room?"

"No, course not. I would have told her that there wasn't any such thing here. Probably not anywhere. Can you imagine running an inn where no smells are allowed? What do you do when other guests are wearing perfume? Or if a child picks a bouquet of flowers? I'm supposed to clean anything without any chemical cleaners? How? It can't be done."

Terry agreed that very few people would probably meet a rigorous definition of being fragrance-free. But other owners might be a little more open to it than Mrs. McClung. If Mavis had talked to her about Mr. Montgomery's environmental allergies, she would undoubtedly have gotten an earful.

"So what if he had a headache?" Mrs. McClung said with a shrug. "I have a headache most of my waking hours. I gave him some aspirin. If he's so sensitive, why doesn't he pack his own? It's ridiculous."

"Maybe he just forgot his at home."

"Or maybe he liked to whine and make people do things for him. I don't like to speak ill of the dead, but the man really was a pain in the neck. And I'm used to dealing with demanding guests. That one really took the cake."

"And then the cake took him."

Mrs. McClung snorted. "You really shouldn't say such things," she declared, fanning herself with her hand as if blushing. "It's very irreverent!"

"Well, some people deserve it and some people don't. It doesn't sound like he was too considerate of anyone else's feelings."

"He was difficult," she admitted. She looked up at the sound of footsteps overhead. "Oh, you see? I was right. She's getting ready to go out to supper now. You've missed your chance to talk to Mavis."

"I'll just ask her a question or two on the way out. Do you know where she is going to eat? I can walk her over."

"Probably the family restaurant. She has tried the Chinese already. And the hot chicken. These foodies, you know. They like to test them all, see what they're like."

Terry nodded. He waited while Mavis walked back and forth a few times overhead, getting ready, and then came down the stairs. She saw Terry and looked surprised.

"Oh, I didn't know anyone was here. How are you doing, Officer…? I don't remember your name."

"Terry Piper, ma'am. I was hoping to ask you a few questions. Maybe I can walk you over to your dinner appointment and we could discuss it on the way."

"Certainly," she agreed. "I always enjoy walking with a handsome gentleman." She smiled. "And his owner, too."

Terry laughed, looking down at his dog. "K9 seems very taken with you, too. And he has very good taste."

"Well, then, let's walk, shall we?"

K9 was looking at Terry hopefully with the repetition of the word "walk."

"Let's go, boy," Terry confirmed, motioning for K9 to heel and leading the way out the door.

He looked back at Mrs. McClung. "Is Olivia here? Or has she already gone out for dinner?"

"Oh, she's already gone out." Mrs. McClung confirmed what Terry had already guessed by the quiet of the house. Since Mrs. McClung didn't serve dinner, guests had to fend for themselves, and the supper hour was well underway. With Mavis out of the way, Mrs. McClung would have the house to herself and be able to relax for a while without worrying about her guests' needs.

"Where did she go, do you know?" he asked, wondering if he might be able to connect with her after talking with Mavis.

"Well, I believe she was going to cook dinner for your wife."

Terry looked at her in amusement. "I'm not married."

"Erin Price. She's your… partner, isn't she?" Her mouth twisted sourly on the word partner. Of course the old biddies didn't like the fact that he and Erin were living together outside the bonds of matrimony.

"Yes, that's right."

"Olivia was going to cook for her tonight. She was quite excited about it."

CHAPTER 43

Olivia reached over and pulled the phone from Erin's hand.

"No phones at the table," she scolded. "That's rude."

So was taking someone's phone out of her hand. Erin stared at Olivia with her mouth open, wanting to protest but unsure what to say.

It was her house, her phone, her dinner.

But as Olivia had said, it was rude of her to talk on the phone while they were eating.

But Erin had only been checking to see who it was. Whether it was something important or just an unknown caller, a sales rep for some kitchen equipment company or a phone company trying to talk her into a new plan. She wouldn't have answered it unless it was really important, and then she would have explained that to Olivia.

Olivia laughed. "You should see the expression on your face."

"Well... I wasn't expecting you to do that."

"We're having such a good time together. I didn't want it to be interrupted by a phone call." Olivia looked down at the phone, waiting for it to stop ringing. "You know, at my restaurant, there was a no phones policy. You couldn't even have it out at the table. When you're eating a special dinner, something that you've paid for and that the chef has put so much time and effort into, you should give it your full attention."

"Of course," Erin agreed, turning her attention back to her meal, showing Olivia that she was willing to immerse herself in the experience and worry about the rest of the world later, when she was finished eating. Olivia put the phone down on the table beside her. It had stopped ringing and the screen was dark. Erin hadn't been able to see who it was before Olivia had snatched it, but suspected it was Terry. Maybe he was on his way home. He could share the dinner with her. There was plenty to go around.

She suddenly felt a little uncomfortable being alone with Olivia and wished that Terry were there to cushion her from Olivia and her intensity.

Olivia was an interesting person. She'd had some amazing experiences with cooking and restaurants, and Erin was fascinated with her encounters with Montgomery, giving her a little window into the kind of person he was. Erin could see that she had dodged a bullet with Montgomery dying before he'd had a chance to review the baking.

If he had come out with as negative a review as he had with Olivia, the results might have been the same. Maybe she would have been ruined, despite being the only bakery in town. She would be forced out and someone else would come in and take over and run a conventional bakery instead of a gluten-free one.

Running a gluten-free bakery had been an uphill battle for Erin right from the beginning. She'd had to fight for the reputation she had. Each and every sale was a win, overcoming people's resistance to eating something different that they considered strange, inferior, or faddish. She had to get people to taste it, to give it a chance.

It would have been much easier for her to open a conventional bakery. With Angela Plaint's death, the timing was perfect for her to take over from The Bake Shoppe, stepping into the void left by Angela's death.

"Everything okay?" Olivia asked.

Erin looked up from her food, forcing a smile. "Yes, I'm fine. Sorry. Off in my own little world there. This really is lovely. You're a good cook. And I love the concept of a simple meal from simple ingredients, but that blends together into something so..."

Erin had another forkful of salad and tried to think of the word she wanted.

"So complex, I guess. The way that all of the flavors and textures go together just the right way. You know, I'm always so tired when I come home from Auntie Clem's that I really don't have the energy to figure out what to make, let alone take the time to do it. I open a can of soup, pull some leftover buns out of the freezer, maybe make a bagged salad and drown it in salad dressing."

Olivia laughed and nodded. "I could teach you a few basic recipes that would help. You can make up batches of salad dressing beforehand so that you have something really nice rather than the bottled dressings full of sugar and preservatives. And a few ingredients can turn a bagged salad into a proper meal: sun-dried tomatoes, seeds, some nice in-season fruit or vegetable. I'll send you a copy of my first book. It contains some really nice base recipes that you can then build on. It doesn't have to take more time if you have your ingredients ready."

Erin nodded. "How about you just stay on as my personal chef?"

"I don't think you could afford me," Olivia told Erin with a chuckle.

"Can I afford *not* to have you? I think that's the real question," Erin asked playfully.

Olivia smiled, appreciating Erin's words even though she knew they were hyperbolic.

Erin looked toward the loft over the garage, wishing Vic were with her instead of looking after Willie. Vic would have handled the situation much more gracefully than Erin, she was sure. Maybe it had even been Vic on the phone, asking whether it was okay to pop by. She usually wouldn't bother to ask but, if she had seen that Erin had a visitor, she might.

"I made dessert, if you're finished with the main course," Olivia said, looking at Erin's plate. She was just toying with what remained, no longer hungry. It was good food—excellent, in fact. But Olivia taking Erin's phone had triggered something. Erin no longer wanted to sit there, visiting and eating with the stranger. Her stomach gurgled and she felt nauseated. Her muscles were tense, even though she was doing her best to relax them. She closed her eyes and thought about doing her tai chi practice in the backyard, her toes digging into the sweet-smelling, soft grass.

"Dessert?" Olivia prodded again, her voice taking on a note of frustration.

It was rude of Erin not to have answered immediately. She didn't know why she was so distracted. She pasted a plastic smile on her face.

"Of course. That sounds delicious."

It was perhaps not the right thing to say, since Olivia hadn't even said what she had made. Olivia frowned, lines appearing between her brows.

"Dessert sounds great, I mean," Erin told her. "I would love something sweet to finish off this excellent meal."

"You didn't eat very much."

"I can't if I want to maintain my figure," Erin protested, putting her hand over her stomach. "I've put on weight since I opened the bakery. Go figure! I'm so short-waisted that every pound is obvious."

"Tell me about it," slim little Olivia agreed. "Tasting food in the kitchen is the bane of a chef's existence. For women like you and me, anyway."

She put her hand over Erin's briefly, affectionate, connecting with her. They were part of a sisterhood—short woman chefs who didn't want to end up shaped like blueberries.

"Well, you don't need to worry about this dessert," Olivia assured her. "I wanted to go with something fresh and local and, seeing as the late summer berries are in season right now, I thought fresh berries with stevia-sweetened, whipped Greek yogurt would be a fresh, sweet, low-cal treat we could both enjoy."

Erin's mouth watered at the description. She nodded. "Yeah, that sounds really good."

Olivia smiled and nodded her approval. She stood up and went to the fridge to pull out the dessert ingredients she had prepared. Erin eyed her phone, wondering if Olivia would notice or would be upset if Erin grabbed her phone back. As long as she only took a quick, covert look and put it in her pocket, Olivia shouldn't mind too much.

She waited until Olivia's back was turned while she filled parfait glasses with layers of whipped yogurt and berries, then reached across the table for her phone and casually slid it across the table toward her, and then into her lap. She exhaled slowly.

It *had* been Terry who had been trying to get her.

Olivia brought the glasses with long-handled spoons to the table.

"Those look gorgeous," she told Olivia. "Almost too good to eat!"

"Almost," Olivia agreed. "But not quite."

Erin dipped her spoon into the yogurt topping, mirroring Olivia's movements. As she brought it up to her mouth, she caught a whiff of something that wasn't quite right. She eyed the yogurt. It looked perfectly fine, of course. White and smooth and rich. What had she smelled? The stevia? Some people swore by it, but Erin had never liked the smell, even though most people said it was undetectable.

But it wasn't the sweet, faintly licorice smell of stevia. It was something else. Unless it was a form of stevia that had been highly processed with other chemicals, and Olivia had professed to use ingredients as close to their natural states as possible.

Olivia raised her brows, watching Erin. "Something wrong?"

"No, I'm just admiring it," Erin said, smiling. "You have to feed all your senses, right? Enjoy the whole *experience*."

"Of course," Olivia agreed. "Just what I was saying."

Erin glanced down at her phone again. She couldn't help it. *Where* was Terry? Was he calling to say he'd be late getting home, or was on his way? He often texted her if she didn't answer but, so far, he hadn't sent her a text to let her know what he'd been calling about.

"Would you excuse me for just a moment?" Erin put down her spoon and rose to her feet, sliding her phone into her pocket as she did so in a movement she hoped was invisible to Olivia. "Sorry."

She headed straight for the bathroom and shut and locked the door. Now what?

She couldn't identify what it was about Olivia's mood and actions that had suddenly put her off. Another time, she would have laughed off Olivia's actions and agreed that it was time to put her phone away. She would have eaten the dessert even though there was a faintly different scent about it.

Olivia had been so kind to come and cook for her, but she was letting her imagination run wild, keeping her from enjoying the meal and showing her gratitude for Olivia's gift to her.

She didn't want Olivia to overhear her talking, so she texted Terry rather than calling him.

Missed your call. You coming home?

She waited for his answer, moving around the bathroom, flushing the toilet, running the water, opening and closing the cabinet, trying to make everything sound normal and natural while she waited for Terry's return text.

She was expecting it to come right away, but maybe he had called her to tell her that he was going into a meeting and wouldn't be able to answer any calls or texts for a while. Maybe he had found something when he had looked into the strawberry emails she had received and needed to present it to the sheriff or other law enforcement officers before deciding on a course of action. It could be good news. He might have made some progress and wanted to tell her in person when he got home.

"Erin, is everything alright?" Olivia inquired through the door.

Erin swallowed. "Sorry, I'll be out in a minute. I just… took a turn. I think I forgot my meds." She tried to make it sound normal and believable, not like something she was just making up on the spot. "I'll be fine in a few minutes."

"Meds? Meds for what?" Olivia demanded.

It wasn't polite to ask someone what meds they were taking. You could discuss it if someone disclosed their medical condition and what they were taking but, if not, it was pretty intrusive to ask.

"Sorry, be out in a minute," Erin repeated.

"Erin, I'm worried. Why don't you unlock this door so I can make sure you're okay? I just don't want you to faint or something while I can't get in to help you. After what happened to Montgomery…"

Erin suppressed a chill at the words: *After what happened to Montgomery.* What if it hadn't been Mavis? Once Erin had started putting all the clues together, Mavis had been the obvious suspect, but what if she had made too many assumptions?

Olivia rattled the door handle. "Erin?"

"I'm fine," Erin told her. "Don't come in."

"Was it something I said or did? Erin?" She rattled the doorknob again and bumped her shoulder into the door. Not hard, just experimentally. Erin looked around the bathroom for something she could use to defend herself. The plunger? An aerosol can?

"Oh, no. I'll be okay. I just need a few minutes."

Terry wasn't answering her text. Erin tried Vic.

Hey, are you busy?

Vic's answer was quick, filling Erin with relief. She had been afraid that no one would answer her.

Just spending some time with Willie. He says hi.

Can you come over for a minute and bring your friend?

She held her breath, waiting for Vic's reply. Her heart pounded hard and fast.

My friend? Vic texted back, *U mean Willie?*

No, your little friend.

She waited for Vic's response, but nothing came through.

CHAPTER 44

Despair welled up in Erin's throat.

She tried to keep herself calm. At the moment, she was in no danger. She didn't even know for sure that there *was* any danger from Olivia. She might just be the concerned friend that she appeared to be. Or a stranger who was trying to be her friend.

Even if Olivia had malice in her heart, Erin was protected for the moment by the locked door. It wouldn't withstand a full-on assault, but it was an obstacle, and maybe Olivia would decide it wasn't worth breaking down the door and showing her hand. She had acted covertly until now, being very careful to cover her tracks and not take direct action. She was not the type to rush in boldly and operate openly.

Erin hoped.

Terry was in a meeting and Vic was with Willie, clearly not understanding what Erin was trying to tell her. Maybe she thought Erin had meant to bring Nilla, her little white dog with her—Man's best friend. Nilla might be able to help. He was a brave little dog and not afraid to attack when he thought his people were in danger.

She should have been clear in her text to Vic, but she was used to referring to Vic's weapon obliquely, since she knew it was not properly licensed. Erin looked down at her phone, wondering whether to send another message, clarifying and encouraging Vic to come over quickly.

"Erin," Olivia banged the door again. "Just open the door, please. I want to make sure you are okay."

Was Olivia armed? Erin hadn't even considered that possibility. Olivia was a poisoner—someone who worked in the shadows. But Erin didn't want Vic rushing onto the scene without being properly prepared.

It had been a mistake to contact her. She should have tried the police dispatcher, even if Olivia did hear her talking to her. That could have been a deterrent in itself.

They both arrived at the same time.

Erin heard the front door open and Terry call her name. And at the same time, the back door opened and closed quickly. There was a moment, Erin imagined, when Terry and Vic both stared at each other, confirmed that Erin and Olivia were not in the kitchen, and then moved into the house, maybe with a hand signal or mouthed instruction from Terry telling Vic to fall back and let him go first.

"What are you doing?" Terry demanded. "Hands in the air!"

"I'm just checking on Erin," Olivia protested in an affronted tone. "She's not feeling well. She said something about not taking her medication, but she won't open the door so that I can confirm that she's okay. I'm afraid she might be having… some kind of episode."

The last was, Erin suspected, an attempt to deflect suspicion if Erin came out with some wild story about how Olivia was trying to kill her and had been the culprit behind Montgomery's death.

"Hands up!" Terry ordered again.

"Officer, I'm not sure what you think is happening here, but you can see I am not armed. I'm just talking to Erin. You can ask her. I haven't done anything."

Terry's voice was closer. "Put your hands up unless you want me to have my K9 secure you."

There was a thump on the wall as he probably pushed Olivia into position and frisked her for a weapon. Erin breathed slowly, thinking about her tai chi and the breath control she had practiced with that discipline. Everything was fine. She could relax.

"Erin?" Terry called. "Are you okay? Everything is secure."

"I'm good," Erin told him, her voice much smaller than she expected. There was no need for her to feel so weak. She forced herself to move to the door. She put her hand against it to begin with. Steadying herself.

Reassuring herself that everything was safe and secure on the other side of the door, just like Terry had told her. As if she were Reg Rawlins, professed psychic, able to feel the atmosphere through the locked door.

With one more fortifying breath, she unlocked the door and turned the handle to open it.

Terry stood in the hallway with Olivia, who had been handcuffed and looked a little stunned at the turn of events.

"You see?" she told Terry, "She's just fine. Now if you would release me, I'll head back to the B&B. This is all a bit much for me."

"Shut up," Terry told her irritably. Not the way he usually talked to suspects. "Erin?" He touched her arm. "You okay?"

Erin nodded. "Did you know…?"

"Mavis didn't get here until after Montgomery died. She wasn't the one playing the loud music. And Montgomery's wallet was misplaced or stolen. Twice."

"Twice?" Erin had thought that Mavis was the most likely suspect for having switched the cards in his wallet. She had been close to him. She had probably been tasked with putting the cards in his wallet in the first place. She would have no difficulty making sure that one of them was the old card without strawberries. Or making certain that they all were and then switching them back again after making sure that he was dead. She would have had access to his room because of her position working for him.

But if the wallet had disappeared twice, then that argued against Mavis being the culprit. Someone had taken his wallet once to put the wrong cards in it, and then again to take them out and cover her tracks. Someone close at hand like Olivia.

"What are you talking about?" Olivia demanded. "What does Montgomery's misplaced wallet have to do with me?"

"Because you were close by to steal it and make sure that his allergy cards were replaced with the ones that didn't include strawberries."

"How would I even have a card like that?"

"Maybe he gave it to you when he visited your restaurant," Erin suggested, "or maybe you had your own fakes made."

Olivia shook her head. "You're crazy." She turned to Terry. "Would you please let me go now? I don't know what you think I've done, but you can see that Erin is just fine and I haven't done anything to her."

CHAPTER 45

$\mathcal{E}$rin moved down the hallway, past Terry, K9, and Olivia. Vic stood here, her gun in her hand, her mouth a grim line. She looked confused about what was happening, but she was there and ready to do whatever was necessary to protect her friend. Erin knew that Vic wouldn't hesitate to use her gun, even if it meant she was arrested for carrying an unlicensed weapon or committing manslaughter.

"Thanks," Erin told Vic sincerely. "I guess the cavalry showed up after all."

"Olivia…?"

"She's the one who killed Montgomery." Erin looked at Olivia. "I thought it was Mavis, but I didn't suspect her."

"But it was the strawberries," Vic protested. She appeared to suddenly become aware of the gun in her hand, and turned away from them briefly to secure it in her bra holster. "How can she be responsible for Montgomery's death when she wasn't the one who gave her the strawberries?"

"Exactly," Olivia said smugly. "How can you charge me with something you know someone else did? I didn't give Montgomery the food that killed him. I didn't tell anyone else to do it."

"If you're guilty of making sure that Erin couldn't know about his strawberry allergy, then you are responsible for his death," Terry said firmly. "If you swap out his allergy cards so that she doesn't have any way of knowing about the strawberry allergy, then you *are* guilty."

She smiled. "Are you sure of that, Officer Piper?"

Terry's expression didn't change. But Erin knew he must be trying to sort it out. Did they have enough to charge her? To prove that she had been the one to swap the cards? Was swapping the cards enough to convict her of murder? Or at least manslaughter?

"There's something in the dessert," Erin told him. "That's why... I think she came here because she knew I was getting too close to the truth. And then... I sort of told her what I had figured out about the emails."

"You should be more careful who you talk to. Are you okay? Did you eat any of the dessert?"

"No."

"What did you put in it?" Terry gave Olivia a little shake by her hand-cuffed arms. "We're going to find out anyway, so you may as well tell me."

"I don't know what you're talking about. Why would I put something in the dessert?"

"We'll have it tested. The lab will find out what you put in it."

She shrugged. "I don't know what you're talking about. If there is anything wrong with the dessert, it must be because someone else put something in there. I didn't. So maybe it was her. Or you. To set me up."

Erin and Terry exchanged glances. They both knew how things could go sideways in court. The problem was that there wasn't a lot of evidence against Olivia, only conjecture. Until it came to the poisoned dessert. And if her lawyer successfully argued that it was planted there in order to convict her because they didn't have enough evidence in the Montgomery case...

"I'll get her out of here," Terry said, his voice still flat and unemotional, not reacting to what Olivia said or the fact that she had tried to poison Erin. "And call in the others to take control of the scene and evidence collection."

It would help if someone other than Terry collected the evidence. But it wouldn't be a slam dunk. The police department was a close-knit group and Terry, Erin, and Vic had been in a position to tamper with the evidence before the rest of the department got there.

"We'd better go outside too," Erin told Vic. "Make sure we're not in the house when Sheriff Wilmot and the others arrive."

Vic nodded her agreement and they all trooped outside.

The air was still warm, though the sun was going down. It didn't take the rest of the police department long to arrive. Bald Eagle Falls was a small town and, unless someone were shopping in the city or on vacation, they were close at hand.

Stayner took custody of Olivia and put her into his squad car. Sheriff Wilmot headed for the house.

"I'll come in with you," Erin offered. "I need to lock Orange Blossom up so he doesn't get out of the house. I wouldn't want to lose him."

She was terrified at the thought of Orange Blossom someday getting out on his own and being hit by a car or attacked by a dog or wild animal.

"I'll take care of the cat," Wilmot said, barring her way.

"He doesn't like strangers. He'll scratch."

He nodded. "I'll be careful. Sorry, you need to stay out."

"You can just shut him in my bedroom at the end of the hall. Hopefully he won't howl for too long and will go to sleep on my bed."

But she knew he would yowl for a good long time. She knew her cat. And Orange Blossom had a singing voice that would keep the whole neighborhood up. Erin looked at the time on her phone. It was getting close to her bedtime, but that would be delayed now.

She retreated and let Wilmot go into the house on his own. Orange Blossom did not escape and come running out, so at least he would be safe, though Sheriff Wilmot might sustain extreme cat scratches and bites.

Vic joined Erin and put her arm through hers. "Are you okay?"

"Yeah." Erin sighed. "I'm fine… no harm done. It was just a bit scary. Only I didn't know whether to be afraid or not. I wasn't sure… whether she had really done anything to Montgomery or not, and whether the dessert was poisoned."

"But you think it was?"

"It smelled funny," Erin explained, not sure that was actually proof of anything.

"Well, knowing your super-smeller, you're probably right, then. If one person could sniff out an odor undetectable to the normal human, it would be you."

"I don't know." Erin rubbed her forehead. "I feel like I might have just made it all up. I mean, I know that I didn't, but… there's no proof of anything."

"Until they test the dessert."

"Well, yes."

"You didn't know that Terry was on his way?"

"No. I couldn't answer the phone when he called me, and I guess he couldn't answer when I texted him back. He was probably driving at the time. But I was afraid he had gone into a meeting; that's why I texted you. I didn't know what else to do."

"Well, she didn't have a gun, so you probably would have been okay. You may just be the baker, but you're pretty tough. She didn't look any bigger than you."

"I hoped that it wouldn't get physical… with her being a poisoner. That she wouldn't dare."

"You need to get one of these," Vic said, touching the spot under her bra where her gun lay.

"I'm not getting a gun," Erin said immediately.

"You would have been able to protect yourself," Vic pointed out. "What would you have done if you hadn't been able to get one of us? If you had a gun, you wouldn't even have to wait for her to break the door down. You could drill her through the door. And even if you missed, she would know you were serious."

"I'm not getting a gun," Erin repeated.

Terry was talking to the other law enforcement officers, then came over to speak to Erin and Vic when he was finished. He shook his head at Erin.

"She insists that it was for you. She did you and all of the other potential victims of Montgomery a favor by 'encouraging him to find another line of work.'"

"She doesn't admit to trying to kill him?" Erin asked. It would have been nice if Olivia just confessed her guilt. Then they wouldn't need so much hard evidence to prove what she had done.

"No such luck," Terry agreed with a rueful smile that suggested that he, too, would have preferred it if she just confessed. "She admits to doing things to harass and annoy him, but nothing with malice. Nothing intended to actually kill him."

"What about the wallet cards? Does she admit to that?"

"Of course not. She knows where to draw the line. Not the act that caused his death. Following him, playing music to bother him, sending him flowers or other things to trigger headaches. But not the big allergies. And not the act of removing the card that included strawberries."

She was smart. Too smart. Erin was worried she would get away with everything.

"What about the emails she sent me to get me to make strawberry muffins for the tasting tour? She did that, right?"

"Not that she will admit to. But the forensic guys have a good start on tracing those. They agree that they were all sent by the same person, not different newsletters. If they can trace the IP address to her home or one of her devices…"

"I sure hope they can get something solid on her."

Terry and Vic both nodded their agreement.

"How would she have known he was coming here?" Vic asked. "No one knew when he was going to be here."

"But a few people knew he was coming to Bald Eagle Falls, even if they didn't know the date. I talked to more than one person about it. His tour route was leaked."

"Well, we've got the dessert," Terry reminded her. "I don't know what she put in there, but the lab will identify it."

"I hope so. And I hope it's something really awful," Vic said emphatically. Then she realized how it might sound. "Not so that it would kill you," she told Erin quickly. "I mean so that they can nail her for trying to poison you, not just a prank or a mistake."

Erin eyed her, laughing. "Uh-huh."

CHAPTER 46

*E*rin was back at the bakery with Vic. It felt strange, as if she had been on an extended vacation instead of just taking a couple of days off to recover from her encounter with Olivia.

As Erin had expected, the police investigation had meant that she was not able to get into her house and get to bed until much later than she normally would have. And even when she was allowed back in the house, she was too wound up to think of going to bed. Every creak and groan of the old house made her jump, and her guts were tied up with anxiety. She hadn't eaten much for supper but, even when she got hungry, she couldn't look at food. The smell of the whipped dessert was still in her nostrils and, apparently, her primitive brain had decided she needed to be on the alert for any other murder attempt, and she wasn't able to settle down for a long time. Even watching a long and boring movie, cuddled up with Officer Piper on the couch, safe and protected, was not enough to convince her body that she was safe and could go to sleep.

It was her usual wake-up time before she was able to crawl into bed, and longer before she was able to get a few restless hours of sleep. Then, her body was awake again, wanting to know why she was off her schedule and when she was going to work. It was one of those days where time was all mixed up, dragging behind and jumping ahead, and she never had any idea what time it would be when she looked at her phone.

But the next day, she forced herself to follow her regular schedule, even though she was tired when she got up. She would get back on a normal sleep and work cycle if she made herself follow her usual schedule. Vic had decided that Willie was out of the woods and that she could leave him alone while she helped out at Auntie Clem's, provided he answered the phone whenever she called. Willie promised to do so to get her out of the house and regain some of his independence and personal space.

"That man just hates conventional structure and roles," Vic said, shaking her head, but there was a big smile on her face. She loved Willie and his ways and was glad to see him acting his old self again, smothered by too much attention. It told her he was healing and getting back to normal. "I swear if he had to work a nine-to-five job, he would explode into a ball of fire. Spontaneous combustion. He just couldn't do it."

"Well, it's a good thing he doesn't have to, then," Erin agreed. She was glad that Willie was feeling better. He had been in pretty bad shape the night they had taken him to the hospital. It was good to see him bouncing back and being feisty about what he would or wouldn't do. "I'm sure glad he's feeling better."

"Yeah, me too. The doctor in charge of his chelation says that, hopefully, this was just because of how quickly his heavy metal levels have been changing and is actually a good sign that his body is bouncing back and able to fight off what it sees as toxins or invaders. And hopefully... we'll see a big improvement in his health and mental state soon. She's adjusted some of his treatments and hopes it will ease the process." She shrugged. "I don't know. Most of it is over my head, so I don't know if I'm saying it right. But here's hoping he gets back to normal soon."

Erin showed her crossed fingers. "Hope so."

Vic went to the front door of the bakery to unlock it and let the morning crowd in. Everyone was concerned about Erin's absence and wanted to hear all about Olivia and what would happen to her.

Erin looked at Vic before launching into an explanation.

"She has been arrested for some charges of harassment of Montgomery and attempted murder of me. They don't know if the attempted murder will hold, but want to start with something high to bargain down from."

Teenage Joshua Cox had come to pick up baking for Mary Lou while she took care of Roger, but Erin knew he was really there as an investigative reporter to get the scoop on Olivia for a story he was writing for the Bald Eagle Falls weekly paper. He had his notepad out and was writing busily away even before digging deeper.

"Why hasn't she been charged with Montgomery's murder? If the stuff that she was doing led to his death, and that was what she had intended, why hasn't she been charged?"

Erin took a breath, inhaling the yeasty smell of freshly baked bread, a soothing balm to her anxious mind.

"Because they need to be able to prove it and, so far, they don't have enough. She admits she was harassing him, trying to drive him away from being a food critic. But she won't admit that she was trying to get him killed by influencing me to make the Morning Sunshine Muffins and changing his allergy card so that no one here would know that he was allergic to them. And I'm sure they'll argue in court that she never thought that her interference would lead to his death and was horrified by what happened."

"Do they know what was in the dessert? The one that you didn't eat?"

"They've done some preliminary testing, and I guess it was eyedrops. Tetra..." Erin tried to get the syllables straight in her mind. "Tetrahydrozoline."

Joshua's pencil paused. "Can you spell that?"

Erin laughed. "I can barely say it."

"Okay, just a second. Say it again, and I'll give it my best attempt. Then I can Google it later."

Erin repeated it for him but had difficulty doing so without mangling it. It never sounded the same when she said it out loud as it did in her head, and she was sure she probably got it wrong. But Joshua would sort it out.

"I've heard of it," Joshua said. "I thought you said that you smelled it. I thought tetra—that stuff—was odorless."

"I guess the scientists never met Erin or another super-smeller like her," Vic contributed. "She can smell a lot of things that I would have said were impossible."

"Maybe something else in the eye drops has a smell," Erin said. "A preservative or other chemical. But I could smell something weird."

"Good thing you did," Vic assured her.

"Does she admit to putting the eyedrops in your dessert?" Joshua asked.

"Initially, she said she would accuse me or the police of setting her up. But after talking to her lawyer, she switched to, 'I didn't know it was that bad. I just thought it would make her sick.'"

"Doesn't everyone know it's fatal?"

Erin shrugged as she assembled the items on Mary Lou's shopping list for him. "I guess it's believable that she might think it would just cause an upset stomach. If you look online, people use it for a prank sometimes. It isn't always fatal. It depends on the dose."

"Well, you can bet that Olivia Morgan didn't just intend to make you sick," Vic declared. "Why would she want to do that?"

"To get me off the case until she could disappear. But I don't think she ever intended to run away and change her name. She wanted me out of the picture permanently so I couldn't cause any trouble for her. Especially once she knew I had figured out the part about the emails. I didn't tell her I had already sent them to the police. I think she was hoping to keep me from pursuing it."

"I don't understand how she could make you make something with strawberries in it and keep you from finding out that he was allergic," Mrs. Peach said, leaning on her walker as she waited for Joshua to be served. He really should have let her go first, but Erin suspected he had been too eager to get his questions answered and had tunnel vision, not even noticing Mrs. Peach with her walker.

"She couldn't *make* me," Erin explained, "but she sent a bunch of emails to try to put the idea of using strawberries into my head. And there were people I talked to in cooking forums online about strawberries, too… they're trying to track down if any of them were Olivia. Or if *all* of them were Olivia."

"But how could she keep you from discovering he was allergic to strawberries?"

"Well, she couldn't be sure, not directly. But the big thing was swapping the wallet cards with his allergies listed. Then, he could have been served strawberries by anyone. But he wouldn't eat them if he could see them. He got so much in just one bite of my muffins because he didn't know they were there, and they were hidden in the middle of the muffin in a kind of sauce. So he didn't know until he got a pretty big dose that they were strawberries, and then because of all of the other factors, even grabbing the epinephrine auto-injector as soon as he could, he wasn't fast enough to stop the allergic reaction."

"It was such a severe reaction that it probably didn't matter how much epinephrine he got," Vic said with a sympathetic glance in Erin's direction. "I don't know all the technical terms, but the reaction was already activated and stopped his heart before the epinephrine could work."

Erin blinked and turned away for a moment. She put the rest of Mary Lou's order into a bag and handed the list to Vic to ring it up.

"I didn't like the guy, and I've heard a lot about the number of people he was horrible to, the careers he ruined… but it still bothers me that I had anything to do with it."

"Well, it's just like with Trenton Plaint's death," Mrs. Peach told him. "You can't help what other people decide to do with your muffins."

There was silence for a few minutes while everyone considered this. Joshua had to put away his pencil and pad to pay for the baking for his mother. He probably had other questions to ask, but he knew better than to hold up the line at Auntie Clem's.

"I'll call you," he told Erin, "If there is anything else I need to follow up on."

Erin nodded. "Okay. I'll talk to you later."

She watched him head for the door and walk out. The bells tinkled, marking his departure.

Mrs. Peach looked around as she pushed her walker forward.

"And where are all of those young people who were throwing around accusations after Montgomery's death?" she asked. "It seems like they've all disappeared into the woodwork now."

"I haven't seen anyone," Vic agreed, "it's been as quiet as a church."

"Maybe they're all over at the jail now," Erin contributed. "Shouting their slogans and waving their signs. I'm glad not to have them here. I'm looking forward to everything going back to normal again."

CHAPTER 47

How is the sale going?" Erin asked Charley after finishing speaking to the last school class.

Charley was manning their booth in the school gym. They were raising money for the food bank in the city.

"Money is still trickling in," Charley confirmed. "We've had a few good runs, but I think that most of the money is in now. It will be a good chunk for the food bank."

"Good," Erin approved. She looked at the time. "School will be out in another hour or so, and then we can knock this down and see how much we made."

Erin turned at the tugging on her sleeve. It was Peter Foster, her favorite customer.

"Hi, Peter. Here to buy a muffin?" Erin suggested.

"No, I already got one."

"Oh, good. What do you think of our little fundraiser and education day?"

"It's been really good!" Peter told her. "I like the talk that you gave. About your sister and how hard it is for people who are celiac or allergic to wheat or other grains."

"Well, I hope it helps people to understand why I do what I do," Erin told him, giving his shoulder a squeeze. "And why I think it is so important to make sure that you and anyone else who is gluten-intolerant or allergic have lots of choices. I think everyone needs to have access to good, tasty baking."

"I'm glad you opened Auntie Clem's here," Peter told her. "It is my favorite, favorite store."

His eyes shone and his cheeks were pink. Erin thought about pictures of the children she had seen in medical journals who had been afflicted with celiac disease in previous centuries. How they had starved to death. Just like she had watched Carolyn starve to death when her system had become so damaged that she wasn't able to absorb the nutrients she needed anymore. Peter looked so healthy and strong.

He was so bright and friendly and would be able to grow up instead of being doomed to fade away to nothing. There was no way she would ever give up her mission to provide him and others like him delicious baking in all of its forms, so that he could have fun and be like his peers and grow up to become a great man.

That was why Erin did what she did.

CUSTARD CREAM
CONSPIRACY

To the heartbroken and grief-stricken
to bring healing someday

It was a perfectly normal day until Erin was bowled right off her feet.

She had finished her shift at Auntie Clem's Bakery and was on her way over to The General Store to see Mary Lou about some more jam. The Jam Lady jams were always a good upsell to go with her handcrafted gluten-free breads, and she felt good about supporting a friend in the community as well. It was a win-win-win. Good for her and her business, good for Mary Lou and her family, and good for the customers, who went home with a yeasty, delicious loaf of bakery-fresh bread and a jewel-toned jar of blueberry jam.

Erin had been hoping that The Jam Lady, whose identity was known to only a very select group of people in Bald Eagle Falls, would be able to start making jam again. She had been excited to receive part of the first batch produced after the Jam Lady's lengthy convalescence.

Maybe Erin's head was in the clouds as she dreamed of a taste of the sweet blueberry preserve and wasn't watching where she was going. But Bald Eagle Falls was a sleepy little town, and she didn't usually have to worry about being run over. It wasn't the big city. And it wasn't like she was walking on the road. She should have been safe from harm on the sidewalk.

And it wasn't a car. *They* all stayed on the street where they were supposed to and, when Erin was blasted from behind, she had no idea, to begin with, what had happened.

One minute, she was on her feet, and the next, she was slammed into the very solid wall of the building next to her. It felt like being hit by a truck. She was hit in the back, and then her face and head hit the wall, followed by the rest of her body.

She was too startled to even shout out in surprise; she just went down in a heap.

Someone else was there, swearing and tangled up with her, their legs flailing to separate and get a purchase on solid ground again. Erin's head hit a solid surface again, this time the back of her head on the pavement. Not really hard, but hard enough that it hurt.

A hoarse voice swore at her, or maybe the other party was just upset by the collision and was hurt himself. Or herself. Erin couldn't really determine the gender to assign to the low growl. She saw a flash of black cloth as the other person involved in the accident extricated himself, and then heard an electric whir.

Then she was by herself on the sidewalk. She was sweating, though it wasn't as hot as it had been lately. Her clothes were sticking to her in the warm Tennessee air. Her purse had been upset, items scattered across the pavement. Erin gathered the bits and pieces together in a daze, jamming them back into the cavernous safety of her shoulder bag. Her planner. Her sunglasses, a compact, feminine items, several pens, her keychain…

"Erin, are you okay?"

Mary Lou hurried up to Erin. Erin had never seen Mary Lou in a hurry or disarray before. Mary Lou was always perfectly groomed and manicured, every line of her shirt and pants lying exactly as it should without a wrinkle, her short blond-turned-gray hair coiffed and styled to perfection. She didn't rush or get upset, even when her personal and family life had been in shambles.

"I saw it all through the window," Mary Lou told Erin, reaching down to her and helping her to her feet. She peered into Erin's face worriedly. "Those contraptions should be banned! I can't believe they are allowed on our sidewalks."

Mary Lou handed Erin her planner, which she jammed into her shoulder bag.

"What contraptions?" Erin asked vaguely, looking around. Everything seemed slowed down and weirdly out of place. Like she was out of step with the rest of the world.

"Electric scooters. They are all over the city now. Part of the whole trend to make the city walkable. How is it walkable when you could be mown down by one of those things at any moment? Are you okay, Erin?"

"Yes, yes, fine," Erin murmured. She looked around herself. "Is that what it was? A scooter?"

"I don't know why anyone would go down the sidewalk that fast. Even if they are allowed, there should be some kind of regulation of the things! Speed limits. Yielding to pedestrians." Mary Lou shook her head. "It's all this tourist traffic. People just don't know how to behave in a small town. How to *slow down*."

Erin supposed that she was partly responsible for the increase in tourist traffic. Ever since Gerald Montgomery had died of an allergic reaction to one of Erin's muffins, his fans and followers had been traipsing to Bald Eagle Falls to try out the breakfast muffin for themselves. The steady stream of visitors had slowed, but there were still a lot of people in Bald Eagle Falls who Erin didn't know, and who didn't know the town or its unwritten rules.

"Sorry," she apologized to Mary Lou. She straightened her shirt and ran her fingers through her short, dark hair to smooth it back neatly into place. She probably looked like a mess. She looked at her wet fingers, sticky with blood.

"You're hurt," Mary Lou observed. "Here, sit back down." She helped Erin to sit on the curb, ignoring her protestations that she was fine. "Where's Vic? Where's Terry?"

Erin shook her head. She usually drove with Vic the few blocks from the bakery to the house she had inherited from Clementine, but Vic had only put in half a day and had gone into the city with Willie for a doctor's appointment.

Terry, her handsome cop boyfriend, was probably out walking a beat as usual, with K9, his German shepherd, at his side.

"I'm fine," Erin told Mary Lou. "I don't think it is anything. I'll just wash up when I get home."

"You hit your face too, I saw when he ran you down. Why would anyone be going so fast on the sidewalk?"

A police car gave a short whir of its siren and pulled up next to where Erin was sitting on the curb.

"Did you see what direction he went?" Stayner demanded, rolling down the passenger side window to talk to them.

"That way," Mary Lou motioned in the direction the scooter rider had taken off in, "I think he turned right onto First—"

Stayner pulled away again with a screech of tires. Erin stared after him, still feeling stunned from the collision. She had expected him to stop to help, to see how she was, sitting there bleeding on the curb. Erin supposed that as a cop, it was important for Stayner to see if he could catch the perpetrator, but it seemed like he should at least make sure Erin was okay first. Maybe he had assumed that since Mary Lou was there, she could take care of anything Erin needed and he didn't have to stop.

Mary Lou muttered something under her breath that Erin suspected was not too complimentary.

"He's not the best with people," Erin commented, putting her face in her hands and her elbows on her knees to steady herself. In that position, she felt stable and wouldn't just fall over at the slightest breeze.

"Officer Piper?"

From Mary Lou's tone of voice, Erin knew that she was calling Terry on the phone, not seeing him approach, so she didn't take her face out of her hands to look.

"Erin was knocked down. She's hurt. I think you should come and see to her."

"I'm not hurt," Erin mumbled. "Just a little bruised. You'll scare him."

"She's scraped up," Mary Lou amended. "It isn't an emergency. Though with how hard that guy hit her, she should probably see a doctor. Make sure there isn't anything serious."

Erin couldn't hear Terry's reply but, by Mary Lou's quick goodbye and no further conversation, Erin assumed Terry had told her he was on his way.

He could drive Erin home, and then she could lie down until she felt less shaky.

CHAPTER 2

"What exactly happened?" Terry demanded as he walked up to Erin. "Erin, are you okay?"

"I'm fine," Erin mumbled through her hands. She knew that she should pull her hands down and let him look at her face, but she felt comfortable in the position she was in and didn't want to move.

"There was a scooter," Mary Lou explained. "One of those electric ones. And the… what do you call someone who rides a scooter…?"

"I don't know," Terry's tone was clipped. "A scooterist?"

"Scooterist?" Mary Lou repeated dubiously. "Okay, the scooterist was going down the sidewalk way too fast. If he's going to go that fast, then he should be on the street, not on the sidewalk. And he ran Erin down. Just came out of nowhere and crashed into her. Knocked her into the wall, and fell and got tangled up with her, and then he took off without even helping her out. I don't think he even said anything to her, did he, Erin? Did he even say he was sorry?"

"He was swearing."

"Oh, lovely," Mary Lou cleared her throat. "This is the generation we are raising now. Kids who swear at someone they knock down instead of apologizing. Zipping around here on those contraptions. It's dangerous!"

"Male?" Terry questioned. "Teenager?"

"I don't know," Mary Lou said. "I assumed so when I saw him, but I didn't get a good look. Officer Stayner went after him; maybe he'll have better luck. I just thought… well, it wouldn't be a woman, would it? Or an older person?"

"Lots of people ride electric scooters," Terry said with a shrug. "Helps people get from one place to another more easily. Especially those who aren't up to walking long distances."

"Hmm."

Erin could feel Terry sit down on the curb next to her. He rested his hand on her back to begin with. A light touch. Warm. Reassuring.

"Erin. Can you let me look at you? See if you're hurt?"

"I'm okay," she assured him. "Just bumps and bruises."

"Let's see. I've got a first aid kit in the car. I can clean you up, get you bandaged up and on your way."

"I'll just go home," Erin told him, finding it more difficult than she expected to pull her face away from her hands and let him look at her. "Have a hot shower and lie down for a while."

"Yeah," he agreed. "That sounds good. Once I've had a chance to look at you. I'm sure you're right and it isn't anything to worry about."

He gently pulled her shoulder back, coaxing her hands away from her face. Erin blinked in the bright light. The sun was getting lower in the sky, but it was still too hot and too bright for Erin's eyes and the headache starting to form behind them. She blinked back tears and rubbed at the corners of her eyes.

"Just hold still a second," Terry advised, holding her chin gently with one big hand. His handsome face took on a look of concern. K9 whined, his head almost at a level with Erin's.

"I'm fine," Erin told K9. "Just a little bump."

Terry prodded the sore spot on the front right corner of Erin's head. "That's not such a little bump. It's swelling up pretty good, and you might need a couple of stitches across there. Where did he hit you? How did you fall?"

"He hit me… in the back and side. Knocked me into the wall. I hit there, and then fell down, and he fell down, and I hit my head—"

"You hit it a second time?"

"In the back," Erin explained. She felt for the sore spot in the back of her head. There wasn't as much of a goose egg there. Not as serious. It was bleeding, but scalp wounds always did.

Terry poked around some more, moving her hair around to get a good look at her scalp. He leaned back away from her again. "I think I should take you to the hospital."

There was no hospital in Bald Eagle Falls, so that meant a trip to the city. Erin didn't feel like going all that way for nothing. She'd had a collision on the sidewalk. It wasn't the end of the world. People had minor accidents all the time. She would go home with a few cuts and bruises and be back at work like she was supposed to be tomorrow.

"Terry… it's nothing."

"You can't see it. I think it is severe enough to warrant looking at it."

"It's just a bruise."

"Exactly how hard did you hit the pavement?"

"I was just walking. So I wasn't moving fast. And I hit the building first, so that absorbed most of the shock. I just hit my head when I landed because it happened so fast and I wasn't braced for it." She cleared her throat. "It wasn't that hard," she asserted. "I didn't lose consciousness. Mary Lou was right here. She can tell you that. I've been coherent."

Terry looked at Mary Lou, who agreed. There was a murmur of voices closing in around them. Erin had a knot in her stomach as she realized people were gathering to watch her, whispering to each other, speculating as to what had happened and how badly hurt she was. She raised her hand as if shielding her eyes from them would prevent them from seeing her.

"Any dizziness?" Terry drilled.

"No. Maybe just a little."

"Double vision?"

"No."

"Nausea?"

"No."

Not really. She wasn't feeling great, but that was because of all the attention, not because of the head injury.

"Tiredness?"

Erin laughed weakly. "Well, yes. I'm tired. I've been up since the wee hours of the morning working. What do you expect? I'm tired and I don't want to have to drive to the city and then sit around in the hospital for hours until a doctor has a chance to look at me, wave his finger around in front of my face, and then tell you that I'm perfectly normal and should go home to bed."

"It would make me feel a lot better."

"Well, not me. I want to go home and have a shower and a bite to eat and then veg in front of the TV until bedtime. How about I do that instead?"

"Someone should be watching you."

"Then why don't you come over and watch me?"

Terry gave her a slow grin, the dimple appearing in one cheek smudged with five o'clock shadow.

"I'm not supposed to be off for a couple more hours."

"And if you had to take me to the hospital in the city, wouldn't you call Sheriff Wilmot and tell him that you needed the time off? And wouldn't Stayner or one of the others cover for you?"

"Of course," he admitted.

"Then tell them that you need to take time off to watch me and make sure that I didn't suffer any ill effects from the accident. It isn't like they won't know what you're talking about. You're not skipping out of work. I *was* in an accident."

Terry had a strong sense of duty that Erin had to work against. He put in more than his share of time with the Bald Eagle Falls police department, and taking a couple of hours off early one evening was not a problem. No one would object.

"You really should take the time off and keep an eye on her," Mary Lou advised, her expression serious.

"Yes," Terry agreed, drawing the word out, still unsure whether he would tell the sheriff he needed to take the rest of the day off.

"Brain injury is nothing to fool with," Mary Lou told them.

And Mary Lou was someone who knew that better than most. She spoke with authority.

"Okay," Terry agreed finally. "I'll let the sheriff know that I'm clocking out early. I'm still around if there is an emergency and they send out a call."

Erin relaxed. It would be nice for both of them to be home for the evening. With nothing to do but cuddle in front of the TV and enjoy each other's company.

CHAPTER 3

*E*rin got the long, hot shower that she had been hoping for. It helped to soothe all the bruises and sore muscles that she was already starting to feel, less than an hour after the accident. She hoped that wasn't a sign of how sore she was going to be for the next few days.

Terry took care of feeding Orange Blossom, who was meowing as piteously as if he had been abandoned for weeks rather than just a few hours. After Erin had finished her shower, Terry examined her bumps and lacerations again.

"I'd like to put some strips across these cuts if you aren't going to go in and get them stitched up."

While Erin didn't want to deal with adhesive suture strips in her hair, she would put up with them if it meant avoiding a trip to the hospital or the doctor in town.

"If it makes you feel better," she sighed.

"It does, actually. I think you should get the one on your face stitched so that it doesn't leave a scar, but… you can think about it. If we at least get it pulled closed tonight, it has a chance to start mending. We'll be able to see tomorrow whether the tape is going to keep it closed or not."

"I'm sure it will be fine. I've hurt myself worse than this before. It isn't anything."

She sat still while he doctored each of the lacerations and then looked over his handiwork.

"I guess that will do," he said finally. "I'll put some bandages over them to absorb any seepage. Maybe some ice would be a good idea to keep the swelling down."

"I don't want anything touching them right now. I'll take an anti-inflammatory."

"Okay." He pressed his lips together and Erin knew he didn't like the idea, but he was going to keep quiet about it and not press her further. He was good that way—most of the time.

Since Erin was injured, it was up to Terry to fix them something to eat, and he had been busy while she was in the shower. The savory smells of roasting meat and warming soup filled the house, and Erin realized she was starving. The knot in her stomach was gone, and she wasn't worried about what anyone thought about her being knocked down in the middle of the sidewalk. It wasn't like she had been careless or clumsy. Anyone could have been run down by a scooter.

"Did Stayner catch him?" she asked Terry as she sat down at the table to eat.

"Hmm? Uh, no. I guess he got away. One of the problems with motorbikes, bicycles, scooters, and the like is that they can go a lot of places that a car cannot."

Erin was reminded of crazy Theresa. And another recent close call with a violent criminal and a motorcycle. She hadn't had any experience with suspects on scooters, but with how popular they were becoming in the city, she supposed it was only a matter of time.

"I can't understand why he was going so fast in the first place." Erin shook her head, then regretted it. Best to keep her head still for a while. "What was he in such a hurry for?"

Terry looked at her for a moment, then continued to bus the food on the table. "Because Rod was chasing him."

Erin had assumed that Stayner was chasing the scooterist because he had seen him knock Erin down, not that the scooterist had knocked Erin down because he was trying to get away from Stayner. She supposed that explained why Stayner hadn't stopped to assist her but had continued to pursue the suspect.

"Why was Stayner chasing him?"

Terry considered. "Well, I suppose you'll see it on the news. There was a break-and-enter in the city, and he matched the description of the perpetrator in the bulletin we were sent. When Rod tried to stop him to question him, he took off. A pretty good indicator of guilt. When Rod pursued him, well, that's when he knocked you down."

Terry flushed a little as he sat down to eat with her. He probably knew that he shouldn't admit to her that the police had been the indirect cause of Erin's accident. She could sue the department for her injuries. Not that Erin was that kind of person, but he certainly left the opening for her when he should have kept quiet.

"So that's why he didn't stop to talk to me. What did this guy steal in the city? I mean, it wasn't something he could have been carrying on the scooter, was it?" Erin pictured the scooterist trying to balance something unreasonably large while on the scooter, like a big screen TV. But of course, it could have been something smaller, like a laptop. Or cash. Or diamonds.

"We don't know whether he had it on him or not. And we don't know whether it was even the same guy. We didn't have a chance to question him yet, so we don't even know his identity. We'll be on the lookout for him, but the chances that he'll continue riding around town on the scooter are… low, to say the least."

"I would guess so," Erin agreed. "It isn't like we have a lot of them around Bald Eagle Falls. He would stand out like a sore thumb. He's probably already ditched it somewhere. In the woods or… a ditch." Erin couldn't think of the word that she wanted.

"Ditched it in a ditch?" Terry repeated.

"Yeah." Erin shrugged. "Something like that. Maybe in a… in the water. It would be impossible to find unless you knew exactly where he had dumped it."

He nodded.

She sipped the soup and let out a long sigh. "This is really good."

"Just what you need after a long, hard day," he asserted, giving himself a self-congratulatory pat on the back. "And then a quiet night together. A good sleep, and you'll be feeling much better in the morning." He paused, considering. "But you are going to be sore. You might want to get someone to cover your shifts at Auntie Clem's for you for a day or two."

"I'll be fine." Erin shrugged. She had weathered worse injuries before.

It was nothing like the head injury she had sustained when she had first arrived in Bald Eagle Falls and gotten wrapped up in the investigation of Angela Plaint's murder. That had been bad. And she had suffered through a number of childhood injuries and had rarely even missed school. A little fall and a few bruises were nothing to be concerned about.

When they were finished eating, Erin got up to help clear the dishes. Her head whirled and she grabbed the table to steady herself.

"Erin!" Terry stepped forward, grabbing her arm. "Are you okay?"

She pulled back from him. "A bit of a head rush. I just got up too fast."

"You don't need to do the clean-up. I'm supposed to be serving you today. You just sit back and enjoy being pampered. I'll walk you over to the couch."

"I don't need you to walk me. I'm just fine. I just took a bit of a turn when I got up too fast."

He stayed at her elbow all the way to the couch. To his credit, he didn't grab her, but he hovered close by so that he would be able to catch her if she demonstrated any unsteadiness.

"I'm fine," Erin repeated, once sitting. She looked at the clock on the wall. "Oh, it's getting late. I was supposed to take Nilla out for a walk."

"Nilla," Terry repeated. "Right. I forgot Vic and Willie were out." He looked toward the loft apartment over the garage where Vic lived, and where Willie had been staying lately, even though he still had a place of his own. He had been undergoing treatment for heavy metal poisoning, and he had not been up to taking care of himself.

The doctor had declared his course of chelation complete, and Vic and Willie had celebrated by going into the city for dinner and a movie, and whatever other entertainment they wanted. And for that to work, they couldn't be tied down to Nilla, the little white dog that Vic had adopted. Erin hadn't foreseen any problems with taking Nilla out for a walk or looking after his other needs. But she hadn't expected to be run down in the street.

"I'll take Nilla out," Terry told Erin. "You stay where you are. I don't want you stumbling around in the dark."

"I would turn on the lights," Erin pointed out in amusement. She could figure that much out by herself, even if she were addled by being knocked down, which she wasn't.

Terry smiled and nodded. "K9. You want to go outside and play with Nilla?" Terry invited. He knew that if the two dogs played together, K9 would wear Nilla down, so that the smaller dog would sleep rather than getting into too much mischief.

"You can bring him in here when you're done," Erin said. "There's no point in us going back and forth with him. He can just stay here until his mommy and daddy are back."

"I'm not sure how Willie would feel about being called the dog's daddy."

Terry shrugged. "I can't help that. Vic may have adopted the dog, but the dog adopted Willie."

Erin had noticed that Nilla seemed much more attached to Willie since he had started his treatment. When Vic had first taken Nilla in, he had been quite anxious around men and had not been happy when Willie was there. But since Willie had been sick and spending a lot of time sleeping, Nilla had apparently decided that his new blanket warmer was okay.

"I'm sorry I forgot," Erin apologized. "I should have taken him out as soon as we got home. I hope he hasn't made a mess."

Terry moved a little more quickly toward the back door. K9 followed closely behind him.

Erin closed her eyes while she waited for Terry to take care of the dogs. She knew he wouldn't be long, no more than half an hour, but she found herself unable to keep her eyes open while she waited for him.

CHAPTER 4

*E*rin was on the edge of sleep for what seemed like a long time before she woke up. She knew that Terry had returned with the animals, and that he had made sure that they were all fed and turned on some TV show. But still, she slept through the activity. Terry touched her when he sat down next to her.

"Erin? Do you want to wake up and watch this with me? Or do you want to go to bed?"

Erin turned her face away from his. She opened her eyes, but found the TV and the lamp too bright. She squinted.

"The light hurts my eyes," she complained.

Terry got up and turned the lamp down one click. "Is that any better? Do you want it off?"

"No." Erin rubbed her eyes. She usually didn't like to have the lights off while watching TV. She preferred to be doing something else while it was on. Working on her planner, reading through Clementine's genealogy files, or something else. But she wasn't sure if she could do any of that today. She was feeling a little woozy, her head thick and heavy. "No, leave it on. I'll... I'll do something..." She couldn't retrieve the right words. She reached for her handbag, unsure if it was at her feet or if she had left it elsewhere.

"What is it?" Terry asked. "What do you want?"

"I just wanted… to get out my planner. There are some things I wanted to do."

"Let me get it for you."

Terry got the dogs settled where they would be out of the way and he and Erin wouldn't trip over them if they got up to go into the kitchen. Orange Blossom sat on the back of the couch where he could look down at the dogs and hiss at them if he thought they were getting out of line. The last member of their furry family, Marshmallow the rabbit, was sleeping behind the couch, but might come out later to lie down with K9 while they were watching TV. Erin wondered sometimes whether Marshmallow considered himself one of the dogs. K9 frequently lay with his head behind the couch in order to be close to Marshmallow. But the bunny might not come out while Nilla was there, since he was quite a bit more hyper and annoying than the German shepherd.

"Erin?"

Erin realized that she had let her eyes close again. She tried to sit up straighter and keep herself awake. She wanted to stay awake until bedtime so that she would be able to keep to her regular schedule. If she fell asleep too early, she might not be able to sleep when her bedtime rolled around, and then she wouldn't be ready to wake up when her alarm rang in the morning. And she needed to be able to get up when her alarm rang in the morning.

"I'm awake," she told Terry.

"How did *this* get into your bag?"

Erin blinked, but Terry was standing too far away for her to see what he was holding clearly.

"My planner?" she hazarded a guess.

"No." He stepped closer, holding the book closer to her so that she could see it closely. "This book."

Erin had never seen it before. It was, from the cover, a recipe book. Vintage, the cover worn and browning, pages yellow. The kind of thing that Erin found fascinating to page through.

"Where did you get that?" she asked. "Can I see?" She held her hand out for it.

Terry handed it to her, looking uncertain. "It was in your bag. Where did you get it?"

"My bag?" Erin tried to laugh. "No, I think I would know if I had something like that in my bag." She opened the book and browsed through the opening pages. The smell of old paper and dust rose out of it. It was a recipe book published by the Bald Eagle Falls Women's League. A community cookbook, comprised of recipes that women in the town had contributed. The kind of thing that was sometimes done as a fundraiser, and occasionally just something to draw the women together, make them feel more like a close circle. Few people would ever publish a book of their own, and appearing in an anthology or a recipe book was the closest they would ever get. It was an accomplishment, something they could hold in their hands, maybe send to family members as a Christmas gift, even if they were back in England or Europe.

Erin turned the pages slowly. It started with Beverages, and then Breakfast. Old recipes, some with short lists of ingredients and just a line or two of instructions, and some that filled the pages with dense writing, laying out complex descriptions of how to pull a recipe together, set places at a table, or cater for a large community event. Erin was enthralled.

The type was blurry and hard to make out in places. Or was it her eyes? Erin held the pages closer to her face, studying them closely.

"You've never seen that book before?" Terry repeated.

"No. This is great. I love vintage recipe books. Where did you find it?"

"This must be the one that was stolen in the city, then. From the museum."

"What?"

"I told you. There was a break-and-enter at the museum."

"Right," Erin agreed, drawing the word out and trying to think of why Terry had told her that and what the circumstances had been. Had he even told her what was stolen? "And this is what was stolen? Why would someone steal a recipe book from a museum?"

If Vic had been there, she would have made a wisecrack. Erin shook her head, imagining it even though Terry would probably not think of it. "And don't tell me, 'Someone hungry.'"

Terry gave an obliging chuckle. "Right. Of course. But seriously, I don't know why it was stolen, only that it was. The book was supposed to be part of an exhibit opening this weekend. Sort of a 'rural communities of Tennessee' commemoration exhibit. But someone broke in and took this." He pointed at the recipe book in Erin's hands.

"And that's who knocked me down?" Erin asked as the connection finally came to her. She was too tired; she didn't seem to be able to put things together like she normally would. "The guy Stayner was chasing because he matched the description of the burglar in the city? He knocked me down, and we got all tangled up."

"Your purse was dumped," Terry suggested, picturing it, realizing at the same time as Erin just what had happened. "And you were picking stuff up and putting it back into your purse. You must have grabbed the book, which the thief had dropped without realizing it."

Erin could remember putting her planner back into her purse, but not the small hardcover book. But they were about the same size. She had been stunned by the accident. Maybe she had just grabbed everything in sight and shoved it into her purse, gathering up the recipe book as Terry had suggested.

"I guess. Maybe. That could be what happened," she admitted.

"Well, the owner will be very happy to get that back, I'll tell you." He reached out his hand to take it back from Erin.

CHAPTER 5

*E*rin didn't hand it over. "Is it valuable?" She couldn't imagine such a little thing would have any intrinsic value. A collector might want it. Someone whose grandmother or great-grandmother had published her family recipes in it. But it was more of a novelty than anything she would have thought had any value.

"I don't know how much it is worth," Terry said. "It is my understanding that stuff like this can be worth anything from a few cents to thousands of dollars."

They both looked down at the fairly nondescript brown cover.

"I doubt this one is worth thousands," Erin said, shaking her head. "I love to look through vintage stuff like this, but I can't see it being worth anything to anyone. Unless it was, you know, grandma's recipes."

"You never know what people will pay for something. It was a big deal that this was stolen, and an alert was sent to the surrounding areas to track it down. So it must be worth something."

Erin was reluctant to hand it back to him. It wasn't hers, of course. She couldn't keep it. But she wanted to spend a little more time looking at it.

"Do you think you could get me an aspirin?" She asked him. "I just want to look at this for another minute, and then I'll be done."

Terry frowned at her. He lowered his hand. "Fine. Just for another minute while I get you a pill. Then we need to call the museum and the investigator on the case to let them know we've tracked it down."

"I'll just be a minute," Erin agreed.

Terry retreated to the bathroom to find Erin an aspirin. She supposed she *should* take something, even if she had only sent him to get her something as a diversion. He was right that she would be very sore the next day, when her bruises all set in and her joints and muscles felt the consequences of the impact.

She laid the recipe book down on the coffee table. It was well-worn enough that it stayed open as she laid it down; it didn't close or flip to a different page. Erin took out her phone, turned the camera to video mode, and turned the pages swiftly, being sure to focus in on each one for a brief instant.

"I can't find any aspirin," Terry called from the bathroom. "Do you want something else?"

"Check the cupboard in the kitchen," Erin suggested.

He obligingly walked into the kitchen. "Which cupboard?"

"The one closest to the sink."

He banged around a little. There were several cupboards that were close to the sink, but none of them held a bottle of aspirin.

"Nothing in here," Terry announced.

"Maybe the pantry, then?"

Terry moved to the large pantry. It would take him a few more minutes to convince himself that there was no aspirin in the pantry shelves either. Erin kept turning the pages in the recipe book. She wasn't sure how good the pictures would be. The words all appeared to be blurred. Maybe a low-quality printer's ink. But she could study it later. See what she could work out and what was too smudged or blurred to be legible. The important thing was to copy it for herself so she could look through the book virtually after Terry took it back.

"Do you even have any aspirin?" Terry asked, standing outside the door of the pantry looking at her.

Erin couldn't hide the fact that she was filming the pages of the book.

"I think there might be some in the drawer beside the bed. On my side. If not, maybe Advil?"

"I'll check," he sighed.

After he found a bottle of pills, he got her a drink of water to wash it down and stood over her while she took two pills.

"And if you're finished with the book, Miss Price…"

Erin giggled at him using his cop voice on her. Maybe she should have felt bad about taking pictures of the recipe book. But chances were, she would never see a copy again, and it would be a huge loss not to have access to those old family and community recipes. A reservoir of recipes and traditional food preparation techniques would be lost to her forever.

She handed him the recipe book. "What are you going to do with it?"

"Take it into evidence for the burglary case. I'm sure the museum will be glad to know it has been recovered, even if it can't be returned to the exhibit yet. At least the owner won't have to make an insurance claim."

"The museum isn't the owner?"

"No, I guess it is borrowed from a private owner for the exhibition and then returned to them after that, normally. Since it was stolen and will be held as evidence until the case is prosecuted, the exhibition will probably be closed by the time they get it back."

"That doesn't seem very fair." Erin leaned back in the couch and looked at the video on her phone, but she wasn't able to make out any of the details of the recipe book on the tiny screen. She would have to transfer the video to her computer at work or tablet. And even then, it might be too blurry to read. "It wasn't the museum's fault that it was stolen. Or the owner's. But they can't get it back until after the burglary trial?"

"Evidence has to remain in police custody. Chain of evidence must be preserved for it to be used in the court case. It's unfortunate, but if they can catch the burglar then it shouldn't take too long to prosecute. Some cases can take years and years."

"But we know this burglar is in Bald Eagle Falls."

"Or he was, a few hours ago. He could be somewhere else by now."

Erin rubbed her temples, trying to clear the brain fog. She must be a lot more tired than she had thought. The accident had taken a lot out of her. "But if the recipe book is about Bald Eagle Falls, and he came back here with it, then chances are, he lives here, right?"

Terry was silent. Erin blinked a few times and tried to focus on him. "That's right, isn't it?"

"It is," he agreed slowly. "I hadn't made the connection. I thought…

we were just lucky to have spotted him here, and he would probably move on quickly to someplace he hadn't been identified. But if there is something specific about that recipe book… maybe he is a Bald Eagle Falls resident."

"Was it the only thing that was stolen?"

"There were a few other items, nothing of great value. Like I said, it is an exhibit about farm life in Tennessee, so they are fairly common items."

"He must have taken the recipe book for a reason. And it's specifically about Bald Eagle Falls. I'm sure he wasn't just using it as a sightseeing guide."

Terry snorted. He disappeared into the kitchen to find a bag to put the book into. He needed to keep it safe until he could take it to the police department. Erin hadn't thought about fingerprints when she had been turning the pages. But she supposed that she and Terry had already handled it before he had realized what she had in her possession. Their fingerprints were already on it. She would have handled it with gloves if she had thought about it. Even if they weren't worried about evidence, she knew the oils in a person's skin would degrade paper over time. Experts wouldn't handle precious manuscripts with bare fingers.

Was the manuscript precious, though? It didn't seem to have that much value, but the thief had apparently thought it important enough to steal. Had he known something about its value that she and Terry didn't? It was certainly possible, since they were only guessing what it was worth. Had it been worth breaking into the museum to get it? Risking imprisonment? It was hard to believe that a Women's Society cookery book was worth serving time for.

"Are you sure you want to stay up and watch something?" Terry asked, reaching for the remote control. "You're looking pretty wiped out."

"I was *wiped out* this afternoon. Right now, I'm just tired."

It took a moment for Terry to get the joke. He shook his head. "I guess you must be okay if you're making jokes, but I'm still worried about you. Do you mind if I look at your eyes?"

He turned his body toward her so that he was facing her instead of shoulder-to-shoulder with him. Erin's cheeks burned at being under such careful scrutiny.

"I'm really fine."

"Then you don't mind if I look…?"

Without waiting for an answer, he took out a penlight like a doctor would use. He started with it beside Erin's face, out of her vision, and then moved it over to flash it briefly in her eyes. Erin knew that he was checking her pupil reactivity, but it was annoying and she pushed his hand away after several flashes into her eyes.

"That's bothering me. Just stop now."

"Bothering you how?" His brows drew down. "You need to be honest about how you feel. I can't assess you if you don't tell me the truth."

The flashes of light had not helped with the sensations of being light-headed and removed from what was happening. Although she had enjoyed the supper Terry had pulled together for her, she wished now that she hadn't had anything to eat. Her stomach twisted with nausea, and she was afraid that if he didn't *stop* shining lights in her eyes, she might just throw up in his lap.

"Just put it away," she told him irritably. "I want to spend some time together. Have a nice evening, not have lights shined in my eyes."

"Okay, okay," Terry agreed, switching off the light and putting it into his pocket. He turned back to the TV and put his arm around her shoulder to give her an affectionate squeeze before turning his attention to finding something for them to watch.

CHAPTER 6

*S*he wandered through the woods, trying to enjoy the beautiful
surroundings as she always had. But nothing seemed to improve
her melancholy this time.

It had been too long since she had seen him. In the beginning, she
had excused his absence, reasoning that he had needed to get away to
think things through on his own without any interference from either her
or his families. And if they were going to be together, he would have to
find a good job. Some way to earn a living. Because neither of their families was going to help him out.

So maybe he was off looking for a job, or had found something and
was already working. He would send her a letter when he could, but he
might be busy in the early stages. Or his letter might have been lost or
delayed by the postal service. Bald Eagle Falls didn't always have the best
service.

But it had been too long now, and she had to wonder if she were lying
to herself. He had seemed excited at the prospect of their being together
but, maybe once he'd had a chance to think about it, his feelings had
changed. They were both young and neither of their families supported
the match. It would be hard for them to manage on their own.

She didn't mind if things were lean for the first few years. They would have each other. And she could stand the privations, knowing that they were building their future life together. That they would be together for many years, like her grandparents. She was willing to sacrifice for their future happiness.

She stopped to watch a squirrel bounding through the long grass and eventually into one of the trees, where it sat on one of the high branches and chattered at her, acting like she was keeping it from gathering the nuts and food he would need when the weather turned cooler.

"Be glad you don't live where it turns cold," she told him, chuckling to herself. "You might think it gets cold here, but up in the tops of the mountains, Uncle Barry says it snows and stays below freezing for weeks."

The squirrel continued to scold her. She smiled and moved along, leaving him to his nut gathering. She should be putting up stores for the winter as well. She had helped Grandma put up her preserves in past years, but she had been too tired this year to help her mother do much canning. Her mother didn't like canning like Grandma did, avoiding it whenever possible.

But if he came back and the two of them ended up on their own during the winter, what would they live off of? She needed to start planning for the future. She couldn't just let events overtake her as they had and expect God to work things out for her.

The alarm rang, startling Erin out of sleep. She groped to shut it off and orient herself to the bedroom, but nothing seemed to be in the right place. The clock was too far away. Her fingers were fat and clumsy. Her head throbbed when she moved. It felt full and congested, like she had a bad sinus cold or had recently had major dental work done. Full and thick and numb.

She knocked something to the floor. Not her phone. Something else that made a terrible racket. She tried too late to stop it, attempting to pick it up afterward, but she couldn't seem to find her way around. It was dark but, even so, she could usually navigate successfully in the familiar room without waking Terry up. He was now stirring beside her, undoubtedly awakened by the crash.

"I'm sorry, I'm sorry," Erin murmured, trying to keep him from getting up or being alarmed by her behavior.

"Erin? Are you okay?"

"I just… can't…" She knocked something else over.

The light on Terry's side of the bed turned on, blinding her.

"Erin, what's wrong?"

"Nothing… nothing, I just…" She looked down at the lamp she had knocked off her bedside table, as well as a water glass and her phone. She swore under her breath. With her luck, she would electrocute herself—or at least brick her phone. Tears welled up in her eyes and a lump swelled up in her throat.

"Are you okay?" Terry sat up beside her, rubbing her back and peering into her face. "Did you have a nightmare?"

"Yeah. Yeah, I did, and I didn't know where anything was when I woke up," Erin tried to explain her mental state. "But I'm awake now…"

He looked over the side of the bed at everything that had fallen. "Let me take care of that. You stay put. Give yourself a few minutes to finish waking up."

"It's time for work," Erin disagreed. "I need to get ready."

"Then let me help you."

He climbed out of bed and went to Erin's side to pick up the lamp and the glass, carefully moving the lamp away from the spilled water. He picked up Erin's phone and wiped the screen off on his t-shirt.

"How wet did it get?" Erin asked as she took it from him.

"Just a few drops on the screen, I think. It should be fine."

Erin shifted to get out of bed. Someone would need to clean up the spilled water.

But her head was woozy and throbbed when she tried to get up. Terry pressed her back.

"You're not feeling well. I think you'd better take a few minutes to see if you are up to doing anything today."

"I'm fine."

"Maybe you're just disoriented by your dream. But you're pretty pale. Just take a few minutes sitting up before you try to stand, or I'll be picking you up off the floor."

"It's too late to find someone to cover my shift. I'm going in."

"If one of your bakers woke up with the flu, would you want her showing up for her shift?"

"Well, no. But I don't have the flu. I'm not contagious. I just have a headache."

He stood looking at her for a minute before speaking. "You've had a concussion before."

"Sure. More than one."

"Then I want you to really think about this. Do you think you might be concussed from your accident yesterday?"

Erin knew that it felt like her head was going to explode if she didn't take a painkiller soon. But that didn't mean she couldn't work.

"I'll be fine once I'm up and around."

Terry shrugged. He turned around and headed for the bedroom door. "I'm going to start the coffee."

Erin watched him leave the room, confused. Terry didn't normally make her coffee in the morning. And he didn't need to be up for his shift for several more hours. He should have been turning off the light and going back to sleep, not making coffee. She had expected a further argument about why she shouldn't go in to Auntie Clem's. She had been marshaling her arguments, getting ready for it.

She waited for a few minutes, sitting and letting her head adjust to an upright position, as Terry had suggested. She rubbed the ridge of bone over her eyes, trying to relieve the feeling of building pressure in her head. But unlike when it was caused by tense muscles or sinuses, rubbing it didn't change anything.

She wasn't feeling great, but she was well enough to go in to work. And as she had told Terry, it was too early in the morning to get anyone to cover for her. She had to go in herself.

Erin slid her feet out of bed and stood carefully. She would prove Terry wrong. He wasn't going to have to scrape her up off the floor. She was perfectly fine. A headache wasn't enough to warrant her skipping out of her shift.

Her head swam. Erin had already stepped away from the bed, so she reached out to the wall to steady herself. It was farther away than she had thought. She stepped closer and rested her head against the wall, waiting for the room to stop swaying. The lurching of the room made her seasick. Her stomach roiled in protest. Even though she hadn't had anything to eat since dinner the night before, Erin knew she was going to throw up. What she didn't know was whether she could make it to the bathroom first. Especially with the way the room was rocking.

"Terry!"

He hurried down the hall toward her. Erin covered her mouth and tried to convince herself she could hold it until she got to the bathroom.

Like that had ever worked.

She made it as far as the bathroom, but not the toilet. She doubled up over the sink. Terry steadied her by the shoulders when her knees buckled, holding her still.

Otherwise, he *would* have been picking her up off the floor.

Gasping, Erin hung over the sink.

"Do you want to sit down?" Terry asked, indicating the toilet.

"I… yes."

He steered her carefully over to the toilet and helped her to sit down on the lid. "Are you going to be okay there for a minute?"

"I don't think… yeah, I guess so." Erin steadied herself with one hand on the counter and one on the edge of the tub. The cool porcelain felt good. She could sit there by herself. And then, when she felt better about it again… she tried to think of what her next step would be. Maybe a cup of ginger tea would set her straight and she would be able to function.

"Who is supposed to be opening with you this morning?" Terry asked.

"Charley."

"Charley can get up this early?" he asked doubtfully.

"No, she comes in at the end of her day. Then she goes home to bed."

Terry chuckled. He left the bathroom, leaving Erin sitting there on the toilet, unable to move anywhere else without assistance.

Maybe he was right and she wouldn't be able to work at Auntie Clem's, no matter how much she wanted to. She could hear him talking on his phone in the kitchen, but couldn't make out what he was saying. Contacting Charley and trying to make alternate arrangements, she supposed. Maybe suggesting to Charley that they close Auntie Clem's for the day. Charley was part-owner with Erin, so she could make that decision if Erin could not be there.

A loud meow in front of her face made Erin realize she had closed her eyes as she tried to regain her equilibrium. Orange Blossom sat directly in front of her, staring at her and asking her why she was sitting there rather than getting ready for the day as she should have been. And filling his food dish, obviously.

Erin tentatively let go of the counter beside her and extended her fingers for Blossom to rub against.

"I'm just not feeling very well today," she told the cat softly. "Everything will be okay. Terry can get you your breakfast."

He purred and rubbed against her. Erin always found it comforting to have him close by when she wasn't feeling very well. He kept an eye on her. He liked to curl up with her when she was sad or not feeling well.

A few minutes later, Terry stood in the doorway, leaning on the frame looking at her. "Are you ready to go see a doctor?"

"I'd rather just go back to bed."

"A concussion can be serious. Don't you think you'd better get some x-rays done to see how bad it is? If there is anything they can give you?"

"I can just take another Advil. It helped last night."

"Do you remember when I had a concussion?"

How could she forget? "That was a lot more serious," Erin pointed out. "You took a really hard blow."

"And your head hit concrete. Twice. Who knows how fast that scooter was going. Fast enough to lose Stayner. Are you telling me that your head hitting the wall at thirty miles an hour isn't enough to cause serious damage?"

Erin looked for an argument.

It would be more convincing if she could get up and walk around unassisted. It was hard to argue that she wasn't injured when she couldn't turn off her alarm in the morning, get out of bed, or walk to the toilet.

And her head really was hurting.

Terry had already vetoed her going to Auntie Clem's. If there had been any chance that she would have been able to make it there on her own, which there wasn't.

"I suppose," she said finally. "Is there someone I could see here in town instead of going to the city?"

"They're just going to send you to the city for x-rays, or MRI, or whatever they have to do. We may as well start at the hospital, since that's where you are going to end up."

"I don't want to go to the hospital."

"Would you rather go to the vet?"

Erin laughed. "Yes." She held her head tightly, because laughing made it hurt more. She really would rather go to Doc Edmunds for x-rays. He dealt with big dogs, so he must have an x-ray machine big enough for humans. A small human, anyway.

CHAPTER 7

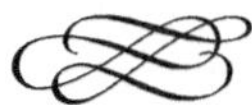

It seemed that even though the vet had been Terry's suggestion, he wasn't actually open to taking Erin to the veterinary hospital instead of going to the city to go to the human one. Which was disappointing, but not unexpected.

Trying to anticipate anything she might need along the way, Terry provided Erin with a bowl, a thermos of tea, a blanket and stabilizing neck pillow, and, of course, her purse and phone. He wouldn't give her an Advil, since she hadn't had anything to eat and didn't think she would be able to keep anything down,

"Anything I'm forgetting?" he asked as he helped her up the step into the truck.

Erin eased herself into the seat, trying to find a position that her head would find acceptable.

"Did you take Nilla out?"

"I took Nilla and K9 out. I fed everyone. Made coffee for myself. Charley is going to look after Auntie Clem's."

Erin sighed. "I guess that is everything, then."

Erin knew she would have to wait to see a doctor. There would be a lot of cases that would be prioritized over hers. She wasn't in critical condition. More than likely, the doctor would make her follow his finger, shine a light in her eyes, and tell her to go home and go to bed and get lots of rest for the next few days.

That had always been the way that it had been in the past if she even went to the hospital or a clinic about a concussion or other bang-ups. She really didn't want to waste her time.

On the other hand, she could see Terry's point. He'd been through a major concussion himself, and he knew how bad it could be. If it were a serious injury. Erin wasn't convinced that hers was, despite what Terry had said about the force at which her head must have hit the concrete. It hadn't exactly been a high-speed accident. She'd been hit by an electric scooter, not a Hummer.

They waited several hours in the waiting room chairs, watching other accidents and illnesses being admitted in front of Erin. People with household injuries, holding bandages, towels, or frozen peas over their injuries. Children wrapped in blankets, faces wan. Elderly people or possibly intoxicated homeless people pushed in, slumped over in hospital wheelchairs.

Erin wished she were at home in bed. She should have been smarter. Arranged to take a day or two off as soon as she had gotten home and stayed in bed instead of trying to get up and prove how tough she was. If she had just told Terry that she was tired and would take a day or two to recover, he wouldn't have insisted on bringing her in. It wasn't until he saw how she couldn't stay on her feet by herself and was throwing up that he'd insisted on bringing her into the hospital.

Next time she was in an unprovoked pedestrian traffic accident, she'd have to remember that.

"Can I get you anything to eat?" Terry suggested solicitously. "I can go to the vending machine or the cafeteria for something. Ginger ale for your stomach? Toast or a muffin for breakfast?"

"No." Erin indicated the flask of tea. "I'll just keep working on this. It helps the nausea."

"You should have something solid."

"No. Not yet."

Terry nodded. He went back to reading or watching something on his phone, and Erin closed her eyes. She couldn't watch anything on her phone without getting dizzy from the motion, and reading wasn't her favorite thing to do, especially when everything on the phone seemed to be so fuzzy. She had probably damaged the screen when she had knocked it and the water and the lamp to the floor. She hoped it could be repaired and she wouldn't have to get a new one. She didn't want to have to learn a new phone. She had everything set up just the way she wanted on her current phone.

She drifted in and out of sleep, not able to rest in the uncomfortable plastic chair, but unable to keep fully alert either, bored with waiting, her head throbbing, eyes sensitive to the light in the emergency room with its long bank of windows.

"How are you doing?" Terry asked, reaching over and taking Erin's hand. But he didn't seem to be taking her hand just to give it a comforting squeeze. His fingers slid immediately to her pulse and rested there.

"Just tired," Erin told him.

"You remember when Willie was here after his accident?"

It seemed like a long time ago but it had only been a couple of years. Erin had still been new to Bald Eagle Falls. She had known Vic and Terry and Willie, but none of them had paired off yet. Vic had been so worried about Willie when he had disappeared. And she had, as it turned out, been right to be worried. He had already been in the hospital when they had started looking for him, but they hadn't known until they came across the blood on the floor of one of his mines and realized that there had been some kind of violence. He wasn't in the mine, wasn't in his truck parked nearby, and there had been no sign of him in the clearing around the mine. With acres of wilderness around it to be searched. But once Terry had put out a call for help and the hospital had seen his report with Willie's picture attached to it, they had recognized him as the John Doe who was currently a patient there. While Willie had been stable, he hadn't been able to remember his own name and had no ID on him, so they hadn't been able to identify him until he was reported missing.

"Yeah. At least I know who I am," Erin commented. She remembered how Willie had called her Clementine at first, confusing Erin's name with that of her aunt. "Clementine," she murmured.

"What?"

Erin didn't feel like she could manage a full conversation. Her headache progressed from pounding to blinding. She pressed her palms to her forehead, hoping it would ease the pain.

"Terry," she groaned.

He tried to take her pulse again, but Erin wouldn't let him pull her hand away from her head.

"Erin, is it worse? Are you okay?"

"Worse," she acknowledged.

Terry swore under his breath. Erin felt him rise from his chair. He called out to the ER staff. "I need some help here. Now!"

There was a lot of commotion and noise, and people were trying to touch Erin all of a sudden. She curled up into herself, just holding her head and trying to keep everything else out, like a rolled-up armadillo.

"Stop," she protested thickly.

"Miss Price, we're going to put you on a bed," a woman with a loud voice said in her ear. "Just relax and we'll take care of you. There's nothing to worry about."

She tried to remain relaxed as several hands lifted her out of the chair and onto a gurney. After sitting in the hard plastic chair for so long, it felt good to lie down. Maybe she should have complained earlier.

She didn't open her eyes to watch her progress as they pushed the gurney from the waiting room. That was sure just to make her feel more nauseated.

The nursing staff asked Terry rapid-fire questions, as if they hadn't already given all that information when Erin had been triaged and sent back to sit in the waiting room. Terry answered, not raising his voice or expressing his frustration at being asked the same questions all over again. He found Erin's hand and squeezed it.

"You're going to be okay, Erin. They'll get you fixed up."

Erin tried to squeeze his hand back, but he pulled out of the grip before she could, and she thought that he was left behind to wait for her somewhere as the staff continued to push Erin's gurney through the hospital hallways.

CHAPTER 8

*E*rin was feeling a lot better the next time she woke up. The blinding pain was gone, and the nausea was under control; there was just a little bit of discomfort in the background. Something that told her she'd better be careful what she ate and how fast.

She had obviously been admitted. She was now in a semi-private room, a sheet pulled out on a rail between her and the person in the next bed, if it was occupied. Terry sat snoozing in a chair next to her. It had probably been a long day for him. Erin had slept through most of hers. She turned her head slowly to look for a window. Her dizziness peaked for a few seconds and then receded. There was a window. And it was still daylight. She hadn't slept the entire day away.

A nurse walked briskly into the room. She nodded to Erin when she saw that she was awake.

"How are you feeling, dear?" She asked as she took Erin's pulse, looked into her eyes, and checked the bandage around her head.

Erin held still during this quick check-up. She didn't want to move too much and risk setting off the throbbing in her head again.

"I guess… okay. Better than I was before. You gave me something for the pain?"

Terry stirred in his chair and sat up straight, rubbing his eyes and face. "Hey, honey," he leaned forward. "How are you feeling?"

"A lot better." Erin looked back at the nurse. "What did you do?" She raised her hand and looked at it to make sure there were no IV lines for her to tangle before raising it the rest of the way to touch the bandage around her head. "Did they do surgery?"

"No, right now they're just monitoring the amount of swelling in your brain. We're hoping to be able to manage it with medication and rest."

"How long was I asleep?" Erin had heard of patients being kept unconscious for hours or even days at a time while they recovered from injuries or illness. How much time had she lost? Days? What about Auntie Clem's? She had a business to run. She couldn't just walk away from it and hope Charley could keep it running in her absence.

"Just for a couple of hours," the nurse reassured her. "Don't get upset; it will just increase the pressure. We want you to stay calm and relaxed, and just let us take care of you." The nurse moved around her, checking the monitor off to the side and taking Erin's blood pressure with an old-fashioned cuff, even though she already had an oximeter on her finger. "I know that a hospital isn't the most relaxing place. You have a lot of other things that you would rather be doing. But for now… imagine you're relaxing on the beach, or in your Zen garden, or something else quiet that you enjoy. This is your spa vacation. We're here to do everything for you."

She gave Erin a smile and a wink.

"As long as we can keep your intracranial pressure down for a day or two, you'll be able to go home and won't need any surgical intervention. And that's what we want."

Erin nodded slowly. She touched the bandage again. "What's this for, if I didn't have surgery?"

"You did have a *small* procedure to put the intracranial monitor in place. It's very quick and provides the medical staff with the information we need to know how your brain is doing. As long as we can keep the swelling down, the surgeon won't have to do anything further."

Erin shuddered at the thought of them having drilled into her skull and whatever else they might have to do to relieve the swelling if the medications were not enough. She really was going to have to stay still and calm. She didn't want to have to go through that.

"I want to ask you about some of your symptoms so that we can track the progress of the injury. You need to be honest with me. Sometimes, patients hide things because they are embarrassed or don't want to look weak. But that doesn't help us and it doesn't help the patient. Understand?"

Erin nodded. She glanced over at Terry, who she knew would be listening in on the questions and might have some of his own when her answers to the nurse didn't entirely square with his questions put to her the night before.

"Any blurriness or double vision at any time since your accident?"

Erin started to nod, but didn't want to aggravate her head, so she held it still. "Uh, yes, some blurriness. Since at least last night. I can't read anything… the type is all too fuzzy. But I thought…" She stopped before explaining that she thought the recipe book was blurry because it was old, and her phone was blurry because she had dropped it and had to be repaired. But she hadn't entirely believed those explanations when she had made them to herself.

The nurse nodded, wrote this information down, and continued down a long list that included many of the symptoms Erin had been feeling since the night before.

"You should have brought her in last night," the nurse told Terry sternly.

"I did my best. She wouldn't let me."

The nurse raised an eyebrow at Erin. She looked away and tried to divert the conversation.

"I had really weird dreams last night. Do you think those were part of the concussion?"

"Probably. Concussion sufferers often do report an increase in vivid dreams."

"Oh. That must be what it was, then. It was weird. I felt like… I was someone else."

"You were someone else?" Terry repeated. He looked mystified. "Who did you think you were?"

"I don't know. I was looking for someone. Or waiting for someone. I don't really know. But I wasn't me… I wasn't thinking about Auntie Clem's, or you or Vic, or baking. I was just… really focused on… whoever it was I was waiting for, and our families." Erin scratched at the edges of the bandage on her head. "I don't have a family," she told the nurse. "My parents died when I was young. Sitting around worrying about what my family would think has never been a part of my life."

"Maybe something you saw on TV lately," the nurse said with a shrug. "You never know what our brains will do when injured. Even when doctors think they can predict what the consequences of damage to a certain part of the brain will be… they are frequently wrong. A bleed or extra pressure on a certain part of your brain… who knows what sensations, memories, or images it might trigger. Have you had any numbness or weakness…?"

She went into another list of symptoms that Erin might have experienced. Luckily, she had not lost the use of any of her limbs. She'd been wobbly a couple of times, but that was the shock of the accident or getting up too fast. Anyone could experience those problems, not just someone who'd suffered a recent brain injury.

CHAPTER 9

The next time Erin awoke, she could tell it was later in the day. The lighting of the room was different, and she knew it was evening before looking at the window and confirming that night was falling.

Terry had been shaking Erin's arm gently. She blinked at him a few times and smiled.

"Hi. You must be getting ready to go home."

"No, I'll stay and sit with you."

"You should go home and get a good sleep. You can't be comfortable sitting in a chair all day."

"I woke you to find out if you are up to visitors. You've been mostly sleeping, and if you want just to go back to sleep, that's fine… it's whatever you feel up to."

Erin massaged the bones around her eyes.

"I guess it depends on who it is," she admitted. She wasn't really up to putting on a show for someone else.

"Vic?"

Erin smiled. "Of course I can see Vic. She's family, not a visitor."

He nodded and smiled, the dimple appearing on his cheek. He was charmingly unshaven. Just sitting there in that chair all day, watching over her. Maybe he'd taken K9 out for a walk and gotten himself something to eat from the cafeteria but, other than that, all he had done all day was take care of her.

"Why don't you go get something to eat while I'm visiting with Vic?" Erin suggested. "You really should get a break. Take care of yourself."

"So that the two of you girls can talk about me?"

"Of course."

He chuckled and walked out into the hallway to talk to Vic and send her in. Vic came in by herself and settled into Terry's chair, looking at Erin with wide eyes. Erin was so used to seeing Vic all the time that she didn't think about her in terms of her age and maturity, her difficult upbringing, or her transition. But looking at the girl's wide eyes, she was reminded of how young Vic really was. Just twenty. She and Erin had known each other for going on three years. Erin felt like it had been forever, but Vic was still achingly young and looked so vulnerable as she looked at Erin with her eyes wide and her lip quivering; Erin felt a rush of affection and protectiveness toward her.

She reached out her hand, the one with the IV attached, and took Vic's hand.

"It's okay," she assured her. "It isn't as bad as it looks. I'm feeling pretty good right now, but they want to keep an eye on things for a little longer. And since I was so stubborn about making the trip to the hospital in the first place, they're worried I might not come back if something changed."

Vic traced a circle with the tip of her finger on the back of Erin's hand around the tape holding the IV line in place.

"What a thing to happen!" she exclaimed, avoiding a show of sympathy that might bring them both to tears. "I swear, those electric scooters are the bane of my existence. If God wanted us to ride around the sidewalk at breakneck speeds, we would have wheels instead of feet!"

Erin nodded. "It just came out of nowhere. Hit me from behind, so I never even saw him coming. And even after I was hit, and we were all tangled up together, I never even caught a glimpse of his face."

"It's a good thing. If we knew who he was, I might just have to go over there and give him a demonstration of what it's like to be knocked off his feet and beaten within an inch of his life."

"Well..." Erin's face warmed at Vic's vehemence, "That's not exactly what happened. I'm sure he didn't mean to hurt anyone, and he didn't beat on me; he just happened to collide with me."

"People like that don't understand an equal and measured approach. You have to take it beyond that, over the top, to really impress it on them. Convince them never to do it again."

"Oh." Erin gave a little laugh. "Well, then. Is that how it is?"

Vic nodded firmly. "That's exactly how it is. So when we figure out who this guy is, I will take care of it." She pounded the fist of one hand into the palm of the other in demonstration.

While Vic had grown up in a home where she had witnessed and been the victim of violence, Erin suspected she would never initiate such a punishment in real life. It was all talk. Blowing off steam. Erin patted Vic's hand.

"So tell me how you and Willie have enjoyed your vacation."

"Well, a heck of a lot better than you have been."

Erin nodded encouragingly. "Distract me from my woes and tell me what a great time you've been having."

"Well, Willie doesn't have his usual stamina back yet, but—"

"Don't you think that's a bit personal?" Erin interrupted primly. "Really, Victoria, you can overshare…"

Vic gave a bark of laughter. "Erin!" Her face turned bright red. "I'm talking about spelunking! Exploring caves, not…"

Erin gave it a beat or two. "Well, what did you think I was talking about?"

Vic laughed helplessly. Erin couldn't help joining in, though she tried to tamp down her mirth to avoid raising her intracranial pressure.

"You are incorrigible," Vic told her. "You're supposed to be lying here on your sick bed convalescing, not teasing me!"

Erin continued to snicker. "So you did get some caving in?"

"Spelunking."

"Call it whatever you like."

"Yeah, we did some exploring. It was nice. And good for Willie to be… doing something normal. Just to be out of the house and doing something he likes to do."

"He had such a hard time with the chelation. I'm sure glad it's over."

"No happier than we are. It's like being released from prison. To see him smiling and joking around again. With the energy to get out of bed and out of the house. That must be what it's like when someone is finished with chemotherapy."

"He'll be glad to return to his mines and other work."

"Yeah. But I'll tell you one thing he isn't doing, and that's the kind of processing he's been doing up until now. I don't even want him to do it himself. He says he still will, but he'll change to more modern processes and wear protective gear. Said he doesn't want to end up in this situation ever again, so I don't need to worry that he's going to cut corners."

"Good," Erin approved. "It will be nice to have the old Willie back. And maybe even better. Who knows how the heavy metals have been affecting him the past few years."

"Well, I don't want him to change too much," Vic said. "I want the Willie I know back. Not... someone else."

"I'm sure he will be."

CHAPTER 10

ic touched the bandage on Erin's head. "Did they shave you?"

Erin hadn't even thought about that. "No—I don't think so. They wouldn't, would they?"

"Maybe a little bit," Vic suggested, "not your whole head."

Erin felt the bandage and slid her fingers along the edges, trying to feel her hair underneath. "It's… no, it's still there. They better not shave anything without asking me first!"

"I don't think they do that when they're cutting you open. They shave whatever they have to."

"Well, they said that the medication should be enough. They shouldn't have to do surgery."

"I hope so. I don't want anyone cutting into your head." She shook her head. "Man, I really would track down the guy who did this to you then. What did he think he was doing going down the sidewalk at that speed? No one needs to do that!"

"Didn't you hear?"

"Hear what? No. I didn't hear anything except what Terry told me. That you were knocked down by a scooter and hit your head on the pavement."

"He was a burglar. Broke into the museum. Stayner was chasing him."

"Chasing him?"

"In his car. So yeah, that's why he was going so fast down the sidewalk."

"He broke into the museum?" Vic demanded.

"Yeah. And you know what he stole? A recipe book."

Vic laughed. "It *would* be a recipe book. Of course. What kind of recipe book do they keep at a museum? Let me guess—" She held up her hands in a "stop" motion. "—an old one."

Erin grinned. "An old Bald Eagle Falls Women's League recipe book."

"For Bald Eagle Falls? Are you kidding? That's so cool."

Erin agreed. She closed her eyes briefly, resting her head against the pillow. She wanted to continue the discussion with Vic, but her energy was flagging.

"I recorded it before I gave it back to Terry. You want to see it?"

"You… recorded it? How? I thought it was stolen."

"It was. But the thief dropped it when we collided, and it ended up in my bag. I didn't realize until later, I was so stunned by everything. Actually, Terry found it. But I had to sneak a peek before I gave it back. And I wanted to be able to look at it later. I didn't have time to look over more than a recipe or two, and I wanted to be able to read the whole thing."

"So you have a copy."

Erin turned her head slightly. "I assume my phone is around here somewhere. Is there a cupboard or drawer with my stuff in it?"

Vic looked around. She managed to find Erin's phone and held it out to her. Erin didn't take it, closing her eyes again. She wished the room were darker so that it didn't hurt her head so much.

"You look at it for now. I couldn't see it well enough when I was looking at it yesterday. I think… I need to look at it on a bigger screen or wait until my concussion is gone."

"Oh… well…" Vic held the phone, unsure what to do with it now.

"Unlock it," Erin urged. "You know the code. It's the last video in my photos app."

"You want me to?" Vic looked excited once more. She had obviously thought that Erin not being able to look at it meant that she wasn't going to get to see it either. She thumbed in the unlock code and tapped quickly to find the video. Her sound was on, and Erin could hear Terry asking her questions about where to find the aspirin while Erin quickly turned pages and paused to focus the camera on each one before going to the next. Vic giggled.

"Didn't he know you were taping it?"

"Yeah, he knew. I couldn't exactly hide the fact. But he didn't make me delete the video." She shrugged. "Obviously."

"This looks really cool. My grandma had one like this. Not for Bald Eagle Falls, but for the women's organization in her town. I guess a lot of little places made them to build community spirit, raise money, stuff like that." She held the phone close to her face while she studied the video. "It looks just like what she had. There are little stories that go with the recipes. About the dish or the person who contributed it. Stuff on how to entertain, where they got it from, how they always served it in Auntie's green soup tureen, or whatever."

"It's a cool way to revisit history."

Vic nodded her agreement. "Do you think we could make some of the recipes from this book? I mean, they wouldn't be gluten-free, so they would have to be adapted, but are you allowed to do that?"

"It's a recipe book. The idea is to make the recipes from it."

"I just didn't know whether it was okay for a commercial bakery or if you had to have special permission."

"No, I don't need special permission. And this book would be out of copyright anyway, if we wanted to republish some of the recipes."

"I'd like to try some of them out. Carrot cookies? Scrap pudding? I don't even know what some of these are."

"That would be fun. And I bet some of the older ladies would be tickled to taste some of the wartime recipes they developed while rationing. Memories of childhood."

Vic paused the video and then resumed it again, leaning forward to read it. "Look, this one is from Moira Cox. And there's one here from a Jackson. I wonder if it is one of my Jacksons."

"Probably."

"That's so cool. We could include the person whose recipe it was in the name. People would think it was neat to have their relative's recipe being sold in the bakery, even if it was adapted."

"Excellent ideas," Erin agreed. Her voice was faint, but she didn't try to speak louder, "I just wanted to read an old recipe book. But you could really bring it alive for everyone."

Vic patted her on the arm. Erin closed her eyes and listened as she watched the video a couple more times, and then Vic put it safely back into the drawer she had found it in.

"Have a good sleep," she whispered. "I'm going to go now. I'll be at Auntie Clem's tomorrow. Have Terry call me if you need anything."

Erin was nearly asleep when Terry walked back into the room with K9 after a brief conversation in the hallway.

"You should go home and go to bed," she murmured to him.

"Shh. Go to sleep." He rested his hand over hers. It was warm and comforting, and she drifted off to sleep.

CHAPTER 11

For the next couple of days, Erin slept a lot. Visits from doctors and nurses were brief, just checking her vitals and advising her to keep quiet and get as much rest as she could to allow her brain recovery time. She was allowed visitors, but had a feeling that Terry was carefully monitoring and controlling them, ensuring that only a few people came each day and that there was plenty of time to sleep between visits. The visits she did have were short, and it probably wasn't worth it for people to drive from Bald Eagle Falls just to see her when they could only see her for a few minutes. If they were in the city for other errands, it made more sense to stop in and see Erin for a bit and then continue with other errands.

Eventually, the doctors said that the danger was past and they were no longer worried that she would need surgery to relieve the pressure on her brain. She was feeling fewer symptoms, though not back to one hundred percent. They said that the peak period for swelling was past and, as long as she kept to quiet activities and didn't get stressed or do anything strenuous, she should be okay.

They prescribed several more days of bed rest. In the beginning, that sounded fine. She had just spent several days in the hospital, and going home was an improvement over that. She would rather be sleeping and resting in her own bed than at the hospital. Terry could go back to work.

People could come to visit her when they wanted to instead of planning a trip to the city.

"You really need to follow the doctors' instructions," Terry told her when she settled into bed at home in comfy clothes with her planner, tablet, and a solicitous orange cat purring beside her. "You remember how hard it was for me when I was recovering. You think you'll be able to do things, but healing takes time."

Erin didn't think that her concussion was anywhere near as severe as Terry's had been, so she took his advice with a grain of salt. She was sure that after a day or two at home on bed rest, she would be ready to go back to Auntie Clem's and jump back into the schedule there. She would be a lot more stressed at home in bed, not able to run her beloved bakery, than she would be putting in some short shifts in the upcoming week.

She would still be careful, but she saw no reason why she couldn't dive back into work.

"I'll do what the doctors said," she agreed. "I'll give it some more time to heal, and then I'll transition back to Auntie Clem's slowly."

She had meant it, but Terry had clearly not believed it.

"I mean it, Erin. You know that if you try to do too much, you'll just set your recovery back. You need to take the time to heal, even if you don't feel like it."

"I'm the one who told you that," Erin reminded him with a smile.

"I know. And you're going to regret it, because I'm going to keep saying the same thing to you."

It had taken Terry months to get back to work, and then to working full shifts. But his work was much more physical than hers, and he had to be in better shape and able to do shift work. All Erin had to do was to bake. She could sit down whenever she needed to. Erin could go home for a nap and come back. She didn't have to be out walking the streets or chasing after criminals. If her vision were blurry, someone else could read recipe instructions to her, and she didn't have to worry about whether she could aim a firearm.

It was totally different.

But she had found it a lot more challenging to rest at home than she had at the hospital, where she'd had nothing else to do. At home, she was thinking about the animals, chores, things that she needed to do at Auntie Clem's, the upcoming promotions they had planned, who was on shift at the bakery, and so many other things. She wanted to be up and active and to get back to the routine.

Vic sat on the edge of the bed, amused by Erin's restlessness. While at the bakery during the day, she had been dealing with Erin's calls to ensure that everything was going smoothly and that they didn't need her.

"What you need is something to do," she told Erin. "You're one of those people who just doesn't know how to relax and enjoy time to yourself."

"I have things to do. I just can't do them from here." Erin wondered whether she could sneak over to Auntie Clem's just to do some work on the computer. It wouldn't be that bad, would it? She would be sitting. She would be out of the way. It wouldn't be strenuous or stressful work. Not the same as standing at the counter dealing with customers.

"Have you read through the new recipe book?" Vic suggested. "There was a lot of cool stuff in there I thought you might be interested in. We could do a whole retro theme for a month or two. People love historical stuff. Things that remind them of Grandma's cooking. Things that they ate when they were kids."

"It's not a *new* recipe book," Erin reminded her.

"I know that. But it's new for us. And I think it would be fun to make some of the recipes."

Erin nodded, something she still needed to do slowly and carefully to avoid aggravating her head. But she could move around more now without getting dizzy or lightheaded. The hospital had given her some medication for headaches, but Erin wasn't sure how much it actually helped. She still had a headache all the time.

"It could be fun," she agreed. "We could get some advertisements designed that look like some of the old ones in the recipe book. Try out some of the old ration recipes in the book. We could even run a contest with people submitting old family recipes or put together our own recipe book. It wouldn't even have to be printed and bound like this one. It could just be online."

"The older ladies would want something printed. You still see lots of those fundraiser recipes around. Spiral bound. They wouldn't cost much, would they?"

"I have no idea."

"Did you transfer the video to your tablet?" Vic asked, motioning to it. "So you can see it in bigger type? You can pause it and take your time to read them."

Erin wasn't much of a reader, but she did love recipe books. She didn't think looking through the recipe book would take much time. Maybe it would take an hour of her time. Then what was she going to do for the rest of the day? She didn't know how she could stay in bed for several more days without something more productive to do. But it was something, at least. So she could show both Terry and Vic that she was trying to follow the hospital's instructions.

"I'm not sure how to get the video from one to the other," she confessed. She would just read it on her phone, but it was far too small to focus on with her concussion. And she didn't want to deal with the frustration of transferring it from one device to another.

"Give it here," Vic held out her hand. Erin gave her the phone and tablet, letting her work her magic.

It was harder to concentrate on the recipe book than Erin had imagined it would be. She loved reading recipe books but, even on the larger screen, the words still seemed to shimmer and needed more concentration to keep them in focus. The headings were in an old-style typeface that was more difficult to read. There were often several recipes on a page, making them cramped. The directions were sometimes obscure, using words or phrases that Erin would have to look up to figure out what they were talking about. The women who had written the recipes had lived in a different world, and their techniques and background knowledge had been lost. What had seemed simple to them often left Erin guessing, even though she'd read other vintage recipe books.

Usually, she just read them for entertainment, not intending to make any recipes for sale to others, so it didn't matter if she didn't understand everything. She might try her hand at one or two for herself, but that was different from having to sell them to others. Especially if she had to convert them to gluten-free recipes, which didn't always work the first time. She would first have to make them as described, ensure they worked out, and then substitute ingredients and see how the gluten-free results compared with the gluten-filled product.

Erin awoke with a start. She hadn't even realized that she had fallen asleep, but there she was with the tablet lying on her chest and drool running down both cheeks. She wiped the saliva away with disgust and looked around. Orange Blossom was curled up against her and trilled in protest when she sat up.

Erin picked up the tablet again and looked at it. She had been reading a recipe for wartime bread. There was an introduction to it by Mrs. Mavis Blake. *While some quarrelsome women refuse to adjust their recipes during wartime or spend long hours complaining about rationing, the capable housewife is creative, frugal, and pleasant as she finds new ways to save on household expenses and ensure that our boys at the front have what they need. It is a blessing for us to be able to help them.*

On the next page was a rich white bread recipe, with a comment by Miss Jane Cox that, *Even in lean times, a certain level of hospitality is expected from a real lady. A house should never under any circumstances be without a white, delicately textured loaf for teatime with special company.*

Erin couldn't help smiling at the dueling introductions. As polite as they were, these ladies obviously had very different opinions on what a "proper" housewife should do during difficult times.

How many more stories were hidden behind the simple introductions to flavorful foods in the little recipe book? Little feuds or jealousies between the members of the Women's League, strong opinions on how to run a household, and all the other petty disagreements that small-town life seemed to encourage. They would all be extra careful of what they allowed into print, but the little comments might provide a picture of early Bald Eagle Falls life that had been lost to the current residents.

She pressed the *Play* triangle to advance the video to the next page.

CHAPTER 12

*L*et's see this recipe book that Vic's been going on about," Charley told Erin, pulling a chair over so they could face each other comfortably instead of Charley sitting on the bed and turning around to talk to Erin. "According to her, it's something special."

"Well…" Erin shrugged. "I guess it is. I mean, it was going to be on display at the museum, so people obviously want to see it. And then it was stolen. But it's just a little book published by the Women's League…" Erin tapped to find it on the tablet and then passed it over to Charley. "I just took a quick video of it before I gave it back to Terry so that I could look it over later."

"That's what Vic said." Charley tapped the video and watched the pages turn. A couple of times, she stopped it and zoomed in for a better look. "This is pretty cool," she admitted. "I like all the little stories and advertisements. It's not just like a dry encyclopedia like some recipe books. And they went all the way to get it properly printed and bound. That must have cost a lot for them back then."

"That's one of the reasons it has advertisements in it," Erin pointed out. "To help to recoup some of the cost of producing the book."

Charley watched the pages. "Jell-O, Coca-Cola, Campbell's Soup. It's funny to see all those familiar brands in olden-day advertising. I didn't realize how long some of them had been around!"

"And Pillsbury flour and Morton salt," Erin agreed. "Have you ever seen pictures of the dresses they made from flour sacks back in the Depression? They were pretty amazing."

"Dresses out of flour sacks? What did they do? Like, cut neck and armholes in them?"

"No, they cut them open and used the material to make dresses. Some feed sack companies even started printing pretty flowers on them and providing patterns for making dresses."

"Huh." Charley shook her head. "You learn something new every day."

"I was looking at some of the introductions or descriptions of the recipes in there. Some of them really got into… political stuff, or little tiffs over how a dish was *properly* made or served."

Charley grinned. "Yeah, I don't doubt it." She watched the screen. "Hey, there are Jackson and Dyson recipes side by side. Who would have thought they would be allowed to put them together in a recipe book?"

"I know they're enemies now. But when did that start? Maybe they used to be friends. Or at least, friendly with each other as part of the same community."

"Not to hear them talk about it! No, sir, Jacksons and Dysons won't walk down the same side of the street. Never the twain shall meet!"

"It had to have started sometime."

"Maybe it was all about a recipe." Charley held up the tablet. "Maybe… the Jacksons put pineapple on their pizzas or didn't brine their chickens in buttermilk!"

"Maybe," Erin laughed. She tried to keep her chuckles soft so they wouldn't hurt her head. "Maybe that's why the recipe book was stolen— so word of their cooking practices wouldn't get out."

"Or the fact that they had once been friends," Charley agreed, looking down at the video on the tablet. "Maybe the Dysons made custard and the Jacksons made cookies, and without both of them, no one could make custard creams." She giggled. "Without both of them, life stopped being as sweet for the small towns on the mountain."

Erin smiled. "What are custard creams?"

"*What are custard creams?*" Charley shook her head at Erin's ignorance. "Well, they're sandwich cookies. But like Peek Freans, not Oreos. A vanilla cookie with a custard filling."

"Like Golden Oreos?"

"Well, sort of, I guess so. But Oreos aren't Custard Creams."

"I don't want to get into an argument here," Erin said, holding her hands up in surrender.

"Custard creams," Charley mused. "You should make some gluten-free custard creams. I know they make gluten-free Oreos, but that's just not the same thing."

"Well, if there is a recipe in there, I'll try it," Erin agreed. "I'll make regular ones first, then try my hand at spinning them into a gluten-free option."

"You have to do it. That would be awesome."

CHAPTER 13

$\mathcal{E}$rin had been wondering what she was going to make for supper. She had been away from home for several days and wasn't sure what was left in the fridge. Or if Terry would allow her to get up to make anything. Or what he would make himself. Or should they order in from one of the restaurants in town?

But she should have known that the Bald Eagle Falls ladies would jump in, especially the ones who came to Auntie Clem's for the ladies' tea after church services every week.

When Vic got home from the bakery, she carried a couple of casseroles with her and informed Erin that she would need to leave the front door unlocked and the burglar alarm off so that Vic could answer the door as several more deliveries were being dropped off.

"That sounds like way too much food," Erin protested. "I'm not an invalid. I'll be able to make something for myself… in a day or two."

"Of course it is way too much," Vic agreed philosophically. "That's the way they do it. They drown you in food. It shows you how much they love you. You can put them in the freezer and take months to eat them. But if they're in casserole dishes, you have to eat them first so you can return the dishes quickly. If they're foil baking pans, you can take however long you like."

"I should have known there would be rules."

"We'll have to keep track of everyone who sends you something so you can thank them."

Erin put a hand to her pounding head. "Can you keep track of them?"

"Of course I will," Vic agreed. "Don't you worry about it. Didn't they do this when Terry was injured?"

"Uh… some. I just thanked everyone when they brought them; I didn't send them notes afterward or anything."

"Probably should have." Vic shrugged. "But if they were for Terry, maybe he thanked them. And men… they don't have to follow all the rules, you know. They can get away with being clueless."

"But I can't."

Vic shook her head. "No. I mean, you're a Northerner. If you want to be considered part of the Bald Eagle Falls community, you'll have to follow the rules."

"Of course. Yeah."

"So what do you want tonight? Macaroni casserole? Potatoes au gratin?"

"I don't know… either one is fine. You put cheese or cream on anything and Terry will eat it. And I'm not picky. I'll take anything if I don't have to make it."

"What time will he be home?"

Erin massaged her forehead. "Uh… seven, probably. If he's done on time and doesn't have too many reports to write."

"I'll put the macaroni casserole in the oven, then, and it will be ready when you guys want it."

"Thanks."

"Go back to sleep," Vic told her. "You still need it. I'll take care of things until Terry gets home."

"We can visit…"

Vic shook her head. "You look wore slap out. Get some more sleep so you can visit Terry when he gets home."

"I've been sleeping most of the day," Erin protested. She had been a lot more tired than she thought she would be. She would get into reading the recipe book, which she had thought would only take an hour or two to get through but, each time Erin looked at it, she would only get a few pages in before she drifted off to sleep again. Then, she would have to find her place again if she left the video playing when she fell asleep.

"You still need it," Vic told her. "Remember when Terry was recovering from his concussion And he was so frustrated because he couldn't go back to work and didn't have the energy to do it."

"Yeah."

"Then give yourself some time to heal. Go to sleep. You can visit with him when you get up."

CHAPTER 14

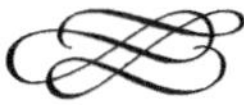

*E*rin was glad she followed Vic's advice and went back to sleep instead of trying to stay up and entertain her. She really did need the sleep. It was probably just because she hadn't gotten enough sleep at the hospital. It wasn't particularly restful to be interrupted by doctors or nurses every couple of hours. Not to mention the noise of people walking and the PA system in the hallway. Even though she thought she had slept enough, it had not been a deep, restful sleep. Once she'd had a couple of days at home, she would feel much better and be able to jump back into things.

It hadn't been that bad an accident.

It had just been one little scooter. Not a racing car. Not a prizefight. Not being hit over the head with a crowbar. The accident was hardly even worth mentioning.

"How are you feeling?" Terry asked solicitously. "Did you get a good rest?"

"I feel like I haven't done anything *but* rest," Erin complained. "Is that what you felt like when you were concussed? That you just… couldn't keep going. You had to sleep?"

He nodded. "That… and the headaches… wanting to get back to work but not being able to. It was frustrating. I'm sure you noticed I wasn't in a particularly good mood most of the time."

And for Terry, it had lasted months. But Erin was sure that her brain would be healed long before that. A few days. It would only take a few days.

"Vic was going to put a casserole in the oven so it would be ready when you got home," Erin told him. "So as long as you got home in good time and it didn't get dried out…"

"The casserole is already out of the oven and ready to be served," Terry told her with a little bow. "If madame is ready for supper?"

"Oh, that's great."

Terry put out his hand for her. Erin thought it was just dramatic gallantry, like his bow and *madame*. But she was also glad to have his steadying hand as she got to her feet and tested her legs.

"I'm just a little wobbly. I've been in bed all day, just like you told me to." It came out a little more accusatory than she intended. It wasn't Terry's fault that she'd had to be in bed all day.

He didn't make any comment, leading her down the hall.

"Just a quick bathroom stop," Erin said, pulling away from him and putting her hand on the bathroom counter to steady herself as she walked in and shut the door on him to take care of business. With the counter and walls to lean on, she was able to make it back out to the hallway without assistance, and she banged along the wall from there to the kitchen, but then she needed another hand across the expanse of tile from the doorway of the kitchen to the table.

Erin could smell the delicious, creamy, homey smell of the macaroni casserole throughout the house. She would be three feet wide if she ate all the comforting, calorie-laden fare the church ladies were dropping off. But for a day or two… maybe her brain could use the extra calories to start healing. After all, hadn't she heard that the brain was sixty percent fat?

Terry deposited Erin in her chair. The animals were unsure what was going on, as Erin was always the one who made supper and fed them their food, and suddenly she insisted on sitting down and Terry was the one carrying dishes and opening the fridge.

K9 lay beside Erin's feet and stared up at her, his eyes not moving, but his ears twisted this way and that like a radar antenna sweeping for movement.

"I should feed Orange Blossom," Erin said, preparing to stand as

Terry made his way to the table carrying the hot casserole dish, Orange Blossom yowling and winding around his legs. "Blossom! Stop that? You'll trip him!"

"I've got this," Terry said calmly. "You stay put."

Erin found that getting out of her chair wasn't quite as easy as she had thought, and relaxed back into it.

Terry fed K9 and Marshmallow first, ignoring Orange Blossom's raucous demands. "That cat needs to learn some manners."

"He's just communicating his needs…"

"You spoil him. You should have been stricter with him from the start."

Erin shrugged. She knew it was probably true. She hadn't thought much about how to train a cat. She'd never owned one before and hadn't really thought about cats being trainable. Orange Blossom had trained Erin more than she had trained him.

Terry got Orange Blossom's food ready for him, but then held the bowl up above him, waiting. Blossom danced around on his hind legs and meowed loudly about it.

"Get down," Terry told him, lowering the bowl slightly and then pushing Orange Blossom down.

Orange Blossom responded by hissing at him and swiping at his hand.

"Just give it to him," Erin urged, "you aren't going to be able to train him now."

"Down," Terry repeated, and pushed Orange Blossom down until he was on the floor trying to claw and bite him. Terry put the bowl down and held Blossom still for a moment, telling him, "Wait," before finally letting him go. The cat jumped at the bowl and started to gobble down his food.

Terry shook his head and sat down across from Erin. "The serving dish is hot. Do you want me to dish it up for you?"

"Meow," Erin told him and giggled.

"Well, you're much better behaved than Orange Blossom. Look at how nice and quiet you are sitting. And you didn't even try to bite me."

Erin giggled again. "Just a little bit, please. I'm not that hungry. But it smells delicious."

"It does," he agreed.

They ate a few bites before Erin thought to ask Terry how his day had gone. It must have been hard for him to go back to work after a few days off, and he had probably worried about how Erin was doing while he was working, wondering whether she was following the doctor's instructions.

He told her a few things about his day and then asked her how her day had gone.

Erin told him about the recipe book and Vic's and Charley's suggestions of how she could use it in promotional campaigns and to capture the interest of the old Bald Eagle Falls families.

"Aren't you better off sticking to modern recipes?" Terry asked. "Do you even have all the ingredients those old recipes call for? And they won't be gluten-free. You'll have to convert everything. Then they *won't* be traditional recipes anymore."

"I know." Erin had another bite of the creamy macaroni casserole. "But I'm used to converting recipes and trying different methods until it works. And it aligns with my goal of giving people with gluten restrictions the range of choices that other people have. Including favorite old family recipes."

"Even though they won't be their favorite old family recipes."

"But they'll be as close as I can get them in taste and texture. And they'll be developed from the authentic recipes."

Terry nodded. "I suppose. And how will people feel about you using their old family recipes?"

"They'll be happy. Happy that they can eat Great-Grandma's old custard creams, wartime loaf, and scrap pudding."

"They won't feel like you stole their family recipes to use them for your own gain?"

Erin opened her mouth to protest. She couldn't find her voice at first. "Stole them?" she finally squeaked, outraged, "I'm not stealing anything. This was a published book of recipes. And they're in the public domain now."

"But that's not necessarily how people are going to feel."

"Nobody is using this recipe book anymore," Erin told him. "I doubt if there is even another copy in Bald Eagle Falls. That's why it was in the museum, right? Because it's an artifact of a bygone era. No one still has this in their kitchen and is cooking from it."

"You might be surprised at how many people have recipes that were handed down from parent to child through multiple generations. Even if they aren't using that actual book anymore, they might still be using Great-Grandma's recipes. And they might not be happy to think that someone else in town is using *their* recipes."

Erin hadn't grown up in a small town like Bald Eagle Falls, so she had to stop and think about it and consider whether Terry, who *had* grown up in town might know what he was talking about. Maybe people were proprietary about Great-Grandma's old recipes. Maybe they wouldn't want her replicating them or making them into some weird, gluten-free substitute. They might think it was some kind of sacrilege.

Though of course if Great-Grandma had known that her progeny would have celiac disease, she would have adapted the recipe for them if it were within her power to do so. How many grannies had learned to give goat's milk to babies who were intolerant of cow's milk? Or had fed their babies a steady diet of potatoes and bananas when they developed "sprue" or "dysentery" from eating bread?

"Do you really think they would mind?" Erin asked tentatively. "I thought people would be happy to taste Grandma's old raisin bread or pasties again."

"You may be right," Terry said. "But you need to consider the possibility that people will not want you using their old family recipes. Maybe ask around and do some market research before you start. You don't want to put all your energy into starting this wonderful everything-old-is-new-again gluten-free vintage recipes campaign. You don't want to waste all that time and energy, only to have it crash because people don't like you 'stealing' their recipes."

CHAPTER 15

$\mathcal{E}$rin sighed. She hadn't even considered the idea that anyone might not like her using their traditional family recipes. If they were in the recipe book, she would have thought that the whole point was to share it with other people and have them make it. However, some of the introductions and notes she had read in the recipe book told her that it wasn't as straightforward as that.

There was no internet social media back then, and some contributors had used the recipe book as a platform to criticize other women's recipes, philosophies, or political views. Maybe there had been more to it than just sharing favorite recipes.

"Have you had any luck figuring out who the museum burglar was? Are you in charge of that, since the thief was apparently from Bald Eagle Falls?"

"We're not in charge of it, but we are obviously involved in the investigation. The burglary took place in the city, so the city's property crimes unit is primary. But we're involved. The fact that the burglar fled here is suggestive that it is someone from Bald Eagle Falls."

"And the fact that the book is about Bald Eagle Falls."

"That too. As you said before, the two things together suggest that our burglar is someone from Bald Eagle Falls."

"Any idea who?"

Terry shook his head. "I couldn't tell you if I did know something. But so far, we are hitting dead ends. Nothing promising in figuring out who it was."

"Do they have surveillance video? Do they know whether it was a man or a woman? Anything about them?"

"From the little surveillance video they have—don't ask me why a museum didn't have better security—it could be a man or a woman. We don't have a face; it was hidden by a baseball cap. And the burglar's jacket obscures whether it is a man or a woman. Slim figure, but that's about all we can tell from the video."

"How did they break in? Was anyone hurt?"

"They stayed in the museum after hours. They probably arrived during the busiest part of the day, found a closet to hide in, and just stayed there until late at night. Came out, smashed the case that the book was in—though they didn't have to, it was actually unlocked. The exhibit hadn't even opened yet; they were still setting up. Exited through a fire door within two minutes of smashing the case."

"Not very sophisticated."

"Most burglaries aren't like the complicated heists in TV movies. Smash and grab is still the simplest, most effective method. Get in and get out quickly, before security can respond or the police have even dispatched a car."

Sometimes, the simplest approach was the best. And the burglar would have gotten away with it if he hadn't knocked Erin down in the street and dropped the precious book.

"Was that the only thing stolen?"

"There were a few other small items as well. Photographs, letters, that kind of thing."

Erin frowned as she toyed with the macaroni casserole still on her plate. "How bizarre."

"You should see this tiny closet the burglar holed up in." Terry shook his head in disbelief. "It doesn't even look like someone could fit in there, standing in front of the shelves when the door was closed. I swear there isn't a gap of six inches. And he would have had to stand there, not moving, for hours."

"I could never do that."

"I don't think very many of us could. But he must have been motivated."

"To steal a recipe book? Some random memorabilia?"

Terry nodded. "It's a mystery," he admitted. "I can't imagine why this book would be so important to him. The book was insured for about a thousand dollars, but I don't imagine the burglar could get that much for it. Where is the market?"

"Maybe he's a collector."

"A recipe book collector? They aren't typically the type to break into museums."

"Maybe… it was a dare. Or some kind of initiation."

"Like a gang initiation? They have to break into a museum to steal a book? I don't think that we have a violent book club initiating their members by having them steal books."

Erin laughed. "No. Probably not." She tried to imagine what the members of such a notorious book club gang would look like. Black jackets and reading glasses on chains around their necks?

"No, this was personal," Terry said meditatively. "It wasn't something that there was a market for. Someone wanted it for himself."

Erin took another bite of her macaroni, savoring the salty and creamy flavors that reminded her of her childhood. Despite the comforting taste, her focus remained on the conversation at hand.

"Speaking of gangs…"

Terry raised his brows. "Speaking of gangs?"

"I was wondering about the Dysons and the Jacksons earlier. If you know how their feud started."

He frowned and shook his head slowly. "I assume that because they are rival crime cartels, it was just a territory thing. They are both fighting for the same geographical territory, trying to be the top dog and control all the drug market and other illegal ventures. So naturally, they are enemies."

"They weren't enemies before they got established?"

"I don't have any idea. They've been rivals for as long as I have been a cop. For as long as I can remember. I don't know how it all got started. Why do you want to know?"

"It was just something that Charley said. When we were looking at the recipe book. There were Jackson and Dyson recipes on facing pages.

She was saying that would never happen now. So I was just curious about when the feud between the two families started and why. Vic was joking about it starting over a recipe. And from reading through that book, there were a lot of jealousies between homemakers in different families."

"I doubt whether the rivalry between the Dyson and Jackson clans started over a recipe."

"I know," Erin agreed. "Me too. It was just a funny thing to say, and I wondered whether you even knew how the whole thing had started in the first place."

"You would have to go back further than I can remember. Even in my grandparents' generation… the rivalry was already well-developed by then. Jacksons and Dysons would never mix."

Maybe it went back as far as prohibition. A lot of criminal gang activity had started during that time. Maybe both clans had been involved in illegal brewing and smuggling. But that was before the recipe book had been published and, if Vic's instinct was right—that the Women's League would never put Jackson and Dyson recipes side by side because of the animosity between the two clans—then the feud had not yet started when the book had been published. After prohibition.

"It would be interesting to know how it all got started. Do you know anyone who would know that?"

"You might ask Willie. Or even Vic. Willie was a soldier in the Dyson gang and still has some dealings with them." Terry's mouth turned down at these words. He tried to have a more open mind toward Willie now than in the past, but he still didn't trust Willie due to his association with the Dysons in his youth. "But… I don't know if I would start digging into that, Erin. If someone gets the idea that you are snooping around about the clans, they might be concerned. You don't want to ruffle any of *those* feathers."

"I'm not… I was just wondering if you knew how it had all started."

"Way before my time."

Erin accepted this. She hadn't really expected to find out. Sometimes feuds had been going on for so long that people forgot what they were all about in the first place. They didn't even know how they had started, just that they had always hated each other.

"How about some dessert?" Terry suggested, watching Erin fiddling with what remained on her plate. "Do you want a cookie? Some ice cream? What do you feel like?"

"I feel like being over this concussion," Erin told him. "I've had enough of it. I just want to be able to get back to my usual routine. I hate lying around here."

He smiled. "I know how that feels."

Erin was struggling after just a few days with her injury. She hadn't given him enough credit for how patient and long-suffering he had been when he'd been dealing with his concussion. She'd been irritated by his moodiness and frustration. She had thought that she understood what it was like for him to have to stay home and not to be able to go to work or do any of the other things he was accustomed to doing. But she hadn't had any idea.

"Can we rewind so I can be more sympathetic toward you during your recovery?" she asked.

The dimple appeared in his cheek. "The thought is appreciated."

"This really sucks."

"It does," he agreed. "At least right now, you are mostly sleeping. But when you can't sleep anymore and still can't do anything else..." He sighed. "You probably won't have to deal with that. You can go back to work when you start feeling up to it, even if it's only for an hour or two. I had to be certified to drive and use a firearm."

"I don't know how you got through it for all those months. I wish I'd been more understanding."

"You were great. I knew you were there for me and would do anything to make me feel better. You took care of me. But you couldn't make me heal any faster."

"I'm just glad we're through it now. For a while there, I wondered if things would ever get better."

"I did, too. But now we both know that it does get better so, no matter how long it takes for you to recover, you can look forward to going back to your bakery again."

Erin appreciated his words. But she knew that not all head injuries behaved the same way. Some people never fully recovered. And she'd had several concussions before and been warned that each one did progressive damage. There was no guarantee that she would ever return to her normal.

CHAPTER 16

$\mathcal{A}$s much as Erin wanted to stay awake and visit with Terry for the rest of the evening, she simply couldn't. By the time she was finished eating, she was ready for bed. She didn't know how merely walking out to the kitchen and eating dinner with Terry could be so tiring. But that was all she could manage, and she needed him to walk her back to the bedroom to ensure she made it without falling on the way to bed.

"I wanted to stay up with you."

"I know. But you'll have to be patient and give yourself more time to recover. Do you want me to stay with you until you can fall asleep?"

"No, you don't want to be stuck in here watching me, waiting for me to fall asleep."

"I would be happy to," he assured her, giving her hand a squeeze. "I wouldn't offer if I wasn't willing to do it."

"I know you're willing, but I doubt you want to."

Terry helped her settle into bed, then walked around the bed and sat on his side, propped with pillows. Erin intended to start a conversation with him and to talk for a bit before she fell asleep, but never got beyond trying to think of an intriguing subject to discuss.

～

She sat in a chair, one hand behind her back, trying to ease the pain. Why did her back have to hurt so much? With everything else she had to deal with, it seemed like the straw that... broke the camel's back. She just couldn't stand it anymore. She wanted everything to be over. She hated being trapped in the circumstances she was in.

And it wasn't like she hadn't been warned. How often had she been given very good advice on avoiding precisely the circumstances she now found herself in? The disappointment of her parents always cut like a knife. She could only imagine how upset they would be if they knew everything.

At first, she hadn't understood how bad it would be. She had been a little excited. She had still thought that it might turn out okay. Other people managed to make things right even after making serious mistakes. Other people were forgiven and were able to go on with their lives just as if they had not screwed it up in the beginning.

She looked out the window, searching the moonlit road for him, even though she knew he would not be there. He was gone. She hadn't heard anything from him. He was gone, just like she had been warned.

She dabbed at her eyes with a hankie. She knew she didn't have the right to cry about it. She had, her mother would say, made her bed, and now she had to lie in it.

A shadow fell across her.

"What are you crying about?"

"My back hurts. I just wish it would stop. I can't do anything anymore without being in pain. I can't sit, stand, or lie down."

"That is too bad."

She sighed. She knew better than to expect sympathy from her mother. But that didn't mean she couldn't long for it. Wasn't there anyone out there who actually understood what she was going through and could be sympathetic about it?

"If it is bothering you that much, you should be lying down in your room. Not wandering around the house."

"I was restless. I thought if I stretched my legs for a few minutes, it might help."

"Back to your room. Young ladies should not be up wandering around the house at night."

She was no longer sure what the reason was, other than to make her miserable. She dabbed her eyes and took one more look out the window, then returned to her room.

~

Erin wasn't sure what had woken her up or what time it was. She reached for her phone and managed to pick it up without knocking anything else down. It was still not late, though the sun had gone down. Erin could hear voices. It took a few minutes to isolate them and determine where they were coming from. Not the TV. Not Terry talking on the phone. There was someone else in the house. For a moment, she was afraid. She had been talking about the Dysons and the Jacksons. She had been talking about the burglar who had knocked her down. How valuable the recipe book might have been. What if the burglar came after her looking for it, realizing that he must have lost it when he had collided with her? What if he didn't know that she had given it to Terry so that it could eventually be returned to the proper owner and thought she still had it in her possession?

But all of that was silly. One of the voices was definitely Terry, and he wouldn't let anyone in the house who would cause her harm. He was a cop. He knew better.

The voices stopped, and there were footsteps. Erin looked anxiously toward the door. It was Terry, of course. He peeked into the room and spoke softly.

"You awake?"

"Yeah. Who's here?"

"Beaver."

Rohilda Beaven was a friend. A strange one, to be sure. One that couldn't be judged by any regular standards. But she had always treated Erin well. She was a federal agent and, while she didn't reveal much about herself, she was always on the right side of the law and had protected or helped Erin in the past. Most recently, she had helped to ensure that a murderer and kidnapper had not escaped. She and Vic's brother, Jeremy, were a couple, though Beaver was older than Jeremy, which, for some reason, Erin always found a little disconcerting. She knew by now that Beaver wasn't just using him or trying to take advantage of him, but Erin

—and Vic—were still not sure what to think of the relationship or whether it would last.

Beaver must have been there to talk to Terry about a case. She was often interested in his cases, even if there didn't seem to be any federal connections. Erin was never sure how much of it was curiosity and how much was professional interest. She wasn't sure Terry knew either, and he was privy to more of those details.

"Did she go?" Erin hadn't heard the door. Maybe Terry was not finished talking to her, but just wanted to check on Erin to make sure she was all right before continuing the conversation.

"No. She wanted to know if she could talk to you. I told her that you were asleep."

"Well, I'm awake now."

"Do you want to see her? You don't have to deal with anyone you don't want to. You're injured; you can bow out of any social obligations."

Erin rubbed her eyes and assessed her body. She felt like she could stay awake for a little while now. Hopefully, that feeling would last.

"I don't mind talking to her."

"You're sure? Beaver can be a little… intense at times."

"No, I'll see her."

Terry nodded his acknowledgment and returned to the living room to talk to Beaver. In a minute, she was in Erin's doorway, chewing her omnipresent wad of gum with vigorous chomps.

"Good evening, Miss Erin."

"Beaver. Come on in. Make yourself comfortable."

Beaver entered and wandered around the room for a long moment before she eventually settled, leaning against a chest of drawers. Erin didn't bother inviting her to sit on the bed or bring in a chair. Beaver had made her choice. She was probably too restless to sit down.

"So, you've been having adventures," Beaver observed.

"Well, if you want to call having a concussion an adventure, then yes, I have."

Beaver chuckled. "Getting knocked down by a burglar fleeing law enforcement. Coming into possession of a valuable artifact. I suppose the trip to the hospital and your convalescence don't exactly count as adventures, although I've always had interesting times at the hospital or in recovery."

Erin would just bet she had. Beaver had previously confessed to being shot. More than once. She was a very strong, fit person. She probably hadn't been willing to wait long to recover before getting back to her training regimen.

"Bad night?" Beaver asked.

"What? No. I've been okay."

"You look like you've been crying."

"Oh…"

"Do you need a painkiller? I can track one down for you. I'm sure."

"No. My head hurts, but I'm not ready for another painkiller yet. I'm hoping that if I stretch out longer between doses… I'll be able to wean off them faster."

"Doesn't necessarily work that way. In the beginning especially, you're better off taking them as soon as you need them, if not a bit before that. The longer you wait, the higher the dose required to bring the pain down again."

"I don't need anything yet," Erin reiterated. She wiped her face, hoping to eliminate any sign of tear tracks. "I was dreaming. I've been having some really weird dreams with this concussion. Like… I'm not even really me."

Beaver raised her brows. "Interesting. Vivid dreams can be a side effect of a concussion. Who knows what functions have been affected by your injury."

That was a pleasant thought. Erin preferred to think of it as a side effect rather than brain damage.

"So I'm interested in this recipe book," Beaver said without further small talk. "Miss Victoria said you had a video of it on your phone or computer. I was hoping to see it."

"Terry has the book. You could probably look at the original."

"He's already returned it to the property crimes investigator in the city. Who doesn't seem very inclined to share? I've seen the pictures that the museum had. Just publicity shots, not anything inside. I'm intrigued by it."

Beaver was, as Erin knew, a treasure hunter as a hobby. When she had time off, she was often looking for some lost or hidden treasure. Sometimes in the county, and sometimes around the world. She said that she had found a few treasures, but hadn't given any detail on what that might involve. Erin suspected Beaver probably didn't give anyone the details of what she had found in the past, and whether she still owned the treasures she had found or had liquidated them.

"There isn't a treasure for you to find, though," Erin pointed out. "The recipe book isn't missing. The police have it now."

"I know. But I am intrigued by it. I'd like to see what it looked like, what was inside. Maybe there are other copies around that might be worth something. People hang on to books, you know. They don't like to throw them out. And especially if they have family recipes in them. There might still be a few copies floating around Bald Eagle Falls."

"I supposed there might be," Erin admitted. "And if they are worth a few thousand each… that's something."

But why not just leave them with their original owners? It made more sense for them to be held by residents of Bald Eagle Falls than in a collection or museum somewhere they would only be displayed once every few years.

Beaver was studying Erin's face. "Why wouldn't I be just as deserving an owner as someone else?"

"I didn't say that." Was her face really that readable? Or had she said aloud what she had only intended to think?

"If I kept it, I would take good care of it," Beaver told her. "And if I didn't keep it, I would find someone who would be a good owner. Someone who really wanted it."

"Of course. I know that. It isn't like it's a kitten that needs to have a home properly vetted. If someone pays for it, they can do whatever they want."

"Even destroy it or throw it out?"

Erin's face twisted at the suggestion. If someone paid for the book, why would they destroy it?

Beaver chuckled. "You are probably more concerned that someone actually uses the recipes in the book," she discerned. "You don't want it to just sit on a shelf or display somewhere without being used."

Erin had to agree with that. "But whoever has a copy right now probably isn't making anything from it."

"Probably not," Beaver agreed. "If they had been using it for decades, it would be falling apart by now. It would only be in good condition if it had never really been used."

Erin had to concede that point.

"What kind of shape was the one that was stolen in?" Beaver asked, one eyebrow raised.

Erin couldn't help feeling like she had been outmaneuvered. She reached for her tablet and brought up the video of the recipe book. Beaver stepped away from the bureau and took it from her when it was offered. She tapped the video and started it playing. Erin watched her face. Beaver studied the footage closely, stopping and starting it a few times, pinching and zooming and manipulating it to get a better look at whatever was important to her.

She watched it several times, then handed it back to Erin.

"Very nice," she said with a nod. "Someone kept it in pretty good shape. And as a baker, you must be drooling over all those old recipes."

"I am," Erin admitted. "That's why I took the video. I didn't want to hand the book back over without getting some kind of record of it. I *wanted* those recipes."

"That was a clever way to get them all very quickly. And you can clip them out and OCR them to get a text document you can manipulate."

"I'm not sure how to do that," Erin admitted. "But I probably wouldn't use them as-is anyway. After trying out the original recipe, I would be converting it to use in Auntie Clem's."

"I'm sure people would love to see some of those old recipes revived. Some things you forget you ever had until you taste it again. And then it brings back all these memories."

"Terry thinks that some people will object to having their family recipes used that way."

Beaver made a noise and waved this away. "You know the saying about not being able to please all the people all the time. You can't *ever* please everyone. Don't even try. You just do what you think is best and carry on."

"But what is best for me isn't necessarily best for everyone. I don't want to step on people's toes, to not even think about how it will affect others."

"It doesn't hurt anyone else for you to use a recipe from a published recipe book. I'm sure you could find any of these in some form on the internet with a quick search. The value of a recipe book is that all the recipes are gathered into one collection, not that they are unique. Even looking through this book, you're going to find recipes that are almost identical, being contributed by several different people. If they had a good editor, he might have weeded out a lot of the duplicates, but you'll still see some repetition."

"What I'm finding most interesting are the little notes people include with their recipes. Where they came from, the traditions that they have in their family, or stuff like how to set the table or get rid of bedbugs. But some of the notes are kind of... sniping at the other women in the community. You know, the sweet sort of, 'Cousin Mary couldn't cook a roast to save her soul, bless her heart.'"

Beaver laughed. "I saw some of those. You could probably learn all kinds of things about the community if you dug into it."

"Yeah. I feel like I know more about them than they knew themselves. Like they told me all their secrets."

"Eighty-year-old gossip."

"Yeah. I'm glad it is that old, though, so I don't have to know anything bad about anyone I know."

"I'm sure you hear plenty of fresh gossip at the bakery. I know I always learn something new when I stop in."

"Well... I try not to listen to it," Erin admitted. But of course it was true that she couldn't help hearing gossip about people she knew and didn't know in Bald Eagle Falls. It was one of the main gossip hubs, especially during the Sunday ladies' tea.

"Thanks for letting me look at that," Beaver said, nodding to the tablet. "I had no idea that vintage cookbooks could be so valuable. Something to think about."

"Are you on the hunt?"

"Maybe." Beaver chewed her gum and gave away nothing. "You never know. You're looking tired, though, Miss Erin, so I should leave you alone. You need your rest."

Erin readjusted her position on the bed. "I wish I wasn't so tired. I have so many things I would rather be doing than sleeping the day away."

"Hopefully, it subsides fast. Some people only have it for a few days."

The rest of the sentence, the part that Beaver didn't say, was the part that scared Erin. *And some people have it for weeks or months.* Or years? Erin hoped that it would only be another day or two. She didn't know how she would manage if it were more than that.

CHAPTER 17

The next day, Erin felt marginally better. Still not one hundred percent, but she could at least walk down the hall by herself and, once during the day while Terry was out, she made herself tea. She had to sit in the kitchen for a long time before she mustered the energy to make it back to her bed, but at least she had been able to get up and do something on her own. That was an improvement.

When Vic came over after work, Erin was awake and able to sit up for a visit. She pushed her hair back from her face. Maybe later, she would be able to manage a shower. Or sitting in the bath. She felt sweaty and greasy like she hadn't bathed in a week.

"Tell me everything that happened today," she instructed Vic. "I want to know everything. If I can't be there, I need to at least hear about it secondhand."

"Well," Vic drawled out her answer, "I dunno, it was just a regular day at the bakery. Everyone wants to see you, of course, so they keep coming by to see if you're back yet. And buying cookies in sympathy. So receipts are good."

"There has to be more than that."

"Everybody is talking about the recipe book and old family recipes. They all want to see it now, but it won't be on exhibit at the museum until after the theft has been all sorted out. Maybe even a year or more. By then, the exhibit will be over, and the book will probably just be returned to its original owner."

"It's really too bad."

"But you have it all on your video. So maybe we can use pages from it in our advertisements. Serialize it or something. Publish a new page each week."

"Do you think I could do that? It is public domain, so I can use it however I like, right?"

Vic shrugged. "It's an old recipe book. Is someone going to come after you and say you can't?"

"I don't know. Does the Women's League still exist? What will they think of it?"

"It still exists," Vic said slowly. "But I don't think they would object to you showing pictures from the old recipe book. Why would they? It's good advertising for them, too. Maybe they can get some new people interested and renew their membership. As it is, it's just old gray ladies. They'll all die out, and the Women's League will have to dissolve."

"Maybe it could be a joint advertisement," Erin pondered. "They could help to pay for some of the space, because it will take more space to display those pages if we want them to be legible. But it could be 'brought to you by Auntie Clem's Bakery and the Women's League' and show a different recipe each week. I don't think I could keep up with converting all of them to gluten-free, one each week, but we could feature a gluten-free version of them… once a month, maybe."

"People could vote on which to convert," Vic said enthusiastically.

"Well, a lot of the recipes are not even baked goods. There are plenty of stews, salads, and things we don't want to make here. But we could make sure that at least one per month is a baked good that we could serve. People can use the original or gluten-free version of the recipe or buy the finished product at the bakery."

"I love it," Vic agreed.

Erin nodded, liking the way that it was starting to work out. She would just need to contact whoever was the president of the Women's League to discuss the project with her to ensure they were onside.

"What else happened today? Who came in? Were the Fosters there today?"

"Not today. But we did have a new friend today."

"A customer?" Erin asked, unsure what Vic was talking about.

"No, a new baker."

It came back to Erin in a flash. "Harold Melville!" she explained. "I forgot about that. Oh, I should have been there today for his orientation. He'll be disappointed. Did you show him—"

"We took care of him," Vic assured her. "We've started other new bakers before. We know what to do. He's been through all the safety and hygiene training, been shown around the store and where everything is, the Bible, the opening and closing procedure checklists, even though he won't be opening or closing for some time."

"How did he do? Did he seem okay with it?"

Harold Melville was one of the kids that Erin had met at the school. He was fairly new to Bald Eagle Falls and was celiac. So he was delighted to have the opportunity not just to have a part-time job, but to learn how to make gluten-free baking of his own, and to take day-old baking home with him.

"He was in heaven," Vic told her. "Honest. He loved it. He was sorry that you weren't there and more sorry that you had been hurt. Like everybody else. He just wants you to get better quickly."

"He's such a sweetie," Erin remembered him telling his friends all about Auntie Clem's and how much he loved Erin's baking. "I'm glad that he asked about getting a job at Auntie Clem's."

"Always nice to have extra hands around that we can call on, too," Vic said. "Those weekend shifts, or if someone calls in sick and we need someone in the afternoon."

"If the boss is injured by a speeding scooter," Erin intoned.

"That too. It's nice to have people we can call on, and I'm sure they're all glad for the extra hours and paychecks."

"I'll be back soon."

"Yes, you will," Vic agreed in a reassuring tone.

Erin sighed. She knew it had only been a few days, but she felt like it had been forever. She wanted to get back to her business. It might sound silly to someone else, but she saw the bakery as her life's work, not just a job.

There was a volley of barking from outside. Erin had been trying to ignore the noise that Nilla was making, but he was getting too loud now. The neighbors would be calling to complain.

"I'd better take care of him," Vic sighed. "He has been so needy lately. He is not happy about Willie going back to work!"

"He misses his buddy?"

"Yeah. It's funny, because when I first got Nilla, he didn't like Willie very much. He avoided him whenever he could, and Willie was always complaining about him getting underfoot or acting like he was being beaten when Willie would push him out of the way or tell him 'no' about something."

"But then they warmed up to each other."

"I guess it was bound to happen with Willie being at home all the time during his treatment, in bed where Nilla could curl up against him so comfy cozy."

"And Willie probably didn't mind having someone around to keep him company when you were gone."

"Another warm body in the bed," Vic agreed. "The old softy."

Erin knew that while Willie looked rough and tough, he was actually very thoughtful and cared about other people. He was fiercely protective of Vic and Erin. It was no wonder Nilla was missing him.

"I'm going to go take him out for a long walk," Vic said. "Nilla, that is, Willie is out. I'll take him—Nilla—through the woods and try to tire him out so that he'll behave and go to sleep when we get home."

Erin nodded at the wisdom of her approach. Nilla was just a small dog. It wouldn't take a long time to tire him out.

CHAPTER 18

*V*ic called Nilla to her and opened the gate from the backyard to the private woods behind the house. It wasn't exactly a wilderness in the middle of the town, but the woods did extend quite a way back and out to the town limits in one direction. It was a good-sized little park area, and Adele, the gamekeeper, did her best to keep it free of trespassers in exchange for being able to live in the little summer cottage. It allowed her to practice her religion, whatever pagan rites that entailed.

Vic preferred to stay as far away from such practices as possible and didn't like to think about Adele being a witch. Not like the ones she saw in fantasy movies, with a magic wand and a bubbling cauldron—a real witch.

Vic wasn't superstitious or gullible, but she hadn't ever taken tea at Adele's cottage. Erin had a few times, but Vic couldn't bring herself to trust that a witch would not poison her or put some curse on her.

Nilla ran back and forth. Vic tried to keep him close to her, but she wanted him to run himself out and expend a lot of energy. He ran here and there after squirrels and crows, tracking scents and looking for deer. He thought he was a much bigger dog than he was. Terriers might have been bred to dig into fox and badger burrows but were not well-equipped to bring down large prey.

Vic saw a streak of dark fur she thought she recognized.

"Nilla!" she tried to call her white dog back to her. "Nilla, you'd better not be chasing Bernt!"

Bernt was Adele's cat, who she refused to keep indoors. Vic had grown up on a farm with outdoor cats, so she understood that they could be independent and some people thought keeping them in the house was cruel.

But it meant that Bernt was in danger from Nilla and large predators. The woods were full of foxes, badgers, raccoons, porcupines, and sometimes cougars or bears. Not exactly a safe place for a cat or a yappy little dog. At least Nilla made enough noise to scare most of the wildlife away. But Vic didn't dare get complacent. A mama bear with cubs, something that was hungry and possibly injured, or even a rabid animal were all possible concerns.

"Nilla!"

She could hear Nilla yapping wildly at whatever he was chasing. He had obviously never heard of sneaking up on his prey. He was a "flush out" dog, not one that would ever surprise his target.

"Nilla!" Vic whistled loudly. "Come back. Come here! Nilla!"

She shook her head, hurrying as quickly as she could through the woods. Of course, Nilla had left the pathway, which meant that she was having to break trail through a wilder part of the woods. The ground was uneven and she couldn't see what might be hidden in the undergrowth in front of her feet.

She had hunted a lot with her father as she had been growing up, and he would have been disgusted with the amount of noise she was making now crashing through the unbroken ground cover. But she wasn't hunting and trying to remain unseen and unsensed by the game. She was trying to catch up to her dang dog before he got himself into real trouble. Or hurt Bernt. But she suspected that Nilla was more likely to be the injured party if the two of them ended up tangling.

"Nilla! You leave that cat alone!" Vic put all the menace into her voice that she could, hoping he would be cowed and come creeping back to her, knowing he was in trouble for some reason. He didn't understand why chasing the cat was any different from chasing a squirrel. And Vic let him chase squirrels. It was easier than throwing a stick or ball a hundred times.

The dog was still barking, but seemed to have stopped moving. Did that mean that he had Bernt cornered? Or maybe that Bernt had escaped, and Nilla was stupidly barking at a fence or hollow tree, thinking he could still get what he wanted? Vic pushed herself a little faster, hoping she could catch him and put a leash on him without having to chase him any farther.

"Nilla!" She whistled again several times.

She pushed through a stand of trees growing thickly together and was surprised to see a building.

There were several outbuildings in the woods. She wasn't familiar with all of them. Besides Erin's house and Adele's summer cottage, everything else had been abandoned long ago. Even the summer cottage had lain in disrepair for years before Adele had started squatting there, cleaning it up and repairing it.

The building Vic saw was barely standing. It was dark gray and weathered, not a speck of paint sticking to it, if it had ever been painted. A few walls. Either a single room shack or one room left of a larger building. She initially figured it had been a barn or storage shed but, when she got closer, the windows and doorknob suggested that it had once been a home. Once cared for by a loving hand.

"Nilla?"

The dog barked from inside the building.

"Oh, good grief," Vic complained. "Really? You had to go inside?"

It was probably filled with rat nests in the cupboards and swallow nests in the rafters. Squirrels in the attic, if there was one. Who knew what kind of trouble the dog could have gotten himself in.

He had gotten in through a broken board on the side of the house. Vic tried the door. It was unlocked, saving her from having to break in.

The inside was, as she had expected, dark and musty. Dirt, dust, and grime colored every surface. Vic fell upon a dirty white mop of fur and quickly clipped the leash onto Nilla's collar. The dog continued to bark and jump at a loft over the main room. That was, Vic assumed, where his quarry had retreated to.

"Just leave him alone," Vic scolded Nilla. "Bernt should be your friend. You shouldn't be chasing him around. Just let him alone now. He'll go back to Adele's when he's calmed down."

Nilla continued to yap annoyingly loudly. Vic squinted up into the loft, trying to see Bernt. She was sure he was okay, but she just wanted to see for herself to be absolutely sure. She'd never even gotten a good look at him when Nilla had begun the chase. It might not be Bernt at all, but another neighborhood cat. Or maybe some other wild animal. A raccoon, even.

She started to direct Nilla out of the shack, but the fact that she hadn't seen what he was chasing niggled at her. She was sure it was just Bernt, and everything was fine. But what if the animal was hurt and was now holed up there, afraid to come down? He could die from shock. Vic certainly did not want to be responsible for the death of someone's pet.

"You wait here," she told Nilla, lashing the leash to the doorknob. "I just have to make sure you didn't do any damage."

The ladder up to the loft looked about a hundred years old. Just because the cat had gotten up it without any mishap, that wasn't any guarantee that a full-grown woman could. Vic tested the first rung, putting her weight on it and then bouncing up and down to see how much give it had. It held and didn't bend or spring to an alarming degree. There was no crack of wood breaking and dumping her unceremoniously back to the floor.

She tried the next rung, bouncing on it the same way. They all seemed sturdy enough, a testament to whoever had built the ladder. Vic climbed it the rest of the way to the loft, trying to ignore the risk. If the first few rungs were sound, then they all were. If she fell, she had a phone on her and could call for help.

There was light from several holes in the roof or the walls of the shack, lighting up the swirling dust motes in the air. A thick layer of dust lay over everything, broken by the tracks of mice, birds, and other critters. Cobwebs swathed the beams in the roof.

There were some old wooden crates and furniture. Long abandoned. Vic was not sure of the soundness of the floor, and didn't step out onto the wooden slates. She made kissy noises to call Bernt.

"Bernt? Kitty kitty? Come on out; I won't let the nasty dog hurt you. Where are you, puss?"

She listened, hearing the birds chirping outside, Nilla padding around below her, waiting to see if she were going to bring a nice juicy kitty down for him to play with.

There was a scritching, scrabbling noise, and then a black cat jumped up onto one of the crates from behind, and stared at Vic unblinkingly.

"Hi, Bernt," Vic said softly. "Are you okay? You don't need to hide up here. I'll take the doggie away and then you can go home."

He didn't move. Vic watched him, but couldn't see any sign that he was hurt. He was perfectly fine. He just didn't want to come out while she and the noisy dog were still there.

"Okay," Vic said softly. "I'll just leave you alone, then, and you can go home when you feel like it. I'm glad he didn't hurt you."

Bernt blinked slowly and made no sound or movement.

Vic turned to look down before descending the ladder, and her eyes caught on something hidden between a beam and the loft floor.

CHAPTER 19

It was getting dark when Vic returned from her long walk in the woods with Nilla. Erin imagined the little dog was probably thoroughly tuckered out. He would sleep well and not keep the neighbors or Vic awake with his whining.

She was surprised to hear Vic at the back door. Erin considered getting up and meeting her in the kitchen, where they could have a cup of tea while they visited, as they had so many times before. But it seemed like an awfully long way to the kitchen. She wouldn't get farther than the bedroom door before Vic met her there. And if she did walk all the way out to the kitchen, she would be tired and might not be able to visit for very long.

Better to conserve her energy and be able to spend longer with Vic in the bedroom.

"Yoo-hoo," Vic called from the door. "Are you sleeping?"

"Come in," Erin invited. "I'm not asleep."

She could hear the jingle of Nilla's leash and collar as they walked through the house. Orange Blossom was lying on the bed with Erin, and he sat up with a disapproving kitty look when he realized that Vic was bringing *that animal* into the bedroom.

"I didn't think you'd be coming back here tonight," Erin observed. "Is everything okay?"

"Yes, everything is fine," Vic assured her breezily. She had smudges of dirt on her cheek that she obviously didn't know about. "I brought you something to do."

"Something to do?" Erin was mystified.

Vic produced a shallow wooden box. It looked very old but was in good condition. Not broken or scratched. The finish was dull. It had tiny hinges on one long side and a latch on the other, like a jewelry box.

Vic sat on the edge of the bed and placed it in the space between her and Erin. Orange Blossom approached to see what it was, deciding to ignore the dog's presence for the moment. Vic flipped up the latch and lifted the lid to display the contents. There were yellowing letters, notes, recipes, and old black-and-white photographs. Thin, angular script covered all of them.

"What is this?" Erin asked, pulling it a little closer to her. "Where did you get it?"

Vic launched into a lengthy description of her trek into the woods with Nilla leading the way. She told Erin about the attic and then the little box that had caught her eye as she descended the old wooden ladder once more.

Erin picked up one of the recipes and looked at it.

"Custard Cream Biscuits," she said with a little laugh. "Charley was just telling me about Custard Creams the other day!"

"How funny!"

"Do you know who these belonged to?"

"I have no idea. I guess your aunt Clementine would know who lived in that little house in the woods way back when. But I have no idea."

"Maybe there is something in her genealogical papers."

Vic nodded. "I would guess so. Has this always been your family property?"

"As long as I know of. I mean, before it was ours it must have belonged to someone… maybe the Cherokee. I don't know if any other European settlers ever owned it. I'm not quite up on my family history."

Vic chuckled. "I couldn't tell you much about the Jackson family going back beyond my grandparents. And this is probably older than that. Back to the 1700s and 1800s… who knows? I couldn't tell you if anyone else ever owned the Jackson farm, either. It's been in the family for generations."

Erin picked up a letter. She feared it would turn to dust in her hands, but it was reassuringly durable. Erin tried to read the tall cursive letters of the sender's name and address. She had practice reading old-fashioned script from Clementine's genealogy papers, but it was still not easy. She tried to read each individual letter and then put them together into words. Then to try different variations to see if any word made sense.

"Hannah?" she tried. "Hannah Dixon?"

"Dixon?" Vic asked. "Are you sure it's not…"

Erin peered at the letters. It was hard to know for sure. It could have been Dixon, but there was a long descender. "Dyson?"

Vic leaned over to study it closely. "I think it is!" she said excitedly. "One of the Dysons living in Bald Eagle Falls?"

"Did they ever live here?" Erin couldn't remember any mentioned in Clementine's genealogy, but she might not have looked at birthplaces for everyone. She might just have associated Dyson with Moose River and not realized that any of them had lived right in her hometown. "Do you think that Hannah lived on the property here?"

"Well, it only makes sense. Why would her papers be in that shack otherwise?"

"Does that mean that I'm related to the Dysons? Or did they own it before the Prices?"

"You're the one with the family trees. Like you said before, anyone who has lived on this mountain for any length of time is kin. The Prices, the Dysons, the Jacksons, the Coxes, we're all related somehow. Although…" her smile dimmed slightly.

"What?"

"Well, you know, the feud between the Dysons and the Jacksons. They wouldn't intermarry if they knew…"

"So everybody would mix unless they knew they were from one of those clans?"

Vic shrugged. "I just know how it was living as part of the Jackson clan. I know that they would never have countenanced me seeing a Dyson. No way, no how. That would have been worse than coming out; you saw how they felt about that. I don't know anyone who ever went against the feud. If someone did… they would be dealt with by the family quickly before it leaked out."

"Charley was a Dyson soldier, until they found out she was related to the Jacksons by blood. Then she was out."

"And lucky they didn't do worse than just kick her out. I think they were easy on her because she'd dated Bobby."

Easy on her. Erin remembered what kind of shape Charley had been in when they had recovered her. She was lucky it hadn't taken another day or two for them to get to her. She might have been dead.

Vic nodded slowly, probably reading this in Erin's expression. She had been there too. She had been instrumental in helping to get Charley away from the Dysons safely. And had suffered at the hands of her father for it. Feuds were nothing to laugh about. TV shows often made them look comical. But there was nothing funny about what Erin had seen of the feud between the two organized crime families.

"So," Vic motioned to the box of mementos to bring Erin's attention back to it. "I thought you might like to go through these things and find out about one of your forbears, if that was what she was. It's something to keep you entertained, at least."

"Yes, thank you." Erin gently laid the letter she had unfolded back on top of the contents. "I am going to have a good time looking through all this stuff. It looks fascinating."

"You can solve the mystery of 'Who was Hannah Dyson?'" Vic chuckled. "Safer than *Rear Window.*"

Erin was baffled by the comment. "What?"

"*Rear Window.*" Vic shook her head. "You've never seen the movie? Heard about it? It's an Alfred Hitchcock."

"No. What's *Rear Window?*"

"Okay, so…" Vic readjusted her position, getting more comfortable on the bed. "James Stewart plays this guy who is convalescing after an injury. He's bored and uses his binoculars to watch people in the apartment building across from him."

"Uh-huh?"

"But, the problem is, he's convinced that this woman has been murdered. And no one will believe him. They think he has just dreamed or hallucinated the whole thing because he's so bored. And he's convinced that this woman was killed. Only he can't prove it."

"That sounds horrible."

"It's a really good movie, if you don't mind oldies."

"No, I mean it's a terrible situation for him to be in. Not that it's a terrible storyline."

They both laughed at that. Erin smoothed the blanket stretched over her legs. "Well, the only apartment that I can see out *my* rear window is yours, so I don't think we need to worry about me witnessing a murder."

Vic opened her mouth to make a crack, and then closed it again. Erin realized belatedly that there had, in fact, been someone killed in Vic's apartment, and both she and Willie had initially been implicated in the murder. It had not been fun and games.

"Well," Erin tried to let the awkward moment pass without commenting, "I think this will be a lot of fun. So, thank you for finding it and bringing it over. And I guess I should say thank you to Nilla for chasing Bernt into that old house so that you would find it."

Nilla stopped nosing around the room and looked up at Erin at the sound of his name, ears pricked forward curiously.

"You're a good dog, aren't you?" Erin crooned.

"Chasing cats is not good," Vic protested. "We don't want him doing that."

"Well, just this once, it was good."

CHAPTER 20

Hannah rubbed her eyes and tried to pretend that she hadn't been crying. Her mother would know the instant she saw her and would want to know why she had been crying again. Even though, of course, she knew why. She didn't want Hannah to have the feelings she did toward Otis and seemed to think that by forbidding it, she would somehow change what Hannah was feeling.

But it didn't. Even if Hannah could stop crying when she thought about Otis, she would still have the same feelings for him on the inside. But her mother wanted her to bury them deep. To say that they were gone and she would just do whatever her parents told her to do from now on. Be the quiet, obedient, respectful daughter they expected her to be.

Rubbing her eyes would not make them any less red or puffy. Maybe if she lay down in her bed in the dark with cucumber slices over her eyes, they would look better. But it wouldn't make her feel any better, and she was more likely to cry more if she were shut in her room alone.

"Hannah, are you finished with your chores?"

Hannah startled. Her mother had the uncanny ability to walk silently across the normally creaky floor and to scare her by appearing out of nowhere.

"Oh, Mama. You scared me." Hannah put her hand behind her back and tried to ease the muscle soreness. She shifted in her seat to turn toward her mother, a tall, hard-faced woman who never seemed to approve of anything Hannah did.

"I asked you whether you completed your chores."

"I… I tried. But I can't do them right now." Hannah rubbed her back, demonstrating why she was unable to. "It hurts too much right now."

"Do I get a break from taking care of this household when I am in pain?" Mrs. Dyson demanded. "No, young lady, I do not. And neither do you. I expect those chores to get done."

"Yes, Mama. I'll do them as soon as I can. I'm sure that in a little while…" She leaned forward, trying to stretch the muscles out the other way. She knew that the pain was not going to go away. She would have to do as her mother insisted and still do her chores whether she was in pain or not.

"A proper housewife does not wait until the end of the day to get the work done," Mama said severely. "You don't know what else might happen during the day that you will need to take care of, so you get the work done early." She allowed herself one swipe across the forehead with her arm to wipe away the sweat collecting at her hairline. "And in the Tennessee heat, you want your physical work to be done before the heat of the day. Leave the afternoon for shelling peas on the porch or knitting in the parlor."

Hannah knew that her mother would not give up until she was moving, demonstrating that she was on her way to do the chores that her mother had set for her. She took a deep breath, trying to gather her physical and mental resources, and pushed herself to her feet. She stood for a moment, swaying with a head rush, before walking slowly to the door.

"I'm sorry, Mama. I'll get started."

"A proper lady does not waste her whole day staring out the window." Her mother had to get one more shot in before Hannah closed the door.

She knew that her mother meant well. She was trying to train Hannah to be a proper lady and member of society. But it was too late for that. She would never be what her mother hoped. She was already a woman, not a little girl, and she had already made the choices that would define her life.

～

Erin awoke to Terry climbing into bed. She rolled over to greet him.

"Hey," she murmured. "Is it that late already?"

"Shh. Go back to sleep."

He knew, as she did, that if she started a conversation now, it might prevent her from being able to go back to sleep. When she had work the next morning, that was a problem. But she didn't have work. She didn't have to be at the bakery in the wee hours of the morning, so it didn't matter whether she lay awake for a few hours during the night. In fact, she wouldn't mind being awake for a few hours instead of sleeping constantly. She didn't like the feeling of being on the edge of sleep all the time, barely able to have a full conversation before nodding off again.

"How was your day at work?" Erin rubbed her eyes and pushed her hair away from her face. She put her arms around him and nuzzled the smooth skin of his neck below the scratchy stubble.

"Mmm." Terry held her close, kissing the top of her head. "No particular excitement today. Just routine stuff."

"Boring?"

"Well… a bit," he admitted.

A cop didn't like things to be too quiet but, on the other hand, he didn't want it to be too crazy or violent, either. A little bit of excitement mixed in with the routine calls. Something more interesting than trespassers and shoplifters. Breaking up domestic squabbles could make him feel like a school guidance counselor instead of a cop, but it could also break out unexpectedly into a shooting or hostage-taking.

So while no cop liked to say that it had been a boring shift, and there was a superstition about using the 'Q' word—quiet—the profession did tend to be dominated by men and women who liked an adrenaline spike and missed it if the job went too long without it.

"How is everyone in the department? Did you see Melissa today?"

"Melissa is fine. Of course, there is no big news for her to spread around right now, but she'll do her best anyway. Still talking about your take-down of the museum burglar."

Erin snorted. "I took him down, now, did I?"

"Apparently, your selfless sacrifice in stepping in front of his speeding scooter to save the priceless, irreplaceable recipe book was both heroic and foolhardy."

Erin couldn't help laughing, even if it did increase the pressure in her head. Terry chuckled along with her.

"You should ask her over for a visit sometime when you feel up to it. I'm sure she would be delighted to have a gossip session with you. Even if it was just over video chat."

Erin nodded slightly. "Yeah. I'll make sure to do that. When I'm feeling up to it."

She wasn't sure when that would be. Dealing with Melissa did take a certain amount of mental energy that she wasn't sure she had yet. She wasn't easy to be with like Vic. Vic could visit any time she liked; Erin didn't feel like she had to entertain Vic or to monitor everything she said to her. And if she got too tired, she could tell Vic she needed to sleep. Though Vic would probably notice even before Erin did that her energy was flagging.

"And in other news…" Terry teased. Erin was alert to what else she might have missed in the community. "There's nothing," he finished. "Like I said, it's been pretty quiet."

"Well, considering some of the excitement we've had in Bald Eagle Falls, that's probably a good thing."

"No disappearing bodies? No clan activity?"

"That's a good thing, right?" Erin pressed.

He played with her hair. "Yes, it is. But I'm left to wonder when the next shoe is going to drop. Because sooner or later… it always does."

"That's a lot of shoes."

"There are an endless number of shoes."

CHAPTER 21

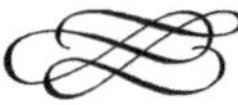

$\mathcal{E}$rin kissed his neck softly. "I had another dream."

"What kind of dream? A nightmare? The doctor did say that you might continue to have vivid dreams for some time."

"About Hannah."

"Who is Hannah?"

"Oh, you didn't hear! Vic found a box of letters and photos in an abandoned shack in the woods, and she brought it to me to keep me entertained for a while. It looks like it belonged to a woman named Hannah. Hannah Dyson."

"A Dyson? That's interesting. It was on your property?"

"Yes. An abandoned building back there somewhere…" Erin waved in the direction of the back of the house. "There are a few old buildings I've never explored. They should probably be knocked down so no one trespassing can claim that they were injured falling through a broken floor or something. But I hate to destroy anything… historical. We might have missed these papers if I had. They were hidden."

"How did Vic find them? What was she doing out there?"

"Chasing after Nilla, who was chasing after Bernt."

"Ah. So what did these papers have to say, and what did this have to do with your dream?"

"I've been having dreams about this woman ever since the concussion. Dreaming that I was someone else."

"That's what you said. The doctor said it was normal."

"Well, I think… this is sort of weird, but I think I was dreaming from Hannah's perspective."

"I thought Vic just brought you this information today."

"She did."

"So, how did you know about Hannah before?"

"I didn't. I didn't know who it was I was dreaming about. And now… I do."

"I see." Terry's tone was skeptical. It was obvious that he didn't see or believe it.

"I know. It's weird. I don't know what to think of it. Maybe I read about her before in Clementine's papers. Or maybe my brain is just trying to make connections between things that don't make any sense."

"You're not talking to ghosts like your foster sister?"

"Reg? No way." Erin shuddered. "First of all, I'm not talking to anyone, just having dreams. Everyone has dreams, and they don't usually make any sense. And Reg has diagnosed mental illness. I know that some of the stuff she spouts is just made up to con people, but she can't help the fact that she *does* hear and see things that aren't there."

"I didn't say that it was her fault," Terry backtracked, trying to repair the conversation, "I'm not making fun of her. But you have to admit that she is… unusual."

Reg was nothing if not unusual. "Yes," Erin admitted. "But don't compare me having dreams to her… issues. Please."

"Sorry. I didn't mean… well, I didn't mean that there's something wrong with you because you're having these dreams. I just mean… you couldn't very well have been dreaming about Hannah Dyson before you even knew she existed. That's just not possible."

"Well… I was. I can't explain it. But when I started reading this stuff left behind by Hannah, it was obvious that was who I had been dreaming about."

Terry didn't say anything for a few long seconds. Trying to compose his thoughts and put them into words.

"Okay," he said finally. "Sometimes things happen that we don't understand. Deja vu. Premonitions. Coincidences. We don't know how they happen, but they do."

"Yeah. We don't know how our brains work. You know I don't believe in religious or paranormal stuff. But sometimes… our brains work in unexpected ways. I'm not going to say that we understand everything. There's still a lot of science that we don't know."

Terry seemed to agree with that. He made a noise of acknowledgment. Had Erin made a mistake by lumping religious phenomena and the paranormal together? She knew Terry had a religious upbringing but didn't know what his thoughts were on miracles, possession by spirits, ghosts, and the like. They'd never discussed it. To Erin, it was all the same thing, but he might not think so.

"So what was this dream about?" Terry asked eventually, after she thought he had fallen asleep. "And what did you learn about her from the papers?"

"I just dreamt… that she was at home. She was waiting for this man she was apparently in love with, but didn't think he was ever coming back. And her mother was there. She was kind of mean. Strict."

"She had a boyfriend but was still living at home? How old was she?"

"It was pretty common for spinsters to stay living at home, no matter how old they were. It wasn't proper for them to live on their own without any kind of supervision or protection. But she was young… a teenager or young adult, I think. She doesn't say in her letters, but she seemed really young."

"First crush?"

"Maybe. But if so… she fell for him pretty hard."

"That does happen."

"Of course," Erin agreed. "Some people are wired that way. Or are introduced to someone new under just the right circumstances."

She didn't exactly believe in love at first sight. Certainly, some people were attracted to each other from the beginning, sometimes even obsessed, but she wasn't convinced it was love. Chemistry wasn't the same thing.

"And what was in the papers? Were they letters to her or from her?"

"From her. Everything was written by her, I think. It all looked like the same handwriting. The letters… I don't know if she wrote them and never sent them, or maybe they were returned to her. Maybe she didn't have a good address, or Otis didn't want to have anything more to do with her."

"That was who they were addressed to? This man she was in love with?"

"Yeah. Otis. I don't have the envelopes, so I don't know his last name. Just 'Dearest Otis' or greetings like that in the letters. Some little notes with 'Hannah & Otis' or little fantasies about him. 'Buy house in Memphis. Four children, two boys and two girls.' Stuff like that."

"Unfortunately, you can't exactly plan out the genders of your children."

"Like I said, they were just fantasies. Maybe they had talked about them, or maybe it was just her daydreaming."

"Any indication this Otis had any feelings for her? Or even knew she existed?"

"I don't know..." Erin had not gotten very far in reading the papers Vic had found. The handwriting was very hard to decipher, on top of her usual difficulties with reading and processing a lot of information. Add a brain injury to that, and she could only manage to read a few sentences at a time. At least the blurriness was clearing up. It would take forever to get through all the papers in the box. But maybe that was the whole point. It would keep her occupied for a long time. Until she was healed enough to go back to Auntie Clem's and her real life. "In my dream, I felt like they both had feelings for each other. But..."

"But that was just a dream. And even if you were feeling what Hannah felt, that isn't necessarily an accurate analysis of how he felt about her."

"Right."

Erin snuggled in Terry's arms. She was happy to be held by him. She spent a lot of nights alone due to his work schedule, which made her savor those nights she had with him that much more. She could imagine Hannah crying during the night as she lay alone in her bed, thinking of the man she could not be with.

"I don't think she was well," she murmured to Terry. "I think she was sick or had something wrong with her. She was arguing with her mother about not getting her chores done and being in pain."

"Did you ever have a fight like that with one of your foster moms?"

Erin couldn't help feeling discomfited by his question. Did he think that everything she had dreamt had just been a reflection of something that had happened when she was a young girl? That she was just reliving something from her own life? That wasn't where the dream had come from. She was not Hannah and was not just reliving disappointments from her own life.

"I've always been pretty healthy. I don't think I ever had an argument about being in too much pain to do my chores."

"You must have been sick sometimes. Or had cramps or something else that kept you from doing your assigned chores."

"No. Not that I remember."

"Hmm."

"And I've never been pining after a man who wouldn't come back to me either. Those aren't my experiences."

"Uh-huh."

Erin closed her eyes. Terry wasn't going to be convinced that it wasn't just her imagination or her brain doing weird things because of her concussion. But he wasn't going to argue about it, either. He had decided not to engage, so there was no way to argue with him. It was not a satisfying way to end the conversation, but she supposed it was better than having a fight and going to sleep with hurt feelings.

She took a few deep breaths, waiting for her brain fatigue to whisk her off to sleep again.

CHAPTER 22

The doorbell rang in the middle of the day. Erin lay on her bed, considering. She wasn't sure whether she had enough energy to make it to the door. And it might just be a salesperson or someone she didn't want to talk to. But it might also be a friend, someone who would help break up the day's monotony. Terry had said that she should call Melissa. Maybe Melissa had decided to call on her rather than waiting for Erin.

She slid her feet off the bed and got to her feet slowly. She stood still for a minute to judge whether she was stable enough to walk to the door. Her vertigo didn't return. Maybe she was healing enough to get around without worrying about falling. Her legs seemed strong and her head steady, so she took a few steps to the door of the bedroom.

Orange Blossom jumped down from the bed to follow her, maybe hoping that she was on her way to the kitchen to fix him a snack. He meowed a couple of times to encourage her to go with him. Did he know that she was sick? Was he worried about her? Or just about his own stomach?

There was a knock on the door. Erin quickened her pace. A doorbell followed by a knock. It wouldn't be long before the caller gave up and decided she didn't want to see anyone or wasn't able to. If it were Erin, she would not have continued to harass someone who was sick. She would just give it one ring and one knock and then she would have left. She would return another time, maybe after talking to the person to ensure she was ready to have visitors.

Erin made it to the door, slightly out of breath but still stable on her feet. She turned the doorknob without looking out to see who her caller was first. She reached for the burglar alarm to disarm it, then paused to see who was on her doorstep. It wouldn't do to ignore all their security precautions just because the doorbell had surprised her.

She looked through the gap in the door and saw it was Mary Lou. She smiled and pushed the door open farther.

"Come in, I just have to do this…"

Erin stared at the burglar alarm panel, trying to remember her code. It became more urgent as the seconds ticked by. If she waited too long, the klaxon alarm would sound, and the security company would be called. She would have to give them her verbal code, and they might still come by to check on her and make sure everything was okay.

"Are you okay, Erin?" Mary Lou asked.

"I just… can't remember the number." Erin shook her head. "I arm and disarm it all the time. How can I not know it today?"

"You have a concussion. I probably woke you up from a sound sleep. Do you want to call Officer Piper? He would be able to tell you what it is."

Erin touched the keypad. She felt like her fingers should know what the keys were. In the back of her brain, she knew the pattern her fingers zig-zagged in when she entered the code. She moved her hand, trying to get it right before the alarm sounded. Her finger went to the final position in the code.

Then something clicked, and she knew what the code was. Her cheeks warm, Erin tapped the number into the keypad.

They both breathed a sigh of relief when the panel beeped and the red light turned green.

"Well, then," Mary Lou said, squaring her shoulders. "I'm sorry to descend on you like this. I should have called first. I was just in the area…"

"No, it's fine. I've been bored, so I'm happy to have another visitor."

"Vic and Charley are running Auntie Clem's, so you don't get to see them very often during the day."

Erin nodded. "Yeah. Come in, have a seat." She motioned to the couch and made her way over to her favorite seat. Terry had left a pile of Clementine's long genealogy binders on the coffee table. Erin had been afraid to go up the stairs to the little attic room while concussed.

Mary Lou looked over the binders. "You look like you're keeping yourself busy."

"Terry just brought those down. I haven't read them yet."

"But still, if you're feeling up to that, you must not be doing too badly."

Erin nodded. "It's getting better. We'll see how much I can actually do when I get to it."

She hadn't finished reading the recipe book or the box of papers from the house in the woods. So why was she starting on another project before finishing those first?

"Bald Eagle Falls has such a rich history," she told Mary Lou. "I was looking at the recipe book, and then at some old letters, and I just wanted..." She concentrated on putting what she wanted to express into words. The concussion had made it more difficult to retrieve the words she wanted than usual and she'd had several frustrating episodes when she had not been able to find the words she wanted at all. "I wanted to fit it into a... framework... in time..."

"A timeline?" Mary Lou suggested.

"Yes. It's hard to visualize how everything fits together."

Mary Lou nodded. "That makes sense. Sometimes these islands of knowledge... we have discrete silos of information, but they don't connect to anything. But to apply knowledge, it needs to fit somewhere."

Erin nodded her agreement, then put her hand to her head. It was easier to move her head without dizziness or pain than it had been, but she still had twinges that reminded her of the seriousness of her injury.

"Are you sure you're up to visitors?" Mary Lou asked. "I can just leave this with you and go..." She indicated an insulated bag that Erin hadn't noticed she was holding before. Another casserole or some other food donation.

"I can visit. For a while."

"Okay. Well, you just tell me when you've had enough. I'll get on my way."

"I will."

"You are surely missed at Auntie Clem's. Your staff is well-trained, but your spirit is absent."

"Oh," Erin smiled. "Thank you for that. For both compliments, actually. I'm glad they're managing without me… but I miss it too. I want to get back as soon as I can."

"And you will be welcomed back when that day comes. But you make sure you take care of yourself. Don't push yourself to come back too fast."

"That's what everyone keeps telling me."

"I'm sure it can't be easy."

"No."

I've been hearing from Victoria about this recipe book you saved. She said you took pictures of it?"

"Yeah. It's been really interesting to read through. I haven't finished yet. My head won't let me. But it's a neat piece of history. Like a time capsule. All about the women in the community."

"Histories are usually just that—*his* stories. It's nice to hear some of the *her* stories sometimes too."

Erin hadn't thought about it that way before. But Mary Lou was right. "I guess they're always there, behind the scenes, but history focuses on wars and science discoveries and politics. Things that women are not as involved with."

"Or *were* not historically."

"It's getting better," Erin acknowledged. But women still didn't have an equal pace in history with men. There was no female President of the United States. Most of the leaders of countries that she saw on TV were still men. Women were becoming more prominent in the medical field and sciences, but most nurses were still women. Enough that she still assumed that the male medical staff at the hospital were doctors or interns, not nurses.

"So, what gems have you found in the recipe book?" Mary Lou asked, gently redirecting the conversation. "There must be some interesting foods you never heard of before, especially since you did not grow up in Appalachia."

"You're right! Some were probably traditional family recipes, and some were wartime recipes, when certain foods were being rationed, and people were being encouraged to grow liberty gardens. They came up with some creative ideas."

"Mock apple pie?" Mary Lou suggested with a smile.

"Mock apple pie!" Erin echoed. "Who knew you could make apple pie with crackers! Obviously, not something I could ever do at Auntie Clem's, but there are a few of the wartime recipes that I think would be fun to adapt to gluten-free. A lot of them are already egg and dairy-free."

"And cheap to make."

"Right." Erin leaned back in her seat and closed her eyes for a moment, getting comfortable. "One of the funny things is all the personal comments in the intros and directions for the recipes. I was surprised at how... *pointed* some of them are."

"Oh? Like what?"

"Well... women complaining about people stealing their family recipes. 'Some people don't respect the hard work of others.' While others were defending themselves with 'you don't own your family traditions' or 'recipes and traditions are not owned by anyone.' It even gets down to outright meanness with stuff like 'a woman's honor and virtue is reflected in the way she treats her family and friends,' or 'someone who is willing to steal from a friend is not a friend.'"

"Huh." Mary Lou gave a bark of laughter. "Who knew women would get so hostile over recipes."

"Well, I have heard celebrity cooks get upset over their recipes being 'stolen' by others. But on the other hand, so many recipes are so similar that you can't be sure someone actually stole yours, unless the directions are word-for-word the same. And even then, if it was Great-Grandma's recipe, then your cousins might have inherited it and passed it on to others, too. The only recipe that's really yours is the one you invent from scratch. And even with those, lists of ingredients can't be copyrighted. Only the narrative instructions."

Mary Lou raised her brows at this. "Really. I had no idea."

"And of course, these recipes," Erin motioned back to the bedroom where the tablet she had been reading the recipe book on lay on the table beside her bed, "they are all in the public domain. So no one can accuse anyone of stealing them now."

Mary Lou gave a knowing smile. "Well, they can certainly accuse. There's nothing to stop them from saying whatever they like about someone else stealing their hard work. Or Great-Grandma's hard work."

"I saw some Cox recipes in there," Erin informed her.

"I have no doubt. There have been Coxes on this mountain almost since the beginning of time. Or at least since the land was settled by the Europeans."

"You must have as many genealogy files and books as Clementine."

Mary Lou looked at the stack of files Terry had brought down from the attic for Erin. "No, I don't think so. I have the ancestors but not the paperwork. Clementine did an amazing amount of work. And almost all of it was done after she got sick. I think she needed something to fill the time when she couldn't run the tearoom anymore."

Mary Lou smiled fondly, remembering the older woman. Erin wished that she had clearer memories of her aunt. But Erin had been a child when her parents had died and she had entered the foster care system, and she hadn't seen Clementine again after that. She could remember "helping" Clementine in the tearoom and showing off her olfactory skills by identifying teas by their smell. But she could remember little else.

"She sure did a lot of work. So are the Coxes related to the Dysons or Jacksons? Did you ever hear of Hannah Dyson, who lived around here?"

"I'm sure we are probably distantly related to both, but nobody would dare claim a close relationship to both clans. It would just cause contention. They would be ostracized from society."

From what Erin had seen of the way the two clans operated, Erin figured Mary Lou was probably right. Years ago, it might have been okay to be related to both families, but not in the last few generations. At some point, a rift had developed between the two clans, and it persisted even though no one probably remembered what had caused it.

"Do you know how it started?" Erin asked Mary Lou, curious whether there were still any rumors about the origin of the fight.

"I really don't." Mary Lou shook her head. "At this point, both families figure that the members of the other are stupid, inbred, dishonorable fools." She shrugged. "Of course, they are all just regular people with normal human foibles. But they have been brought up to hate and violence. I would never try to get between the two, even to help them to reconcile."

"Just too dangerous?"

Mary Lou nodded her agreement. "When both sides of a quarrel wield guns, it is best not to get caught between them."

"Yeah."

"And this woman you were asking about?"

"Hannah Dyson."

Mary Lou shook her head. "Not a name that is familiar to me. Someone's great-grandma, I assume?"

"I don't know. I'll look through the family trees and see if I can find her. I hadn't ever heard of her before. But that doesn't mean anything. I don't have the generations memorized." Erin leaned forward and straightened the pile of files. But she found she needed to stop to steady herself, leaning on the coffee table.

"Whoops," Mary Lou commented. "Careful, there. A bit dizzy?"

"Yeah, a little. It's okay."

"You've got some lovely bruises."

Erin had barely even looked at herself in the mirror, not wanting to see the ugly black, blue, and green bruises. She should probably have tried to cover them up with concealer instead of frightening any visitors with her ghoulish appearance. She touched the bump on the side of her head that had reduced considerably in size since the accident.

"It's not as bad as it looks. Or as bad as it was."

"You certainly took a beating. It's as bad as a car accident."

Erin had escaped car accidents with far less severe injuries.

"Maybe you'd better head back to bed," Mary Lou said. "I've worn out my welcome. Can I help you?" She gestured toward the bedroom.

"No, I'm pretty sure I can make it on my own now. I'm getting better. Be back to normal in no time."

"I certainly hope so." Mary Lou's lips pressed together into a thin line. If there was one person in Bald Eagle Falls who knew about brain injuries and the consequences they could have on life, it was Mary Lou. But Erin's injury was nothing like Roger Cox's. If things ran their normal course, her injuries would heal and she would be able to carry on normally without any ill effects. She would not be permanently affected or disabled by it.

"Shall I put this in the kitchen for you?" Mary Lou gestured to the bag she had brought with her. "Just a little something for supper for you and Officer Piper."

"Sure," Erin agreed. "That would be great."

She could get to the bedroom, she was sure. But she wasn't sure she could carry something to the kitchen, get it from the counter to the fridge, and then get from the kitchen to the bedroom. That might be a little adventurous for one trip.

"All right, dear. You take care of yourself. I'll let myself out."

CHAPTER 24

*E*rin slept for a short time, but then found herself unable to go back to sleep. Maybe she was starting to get more of her energy back. Maybe the worst of the concussion symptoms were receding.

She remembered the stack of binders in the living room and decided she could curl up on the couch to browse through them. If she got tired, she could just stretch out and go to sleep. If she wasn't that tired, she could make some progress on finding Hannah and some record of her family in the genealogical records.

She had asked Terry to find the files for several of the family names she had seen in the recipe book, so that she could establish who they were and their relationship to the current Bald Eagle Falls residents. While there were people in Bald Eagle Falls that she didn't know, or only knew in passing, she knew the most common names from the church ladies, her most frequent customers.

If she could show them the recipes in the book that had come from their families, she could tell them how she would honor them by baking their recipe—assuming it was a baked good—and get permission to feature the new item with their family name. No matter what anyone else thought, she was sure that would help to promote good feelings in the community and draw the members closer together.

There had been Coxes in the recipe book, as Erin had told Mary Lou, so she flipped through the genealogy binder for a few minutes, looking for Charlotte Cox and Hitty Cox, the women who had contributed the recipes. She had to go back several generations to find them, but she eventually found the two sisters. Charlotte had a number of children and grandchildren. Erin would have to sort through the various lines to see if she could find Mary Lou's parents. Hitty had, it appeared, died a spinster. She had still been a young woman. Had she fallen victim to the typhus or polio epidemics? It was easy to forget how far medicine had advanced since those days, how much shorter the average life expectancy was. Young people died. Children. Infants. People had not expected that all their children would survive until adulthood. It was a very different world.

Erin turned to the Dyson binder. After hearing all the clan feud stuff about the Dysons and Jacksons, it felt a little taboo to be in possession of a book of their genealogy. It didn't contain any clan secrets, of course. Everything in there was stuff Clementine had discovered in the public record, going over microfilms of old newspapers, censuses, and vital statistics records. But Erin still felt like she could be in trouble for owning such a thing. If someone from the Dyson clan found out, would they really be upset? Of course not. It was just genealogy, stuff they already knew, and it would not disrupt the business of the clan. It wasn't anything to do with the crime syndicate's unsavory activities.

Going by the dates on the letters, Erin flipped through the pages looking for the right generations, and then skimmed for Hannah Dyson's name. She was looking for the recipe contributors' names, but Hannah was on Erin's mind, and it wouldn't hurt to find out where she fit in the family, too. Erin was curious about anything to do with young Hannah and how her life had turned out.

Had she met a good man and raised children with him? Watched her grandchildren grow up?

Eventually, she found a Hannah Dyson, daughter of Peter and Lucy Dyson, who seemed about the right age. She knew better than to assume that it was the same Hannah Dyson. Sometimes names were repeated throughout a family, with several cousins being named after the same grandparent or great-grandparent, or being given a biblical or other name that was popular at the time. There might have been several Hannah Dysons living around Bald Eagle Falls at the same time.

But it was a possibility. Hannah Dyson, daughter of Peter and Lucy Dyson.

If it were the same girl, then the answers to Erin's questions were not happy ones. The girl had died at the age of seventeen—no chance at marriage or children. No descendants of Hannah's were still living in Bald Eagle Falls, Moose River, or any other nearby towns.

Like Hitty Cox, she had been struck down in her youth. The two of them might have even been friends, gone to school together, and died in the same outbreak of fever. Erin would look for an obituary later. If she were lucky, it might mention how the girl had died.

The little box of mementos was probably all that was left of Hannah now. Her parents hadn't even known where to find it.

Erin turned on her tablet and looked through the video for the Dyson recipe that Charley had mentioned. She was startled to see that it had been contributed by Lucy Dyson. Hannah's mother? Or another Lucy Dyson?

The recipe was for vanilla sandwich cookies. Lucy had included a little note at the top of her recipe, as many other women had. Hers read, "Family is more important than any other relationship, including community, religion, or romantic partners."

Was it just a homily or a pointed accusation or criticism, as some of the other comments in the recipe book clearly were? Was it aimed at someone in the community who had betrayed their family in some way? Maybe someone in her own family? Another Dyson? Had someone betrayed the close-knit clan?

She had fallen asleep. She struggled to wake herself up, feeling that she wasn't supposed to be sleeping, but stuck in a dream and unable to pull herself out of it.

Was she Erin or Hannah?

Everything was black and dark. She could feel a presence in the room. A menacing, dangerous presence.

Who was there?

"Who is it?"

She reached out her arms, trying to feel around her and figure out where she was.

"Is everything okay?" a familiar voice asked.

She finally broke out of the dream world, opening her eyes and finding the room filled with sunlight.

There was another figure in the room with her, but not someone who was a danger to her. The man, rough-looking at first glance, was a friend.

"Sorry, did I wake you up?"

Erin rubbed her eyes. "Willie. No, it's okay. I was kind of stuck in a dream." She swallowed and looked around for a drink to moisten her dry mouth and throat. But there didn't seem to be one close by. "I'm glad I woke up."

"What do you need?" he asked, studying her.

"Just… water." Erin licked her dry lips. When was the last time she'd had something to drink? She knew that at the top of the list of advice for dealing with any illness was getting enough to drink and not allowing herself to get dehydrated, and that included treatment of a concussion. It was on her list of ways to help herself heal. *Get enough fluids. Don't get dehydrated, it may worsen your symptoms.*

Willie walked into the kitchen and ran water in the sink for a minute before filling a glass of cold water for her. He returned and watched as she gulped down the first few swallows, then sipped it more sedately.

"How about some tea?" he suggested. "And when was the last time you ate?"

"I don't know. Terry will make dinner when he gets home. He's been taking good care of me."

"Not well enough," he chided. "He should have left you with plenty of water or tea within reach and something to eat for lunch. He knows how sick you are."

"I've mostly just been sleeping."

"Are you up to a sandwich? Soup? Cookies? What would you like?"

"I'm fine until Terry gets home, really. You don't need to do that."

"I'm going to do it. So what do you want?"

It was nice to see Willie on his feet again. If there was anyone who could empathize with Erin having to sleep the day away while healing from her concussion, it was Willie. The grueling course of chelation had kept him off his feet and in bed much of the day, too. Now, he was finally finished and feeling better. From what Vic said, he wasn't quite one hundred percent yet, but he was so much better he seemed like a different person.

"You really don't have to," Erin tried again.

"What are you in the mood for? I'd hate to make something that you don't like."

"I like anything," Erin brushed his concern aside. She had learned growing up in the various families she had been placed with to eat whatever was placed in front of her, and she wasn't picky. She was very selective about her baking and judging how each new recipe turned out but, when someone else was cooking for her, she would eat anything.

Except fish. She couldn't eat anything that smelled the least bit fishy.

"Maybe… some soup," Erin finally relented. What was the point in telling him not to make her anything? Opening a can of soup and warming it up for her was simple and would take only minutes. He would feel good for having served her, and she really could use something in her belly. Or at least the extra liquids. She should have had a bottle of water beside the bed or couch to keep her from getting dehydrated.

"Soup," Willie agreed, happy to be given some direction. "Let's get you some soup."

He went into the pantry and checked out what they had in stock. "Mushroom and rice?"

"Sure," Erin agreed. She liked anything that was stocked in the pantry. He wouldn't find anything in there that she didn't like. Other than the pet food.

Willie made himself useful in the kitchen, opening the can and dumping the contents into a saucepan. Erin made her way into the kitchen, her legs steady but her head still swimming a bit when she walked unaided. She sat down at the table while Willie whistled cheerily, whisking the ingredients around as the soup heated. The comforting smell began to fill the kitchen.

"So, Vic said she left a box of mementos over here?" Willie suggested. "Could I get those back?"

Erin looked at him. "What?"

"That box she left. If we could get it back again…"

"But… it's not yours. Vic gave it to me."

"To look at. But you really aren't the rightful owner. I would like to preserve it properly."

"The rightful owner? The rightful owner died years ago. I even looked it up in Clementine's genealogical records. She didn't have any children. So there is no heir. It was found in my woods. The woods are my property, and anything in them."

"I'm not sure that argument would stand up in court, when you are talking about historical objects. There are laws about artifacts and they can be very complex. And you weren't the one who found the objects. Vic is."

"And she gave them to me."

"But she didn't realize when she gave them to you that they belonged to the Dyson family. She didn't really have the right to give them to anyone else. The Dysons should have control and ownership of any of the family's historical artifacts."

Erin could see an argument to be made for this. The papers had, after all, belonged to Hannah Dyson, and Vic had obviously told Willie this fact. Willie claimed not to have anything to do with the Dysons anymore other than legitimate business installing computers, network equipment, security systems, and so on. But that was still a connection. He could talk to Nelson Dyson and see how he wanted Hannah's mementos handled.

Willie brought a bowl of soup to the table and handed Erin a spoon.

"So you don't mind if I take those things…"

"I'm still looking at them. Vic said that I could hang on to them. I don't think anyone else has the right to them."

"The family…"

"Her family died a long time ago. She didn't have any children. Maybe somebody in the Dyson clan has a claim, but I don't know who that would be. I'll have to talk to someone and see what my options are."

"I'm sure someone would take care of them. Keep them with the clan records or inter them with her body."

Erin shook her head. She wasn't sure why Willie was so intent on getting them back, but she wasn't about to be talked into anything without having a chance to think about it and talk it over with a lawyer first.

She sipped the hot soup slowly, enjoying the warm, comfy atmosphere of her kitchen and being cared for by a friend. Willie sat watching her, leaning against the counter.

CHAPTER 25

*I*t was a long walk out to the mailbox, but checking it at least once a day was not a chore that Hannah had to be talked into doing. She would have checked it three times a day if it meant she got a letter from Otis. Every day she faithfully checked, and each day, there was only correspondence for her parents and nothing for her.

Hannah walked slowly and determinedly. Maybe this was the day. Maybe this time, she would find something there with her name on it. Otis wasn't a big writer. That was okay. All she cared about was a few words on paper to show her he was thinking about her. He was making plans and pulling things together so that one day they would be able to be together again like he had promised.

The birds were singing a happy song in the trees. She could hear her father chopping wood in the distance. Hot work, but they needed fuel for the stove for cooking and preserving the land's bounty. Her mother was using the summer kitchen so that it would not heat up the house, and they would have somewhere cool to sit and read or go to bed at the end of the day.

Hannah knew she would have a list of other chores to do when she returned to the house after checking the mail, but she wasn't sure how much she would get done. It seemed like she got slower and clumsier with every day that passed. Tasks that had seemed easy a few months ago now took all day—or never got done. Her mother was not impressed with this change in her behavior.

"You are a sluggard," she told her daughter roughly. "A lazy, slovenly woman. Is that how you want the community to see you?"

"No." Hannah didn't leave the homestead. The closest she came was her walk to the mailbox. And no one saw her doing that. No one could see what she had become.

"Then you need to pick yourself up and act like a decent, respectable woman."

And so it went, on and on. Hannah wished she could do what her mother suggested, but it was impossible. Some mornings, she could hardly even get out of bed in the morning, despite both parents shaking her and calling her down to repentance. When she did get up, it was to sit in the chair by her bed and write letters to Otis, to leaf through what she had written before, and to stare out the window, pining after him. Even the needlework and mending her mother tried to get her to do was too much.

She walked down the winding road, putting her hand on the arch of her back to ease the pain, and taking one step at a time toward the mailbox that could hold the answer to her prayers, but was unlikely to.

"Erin? Are you okay?"

"I'm fine," Erin called back. She could hear Terry moving around restlessly in the bed.

"Are you coming back to bed?"

"No. I'm going to go in today."

Terry groaned, and she heard him getting up. She had known that he would object, telling her that it was too early and she was being foolish by trying to return to Auntie Clem's too soon. But she needed to be there, even if it was only for an hour. She needed to see her kitchen and her store and to see that everything was running smoothly. And to breathe in the smells of the yeast and the spices, hear the bells on the door and see her favorite customers.

"Erin." Terry padded down the hallway and stopped in the bathroom doorway to watch her get ready for work. "It's too soon."

"I knew you were going to say that. But I have to get in today. Just for a little bit."

"Why don't you sleep in and see how you feel when you get up…"

"I'm up now, and I want to go in and make bread before we open. I want to mix batters and turn on the ovens and smell everything baking."

"Yesterday, you were just barely able to walk around on your own. How are you going to handle work today?"

"Today, I'm not having any trouble walking around. And when I get tired, I'll come home and sleep. It isn't like when you were recovering from your concussion. You had to worry about what would happen while you were on the job. How you would protect people, see to shoot straight, and all that. I just need to be able to walk around a bit, wipe down the counter, and throw some bread in the oven."

"You could do that here. For a trial run. Before going all the way to Auntie Clem's—"

"All the way? It's a few blocks."

"You can't drive."

"Why not?"

"You have a concussion!"

"I can see just fine. The blurriness is gone. No double vision or dizziness."

"You still can't drive until you're cleared by a doctor."

"He never said that."

"It's common sense."

Erin looked away from the mirror to meet Terry's eyes, to show him she was serious.

"If I can't drive, then I'll walk."

They both knew that just walking across the house had been an ordeal yesterday. Walking a few blocks today might be too much to expect from her healing body and brain.

"Erin," Terry said in exasperation. "You can't walk that far today. Why are you so set on getting to work today? I know you were bored yesterday, but you still needed a lot of extra rest. Why are you pushing it so much?"

"I just need to get in. I can't keep lazing around at home. I need to show everyone that I'm not a… a sluggard."

"A sluggard?" he repeated. "Who even says that?"

"I need to get in today."

He sighed deeply. "I'll drive you, then. And you'll have to call me when you're ready to go home. I'll get there as soon as I can."

"I don't want you to have to…"

But Erin knew that it was the only solution that Terry would likely agree with, unless Willie offered to drive Erin and Vic in. And he didn't usually keep baker's hours, but waited until later in the morning to rise and start in on his workday.

Terry returned to the bedroom to dress. Erin was surprised he wasn't muttering under his breath about what a demanding woman she was.

It wasn't very nice of her to spring it on him like this. But she had awoken at the usual time, like a switch had turned on in her brain, and she had known that she had to get to work today. She knew it was inconvenient for Terry. And inconvenient to everybody else she worked with, as she would be moving slowly and probably getting in everybody's way in the kitchen.

But she had to be there. She couldn't explain it to Terry. The dream, to him, was just that. A dream. Not something that spoke to him. Not something he had to do.

Vic came over when she saw the light on in the house.

"What are you doing up?" she demanded after letting herself in. "Aren't you still supposed to be in bed?"

"I'm going to work."

Vic looked at Terry, who undoubtedly gave her a look of frustration and disapproval while Erin's back was turned to him.

"Well," Vic smiled brightly. "We sure will be glad to have you back today, boss. Even if you don't end up staying for very long. You don't want to overdo it."

"I know. I'll do my best, and when I get tired, I'll go home." Erin turned her head toward Terry. "Terry said to call him and he'll take me home."

"As soon as I am able," Terry clarified. "If I am at an accident scene or something else prevents me, I might be a little while. You can just sit in your office and relax until I can get there."

Erin smiled as if this were perfectly acceptable. If she wasn't allowed to take her own car, then it would have to do.

~

Erin felt like she was returning to the bakery after years of being away. It was almost like when she had first arrived in Bald Eagle Falls for the first time since she was a little girl, and everything was fresh and new, and yet completely familiar, too. Other than the things that had changed.

But nothing had changed significantly since Erin had been knocked down by the scooter a week before. Nothing big, anyway.

Vic opened the door for her and flipped on the light, turning slightly to allow Erin to enter ahead of her.

There wasn't any "welcome back" party or banner. But Erin felt a rush of emotion as if she were finally coming home after a long absence.

"It's so strange," she told Vic as they walked in together and went through the usual opening routine as if Erin had never been away. "It's so nice to be back."

"Nothing strange about that," Vic declared.

They worked in tandem as if Erin had never been away. A few minutes after their arrival, the door opened again, and the newest employee joined them.

Harold's eyes widened. "Miss Erin!" His voice was high with surprise. "You came! Are you okay?"

Erin smiled. "I'm on the mend," she affirmed. "Not one hundred percent, but I'm working on it. How are you doing? I'm sorry I missed your first few days. I intended to be here to help train you."

"Oh, that's okay. Miss Victoria and Bella helped me out. It wasn't that hard. Everything is written down in the binders so, even if I was in the kitchen by myself, I could still figure it out."

"Well, I certainly appreciate you stepping up and putting in even more hours than expected with me being away. Everyone has had to sacrifice a bit to cover for me."

"I don't mind a few extra hours. It means more money!"

"Well, it does at that. Mostly, I think it's Vic and Charley who have had to deal with all the extra hassle."

Vic shrugged. "You have to deal with it all the time. What does it hurt us to step up for a few days to give you a bit of a vacation? Not that it was a vacation, I mean. I know it hasn't been fun or relaxing for you."

"No," Erin admitted. "It's been kind of tough. But I'm feeling a lot better today, and I think I'm almost there. There's been a big improvement the last couple of days, so I think the swelling is going down and I'm well on the road to recovery."

"Don't work too hard today," Harold cautioned, pushing his glasses up and looking at her seriously. "Tell someone if you need help or need to take a break."

Erin smiled at his advice. If a teenager knew enough to tell her that, she should take it to heart and not be stupid about trying to do too much.

"I'll try to take care of myself," she promised.

By the time they were ready to open the bakery, Erin was tiring. Her energy was flagging and her eyelids starting to droop. She stayed out front long enough to say good morning to the early morning customers, Mary Lou among them, and then she retreated to the kitchen and sat on one of the stools to take a break and recover her strength. Vic stayed out at the front of the store to serve customers, and Harold was busy in the kitchen getting more muffins into the oven. He followed the instructions meticulously and set the timers.

"Should you be sitting on a stool if you're getting tired?" he asked solicitously. "It doesn't have a back or any support. If you aren't steady, you could fall off."

"I'm okay for now. If I don't start to feel better just sitting here, I'll call Officer Piper to pick me up. I'm under strict instructions not to overexert myself or to try to go home on my own."

Harold nodded his approval at this plan. He put the mixing bowls into the sink to wash.

"I heard about... the photos and letters and stuff that Miss Victoria found."

Erin supposed Vic had probably been excited by the find and told everybody at Auntie Clem's about it.

"Yes. Some pretty interesting history."

"She said that it was... clan stuff."

"Well, no," Erin turned her head to look at Harold, but his back was to her while he washed the bowls. "They belonged to a girl, a teenager like you. About her thoughts and dreams... the boyfriend she was hoping would come back to her. Stuff like that."

"But she was a Dyson."

"Yes. She was a Dyson. But that doesn't mean it has anything to do with the Dyson organization."

Willie seemed to think the papers should all go to the Dyson family, but Erin wasn't convinced that was the right choice. They would probably just throw them out or incinerate them, after ensuring they didn't contain any family secrets.

"If she's family, then you should stay out of it," Harold cautioned. "They don't like people poking their noses into family business. You should know that." He stacked the overturned bowls into the drying rack and looked over his shoulder at Erin. "I don't want anything to happen to you."

"What do you know about the clans, Harold? You and your family just came here from Nashville, right? That's a long way away from the Dyson and Jackson clans. Maybe you've heard about them from the other boys in school, but… you can't believe everything you hear from them. You know how things get exaggerated."

"It's not stuff I learned from the other guys." Harold wrung out the dishcloth and draped it over the faucet. "Being from Nashville doesn't mean I don't know anything about it. I know all about it."

He didn't say how he knew it, but Erin realized with a sigh that one of his parents must be in one of the clans. She didn't recognize the name Melville from her genealogy, so maybe his mother hailed from the area and was part of one of the extended families. Since Harold was talking to her about the Dysons' right to Hannah's papers, they were probably from the Dyson clan. And how was she supposed to deal with that?

Willie, Vic, and Charley all had roots in the clans. But since they were not a part of that world anymore, it all seemed remote and unreal until something landed right in her lap. Like hiring a member of the Dyson clan and being warned off by him.

How was she supposed to take that?

CHAPTER 26

"To be honest, I didn't think you would call me," Terry said with a chuckle. "I figured we would have to pry you out of that bakery."

"I told you I wouldn't work for too long."

"Yes, but you've told me things like that before. You tell me what you think I want to hear, and then go ahead and do your own thing."

Erin looked for a way to argue with Terry, but she couldn't think of what to say to excuse herself. She knew it was probably true. As a child, she had learned to be obedient and compliant on the surface, but then to take care of her own needs. It was the safest, easiest route to go. She thought she had overcome this as an adult. But her upbringing still showed through.

"Well... I don't mean to do that to you. I guess... I'm just used to looking out for myself."

He nodded and didn't comment on this. "How did you feel working at the bakery this morning?"

"Really good. I really had to get back there. I've been missing it so much."

"You would think you had been kept away from it for a year."

"I know." Erin smiled, amused with herself. "Maybe the concussion has made me overly emotional about it. But I am feeling a lot better this morning. I wasn't making that up. I didn't have enough energy to make it through the day, but I didn't expect to."

"Just being able to stay on your feet for an hour is an accomplishment at this point."

"Yeah, I guess. It felt good. But I did get tired." She rested her head back against the headrest and closed her eyes. "Tomorrow, I'll be able to stay longer."

"Don't push it too hard. You might need a recovery day tomorrow. Wait and see how it affects you."

"I suppose."

She didn't want to think about having a setback because of the work she had done today. She wanted to believe it would be a straight shot to recovery. That every day would be better than the last, getting in another hour or two longer each day until she was back to her normal schedule. But Terry was probably right. She needed to be prepared for down days if she overexerted herself.

"You'll get better," Terry assured her. "Just remember that it will take a while."

Hannah walked back from the mailbox, trying not to let her dejection show. What had happened to all his promises? Why would Otis say all the things that he had and then just disappear? She worried sometimes that something had happened to him and, other days, she was angry he had abandoned her. Was she just an inconvenience to him? A problem that he had to solve? So he had left her there while he went on with his own life, pursuing his own dreams rather than the ones they had discussed together.

Had he just been stringing her along? Telling her what he thought she wanted to hear in order to get what he wanted from the relationship, and then tossing her aside when he got tired of her?

At the house, she laid the mail on the table. Letters addressed to her mother and father. A catalog for her father. Correspondence to be dealt with. But nothing for Hannah. Why would there be? She was just a little girl. No one of any consequence.

"Why are you walking around here with a storm cloud over your head?" Mama demanded.

Hannah tried to wipe the scowl from her face. She didn't smile, as she knew her mother expected her to, but she could at least try to keep her expression neutral.

"What's the matter with you?" Mama persisted.

"I'm just not feeling very well."

"You need to be pleasant and well-mannered. Put your own concerns away and focus on others."

"Yes, ma'am," Hannah murmured, walking toward her bedroom.

"I know what your problem is."

Hannah swallowed. There was a big lump in her throat. Her mother knew? Did she know everything? How could she?

Hannah opened the door to her bedroom. "I'm going to lie down. See if that helps."

She entered her room, shut the door firmly behind her, and went over to the window to look out. She knew she wouldn't see Otis coming down their secret pathway toward the house, but she desperately wanted to. Maybe he would come back to town. Maybe the reason he had been gone was because he was getting things ready for her. Making sure that he had everything in place to take her away and make her happy. Then they would live out the dreams that they had planned together.

Hannah sighed.

They would live happily ever after. Just like in a fairy tale.

The door opened behind her, and Hannah whirled around to look at her mother, startled.

Lucy Dyson stood in the doorway, tall, thin, severe. For a minute, she just looked at Hannah and didn't say anything. Then she finally spoke.

"You may as well cheer up and get on with your life," she said in a low, reasonable tone. "Otis Jackson is never coming back."

~

Erin sat bolt upright, gasping.

"Whoa." Terry patted the bed, looking for her. "It's okay. What's wrong?"

"I can't believe it." Erin didn't know what to do. Turn on the light?

Grab her phone? She felt the need to do something, to mark this occasion. She hadn't known. She hadn't even guessed. And now…

"Can't believe what?" Terry asked, his words still mushy with sleep. "You had a dream. Lie back down."

"I can't. I can't believe this!"

"What are you talking about?"

"Hannah Dyson. I just had another dream. And the man that she was with, the man she had been pining over, dreaming of, worrying about. He was a Jackson! Otis *Jackson*!"

Terry moved around beside her, turning over to face her directly. He rubbed at his eyes. "What?"

"Romeo and Juliet," Erin exclaimed. "He was a Jackson!"

"How could you know that? It was just a dream, Erin."

"But he was a Jackson! I know that now. I don't know why I didn't figure it out before."

Terry groaned. He still didn't understand that it wasn't just a dream. It was the truth. Erin's concussed brain had been working on the problem subconsciously and had come up with the solution. It wasn't paranormal. She wasn't hearing voices like Reg. She had just gathered all the details and now knew, and her brain had provided the answer.

"It's the truth! It all makes sense."

"Erin, you couldn't know that. Go back to sleep, and we'll talk about it in the morning…"

"I can't sleep now!" Erin made her decision. She grabbed her phone from the bedside table and unplugged it from the cord.

"Where are you going?"

"I need to look it up in the book. And see what else it says in the papers."

"You can do that tomorrow."

"I'm not going to be able to go to sleep now. Not after figuring all of this out."

CHAPTER 27

$\mathcal{E}$rin turned on the lights in the living room and sat down with Clementine's genealogy binders and the box of Hannah's mementos. She pored over them feverishly, seeking confirmation of what she had dreamed.

She turned the pages of the long genealogy binder for the Jacksons, looking for Otis Jackson. He was a contemporary of Hannah's, probably a little older. She just had to find the right page…

All this stuff was probably on the internet. Clementine had worked strictly with hard copy records, but it would be much faster to do searches through one of those genealogical databases than it was to find Otis's name on the family tree.

But she would have to figure out which database to use, set up an account, and figure out how to save stuff once she found it. Or she could print it out, she supposed, and keep it in physical files like Clementine.

A name jumped off the page at her and Erin stilled, freezing with the book open to that page.

Otis Jackson

A birth date, but no death date.

Did that mean he was still alive, or just that Clementine had been unable to find a death date in the public records?

Erin calculated back. That would make him more than a hundred years old. Not still alive.

Terry shuffled out of the bedroom, squinting in the assault of light. "Erin."

"Look. I'm not just imagining it." Erin turned the book around for him to see. Terry leaned over for a look at it. He shrugged.

"Okay, so there was an Otis Jackson. Maybe even several of them. It wasn't an uncommon name a few generations ago." He shrugged. "But I don't see a connection with Hannah. No marriage or children."

"But he's here. I know they were a couple. That's who Hannah was waiting for."

Terry shook his head. "So now that you've looked him up, will you come back to bed?"

"No, I need more." Erin checked a couple of pages before and after the family tree with Otis's name on it, but didn't see anything else relevant.

Of course they hadn't put anything down in writing. The two families were at war with each other. They wouldn't acknowledge the couple's relationship on paper.

Erin put the book to the side, open to that page, and picked up Hannah's memento box. She took papers out gently, not wanting to handle them more than necessary. They were treasures. She should video them as she had the cookbook, so she could look through them as many times as she wanted to without damaging them or leaving the oils from her fingers on the pages. Hannah hadn't had archive-quality paper. She just had notepaper from the general store. Maybe some given to her by her mother, swapped with school friends, or ordered through the mail. They were yellow, some of them already brown and unreadable in places.

"You probably saw that name as you were looking through the binders earlier," he pointed out. "You just absorbed it subconsciously, and it came out in your dream."

Erin nodded. "Probably."

Terry seemed taken aback by her agreement.

Hannah's handwriting was still just as difficult for Erin to make out as it had been before. But this time, she knew what she was looking for. The round O of Otis and the swooping descender on the letter J. Some of the letters were to him, but Hannah had never addressed him by his full name, and Erin didn't have any envelopes. Erin suspected Hannah had never actually mailed them.

There were other papers, not just letters: poems, school practice, recipes, notes about the community. Erin skimmed them all, looking for just one piece of paper that would confirm her suspicions.

Terry navigated around the coffee table and sat on the couch next to Erin, looking at the papers as she shuffled through them.

"There, stop." He pointed to one of them. Erin stared down at the page. Her eyes skimmed over the words until she saw, "Can't wait to become Mrs. Otis Jackson."

Erin looked at Terry triumphantly. "See? I told you it wasn't just my imagination."

He nodded slowly. "You must have seen this before and absorbed it, but not consciously."

"The concussion makes it hard. I start reading something, and then I fall asleep, and when I wake up, I don't know where I left off."

"So you forgot you read it. Didn't know it was even here to look for. And your brain had to figure out another way to tell you."

Erin thought about the vivid, emotion-filled dreams from Hannah's perspective. She'd never had dreams like that before. And they had started before she even got the papers from Vic.

Were they just caused by the concussion? It seemed like such an ordinary explanation for the extraordinary visions.

"Can you believe it?" she breathed. "A Dyson and Jackson romance."

"Maybe not the only one," he said with a smile and a shrug. "Small towns like this… kids meet each other… but they would keep it quiet. I'm sure it's not the only illicit affair."

Erin looked down at the family tree with Otis Jackson's name on it. "I wonder what happened to him?"

"What do you mean?"

"Where he went and what he did. Did he ever come back to Hannah? They didn't get married, so I guess the romance was over. She died young. Maybe he eventually came back, but she was already dead."

"There isn't anything about him in the history?" He nodded toward the book. "No stories?"

"I don't know. I haven't read through all of it." Erin flipped through a few pages to examine the long, typed passages. That was going to take her a lot of time to read through. Easier to read than Hannah's cursive writing, but there was a lot more to go through.

"You should scan it," Terry suggested. "Then you could use the computer to search it for keywords."

"Oh, that's a good idea." Erin paused. "If I knew how to scan it."

He chuckled. "Well, you need the proper equipment. Or else to send it to a place in the city that does that kind of thing. Digitizing documents for people. I have no idea how much something like that costs."

"Probably more than I want to spend finding out if anyone knows what happened to Otis Jackson."

"Maybe it's a name Vic will know. Sometimes, there are legends in families. Or somebody knows somebody who has that knowledge. Often just oral traditions."

Erin reached for her phone, then realized it was still the middle of the night.

"Now will you come back to bed?" Terry asked.

"Well…" Erin was still hyped up about the discovery. She didn't know if she would be able to sleep, but she also didn't know what else to do. There was a lot of reading involved in pursuing the project any further, and she wasn't up for a few hours of research before it was time to go to work. "Maybe I'll just put something on TV. I don't think I can relax and go back to sleep."

"You need your sleep to heal. And especially if you're still thinking of going in to work."

"I am… But I can't *make* myself sleep when I'm in this kind of mood. I know from previous experience that it just won't work."

"So you're not going back to bed."

She shook her head. "No."

"I think it's a mistake."

"I know. But you didn't always sleep well when you had a concussion either, did you?"

She had often found him asleep on the couch with the TV playing. And it had worried her. Now, the roles were reversed. She understood his concern, but there was nothing she could do but work with her recalcitrant brain the best she could.

Terry put his hand on her knee. It was warm and gentle. "Well, if you start feeling tired, come on back in. Don't worry that you are going to wake me up. I sleep better with you there."

"Okay." Erin kissed him on the cheek, and he went back to bed.

CHAPTER 28

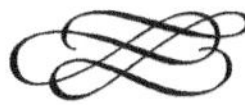

*E*rin surfed channels on the TV but couldn't find anything interesting. Late-night TV wasn't all it was cracked up to be.

She leafed through Hannah's papers, not taking a video, but snapping a picture of each item, carefully centered and focused. She was happy she could see the images on the phone clearly again. She didn't need a new phone. She had just needed to heal from her concussion.

She didn't try to read everything. She let her eyes move lazily over the curves of the words without taking anything in. Sometimes her eyes focused on a word or phrase and she stopped to read it.

The words on one letter written on soft pink stationery stood out to her, and she focused on them. It was only a portion of a letter. She didn't know if she had the first page in the stack of papers or if it had been lost in time.

He is so perfect. A miracle. Please come and visit us. We need you to come home.

It was signed by Hannah, with a little heart drawn next to her name.

CHAPTER 29

*E*rin climbed back in bed with Terry. He made a noise and turned over to face her. "Feeling better?" he asked. "Decided to try to sleep after all?"

Erin cuddled up close to his warm body. At the rate her heart was hammering, she didn't know whether she would be able to sleep or not, but she needed to be with him and to tell him her new discovery. She couldn't wait until morning.

"There was a baby."

"Mmm. What?"

"Hannah and Otis had a baby."

Terry propped himself up on his elbow. "They did? Out of wedlock?"

"Yeah."

"Oh, boy. I don't imagine that did much for the feud."

"I'm thinking maybe there wasn't a feud before that. Maybe that was the trigger."

"Why?"

"Well, there were Jackson and Dyson recipes beside each other in the recipe book. Charley said that would never happen with the feud. And in my dream, when Hannah's mom said that Otis Jackson was never coming back, she didn't say it like they were enemies. Like he wasn't allowed to see her. It just sounded like… he was irresponsible. That he wasn't someone Hannah could rely on."

Terry stroked Erin's hair. "Your dream isn't evidence of anything."

"The dreams have been right until now."

"Maybe so… but that just means that you've intuited what happened. Not that you saw what actually happened. Your dream is… an extension of your imagination. A trick of your brain."

"And it has been right."

Terry opened his mouth to object again, then shook his head. "It doesn't matter. We don't know whether the feud existed yet or not. Maybe you're right. Maybe this relationship and out-of-wedlock baby triggered the bad feelings between the families in the first place. It's certainly not outside the realm of possibility."

"It was a baby boy."

Terry breathed softly and evenly beside her and she thought he had fallen back asleep or was about to. "What was his name?" he asked.

"I don't know. I haven't found out yet. He wasn't on the family tree that Clementine filled out."

Hannah lay in her bed, completely drained. She drifted in and out of sleep a few times, but she was afraid that if she slept, she might roll over on him. She had heard of that happening and was terrified it could happen to her. Hannah had brought a new life into the world and she was responsible for him. She had to protect him. She couldn't let anything happen to him. She sat up to keep herself awake. She could still rest. It wasn't yet dawn. But she couldn't let herself sleep deeply enough that she smothered him. She had to be vigilant.

She picked him up. Wrapped in a blanket she had crocheted for her hope chest when she was just thirteen. She had not expected to use it before the wedding linens, but her life had not unfolded exactly as planned. Maybe it did for other girls. Maybe for them, things had worked out the way that their mothers had planned.

But for Hannah, there had often been unexpected events. She had become one of those girls her mother had warned her not to hang around with. Girls who disobeyed their parents and went against society's expectations and who didn't guard themselves with the boys.

She had seen Otis without a chaperone. They had spent time alone together, wading in the stream, having a picnic, lying on a blanket looking up through the dappled light in the green leaves. They had pledged themselves to each other, made plans together, talked about their future together.

And then he was gone.

The bedroom door opened unexpectedly. Hannah clutched the baby to herself, trying to think of what to say or do as her mother's silhouette was framed in the doorway. She had agonized over how to tell her parents, what to say to them, and how she was going to survive this crisis. For many long months, she had tried to find ways to work it into the conversation and, despite binding her belly to hide her condition, wanted them to notice so she didn't have to say the words "in the family way."

"Hannah, there is—"

Hannah was never to find out what her mother had come to her room before dawn to tell her. Instead, Lucy stared at the bundle clutched to Hannah's chest, took in the smell and condition of the room, and stood there as if thunderstruck.

"Mama," Hannah squeaked, still not sure what to say.

For a long time, they just stared at each other, the sun starting to peek over the horizon.

"The shame!" Mama said finally. "How could you bring this shame upon your family?"

Hannah kissed the baby's forehead and stroked his still-damp hair.

"He's beautiful," Hannah told her. "He's perfect. How could God create something ugly and shameful?"

"God didn't create this," Mama growled. "You did! You and that Jackson boy."

Hannah started to cry. Not because she was afraid of her mother or the humiliation she would face in the community, but because Otis was gone. Where was he when she needed him the most?

If he had come back, she could have eloped with him. They could have started life anew, somewhere else, and no one would know their secret. But he had gone away before she could even tell him the news of what was happening to her, how her body was changing with the seed he had planted.

She told herself that he had gone to earn money, buy a homestead, and build a house. That it was all part of the plan to make her his wife and raise a family together.

"Wipe your tears," Mama snapped. "You made your bed and now you can lie in it!"

Her eyes went to the sheets that Hannah had bundled up to be washed—or maybe burned—after the birth. The room was still a mess, but Hannah was not going to lie in sheets soaked from birthing. She *had* made her bed.

"You are shameful. Shameful! To think that you would bring this horror upon our family. Have I not taught you right from wrong since the moment you were born? Have I not trained you up in the way? And instead, you choose sin and shame."

"I'm sorry," Hannah told her in a low voice. "Sorry that we were not able to get married before this happened. I don't know where Otis went. But what happened, happened, and I am left with his child."

"He left because he was an evil man. The kind of man who leads foolish women astray and then abandons them when he has satisfied his animal desires and begot shame upon them."

"No!"

"Here is the evidence of it!" Mama gestured to the baby in Hannah's arms. "How can you argue with that? You know what you did. You know how he led you into sin. And to bear this baby in sin and shame!" She gestured at the room as if Hannah could have had it anywhere else.

Hannah gulped, trying not to sob.

Mama shook her head briskly, her mouth a thin, angry line. "I will talk to the priest, and he will know who will get rid of this problem for us. I cannot believe that my own daughter would do such a thing. I have always been an example to you. Do you think I would have done such a thing before I was married? I never let any man touch me. I was never unsupervised. I knew how to be a good and proper girl!"

Hannah wondered fleetingly whether those choices had brought Mama happiness. She did not show it. She was a woman as bitter and sour as poison. If she was happy, she let no one see it. She and Papa were never affectionate with each other in Hannah's sight and slept in separate beds in separate rooms. Despite the scriptures about being the joyful mother of children and in bearing a quiver full, Hannah was the only child of their union. Not even a boy to carry on her father's name. It must have been a bitter disappointment for both of them.

"I am not giving this baby away," she told Mama calmly. "He is all I have of Otis, and I am going to keep him."

"You cannot keep this baby. Everyone will know our shame! The very thought! You should have used pennyroyal or made sure he did not draw breath."

Hannah was horrified at the suggestion. "I will not give him away."

She had thought once that perhaps Mama would want to raise the baby as her own. If Hannah had told them early enough and Mama had bundled blankets and heavy clothing around her waist, people would have believed she was in a delicate condition. But on further thought, not only did she not want to give the baby up, but she also would not want to sentence any child to be raised as she had been.

"You must cast off this sin," Mama said firmly. "How will you ever get married if everyone knows you gave away your virtue?"

"I won't get married. Unless Otis comes back, and then I will marry him."

With her face a tight mask of fury, Mama swept out of the room and slammed the door behind her.

CHAPTER 31

*E*rin was more exhausted when she got up in the morning than she had been when she had woken in the night.

It had been a night of revelations, and she felt like she had been living two lives, both of which had drained the energy out of her.

Vic came into the kitchen when she saw Erin's light on, and raised an eyebrow at Erin's mug of coffee.

"First cup or second?"

Erin cleared her throat. "Second."

Vic would know that this was serious. Erin rarely had a second cup, and never before Vic got there. Erin usually dripped her coffee directly into her travel mug, which she nursed all throughout the morning at Auntie Clem's.

"You should stay home if you didn't get any sleep. You know we've got it covered today. Yesterday took a lot out of you."

"Actually… it's Hannah's fault."

"Hannah's?" It took a moment for Vic to figure out that Erin wasn't talking about someone in Bald Eagle Falls harassing her. "Hannah Dyson?"

Erin nodded. "Do you know what I figured out?"

"What?" Vic helped herself to a mug of coffee.

"Her lover was a Jackson."

Vic froze with the mug halfway to her mouth. Her eyes were wide. "A Jackson? Are you sure?"

"Otis Jackson."

Vic let out a low whistle. "That's crazy. I can't even imagine what would have happened to them if someone found out. Even today, with how 'civilized' the clans have become… one or both would probably be killed."

"Do you know when the feud started? How long ago? And do you know anything about Otis Jackson?"

Vic shook her head slowly. "Not a name I know. I can ask Jeremy, see if it rings any bells for him. Other than that… there's not much I can do to find out about him. I am *persona non grata* with the clan."

"And—they had a baby. Or Hannah did."

"That must have been six kinds of scandal! Hannah and her family would have been ostracized. Did they marry?"

"Otis apparently disappeared before the baby was born. And there's no death date for him on Clementine's family tree. So he must never have returned, even when he was old."

"I would disappear too," Vic agreed. "Get on a fast train out of here. What happened to Hannah?"

"I don't know yet. I have to look into it a little more. According to the family trees, she died quite young. Never had any other children. At least, not as far as I know. It isn't like the baby is listed in Clementine's family tree."

"It would have been a terrible disgrace back then. They probably sent her away to an auntie's or a home for wayward girls to have the baby. And then she would have returned home with no one the wiser."

"There wouldn't have been rumors?"

"Oh, I'm sure there were rumors. But if there was no *evidence*, she was probably safe." Vic shook her head. "As safe as any Dyson dating a Jackson could be."

"Well, she wasn't seeing him anymore at that point."

"Clans have long memories."

Erin didn't tell Vic about her dream of Hannah delivering the baby at home on the homestead after keeping her pregnancy a secret from everyone. That was just a flight of fancy, something that her brain had made up to fill in the cracks because she didn't know what had happened.

And it wasn't very likely. What girl in that delicate condition would have stayed home, where everyone would learn about her pregnancy? As Vic had said, girls like that were sent away.

She wouldn't have insisted that she would keep the baby as the Hannah of Erin's dream had. That would have been shocking. An unmarried girl did not keep her baby. Maybe the occasional case where a baby was raised by the grandparents and no one outside the family was the wiser. But even that had to be rare. It would have been easy for the townspeople to tell that rail-thin Lucy had not been pregnant before the arrival of the baby.

But there was no other child on Clementine's family tree. No supposed sibling to Hannah. No child at all in evidence.

So what had happened to the baby? And what had happened to Otis?

Terry joined them in the kitchen. His eyes were red, and his cheeks were still rough with whiskers. Erin felt bad about dragging him out of bed when he clearly still needed more sleep.

"I really could drive," she told him. "My vision is fine now and it's only a few blocks away."

"I'm not comfortable with you driving yet. You're still having a lot of symptoms. And if you drive there, you will want to drive home. You're not going to want to leave Auntie Clem's until you're dead on your feet, and you can't drive in that condition."

Erin was disgruntled, but could not argue his logic. He was probably right on the money, and it would not be a good idea for her to drive if she was too tired to continue working at Auntie Clem's. She could vow to leave the bakery before she got that tired, to only work until her energy started to flag or she started to get sleepy, but she knew herself. She was far more likely to ignore those initial feelings of fatigue and keep working until she was ready to drop. It was just in her nature.

"I could drive," Vic suggested.

Terry just looked at her and said nothing about her possibly not having a license. He had not admitted to knowing that she did not have one and that he had overlooked other cases where she had driven without one. Erin would have to talk to Victoria about getting properly licensed when they were out of Terry's hearing. It was a failing that should be rectified.

"Well, we should be heading out," Vic said, looking at the clock on the wall.

Erin filled her travel mug with coffee. She was going to come crashing down in the afternoon if she wasn't careful. But maybe she would be ready for a nap at that point anyway and it wouldn't matter.

Terry got one for himself as well, which meant he wasn't planning to go back to sleep after dropping Erin off.

"Are you sure you should stay up? I kept you up half the night."

"I need to be at the office this morning. I'd rather be able to relax with my coffee and the news before work than to be rushing because I went back to bed. You know how restless you can be when you're trying to go back to sleep after a rough night. You end up more tired than if you hadn't tried to sleep at all."

Erin had always been amazed at how easily Terry seemed to be able to get to sleep no matter how much he was changing shifts. If he said that he wouldn't get any rest going back to sleep after dropping Erin off, he was probably right.

They traipsed out to the truck together. Terry sipped his coffee.

"You told Vic about your… theory?" he asked.

Erin opened her mouth. It was more than a theory. She knew that Hannah had been in a relationship with Otis and that it had resulted in the birth of a child.

But she could only prove the first part. That Hannah had been in a relationship with Otis Jackson. Or that she had written that she was. She didn't have any proof that a baby had been produced by the union.

"Yeah, I've been telling her about it," she agreed.

"A Dyson and a Jackson, hey?" Vic contributed. "The forbidden love. A tale as old as time."

"They weren't exactly the Capulets and the Montagues," Terry said dryly.

"What's that supposed to mean?" Erin demanded.

Terry climbed up into the cab of the truck, followed by K9, who was consigned to the back seat. Vic sat beside K9 and Erin beside Terry. They all settled their coffee cups into the cup holders.

"I just mean," Terry said slowly, "that this isn't some fairy tale romance. This isn't… some dramatic story written for entertainment. We don't know all of what happened, but these were real people."

That wasn't the direction Erin had thought he was going with his argument—quite the opposite. Rather than brushing it off as a simple teen romance with no more importance or drama than two modern-day kids kissing behind the school, he meant it was more serious and real than Shakespeare. That they were talking about two real people caught in a real feud with real consequences.

"What do you think happened to them?" she asked. "I mean… Otis disappeared and Hannah died. There is no mention of the baby. It's a tragedy just much as Romeo and Juliet." Despite what Terry had said, Romeo and Juliet wasn't a fairy tale. They didn't live happily ever after. On the contrary, they hadn't even had the time together that Hannah and Otis had—a couple of brief encounters that hadn't led anywhere but to their deaths.

"There's nothing romantic in death," Terry said. "Otis probably left town when he found out there was a baby on the way. Or his family sent him away when they discovered who he was mixed up with. Hannah and the baby probably died of some childbirth infection or a virus that spread through the area. There was a short life expectancy and high child mortality rate back then."

Erin was quiet, thinking about it.

It wasn't romantic, despite all the little notes and dreams Hannah had written down. Life was ugly. Hannah hadn't had the support of her family or the option of going to social services for help in raising a child on her own. Otis hadn't come back to her rescue and carried her off like the handsome knight or woodsman of the fairy tales. Instead, she had been abandoned. In a home that did not welcome a new life into the world as the momentous occasion it was. It was not celebrated as joyful or wondrous, but as a curse and a shame brought down on the household.

Erin's heart ached for Hannah.

CHAPTER 32

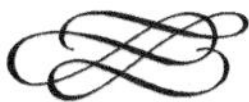

$\mathcal{E}$rin had hoped to be able to put in more hours than she had the previous day, but she ran out of steam at about the same time, despite the amount of caffeine she had consumed. Or maybe due in part to her caffeine consumption. It had burned through her energy quickly.

Terry picked her up and took her home as he had the previous day, making no comment about how he felt about her wearing herself out at Auntie Clem's rather than staying at home and getting all the rest that she needed.

Maybe he understood her need to be there at her business to ensure everything was running smoothly and to put her idle hands to work, even if it was just a couple hours.

Or maybe he just knew there was no point in trying to change her mind about it.

"Have a good rest. Take care of yourself," he told her. "Do you need anything?"

Had Willie said something to Vic or Terry about how he thought Terry wasn't taking good enough care of Erin, leaving her to fend for herself and not making sure she had something to eat without preparing it for herself?

"No, I'll be fine," Erin assured him. "I'm just going to sleep."

"You won't sleep the whole time I'm gone. Do you want me to make you a sandwich or something when you get up?"

"No, it's okay. You've got a job to do. I can manage a sandwich."

He studied her. Erin tried to sit up straight and look strong and capable, like she normally was. When she didn't have a concussion to deal with.

"Okay. Call me if you need anything. I can stop in, unless I'm out at a scene."

Erin nodded. "I will."

He kissed her at the door, then headed back to his truck.

Despite her fatigue, Erin found she could not sleep. She eventually gave up on bed and moved to the living room, sitting down again with Hannah's papers and Clementine's books.

Clementine's Jackson genealogy book was not as thick as the Dyson one. Had it been harder for her to find the information she needed? Or were there just fewer people in the family? Erin had assumed that the families were similar in size, or one of them would have won the feud and eliminated the other generations ago. There had to have been some kind of balance of power over the decades.

The doorbell rang. Erin was already in the living room and it was not as challenging to get to the door as it had been the last time, when Mary Lou had called. She had more energy, and her sleepiness after the morning shift at Auntie Clem's Bakery had fled. She was okay with having a visitor; eager, even.

She stood up carefully, ensured she was steady and had no vertigo, then went to the door. She had not armed the burglar alarm this time, so she didn't have that frozen moment of panic when her brain couldn't recall the correct passcode. She saw Joshua Cox on the doorstep and smiled at him in welcome.

"Come on in," she told him. "Did you come for Mary Lou's dish?"

Joshua was Mary Lou's younger son. He was still in high school, probably his last year in school, though he had missed a semester or two, so he might need to take another year. Joshua aspired to be an investigative reporter. In fact, he was already well on his way to establishing his career.

Josh flushed a little as he entered the house. "Well, I was hoping to talk to you, actually."

Erin went into the kitchen to retrieve the cleaned casserole dish from the counter. She handed it to him in the living room and motioned to a chair for him to sit down.

"I wouldn't mind a visit."

"Mom said you were pretty wobbly. You must be feeling a lot better than when she came."

"I am. I was still in rough shape when she came by. But now… I feel like I'm back to normal, except for my energy level. I feel like I should be able to do all the normal things, but I get tired too fast. My body does want to get back to my normal routine; I felt good when I got up this morning… but I fade pretty fast."

"I wonder if you would help with a story about the accident, and the recipe book and everything. Since you're all about recipes, I thought it would be good publicity for the bakery."

It was a good line to elicit her cooperation, anyway. He knew where Erin's interests lay.

"It's an intriguing story," she told him. "And… becoming even more interesting as I have run into some connections with one of the women who contributed to the recipe book."

"Connections? What kind of connections?"

"Vic found a little box of letters and mementos a few days ago that belonged to her daughter. It's all very… mysterious."

Erin knew where Joshua's interests lay, too. She could see his curiosity pique. Going from trying to craft an interesting narrative from a fairly minor traffic accident to something that could be a *real* story.

"A mystery? What kind of mystery could be connected to a recipe book?"

"Well, the recipe book is only adjacent to the mystery. Charley noticed when she looked at it that there were recipes from a Dyson and a Jackson on adjacent pages. She joked about how that wouldn't be counte-nanced now, with the feud. How much do you know about how and when the feud between the two clans started?"

"Well," Joshua's mouth twisted as he thought about it. "Not very much, I'll admit. It isn't like the Coxes were involved or we took clan history in school. I know a little bit from people I've heard talking over the years."

"When was it, do you know that? It seems like it couldn't have started yet when the recipe book came out, or wasn't very bad yet, if they could put both recipes together without anybody thinking anything of it."

"I don't know. I think it was like... wartime or sometime around then."

"World War II?"

"I guess. I didn't really think about it."

"And you don't know what triggered it?"

"I don't know if it was just one thing. I think that things built up... until it got bad and they wouldn't have anything to do with each other."

Erin nodded, a little disappointed that Joshua didn't have any insight into it.

"Why? What did you find?" he asked.

"Well, I found a couple. A Dyson and a Jackson who had a secret romance. Things went badly for them. There was a baby. He disappeared. She—"

"The baby disappeared?"

"No, the man. He disappeared while the woman was pregnant and never saw the baby. And then she died within a couple of years."

"Murdered?"

"No! At least—not as far as I know. I haven't found anything that would suggest she was murdered. Why would she be murdered?"

"I don't know." A shrug. "I just thought if all of this happened and then she died... then maybe one had something to do with the other."

"I don't know what she died from yet. Probably just fever or something like that. Medical care back then, out in the sticks... there wasn't much you could do with someone. Give them fluids and rest, and hope they pull through. They didn't have access to modern medicine."

"So what is the mystery?"

"Just... what exactly happened between them. Where the man went. What happened to the baby."

"The guy just disappeared?"

Erin nodded. "He left and never came back. Hannah hoped he was getting things ready for them, getting a job or a house and then coming back for her, but he never returned. She had the baby without him. I have her death date, but not his."

There were certain parallels to Erin's own parents and what happened to them. How puzzled she had been by the death dates on Clementine's family tree the first time she had seen it, the records she'd had to request and research she'd had to do to get the true story. And in the end, the truth hadn't come from any of the vital statistics records, but from a secret keeper. Someone who had known all along and kept anyone else from finding out. Until Erin had come digging decades later into their secrets. On one hand, she felt sorry for what had happened, the pain she had caused, and the loss of Bertie Braceling, whom she had considered a friend. On the other hand, she had finally uncovered the truth, and that discovery had led to her finding Charley, her half-sister.

Who knew where the information about Hannah Dyson and Otis Jackson might lead?

Probably nowhere. It didn't seem like there were a lot of leads. She would keep looking through Hannah's papers and Clementine's books and the files where she had kept the primary materials from which she had gathered the information for the family trees. But if Otis had never come back to Bald Eagle Falls, then what were the chances that anyone there had recorded what happened to him? If there was a death certificate somewhere, it might be in a different state. In a different name. They didn't have any interconnected databases to track where someone had come from back then. Social Security Numbers were just coming into use and were not yet being used to track births and deaths.

"Well," Joshua tried not to make it obvious he was disappointed with her lack of information or an exciting story. "I'll make a note of that. I don't know if it will branch out to anything of interest to the paper."

He made a show of taking out his notepad to write the information down so that Erin would see he was following up on her suggestion and be more likely to answer his questions.

"I don't know that there's really much interesting to do with the scooter accident," Erin told him. "I mean, the museum burglary is the most exciting part of the story. And the fact that they haven't caught the culprit yet."

"You're underestimating how interested people are in what happened to you. Getting knocked down and concussed by an escaping criminal is pretty exciting."

Erin shrugged. From her perspective, it had been irritating, and who knew how long it would continue to affect her? It didn't benefit her in any way, other than a few more visitors coming to Auntie Clem's to check up on her and a few casseroles in the freezer.

"The story I'm really interested in isn't the burglary. It's what happened before that. Before the recipe book was even sent to the library."

CHAPTER 33

There had been many arguments. Or maybe "arguments" was too generous of a term for what had taken place. It wasn't like anyone listened to what Hannah had to say. Nothing she said made any difference to either of her parents.

Her father hadn't even come to the door of the bedroom, let alone come in to lay eyes on the baby. Hannah supposed he was in denial. If he didn't see the baby, it didn't exist. If Hannah came out of her room and sought him out, he grumpily told her to go back to her room. She was sick and needed to sleep. She begged him to talk to Mama, but he just turned away, ignoring her as if she were invisible.

Mama had laid down the law. Hannah was not going to keep the baby. She was not going to leave the house. She was not going to talk to anyone outside the house. *Otis Jackson*—Mama's nose wrinkled in disgust when she said his name—was a wicked man who led silly girls astray, and he would not be coming back to take Hannah away. If Hannah thought that men like him ever came back to repair the damage they had done, she had better think again.

There was nowhere Hannah could go and nothing she could do, and yet she made plans anyway. When she was recovered, no longer confined to bed, she would find a way to leave. She would bundle the tiny infant up like the Christ child in Mama's nativity picture, and she would walk out of there. She would wait until night so no one would see her go, and she would walk right out of there. By morning, when they started looking for her, she would be miles away. She would hide in a cave or a hollow tree while they looked for her. She would only travel at night, getting farther and farther away until she was sure she and the baby were safe.

Until then, she thought it advisable to keep him as quiet as possible. That wasn't too hard; he seemed to be much quieter than other infants she had dealt with, crying only when he was hungry or wet, and quieting as soon as she picked him up to take care of the discomfort. A well-stocked hope chest ensured she had enough diapers for the first few days; then she would have to get up and take them down to the creek to wash them herself since no one else in the house would help her. That would be a good way to gauge her physical condition and see how far she could walk when she was ready to leave.

But the best-laid plans went oft awry, as Mama was fond of saying.

Hannah slept as much as possible, hoping to speed her healing and get strong enough to walk the miles she would have to. Her body was sore and exhausted. It hurt to get up and down, to shuffle out of her room. She used the hated chamber pot because walking to the outhouse was still too difficult. When the bleeding slowed, she would be able to walk farther.

Mama brought Hannah a hot toddy to ease her pain and help her sleep, and the unexpected service brought tears to Hannah's eyes. The gruel that Mama had brought until then was thin and room temperature and was supplied without a smile or kind word, the empty bowl taken away the same way. As much as Hannah vowed that she wouldn't, she felt the shame her mother had pronounced. She felt dirty and guilty and outcast.

The hot toddy made her sleep for a long time. She didn't wake up to feed the baby in the night. When she awoke in the morning to the sound of a departing vehicle, it was already full light outside. Hannah opened her eyes, listened for a moment to see if she had been wakened by the baby fussing, and then closed her eyes again, lying on her side and dozing in the sunlight.

As time passed, worry welled to the surface. Why hadn't the baby awakened for his morning feed? Had she slept through his nighttime feed, or had she fed him and forgotten, muzzy from the hot toddy?

Things could happen to a baby. Many did not survive infancy. He hadn't seemed unwell, but he had never cried as loudly as a normal child. Did it signify some kind of illness? A weakness in his heart or lungs? Had a fever come upon him in the night?

Hannah pushed herself to a sitting position, ignoring the pain in her pelvis and back, the shakiness in her legs. She reached for the spot where she had laid the baby, in the cradle she had used for her dolls since she had outgrown it herself.

It was empty.

Hannah's heart pounded. She pushed the blankets aside as if he might be hidden underneath. She pushed the cradle aside in case he had fallen behind it. She searched bedclothes tangled around her in case she had laid him beside her in the night instead of putting him into the cradle.

He was not there.

"Mama!" Hannah called, panicking. Had her mother picked up the baby to feed him while Hannah slept? Was she walking him, trying to keep him quiet so her daughter could sleep? "Mama, he's gone! Where is he?"

She dragged herself out of bed and pushed through the pain, staggering to the door.

"Mama! Mama, do you have the baby?"

She held the wall for support as she walked to the kitchen, where her mother stood at the counter kneading bread dough.

"Mama! Where is he? Where is my baby?"

Mama turned to look at her, eyes as cold as ice. Of course, she had not taken the baby to feed him or walk him to comfort him. Hannah had seen no softening in her behavior since he was born, other than to give her the hot toddy the night before.

The hot toddy that had kept her asleep late into the morning.

"What did you do with him? Where is he?" she shrieked, unable to control the tenor of her voice. "Where is my baby?"

Mama blinked at her slowly. "You have no baby."

"I do! Where is he? What have you done with him?"

"There is no baby here. There never was. You are a good girl. You would never bring such shame upon us."

"What did you do?"

"I didn't do anything. I am making bread, just like any other morning."

But it was late for her to be making bread. She liked to get it into the oven before the heat of the day and it was already getting stifling hot.

"Who was here? Who did you give him to?"

"There is no baby here," Mama repeated firmly. "As I told you. I would not let you bring shame to this family."

Hannah fell to her knees, weeping, pulling on her hair. She wailed wordlessly. She held her mother's feet, pleading for her to return the baby. The baby was her only solace since Otis had failed to return. If she didn't have Otis, at least she had a part of him. The thing that the two of them had created out of their love for each other.

And now, he was gone, too.

CHAPTER 34

*E*rin. Erin, wake up."

Erin clutched at him, tried to pull him closer, to disappear into his embrace, the pain in her heart all too real and all-consuming.

"No, no, no!"

"Erin, it's okay. Wake up. It's just a dream." He kissed her forehead, smoothed her hair, and tried to bring her gently out of the dream. "Sweetheart," he whispered. "Oh, honey, it's okay. Shh."

He wiped at her tears with his thumbs and pressed her against his chest, his arms encircling her firmly. "Shh. It's just a dream. It's okay. Finish waking up. You'll see that everything is okay."

Erin continued to weep, but less violently now. Her own screams still rang in her ears. Had she really done that? Shrieked out in her dream from the pain and grief Hannah felt? It had been real. It had all been too real.

Terry withdrew Erin slightly from his chest and kissed her again, gently, searching her face.

"Are you okay now? Are you awake?"

Erin sniffled. She pulled back from him. He let her go. Erin turned over, feeling for the lamp, and eventually found it. She turned on the blinding light and squinted her eyes tightly shut until she could recover from the brightness and look around the room.

Her room, not Hannah's. She had expected to see the empty cradle and other things that had been in the dream. She had truly thought that she was there, that it was real.

"Are you okay?" Terry asked again, holding his arms out for her to return. Erin obliged, pressing herself to him and clasping him tightly to convince herself of his solidity, his realness. *This* was real. Not *that*.

"I'm okay," she whispered.

"Thank goodness." He breathed heavily into her hair. "I thought that something had happened. A stroke or a seizure. You've *never* had a dream like that before."

"No."

Erin didn't know how she would have managed it if that were how she felt after a normal nightmare. She would be afraid to ever go to sleep again.

They both lay there, holding each other, waiting for their heart rates to slow and their muscles to relax and to get back to that sleepy, comfortable place where they could talk and eventually drift off to sleep again in each other's arms. Terry was warm and solid. More real than the dream.

"The baby is gone," Erin told Terry brokenly.

"The baby? You had a dream, Erin. It's okay. It wasn't real."

She didn't know if she could handle the thought of it not being real. Of course it had been real. All those feelings had to be real.

"The baby. Hannah's baby. They took it away. They stole it while she slept!"

He rubbed her back slowly, soothingly.

"Just a dream, honey."

"How could anyone do that? How could they just steal it away from her?"

"They didn't. It's just something that your brain invented. It didn't really happen."

"It did. Just like the other parts that I dreamed. I don't know how it is coming into my head, but it is real. I know her. The way that she lived, the things she thought and feelings she felt. I know it is real."

He didn't say anything for a long time, just holding her, rocking back and forth slightly. She knew that he didn't believe her, didn't understand how it could be happening to her any more than she did, and she appreciated his holding his tongue. What good would it do to argue about where the dream had come from? She didn't understand it. She didn't believe in holy visions or psychic phenomena. But she couldn't deny that some things were inexplicable, and this was one of them.

"I'm worried, Erin." Terry spoke gently. "I think we should take you to the hospital. Make sure that everything is okay. What if this is being caused by a bleed in your brain? Or something else we need to be aware of? A kind of a seizure?"

"They said I could have vivid dreams."

That couldn't even begin to describe how Erin felt about the Hannah visions. "Vivid dreams" was completely inadequate to describe the rich experiences, lived through Hannah's eyes, felt by her tender heart.

"But this? I was afraid I wasn't going to be able to wake you up. You were so... far away."

"I know. But I'm awake now and it's fine. Nothing hurts. There are no aftereffects. Just a memory."

"I still think we should go to the emergency room."

"To sit in a cold, hard chair for the rest of the night and have them send us home in the morning? No. No, thank you."

"I'd feel better if we could talk to a medical professional about it."

"Then call him." Erin didn't move to get her phone. "They said if we had questions or concerns, we could call. They can beep him if he's not at the hospital."

"I don't know about waking him up in the middle of the night..." Terry said doubtfully.

"If you think it is an emergency, then wake him up. If it isn't an emergency... wait until morning."

If he was willing to drive her all the way to the hospital and wait in the chairs for hours on end, then he must consider it an emergency.

"Okay," Terry said finally. "Do you have the number to call?"

Erin sat up slowly. She was surprised that her pelvis and back did not hurt. She had expected to feel the pains of Hannah's body, but she did not. She found the phone, unlocked it, and found the number of the neurologist for Terry. She handed it to him. "You call. You're the one who thinks something is wrong."

He didn't like it, but he didn't argue. He tapped the name and waited for it to be answered. The whole exercise involved tapping through automated messages and then speaking to an answering service, then some kind of medical professional on duty, and then finally, his call was routed to the neurologist.

Terry apologized profusely. So profusely that Erin wondered why he had called at all. If he didn't think it was necessary to get an answer right away, to wake the neurologist up from a sound sleep, then why had he called?

Terry then explained the problem. Erin's vivid dreams, her emotion, her screams, the difficulty in waking her from the dream. On speaker-phone, the doctor talked to both of them, asking Erin endless questions and asking Terry to look at her eyes to perform simple neurological tests. He finally made a decision.

"It doesn't sound like a seizure or an emergency," he told Terry. "She seems intact neurologically. I don't hear anything that indicates a stroke or seizure—just a dream. If you would like to come in tomorrow, I will schedule a CT scan and EEG, and we'll have a little look to see if anything is wrong. I don't think there's any need to rush to the emergency room."

Erin nodded her agreement. Terry stroked a lock of hair back behind her ear and tenderly brushed the corners of her eyes where the tears had collected. "Okay," he agreed. "Will you go in tomorrow? Just to make sure? I don't want to lose you, Erin. I need to know that everything is okay and you don't have a bleed or a clot or anything else that could do more damage. Will you go in?"

"Okay." Erin couldn't deny him. Hannah's feelings toward the baby had transferred to Erin's tender feelings toward Terry and she couldn't tell him no. If he felt that strongly about it, she would take the day off and get her head examined. Again.

"Thank you."

"Try to get some more sleep," the neurologist advised. "You're going to need it."

CHAPTER 35

$\mathcal{M}$orning brought with it the certain knowledge that Erin would have to make another trip to the hospital. She hated having to go back to the city. Back to the hospital. Sitting and waiting in one room or another. The indignity of having her head examined. Not just the simple neurological tests proving that she could count three fingers or follow an object with her eyes, but a CT scan and an EEG. She would have to wait for both, of course, in different places, and then she would have to wait for the neurologist to look at the results and decide whether it was safe to send Erin home again. Which of course it was, because she hadn't had a seizure or a stroke, just a dream.

She had hoped that Terry might change his mind and back off upon seeing how well she was in the morning. She had no trouble waking up. In fact, she got up earlier than Terry. She didn't have any cognitive problems. She made coffee and toast and fed the animals, even bending down and straightening up without any vertigo or throbbing pain. She could carry on a conversation and talk logically about the dream of the night before and what it might mean.

She knew that one of the reasons he was still worried, aside from the fact that he'd had such a hard time waking her up the night before, was her insistence that the dream about Hannah was true. That this was *actually* what had happened to Hannah, not just her brain trying to fill in the gaps left by the letters and notes. She couldn't know, and she knew she couldn't know, but she was nevertheless sure that her experience of the night before was what Hannah had experienced. That somehow, inexplicably, that knowledge and experience had transferred into Erin's brain. She didn't believe it was possible, yet she knew it was.

And that was what concerned him. If Erin had been a person who believed in miracles, telepathy, reincarnation, or some other phenomena, he wouldn't have been alarmed at her position. But the fact that she didn't believe in any of those things and yet was convinced that the dream was true was something that concerned him deeply.

And it should have bothered Erin too, but it didn't.

"Do you want to take that to go?" Terry suggested, nodding to the coffee when he made it out to the kitchen, bleary-eyed and unshaven, smelling musky and sweaty. He did not like getting up as early as Erin and, under normal circumstances, usually slept in several hours after she got up.

"You still need to get ready," Erin pointed out, "I'll be finished by the time you're ready to go. And I don't know yet what time the doctor set up the tests for. I'm still waiting for an email. I don't want to go over there early in the day if they're scheduled for later in the day."

"They might be able to get you in earlier."

"The hospital can't ever fit anyone in earlier," Erin pointed out. "Everything is always later than you think."

Terry sighed and bent over to scratch K9's ears as he rubbed his nose against Terry's leg for attention.

"You probably don't even need to get up yet," Erin pointed out. "Why don't you get a few more hours of sleep?"

"I want to be ready when you get the email. And if you don't have it by the time I'm out of the shower, you should call him to push things forward."

Erin shrugged. "I'm sure I'll find out as the departments open and start their days. He probably can't schedule them in the middle of the night unless they are emergencies."

"I still think it is urgent."

Terry eventually retreated to the bathroom to shower, shave, and get himself prepared for the day.

Erin sat down once more with Hannah's notes and continued taking pictures of them all, starting where she had left off previously. She kept her eyes open for anything that might refer to the baby. Anything that Hannah had said openly would probably have been destroyed. Even though the memento box had been hidden in the wreckage of the shack in the woods, she couldn't assume that Hannah had been able to keep them from her parents while she had been living with them. At some point, she had snuck off and hidden them but, before that, she'd had them in her room. The building that Vic had found them in was too small to be the one Hannah described in her letters and notes and that Erin had seen in her dreams. Hannah had slept in her own room and her parents in theirs. There had been a separate kitchen and dining room.

She eventually received confirmation emails for her CT scan and EEG, as ordered by her neurologist. Several hours apart, of course. Why would they schedule them closer together? They didn't care if Erin had to sit around the hospital all day.

She was surprised, as she sat in an uncomfortable chair waiting to be called to her CT scan, to see Beaver and Jeremy. Her mind started going through all kinds of scenarios to explain why they were there before they approached and greeted Erin warmly. Jeremy gave Erin a quick hug. He had long, shaggy blond hair and a stockier build than Vic, but they had a number of similarities in their facial structure. A strong family resemblance.

"Vic said that you were stuck here all day," Jeremy told her, releasing her. "And since we were in the city, I thought we would come by and visit for a while. Break up the monotony."

"That's great," Erin told him appreciatively. "It's really boring just sitting around here waiting for them to get to me. What am I going to do? Go shopping for a couple of hours and come back again?"

"You could," Beaver pointed out, chewing.

"I don't have that kind of energy. The concussion is still taking too much out of me. I can only work at Auntie Clem's for a couple of hours at a time."

"Ah, makes sense."

"So here I sit!" Erin motioned to nearby chairs, inviting the couple to join her.

The conversation turned quickly to Hannah, the notes and other mementos Vic had discovered, and how Erin's delving into them had triggered the vivid dreams of Hannah's life.

Erin didn't mention that she had started having the dreams before she had begun reading the notes. That would just muddy the waters. It was better not to complicate things too much.

As Erin told Beaver and Jeremy about Hannah's baby, she could see Terry's lips tighten and his expression go blank. He didn't jump in and tell Beaver and Jeremy that the baby was all in Erin's imagination. He just sat by quietly, listening to Erin's exposition about the Dyson-Jackson union and the baby born to Hannah after Otis disappeared.

"That poor girl," Jeremy said, shaking his head. "It would be hard for a modern-day teen to deal with. But the way things were handled back then? All the religious prohibitions about extramarital relationships… ending up as a single teen mom. She wouldn't have had any kind of support from the government. A pariah in the community. Seen as a bad girl, a fallen woman."

Erin nodded. "Her parents were the only ones who knew. And it was a surprise to them; she didn't tell them she was pregnant before the baby was born. I'm not sure exactly where they lived, but the homestead wasn't right in town. So she was more isolated from the community."

Beaver nodded, her eyes bright and interested, while the rest of her body appeared languid and relaxed. Erin knew that Beaver's apparent laziness was all show. Part of her cover.

"I don't understand why marriage was such a big thing for religious types," Erin said. "And still is, to some of them. Do people really think that God or some power in the universe cares whether people have a marriage certificate or not? Look at all the people who live together now. Are they all going to be punished because they choose to live with each other without seeing a priest or judge to get it 'approved' somehow? How are they supposed to know whether they are compatible and will be able to get along and live together longer term without a trial run? Maybe they're completely incompatible. What then?"

"Then they get divorced," Beaver acknowledged.

"Which is also a sin, right?" Erin looked at Jeremy, who she suspected was the more religious, or at least the more knowledgeable about religious matters. She had seen the way his parents had reacted to Vic's transition.

Jeremy nodded his agreement. "Yeah. Most religions will allow divorce, but still consider it a sin on some level."

"So you're just supposed to commit for life to someone you don't really know very well, assuming that you will be compatible. Because that's what your religion says to do."

"Everyone has a different perspective," Jeremy said uncomfortably. "That's sort of a simplistic analysis."

Erin shrugged. "I'm not looking for a debate. I'm just saying… it seems like the purpose of marriage is to *force* a woman to stay with a man. And traditionally, a man could fool around on the side and that was fine, but for a woman to do the same was wicked."

Terry shook his head at Erin. A warning to let it go. She knew better than to discuss religion—or to criticize people's religious beliefs.

"Blame it on my head injury," she sighed. "I don't usually speak my mind on these things."

"There's nothing wrong with having an opinion," Jeremy said. "It's just that… there's no right answer. We can't change the way that women have been treated historically, or even the way that they're treated today or the way that religious or non-religious people see their behavior… All we can do is watch our own behavior. And I think…" he looked at the others, "I think that all of us here do a pretty good job of treating people fairly, no matter what gender."

Beaver chewed. Terry nodded. Erin rubbed the center of her forehead, where a headache was gathering, and nodded her agreement slightly.

"Yeah," she agreed. "Even in tricky cases, like changing how you think of Vic. I guess I'm still all wrapped up in that dream last night. The unfairness of it. I knew that single girls were forced to give their babies up for adoption. But to have him stolen from her like that? I guess it just made it even more… reprehensible. It just makes me sick to think of it."

"There were some pretty infamous baby brokers," Beaver said after consideration. "One of the most well-known operated here in Tennessee, Georgia Tann. It's estimated that she stole over five thousand babies and then sold them to adoptive parents. And many died in her children's home or were abused in horrible ways."

Erin had heard the name before. As a foster child herself, she had always been attuned to news or rumors about children taken from their parents and fostered or adopted. She had imagined that her parents were still out there somewhere, looking for her, hoping she would come back. Even though she had been told by the social worker that her parents had been killed instantly in a car accident, many people involved in selling the babies of unwed mothers lied to all parties involved. The mothers who were told that their babies had died. The children who were told that their parents had died. And the adoptive parents who were told that the birth mother had died or had been eager to give her baby up to a family that could raise him properly.

But she hadn't heard the numbers associated with Georgia Tann. Five thousand babies? How could she have accomplished that?

"How? How long was she doing this?" she demanded.

Beaver shifted the wad of gum in her mouth. "Twenty years or more. She was kicked out of a couple of places before she started operating the Tennessee Children's Home. Who knows how many children she had dealt with in that time? By the time she started working there, the operation was pretty sophisticated. She had a lot of people working for her. Social workers, policemen, judges, they were all onboard, either thinking that they were saving children from a desperate situation or greedy for the payoffs."

"How can they ever find out what happened to them? How can the adopted children find out where they really came from? Or the parents get in touch with them again?"

"At this point... they are too old for reunions. There were some in the eighties. But by now, those babies are seventy, eighty, ninety years old. Their birth parents aren't around anymore. And most of the children's home records were destroyed. And the rest was falsified. False backstories, changed ages. The court documents were complete lies. Children were stolen off the street, out of their front yards. It wasn't just children of unwed mothers or families that couldn't afford to keep them."

"Maybe DNA analysis," Terry suggested. "It's becoming common enough now. A lot of people will discover that their grandparents did not come from where they thought they did."

Erin's head spun.

How was she going to find Hannah's baby?

She hadn't realized until then that she had decided to track down

Hannah's baby. She would find out for Hannah what had happened. Even though Hannah had died years ago and Erin didn't believe in an afterlife or that she would ever know that Erin had tracked down her baby, she was determined to do it. To right the wrong, even though Hannah Dyson would never know it. She had been victimized. By her own parents. Maybe by Otis, too. Things needed to be set right.

"Are you okay, Miss Erin?" Beaver asked.

Terry put his hand on Erin's back and rubbed it soothingly, but she didn't want to be touched. She pulled away from him.

"It's not right," she told Beaver. "It's not right that they took her baby away and that she died without knowing what had happened to him or whether he had ended up with nice people."

"No," Beaver agreed. "It's not."

"But we can't do anything about it," Terry pointed out. "That happened decades ago. There's no way for us to right the wrongs. Hannah is beyond being hurt now."

Erin believed it and didn't believe it. She knew Hannah was dead and gone long ago. But Hannah had also been in her head just the night before, her anguish fresh and real to Erin. The Hannah that had been a part of Erin was not beyond being hurt, and Erin had to find justice for her.

CHAPTER 36

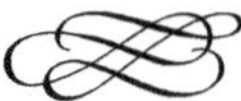

They didn't find any bleeds or clots. The technician who looked at Erin's EEG raised his brows as he looked at her results before calling the neurologist. Erin was not satisfied with the neurologist's report at the end of the day.

"Everything falls within normal parameters," he told her. "There is no indication of brain damage, which is what we were looking for."

"What does that mean?" Erin demanded. "No seizures? Nothing?"

"There is… a lot of electrical activity. Since we don't have a copy of an EEG from before your accident, we don't have anything to compare it to. It may be that this is your 'normal.' There is no indication that there is anything *wrong* with your brain."

Erin looked at Terry for help. Sometimes, she had found, professionals responded differently to men. They didn't even realize their biases, but they automatically had a better opinion of men's intelligence level and professionalism, and dealt with women by brushing them off and giving them the equivalent of, "There, there, dear. Don't worry your pretty head."

"What does 'a lot of electrical activity' mean?" Terry asked. "Is that unusual? What does it usually signify?"

"The brain has areas with more activity and less activity… certain areas 'light up' only under specific stimuli. Others only go dark when there is a learning disability or brain injury. The amount of activity in Miss Price's brain right now…" He made the briefest of glances in her direction. "May explain why she is having such vivid dreams. A lot of areas are lit up right now that… typically aren't. In my experience, that's just her brain trying to establish new connections. To heal anything that has been disrupted. We don't know as much about what is going on in the brain as we do in, let's say, the heart. We can see the blood vessels and the electrical activity, but we can only guess at what else is going on."

What had been the point in spending all day at the hospital to have them run those tests?

"I'm left-handed," Erin said. "I've heard that people who are left-handed have more learning disabilities and that their brains are organized differently."

"Yes, that's true. We don't know exactly why. There is a lot of research being done in that area."

"So these areas of activity, they could be why Erin is having the dreams?" Terry asked. "The accident and concussion have disrupted things somehow, and that's why she's having such disturbing dreams?"

"That is one possible side effect of a concussion," the doctor affirmed.

Terry gave Erin a look that she interpreted as meaning he had proven that her dreams were just her diseased brain acting up and not anything significant. They didn't mean that what she was dreaming was true.

But none of this was news. Erin had known from the start that her concussion was causing the dreams. She had told him so.

But that didn't mean that they *weren't* the truth. It didn't mean that they weren't reflections of something she had read or absorbed that was real. A truth that she just hadn't been able to come to consciously.

Maybe tonight, after having talked to Beaver about Georgia Tann, Erin's brain would be able to put more together, and she would understand more on waking up.

The night passed uneventfully. Erin did not dream of Hannah or her baby. She was exhausted from the day at the hospital, fell into bed when she got home, and slept through dinner and all night.

"How are you doing?" Terry asked when Erin started moving around in the morning. "Did you have a good sleep?"

"Yeah. Good," Erin agreed. She was a little irritated that she hadn't dreamt any more details about Hannah but, on the other hand, she was glad that she had gotten a good night's sleep and not been awakened by a nightmare. She knew how Hannah must have been feeling after the baby was stolen from her.

She had felt Hannah's devastation when she had woken up and the baby was gone.

At least Hannah didn't believe that the baby was dead. She knew that her mother had taken the baby and had arranged it so that someone would come while Hannah was asleep and take the baby away. So the baby was alive, and not dead, and maybe that meant that she would be able to see him again someday.

Erin had heard horror stories about cases where unwanted babies had been disposed of in other ways. While what Georgia Tann and the other baby brokers did was despicable, at least they were not committing infanticide.

"Are you going into Auntie Clem's today?"

She knew that Terry would prefer that the answer were no, and she thought about it for a bit, testing out how her body and brain felt and whether she would be able to get anything productive done at the bakery. She had been helping with opening the last couple of days, but that probably wasn't the best use of her time. The others could open, but Erin was falling behind on her marketing and accounting, things that only she could do. She should go in and make sure that she got her advertisements ready for the next paper. And check the store email for any invoices, orders, or correspondence that needed to be handled.

And she really didn't feel like doing any of that. It was one thing to force herself to take care of such necessities when she was feeling like herself. Doing it while she was concussed was ten times harder.

She groaned. "I need to do computer work."

"Can you do that from here?"

"Well… not really. I can check my email from here. But my advertisements for the paper…"

"Can you just call them and tell them what to put in?"

Erin always worked on her graphics and holiday promotions and got everything *just right* before sending them to the paper to put into her advertising space.

But they had previous ads and graphics she had used other weeks. Erin liked to refresh them and change them a little so they weren't identical from one week to another, but what difference did it really make? If the ad for apple pies were the same graphic this week as it was two months ago, did that matter? Would anyone care?

"I guess… yeah, I could have them reuse old graphics. But I have accounting to do…"

"Bills that must be paid today? Or entering information into your system?"

"Entering information. Most of my vendors give me thirty days to pay so, even if I don't send money this week, I can catch them next week. But…"

"You don't normally put them off. It isn't procrastinating if you have a brain injury and can't manage it this week. You can do it next week. Or if you still aren't feeling up to it, you can give Charley instructions so she can do it. It can't be that hard to make a payment."

"No… it isn't."

"Then why don't you do that? Check your email, call the newspaper, and then rest, get back some of your energy. I'm sorry for insisting on the hospital yesterday, but I was really worried about you. If there had been a clot or a bleed… that's not something you can mess around with. They have to catch it immediately to avoid further damage."

"I know. I'm not upset that you made me go. Irritated with the doctor, but it isn't your fault that I'm tired. You were just looking after me."

They lay together in bed for a while longer, just talking about little things, thoughts that crossed their minds. They didn't normally have a lazy time in bed like that except on the occasional Sunday morning, if Terry didn't have a morning shift and Erin had someone else taking care of the ladies tea.

"This is nice," Erin admitted. "I don't like lazing around, but…"

"I could get used to this," Terry murmured, running his fingertip along Erin's white, smooth upper arm. She shivered and laughed, covering it up with the sheet so he couldn't get it again.

"I should get up and—"

"No. I made you go to the hospital yesterday. I'm making it up to you by making you stay in bed late today. I will make you some tea and toast. I'll let Vic know that you will work remotely today and to let you know if she needs anything. And you will not move out of that spot."

It *was* a deliciously warm and comfy spot.

"What if I have to go to the bathroom?"

"You may go to the bathroom. But you may not go *past* the bathroom. You will return immediately to this spot." He pointed, giving her a stern face.

"Am I under house arrest?" Erin teased.

"Yes, exactly. So you'll stay there and behave yourself."

Erin chuckled and closed her eyes. She listened to Terry get up and use the bathroom himself, then go to the kitchen to take care of the tea and toast. Orange Blossom ran into the kitchen meowing for breakfast, and Terry took care of the animals too. Erin wondered how Bernt was doing. Would he catch his own breakfast or go back to Adele's and beg to be let in and fed commercial cat food?

Since she wasn't allowed to go to the living room, Erin picked up her phone from the side table and unplugged the charging cable. She had finished taking pictures of all the letters, notes, and photographs in Hannah's mementos box, so she had both the recipe book and the mementos at her fingertips. Erin flicked through the photos, looking for anything indicating Hannah knew where her baby had been sent. She might have managed to get information from one of her parents with the promise that she would not try to go after the baby to reclaim him. Or she might have overheard them talking to each other, or someone might have let something slip without realizing it. The baby brokers might be able to operate with impunity, but that didn't mean that everyone else was blind to what was going on. There would be other people who knew pieces of the puzzle.

The cursive writing was still difficult to read. It wasn't like flipping through web pages where everything was clear and the documents were split up with headings and bolded type. It took all her concentration to work every single word out and, even then, she wasn't sure she got them all right.

Terry brought in a tray with Erin's tea and toast, some local honey, and a small jar of Jam Lady strawberry preserves.

"This is wonderful. I could get used to being served like this every day," she teased.

"Well, as I'm not here every morning, and you get up earlier than I do most days, that could be difficult. But if you wanted to give up being the baker and just stay home all the time and follow the same schedule as I do, I will see what I can do…"

"No way!" Erin laughed. "I could never do that. I love Auntie Clem's too much. I love being the baker and providing nourishing and delicious food for everyone, especially those who don't usually have much choice of what to eat."

"You love what you do," Terry acknowledged. He had known there was no danger in her taking him up on his offer.

"Who is the oldest person in Bald Eagle Falls?" Erin asked as she spread jam on her first piece of toast. "Who would remember Hannah's parents and other people in that generation?"

Terry cleared his throat and considered. "We have a few people who are ninety-five or older, but not many of them. And I'm not sure if any of them can remember that far back. That's asking a lot."

"I know."

"Mrs. Ford would probably be your best bet. She seems to be very sharp still. I don't know if she can remember that far back or if she even lived in Bald Eagle Falls as a child. But maybe she would be able to tell you something about them."

He sat on the edge of the bed, watching Erin eat. "But you have to be careful not to harass her. I don't want to get complaints that you are stirring things up and causing problems about this. Whatever happened took place decades ago. I understand you want to know what happened, but you might never find out more than you can divine from that box of papers."

Erin nodded. She nibbled the toast, enjoying the sweet, tart jam. The Jam Lady knew how to make the most luscious preserves.

"I know. And I know you don't think that the dreams mean anything and that there even was a baby."

Terry looked away as if ashamed to admit it. Erin knew he wanted to believe. But that was different from actually believing.

"They're dreams," Erin said flatly. "And normally, you forget about dreams within a few minutes and go on with your life. But you've never had dreams like this before, that have seemed so real, and so meaningful and stuck with you like this. If you had, you would understand why I have to do everything I can to find out the truth. Even though… I can't help Hannah or even tell her what I figure out."

"Just be careful," Terry repeated. "I don't want complaints that you've upset someone's granny."

"I'll try not to upset anyone's granny."

In a couple of hours, Terry had to shower and dress and head to work. Erin waited until he was gone to get up. Then, she showered and sat back down on the bed to take care of her emails. While she couldn't deal with everything on the spot like she would be able to at the office, Erin was able to respond to the important messages, clean up a few things that she had missed since the accident, and assure concerned vendors and customers that she was on the mend and would be back soon.

Then she had a nap.

Another half hour was spent making phone calls to deal with the newspaper, making sure that Charley and Vic knew what the upcoming specials for the week were, and catching up with a couple of other phone contacts.

Then it was lunchtime and another nap.

CHAPTER 37

The attendant escorted Erin to Mrs. Ford's tiny room. It was better than a hospital room, Erin supposed, but not by much. There were some personal effects on the dresser and on the wall, and the bed was made with blankets and coverlets that were lovingly handmade. Maybe by Mrs. Ford herself, and maybe by family members or friends who wanted her to be comfortable and to have something of home and family in the bare little room.

It was the same kind of bed one would find in a hospital, with rails on the side and a head that raised and lowered with an electric control.

Erin had done enough elder care to know that sooner or later, at some point, the elderly needed to go somewhere they could be taken care of. They reached a point where they couldn't do it on their own anymore. She was glad Mrs. Ford had people to look after her, though sad she could no longer live at home.

She was a wizened old lady, skin and bones and a little gristle. Her curly gray hair was thin but carefully maintained. She wore a red caftan that hung off her loosely. A little powder and lipstick made her company-ready.

"Mrs. Ford, this is Erin Price," the attendant told the woman in a loud voice intended for the nearly deaf. "She is here to visit you."

Mrs. Ford nodded. She reached for Erin's hand. Erin gave it to her, not sure if she was expecting a handshake or something else. The old woman squeezed her hand and then held it warmly between her two thin, wrinkled ones.

"It's so nice to see you, dear," she told Erin.

The attendant nodded and left Erin there to visit.

Erin sat down in the chair next to the bed. "It's nice to meet you, Mrs. Ford," she said loudly, hoping the woman would understand they did not already know each other, in case she thought Erin was a grandchild or someone else she should know. It was hard for some elderly people to keep track of all the family members they should know. They would pretend while trying to figure out who it was, sometimes never able to figure out who it was.

"You don't need to yell," Mrs. Ford told her. "I'm not that deaf. The hearing aid boosts the tones I can't hear so well anymore, but I'm perfectly able to understand a normal speaking tone."

"Oh, I'm sorry."

Mrs. Ford waved her hand toward the door the attendant had exited through. "They think everyone here is deaf. They yell at everyone."

Erin laughed. "Well, I'm sorry about that. I'll try not to yell."

"They do their best. I've been lucky to have good people here, I suppose. You hear horror stories about some of these places."

Erin knew some of those stories. Had dealt with some of the men and women who had originally been incarcerated in places where they had been abused and neglected. Dealing with the fallout of traumatized elders who behaved erratically, not knowing what to expect from their caregivers.

"Yes. Sometimes they just want to warehouse old people… or enjoy hurting them." Erin shook her head gently. "I'm glad you lucked out."

Mrs. Ford patted her hand. "So… to what do I owe the pleasure of a visit from such a pretty young woman?"

Erin's cheeks warmed. She considered herself plain rather than pretty. Not ugly or unpleasant to look at, but she was no beauty. Maybe Mrs. Ford had cataracts.

"Well… I wanted to ask some questions about people who lived in Bald Eagle Falls a long time ago. And I was told you were probably the best bet."

"Not many of us oldsters around anymore."

"No, and not many who still have their faculties."

"I've been lucky. Clean living."

Erin nodded politely. Mrs. Ford cackled. "That's a joke, dear. Smoked for years. Had a glass or three of wine every day. Red meat whenever we could afford it. No exercise routine, just everyday work. Not 'clean' by today's standards, but back then… people were more concerned about moral behavior than all those things. We didn't understand health and nutrition the same as we do now."

"Even now… it seems like it changes every day. A glass of wine every evening is good. No, it's bad. I just try… not to eat so much of my own baking that I gain weight."

"Oh, you are a baker!"

Erin produced a small box and opened it for Mrs. Ford. Six small chocolate chip cookies. "I didn't know if you were on any special diet, but the nurse said I could give them to you."

"Oh," Mrs. Ford peered at the cookies, considering. "Well… I do love something sweet now and again. Here they give me Jell-O." She rolled her eyes. "Artificial colors, flavors, and sweeteners. A delightful chemical concoction. But cookies…" She selected one from the box and held her other hand under it to catch crumbs while she took a bite. "Ah. Perfect. This is what dessert should taste like. Thank you."

"You're welcome. I'm glad it was something you could have. I run Auntie Clem's Bakery. It is a gluten-free and specialty bakery."

"Oh, you're the baker. Well, I'm glad you make regular stuff too. So…" Her eyes were quick and intelligent. "What do you want to know from Adelaide Ford?"

Erin smiled. "I know it was a long time ago. But do you remember Hannah Dyson? I think she would have been around your age."

"Hannah. Now there is someone I haven't thought about in years. Yes, we went to school together. I think she was a year older than me, maybe. We didn't do things together, but I remember admiring her, like younger girls do."

"She went to school here in town?"

"Most of the time. When her parents would let her go."

CHAPTER 38

$\mathcal{E}$rin raised her brows, surprised at this. Why wouldn't her parents let her go to school?

"It wasn't like it is now, when you are expected to send your children to school every day from kindergarten to grade twelve, and maybe even to college," Mrs. Ford explained. "Kids were expected to help on the farm, so they wouldn't be at school during harvest. And if it got too cold in the winter up the mountain, they wouldn't bother to come down."

Erin nodded. And, she supposed most girls probably stopped going to school around age sixteen, when they were considered adults and expected to be working on other pursuits.

"So school wasn't such a big deal... especially for girls. And some families just educated their children at home."

"But Hannah's sent her to school."

"She came to school most of the time. But her parents didn't consider it important. Not like now. She could read and write. Girls didn't need much more than that. So she came when she could, and the rest of the time... just stayed out on the homestead."

"Did you know the young man she was seeing? Otis Jackson?"

"Otis." A smile flitted across Mrs. Ford's face. "Oh, I remember him. He was very handsome. A lot of girls liked him. But Hannah was the one he was interested in. For a while, anyway."

"Then what happened? He got bored with her?"

"Oh, I don't think so. He didn't start seeing someone else. He just… I stopped seeing him around town anymore. I thought he had probably gone north to find work. Or he had enlisted. A lot of the boys went off to war."

Erin hadn't thought much about the war, even though Hannah had mentioned it a couple of times in her letters. Another thing that Hannah and Otis had been dealing with that she didn't have to worry about. The world had been a very different place.

"You never heard for sure where he had gone? No one ever mentioned or speculated?"

She frowned, the lines around her mouth deepening. "I wouldn't like to say. I was never one to carry tales."

"I don't think you could be accused of carrying tales now, so many decades after it happened. You're not saying anything bad about him. Just what you thought might have happened. Like he might have gone to war. Or he might have…?" She waited for Mrs. Ford to fill it in. He might have been interested in another girl. Gone to Canada to avoid the draft. Become a bank robber.

"I don't know," Mrs. Ford said, shaking her head stubbornly. She wasn't going to give it up easily. Erin might have to take the conversation in another direction and then try to circle back to it.

"And how about Hannah? Did you see her much after Otis left?"

"No. She was busy on the farm, I guess. Or maybe her parents sent her off to work or stay with an elderly aunt. People did things like that back then."

"She had an aunt?"

"Everybody had an aunt. Plenty of them. Families were much bigger then."

"Hannah was an only child."

"Well, I don't think her parents got along, to be perfectly honest."

Erin nodded in agreement. She hadn't seen any affection between the two of them. They had stood together on the issue of Hannah not keeping the baby, but that was the only time she had seen any sign of solidarity between them. Otherwise, they kept to themselves, doing the work that needed to be done to keep the farm running, barely even talking to each other.

"But they had siblings that she might have gone to? She didn't just stay on the farm?"

Mrs. Ford thought about that for a while. "I suppose. I never heard anything one way or the other. They were… standoffish folk. The Dysons always were. Kept themselves to themselves. Whether they kept Hannah home or shipped her off to someone else… well, I never heard."

"Did they have a reason to ship her off to someone else?" Erin pressed.

"They might have thought she was getting too involved with the Jackson boy. Girls married at her age, but if they didn't approve of him or didn't think he was ready to make a match, they might have sent her away to get her away from him."

"But he went away too. You didn't think they might have any other reason to send her off?"

"Well, she was that age… sometimes girls her age went off to finishing school or to apprentice at a store or help a relative."

"Or for other reasons."

Mrs. Ford nodded, but she didn't say the words out loud.

"Did you ever think that she might be in trouble?"

"I never heard that she was."

"But with her spending time with Otis, they might have gotten too familiar."

"I don't know," Mrs. Ford insisted. "Really, you can't force me to say anything bad about Hannah or Otis. They were two children. Young adults. It was wartime. Sometimes, we felt like… the world might end every day, so why be so careful? Why not show our feelings and do the things we were dreaming of? Not just in relationships, but in everything. Jobs opened up that a woman would never have been able to do before. People needed help to keep their farms, stores, or households running while the men were away. Women wore pants. Played baseball. But places like Bald Eagle Falls were still very conservative. They didn't welcome the changes that were happening all over America."

"What happened to girls who had babies after their boyfriends went away to war?"

Mrs. Ford looked away. She fidgeted with the blankets around her, pinching and straightening them and avoiding Erin's gaze.

"Being common did not make it acceptable," she said finally. "Girls today think it is romantic, a baby born and Daddy never returns from war. But it was tragic. Doubly tragic for those girls who did not manage to get married before sending off their young men. Because they couldn't keep their babies. They couldn't pretend that it was a legitimate birth and that they were married. People knew better, especially in a small place like this. They didn't believe that you were married or widowed just because you said so. You needed a ring, a dress, witnesses, pictures, a wedding certificate. There were women who made it their business to root out the... offenders."

Erin had wondered earlier why Hannah hadn't simply tried to pass herself off as having eloped with Otis. But if there were people who were that intent on disproving such stories, that explained why she hadn't tried. As well as the fact that she would have had to get past her parents. She hadn't had her own means of transportation and lived out in the sticks.

"What would happen to girls who had... surprise babies?" Erin asked, trying to be delicate in her language so that Mrs. Ford wouldn't be offended and refuse to talk to her.

"They couldn't keep them," Mrs. Ford said flatly, shaking her head. "It was not allowed. An unwed girl could not raise a baby. There were a lot of adoptions. It was very popular. Women everywhere were adopting. There were pictures of babies and children in the paper, like pet adoptions now. Famous people adopted 'unwanted' babies. Joan Crawford. Other actresses and actors. It became very *vogue* to rescue these unfortunate children."

"I've heard of... people stealing babies to sell them for adoption."

"I don't know if that ever happened," the old woman's voice was cautious. "Girls who found themselves in the family way knew they could not raise their children. It was just the way things were back then."

"You didn't know any girls who said that... they'd been forced to give their babies up."

"That's different from stealing them," Mrs. Ford pointed out.

"Not very. If she wouldn't agree, they took the baby."

Wrinkled hands smoothed the sheets. "I suppose they probably did."

CHAPTER 39

*D*id you know of anyone in Bald Eagle Falls who adopted babies?"

"Oh yes, there were a few that I knew about. Sometimes, you didn't know because they went away, or you hadn't seen them for a while. Or some mothers wore a belly under their dress. A fake belly," she tried to explain to Erin, "so that they looked pregnant."

"But you knew some in Bald Eagle Falls?"

Mrs. Ford nodded. "A few," she agreed again.

Erin didn't dare ask for names yet. Mrs. Ford was still not sure of her. Still being careful not to say too much, to give away the secrets of Hannah, Otis, and the other people of Bald Eagle Falls. Maybe as they got to know each other, Mrs. Ford would entrust those names to her.

If she were very careful how she approached it.

"So… Hannah was a Dyson and Otis was a Jackson." She shifted the conversation to the feud between the Dyson and Jackson families.

Mrs. Ford looked at her with sharp eyes and quick, birdlike head tilting. "Yes, that's right."

"Was that *before* the feud between the two families?"

"What do you know about that?"

"Not as much as I would like to. I know there is a feud, and the two families… are involved in criminal enterprises. The clans operate around here like the mafia."

Mrs. Ford rubbed her nose. "Could I have another of those cookies? They are very good."

"Of course."

Erin held the box out to Mrs. Ford again, giving her time to think about it and decide what she wanted to say.

"They are very good," Mrs. Ford repeated. "Did you get the recipe from your recipe book?"

"*My* recipe book?"

"The Women's League book. You got the recipe book, didn't you? That's what I heard. The baker got the recipe book."

"Yes…" Erin wondered what the recipe book had to do with the feud. But it wasn't the first time they had both come up in the same conversation. "I have copies of the recipes from the book because it fell into my hands after it was stolen from the museum. How did you know about that?"

Mrs. Ford giggled. "Well, it was *my* recipe book before that."

"You're the one who loaned it to the museum?"

"Yes. I thought it would be nice for people to see the old recipes. Our family recipes and the ones we relied on during the war when we were trying to support the boys overseas. It is a piece of history many people don't know about and will never see."

"Well… to answer your question, these cookies are not from a recipe in the book. But I am going to make some of those recipes. Or adapt them so I can make them and sell them in Auntie Clem's Bakery."

"Back then… recipes were very important. Part of a family's legacy. Passed down through the generations, nourishing the children and grand-children, a way to make money in boarding houses and restaurants. They were traded like currency or collector's cards. People were very possessive."

"But then they published them in a book. They obviously couldn't keep them a secret anymore."

"A lot of those recipes are missing ingredients." Mrs. Ford gave a sly smile. "They won't work if you don't know what that ingredient is, or how much to add."

"Then why put them in the book at all?"

"To tease people. Your pot roast stew is famous across the county, so you agree to put it into the recipe book. But no one who uses the recipe in the book can replicate your success, so your real recipe is safe, and people still keep coming back for it."

"Free advertising?"

She nodded, smiling.

"There were Dyson and Jackson recipes in the book. My sister Charley noticed that they were even on facing pages. Right beside each other."

"Lucy Dyson and Eleanor Jackson. They were once great friends."

"What happened?"

The woman stared out her window, most of which was covered by blinds, with just some glass and blue sky showing around the edges.

"There were jealousies. Accusations. Petty things but, every time something happened… it escalated. They weren't friends anymore. But their children…" Mrs. Ford trailed off.

"Hannah Dyson and Otis Jackson."

"Yes."

"They stayed friends?" Erin suggested.

"Oh, yes. And I suppose Mrs. Dyson and Jackson were okay with it to begin with. They had problems with each other, but I don't think they said anything to their kids or husbands about having to stay away from the other family. It was just the two women, to begin with."

Erin thought about the scenario. Two women fighting with each other. Then, the children's romance blossomed, with Hannah becoming pregnant and Otis disappearing. Each mother had probably blamed the other's child for their problems. She didn't know whether Otis had told his parents where he was going and kept in touch with them, but if Mrs. Ford hadn't even heard rumors of where he had gone, then she doubted if the Jacksons knew. Things like that tended to spread through a small town, even if they were supposed to be kept secret.

"And the feud? It started after that?"

"Sometime around then," the old woman agreed. She licked her lips and reached for a cup on the side table with a straw. Erin handed it to her and waited while she drank. "I suppose it was probably the children who triggered the bad feelings," she admitted. "Mrs. Dyson and Jackson were having an argument, upset with each other over a multiplicity of little wrongs. And then the children… Otis leaving like he did, there must have been bad feelings. Mothers try to protect their children from hurt, especially an only child like Hannah. They are spoiled and cosseted."

If what Erin had dreamed had been spoiling and cosseting, she sure didn't want to see abuse. She had hardly seen anything to indicate that Mrs. Dyson even liked Hannah. She had been more concerned with chores and the family's reputation. How things looked had obviously been very important to her. It was no wonder Hannah had been too afraid to tell her what was going on in her body, despite the danger of an unattended birth.

"And you think that was what started the feud?" she prodded.

"Suddenly, it is not just two homemakers angry at each other for little slights and wrongs. Now there is a problem with the children as well. Problems that might have been perceived as major issues. Jilted lovers, especially if promises had been exchanged... one family bringing shame on another. Each placing blame on the other for their child's part in the relationship and the breakup... We didn't have TVs, you know. We watched each other. There was no *Father Knows Best* or *Leave It to Beaver*. People learned parenting from their own parents, and most parents were strict. Not like today, when it's okay if kids make decisions the parents don't like."

"But you don't know if Hannah ever had a baby."

"I never heard that she did." Mrs. Ford shook her head solemnly. "Never a peep."

"And the families that might have adopted children back then? When you were a teenager? Can you tell me who they might have been?"

"It was such a long time ago, dear. And I don't want to accuse anyone of anything."

"There isn't anything wrong with adopting a baby. And if it was the adoption of a baby who was taken away from her mother by trickery or force... that's not the fault of the adoptive parents. It's the fault of whoever brokered it."

Mrs. Ford shook her head. "You make it sound like they were selling babies. No one was selling babies."

Erin kept her mouth shut about people like Georgia Tann. There were many people in the adoption community who only wanted to help. Who had tender hearts and wanted to ensure all the children were cared for.

"I'm sure it was done for the good of the children," she said, forcing the words out. She tried not to let strain enter her voice. "Those poor, helpless children in need of homes. The people who took them in were very kind. Very special."

"Yes. Children were not regarded the same way back then as they are now. They were expected to earn their keep. It was a difficult time to fill extra mouths. Those willing to open their homes to unwanted children were very special."

Erin nodded her understanding. "They surely were," she agreed. Despite Mrs. Ford's assertion that things had been different back then, Erin had heard such things said about children during her time in foster care as well. Children needed to help and be productive. Contribute to the home. Children were expensive, and the people who took them in were saints. Oh yes, she'd heard it all before.

"Well… I remember John and Hope Andrews. Irma Montgomery, I can't remember her husband's first name. Richard Mans and… Chastity, I think her name was." Mrs. Ford pressed her lips together. "There are probably others that I can't remember. I am sure there were. And other babies that I never knew were adopted. Though, by the time I was that age, I think I was pretty aware of when babies were… surprises."

Erin pulled out her phone and tapped the names in. It wasn't much to go on, but it was more than she'd had before talking to Mrs. Ford. And she was a nice old lady, pleasant to talk to. Not like some of the crankier clients she'd had.

"I really appreciate that, Mrs. Ford. Thank you for helping me out."

"Are you doing your genealogy? I remember your Aunt Clementine was into genealogy."

"Yes, she was," Erin agreed. "I've been looking through all her files. She did a lot of work! You wouldn't believe all the binders and files she filled with her research."

"She would be happy that you are taking an interest in your family history. Family was important to Clementine."

CHAPTER 40

$\mathcal{M}$rs. Ford was frail, but Erin was exhausted after the interview. Mrs. Ford still looked fresh, and Erin felt her bed calling.

She got home safely and headed back to bed. Soon she would be strong enough to get through a day of work at Auntie Clem's. But that day was not yet.

At least she knew there was no bleed deep in her brain, draining her strength away. She only needed time, and then she would be fine.

Vic stopped in once Bella arrived at Auntie Clem's for her afternoon shift. Erin was ready to get up again. She sat on the couch with a blanket around her and a cup of tea that Vic had prepared.

"I know that you're still not feeling well," Vic observed, watching Erin. "There is no way you would be wrapping up in a blanket if you were yourself."

Erin cuddled up inside it. She had been thinking that it was an unusually cool spell for a Bald Eagle Falls summer. But maybe it was just because her body was putting so much energy into healing. "I guess," she admitted. "I'm getting better. A lot better than I was. But I'm not quite recovered yet."

"These things can take time," Vic consoled. "Months, sometimes."

Erin glared at her. "Do you think that is going to make me feel better, somehow?"

"Oh…" Vic got red. "I didn't mean it to sound discouraging. I meant that… you shouldn't worry that you're not fully recovered yet, because sometimes it can take months. It doesn't mean that you're stuck like this forever. But… I guess it came out wrong."

"What I want to hear is that it will definitely be better this time next week. I'll be able to go back to Auntie Clem's and do all the things. That's what I want to hear."

"Sorry."

Vic did *not* tell her that it would only be a week. Erin didn't think it should take more than a couple of weeks to recover from a concussion. That seemed like plenty of time. She sighed and sipped her tea.

"So, any news? Who was by today? Did you see the Fosters?"

Peter Foster was one of Erin's favorite customers, along with his little sisters. And now another little brother, too. Alan, teething and toddling, was a going concern. Mrs. Foster had her hands full with her little brood.

"I think Mrs. Foster was by yesterday," Vic said. "But not all the kids. Just her and Allan."

"How are they doing? Everything okay?"

"As far as I can tell. Mr. Foster is still working at the Book Nook, so I think they're more comfortable."

"It's hard for moms who want to stay home now."

"Yeah. Everyone says you need two incomes. At least."

"Not that things weren't hard back in the depression and wartime." Erin thought about what she had learned about the Dyson and Jackson families and what little she knew about the hardships of working a farm during that time. "A lot of people didn't have very much at all."

She started to tell Vic of all she had learned from Mrs. Ford.

"She sounds like quite a character," Vic observed with a smile. "I don't know her. Or if I met her, I don't remember her."

"She's the owner of the recipe book!"

"What made her donate it for their exhibition?"

"Just… wanting people to know about what their lives were like back then—not wanting everything to be forgotten. She was glad I was going to try making some of the baking dishes for Auntie Clem's. Although I don't think she understands about it being gluten-free and me adapting the recipes so that I can sell them."

"Well, it's hard to understand for someone whose staple food was wheat."

"She knew Hannah Dyson. They went to school together. And she remembers Otis Jackson, the boy who was courting her."

"So he really was a Jackson?"

"He was."

"Wow. A Dyson-Jackson pairing. Who would ever have thought? I'll bet the families are glad that relationship did not survive."

"If it had gone well, maybe there would never have been a feud. It sounds like it might have been the straw that broke the camel's back."

"Because their families didn't want them to have anything to do with each other?"

"Because he left her. Disappeared without explanation. Mrs. Ford thinks maybe he enlisted and went overseas. I'll have to see if I can find any record of his serving in the army. Maybe the reason he never came back was because he was killed in Europe."

"It's possible, I guess. But wouldn't his family have been told about that?"

"If he gave the army the right information about his family and next of kin. But maybe he didn't. Maybe they didn't know who to inform. He might have even used someone else's birth certificate and enlisted under a completely different name."

"How are you going to find him if that's what he did?"

"Well, if he did that, then I won't be able to find anything. But I have to look. I need to know why he left. How he could leave Hannah without a word, and what happened to keep him from returning?"

"You don't think that he just abandoned her? Got what he wanted from her and then moved on to something else?"

Erin sighed and sipped her tea. "She loved him. I don't know how he could do that if she really loved him."

CHAPTER 41

*E*rin had not been doing her tai chi practice since her accident. Not only because her body was so bruised and sore from the collision with the scooter, but because of the unsteadiness and fatigue that had come with the concussion. She had come a long way in her tai chi since she had first started it, and had good control and balance now, but that was shot when her brain swelled up. She'd felt as unsteady as a new toddler those first few days.

But she was starting to feel better, and her body ached for the familiar forms. She had come to rely on the focus and centering that the tai chi discipline brought her. She knew that others in town considered her tai chi a heathen religious practice, something that was just as bad as, if not worse than, her atheism. But Erin just liked it for how it felt and helped her stay centered and focused.

A car approached as she worked through her routine, barefoot in the grass in the backyard. Erin valued her privacy, especially while she was trying to meditate and sort out the various threads of Hannah's life and that of her parents and others who had been involved in Bald Eagle Falls around the time Hannah's baby was born.

She recognized the car. It was Jeremy. There to visit his sister, no doubt. She appreciated how he supported Vic. None of the rest of the family did, so his relationship with her was particularly valued. Vic had been disowned when she had come out as transgender, and her encounters with her other brothers and parents since then had been hostile. Erin didn't like to think of the abuse that Vic had likely faced growing up in that household. And maybe Jeremy, too. Chances were that Vic was not the only one who had been abused, though her feminine leanings had undoubtedly made her a larger target.

Jeremy climbed from the car. Erin expected him to wave and go directly up the stairs to the loft over the garage to visit with Vic.

Instead, he lifted a hand in greeting and stopped in the backyard, watching Erin, obviously waiting for a moment in her workout that would be more convenient for him to speak. Erin shifted her focus to him.

"What's up?"

"I thought we should talk."

Erin gave a slight nod. "Okay. What about?"

"I couldn't say much when we were at the hospital. Too much of a danger of people overhearing. And I really didn't want to say anything in front of Terry. Or… Ro."

"Beaver?" Erin was surprised he didn't want to speak in front of her. She could understand that there might be things he might not want to reveal to Terry, one of the town cops, but Beaver was his partner, and her views on law enforcement seemed to be… more fluid than Terry's.

"This needs to just be between you and me," Jeremy told Erin.

She experienced both anticipation and dread at the same time. What information did Jeremy have that she wanted? And why couldn't he talk about it in front of law enforcement or even his sister, keeping it strictly between him and Erin?

"Should I be sitting down for this?" she teased.

Jeremy's serious expression remained firmly in place. "It might be a good idea," he admitted.

Erin had only been joking. She was feeling much more solid on her feet and wasn't likely to faint dead away at whatever Jeremy had to offer her.

"What is it?"

He looked around. "Maybe we should go inside where we won't be overheard."

There was no one else around, but there was always the danger that

Adele would be in the woods nearby. Or someone else. Or maybe he was worried about Vic coming down from her apartment to talk to them.

"Okay, just give me a minute." Erin switched to her wind-down sequence. She hadn't had as much time as usual for her practice, but maybe that was a good thing. Start small and work her way back up again.

She finished the forms and stood for a moment to center herself, then turned toward the house. "Come on in, then, we'll defrost some cookies."

"All right!" Jeremy approved. "I love coming to your house."

Erin laughed. In the kitchen, she pulled a few cookies out of the freezer and put them on a plate before popping them into the microwave. She and Jeremy sat at the kitchen table with cookies and milk. Jeremy approved of the cookies and they nibbled at them in silence for a few minutes before Jeremy managed to get his mind around what he wanted to discuss with Erin.

"You know, don't you, that spreading gossip around town about this alleged Dyson-Jackson baby is dangerous?"

Erin raised her brows, surprised. "This happened decades ago. Why would that be dangerous? It isn't like I'm talking about someone who is still around."

"Neither clan wants there to be a Dyson-Jackson baby."

Erin turned this over in her mind. She shook her head. "I don't understand why it matters."

"You know how much animosity there is between the clans. Or maybe you don't *know*, but you've seen some of it. You know that they would like more than anything to wipe each other off the face of the earth?"

"You don't think… that's exaggerating things just a little?"

Jeremy shook his head, saying nothing.

"I know that they have a rivalry, that they don't want anyone in their family to have anything to do with the others, but they've each got their own businesses, their own territories, and they've lived with each other operating in Tennessee for decades. If they wanted to kill each other off, then wouldn't they have done it by now?"

"There have been many casualties. You might think they are just small-time crooks with an ongoing rivalry, but you're wrong. They have always been sworn enemies. You've been lucky in your dealings with them so far. You think they have some kind of respect and tolerance for each other and won't do anything to you when you get between them except warn you off. But that's not the way it works. There is no 'honor among thieves.' They haven't agreed to leave each other alone and let the others operate in their own territories. They will kill anyone they see as a threat to their way of life or who could upset the balance that currently exists."

Erin shook her head. "What does that have to do with me? What am I doing that poses a threat to them?"

"A Dyson-Jackson baby will upset the balance. Digging up the old relationship between Hannah Dyson and Otis Jackson will rekindle old resentments. You don't understand how deeply those resentments run."

"So you *do* know something about Hannah and Otis."

CHAPTER 42

Jeremy shook his head. "I know the stories and the rumors around them. I know the old family legends. And the Dysons will have their own spin on what happened. This runs deep, Erin. This runs right to the heart of the feud."

"So it *was* what started everything."

"It didn't start everything, but it brought it all to a head. It caused the breach. Took the situation from a few people with resentments to a full-blown war."

"Because Otis left Hannah?"

"Did he?" Jeremy challenged.

Erin was taken aback. "Well… yes. He left and never came back. Hannah was left to have the baby by herself. She kept waiting for him to return, but he didn't. Mrs. Ford said she thought he might have enlisted. Or maybe he just left town and worked for an uncle or something."

"He left? Do you have evidence that he enlisted? That he got on a train and went somewhere else?"

"No," Erin admitted. Her cheeks got warm. "I'm doing what I can to figure it out, but it happened so long ago. I should be able to search military records to find out if he was a soldier, as long as he signed up under his own name. But if he just went somewhere else to work, or went to

"

look for a house and didn't come back… Maybe he met someone else, I don't know."

"What makes you think he *chose* to leave?"

"Well, I don't know. I guess he might have been coerced into it. If his mother didn't want him to be involved with Lucy Dyson's daughter. Maybe they told him he had to leave. Or paid him off."

"Or maybe someone stopped him permanently," Jeremy said flatly.

Erin swallowed. "Stopped him permanently?"

"It never occurred to you?" Jeremy leaned forward and stared hard into Erin's eyes.

Erin was used to the laughing, good-humored Jeremy. To a laid-back, fun-loving young man who didn't take anything too seriously.

"You think someone killed him?" Erin asked breathlessly. "Really?"

"You think that he had no honor and would just leave behind a woman who was in trouble? That he would offer to make an honest woman out of her, make plans for their life together, and then just leave?"

"It *does* happen."

"Not a Jackson," he disagreed. His voice turned hoarse whisper. "Not Otis Jackson."

Erin took a long sip of her cold milk and tried to swallow the lump in her throat. "He was killed?"

"That boy did not run away. He didn't misuse Hannah and then toss her aside. Only one thing could have kept him from going back to her."

"How could you know that?"

"You know what *you* know. You've seen the evidence of what Hannah suffered. Hard evidence and… other knowledge. And I know about Otis."

"Things you've heard through your family? His papers? A journal?"

"It doesn't matter how I know. But if you keep it up, if you keep making noise and telling people what you know and what you have, someone will see to it that evidence is destroyed. And maybe you with it. You're putting yourself in the path of a speeding car, Erin."

She already knew what it felt like to be in the path of a speeding scooter. She would not survive an encounter with a speeding car. Or a speeding bullet.

She shook her head wordlessly, her mouth as dry as a desert. She couldn't raise her voice to ask the further questions she had. She was finally talking to someone who knew the answers, and she couldn't ask.

"There has already been trouble over the recipe book," Jeremy pointed out. "A couple of recipes and a few cryptic words back and forth between them, and for that, the families want it destroyed. How much more do you think they would want to annihilate the evidence that you have from Hannah? Why do you think it was hidden in the first place?"

"What do you mean they want the recipe book destroyed?"

He raised his brows at her, waiting for her to think about it. It wasn't hard to understand what he meant, just to believe that anyone would care about a decades-old community cookbook that no one had even cracked open in years.

Maybe that was the point. No one was looking at it until the suggestion that it was going to be displayed in the museum's exhibit. And then it had been stolen. Someone had thought it important enough to burglarize the museum and steal the recipe book. They had thought it might be because it was valuable. Terry had said that it might be worth thousands of dollars. As a treasure hunter, Beaver had wanted to see it and wondered whether there were other copies still in the community.

Unless Beaver didn't really want to see it as a treasure seeker, but as a government agent involved in an organized crime investigation. Surely she could have gotten her eyes on the original, if that were the case, and wouldn't have bothered to come to Erin to look at the video she had taken of it?

Unless she was being cagey and didn't want to tip anyone off that she was looking at it.

Was it possible that the book had been stolen, not because of its intrinsic value, but because of the words that were inside? Because the families' recipes were side by side, preserved for all to see that they had once been friends? Because of something cryptic that had been written in one of the introductory remarks for the recipes? Erin had read through some of them but not nearly all of them. Could she have missed information about the relationships between the Dysons and the Jacksons? Was there information there about Hannah or Otis or what they had done? A coded message between the two of them?

All Erin had been interested in were the recipes.

"I'm not trying to cause any trouble here," she told Jeremy. "I just want to find out what happened for Hannah. I want to know what happened to her baby and if things turned out okay for him. I want…

justice for her. I know that's not possible because it happened so long ago, and she isn't going to care either way because she's dead and gone. It's just that…"

Jeremy's eyes were steady. He waited for her to finish her thought. Eventually, he prompted her. "It's just what? You need to let this go and be safe. I don't want you to stir anything else up. I don't want you starting an all-out war between the clans. Things are quieter right now than they have been in years. You want to see drive-bys? Mass murders?"

"No, of course not." She gulped and broke out in a sweat. "Do you think—"

"I don't know what would happen," he admitted, holding his hands up. "There's no way to know just what your questions could trigger. Maybe the powers-that-be will just laugh it off and wait to see if there is any blowback before starting anything. But do you really want to take that chance? For no reason? We don't know what the cost could be."

Erin rubbed her head. She was drowning, and his words washed over her, but they were distant and muffled. She was overwhelmed. All she wanted was to discover what happened to Hannah's baby. No one could care about that. It had happened decades ago. The baby himself was probably gone. Hannah and Otis were. It was just genealogy, not gang activity. Family origins.

"You're still not feeling very well, are you?" Jeremy asked, his voice sympathetic.

"No. I'm doing better. But all of this is just hurting my head. It doesn't make any sense. Why would anyone care about recipes in a book? Why would anyone care what happened to one kidnapped infant decades ago? Or what had happened to Otis?"

She already knew what happened to Hannah. Hannah had died before her eighteenth birthday.

"These people are all dead," she told Jeremy. "I'm just writing dates on a family tree."

"You promise you won't talk to anyone else about it?"

She thought about Mrs. Ford. She definitely couldn't tell him about that conversation. Mrs. Ford was probably the only one in town who could remember Hannah personally, who had recollections of what had happened between her and her young man.

"I… won't talk to anyone else about it."

"If people hear you have been asking questions… I don't want to predict what could happen. You understand that? You got knocked over by a scooter. You gave the police the recipe book that burglar dropped. That's *all*. You don't say you took pictures of it. You don't talk about Hannah's papers. We don't want any of this spreading any further than it already has and, if anyone asks you about it, you tell them that it's all been exaggerated. You put them off. Make them believe you don't know anything about any of the Dysons or Jacksons, especially Hannah and Otis."

Erin took another drink of her milk, swallowing hard. "Okay."

Jeremy looked at her searchingly, trying to discern the truth of her words. Erin put her hands over her eyes. She didn't want to meet his eyes. She didn't want to get emotional over the whole thing. The last thing she wanted to do was cry. She could brush it off as the pain of her headache, but then Terry would want to take her to the hospital again.

Jeremy looked away. He glanced around the kitchen as if there might be mobsters hiding in the corners, listening in on their conversation.

"I'm sorry you got mixed up in this. But if you live in this part of the country… you will run up against issues with clans at some point. It's inevitable."

"I have before."

He nodded. "Yeah," he said softly.

She wondered how much he knew about what had happened with Charley's rescue and other encounters she'd had with the Dysons. He knew about her meetings with his parents, though he hadn't been there the first time she had met them, when Vic's father had whipped her—his own child—with his cane. It was the first time she had seen how vicious the man could be. How Vic and her brothers had been raised and what could happen if one of them stepped out of line. Erin had feared for her life and Vic's that day.

She knew Jeremy was right. She did not want to be mixed up with the clans.

CHAPTER 43

Terry pulled a double shift, making up for the shift he had missed while he had been at the hospital with Erin. She felt bad that he had to pull a double shift because of her. But it really was his own fault; he was the one who had insisted she had to go back to the hospital, even though she had told him that she was fine. And she had been right.

Of course, if he had been right and the tests had discovered a bleed, clot, or something else going on, she would have been singing a different tune. She would be grateful for his insistence.

That was the way life worked.

"I thought you would be in bed," Terry said, bending down to kiss her sitting on the couch. "Aren't you tired?"

"I've had about ten naps today. So I'm awake now, but I slept before you got home." Erin yawned. "And I'll sleep again. Just not at a predictable time."

"It will even out sooner or later."

"I hope so. Did you know that sometimes head injuries can alter your sleep patterns forever?"

He cupped her chin and kissed her again. "I promise it will get better."

"You can't promise that."

"I just did."

Erin laughed despite herself. "How was your day today? It was a long one."

"It was, at that. I just kept in mind that I would see you at the end of it, and I was able to muscle my way through it."

Erin thought about Hannah waiting for Otis, sure that he would come back to her as soon as he could. But he had never come back.

"No need to look so serious," Terry told her.

"Sorry. Just thinking about… something."

"Hannah?"

Erin wasn't supposed to be talking about her. "I guess. Yeah. It's just… hard to forget her, when I felt like I was inside her head. Or she was inside mine. Those dreams were so vivid. I can't forget."

"They'll fade eventually."

"I hope so."

"I don't want you to get too excited about this… but I may have found something."

"Found what?" Erin's interest was piqued. The fact that he didn't want her to get too excited meant she was immediately.

Terry plopped down onto the couch next to her. He pried his shoes off with his toes and K9 lay down on the floor, sighing loudly. Erin grinned at him. "I know, boy, you had a long day too, didn't you?"

"Yeah, and my partner didn't even get to choose whether to go with you to the hospital or to go on his shift."

"What did you find?" Erin repeated, not about to be distracted.

"Well… You talked about Otis Jackson leaving and never coming back, so I thought I would do a little bit of historical research. It isn't like doing an internet search because, of course, none of the information from back then has been properly digitized. It means going to the paper files and searching them by hand."

"That must be a lot of paper."

"Not as much as you would think. We produce more paper now than they ever did back then, when they had to type and review everything manually. And probably a lot of stuff that was investigated was never actually written up. Just the big cases and stuff that led to arrests."

"What about black mold? That's all you hear about old paper archives now. How much stuff had to be destroyed because of killer mold."

"Well, I'll admit that it didn't all smell very good, but I don't think we have any killer mold. It's just dusty and musty from sitting there for so long. Luckily, no mice or squirrels. That's something else that destroys paper."

Erin nodded. "So, was there ever any investigation into where Otis had gone? Was he reported missing?"

"No. Nothing like that. People could pretty much come and go as they liked back then. There wasn't any surveillance. Maybe people saw you, and maybe they didn't. They just assumed if someone was gone that they had walked away under their own power, unless there was blood or obvious signs of violence. And there's no crime in walking off, even if you leave a pretty girl behind."

Erin waited. If there wasn't a missing person report, what had Terry found?

"What I did find wasn't discovered until after Hannah's death," Terry said. "So we're talking a couple of years later. There was a body discovered. In the wilds. Not far from here."

"A body?"

"They were unable to identify it. No facial reconstruction. No DNA or dental analysis or other fancy tricks. Things were much more basic then. If it didn't have a face, there wasn't much they could do."

"If it didn't have a face?" Erin repeated faintly.

"Well, of course there was one to begin with… but as the body decomposes…"

"Oh. I see. So what they found was… bones."

"Mostly, yes. A few bits of clothing and personal possessions, but not enough for them to identify him."

Erin thought about this, not letting herself picture what the remains must have looked like at that point or how they had found him. Just pondering what they did have.

"So you're telling me this because… it was a young man. Someone who could have been Otis."

Terry nodded. "There is nothing to indicate that it *was* him at this point. We'll have to see if there is enough evidence to identify him now. The bones were interred. There is some photographic evidence. I don't know if it is enough to do a forensic analysis and build a face now. Or if there are any photographs of Otis Jackson in existence for us to compare one to. Those are things that will need to be considered."

"Do you have pictures of the other things that were with him? The… bits of clothing and possessions?"

"Yes. Old photographs. Not the clearest, and we don't have the original evidence. But it was investigated by the police, at least. We have a record, even if it is not as complete as we would like. I don't know if there is enough to ever identify the deceased as Otis. But it is possible that Otis didn't return because he couldn't. He was dead."

Just as Jeremy had suggested. Erin was reluctant to ask the next logical question. "How did he die?"

"There is a clear bullet hole in the skull. It would appear that he was shot." Terry held up both hands in a warning. "We don't know that it was murder. There may have been an accident. A hunter that mistook him for a deer. Suicide. Mishandling of a gun. We don't know enough to say exactly how he died. Just that it appears to have been a gunshot wound."

Erin closed her eyes, thinking about this. Thinking about Hannah staring out the window, waiting. Thinking about her walking all the way out to the mailbox, hoping there would be something from Otis. Something that would tell her what he was doing and that he was still coming back to her. And all the time… Otis's body was in the woods, subject to predation and decomposition, gradually returning to nature.

"Poor Hannah. I wish she had known what happened to him."

Terry nodded his understanding. "It must have been difficult for her, not knowing what had happened. If he had just abandoned her, if he was ever coming back. The communications systems were not the same as they are today, so she might think that he was just unable to reach her. That his letters hadn't gotten through. That there was some explanation for him being gone but that he would return. But sadly for her… all the hoping and wishing in the world would not bring him back to her."

"And she had his baby without him. She didn't have anyone to take care of her."

"Except her parents."

"Yeah. The parents who stole her baby. The only thing she had left of Otis. And I think that Otis's disappearance is what caused the feud." She didn't tell him she had gotten this from Mrs. Ford or Jeremy. She knew from what Jeremy had said that she needed to keep quiet, not to say that anyone had told her anything. Terry might repeat it to the wrong person. Or someone else in the department might read and leak what he had written. The Bald Eagle Falls police department was not well-known for being able to keep secrets.

Terry tilted his head. "Why would Otis disappearing cause the feud? I can understand that his taking up with Hannah and getting her pregnant could cause resentment. But leaving her? Wouldn't her parents be happier that he was out of her life? And wouldn't his parents be relieved that he had cut her loose and might be available for a more suitable match?"

"He broke her heart when he left her."

"But would either set of parents be concerned about that? From what you have said about her parents, I would think that they would have been happy about it. It didn't sound like they were that concerned about her happiness. Just their reputation. Which would be better if she was not seeing him and breaking society's rules about how a good girl behaved."

"Well… yeah. I don't know. Maybe one of them cared, even though she didn't think they did. Maybe they argued about it when she wasn't in the room."

Terry pursed his lips, not finding it believable. Erin had to admit that it was a stretch. From what she had seen in her dreams, neither of Hannah's parents had been concerned with her heartbreak after Otis had left. It was her mother who had told her that he was never coming back.

Did she know that? Or was she just trying to get Hannah to give up on him and get on with her life?

CHAPTER 44

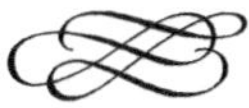

"GET OUT OF BED, YOU LAZY LUMP!"

*H*annah pulled the pillow over her head, shutting out Mama's voice. Or trying to. It didn't actually work, and they both knew it.

"You have chores to do. You are still a part of this family, and you need to do your part around the farm. Get up now. We don't sleep all day in this house. Who do you think you are, the Queen?"

Hannah might have gotten out of bed and done chores if she could have. She might have found it easier than lying in bed remembering, mourning for her lost boys. Otis and the baby. How could she have lost everything in such a short time? Her heart felt broken. Wrung out and shattered and stomped on, all at once.

Going on with her life would have been easier. Forgetting the shame that she had brought upon her family. Forgetting the life she had labored to bring into the world. Pretending she was just like any of the good girls she had gone to school with. Going on to help take care of the farm.

Maybe to think about going away to college, where she could learn a trade, since she was never going to marry. She could learn to type, cook in a boarding house, or teach children at school. Any of the respectable jobs that a spinster could get. She didn't have to worry about finding her own house or feeding herself. She would be expected to live at home until she or her parents died. She would contribute whatever she earned to the household income so that her parents could get nice things and maintain the house and the farm equipment.

She could be the perfect daughter that they had wanted. She wouldn't give them the joy of grandchildren, but she could at least pretend to be respectable. She didn't have to let the rest of the world see the depths to which she had fallen.

But all of that would presuppose she could get out of bed. To drag herself up by her bootstraps, get dressed, and leave the house. But she had no energy or desire to do that. She simply couldn't.

Mama banged the door open and stomped over to the bed where Hannah lay. She slapped Hannah's arm, which was sticking out from the covers. It stung for a few seconds, then subsided to a dull burn.

"Get up," Mama insisted, grabbing her shoulder and shaking her violently.

Let her. What did it matter? What more could she do?

Mama tried to drag her from the bed, but Hannah was a grown girl, not a little child anymore. She was more solidly built than her spare, straight mother and had gained a certain amount of weight during her illness. Mama could no longer pick her up or drag her out of the bed. Maybe she and Hannah's father could do it together, but that would mean they had to agree on a course of action, and Hannah doubted they would cooperate for long enough to achieve it.

"You big, fat lump," Mama sneered. "Do you think we're just going to let you sleep all day?"

Hannah didn't answer. She just closed her eyes and turned her back to her mother.

~

In the morning, Vic found Erin poring over the genealogy binders at the kitchen table.

"Mornin', sunshine," she greeted, looking the piles of books over. "What's all this? Have you been bitten by the bug?"

Erin tried to drag her attention away from the books to her friend. "Bug?"

"The genealogy bug. I know some people get it pretty bad..."

Erin rubbed her eyes and looked at the mess she had made, books piled on top of books, paper files strewn everywhere. "Oh… well, not exactly. I've been looking for information on some babies…" Erin trailed off, not wanting to say too much. Jeremy had warned her. It could be dangerous to say too much about the baby.

But Vic knew better than to say anything to anyone. It wasn't like passing information on to Melissa Lee, who would have spread it all over Bald Eagle Falls in a matter of hours. Vic knew how to keep her mouth shut, and she knew more about how the clans worked and what was important to them than Erin did.

"Babies?" Vic went over to the coffee machine, sniffing the coffee in the pot to gauge its freshness. She poured herself a mug. "What babies? And how long have you been up? I thought Terry was home."

"He is." Erin didn't know what Terry being home had to do with anything else. "And I've been up… I don't know how long. My sleep is so disrupted now that I can't keep track of what time it is." She looked at the clock on the wall, noting that it was time for her to get ready to go to the morning shift at Auntie Clem's if she had been going. But she had been up most of the night, and it probably wasn't a good idea to get her fingers anywhere near moving beaters or hot pans in ovens. "I don't think I can go in today."

"That's okay," Vic assured her. "You have to take care of yourself. It might take some time to get back into a regular schedule. I think you tried to do too much too early, and your body still needs more rest."

Erin nodded, her mind on other things. Vic sat down across the table from her. She wouldn't be able to stay for long, but she could have a sip of coffee and discuss a few things with Erin before heading off to Auntie Clem's.

CHAPTER 45

So what's this about the babies?" Vic asked, looking at the stacks of paper. "Is this to do with Hannah Dyson's baby?"

"Maybe," Erin admitted. She hesitated about what to say. Vic already knew about the Dyson-Jackson baby, so Erin wasn't going against what Jeremy had told her. She wasn't telling anyone anything they didn't already know. "I got some leads on the families that a baby might have gone to back then and I was just trying to track down all of the family trees so I can see if the timing is right."

"Do you know when it was?"

"Some of the letters and other things from Hannah are dated, so I have a pretty good idea. Down to a couple of months."

"Well, that's pretty good. There can't have been too many adoptions done in a place as small as Bald Eagle Falls in a two-month period."

"No. I think I have it nailed down. The problem is that it isn't a family Clementine had a lot of information on. I think they left Bald Eagle Falls shortly after the adoption, so trying to trace the line down to someone more modern is proving to be difficult."

"Why do you need to trace it down? I thought you just wanted to know where the baby went. So that Hannah could… be at peace."

That wasn't how Erin would have put it, but she supposed it was close enough. It was hard to describe how she felt she needed to know these

729

answers when Hannah and everybody else involved were dead and gone. She didn't believe that Hannah's restless ghost was wandering around anywhere. Or that she was in heaven—or somewhere else—still mourning the loss of Otis and her baby. She believed that Hannah had ceased to exist. So why did she need to do anything to prove to herself what had happened to the baby?

"I guess I just want to know what kind of a life he had. Hopefully, after he was adopted he had a good life. People only adopt babies when they really want them, right? So they would be good to him. He would be better off there than with an unwed mother. Than living with her on the Dyson farm, with her parents…"

"Yeah, probably," Vic agreed. She rolled her eyes. "Anything would be better than living with the Dysons, right?"

That was how she had been raised. That there was nothing worse than the Dyson clan. She acknowledged in her body language and tone of voice that she knew she had been indoctrinated by her own family to be biased against the Dysons. That she knew it wasn't the truth, even if it was her first instinct.

"So what have you found?" Vic motioned to the genealogical records.

"Well, it looks like he went to John and Hope Andrews. An older married couple who didn't have any other kids yet, so they probably couldn't get pregnant. But then they moved away. They called him Jesse. I've been looking on some of the genealogical sites to try to find him and his descendants. Maybe I can talk to them… a grandson or someone will be able to remember him and tell me about him. How things turned out for him."

Vic frowned. She took a sip of her coffee.

"Are you serious? It's a bit late in the year for April Fool's Day."

"What do you mean?"

"I haven't got enough caffeine onboard yet, so maybe I'm not getting the joke…"

Erin shook her head. "It's not a joke."

"Andrews? Like Willie's family?"

Erin opened her mouth and closed it again. Willie? How could she not have thought about him as soon as she had heard the name Andrews?

"Blame it on the concussion," she said, her cheeks heating in embarrassment. "I didn't even think about Willie. But Andrews is a common name. They're probably not actually related. Willie grew up in Bald Eagle Falls, didn't he? So if these Andrewses moved out of Bald Eagle Falls, it wouldn't be the same family."

"Could still be related. Uncles, cousins, whatever. And you're going back a couple of generations, right? This would be his grandfather's generation? Great-grandfather's?"

"Grandfather's, probably," Erin said, looking at the dates.

"So we can just ask him. What his grandfather's name was, if he had a brother named…?"

"John. But that's a pretty common name too. John Andrews—there are hundreds of them when I do a search."

"It's still worth a try, though, don't you think?"

"I guess, but what's…" Erin shook her head, trying to get her thoughts into order. Just how much was the concussion muddling her thinking? "What are the odds that he's from that family? And that they moved back here after they moved away? They must have had a reason for moving."

"People move back and forth all the time," Vic laughed. "Trust me. I don't know how many friends I have who moved away for a few years and then came back. Especially if someone dies and leaves you their house…" Vic laughed. "Like someone else I know."

Erin was about to ask who she was talking about before realizing that she had lived in Bald Eagle Falls for a short time before her parents had left town and been killed and she had entered foster care in another state. She had been raised up north, all over the eastern seaboard, and then had returned to Bald Eagle Falls when Clementine had died, leaving Erin her shop and house.

So why couldn't the same have happened with Jesse Andrews's family? They left to pursue a job opportunity or something else. Then a child or grandchild returned to Bald Eagle Falls when a grandparent had died or grandmother had been sick and needed someone to take care of her, or some other scenario requiring them to go back to the family home or be available in the area.

Erin tried to remember what Willie had told her about his past. "Willie said his parents moved to Bald Eagle Falls before he was born. Because they wanted to…" she trailed off.

Vic blinked at her, apparently not remembering. It had been a difficult time. They had been under a lot of pressure, trying to figure out how to rescue Charley and to avoid getting in any trouble themselves. Willie had known from the start that Vic was a Jackson, even if she didn't go by that name anymore. But she had not known that Willie was a Dyson. And not just a Dyson by blood, but that he had served as a street-level soldier for them for five years, the initial indenture period that every recruit had to agree to. It was rare for anyone who survived the first five years to decide to leave when that period was complete.

"He said they had left Moose River and come to Bald Eagle Falls to escape the clans. From the Dysons. Remember that?"

Vic shook her head slowly. "You have a better memory than I do. I don't remember that detail. But I'll trust you on it. So that's your answer. Jesse Andrews left Bald Eagle Falls and went to Moose River, probably, to be with the clan. But Willie's parents didn't want to be part of that whole scene, so they moved away. Moved back to Bald Eagle Falls, where grandpa had come from. Maybe he still owned a house here that they moved into."

"Willie went back to Moose River for those five years, and then he came back here when he was done and realized that wasn't the life he wanted to be in."

Vic nodded. "I can understand a stupid teenager deciding to be part of a powerful clan. He wants the money, the power, the prestige. But I have a hard time reconciling that with the Willie I know."

"I'm sure he has changed a lot since he was a teenager."

"Yeah. I guess so."

"I guess… I should ask him if he is related to Jesse Andrews. See if that's his grandpa and if he ever met him. If he knows anything about him and the life that he led." Erin pressed her lips together, thinking. "I hope I don't find out that he went to Moose River to become a don in the family. Hannah would not be happy about that."

"The clan wouldn't have been organized like that so long ago. If they had just started feuding… then it was probably just one family, one extended family against another. They wouldn't have had an organized power structure like now. Whoever was the oldest in the family would have been the leader."

"How does a family end up becoming… an organized gang?"

Vic shrugged. "I can't tell you much about that. The Jackson clan was

already big when I was old enough to know anything about it. I guess…
they recruit extended family members to join them for protection, to try
to get more people on their side. Each of them wants to get enough power
to overcome the other. Or as time goes on… just to maintain what power
they have. You hire talent. Recruit professionals. Have children, and
grandchildren, and great-grandchildren, and try to keep them all as part
of the organization, if you can."

"Keep growing the power structure. But Jesse probably just lived a
normal life," Erin repeated tentatively.

"Hopefully, yeah," Vic agreed.

"Is Willie home?" Erin nodded to the loft apartment across the yard.

"No. He was up in the wee hours this morning. Going fishing,
maybe. Or to check on a mine that is farther away."

"When will he be back?"

"Didn't say when he would be back, so I assume it will be around
supper like usual." She nodded in anticipation of Erin's question. "I'll tell
him that you want to talk to him."

"Thanks."

Erin smoothed the page of one of the family trees. "Wouldn't it be
funny if the descendant of Hannah's baby was right here under our
noses?"

"This is a small town. And everyone is related to everyone. It's not that
unexpected."

CHAPTER 46

$\mathcal{E}$rin was on pins and needles all day, waiting for Willie to get back home so she could ask him about his ancestors. Maybe he would know nothing about them. Erin certainly didn't know anything about her grandparents on either side. She could be a descendant of Hannah and Otis herself, and she would not know it. Maybe she should get into the genealogy a little bit herself. So that she at least knew her grandparents' and great-grandparents' names. And some stories about them and the kind of people they were.

But as the afternoon progressed and she watched for Willie to return, time stretched on, and he didn't put in an appearance. She had hoped that with such an early start, he would be back well before supper.

Her phone rang. Erin picked it up and saw that it was Terry. She didn't have anything on the stove for supper. It hadn't even occurred to her to get something started.

"Terry, hi!"

"I thought I'd see how you were feeling. We haven't talked since this morning."

"Oh, I'm okay. I just realized what time it is, though. I haven't got anything on for supper."

"You want to go out to eat?"

"I don't know. If people see me out and about, they'll think I'm just faking about still being too injured to work."

"Who cares what people think?"

Erin seemed to remember that he had cared what people thought about him when he was disabled by a head injury. But she didn't point that out. "Could we do takeout?" she suggested. Then she wouldn't have to put up with people staring at her or thinking she was well enough to be gallivanting around town.

"Sure," Terry agreed. "Do you want to come to the police department offices to eat? I have some things to show you."

"Oh? Yeah. That sounds good."

"Good. I'll pick you up, we'll grab some burgers or ribs, and then we'll go eat at the office and I'll show you what I've got."

"Should I get ready now?"

"Yes. I'll be there in a few minutes."

Erin was glad to have something to do other than waiting for Willie to get home. Sometimes, he was away for several days at a time if he had a lot of out-of-town work to do. He would probably let Vic know his schedule if he wasn't home for supper but, until then, they had no idea if he was even planning on coming back to Vic's for the evening. No specific plans had been discussed.

Erin got ready, made sure everything she would need was in her purse, and waited at the door for Terry to pull up. Orange Blossom started fussing about Erin going out without feeding him first, so she went back to the kitchen for long enough to feed him and Marshmallow, then returned to the living room to see Terry waiting at the curb.

Terry leaned over to kiss her when she climbed up into the cab of the truck. "How are you feeling? I didn't ask."

"Not bad. Maybe I could have gone into Auntie Clem's for a little while, but I was back and forth on it all day… I'd have energy for an hour or two and think I should really be at work, and then it disappears, and I have to take a nap. It's really irritating, you know?"

"I know," he agreed.

"Will it ever stop?"

"If your recovery progresses the same way as mine did, then yes. I hardly ever have anything I would consider an after-effect of the concussion anymore. I wouldn't say I suffered any permanent damage."

Erin nodded. She felt like she would never recover, but she had felt the same way dealing with a cold or flu before, too. Sometimes, it felt like it would never end, and she would return to the state of health she had been in before. But sooner or later, even if it took longer than she thought it should, the virus would run its course and she could get on with life.

She just wished that the progress of a head injury was as predictable as a cold.

"Give it time," Terry advised. "If it were a broken leg, you wouldn't be expecting to walk on it in two weeks."

"No."

"Give it some more time."

They agreed on hot chicken instead of burgers or ribs, ordered extra for anyone still hanging around the office, and then returned to the police department offices in the Town Hall. Terry put their food in one of the interview rooms and the extra in the break room. Erin arranged things while she waited for him to return.

"Should I leave the photos until after we eat?" Terry asked as he came back into the interview room.

"No!" Erin told him emphatically. "You don't tell me you have something to show me and then make me wait!"

He grinned, and Erin figured he had probably anticipated her response to his suggestion. He brought a folder into the interview room and removed some modern copies of old photographs that had been on the original investigation file. They could handle copies all they liked without worrying about degrading the originals.

He had not included photos of any bones or other tissue that remained. Just the tattered, weatherworn clothing and the items on or around the body. Erin studied each picture in turn.

They were not high-definition photographs like they would have taken today. They were fuzzy and brownish. The police investigators had done their best to show the details of the items they had found. Maybe they'd had fancy new cameras that they had wanted to test out and it seemed like a good time to do it.

A few coins. Any paper money or train tickets had dissolved and disappeared. Would a young man have had paper money back then? Or had the few coins been the extent of his wealth? The fact that he had any money on him probably meant that it was not a robbery gone bad. He had a pen but no paper. They had recovered a few buttons from his clothing, but Erin couldn't divine anything from that.

There was a pocketknife. It had been opened and each blade and attachment carefully documented. It appeared to be well-used, but in good shape. It was not dull, nor were any of the blades nicked.

There was no gun. If he had fallen or had some other accident and ended up shooting himself, then where had the gun gone? Had it been picked up by someone else who had happened to find the body? If so, why had they taken the gun and not reported the body? Surely most people would have at least wanted to give the family the opportunity for a Christian burial.

"Is this a lighter?" Erin asked, looking at a small silver box. There was also a cigarette case, devoid of any cigarettes.

"Actually, it is a music box. Maybe a family heirloom or something he intended to give as a gift."

"But why would he be carrying around a family heirloom? It's pretty." It was actually dirty and tarnished, but Erin could see the quality of work that had gone into it. It was a nice piece. "What does it play?"

"Ode to Joy."

"What is that?"

Terry hummed a few notes of the melody. "It's a hymn."

"Something you might give to a lover?"

"Yes, it certainly could be."

Erin imagined the young man, the handsome young man that Mrs. Ford had described, taking the small music box home to Hannah. The girl he was in love with. Why else would he be carrying it around with him? He must have been on his way to see her when the accident had occurred.

"Do you know when he died? Could the police back then make an educated guess?"

"They figured it was a couple of years. Which, according to you, is around the time he was seeing Hannah, but then he stopped coming."

"So he didn't run off. He wasn't just using her. The reason he didn't go back is because he was killed."

"That would appear to be the case. If this was Otis. Do you see anything that would identify him?"

Erin gazed down at the random items. Buttons, pocketknife, empty cigarette case, music box, change. How could any of it identify him?

"The only thing really unique is the music box. If he was going to give it to Hannah… where did he get it? Did he buy it at a store? Mail order? Was it a family heirloom?"

"I'm afraid we don't know any of those things."

"It wasn't an accident. He didn't just kill himself mishandling his gun. There is no gun."

"None that was apparent to the police at the time his body was found, no. There doesn't mean there never was."

"Someone who took his gun would have taken his money. Probably his knife, music box, and cigarette box, too."

"Maybe. The death is suspicious, whether it was homicide or not."

"Is that what the police said back then?"

"It doesn't seem to have gathered much attention. No one identified him. Unknown remains. They figured he was just a vagrant passing through who came to harm. They left it undetermined."

"What about his parents? They didn't identify him?" Erin rubbed her head. How many people had gone missing from Bald Eagle Falls? Surely, when they had discovered the body of a young man, they would have compared it to a list of men who had gone missing. "Wouldn't his parents have looked at these things and identified him?"

She gestured to the pictures of the items found on the body.

"As you said, only the music box was unique. The knife and the cigarette case were commonplace. Nothing special about the buttons or the money."

"Did his parents look at them?"

Terry nodded. "They said it wasn't him."

Erin made a noise of disgust. "You weren't going to tell me that part?"

"They might have been mistaken. All they saw was some random items found on or around the body. There was nothing left of him but bones."

"They couldn't identify him from his dental records?"

"There apparently weren't any."

"People had work done on their teeth!"

"Yes. But not everyone had x-rays. Or work was done by dentists who traveled through town and didn't have an office here. Or he was taken into the city, but no one knows what doctor he saw. Even now, finding enough of a person's records can be tricky to make a definite identification. There is no central database. People go to different dentists for different things. Even go out of the country to have work done."

It always sounded so neat when they did it on TV. Everything was quick and easy to search, and the results were practically wrapped up and decorated with a bow.

"But you think this was Otis."

"I think it might have been. The height and age are about right. The timing is right. His body was found close to the place where Vic found Hannah's things. I think… they probably met there on occasion. That's why he was there and why her papers were found there. You can bet that if she had left them at her house, her mother would have destroyed them after her death. Records of a young mother pining after the boy she was not married to… From what you say her parents were like, I assume they would have gotten rid of every trace of her embarrassing behavior."

"Yeah," Erin agreed soberly. "I think you're right."

CHAPTER 47

It was late when Erin heard Willie's truck pull in back. Normally, she barely even registered the sound of the truck's engine. He belonged there and she didn't monitor his comings and goings.

But she had fallen asleep after getting back from supper and, once she woke up, it was hard to get back to sleep again. As she had told Vic, her whole sleep schedule was thrown off. So she was lying there, restless and awake, when she heard Willie drive in.

She got up quietly and pulled a housecoat around her before going to the back door. She turned on the lights so she wouldn't startle Willie out of his wits, and opened the door.

"Psst. Willie!"

He stopped, turning his gaze towards her. "What are you doing up, Erin? Is everything okay?"

"Yes. I wanted to ask you about something, though."

He walked slowly toward her. "Yes… Vic said that you wanted to discuss some family history stuff. I'm not really into family stories, Erin, and it's late."

"I just wanted to ask you a couple of quick questions before you go to sleep. I can't sleep with everything on my mind…"

"Everything on your mind?" he repeated.

"Well, I've just been thinking…"

"Did you decide to give those mementos back to the Dyson family?" Willie asked. "You know they're not yours. They really should go back where they belong."

Erin had almost forgotten that he had tried to talk her into giving up Hannah's papers.

"Uh… maybe when I'm done," she agreed. If he was one of Hannah's descendants, she might give them to him. She wouldn't feel so bad about that. She knew Willie would take care of them.

"Done what?"

"The research I've been doing. I wanted to… make the record complete. Of her family, her history. Her… posterity."

"Oh." He shifted and looked away. "I thought Vic said that she was a young girl. Died as a teenager."

"She did. But she had a baby."

"Oh. I see."

"Vic didn't tell you… what we figured out about the adoption?"

"I've been away since early this morning. It has been a long day, Erin. Maybe we could do this some other time."

"Hannah's baby was adopted by an Andrews."

"It's not an uncommon name."

"No. I know that. That's what I said to Vic. But he was adopted by a couple that lived here, in Bald Eagle Falls. This is where your family was from, isn't it?"

"Yeah, sure."

"Did you have a grandfather named Jesse?"

He didn't answer at first, staring across the yard toward Vic's apartment, where a friendly light burned, waiting for his arrival.

"Jesse Andrews?" Erin prodded. "Was he your grandfather? Or great-grandfather?"

"Grandfather," he said finally, and turned his eyes back to her. He sighed. "And really, I would prefer you didn't spread anything around about him being adopted."

Erin didn't understand. "There's no shame in being adopted. I know that back then, it was sometimes kept quiet, but that's not the way it is anymore. It isn't a shameful secret anymore. People are interested in finding out things like that about their ancestors. Don't you think it is interesting?"

"I think... that I told you those papers were not yours and that I would like this kept quiet."

"Why?" Erin demanded, baffled.

"Because old secrets... can still cause harm. This is not a can of worms you want to open."

"I don't see the harm in it." Despite the warning from Jeremy, Erin couldn't see the problem with talking to a Dyson about a Dyson. Or an Andrews about an Andrews. "It's just finding out where you came from. Don't you want to know where you came from? Who your people are?"

"I already know who my people are," he said in a low growl, "And trust me when I say they are not people that you want to exchange gossip with."

A cold wind blew through the open door. Erin shivered and pulled her housecoat closer to her.

Willie knew that he was a part of the larger Dyson clan. He had served as a soldier in that clan and had seen blood and violence that he did not want to have anything else to do with. So he had broken with them. Was he worried he was going to find more of the same when she told him about Hannah and Jesse?

Hannah's story was not like that. She was a young farm girl, not the member of an organized crime family. As far as she could tell, the violence and the organized feud between the two families hadn't started until after Otis disappeared.

"Jesse Andrews was Hannah Dyson's son," Erin told Willie, thinking she hadn't been clear enough, that Willie didn't understand what she was trying to tell him. "The son of Hannah Dyson and Otis Jackson."

Willie leaned in closer to Erin. They were friends, and she hadn't been so uncomfortable with his physical presence since the first day she had met him, when he'd tried to help her with her groceries and she had thought him a pushy homeless man looking for a handout.

"Erin. I don't want you to repeat that to anyone. Those words must never cross your lips again."

CHAPTER 48

*E*rin gaped at Willie.

"What?"

She had heard him clearly, of course, but she couldn't believe what he had said. Not only was he not surprised by her revelation, but he didn't want to talk about it. Never wanted to talk about it or for her to mention it to anyone again. She had thought he would be interested and excited by the news of his heritage. Intrigued or interested, at least.

"Did you already know?" she demanded, trying to take it all in and process it at once.

She had expected shock, but on Willie's part, not her own.

Willie flicked his fingers toward the interior of the house. "Shall we go in? I don't want to be discussing this out in the open."

There was no one else in the yard. No one was going to overhear them. Terry was asleep in bed. Vic was in her apartment, either sleeping or awaiting Willie's return. Who did Willie think would hear them discussing it in the yard?

But she didn't have any reason to argue with him about it. In fact, she should be sitting down rather than propping herself against the doorframe for support. She stepped back and led the way to the table, where she and Willie sat down. Erin looked at the counter, wondering whether she should make tea.

"You want something?" Willie asked, following her eyes.

"No. I wondered if you did."

He shook his head. "I don't need anything."

Erin took a deep breath in and exhaled. "You already knew about Jesse?"

"How did you figure it out? Something in those papers?" His eyes were piercing. "You should have given them back to me when I asked. Why did you have to go digging?"

"I just wanted to know the truth. Ever since the accident, I've been dreaming about Hannah. I had to know the truth about her. About her and Otis and the baby. I couldn't just let it go."

"You had to know that it's dangerous to go digging around in the Dysons' business. Haven't you learned anything about the clans and how seriously they take any intrusions into their business?"

"I didn't think it was anything important. Why should anybody in the clan care about what happened to a teenage girl generations ago?"

"Everything matters. Traditions. Origins. Family relationships. You are talking about the foundations of the feud between the two clans. How could that *not* be important?" Willie demanded, his voice rising.

Erin glanced toward the bedroom. She didn't think Willie wanted to wake Terry up and invite him into this conversation.

"I didn't know about any of that," Erin fumbled with her explanation. She pressed fingertips to her head where a headache was taking root. "I thought it was interesting that a Dyson and a Jackson had gotten together. When I looked into it and talked to people, it was before the feud, or before it was really established, if it had already started. I didn't think that would matter."

"You were wrong." Willie shook his head. "I thought you were smarter than this. But you are always a bulldog with mysteries and clues, aren't you? You think this is another mystery you could solve, another one to tally up in your planning binder?"

"Are you talking about Otis's death?" Erin asked. "He was shot. I don't know how they could pass it off as an accident."

He opened his mouth to say something, and then changed his mind and closed it, reconsidering.

"What do you know about Otis Jackson's death and how did you find out?"

"Well, Terry pulled the old file—or the investigation into the death of a John Doe that he thinks was Otis Jackson. That's why Otis never came back to Hannah; he was killed."

"You've involved the police in this?"

"No, just Terry… I didn't ask him to look it up. He did that on his own. Decided to see if there was a reason Otis didn't come back…"

Which was precisely what Willie did not want revealed. Why not? Wasn't it better if people knew the truth? It wasn't like anyone even cared anymore. Erin was the only one interested in what happened to the young couple so many years ago.

Willie looked toward the living room, where Erin's genealogy books and papers were stacked untidily. "Do you have copies of the information from that John Doe file here?" he demanded.

Erin shook her head. "No. Terry and I had supper at the police department and he showed me the pictures from the file. Nothing gruesome, none of the body, just the stuff he had in his pockets."

"Identifiable?"

"No. Nothing identifiable. No papers, wallet, or ID. Just pocketknife, cigarette case, that kind of thing." She left off the music box. So far, she knew of no way that it could identify him as a Jackson. Anybody who would have been able to recognize it if it was a family heirloom was dead and gone, just like Otis.

"So no one can prove that was Otis Jackson."

Erin shook her head.

"We need to keep it that way, Erin. And you need to drop this."

She stirred uneasily at the memory of the warnings that Jeremy had given her. It seemed like a long time ago that she had talked to him. It was like his words were far away. Underwater. He had told her not to look any further into what had happened to Otis. And she hadn't. That had been Terry. It had been his initiative.

And then there was Mrs. Ford. No one knew that Erin had gone to talk to her about Hannah. Erin should go back to the nursing home, maybe with another little box of cookies, and warn her not to talk to anyone about it or let them know that Erin had been there.

She didn't know how to cover up everything she had already done.

She could give Hannah's papers to Willie. She had them on her phone anyway, along with the recipe book and pictures of Terry's photographs.

Maybe giving them to Willie would convince him she wouldn't pursue it any further.

"I'll… I'll get it all for you," she told him. "You can take it now. And if the Dysons want it, or whatever…"

Willie nodded, his eyes sharp. "Yes. Give it to me."

Erin went into the living room, made sure that everything was gathered together, and returned it to the box. She stroked the warm, worn wood of the little treasure box. She walked slowly back to Willie and handed it to him. Willie didn't open it to look at the letters and other materials. She wondered if he would later, or if he would just incinerate the whole thing without ever opening it, to make sure that no one else could follow the story, as Erin had.

"Thank you."

"I just want to know… what you can tell me about your grandfather. What kind of life he had. I guess he got married and had kids," that much she had learned from the genealogy books, "and they all had kids… I just need to know for Hannah."

Willie frowned and shook his head, but he wasn't refusing.

"I think he had a good boyhood. As much as anyone growing up during that time did. People didn't have much money, but he had enough to eat, went to school, had friends. He always had an interest in me… the oldest grandchild. He would take me aside, and we would talk. More like a job interview than a grandfatherly chat. He wanted to know what I had been doing, if I was living up to his name."

"Jesse Andrews."

He didn't respond at first, then gave a brief nod.

"Did he know… his heritage? Where he came from?"

Some of the people adopted in those days didn't even know it. But Mrs. Ford had known.

"There were other children in the family. They told him. Acted like he didn't belong. Like he was just a foundling that their parents had picked up out of Christian charity. He was always sort of an outcast from his family."

It seemed to contradict his claim that Jesse had a good childhood. But then, Willie had always been something of an outcast in Bald Eagle Falls. So for him, maybe that was normal and seemed fine. She wondered if there was a connection. Had they all been outsiders in their own family or community? Jesse, Willie's father, and Willie himself? Because of Jesse's status as an adoptee?

"Did he know who his birth parents were?"

Willie's gaze slid away. "I grew up with a lot of family secrets. Things that were kept from me and things that were told to me."

Erin had no idea whether that meant that Jesse had known or not. And whether Willie had known or not. Had he known all along that he was Jackson as well as Dyson? Had he known that growing up in Bald Eagle Falls, where he was ostracized? When he had gone to work for the Dysons for those five years?

Or was it only a recent discovery, maybe just before Erin herself had figured it out?

"Willie…"

"You know too much already," Willie told her. "I'm not going to tell you more. You need to leave this alone. You gave the recipe book back to the police. You gave me Hannah's papers. You didn't get copies of the pictures that Officer Piper had. So you don't have anything. Put your head down and stop asking questions. Let people know that you were just a little off your head because of the concussion. And don't ever mention any of these people again."

Erin wanted to argue, to explain to him that she was the only one who cared about Hannah and what had happened to her and her baby. No one else had any interest in it, and Willie was just being paranoid, thinking she was going to bring the ire of the entire Dyson family down upon her if she continued to investigate something so innocent and unimportant. A girl who had lived and died decades before didn't matter to anyone else still living. Except maybe to Hannah's old school friend, Mrs. Ford.

"Please, Erin," Willie importuned.

"Okay," Erin agreed. "I won't ask anyone else anything about her."

"And you don't go to the library and read microfiche looking for her. Or go to adoption reunion or genealogy sites. You stop. Now. You learned what you set out to, and now you need to forget it."

CHAPTER 49

*E*rin tried to give the impression that everything was back to normal. Or as close to normal as it could be. Despite not having slept, she got up at the usual time in the morning and got ready to go to Auntie Clem's. She didn't give Terry or Vic any reason to think that there was anything to be concerned about. Just their usual concerns about whether she was up to it or not.

Terry dropped them off and again promised Erin that he would come and pick her up when she reached the end of her energy and was ready to go home. She had only to ask.

She put in a couple of hours before opening, said hello to the early birds, and called Terry. He took her home, properly sympathetic to her inability to put in a full day yet.

Erin was exhausted. She had a nap, but she set an alarm so she would remember to get up in a couple of hours and not sleep the rest of the day. When she woke up, still bleary and tired, she made herself get out of bed and she puttered around cleaning up and doing minor jobs until she was focused enough to go see Mrs. Ford at the nursing home. She felt better after her short nap than she usually did after a long one. Maybe she had been sleeping too much and needed to get up and do things even if she didn't feel like it.

Even though Terry didn't think she should be driving, she did. She drove herself over to the nursing home so that she could tell Mrs. Ford to be careful and not say anything about Hannah to anyone else. Even if she had already talked to someone about Hannah, she could use her age as an excuse and pretend to have forgotten everything she knew on the topic. Old people sometimes brought up memories of things that had happened as a child with great clarity, but a day later might not even remember it had happened. She had a built-in excuse for not discussing it with anyone.

Erin smiled at the receptionist in the lobby.

"I'm just here to see Mrs. Ford," she announced, and took a step toward the elevator.

"Mrs. Ford?" The woman straightened in her seat. "Wait a minute, please."

Erin paused. She didn't think she needed any special permission to be able to get in to see Mrs. Ford. But maybe she had someone in with her giving her a bath or taking care of other physical needs. Or maybe she had the flu and couldn't have visitors who might catch it or spread it to other seniors.

"I just thought I would go in," Erin said, motioning to the elevator. "I know where she is. Is there a problem?"

"If you would please just take a seat for a moment." The receptionist nodded to the small grouping of chairs.

Erin sighed and walked over to the waiting chairs. She had hoped to avoid any needless bureaucracy. She knew from experience that in a place like a nursing home, the trick was to appear as if she belonged there and knew what she was doing. If she acted confident, people didn't stop to think about who she was or whether she had permission to be there.

She sat down and looked at her phone, scrolling through the pictures and videos she had taken over the past few days. Maybe she could show Mrs. Ford the tiny music box and ask her if she recognized it. She knew Willie didn't want her to ask any more questions, but if she could just confirm to herself that the John Doe found in the woods was, in fact, Otis Jackson...

Of course she would warn Mrs. Ford not to repeat the information to anyone else.

"You're here to see Mrs. Ford?"

Erin looked up at the woman who had approached. An administrator in a blazer and crisp white shirt, not a nursing smock.

"Yes. That's right. Is there a problem?"

The woman sat in one of the other chairs in the grouping, leaning toward Erin. "Are you a friend of Mrs. Ford's?"

"Yes." Erin didn't try to explain that they had only met once. The woman didn't need to know the exact level of their friendship. She just wanted to ensure Erin wasn't a family member or someone who had a professional relationship with her.

"Have you seen her recently?"

"Just a couple of days ago. Why are you asking? What's going on here?"

The woman gave her a sympathetic look. Her hands twitched, as if she were trying to decide whether to hold her hand or not. Erin stood up, alarmed.

"What's happened?"

"Well, I'm sorry to have to break this to you," the administrator rose to her feet as well, reaching out to stop Erin. "But Mrs. Ford passed away."

"What? When? I just saw her."

"I know. I'm sorry it's such a shock. But she was very elderly. Sometimes... we're not prepared for the inevitable..."

"This is crazy. How? What happened?"

"Oh, nothing happened. She passed away peacefully. It was just her time."

Was it?

Erin didn't know what to do with herself. She had involved Mrs. Ford, had come here asking questions about Hannah, which Willie told her was dangerous, and now she was dead? Could that just be a coincidence?

"Are you sure?" she demanded. "I mean... not that she's dead, but that it was natural? There wasn't... any foul play."

"Foul play?" the woman repeated in disbelief. "Of course not. Mrs. Ford was very elderly. One of Bald Eagle Falls's oldest residents. It was inevitable, I'm afraid..."

"How did she die? Are you sure?"

The woman shook her head, frown lines between her brows. "I don't know why you would say such a thing. We take good care of our residents here. Nothing could have happened to her. It was just her time."

"She just died in her sleep?"

"Yes. That's all. Trust me, she wasn't in any pain. I'm sorry you were taken by surprise, but these things do happen. Sometimes you can see the end, and sometimes you can't."

Erin put her face in her hands as she tried to work it out. It could be purely coincidence that Mrs. Ford was dead. She had been old. She had been very near the end of her life by anyone's calculations. So what if she had died within days of talking to Erin? That didn't mean that she was killed for what she had told Erin, or to prevent her from saying anything more.

Willie had said that no one but the oldest residents of Bald Eagle Falls had known about Hannah and Otis. Mrs. Ford was certainly one of those he had been referring to. Perhaps the only one who could still talk about what was, to everyone else, ancient history.

But she had just died in her sleep. The doctors who attended at the nursing home were surely capable of telling whether a death was natural or not. They had seen what death looked like. They were intimately familiar with it.

But Erin had seen true crime shows on TV where deaths that had been declared natural by a medical examiner were challenged by someone else, and the manner of death was subsequently changed. There were plenty of murders that had initially been ruled accidental or natural deaths. A pillow or piece of plastic over an old woman's face… there wouldn't be much of a struggle, and she would be gone in seconds. The faster she died, the fewer indicators there would be on the body that it had been murder.

CHAPTER 50

"I'm sorry," the administrator repeated, comforting the mourning friend. "Can I get you anything? A glass of cold water? Maybe a private room until you can collect yourself?"

Erin wondered if she could ask to sit in Mrs. Ford's room for a few minutes to commune with her spirit there. People did that kind of thing. Would there be anything in the room that would provide a clue as to what had really happened?

But it would probably be better to get the police to secure the scene and see if they could find anything. Better than Erin being accused of interfering with the scene or planting evidence.

"Could I... I need to make a few calls..."

"Of course. Come with me, I'll find a meeting room for you."

She led Erin to a suite of meeting rooms in a hallway Erin had not been to previously. There were panels beside each door with a place for the name of a party to be displayed and a slider to swap between Vacant and Occupied. Each had a narrow window filled with mini horizontal blinds so that no one could see in from the hallway. The administrator found a key in her pocket and unlocked one of the doors for Erin. It was neat and clinical. A round, easy-wipe table with several seats around it. Not rolling boardroom chairs, but tubular steel and blue upholstery sprinkled with a yellow and orange pattern. There was a whiteboard on one wall and a conference phone in the middle of the table.

"Thanks," Erin murmured.

"Use it as long as you like. Just pull the door shut when you leave." The woman flicked the sign to Occupied and shut the door.

Erin collapsed into the chair and sat in silence for a minute, gathering her thoughts and trying to figure out what she would say. It was one of those conversations that was extremely difficult to script.

Eventually, she pulled out her phone and tapped Terry's contact short-cut. He answered after two rings.

"Erin. How are you doing?"

Erin swallowed and took a deep breath. He probably thought she was calling him about supper or to see what time he was coming home. Or to ask him to pick something up on the way home.

"Mrs. Ford is dead, Terry."

There was a moment of silence while Terry took this in. He didn't go immediately to "Are you kidding?" which was how Erin found most people responded to unexpected news of a death.

"Mrs. Ford. What happened?"

"They said it was just natural causes, that she died in her sleep. But I don't think that's what happened. Or… I'm afraid that it's not."

"Why is that?"

"I just talked to her about Hannah… I just talked to her two days ago. Do you think that's a coincidence?"

"Well, yes, I do."

"It can't be! Willie told me not to talk to anyone about Hannah or something could happen. He said that it was dangerous. And he said that the only people who knew what had happened back then were Bald Eagle Falls's oldest residents."

"Well, that's true. When did you talk to Willie about her?"

"I didn't tell him that I had talked to Mrs. Ford. I was just talking to him about Hannah. I didn't tell him that I'd already talked to her. I came here today to tell her to be careful not to talk to anyone about it, not to tell anyone that she remembered Hannah or had talked to me about her. I didn't want her to be in any danger. But now…" Erin's voice was cracking. She was trying to hold it together, but she couldn't help the emotion that rose up with the certain knowledge that she was too late. She had tried. Good for her for trying to do the right thing and keep Mrs. Ford safe, but she was too late. She had taken too long to get there.

She shouldn't have talked to Mrs. Ford in the first place.

"When did you talk to Willie?" Terry repeated.

"Last night, when he got home. You were asleep."

"And he threatened you?"

"No! No, he didn't threaten me, but he told me that it was dangerous to talk about Hannah and that I couldn't say anything about her to anyone. I just had to… let it cool. Let people forget I'd ever had questions about Hannah or her baby. Or Otis. You have to put the investigation into that John Doe back away, Terry. I didn't mean to stir anything up with this. I never meant for anyone to be killed!"

"Mrs. Ford's death is not your fault. You are probably overreacting. She was an old lady. She was going to die sooner or later. Well, sooner, to be honest. She didn't have a long time left on this earth. I understand why you're upset, but I don't think you need to blame yourself. It wasn't because of Hannah Dyson or her history. What did the nursing home staff tell you? I haven't seen anything come across my desk about a death at the nursing home."

"No… they said it was just a natural death. They wouldn't report it to the police if they thought it was natural. But what if it wasn't? What if she was smothered because of what she had been telling me or what they thought she might reveal?"

"Why smothered?"

"I don't know. Because that's what I've seen on TV. Sometimes, it is missed. I'm talking about real crime TV," she clarified, "not the made-up stuff. In police series, they always find a fiber in the lungs that proves the person was smothered."

"That's true."

"I think you should check her room before they can clean it up and get all her possessions boxed up. What if there is evidence that something happened to her, and you lose your chance to find it?"

"But if it was a natural death, then we are going to upset a lot of people and stir things up for no reason. If you want to keep Hannah's name out of this, we should just let it go. If we process it as a crime scene, we will need to explain why and what evidence we have. If you're trying to keep it out of the paper and not have people gossiping about it, that's not the way to do it."

"But… if they did kill her…" Erin's sense of justice would not allow her to consider the police not pursuing an answer. They couldn't just let an old woman be murdered because they didn't want the trouble of explaining to people that some of the circumstances surrounding her death were suspicious.

But did Erin want people hanging around her house? Following her to work? Sending her threatening notes? Because they would. And if Willie was right, she had more to fear than a campaign of harassment. She could end up like Mrs. Ford.

"Terry… I really think you should look into it."

"Have you received any threats?"

"No… well, warnings, but not threats."

"Warnings from who?"

Erin cleared her throat. "Um… a few people. But it's all muddled. The concussion is messing with my memory a bit. Willie said I needed to stay out of it, not even say Hannah's name to anyone. And…" Erin pressed a knuckle against her forehead, as if she could press the information out of it. "Beaver? I can't remember if she said anything. She asked me about the recipe book when she visited."

"She did?"

"Yes. She was really interested in it."

"Why wouldn't Beaver come to me if she had questions about the recipe book?"

"I don't know. She wanted to look at the video I had taken. She said she was just interested in how valuable it was… she said there might still be other copies in Bald Eagle Falls."

Had Beaver given her any warnings about leaving it alone? Erin couldn't remember for sure.

"Hmm." Terry considered, but didn't tell her what he was thinking about or if he would call Beaver about it later. "But no threats. No letters, phone calls? Hang ups? Who knew that you were going to see Mrs. Ford?"

"No one. I didn't tell anyone. I just went over to see her. You said she would be a good person to talk to about Hannah, so I went over and visited with her."

"Anyone follow you?"

"No… not that I noticed."

Would Erin have noticed? She wasn't exactly trained in countersurveillance. She had just been driving over to see an old lady. She hadn't expected anyone to object or be concerned about it.

"And who did you see at the nursing home? Anyone you knew? Anyone who might know you?"

"I don't think so. I just talked to whoever the receptionist was to find out where to find Mrs. Ford and if I could visit with her. I didn't see anyone I knew. I don't think I did. I wasn't really paying any attention. Someone might have seen me and recognized me. Lots of people know me from Auntie Clem's, even if they don't shop there often enough for me to recognize them."

"Okay. Where are you now?"

"I'm at the nursing home."

"I'm going to come get you."

"I have my car here. I'll drive it home. Are you going to search Mrs. Ford's room?"

"I don't have any cause."

"Can't you just ask them? If they give you permission, you can look at it and don't need a warrant or anything."

"No. Especially not if we don't want to attract attention to this death. I would rather err on the side of caution. Not draw attention to your visit here and the fact that you talked to her before she died. If it was a homicide, and they don't know that you got there to talk to her already, I'm not about to tip them off and paint a target on your back."

And what would a cop coming to the nursing home to pick her up do?

"I'll drive home. I don't want to leave my car here."

"I'd like to make sure you're safe. And I don't think you should drive while you're so upset about this."

"I can drive. I don't want you coming here if you're not going to investigate Mrs. Ford's death. Then you'll attract attention. Right now, only a couple of people know that I came here today. We don't want to tip them off." She used his words, figuring he couldn't very well argue with his own reasoning.

"Erin…"

"I'm not some hysterical woman. I'm fine. I can drive a few miles to get home safely. It's not like there's a lot of traffic to navigate."

"Can we meet at the house? I want to make sure you're okay."

"Yeah, of course. When do you get off work?"

"Right now," he told her tersely.

Erin nearly laughed at that. "Okay. I'll see you at home in a few minutes, then. I'll start dinner."

CHAPTER 51

*A*s it turned out, Erin was not to start dinner before Terry got home.

She left the nursing home, worrying over everything that had happened. Or what she feared had happened. Was she jumping to unwarranted conclusions? Was Mrs. Ford the victim of foul play or had she just passed away peacefully in her sleep as the administrator had told her? They would know more about her health than anyone else. Maybe they were right.

She looked around as she left the building and walked to her car. There was a prickling at the back of her neck. Was someone watching her, or had Willie just made her paranoid?

What did it matter what stock Willie came from? Why did anyone really care whether the story was revealed now, generations later?

Nothing changed just because a Dyson-Jackson baby had been born.

Telling herself that it was silly and that she was just letting her imagination run wild did not help. It did not change the feeling that she was being watched.

Someone had seen her there. Someone now knew that she had talked to Mrs. Ford. Anyone with eyes could see by her reaction to the news of Mrs. Ford's death that they were not strangers.

Could one of the staff members at the nursing home have been the one to administer death? A nurse or aide could have smothered her, given her a drug, or knocked her over the head. No physician was going to examine the body to find out.

Erin looked back at the nursing home to see if anyone were watching her go. She couldn't see through the reflections on the glass.

She hurried to her car, scanning for any shadow or figure hanging around, watching her in the parking lot. She should have known better than to come here. She should have known from what Willie had said that it could be dangerous. He had said to talk to no one. But he didn't know she had already talked to Mrs. Ford and needed to warn her to stay quiet. If he had known that, he would have told her to go.

The car started without a problem. As much as she missed the old Challenger she had driven into Bald Eagle Falls for the first time, Clementine's VW Bug was much more reliable. Despite its age, it had been well maintained during the years that Clementine had driven it, and nothing but a minor tune-up had been needed when the Challenger met its fate and Erin needed something to drive.

And it was a fun little car. People certainly knew who she was when they saw the yellow Beetle coming.

It was very visible. Very easy to follow her progress as she went through the few streets of Bald Eagle Falls back to her house.

But it was too late to get something less easy to pick out of a crowd— a little white compact favored by all the rental companies.

Then again, if someone knew that Erin was at the nursing home, chances were they knew where she lived. They wouldn't need to follow her progress through town. They would just go back to her house and wait for her there. She would return sooner or later, even if she went to Auntie Clem's first or made a run into the city to deal with the doctor or do some shopping. Sooner or later, Erin would return home.

And that was where Terry would be, so it would be the safest place for Erin, whether she was being observed or not.

She hit the gas, navigating quickly. She wasn't being chased by anything but her own demons, but she wanted to get home without giving herself any more time to think about it.

In a few minutes, she was home. Following the same principle of not allowing herself time to think, she parked in the garage and made her way immediately into the house.

She would focus on dinner. Terry would be there in a few minutes. He would reassure her that she didn't have anything to worry about; he would be there to protect her if there were anyone unsavory gunning for her.

But Erin couldn't focus on making any food. She opened and closed the fridge and cupboards mindlessly, without any idea what they contained. She was listening for Terry's truck. He had said he wouldn't be long, and she expected him to be home within a few minutes.

Unless he got distracted by something else. Unless there was an emergency call that he had to follow up on. There were too many things that could have taken him away.

Orange Blossom was underfoot demanding food, so she went through the motions of playing with him for a moment and then feeding him.

She heard the truck engine as it pulled in front of the house and then went quiet. She looked out the front window to verify that it was Terry's vehicle rather than anyone else and was reassured by the sight of the big black truck. Terry and K9 got out and walked up the sidewalk. A woman joined them whom Erin didn't recognize immediately. Terry stopped to greet her and let her walk with him. She was an older, plump woman, maybe in her late sixties, wearing a shapeless dress that didn't do her figure any favors. She was carrying a casserole dish wrapped in a towel.

Maybe Erin wouldn't have to make supper after all. They could eat whatever the woman had brought while they talked things over.

Erin disarmed the burglar alarm as Terry walked up. He unlocked the door and entered first, looking at the alarm panel to see that she had disarmed it, and then inviting the woman to come in with him.

K9 was sniffing the air, watching the woman with great interest. Maybe he wanted some of the tuna casserole or whatever she had brought.

"Someone to see you, Erin," Terry said unnecessarily.

Erin still didn't recognize the woman's face. She looked vaguely familiar, but nothing that Erin could place. Maybe she had met a relative and saw a family resemblance.

"Let me just put this on the table for you," the woman said pleasantly. "It's hot."

Erin and Terry both stepped aside so that she could do so. She placed the casserole dish on the table, removed the towel, and turned around with a large black gun pointed at Terry.

CHAPTER 52

*E*rin's mouth hung open. She stared at the gun and didn't know what to do. She turned her head ever so slightly to look at Terry for his reaction. He was frozen, hands nowhere near his gun. He didn't have time to move and draw it.

"Put the dog in his kennel," the woman told Erin.

K9's teeth were bared and his ears back. He was ready to attack, given the command. But Terry didn't say anything. K9 was close to Terry's side and maybe Terry knew that the dog wouldn't have a chance to take the woman down before getting shot. No cop wanted to make the wrong move and take the chance of his partner getting killed.

"Do you want me to do it?" she asked Terry, unsure if she should follow the woman's instructions.

Terry's eyes were focused on the woman, evaluating everything about her. Erin was no expert but, to her, the woman looked like she was familiar with guns and knew exactly what she was doing.

"Yes," he agreed finally, his tone angry but under control. "K9. Kennel."

K9 gave a high-pitched whine. He did not want to leave his partner with this suspect. He had been trained in weapons, trained to disarm someone. But the situation was apparently too dangerous. They were all in close quarters, and Terry was obviously worried that one of them would be seriously wounded if they allowed K9 to attack and try to disarm her.

"Go," Terry ordered firmly.

K9 whined again, but he walked down the hall to the bedroom where his kennel was. With a glance at the woman, Erin followed K9 to latch the door once he was inside.

K9 went inside his kennel and lay down obediently. He was tense and confused. Erin could sense that he wanted to go out there and take the woman down, not to leave his partner in danger.

"I'm sorry, boy," Erin told him.

She fiddled with the latch, lifting it up and down to sound like she was locking it. She left the door resting in the closed position, but without the latch locking it into place. She didn't know if K9 would have a second chance to disarm the woman later. Maybe all he would be able to do was to raise the alarm if something happened to them. But it was something. It was the best she could do.

She trudged back down the hallway to where Terry and the strange woman stood.

"Who are you?" Erin demanded.

"You should have stayed in there, Erin," Terry told her.

That probably would have made more sense. She had been out of sight. She could have called the police. Let someone know that they were in danger. Instead, she had been too focused on figuring out who the woman was and why she was there. It hadn't even occurred to her to hide or use her phone.

"She has some sense," the woman said. "There's no point in cowering in the other room. I could just shoot you and then go and get her. This way, I didn't have to shoot you. She's better off doing what she's told than looking for ways to outmaneuver me."

"What is it you want?" Terry asked, in the calm, measured tone Erin had heard him use with offenders before. De-escalate the situation. Find out what the person wants and talk them down. Establish a relationship. A rapport.

"I want the two of you to stay out of family business; that's what I want."

Terry looked at Erin, then back at the woman. "Family business? What family business?"

"Don't try to pretend that you don't know. A sleepy little town like this doesn't have that much going on. You know exactly what I'm here about."

"We haven't had much of anything lately," Terry agreed. "Just routine, domestic, small-town stuff."

Of course, "family business" could only be one thing. She was from one of the clans and didn't like the way Erin had been digging into old clan business. But Erin didn't even know which clan she was from.

What Terry said was true. The only big, unusual crime recently had been the museum burglary, and the property had been recovered. They might not have caught the burglar, but any further investigation was being done in the city, not Bald Eagle Falls. Everyone was assuming that was where they would find the clues. The recipe book didn't lead to anything.

Or maybe the recipe book revealed more than they had thought. Maybe the burglar lived in Bald Eagle Falls and was still hiding out there.

But this woman was obviously not the person who had stolen the book and knocked Erin down in the street. She had not stood for hours in a tiny cupboard. She had not been riding down the street on a scooter.

Why did she care anything about the recipe book or the Hannah-Otis mystery, if that was really what she was there about? Erin couldn't understand why Willie said it was dangerous to even mention their names around anyone else. The long-ago deaths of Hannah and Otis didn't have anything to do with modern Bald Eagle Falls.

"Who are you?" she asked again.

"You don't know?" the woman asked. She looked at Erin with dark, glittering eyes. "Maybe you're not as smart as I gave you credit for."

"I don't know what this is all about. So maybe you can just let us go. We can't identify you or know what connection you have with any open cases, so…"

The woman gave a short, harsh laugh.

"So why don't I just let you go? No, I don't think so, my dear."

"Whatever this is about, I think you've gotten things turned around. I don't know who you are or why you are here, or why you have anything against me or Terry. We came home for supper… but I gather we're not having tuna casserole." She nodded toward the untouched casserole dish on the table.

The woman's gaze didn't shift.

"There are plenty of casserole recipes in that recipe book. Why don't you make one of those?"

"I don't have the recipe book anymore. I only had it for a few minutes. Then I turned it over to the police. I assume it's gone back to the police searching for the burglar, and then after they've caught and convicted him, it will go back to the original owner."

It wasn't until then she remembered that the original owner was Mrs. Ford. It wouldn't be going back to her. To one of her children? Grandchildren? Or maybe whoever had stolen it from the museum would follow up and find a way to make it disappear permanently.

"I don't care if you don't have it anymore. You read it. You know what was in it. And that is enough."

"This is all about a recipe book?"

"After you found the recipe book, you sent the Jackson girl to get the papers from where they were hidden. I don't know how you tied what was in the book to those records. I don't know how you knew where they were. But now you know the whole story. Don't pretend that you don't."

Erin opened her mouth to argue. But the woman had just told her not to, so she closed her mouth again and looked at Terry. What was their best course of action? To bluff the woman into thinking they knew what was going on? Pretend to know more than they did? Erin was sure that would backfire. But telling her the real story, that Vic had just happened to stumble upon those papers when chasing a cat, was not likely to pass muster. It sounded stupid.

"What does Vic have to do with anything?" she asked. "Those were my papers, on my property. That doesn't have anything to do with anyone else."

"I don't know how you convinced her to give them to you. You must hold something pretty good over her. Because as a Jackson… they were priceless."

"They were a few love letters written by a heartsick teen," Erin said. "They weren't important to anyone."

"You don't believe that."

Erin knew better now. She knew they were valuable but didn't know how or why. Someone was willing to kill for them. Or if Mrs. Ford had just died naturally in the nursing home, then someone was at least willing to hold a cop and a concussion victim at gunpoint over them.

She took a breath and let it out slowly. The one truth that had gotten the biggest reaction out of Willie. The thing that had surprised them all, even though it seemed innocuous to them…

"Hannah Dyson and Otis Jackson had a baby together," she told the woman. "Is that what you're talking about? That's the truth you don't want spread around? That someone around here carries the blood of both the Dysons and the Jacksons? I'm sure Jesse Andrews wasn't the only one."

"You know that the Dysons and Jacksons don't have any dealings."

"Not officially,"

"They don't!" she shouted. Her finger tightened on the trigger. Then she pulled herself back. Tamped down the emotions and faced Erin without any sign of the anger that had flooded her face an instant before.

"I wouldn't take a bet that no lovelorn teenage Romeos and Juliets ever got together, would you?" Erin asked the room in general. The woman didn't answer, and neither did Terry.

"You'll regret suggesting that."

"So that's all this is?" Erin asked. "You don't want anyone to know that Dysons and Jacksons could mix? Like you're two different species?"

"Quit playing ignorant. That is more aggravating than trying to fight me or get away." Her finger was still tight on the trigger. "Neither of which you are going to do today. Not if you want to live."

Erin's heart was pounding like a train engine, so fast that it hurt, but she tried to keep her reaction hidden and to respond coolly. "Is there a scenario where we *don't* die here?"

The gunwoman considered this for a moment, then shook her head. "No, there probably isn't. I can't think of a thing you could say or do that would convince me to let you go. You're too much of a danger to the clan."

Erin thought she saw Terry move just an inch out of the corner of her eye. He knew now that the woman didn't intend to let either of them live under any circumstance, and that probably changed his outlook on how to handle the situation. If they were both going to die anyway, then he would take a bigger risk if it meant they might escape with their lives. She didn't look toward the bedroom where K9 was in his kennel. Could Terry signal him without the woman realizing what he was doing? K9 wouldn't budge from the kennel without Terry telling him to.

Erin had not rearmed the burglar alarm when Terry and the visitor had come in the door, which was why she didn't hear Willie come in the back door. Willie might not look like it, but he could walk as silently as a ghost. Erin had been in various situations with him before, both inside buildings and out in the wild, in a forest or a cave, and Willie walked like a cat.

CHAPTER 53

"Leave them alone," Willie said in a low, measured tone.

The woman jumped and looked at him, glancing away from Terry and Erin for an instant. But Terry did not jump forward and try to wrestle the gun out of her hand like a TV show cop. He put his left hand on Erin's arm, his touch telling her to stay still and not try anything, while his right slid a little closer to his holster.

Willie was holding a gun pointed at the woman, his hand steady and no tension or stress showing in his face or stance. He nodded at Terry and Erin but didn't speak to them directly.

"Mona," Willie said. "These people have not done anything."

"They haven't done anything?" Mona snapped. "You have no idea how hard we have worked to keep rumors like this from spreading. You have no idea the kind of surveillance and networking needed to stay on top of every hint or whisper that might grow into something more substantial. This is a huge breach! It cannot be allowed to go on."

"You are not to do anything to harm them." Willie's voice was steel, brooking no argument.

Erin blinked at him in astonishment. She knew Willie. She knew he wasn't involved with the Dyson clan anymore. Terry thought he might still be, but Erin knew in her heart that he wasn't. His involvement with them was clean and professional. Working on computers, networking, security systems—technical support. He wasn't involved in any of their criminal ventures.

The woman, Mona, did not change her stance or say anything to indicate that she intended to obey Willie. Another confirmation that he had absolutely nothing to do with the clan.

"You think you can give orders now?" Mona snapped. "All these years, you have refused to take a position, and now you think you can?"

"I don't want to be involved. But I will not stand by while you do anything to harm Erin and Officer Piper. I've already talked to them to see what they know. Erin has given me the papers. She gave the recipe book to the police back in the city. Officer Piper has looked over the old homicide file and has not found anything new. The identity of the victim cannot be confirmed. Neither can his killer. Whatever happened all those years ago rests in the past." He moved a couple of steps closer to Mona. "There is no need to do anything drastic. Just put it to bed and forget about it."

"Are you stepping up? Identifying yourself and taking your place?"

Willie was silent for a long time. Erin waited for him to say yes. To do whatever he needed to do to help Erin and Terry escape the woman. She didn't follow the conversation entirely, but could see no reason why Willie should not identify himself, explain how he was related to the family, that he was one of them.

"Is that the only way you will stop?"

She snorted. "I'll stop if you shoot me."

"I don't want it to come to that. I'd have a target on my back for the rest of my life."

"It wouldn't last long," she consoled, sarcastic.

The silence stretched out still longer. Erin could feel every beat of her heart pounding in her temples. She really needed to lie down and have a nap now. She had been up for too long.

Willie exhaled. "Fine. As you already know… I am the heir."

CHAPTER 54

*E*rin looked at Terry, confused. He didn't seem any more enlightened than Erin was on the matter. She could only guess at Willie's meaning.

"You are the heir?" Mona repeated.

"I am the grandson of Jesse Andrews. Great-grandson of Hannah Dyson."

"The oldest grandson of Jesse Andrews?"

Willie's voice was tired. Resigned. "Yes."

"You have denied your lineage before. Refused to take your place in the family. Unless you do that, you can't give me orders. You're just as much a threat to the family as these two are, operating as a lone wolf with no allegiance to the family."

Willie was a step closer to them. Erin could see him swallow hard before answering her again.

"Yes. I acknowledge my name and line. And I have the proof."

Mona's gun slowly lowered. She turned to look over her shoulder, directly into Willie's face. Erin couldn't interpret the expression on her face.

Terry's gun cleared its holster and he held it pointed at Mona, with one eye on Willie, who still had his gun aimed at Mona.

"Put it away, Officer Piper," Willie said, his gun hand still not wavering even a hair. "Let's keep this all civil. Allow me to introduce you to Mona Dyson, matriarch of the Dyson clan."

Willie's grandmother? Aunt? Erin hadn't retained enough of the family trees she had been studying the last few days. All the names seemed to have flown right out of her head. She blamed it on the concussion, but she could remember her schoolteachers criticizing her for being so empty-headed. She had never been a very good student.

"I thought Dwight was the head of the clan," Terry said, frowning. He hadn't lowered his gun yet, but he didn't seem intent on using it. His eyes moved between Mona and Willie, trying to monitor them while sorting out what Willie was saying.

Willie looked at Mona as if for permission to talk to Terry about it. Mona just pressed her lips tightly together. If Willie's declaration now made him her superior, then the decision was his. He didn't need her consent.

"The Dyson family has always had men as their figureheads," Willie explained. "One of the reasons for that is to protect the actual authority over the clan. Which has always been a matriarch."

Erin was stunned. The Dyson clan was run by women? And had been for decades? Ever since the feud had started?

Willie read Erin's face and nodded his agreement. "Starting with Lucy Dyson. Only her daughter did not survive, so the authority passed to her sister rather than to Hannah."

"But she made it clear from the beginning that when Jesse Andrews or his heir were ready to take over leadership of the clan, that authority would pass to him," Mona explained. "Jesse himself never had any desire to involve himself in… women's petty jealousies," Mona sneered the words. She rolled her eyes and shook her head at his foolishness. "He would never acknowledge the power of the clan. What we could be and what we could do. He asked how he could love his mother's family and hate his father's family, as if there were any comparison."

"Maybe to him, there wasn't," Erin said, though she knew she should just keep quiet and wait for it to all blow over. Willie had stepped up and would straighten everything out. Mona would go home, and Erin and Terry could continue their lives as usual.

"No difference between the womb that bore him and hand that rocked his cradle and the man who abandoned him when he was his most vulnerable? The man who didn't even have the honor to stay and give him a name? How could a person *like that* be considered equal to those who brought him up, who fed and clothed him and raised him to be a strong man?"

"If Otis was the young John Doe that Terry found mentioned in the files, then maybe it wasn't his fault that he never went back to Hannah and the baby," Erin argued. "Any more than it was Hannah's fault that the baby was taken away from her or that she died before she was even an adult."

"The heir had to go to a family who would be able to raise him properly. Hannah was too young and had already shown herself to be a poor judge of character and her propensity for making wrong choices. Lucy did that for Hannah's own good."

"And if Otis was killed," Erin persisted in trying to make her point.

"There is no proof he was the young man who was killed," Mona pointed out. "You have looked at it again and found nothing to indicate who he was or that he was even local. He was some wandering waif from the train. Trash. Someone no one even cared about enough to identify."

"The remains were too decomposed for identification," Terry told her. "It wasn't because no one cared. They didn't have the forensic technology that we have now. Being able to produce a sketch from a skull or DNA."

Mona just stared at him as if his very existence were offensive to her. And maybe it was. She had been planning to kill him, after all, and Willie had insisted she leave him alone.

"Put the gun away, Terry," Willie prompted. "No one is going to be shot here tonight."

But he still hadn't put his away, and Mona's was still in her hand, even though she had lowered it at Willie's command.

Terry weighed the situation and eventually lowered his gun and secured it in his belt.

"Mona, you're done here. Go home," Willie told her.

A wave of red spread over her face. But she kept her rage under control. She swept past Erin and Terry out the front door, slamming it behind her.

The three of them stood there frozen for what seemed like a long time, listening for her to return or for the sound of a vehicle driving away. Eventually, Willie moved. He went to the window and used the tip of the gun barrel to twitch the curtain to the side slightly and look out to the street. He stood there for a moment, then turned back to them.

"She's gone."

Terry armed the burglar alarm.

Erin whistled and called K9, and he came racing down the hall, then stopped and looked at them, confused, his ears moving back and forth as he analyzed the situation. He settled on baring his teeth at Willie, the only one still holding a gun.

Terry looked at Willie, his jaw clenched. "So now the truth comes out," he said. "After repeatedly saying that you have nothing to do with the Dysons."

"I didn't. You heard her. I've turned down any position in the clan multiple times."

"Until now."

"It was the only way I could see to get you and Erin out of this situation safely. Nothing has changed. I'm still the same person I was."

"Nothing has changed? Except that you are now the leader of the Dyson clan?"

Willie cleared his throat. "I will do what I can to unwind it tomorrow." He sighed. "It isn't going to be an easy task. They do not like to be trifled with."

There was the sound of the back door opening, and everyone turned quickly toward it, expecting to see the angry Dyson woman there again. But it was Vic, tapping her security code into the burglar alarm so it wouldn't go off, and then looking at the three of them.

"Hey... what's going on?" Her eyes went from one to the other and lingered on Willie's gun, which he slid into a holster inside his jeans. "What is all this?"

CHAPTER 55

*I*t took a while to explain everything to Vic, trying to sort out all the threads of what they had discovered, while at the same time trying to keep Willie and Terry from each other's throats. They were growling at each other like dogs guarding their territory, cop and crime boss being natural enemies. Erin defrosted some cupcakes and tried to keep everything civil.

Willie did not want her to talk about his direct line to Hannah Dyson and Otis Jackson, but Erin ignored his growls of protest and did anyway. He had already defended her from a Dyson with a gun; did he think that telling Vic was really a risk? He should have told her the details himself.

Vic gaped over the confirmation that Willie was, in fact, the direct descendant of the two rival families. But that wasn't the biggest surprise to her. She barely turned a hair at the news that Willie had claimed his place as the heir to the leadership of the Dyson clan, focused instead on the fact that Mona had been the de facto leader of the clan and the various Dyson men that she had known to have led the Dyson clan over her lifetime had simply been figureheads, there to protect the matriarchs who had the actual authority within the family.

"The Dyson women lead the gang?" she asked in disbelief. "How could that be? It's always been the men."

Willie shook his head. "It's always been the women. It was the women who started feuding over recipes and jealousies and social standing. It was Lucy Dyson who decided that a Jackson was not good enough for her daughter. The women preserved the feud for generations, making sure that there would never be any reconciliation or truce between the families."

Vic shook her head in disbelief. "The only thing that would surprise me more is if you told me that the women are actually the leaders of the Jackson clan, too."

"They followed a more traditional structure," Willie said with a smile. "At least, as far as I know. But who is to say? Unless you are inside the elite levels, you wouldn't know."

Erin was troubled by the idea of Willie now sliding into place as the heir to the Dyson power structure. He was not suited to it. He had left the Dyson organization after five years of service. It wasn't what he wanted to do. He had no interest in the power of the position. He was a loner. And he was generally a law-abiding person. He didn't like violence. She was relieved he had been able to stop Mona without anyone getting hurt, but what would the consequences be to him?

Eventually, Willie and Vic returned to Vic's apartment, and Erin and Terry headed to bed.

"It's been quite the day," Terry murmured in Erin's ear. "Try to get some rest. Don't worry about anything. Tomorrow will take care of itself."

Which was nonsense, as far as Erin was concerned. Things didn't just take care of themselves. There was plenty to be concerned about.

But her concussed brain was worn out and, despite her worries, Erin fell into an exhausted sleep soon after her head hit the pillow.

Hannah looked out the window, wondering when she would be able to see Otis again. The flag was not up on the mailbox, so there was no letter from him waiting for retrieval. She looked forward to the next opportunity she would have to nestle in his arms, touch his face, and kiss his lips.

While she knew her mother disapproved, she couldn't help herself. She had to be with him again. They were in love, and she believed that God would forgive any trespasses they made, as long they were faithful to each other.

Mama had been baking pies all morning in the summer kitchen, and Hannah found herself wandering over to the kitchen to see what she had made and what they would have for supper. While she was frequently queasy in the morning, her appetite in the afternoon and evening more than made up for it, and it was difficult not to overindulge.

There was the crack of a rifle in the distance. A hunter on their land? Her father had taken the train into the city, so she knew it wasn't him. Just someone on one of the adjacent properties,

Mama wasn't in the summer kitchen. She had probably taken a break to cool down, or to feed the chickens or do some other chore that Hannah had neglected to perform. The difficulty of getting up and getting moving in the morning had impacted Hannah's ability to complete the chores that she had been tasked with since she was a child.

The pies looked delicious, lined up on the counter to cool. The tops all golden brown. The summer berries would be delicious. And she looked forward to the apple pies that would come in the fall. Apple pie was one of her favorites.

As she turned to leave, she saw a stack of mail at the end of the counter. Mama had picked it up earlier. Hannah moved closer to look at the mail, dread growing in her heart. Had Otis left a note for her? Mama would want to know what it said. She would not be happy about Otis meeting Hannah alone, rather than just attending dances or community functions with him. Young people should be supervised and prevented from falling into transgression. Hannah understood why now better than ever before. Her forays into romance with Otis had confirmed just how strong the temptations of the flesh were.

Hannah thumbed through the envelopes and found one addressed to her in Otis's spiky writing. She was relieved at first and happy to have received a communication from him.

But then she noticed that the flap had been opened. It was not torn, but it was open. The glue must have been too scant.

The dread reasserting itself even more strongly, Hannah drew out the note and unfolded it.

Dearest Hannah…

She had never seen him again.

CHAPTER 56

he difficult days of pregnancy and birth had followed. Then Hannah held the baby in her arms and was comforted that even if Otis never returned, she at least had a part of him. Something she could hold and cuddle and remember Otis's gentle touch and whispered words to her during their stolen moments. A balm to her broken heart.

Until she woke up one morning and the baby was gone. Mama had stolen that one solace from her, and her broken heart was ripped out of her. For days, she lay in bed. The days stretched into weeks and months, and although she was physically able to get out of bed and resume her chores, she didn't have the strength even to read the book that lay in her lap for long hours as she stared out the window at the empty road.

Eventually, she could no longer stand to be there. In a place with no love. She left without telling anyone and with no destination in mind. She took with her the small box of keepsakes. Hannah didn't want her mother finding them, reading through her private things. She would hide them. Burning them would be better, but she wasn't sure she could do that.

She just walked, letting her feet take her where they would. And where her feet took her was their old meeting place. The place where Otis had told her to meet him that last day. But she hadn't gone. Knowing that her mother had read the letter, Hannah had decided she would rather not be caught in the act of meeting her lover. She would stay away, and Otis would know they had been discovered or something else had happened to keep Hannah away. They would make other arrangements in a day or two when the coast was clear.

But that day had never come. She had never received another communication from him. Never seen or heard from him again. She was afraid he had been hurt and left her. And afraid that something had happened to keep him away.

It all seemed like a lifetime ago. Like it had happened to someone else. A younger, happier girl. An innocent who didn't know what love or heartbreak felt like.

She walked restlessly up and down, pacing as if expecting him to come. But of course, what her mother had said had been true. "Otis Jackson is never coming back."

She weaved in and out between the trees, not wanting to trample the grass down by walking back and forth across the same patch of ground a hundred times. She wanted the wilderness to stay the same. Serene. Pristine. It was as if no man or woman had ever walked through it or met together.

Behind the old tumbled-down cottage where, rumor had it, a witch had once lived, she saw a bundle of clothes left there to rot. With the poverty of so many of the residents of the county, why would anyone waste clothes that way? If they didn't want them, plenty of people did.

Hannah moved in for a closer look. Maybe a transient had left them there while he went for a dip in the nearby stream. Or as he went to pick up an animal he had shot or check a trap. The clothes might not be abandoned.

She saw that they were not, in fact, abandoned, but that the owner was still there with them. Wearing them. Someone who had been lying there for a long time.

The march of time was slow, and he was still, horribly, recognizable. At least to her. Despite the processes of decomposition and predation, she knew the clothing and the height and build of the body, though he now appeared deflated, as if he were melting into the ground beneath him.

Crying out, Hannah knelt at his side. Though she was initially afraid to touch him, she forced herself to. Didn't she love this man? Hadn't she said that nothing would ever change that? He was still her Otis and she had been granted one more chance to see him.

She searched his pockets, looking for a keepsake, and found a ring. It was plain silver, with no markings, but what more could she have expected from a young man still finding his way in the world? Until he found his way out of it. She slipped the ring on her finger. It was a perfect fit.

He had kept his promise to her, or had tried to. He had never intended to abandon her.

Hannah wanted to leave something for him. They would meet at the judgment bar on the other side. She no longer had to mourn his absence. But she wanted to mark the occasion.

She opened her keepsake box, unsure what to do. Leave a note in his pocket, one last profession of love? It would rot away with the rest, and she wanted something that would last.

The only thing in her box that fit the bill was a tiny music box. It had charmed her as a child. She had played it over and over again as she went to sleep. It was fitting that it would play Otis to sleep this last time.

She wound it and placed it in the pocket from which she had removed the ring. As it played, she found a pretty sheet of paper in her keepsake box and wrote one final note before hiding the box. She wondered who would find it, and when, or if it would just turn to dust in the abandoned shack as the years passed.

Erin awoke with a gasp, as if she had been holding her breath for a long time. She sat up, trying to calm her rapidly beating heart, and reached for her phone beside her bed.

"Erin?" Terry murmured. "Are you okay?"

"She wrote a note," Erin told him. "She wrote me a note, and I have to read it."

Terry turned over. "What?"

Erin turned on the phone and went to her photos, where she had saved a picture of each of Hannah's notes, letters, photos, and clippings. She went through each carefully, looking for Hannah's final words.

"Erin," Terry asked again, propping himself on his elbow to see what she was doing. "What did you say?"

"Shh. Just give me a minute. I have to find it."

At last, she found the little note penned in Hannah's neatest writing.

Neath summer's sun, two hearts beat as one,
Melody of love, heavenly song.
Baby's laugh rings, pure and true,
Bond unbroken, we bid adieu.
Soon shall we meet face to face,
Join in a dance, a sweet embrace.
Music box plays, our hearts will sing,
Our timeless tune to heaven bring.

"It's here," Erin told him, pushing the phone into his hand so he could read it. "There is your proof that the John Doe was Otis Jackson. Read it."

Terry rubbed his eyes and stared at the screen. He took a long time to read through it, then shook his head.

"It mentions a music box," he admitted. "But I don't know that it is proof of anything."

"She found him and left her music box with the body. That's why his parents couldn't identify him by the music box. Hannah gave it to Otis, he wasn't giving it to her."

"It's possible, but I don't know how—"

"She was so depressed after the baby was born and they took him away. I think when she found Otis's body, she just gave in. After leaving him with the music box and writing the poem, she went home and died."

Terry didn't bother trying to tell her that it was all speculation. He just put his hand on her knee and let her go on.

"And do you know what the worst part is?" Erin asked. "I think Hannah's mother is the one who shot Otis."

Terry didn't try to cover his surprise at this statement. "Why would she do that?"

"She saw the note Otis had written Hannah and left in her mailbox arranging for a tryst. She probably already knew Hannah was pregnant because of her morning sickness. So Lucy went out to meet him. Hannah heard the shot in the distance but didn't know what it meant until months later."

"When you believe Hannah found the body."

"Found him, and left him with the music box, wrote the poem for him and hid all of her papers in the shack."

"Why would she do that?"

"Because she didn't want her mother to find them. She was heart-broken and could see no other way out."

Terry took his hand from Erin's knee and massaged her back in slow, soothing circles. Erin rubbed her burning eyes, put her phone down, and lay beside him.

She curled up against his body and thought about Hannah.

EPILOGUE

$\mathcal{E}$rin finished arranging the cookies in the display case and stepped back so Vic could match the hand-printed cards to each variety. She took a deep breath in, inhaling the sweet smells of fresh baking.

"Lucy's vanilla sandwich cookies," Vic said as she placed the last card.

"But you didn't put Lucy's name on the card, did you?"

"No," Vic agreed. "And they're right next to Eleanor Jackson's carrot cookies. Just like in the recipe book."

Erin smiled her approval. Maybe she couldn't reconcile the Dyson and Jackson clans with each other, or use their names on the new gluten-free recipes she had created, or prove to the police department's satisfaction that the old John Doe remains were those of Otis Jackson. But she could put Lucy and Eleanor's cookies together, side by side, once more. Old friends reunited and reconciled.

Mary Lou, one of the first customers in the door, smiled to see Erin there.

"How are you feeling, Erin? Back to yourself?"

"Nearly," Erin agreed. She had been putting in longer and longer days, shaking the last few effects of the concussion. She almost felt normal again.

Mary Lou looked into the display case and her eyes went immediately to Lucy's cookies. Her face lit up.

"Vanilla sandwich cookies! Well, I do declare! Do you know what we used to call these when I was a child? Custard creams. It has been ages since I had homemade custard creams. I'll take four of those, please. And… two of the carrot cookies. I haven't even seen those since I was a little girl."

Erin guessed that the carrot cookies were for Mary Lou herself, even though she rarely indulged in sweet treats. Erin put the six cookies together into a small box for Mary Lou, once again feeling a little thrill at daring to put them together after all that had happened.

She smiled at Mary Lou. "Y'all enjoy those cookies."

Did you enjoy this book? Reviews and recommendations are vital to making a book successful.

Please leave a review at your favorite book store or review site and share it with your friends.

Don't miss the following bonus material:
Sign up for mailing list to get a free ebook
Read a sneak preview chapter
Other books by P.D. Workman
Learn more about the author

Your First Bite – Cozy Mystery Starter Pack

Get Your First Taste of Murder and Muffins at pdworkman.com! Start your cozy escape with a free ebook + audiobook, printable recipe cards, and more.

MOCK APPLE ALIBI

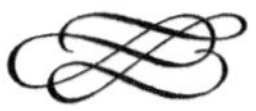

PREVIEW CHAPTER 1

*E*verything was quiet in Bald Eagle Falls. Erin stood at the front window of Auntie Clem's Bakery, looking out at Main Street. Trees and flowers bloomed along the road. A gentle breeze carried the light scent of dogwood into the bakery.

It was too quiet.

The town looked just as it had the first time she had rolled into town to claim her inheritance from Clementine after an absence of twenty years. When her mother had taken her away from Bald Eagle Falls that fateful night, Erin had not had any idea that it was the last time she would see the town until she was an adult. Driving by the charming storefronts with their colorful sunshade canopies, she had thought that it was just a trip like any other. They were going into the city. Maybe for shopping or visiting a friend, she hadn't really had any idea then. Her parents were not in the habit of consulting with her about their plans.

Returning to Bald Eagle Falls had been like coming home, even though it had never been her permanent home. Just where they visited Aunt Clementine and crashed at her place for a while. Much like they had crashed with many other friends and relatives during Erin's short lifetime, living a somewhat nomadic existence as her parents moved from one short-term job to another.

Erin had loved staying with Clementine and going with her to work in what had then been a tea shop. Erin had been a mature child and enjoyed helping Clementine with the tea orders and baking cookies, but she must have gotten underfoot sometimes. She couldn't imagine having a seven-year-old working alongside her at Auntie Clem's Bakery. But Clementine had always been kind and patient with her and Erin couldn't remember her ever getting angry or impatient about her mistakes or clumsiness.

Main Street seemed to be frozen in time. The cars and clothing styles had changed. Some of the storefronts had changed. Auntie Clem's was now across the street from the storefront she had inherited from Clementine. But in other ways, it looked and felt just the way it had when Erin had been there twenty years before.

"Is everything okay?" Harold asked. He leaned on the top of the display case, his lanky teenage body relaxed, acne-pocked face curious.

"It's too quiet," Erin said, looking up and down the street again. "I don't like it."

"You're worried about not getting enough business?" Harold asked.

"No…" There was a momentary lull in the arrival of customers, but Erin knew it would pick up again as people left work and started to think about what they wanted to make for supper, or for breakfast or lunch the next day. "It isn't customers I am worried about. It's… I was expecting everything to change. I thought that with Willie claiming leadership of the Dyson clan, there would be a lot of… unrest."

"You're worried that there *isn't* a gang war going on in front of the store?" Vic asked as she came out of the kitchen with a tray of muffins. "You were hoping for gunplay?" As usual, her long blond hair was neatly tucked away in a baker's hat, and Erin's shorter dark hair was forever escaping bobby pins and getting in her face.

"No!" Erin's cheeks got hot. If anyone should be worried, it was Vic. She was the one who had belonged to the opposing clan, born into the Jackson family, and whose romantic partner had just claimed leadership of the Dysons.

Maybe because Vic had already been disowned by the Jackson family for being transgender, she thought she was safe from anyone targeting her for her choice of partner. Or maybe she felt that because Willie was now the leader of the Dysons, no one would dare lay a finger on her.

But she was the one who had the most to worry about. The Jacksons could easily target her because she was important to Willie. Or because she had turned traitor and joined the Dysons—even though she hadn't. Vic didn't want anything to do with either clan. Raised to hate and fear the Dysons, she had been pretty upset when she had first found out that Willie had neglected to mention his history with the clan to her. It had nearly broken them up for good. But Vic had eventually accepted that Willie had done his time as a Dyson soldier and wasn't involved in clan business anymore.

Until now. Erin had expected her young employee to blow up when Willie accepted the leadership of the clan, even though the only reason he had done it was to prevent Erin and her sweetheart, Officer Terry Piper, from being killed. But Vic hadn't had much to say about Willie's claim on the leadership of the Dyson family as a direct descendent of Hannah Dyson.

"Why aren't you worried?" Erin asked Vic. "Aren't you concerned about Dyson members gunning for Willie because they don't like someone who has previously turned his back on the clan suddenly taking over? Or about someone coming after *you* to hurt him?"

Vic was silent as she arranged muffins in the display case with practiced ease. She looked back over her shoulder at Harold. "Shouldn't you be doing the washing up back there?"

Harold straightened up and nodded, agreeing that he should get back to his duties.

"Yes, Miss Victoria." He walked through the door into the kitchen to do as he was told.

"Of course I'm worried," Vic admitted. "I know that sooner or later, something is going to happen." She looked out the front window, scanning up and down the street to reassure herself, as Erin had, that it was still quiet. "But I don't think there is any point in scaring Harold about it. Or saying anything to any of the customers. For now, just... wait..."

"Pretend there is nothing to be worried about?"

"What good is it going to do to fuss about it?" Vic challenged. "Is that going to stop it from happening? Is it going to make you feel better? Make you better prepared?"

"Well, no," Erin admitted. Vic was barely out of her teens, but she had been raised with clan warfare and politics, and had wisdom beyond her years as a result. "Although, if there is something I can do to be better prepared for what's coming… I would like to do it."

Vic nodded her agreement and understanding. "We'll talk about that later. For now, since there are no customers, why don't we take the opportunity to talk about your mock apple pie?"

She said it as she turned around and walked back into the kitchen, raising her voice so that Erin could still hear her with her back turned.

Erin left her place at the window. Vic was right, of course, standing around looking out the window, worrying that when something terrible was going to happen, wouldn't do anything but give her an ulcer and keep her from her work. The actual running of the bakery was her life's work. A clan war wasn't going to change that. No matter what happened, people would still need to buy bread. The clans didn't have any reason to target the bakery. It would stay open and keep running no matter which clan had the upper hand in their ongoing, generations-long feud.

"What exactly *is* a mock apple pie?" Harold was asking as Erin followed Vic into the kitchen.

"It is an apple pie made without apples," Vic told him. She took a binder out of the niche under the upper cabinets where they stored several binders of information on procedure, ingredients, and vendors. The slim binder contained copies of the recipes that had been in the vintage recipe book published by the Bald Eagle Falls Women's League, the original of which was no longer in Erin's possession.

Vic flipped through the binder to find the recipe for mock apple pie.

"It doesn't have apples in it," Harold repeated doubtfully.

"Nope. No apples."

"Why would anyone make apple pie without apples?"

"Because sometimes, historically, apples were very expensive to ship across the country and spoiled faster than something like crackers, which could sit on the shelf for months."

"Crackers?"

"Ritz crackers. There was even a recipe on the back of the cracker box."

Harold looked at Vic, his brows furrowed, then turned to Erin, waiting for her to tell him it was all just a joke.

"It's true," Erin said. "During the depression and wartime, women made apple pie with Ritz crackers."

"And no apples," he said.

"And no apples."

Harold shook his head like it was the most bizarre thing he had ever heard, and Erin had to agree with him. When she had first heard of mock apple pie, she hadn't believed it either. But she had talked to several women who had eaten it and assured her it was a fairly convincing fake.

"It has to do with the spices," she told Harold, "and lemon juice for tartness. Apparently, the way you prepare the crackers in the filling gives them a texture that is like cooked apples."

Harold shook his head slowly. "Ain't that something!" he declared. "And how are you going to make gluten-free mock apple pie? Ritz crackers are not gluten-free, and if you get the gluten-free crackers, won't they just dissolve without any gluten to hold them together?"

Vic turned and looked at Erin, raising her brows. They'd already had this discussion, and Erin had been researching different approaches to the problem. Make her own gluten-free crackers that would stay together better? She was sure that the texture still wouldn't be right.

"Okay," Erin got closer to Harold and Vic so that it was easier to hold the conversation without raised voices and the possibility of anyone who came into the bakery overhearing them. "I've been working on it, and I have a few ideas about the direction to go…"

The bells over the door jingled and Erin hurried out to the front to greet her customer. It was a face that she didn't recognize, which instantly sent her heart racing. The twenty-something baby-faced young man did not look dangerous, but as with mock apple pie, looks could be deceiving. Young men were recruited as street-level soldiers in both clans, and this fresh-faced stranger could be there looking for trouble. Plenty of people knew Willie's girlfriend worked at the bakery.

Erin forced a smile to her lips and inquired pleasantly. "Welcome to Auntie Clem's Bakery. How can I help you?"

The man pulled something out of his pocket, and for an instant, the sun's reflection off a metallic surface convinced her it was a gun. But before she could react, the young man held a phone out in front of him, and the shutter-click whir told Erin that he had snapped a picture of her. She kept her smile steady.

The customer stepped up to the display case and scanned the rows. The camera tipped Erin off as to what he was looking for.

"Morning sunshine muffins?" she guessed.

His face lit up. "Yes, how did you know?"

The late Gerald Montgomery's social media followers were still making pilgrimages to Bald Eagle Falls to eat the last thing he had sampled before his death.

It still bothered Erin that the strawberry compote surprise at the center of the morning sunshine muffins had given Montgomery an anaphylactic reaction that had killed him within minutes. But she wasn't about to stop making them as a result. Not when people traveled across the country and around the world just for the chance to eat one of the muffins.

She took a muffin from the display case and placed it on one of the garish gold paper plates they now stocked for just such an occasion. If people were going to make the purchase of a morning sunshine muffin a social media event, Erin was going to get as much mileage as she could from it. She inserted a toothpick mounted with the words *Auntie Clem's Bakery* into the top of the muffin. She set it in the best position for the Instagrammer to take pictures from the most advantageous angles.

He snapped a few more pictures, but as the young man reached out to take it, Erin removed it from the top of the display case and put it on the counter beside the till. "Payment before tasting," she informed him, and rang it up. He paid with a twenty-dollar bill and a smile, telling her to keep the change. Erin put the change into the tip jar to be divided among the employees.

He recorded himself taking a big bite of the infamous muffin, pausing a dramatic moment to see if it would kill him, then declaring how delicious it was and giving a thumbs-up and a challenge to his followers to make the trip to Bald Eagle Falls in Tennessee to taste it for themselves.

Erin smiled and nodded and saw the customer out the door. As much as she disliked the morbidness of people's fascination with the "murder muffins," she couldn't deny that she made a very good profit on them—this latest customer was not the first to give her twenty dollars, or even more, for a single muffin—and the muffins attracted a lot of customers to Auntie Clem's that would not otherwise have even been in the vicinity. They often stayed at the bed and breakfast and came back again to sample her other wares.

"Erin, have you heard anything from Charley?"

Erin turned to look at Vic, who was standing in the doorway of the kitchen, frowning.

"Uh, no, I haven't heard anything." Erin looked at the clock on the wall. Charley was on the afternoon shift and should have been there twenty minutes ago. "She must have slept in. Can you give her a call?"

"I already have. There's no answer."

"Oh, good grief," Erin snapped. She wasn't irritated at Vic, but at Charley. Her half-sister had been a much more reliable employee than Erin had expected her to be, but occasionally she still flaked out and didn't show up on time for her shifts. They only scheduled her for the afternoon shift so she could sleep until noon and still get there in time. If they were really stuck for help with the early morning time slot, Charley would arrive at the end of her day, after partying or whatever else she did past midnight, and would put in a few hours before going home and going to bed.

Erin wanted to gripe about this not being a good day for Charley not to show up for work, but in truth, it wasn't any worse than any other day; she was just tense and wound up.

That was just Charley. She would end up calling them at three o'clock, embarrassed that she had slept in and asking whether they needed her to help with the last few hours.

Erin relieved her stress by swearing quietly under her breath, and she addressed Vic in a calm, cool voice. "Would you see whether Bella is free? I think she only has morning classes on Wednesday."

"Sure," Vic agreed. "No problem."

She returned to the kitchen. The bells tinkled and Erin turned her attention back to her new customer. Mary Lou usually came either first thing in the morning when the bakery opened or at the end, just before Erin locked the doors; it was unusual for her to be there in the early after-noon. Mary Lou worked down the street at the General Store, so she usually worked the rest of the day and didn't come to the bakery on her break, if she took one.

"Hi, Mary Lou," Erin greeted her warmly. "It's nice to see you."

"Good afternoon," Mary Lou returned. She smoothed her unwrinkled pantsuit over her hips and perused the display case. "I only have a minute, but I just found out that Cam will be coming for supper and wanted to make sure I had something nice for dessert. I think maybe… a variety of cookies?" she suggested, with slight frown lines between her eyes. "Yes… a selection of twelve cookies. Then everyone can be sure to have one of their favorites."

"Sure," Erin agreed. She got out a box and selected several different kinds of cookies for the Cox men. Mary Lou's husband, Roger, and sons

Joshua and Campbell, would enjoy the sweets. However, as this order was over and above Mary Lou's usual carefully budgeted order, she worried it would strain the family's meager finances. "Can I unload some day-old goods on you?" she asked. "My freezer is full to bursting, and I'm going to have to start throwing stuff in the garbage. Maybe… some rolls for dinner tonight, bagels for breakfast? I know you always plan your menu before-hand, but if you could see your way to taking some off my hands, that would be helpful. Maybe Cam will stay over for breakfast?"

Mary Lou glanced over her shoulder to verify that she was the only customer in the store and none of her friends would hear about her accepting charity. Then she gave a quick nod. "Rolls and bagels would be lovely," she agreed.

"And maybe a couple of pizza shells?" Erin suggested, "Just in case Cam is looking for a midnight snack?"

"Okay," Mary Lou agreed. "Thank you, Erin."

"I'll just be a minute," Erin promised, and hurried into the kitchen to grab what she had promised from the day-old freezer. She wanted to make sure she handed it to Mary Lou and gave her a chance to get out of the store before anyone else arrived. Returning to the front, she bagged every-thing and rang up the cookie order at the till.

"You know you can always pop in the back door if you know of anyone who needs help," Erin reminded Mary Lou tactfully. "We always have day-old available, no questions asked."

"Of course," Mary Lou agreed with a nod. "You are very generous for caring for the community as you do."

She counted out change to pay her bill to the penny, and then was gone, headed back to the General Store.

Bella came in the front door just as Mary Lou left, turning her head to look at Mary Lou's retreating figure. She knew Mary Lou's schedule as well as Erin and was obviously surprised to see her.

"I thought I saw Campbell earlier," she said to Erin. "I guess that *was* him, and Mary Lou needed a little something extra for supper tonight."

"You guess correctly," Erin confirmed. "Thank you for coming in. I don't know what happened to Charley."

"Sure, no problem. Luckily, I was in town already, so getting here didn't take long."

Bella and her mother lived on a farm outside Bald Eagle Falls, and it would have taken her at least another half hour to get in if she'd not already been there.

"I appreciate you being able to drop everything to help us." Erin sighed. She moved back to give Bella room to pass her so she could wash up and get her apron on. Erin poked her head into the kitchen to talk to Vic. "Did Harold get on his way already?"

Vic nodded. She looked at her watch. "He should have made it back to school in time."

Both Harold and Bella were still in school, and worked around their class schedules. Harold had relief time for work experience some mornings, and Bella had organized her class schedule to give herself afternoons off a couple of times a week. Both were able to put some time in after school dismissed or on weekends. Erin enjoyed the younger employees' energy and interest level. Bella was a business student and hoped to run her own business after college. Not a bakery, but she hadn't decided what kind of a business it would be yet.

"Great. We're good for this afternoon, then."

Mock Apple Alibi, Book #25 of the *Auntie Clem's Bakery* culinary cozy mystery series by P.D. Workman can be purchased at pdworkman.com

ABOUT THE AUTHOR

P.D. Workman is a USA Today Bestselling author and multi-award winner, renowned for her prolific output of over 100 published works that span various genres. With a knack for crafting page-turners, Workman captivates readers with everything from cozy mysteries like the Auntie Clem's Bakery series to gripping young adult and suspense novels.

A prolific reader and writer since childhood, P.D. Workman crafts emotionally powerful stories that don't shy away from hard topics. Her books tackle mental illness, addiction, abuse, and trauma with raw honesty and compassion, giving voice to the often unheard. If you crave authentic, character-driven page-turners that hit deep and stay with you long after the final page, you're in the right place.

With each new release, fans eagerly anticipate another thrilling blend of thought-provoking storytelling and relatable characters that define P.D. Workman's brand as an author of unforgettable page-turners—gripping tales that leave a lasting impact long after the last page is turned.

> P. D. Workman, does not shy from probing the deep psychological scars of childhood trauma, mental illness, and addiction. Also characteristic of this author, these extremely sensitive issues are explored with extensive empathy, described with incredible clarity, and portrayed with profound insight.
>
> ——KIM, GOODREADS REVIEWER

Some of Workman's titles have been translated into Spanish, French, Portuguese, German, and Italian.

Workman began writing at an early age and is a prolific reader as well as writer. She is also passionate about teaching and learning, expresses her creativity through art and cooking, and loves exploring the Calgary parks and green spaces where the Parks Pat Mysteries are set. She was a legal assistant for many years and has done extensive charitable work.

Workman was born and raised in Alberta, Canada, and is married with one adult son.

~

Please visit P.D. Workman at pdworkman.com to see what else she is working on, to join her mailing list, and to link to her social networks.

~

If you enjoyed this book, please take the time to recommend it to other purchasers with a review or star rating and share it with your friends!

tiktok.com/@pdworkmanauthor

facebook.com/pdworkmanauthor

x.com/pdworkmanauthor

instagram.com/pdworkmanauthor

amazon.com/author/pdworkman

bookbub.com/authors/p-d-workman

goodreads.com/pdworkman

linkedin.com/in/pdworkman

pinterest.com/pdworkmanauthor

youtube.com/pdworkman

Find P.D. Workman's books at

PDWORKMAN.COM

Scan the QR code below